Sweet Surprise

Romance Collection

Sweet Surprise

Romance Collection

Wanda E. Brunstetter, Kristin Billerbeck,
Kristy Dykes, Aisha Ford, Birdie L. Etchison, Pamela Griffin,
Joyce Livingston, Tamela Hancock Murray, Gail Sattler

BARBOUR BOOKS

An Imprint of Barbour Publishing, Inc.

Print ISBN 978-1-63058-457-3

eBook Editions:
Adobe Digital Edition (.epub) 978-1-63409-136-7
Kindle and MobiPocket Edition (.prc) 978-1-63409-137-4

Published by Barbour Books, an imprint of Barbour Publishing, Inc., P.O. Box 719, Uhrichsville, Ohio 44683, www.barbourbooks.com

Our mission is to publish and distribute inspirational products offering exceptional value and biblical encouragement to the masses.

Member of the
Evangelical Christian
Publishers Association

Printed in Canada.

Contents

SWEET AS APPLE PIE
by Kristin Billerbeck

*Be kindly affectioned one to another with brotherly love;
in honour preferring one another.*

ROMANS 12:10 KJV

Chapter 1

Watching the door isn't going to make him appear." Kayli Johnson laughed, but she didn't tear her gaze from the bakery storefront. "Maybe not, but I don't want to miss him. I'm going to smile at him today, and maybe he'll come in." Kayli's stomach churned at the very thought of such uncharacteristic boldness.

"In my day men came calling properly. There was none of this spying out the window business." The stout older woman wiped the glass countertop with vigor. Kayli feared being a dirty appliance in Mrs. Heiden's path.

She plopped a fist to her hip. "You never had a crush on anyone? Come on, Mrs. Heiden. There was never anyone who set your heart aflame?"

"Never."

"Then how did you meet Mr. Heiden?"

"He was just lucky, I suppose."

Kayli let out a short laugh. "I suppose he was at that." Rearranging the apricot Danish into a more elegant design, she spoke again dreamily. "But this man, Mrs. Heiden"—she erupted into a long sigh—"he is unlike anyone I've ever seen around here. I can't explain it. I want to know who he is and ask him all sorts of questions. Maybe we're soul mates." She immediately regretted adding the final bit.

"Rubbish! Maybe you spend too much time watching old romantic movies. A girl your age should get out more, not daydream constantly."

"I was born a hundred years too late." Kayli shrugged. "Going out doesn't interest me much. I would have been perfectly content to pad around my sitting room and wait for suitors to call."

"You were born at the right time, Kayli. May I remind you a woman wouldn't have owned a business like this? If she did, a man would be fronting it."

"So what do you suggest, Mrs. Heiden? Should I accost this man on the street and introduce myself?"

"I suggest you get your dreamy eyes off that window and worry about your chocolate molds. They are nearly ready. Love will come calling when it's time."

Kayli gasped. "There he is!" Her heart thumped against her chest, and she closed her eyes. "Please come in—please come in," she repeated to herself.

Before opening her eyes she heard the jingle of the store bell. Shaking, she blinked several times. He stood before her, in all his masculine splendor.

Light brown hair shorn close to his head and incredible clear green eyes, like the finished edge of glass. She heard herself exhale. His set jaw exuded confidence, and his towering height, probably about six-three, rendered Kayli speechless. Sincerity was in his eyes, and a warmth emanated from him. Something told her immediately he would be a good father. She chastised herself for mentally sharing children with a man she hadn't yet spoken to. What was wrong with her?

"Hello?"

He waved his hand in front of her dazed eyes, and she nearly collapsed from embarrassment. Where was her voice? She swore she'd talk to him, and now nothing came from her mouth except gurgling noises.

"Good morning." Mrs. Heiden finally rescued Kayli. "What can we get you?"

"Coffee."

Kayli had to say something. "How about a cappuccino? It's on the house today." She forced the words and they sounded completely unnatural, as if they'd been thrown at her and she were a puppet fronting the conversation.

"Cappuccino?"

"Italian espresso with steamed milk. I make the best in Palo Alto."

His eyes narrowed. "Is this how you get customers hooked on three-dollar coffees instead of the regular stuff?"

"You'll try it." Mrs. Heiden ordered. "You can order the plain stuff anywhere. This is a European bakery. Kayli is trained as a renowned pastry chef. You'll not drink standard fare with her delicacies."

"This is a European bakery?" He looked confused for a moment, then flustered, and focused on the backward words on the window.

"Yes, why?" Mrs. Heiden inquired. "Didn't you read it on the glass?"

He shook his head. "Never mind. It's not important." He looked back toward the window for a second. "I didn't realize a European bakery was already here."

"What do you mean 'already'?" Mrs. Heiden asked.

"Nothing. I'll try one of those cappuccinos." His clear eyes gazed directly at Kayli. She froze in the moment, and her stomach fluttered. *Does he know what I'm thinking? Does my face give it away?*

"Single? Tall?" Kayli stammered.

"Yes, I am." The stranger held open his hands. They were strong hands, if a bit rough-hewn. "Is that a requirement for the free coffee?"

Kayli blinked rapidly. "No, I meant do you want a single cappuccino or a double? A standard cup or a tall? You know, small or large?" Mortification settled over her as she rambled endlessly.

"Ah, so this is how you do it. You get people so confused about ordering a cup of java that we leave totally confused and satisfied we've gotten our three dollars' worth because we figured something out." His eye held a sparkle, and Kayli noticed he winked at Mrs. Heiden.

"No, I only meant to offer you a free cup since I see you walk by each day." She bit her lip.

"You're very observant."

"You're hard to miss." Kayli wiped her hands nervously on her apron. "Being so tall and all." She turned on the espresso steamer, thankful it drowned out her ridiculous babbling.

"I'm building the restaurant up the street!" he yelled over the machine. "I did the owner's house, and now he asked me to work on the restaurant. It's almost finished, and then I can head home. To a place where the coffee comes only leaded or unleaded."

"Home?" Kayli stopped the machine.

"Montana, blue sky as far as the eye can see." He waved his large hand in the air. "And the closest neighbor has an udder."

Kayli heard Mrs. Heiden laugh, and she shot the elder woman a grimace. "Why would you want to move away from all this?"

He looked out the shop windows again. Several impeccably dressed business people passed, a few foreign cars stopped at the light, and a woman strode by, looking as though she belonged on a soap opera rather than walking down a city street. "What part do you think I'll miss?" He crossed his arms across his wide chest.

"For one thing, I imagine not many people want luxury homes or restaurants there. What will you do?" Kayli wiped the extra foam from the outside of the cup.

"Whistle Dixie if I have to. Maybe I'll raise llamas."

Kayli handed him his coffee; her heart slowed. He was a cowboy let loose on the city streets. He wasn't her soul mate at all but a gorgeous impostor. Kayli sniffed. "If that's your true calling, I wish you luck."

"Mmm," he said after his first sip. "This is incredible coffee. I've never tasted anything like it. I'm beginning to think the three dollars might be justified. Maybe the Europeans know something." He winked again.

"Do you want anything else?"

He looked into the glass counters, his eyes brightening. "Do you have any apple pie?"

"Apple pie?" Kayli was almost offended. "This is a European bakery."

"So you said."

"I have tiramisu that will melt in your mouth and make you forget you ever ate such a trite dessert like apple pie."

"I have no idea what tiramisu is. Apple pie is American. What kind of American are you, running a European bakery?"

"A European-trained pastry chef." She squared her shoulders. "And a patriotic American. Tiramisu is a delightful Italian dessert made with marscapone cheese and lady fingers soaked in espresso. The word means 'to lift you up,' and it does just that."

"So pastry chefs can't make apple pie?" He shook his head. "What a waste of talent. My mother," he groaned, "could make an apple pie crust that would disintegrate in your mouth. You never tasted anything like it."

"I can make a piecrust that would do the same thing. I just choose not to." She crossed her arms. "There's not a lot of money in apple pie around here. I have to make a living."

He seemed unimpressed. "You know, it's easy to say you can make an apple pie like my mother's, but why should I believe you? You might be like those gourmet chefs who can't microwave a hotdog."

"I studied pastry for years. I think I could take on your mother's crust." Kayli shook her head. An apple pie. . .really!

"Do you?" His eyebrow lowered. "I'd like to see you try."

"You come back Friday afternoon. I'll have an apple pie that will knock your socks off."

"I'll believe it when I taste it."

"And you'll pay for it this time."

He laughed. "I think I already have. But I'll see you Friday. You'll have my pie ready." The jingle of the bell annoyed her.

"How dare he!"

Kayli picked up her chocolate molds with force, and a few of them collapsed under the pressure. Mrs. Heiden took the tray from Kayli before any further damage was done. Her assistant's bent frame shook with laughter, and Kayli felt incensed.

"Just what is so funny?"

"Kayli, my dear. I can't help but giggle at the notion that your soul mate, as you so romantically put it, lives next door to cows. Have you even seen a cow?"

Kayli stood tall. "I have. We went to a working dairy when I studied milk chocolate in Switzerland."

"I certainly hope there's another soul mate out there for you because that one sounds distinctly like Annie Oakley's soul mate. His America is far different from yours."

"I'll grant you that. An apple pie! Honestly, I think he's looking for a diner on Route 66, not Les Saisons Bakery."

"So will you make this apple pie?"

"You bet I will, and it will leave him wondering how he ever stomached his mother's."

"You're cruel, Kayli, and far too competitive. You'll never get a husband that way."

Kayli grinned. "Maybe not, but I didn't study for six years to make apple pie either. I can't believe I ever found that man attractive. Perhaps I should have kept believing in my dreams and let him keep walking by."

Adam Harper exited the fancy bakery with a heavy heart. Mike Williams never told him a European bakery already existed on University Avenue. Adam might not have noticed if he hadn't seen the beautiful owner. That forced him into acknowledgement, made her real, and guilt weighed heavily on him. A ruthless businessman, Mike Williams would undercut this elegant little bakery until it couldn't afford to operate; then he'd raise his prices and force rents up in the neighborhood. The bakery owner's big brown eyes resonated in Adam's memory. He would remember them always and what he'd done to remove some of their sparkle.

Adam sighed. Taking money from a man with no morals, he supposed, made him just as bad. He brought out the wrinkled picture of his Montana property. Was it worth it? He looked back to the tiny bakery, thinking about those wide, innocent eyes gazing at him.

"You ought to be ashamed of yourself, Adam," he muttered. *You're as bad as them and worse. You know better.* The faster he was out of California, the better. Before he gave up everything he believed in.

"Hey, you checking out the competition?" Mike Williams met him on the sidewalk, nodding toward Adam's coffee cup.

"You didn't tell me there was any competition."

"All you had to do was pay attention, Adam. You walk by the shop every day." Mike waggled his eyebrows. "Did you get a load of that pretty little owner?" He motioned an hourglass in the air. "I'd like to get her on my payroll."

In Montana, Adam would have hauled off and socked the guy, but here in California he just clenched his teeth, quietly enduring the immorality. *Only a few more months, and I'll be out of here.*

"She seems like the kind of woman who wouldn't give you the time of day. Too sweet."

"Until she finds out about my mansion." Mike winked. "Women are more open to me then."

"Not this one, Mike. I think she's beyond your standard money-grabber."

"All women have their price—some are more expensive than others."

Adam's eyes narrowed. "If you believe that, you're more pathetic than I thought. What does your wife think of this opinion?"

"Careful, Boy. This job ain't over yet. You got a plumber that hasn't shown up and a problem with the inspection on the stoves. I suggest you get to it. Swallow that sissy coffee and get a move on."

Adam clenched his lips between his teeth to avoid replying. In less than three months, he'd take his payment from Mike Williams and be long gone. He held to that with fervor. It felt like all he had right now.

Chapter 2

Friday came quickly, and Kayli manipulated the dough in her hands then rolled it out into a flat circle. She cut a perfect circle, tossing the scraps aside for later. She held up a pippin apple, crowned to perfection. "I really hate to dash your mother's title, but, alas, my pride has been wounded."

"Are you talking to yourself again?" Mrs. Heiden entered the back room. "My stars! You look like the wicked queen with that apple in your hands."

"I was talking to my former soul mate. I'm feeling sorry for his mother. Soon my pie will show her pie for what it is. A pale comparison." Kayli felt the corner of her mouth turn, and she tossed the apple playfully.

"You are a prideful thing—do you know that? And you know what they say about pride." Mrs. Heiden grinned. "It goes before the fall."

Kayli grimaced. "Mrs. Heiden, really. Do you honestly think some backwoods Montana mom could hold a candle to my baking expertise? I was born with gifted taste buds."

Her eyebrow raised. "And tiny hips. Life isn't fair, and, yes, I do think his mother's pie could outrank yours. Taste is subjective." Mrs. Heiden removed her red apron and hung it on a wall hook. "More important, I think it hardly matters. You should be doing something constructive to assist your social life, not baking pies for a man moving out of town. To get away from the likes of you, no less, and move back to the cows."

"Now you're being ornery. He is not moving to get away from me. He doesn't even know me."

"He knows all about your princess ways. They're not hard to see. What is that on the piecrust?" Mrs. Heiden bent over Kayli's pastry.

Kayli used her pastry brush to "glue" the decoration to the top of the shell. "It's a cow. See?"

"You put a cow on the piecrust." Mrs. Heiden shook her head. "You know, in some places, they would lock the likes of you away."

"I thought it was cute. A going-away present, you might say, to remind him of home and his America."

"Your friend Robert is here, and it's nearly time to close. I'll see you in the morning. I don't want to be seen here late in case they haul you off."

" 'Bye, Mrs. Heiden. Thank you for your help today. I'm going to bake this, and it will be ready when our cowboy comes. Fresh and warm, just like his mama makes, only way better." Kayli shrugged.

Mrs. Heiden clicked her tongue. "Get a life, as you young people say."

Kayli laughed and slid the pie into the oven. Then she emerged to the front counter. "Hi, Robert. How are you?"

"I'm good. Listen—a few of us are doing dinner tonight. A barbecue at my house— you interested?" Robert pressed his glasses to his face with an index finger. He crinkled his always-sniffling nose and smiled.

Kayli checked her watch. "I'm waiting for a customer pick-up. What time?"

"Not until six, but that isn't all I came to tell you." Robert pulled her around the counter by her elbow and sat her down at one of the two tables in the bakery. "You know that big restaurant going up down the street." He looked around the store, en- suring no one was around. "I could lose my job for this, so you didn't hear it from me."

"Well, tell me, Robert. I didn't know you had this mysterious side."

Robert grimaced, in his annoyed bureaucratic way. "I did the paperwork for it downtown. It's not just a restaurant. It's a European bakery during the day. They plan to sell out of a shop up front."

Kayli hunched over. She felt the blood drain from her face. Shaking her head, she finally looked up. "It's a restaurant, open for dinner—right? It has nothing to do with me."

"Right, a restaurant. But during the day they bake bread and desserts for the res- taurant. They're going to open a bakery café."

Kayli shook her head. "No, Robert. The builder was here. He would have said something." Her hands trembled. "I can't go back to the hotels again. I've worked too hard for this. But if my business is split in half, what will I do?"

"I don't know, Kayli, but I thought you should know. I heard the Royal Court is looking for a pastry chef."

Kayli's head swayed violently. "No, never again! I'd rather be a dishwasher than work in a fancy hotel again. The hours are stifling, and the rewards are null. Half my desserts ended up in the hotel cafeteria, stale and unappreciated. No, I can't do that."

"Mike Williams is building this restaurant. He plays to win. I'm not trying to scare you, but I want you to be realistic. We in the city have seen him take out a lot of mom- and-pop shops."

Kayli's heart sank. Robert supported her in nearly every endeavor. He'd even loaned her a small bit of money to get started. If he thought her chances were slim, they were probably impossible. "I don't mean to shoot the messenger, Robert, but I need time to assimilate this information."

"Join us for the barbecue—you'll feel better." His brown eyes widened, and she smiled at his sweetest grin. Robert, as fine and decent a man as there ever was, and yet Kayli felt nothing when she stared into his eyes. Why was that? "Kayli?"

"I'm sorry, Robert. I'm still digesting what you've told me. I don't think so on dinner. I wouldn't be good company anyway. But wait a minute—let me get you a tiramisu to serve." Kayli went behind the counter and retrieved her signature dessert. She boxed it in an elegant gold box and placed a sticker on it. "Here, Robert—enjoy it with my compliments."

He reached for the box, grasping her hand as he did so. "I'd rather have you there," he whispered. "The dessert isn't nearly as sweet."

Kayli pulled her hand away. "Thank you, Robert, but I've got to be proactive. If I plan to beat Mike Williams at his own game, I'd better think of a plan. I wouldn't be able to concentrate on small talk."

"Maybe Mr. Williams is looking for a pastry chef."

"I like having my own business. Besides, if I can't handle a little competition, I'm not really that good—right?"

Robert brushed her face with the back of his hand. "You are awesome. Don't you forget it. I'll see you at church this weekend."

Kayli forced a smile. "Sure. Have fun tonight."

"Not nearly as much without you." He winked and turned.

Kayli sat for a long time with her chin in her hands. Wasn't this always the way? She rejoiced in having her own business, just finished bragging about it, and it might be snatched out of her very hands. Sometimes she didn't understand God. Hadn't she paid her dues? Wasn't this justification for all she'd missed in life? Kayli laughed out loud. This time she'd wrestle with God. She was sick of having to grin and bear it, and her business wouldn't go without a fight.

"You look heavy into thought. Is this a bad time?" The tall cowboy made his way into the shop. The bell announcing him didn't do him justice. She thought he should have his own special sound, maybe a bullhorn calling attention to his entrance. Though she doubted he had any trouble getting attention. Her eyes narrowed, thinking of all the information this man had kept to himself. That he had the nerve to walk into her shop.

"I've only just heard what you're building. Won't Mike Williams have your head for consorting with the enemy?" Kayli tried to sit tall, but her shoulders slumped again, and she felt the beginning of tears. She wiped away an escaped tear and looked away. "I'll get your pie, and then I'd appreciate it if you'd just let Mike's bakery serve your penchant for pie."

"No, wait." He grabbed her hand, and she turned to look up into his tropical green eyes. Her troubles seemed momentarily forgotten. What was it about this man? Why did she feel she'd known him for years? "I didn't know there was competition in town. Not until you handed me the cappuccino the other day. I wouldn't have done this knowingly."

"I should make you pay for the coffee now." Kayli sniffled. "So you think I'm about to go out of business, too?"

"I didn't say that," he whispered in a hoarse voice, and she felt herself swallow. Her hand was still in his. Such familiarity with a stranger was unknown to her, but she didn't pull away. Anger mingled with interest.

"How could you do this? Build something for that monster and harm a small business. My small business."

"I didn't know. Honestly I didn't. I'm not what you'd call an observant man. I passed by here every day and never bothered to notice."

She blinked away fresh tears. His guilt only confirmed her worst suspicions. Mike Williams would put her business under; it was only a matter of time. "When will the bakery open?"

"Three months."

"I'll get your pie." She turned to the back, but his hand squeezed hers. Suddenly she smelled something burning. "The pie!" She ran toward the back and opened the oven to see smoke. She fanned the fumes away, donning her oven mitts and coughing in the midst of gray clouds. She pulled out a blackened pie. It looked worse than it smelled.

The builder walked up behind her. "Is that a little cow on the pie?"

She nearly kissed him, so beautiful was his gesture to ignore the blackened pastry and focus on her handmade cow. She nodded.

"It's a lovely cow. Reminds me of home. Thank you." He took twenty dollars from his wallet. "You sure know how to impress a guy."

"You don't think I'm actually going to make you pay for this, do you?"

"I appreciate the effort. I imagine this hasn't been your best day, and I wouldn't do anything to make it worse. You take the money and buy essentials for another pie. I'm still dying to know if it beats my mom's."

Her tears started to roll again. Since when had she been so emotional? She shook her head, sniffing every few seconds. "I really can make an apple pie."

He laughed. "I know you can. In fact, I'm certain there's no end to all the things you can do. Have dinner with me. I want to let you know how sorry I am."

"Tonight?"

"Now. We'll go somewhere that Mike Williams doesn't own. You'll get to know me. I'll get to know you, and we'll share our contempt for everything Williams. Please. I could use a friend here."

"Shouldn't I know your name?" Kayli realized she didn't even know this stranger. She only felt as though she did. His regular jaunts past the storefront provided a familiarity with him that didn't extend into reality.

"Adam. Adam Harper."

"I'm Kayli Johnson."

"We'll leave my business card here on the counter, Kayli. That way, if you have any fears of walking up the street with me, someone will know how to find us. My cell phone number is on there. I don't think your assistant would think too much of your taking off with a stranger. She doesn't look like the type of woman I want to mess with."

She smiled. "Believe me—she's not. Let me turn off this oven and clean up a bit." Kayli left the door unlocked. No sense in turning away business today. She'd need customers more than ever if competition loomed.

She brushed away the remaining flour from her work table and tried to forget that the man she'd admired from afar stood in her shop, waiting to take her to dinner. She checked her reflection in a tiny compact and sighed. She looked worn and pale, covered by a light dusting of flour. Kayli shook out her long, dark tresses and applied a bright red lipstick and a little blush. She puckered up, matting the lipstick, and drew in a deep breath.

The bell at the door jingled, and Kayli emerged to Robert's questioning glance. He looked toward Adam and back at Kayli, and Kayli felt her eyes drift shut. She opened them to Robert's sad brown eyes. "I thought you might be hungry for something. I got you a little soup up the street. I'll just leave it here." He placed a white bag on the counter and immediately left.

Kayli felt Adam's glare and avoided looking in his direction. "A friend from church," she finally said.

"A good one obviously." Adam searched the room.

"It's not what you think. He's having a group over for dinner and asked me to join them. I didn't feel like being in a group tonight, and I still don't. But I'd like to get to know you, Adam Harper, if you're still willing."

Adam brushed his chambray shirt. "Something tells me by the look in that man's eye, you're trouble, Kayli Johnson."

"You're probably right."

"You'll break my heart, won't you?" His gentle green eyes narrowed. He had mirth in his gaze, but also a sobering severity.

"Not over dinner, I won't."

"Fair enough."

Adam took her arm, and they entered the busy sidewalk together. She feared looking into those clear eyes again, but she felt his large presence even without gazing toward him. Adam Harper would not be easily forgotten, and she had little doubt that it would be her heart broken in two. Still, his invitation proved as powerful as any web. She was drawn to him and hoped an evening in reality would put aside this ridiculous crush on a myth.

Chapter 3

University Avenue bustled with the wealthy of Palo Alto's elite, next to the backdrop of sweatshirted Stanford students on bicycles. Kayli's stomach churned from being on the arm of this man she had idolized for so long. He was real and, for the moment, unaware that Kayli Johnson was not his type. Neither glamorous nor into cows, Kayli tried to forget this man would bring about her ruin in business. Indirectly anyway.

"Do you know how long I worked to get my own business?" Kayli heard her voice speak. It wasn't like her to accept the invitation of a stranger, much less one with whom she obviously shared so little in common.

Adam turned and focused on her. His crystal green eyes narrowed, and she felt their weight. "I didn't know, Kayli. You had to realize that if you were doing something well in Palo Alto, someone might come in and try to do it better. All you have to do is look at the countless expensive retailers here to realize that. The shopping compares with New York. You're not that naive."

Kayli frowned. "I think I was."

"Did you come out with me to bust my chops all night?" He stopped suddenly on the street, and Kayli gulped.

"Well, no."

"Come on—we're going in here." Adam opened the door to a quiet, Italian restaurant. The setting felt romantic, and Kayli felt a bit of her anger dissipate under the soft lighting and gentle music. They were seated at a quiet table in the corner by the window. The waiter handed them menus and set a wine list on the table. "Do you drink?"

Kayli shook her head.

"You can take this away." Adam handed the waiter the leather-bound drink menu.

The waiter sniffed and removed the wine list and the glasses with an angry clink.

Kayli opened the menu, and her eyes widened. She didn't partake of restaurants very often, and this one was certainly above her price range. "So what does a cowboy think about paying twenty-seven dollars for a steak?"

Adam grimaced. "Don't get me started. The same thing I think about paying three dollars for a cup of coffee—that's what I think. Is there anything that justifies these California prices?"

"The weather tax. That's what we call it. You get sunshine about three hundred and fifty days a year. No snow to shovel, and the ocean a rock skip away. So we call the prices the weather tax."

"Well, it's disgusting."

"Have you tried to pay the rent here? There's a reason we charge those prices, Adam. Someone charges us. Though I must admit the price of a steak makes me wonder if the cows live in a fancy hotel suite until their demise. Still, the rent is quite overbearing for most."

"Yes, my two thousand a month is buying me a lovely little one bedroom up the street, built in the forties. I'm praying we don't have an earthquake before I get out."

Kayli laughed. "Welcome to California, huh?"

"It's not exactly the most welcoming state. But judging by all the people here, there must be something people want."

"Have you walked Stanford's serene campus? Or taken a hike in the mighty redwoods? Have you felt the ocean waves lap at your bare feet? Have you stood on the floor of Yosemite Valley? God's creation is so apparent in California." Kayli laughed. "I sound like a praise song, but some things are worth their price."

He looked away from her and focused on his menu before lifting his gaze back to hers. "You're a Christian." It sounded more like an accusation than a question.

"I am," Kayli answered. "How did you know?"

"I saw the fish sign on your window. That's what pulled me in your shop that day. Almost like it was a sign."

Kayli looked away. Yes, she was a Christian, but little good that seemed to do her. While heathens like Mike Williams built bigger tributes to themselves, little Christians like Kayli struggled to make ends meet. Where was God in all this? And why was she facing her old life and those vicious questions again?

"I haven't been a Christian very long, and this is not the first time I've questioned my faith." Kayli shot a hand toward her mouth. Had she really uttered her fears?

Adam laughed, and Kayli bristled. "Life ain't fair—that's for sure. God never promised us it would be. When I get back to Montana, my faith will be restored. Clean air, blue skies, and honest people. It's easy to get lost in all the hustle-bustle here. You hold on. It won't always be this way."

"Easy for you to say. I'm glad it's perfectly acceptable for you to come here, take our money, build a monster restaurant, and go home with no guilt whatsoever. Is that His plan for your life? You can take people down as long as they aren't from your home state?" Kayli hated the sound of her voice. It sounded edgy and bitter.

Adam dropped his head, blinking quickly. His expression sent a pang of guilt through Kayli, and she instantly regretted her words and her tone. "Montana is no picnic, Kayli. There are no free rides. We all have our own crosses to bear. I'm sure you wouldn't want mine, and I wouldn't want yours."

Kayli opened her mouth to speak but closed it upon seeing the severity in Adam's eye. She breathed deeply before speaking.

"I envy your escaping your troubles—that's all."

"Montana is no escape. Responsibilities can be painful no matter where you're placed."

Kayli swallowed hard. Something about the grievousness of his expression told her something more went on in Montana, but she feared the answer. "I'm sorry. I plan to win this war with Mr. Mike Williams, Adam. You tell your boss that."

"No, I don't think I will. I'll let you prove it to him. He doesn't need the added challenge. It's better he looks at you as a fly to be swatted away."

"You don't think I can take him, do you? You think his bakery will do me in within a month?"

"Kayli, I've built enough for Mike Williams to know he is not a man I'd mess with. Do I respect him as a person? Not on your life. Do I respect his mind for business? Absolutely, and I wouldn't toy with him like a kitten's ball of yarn. You'll only hang yourself."

"Speak of the devil." Kayli nodded toward the door where Mike Williams had just come in. She noticed Adam shift uncomfortably. "Do you want to leave?"

Adam shook his head and crossed his arms, as though bracing for Mike's approach.

"Well, if it isn't my builder with Miss Johnson." He whistled, and the waiters looked angrily their way before noticing it was Mr. Williams and consequently ignored the breech in peace.

"Do I know you?" Kayli asked.

"Mike Williams." He held out a hand, which Kayli ignored. "I'm building the new restaurant and bakery up the street. Hasn't my trusty contractor spilled the beans yet?"

"No, actually, he hadn't, but your reputation precedes you regardless." Kayli narrowed her eyes, staring into Mike's cold gray ones. "I hope you're prepared with that bakery, Mr. Williams. I was trained at all the finest hotels in Switzerland. You'll have a hard time competing with me."

"I don't plan to compete. I plan to hire you, Miss Johnson. I can pay you twice what you must be earning in that little sweatshop of yours." He opened a palm pilot, studying the calendar before placing it in front of her and pointing to the date. "One year from today, Miss Johnson, and you'll be begging me for a job."

"I sincerely doubt that." Kayli forced her gaze from the PDA.

Adam cleared his throat. "This is a date, Mr. Williams. You know—a guy-girl thing. Do you mind? I'm not on the clock."

Mike laughed. "Okay, okay. I know when I'm not wanted."

Doubtful, thought Kayli.

"Just so you know, Miss Johnson—I don't take any offense at your refusal. I know that down the road things will look different. I'm a businessman. I don't let my personal feelings get in the way. Enjoy your dinner." Mike pulled at his sleeve and disappeared from the restaurant.

"Charming, ain't he?" Adam smirked.

Kayli tossed a hand. "It's not worth thinking about. Let's order." She looked up at him. His eyes were filled with pity. She felt her stomach turn. "I will win," Kayli said again, but this time her voice quavered.

"When I'm gone to Montana, you'll have to write and let me know how it goes."

"Why are you so eager to get back?" Kayli bit her lip.

"Someone waits for me in Montana. I must go back, and I must go with money. I have no more options than you do, Kayli. I hoped I'd see a friendly face when I saw your fish sign in the window. I hope I was right."

Kayli straightened. "I'm not at the mercy of Mike Williams, and neither are you."

"Oh, but you are." Adam's firm jaw hardened. "You're like a calf being dragged to the branding iron. You don't realize it yet. Excuse my pessimism, but I'm beginning to wonder if I'll ever cut loose."

"Well, I'm sure whoever waits for you back in Montana will wait a little longer." *I would,* Kayli wanted to add.

"I have to go to a dinner next Saturday night. Mike is celebrating the grand opening of his luxurious home. Would you care to come?"

"Will this affect whoever waits in Montana?"

"Not in the least, unfortunately. Come with me. You can infiltrate the enemy's camp." Adam laughed.

Kayli was about to answer when the waiter returned. He rambled off specials in some barely discernible English and waited for the two of them to order. Kayli ordered a modest ravioli dish, while Adam opted for rigatoni. Neither ordered an appetizer.

"How did you come to work for Mike Williams?"

"His wife was an old girlfriend of mine during high school. She's from Montana. She knew I was struggling in Montana and called to help."

Kayli heard herself sigh aloud. "You're still friends?"

"What better way to show me how much wealth she has and how successfully she married? Can you think of a more elaborate plan to disregard an ex than to offer him a job working for your husband?" Adam sat back in his chair.

"Surely you didn't have to take it."

"Oh, but I did, and Andrea knew it." Adam's eyes flickered, and Kayli pondered his conversation. So free with some pieces of information, so private about others. He seemed a man rooted in turmoil, and yet she felt even more attracted to him. As complex as he seemed, there appeared a simplicity, a line so true that she couldn't run. But she knew she probably should have.

"I'll go with you next week, if you're not embarrassed to have me in front of Andrea. I imagine she's quite glamorous."

"She's that and more. But I won't say anything else. I'll let you decide for yourself, and you could show up in a sack and be perfectly beautiful."

Kayli ignored the comment. "Are you over her?"

"I'm that and more." Adam grinned. "Somehow I suddenly have the heart for three-dollar coffees and French pastry." He winked.

"I thought you were an apple-pie man."

"I'll wait for my mother's."

"No, you don't. You promised you'd give me another shot. Next Friday evening you come in after work. I'll make you an apple pie you won't soon forget."

"I think I'll have a hard time forgetting you anyway, Kayli. With or without a pie." He smoothed the tablecloth before him, avoiding her gaze. Whatever secrets Adam Harper held close to his heart, Kayli longed to discover them. Even if it cost her, and it surely would.

Chapter 4

Kayli set about her apple pie with renewed fervor. She nibbled on her bottom lip as she focused on getting the consistency of the dough right. She covered her marble roller with flour and smoothed the pastry to a delicate thickness. Mrs. Heiden's sigh interrupted the careful operation. Kayli placed a fist on her hip. "What?"

Mrs. Heiden put her head down, shaking it while wiping down the countertops. "What was this big plan you had to steal all the business from the new restaurant? Free samples, advertising, promotion? It's been a week."

"I'm working on it." Kayli pointed to her head. "But first I have to finish this pie."

"I think you've finally gone crazy, Missy. In a few short months, a monster bakery is opening, and yet you're competing with an unknown house frau from Montana."

"I am not competing. I'm only trying to prove myself as a baker."

"To whom? This is the equivalent of a dog marking his territory. Nothing more." Mrs. Heiden's sour expression erupted.

Kayli giggled aloud. "You're right, Mrs. Heiden. I am avoiding the inevitable. Let me top this pie and slip it in the oven. I'll get started on the ad blitz."

Mrs. Heiden looked over the pie, her eyebrows raised. "What, no cow?"

Kayli crinkled her nose. "A bit over the top, didn't you think?" Actually Kayli thought the cow was cute, but she didn't have time for such frivolity. The pie's taste would speak for itself this time.

"As if you ever listened to what I think. Seventy-two years of living I've done— you don't think I learned something?"

Kayli embraced Mrs. Heiden loosely. "I think you've learned a lot, probably more than you'll ever teach my hard head."

"You can say that again." Mrs. Heiden rearranged the remaining pastries from the morning, making the display appear fuller and fresher. "I've spent ten years alone now. And I liked being married better. I want the same for you, Princess. You'll work yourself to the bone on this bakery and have nothing to show for it in the end. You only think you've received what you want by quitting the hotel, but this business will never satisfy. I know you, Kayli. You want it all. Ask God for it."

That was as close as Mrs. Heiden would ever come to true warmth. It brought a lump to Kayli's throat. The elder woman set about helping a customer until he ordered a cappuccino, and then she complained about the newfangled machinery that only young people could operate.

Kayli prayed silently that she would learn to concentrate on the things that mattered. Competing with an unknown baker in a far-off state seemed much easier than planning for the possible demise of her business. Kayli determined she must seek God more about His plans.

She wished to be married. Someday. But not to just anyone. Not to the first man who courted her properly, as Mrs. Heiden would suggest, but someone who set her heart ablaze. Someone God ordained as her life partner. Kayli wanted to start with fireworks and explosions and work into faithful and loving. Was that too much to ask?

The front bell rang, and Kayli looked up to see Adam's towering frame. His smile set her heart pounding, and she took an audible breath. This is how she wanted to feel when she looked at her husband. His clear green eyes spoke to her, saying things his mouth might never utter. Whatever secrets Adam held close to his heart, his eyes didn't lie. Honest and shining, the emotion in his eyes connected with her. He didn't speak, and neither did Kayli. She took it all in, allowing this moment, this silent union, to continue. He'd been in for several cappuccinos during the week, and they barely spoke but still expressed volumes.

"I hope you are not here for your pie yet," Mrs. Heiden barked.

"No." Adam shook his head. "Actually I came for the coffee. The normal stuff."

"Good. I can get that." Mrs. Heiden took a paper cup while Adam stared at Kayli. She didn't realize how much she was looking forward to Saturday night until she saw him again. Her instincts told her this was the man for her while her head told her otherwise, for how could he be if he was leaving town? Kayli had a thriving business. At least she did for now. Adam Harper had come to California to make his money and leave. He couldn't be the one, no matter how much wishful thinking Kayli might do.

"Tomorrow night still okay with you?"

Kayli nodded. "I'm looking forward to it. I bought a new dress," she blurted out.

"Mike's house is grand. I'll enjoy showing you my handiwork there. He spared no expense, and it was a contractor's dream to have free rein."

"So Mike isn't all bad."

Adam shook his head. "He's made his money in this corporate culture. He wants every town across America to look the same." Adam shrugged. "A lot of people agree with him. I happen to like towns with individual personality. I like the little mom-and-pop shops, not the same menu everywhere. It comes down to having options, which people are quickly eliminating with the box-store culture." Adam frowned.

Kayli searched Adam's eyes, willing the butterflies in her stomach away. "I'm glad. I bet it's the same with houses for you. It's like building a tract house over a custom home, I imagine."

"Now you understand."

"Your pie is baking. About another hour I'd say." Kayli lifted out a small mansion she'd created of chocolate. "This is for another millionaire celebrating his new home." She longed to turn the conversation to something she didn't have to stumble over.

"No shortage of egos in this town." Adam clicked his tongue. "Your work is beautiful though. I'd never thought I'd meet my equal in building, but your chocolate creations put me to shame." He laughed. "Shall I pick you up here tomorrow night?"

"No, I'll start doing something if I wait here. I'll probably end up with flour on my gown, so why don't you come by the house?" Kayli wrote her address on a scrap of paper.

"Here's my card again, in case you lost it." Adam reached into his pocket. She grasped it tightly, brushing his hand in the process. A current ran through her arm, and she saw the same question in his eyes that she heard swirling in her own head. Perhaps this attraction was too powerful. He took the cup of coffee and placed the money in Mrs. Heiden's hands. "I'll see you at the end of the day for my mouth-watering pie."

Kayli nodded, watching as he strode toward the door.

"That is not good," Mrs. Heiden said. "No good can come of that. You two have too much fire. Robert is a nice steady man. You need to find one like him. Adam is too dangerous for you."

"Adam's a Christian, Mrs. Heiden."

"He's dangerous. Too good-looking. You find a nice, homely man, Kayli. They make good husbands."

Kayli laughed. "I don't want a lap dog. I want a husband. What if I don't have a choice?"

"You always have a choice, Kayli. You go and have a nice evening tomorrow with Mr. Fire. Then you find someone worth having for a lifetime."

"Is someone worth having if you don't want him?"

Mrs. Heiden tossed a hand. "You young people! You're too spoiled for your own good. In my day we didn't expect so much."

Robert ambled in, and Kayli felt guilty, as if he might have sensed the conversation. His squared glasses complemented his innocuous face. *Loving a man like Robert would be easy,* Kayli thought. *He'd love you back—you'd get married—end of story. Why must I always take the hard route?*

Robert scratched his beard. "You look guilty."

Kayli brushed the flour from her apron. "Why should I?"

He cleared his throat, and Mrs. Heiden stepped into the back room. "I have a date on Saturday."

Robert had a date? Relief flooded Kayli. Robert must finally understand that friendship was all the two of them would ever share. She hoped so; he was far too sweet to hurt.

"That's wonderful, Robert."

"She has a brother. Thought you might be interested in joining us. It might not be so uncomfortable. It's been a long time since I went on a date. I know if you went along, I'd be my charming self."

Kayli groaned. "Oh, Robert, I'm sorry, but I have plans. I've been invited to Mike Williams's new house with the contractor. Can you believe I finally have something to do on Saturday night?"

"The cowboy?"

She nodded.

"Well, this guy is an engineer. He's a solid Christian and taller than you. What more do you need? Surely not some backwoods builder who has nothing in common with you. Cancel your date—it'll go nowhere. Come out with me. I'm a good judge of character for you."

Kayli laughed. "Your engineer sounds great. This isn't really a date on Saturday. I'm going to see the work he's done on the house and maybe get to know Mike Williams more. Maybe if I just talk with Mr. Williams, we can come to some type of agreement on the bakery. He can't want to divide the business either." Kayli wished she could believe the words, but saying them aloud almost made things worse. Robert seemed to realize it immediately.

"I think you're beyond optimistic if you think you can reason with him. He has a reputation in the city, but I understand your need to try. Maybe we could reschedule. The engineer sounded very interested in meeting you."

"Yes, that would be good. Adam will be returning to Montana in about two and a half months. Maybe we could do it then."

"You're not going to put your social life on hold?"

"No, of course I'm not. I thought I'd like to be with him while he's here. It's lonely in the city. Hard to get to know people. I thought I might invite him to the singles' group at church. Does this engineer have a name?"

"John Hanson. He's a nice guy, Kayli."

"Well, tell John for me that I'm sorry I already had plans. It sounds like a wonderful evening out. Where'd you meet John Hanson's sister?"

"At the opera in the park. She was walking her bulldog. It caught my attention. Her brother seems like a real catch, Kayli. Stop chasing after the next Mel Gibson. You don't get married only on feelings."

"Good advice!" Mrs. Heiden called from the back room. "Your pie is burning."

Kayli gasped. "See you, Robert! I have to run." She sprinted to the back ovens and opened to see her pie a perfect golden brown. The pie had bubbled over and spilled onto a protective cookie sheet, filling the room with a luscious caramel aroma. "Perfect."

Mrs. Heiden came behind her. "Yes, it looks fine, but I miss the cow."

"I did these fall leaves instead. Don't you think that's pretty?" Kayli tilted the pie toward Mrs. Heiden and with dread watched as it slowly slid off the cookie sheet. Kayli tried to grip it but screamed at the searing heat. The pie landed with a hot splat, erupting with volcanic force, leaving its golden lava on cabinets and in droplets on their pant legs. Kayli sucked on her finger then placed it in a pat of butter on the counter.

Mrs. Heiden said nothing. She lifted her eyebrows in her familiar way and walked off to clean her slacks. Kayli surveyed the mess, unable to believe she'd destroyed another pie. She reached down to clean the counters but realized the filling was still too hot to clean. Sliding to the floor, she decided to wait beside the mess.

"He's going to think I'm a complete idiot." Her forehead fell into her hands. "Why am I trying to impress this man? He's leaving, he's too good-looking for his own good, and he's building my doom. Could I have worse taste in a man?"

"Kayli, I have seen you talk to yourself more this week than in my entire five years of knowing you. This man is making you crazy. That's the first sign you need to move on. Meet the engineer. He sounds nice. And stable."

"Stable. That's what you want in furniture, Mrs. Heiden. I want something a bit more exciting in a husband." Kayli felt a tear escape down her cheek. She looked at the pie like the remnant of her social life. "Do you really think I'm not capable of meeting a man who sends me soaring? You don't believe there's a soul mate for me? I'm just supposed to settle down with a good selection of sturdy male?"

Mrs. Heiden bent and put an arm around her. "Sure I think someone is out there for you, Sweetheart, but soul mates aren't built on mutual attraction alone. That's all I'm trying to say. I don't want to discourage you, but certainly this pie fiasco is a bad omen."

Kayli began to laugh. "What am I going to tell him?"

"Tell him you have a dynamite tiramisu on special."

After scraping the cupboards clean and scrubbing the tiled floor, Kayli had worked herself into a sweat. She brushed away her damp bangs with the back of her hands and tossed the final rag into the mop sink. The bell jingled again, and Mrs. Heiden harrumphed. It had to be Adam.

Kayli decided against checking her reflection and made her way to the front counter. Her pants were still splattered with apple remains, and she pulled herself up at the shoulders. Adam's eyebrow lifted, and he crossed his arms.

"I'm taking it this means my pie isn't ready."

"It's been postponed." She jutted her chin forward, forcing a confident stance. "There was a little trouble with the oven." *I put an apple pie in it,* she added silently. "I have incredible chocolates available. Why don't you take a truffle or two?"

He shook his head. "I'm not much of a sweet eater anyway. It's just that apple pie brings thoughts of home. I thought it might be nice to try yours."

Yes, wouldn't it, though?

"It's not a big deal, Kayli." Adam shifted uncomfortably. "I'll be going home soon for a visit. I can have one then."

Kayli stamped her foot. "I'm determined to make you an apple pie."

"Even if it blows up your business?"

Kayli squinted. "I have a beautiful apple and peach tart here. It's certainly not me. It's your order that's jinxed."

"You know, there's a Baker's Corner up the street. I can pick up a pie there."

Mrs. Heiden gasped. "You're throwing pearls before swine, Kayli. He isn't good enough for your pie—if he could eat a corporate pie and compare the two."

Kayli looked at her employee, thankful for the offered support. But at the sight of Mrs. Heiden's cuffs filled with apple sludge, the comments did more harm than good. It only brought attention to the fact that Kayli had painted everything a sticky apple brown.

Adam laughed. He tried to cover his mouth, but his shoulders started to shake. He put a palm in the air. "I'm sorry," he said between choking laughter.

"You are taking home chocolate, and I don't care if you're allergic to the stuff. You are going to eat it, praise it, and know I am the finest baker in Palo Alto." She watched him through her narrowed eyes, daring him to continue laughing.

His shoulders soon stilled, and he took out his wallet.

"Put it away. This is on the house. The compliments, however, will cost you. Write them down if you have to."

He shook his head rapidly. "That's okay. I'm sure I'll remember them."

Kayli took out a gold foil and wrapped a slice of tiramisu and one truffle. "There's enough fat in here to keep you going for a week. I expect you to eat both."

"Are we still on for tomorrow night?"

"Absolutely. You owe me, Adam Harper. I have made exact replicas in chocolate of the Eiffel Tower, Mount Rushmore, even the White House. Your pie will not beat me—do you understand?"

"I think so. Am I going to get the red earth of Tara speech now?"

"Adam Harper, you take this chocolate and devour it. Then pick me up tomorrow with compliments at the ready." Kayli raised her eyebrows playfully. "I'll get your pie one of these days."

"I will wait until I go home for Thanksgiving. It's not important."

"Oh, yes, it is. It's very important now that you think I can't do it."

"Andrea couldn't make an apple pie. I almost married her."

"I can make an apple pie, the best pie you ever tasted, in fact. My timing is just off. This has undermined my confidence. But I'll get it back, and you'll be begging me for another slice."

He came around the counter. Mrs. Heiden threw him daggers through her glances, but Kayli noted Adam didn't appear to notice. He placed his solid hand on Kayli's shoulder, and she gulped at his touch.

"I'm terrible with words, Kayli. That's why I work with my hands. I don't care about the pie. I only ordered it so I could see you again."

"But I really can make an incredible pie. I want to prove it to you."

"How about you prove that you're there under all that sticky film? Would you do that for me?" His green gaze upon her caused her heart to stir again. She closed her eyes.

An engineer would be so simple, a man who wanted to settle down, have a dog, maybe a couple of kids. Adam Harper wanted too much: a life in the country, corporate money to build his cabin, and a woman like his own mother. Kayli could fulfill none of that criteria, so why didn't she end this here and now?

"Kayli?" he whispered.

"I'll clean up. We'll enjoy ourselves tomorrow night. I'll get into Mike Williams's command center, and we'll get out for an evening. One night out of our lives—it's a fine deal."

He frowned. "That's not exactly what I meant."

"No, but it's best for both of us." Kayli watched as Mrs. Heiden turned the open sign around in the shop window and locked the deadbolt.

"I suppose you're right about that." Adam looked back to the door, taking his hand from her shoulder. "I'd better go. I'll pick you up tomorrow at six."

Mrs. Heiden stood at the door, a warden in the waiting. Adam strode toward the door, and she unlocked it with a grimace. She closed it again with fervor behind him. "Good riddance to him."

"I think you like him, Mrs. Heiden. You're as taken in by his charms as I am."

"Tsk." She clicked her tongue. "That will be the day. If you go out with him tomorrow night"—she wagged her forefinger—"well, you deserve to fall in love with the likes of him."

Kayli grinned.

Chapter 5

Adam adjusted his tie and buttoned the lower button on his sport coat. Satisfied this was as good as it would get, he started toward his Jeep. He had thought the rugged vehicle would be out of place in high tech Silicon Valley, but plenty of engineers were driving Jeeps and foreign SUVs. Most had leather interiors and never touched a dirt road, however. Adam had seen plenty of mud on his four-wheel drive, and the shredded seats were testament to the fact that his vehicle had visited plenty of job sites in its day. He hoped Kayli wouldn't be embarrassed to show up at Mike Williams's mansion in such a chariot.

Adam sighed thinking about Kayli. Her fresh-looking skin and dark hair mesmerized him. Her dark brown eyes were almost a russet color, big and wide and completely unaware of their effect on him. When he first looked into those eyes, he nearly forgot all his reasons for being in Silicon Valley, casting aside the fact that he would be going home someday soon. The warmth in those eyes arrested his attention and wouldn't let him go. Even though he knew he should before he got in too deep.

He smiled about the pie. He never doubted her abilities, but it touched his heart she couldn't complete the task, which had to be simple to her. For every pie she annihilated, Adam had one more reason to come back to her pleasant European bakery. He would have known Kayli was a believer even without the fish in the shop window. Adam's spiritual gift of discernment told him the Holy Spirit dwelled within that shop. Comfort and a feeling of home emanated from the place, something Mike Williams's monster restaurant would never be able to duplicate.

He drove up to Kayli's apartment. It was obvious which was hers. A small cluster of lights lined the walk, each of them a cappuccino cup holding a tiny bulb. The stone path led to a bright red door with an intricate beveled glass window at the top. He rapped on the door, and Kayli opened it immediately.

Adam felt his jaw drop at the sight of her. He groped for words, trying to take in her beauty, which was so contrary to fashion. Black seemed to be the only color a woman wore out at night in the Bay Area, but Kayli wore a simple linen sheath in bright apple green. It wasn't a color most women could wear, but on Kayli it looked radiant. She would be the envy of every woman in the room, with her slender figure in the simple dress. Neither sequins nor diamonds nor designer labels would equal the picture Kayli created.

"Excuse my stunned silence. You look amazing." He stammered over the words. How many men with fancy words must have told her the same thing? He probably sounded like some backcountry farmer to her. He felt perplexed by her beauty, unable to wrestle his tongue free to say what he thought. He swallowed hard and forced a shaky grin.

She blushed, turning away. "You mustn't spoil me with such sweet words. I may begin to believe them, and then where will you be?"

"I hope you do believe them. I can't be the only man who's ever told you, but I am the most sincere."

She turned her chin upward, gazing at him with a look that nearly stole his breath. "I wish I could believe you, but you have all the charm of William Holden." She fiddled with her hands. "William Holden starred in *Sabrina*. I'm an old movie fan." She cleared her throat. "I'll get my sweater." The closet door swung toward him.

It took all his will not to reach out to her and put her at ease. He planted his feet in the doorway, determined to fight the rising feelings within him. He longed to kiss her, to take her away from California forever, and bring her back to his Montana home. But that was barbaric and ridiculous. He barely knew her, and when she found out his reason for going home, she would disappear like the loose flour in the bakery. Yet he saw them together, watching classic movies and growing old together.

"Are you nervous about seeing Andrea tonight?" she asked.

"No, as a matter of fact, I hadn't thought of it until you brought it up. I loved Andrea once—for all the wrong reasons. The next time I fall in love, it will be for the right reasons."

"Which are?"

"A woman who loves me despite my bank account. A woman who can deal with what I must grapple with in Montana, and one whose beauty lies both inside and out."

"I hope such a woman exists."

"I'm sure she exists. The question is, would she have anything to do with me?" They both laughed.

Kayli came close to him, turning her back to him and handing him her sweater. He felt the electricity from her. It was as if being next to her created its own current. He placed the sweater around her shoulders, leaving his hands there for a moment longer than necessary. Almost unconsciously he embraced her, putting his head beside hers, and whispered in her ear. "I wish I could explain what I feel for you so suddenly, Kayli, but I think that might be hazardous."

He heard her swallow. "We should be going." She walked quickly, her heels clicking on the entryway's tile. She waited for him to exit and locked the door behind them, keeping her gaze from matching his own. Why had he been so forward?

Once in the car, their conversation stalled. Adam didn't know what to say, but he also didn't feel it necessary to speak. Kayli beside him said enough. A short drive deposited them on the tree-lined streets of Los Altos Hills, an elegant enclave of mansions. Each bigger and more elaborate than the one built below it on the hill. Even in the dark night, the city was lit up like a thousand stars.

Driving up the long drive, Adam's stomach churned. Kayli would only realize how different he was from her, how he didn't belong here. He hoped she wouldn't hold it against him—at least not for the evening. He wanted tonight to go perfectly.

The house lay before them like a mighty Mediterranean fortress. A rose pink, it practically glowed in the carefully planned landscaping, even though night had descended. Sixteen million the house cost to build, and not nearly enough of it had gone into Adam's pocket. He felt almost ashamed he'd been part of its construction. Once he thought it would be the flagship of his company, a testament to his building skills. Now it felt like disgusting excess.

"There it is, Silicon Valley's newest tribute to the almighty dollar."

Kayli placed a hand on his. "It's a beautiful house, Adam. You should be very proud of your work."

He didn't feel proud; he felt mortified, but he tried to justify himself. "I'd like you to see the inside. Outside is quite tacky, but not a detail within has been left unturned. I used every bit of experience I'd gleaned to build this house. If you can overlook its size, you'll see it really is very homey—once you get into the actual living area, the parts of the house that aren't for show."

A hired man opened the car door and let Kayli out. Adam pulled the tie loose from his neck and came around to grasp her arm. "You're shaking."

"I'm a bit nervous. I've never been in such a mansion as this, and I'm fearful of meeting Andrea. What will you tell her about me?"

"I'll tell her how fortunate she is to live in such a well-built house and to excuse me for bringing in a woman who will outshine her."

Kayli playfully hit him. "Oh, stop. You will do no such thing."

"I won't, but I should. You'll surpass every woman here in that dress."

"It was twenty-nine dollars at the clearance store," Kayli whispered. "The sweater was free with purchase."

He laughed. "A woman after my own heart. It goes to show you—beauty can't be purchased."

"From the looks of this house, I'd say it can."

"You can't buy taste, Kayli. This house, though big, is tacky. Admit it."

"No."

"You'll admit it when you see the brass and beveled glass elevator inside."

"Tell me you're kidding."

"Apparently carrying the poodle up the stairs got to be too much for them." Adam shrugged, and Kayli giggled. The sound of her laughter carried infectiously into the night air. He couldn't tear his gaze from her, until a familiar voice broke the spell.

"Adam, what a pleasant surprise." Andrea met them in the elaborate foyer and held out her diamond-laced fingers. "Who's this?" Her voice held a tinge of disapproval, but Adam shot her a look of warning.

"Andrea Williams, meet Kayli Johnson. Kayli is a European pastry chef in Palo Alto."

Kayli shook hands with Andrea, gripping the jeweled hand in both of her own. "Your gown is exquisite, Mrs. Williams. I appreciate the honor of being able to see your new home."

"Be sure Adam shows you everything. He's full of surprises."

"Hardly," Adam quipped. "I'm pretty stagnant. You've said so yourself, Andrea."

"I think you're full of surprises, Adam." Kayli's voice told him she believed it with her whole heart.

"Mike is around here somewhere. You wouldn't be the little baker on University Avenue, would you, Kayli?" Andrea craned her neck, searching the small crowd. "My husband says he intends to hire you."

Much to her credit, if Kayli was reacting within, she gave no outward sign. "I think your husband intends to hire everyone at some point, Mrs. Williams." Kayli smiled sweetly. Too sweetly.

"How is Rachel, Adam?" Andrea looked to Kayli and this time got a reaction.

Adam winced at how the words affected Kayli. She questioned him now. Why shouldn't she? He hadn't been exactly forthright. Maybe he was full of surprises.

"Rachel is doing fine. Thank you for asking." Adam placed his palm at the center of Kayli's back, guiding her away from Andrea and her meddling ways.

The strained look in Kayli's expression made him want to spill everything. But what good would that do? In two months' time he would be gone from California for good. This was a date. Nothing more. So why did it feel different? Why was he so drawn to this beautiful pastry chef?

"You have an interesting taste in women," Kayli said from out of nowhere.

Adam laughed. "I suppose you mean because I dated Andrea, but that was a long time ago. I've grown up a lot."

Kayli lifted her eyebrows. "So I see."

They entered the main area of the home. The expanse was incredible, with marble making up nearly every surface. He processed thoughts of how troublesome the heavy material had been to move. All of the furniture had that distressed look, making him feel as if he'd entered an ancient tomb. He should feel proud of his work, but in reality he felt humiliation for building a circus tent.

Well-dressed people milled about, sizing up Kayli and Adam, deciding if they were worthy of a conversation. Most would have probably decided no, but Kayli had an aura about her, a light that shined outward, attracting people easily, especially the single men.

"Hello. Alexander Peyton." A hand was thrust toward Kayli. She grasped the hand and returned the greeting, which technically should have been extended toward Adam, but chivalry was dead in Silicon Valley.

"Hi, I'm Kayli Johnson, and this is Adam Harper. He built this beautiful house."

"It's very nice, and what a coincidence—I did all the art." Alexander nodded toward him. "Adam, would you mind if I showed Kayli my work? I'm so proud of the gallery. Come with me." Alexander Peyton gently guided Adam's date away.

Adam blinked in surprise before noticing Andrea grinning proudly. The tap of her heels echoed on the marble flooring, and the crowds around him felt nonexistent. Like a caged animal he longed to rip off his tie and escape before this hunt continued.

Chapter 6

Alexander Peyton appeared to have little interest in whether Kayli enjoyed art. It didn't take a genius to figure out Alexander's tour had ulterior motives. Andrea Williams had a distinct and current interest in Adam Harper, and Kayli was merely a barrier. The gallery owner, Alexander, represented nothing more than a pawn sent to do Mistress Williams's bidding.

Kayli eyed Adam warily. Was he a part of this? He didn't seem like the type to use a woman, much less carry on some type of affair with a married woman. Whatever secrets Adam held, Kayli couldn't believe they had anything to do with Mrs. Williams. But maybe she was only casting wishes. His handsome features blurred Kayli's reality a bit.

"Have you known Mrs. Williams long?" Kayli asked the hulky gallery owner.

He spoke in a foreign accent Kayli couldn't place. He was incredibly handsome but appeared very aware of that fact with silver blond hair and brilliant, icy blue eyes. While he explained each art selection in the home, his attention seemed to drift continually to his preferred piece: the mirror.

"Mrs. Williams began shopping my store before she had the husband to pay for such works. She has a fantastic eye, and it's only right she should have the money to pay for such beauty. Do you like this one?" He stopped in front of a large painting. "It is my favorite."

Kayli focused on the artwork before her. She cocked her head, trying to make heads or tails of the colors. Surely the artist was trying to say something, but Kayli thought it must be something about misery because that's what she felt staring at it. "I'm not an art critic, but the colors depress me. I studied quite a bit of artwork when I lived in Paris, and I never was too fond of the abstracts. I guess my taste runs to the more simplistic landscapes and portraits."

"All people say that at first. It is not for everyone to understand, but with time and depth, you would understand."

"What should I understand about this piece?" Kayli moved closer to the barrage of color. She eyed it thoughtfully, trying to see the message.

"Besides that it's worth twenty thousand?" he asked with a haughty laugh.

"Yes, besides that," Kayli answered, unimpressed that anyone would waste money on this callous piece of art when they could have fed thousands with the money.

"What do you think the artist was trying to convey?"

"Well, I don't know, Kayli. What does it say to you?"

Kayli crossed her arms and drew in a deep breath. "I find it simplistic and drab. I believe the artist must have been saying he's at a low emotional point in his life, and he needs some spiritual guidance. Perhaps you might lend him a Bible."

The gallery owner exploded into laughter. "And you say you aren't a critic. It goes to show you that everyone's a critic. Mrs. Williams finds this piece contemplative and earnest."

"I think I would be more contemplative about spending twenty thousand dollars on a piece of art. No offense—I realize that's what you do. I hear all the time how ridiculous it is that a truffle should cost two dollars."

Alexander grinned. "I think, my dear Kayli, that this ex-boyfriend of Mrs. Williams has done far better for himself. But you didn't hear that from me. But I do hope to see you in my gallery one day." He excused himself and went to greet more potential buyers.

Kayli turned to see Andrea whispering in Adam's ear. Kayli felt the hair on the back of her neck rise. Whether or not Adam had any interest in Kayli, she wasn't about to sit back and watch him carry on with a married woman. As a Christian she answered to a higher authority. At least that's what she told herself was the reason for interrupting the tête-à-tête.

Marching deliberately toward the cozy couple, Kayli watched Adam straighten and pull away from Andrea. He pulled at his sleeves and jutted his squared jaw toward Kayli. Her resolve weakened a bit watching the action. He was uncomfortable and appeared almost grateful for her presence.

Kayli put a smile on her face. "Mrs. Williams, I've had quite an interesting encounter with your gallery owner. Alexander is a fascinating man and went on about your impeccable taste. I find it very different from mine but can appreciate your theme here." Kayli grasped Adam's arm and tugged him slightly away from Andrea. "Clearly we have the same taste in some things."

Andrea's eyes flashed. "Alexander failed to show you the gallery up on the landing. That is where his work is seen at its finest. Why don't you run along and catch him?"

"While I love the art of an artist, there is no artist like God. Don't you think? The human biceps are a work of magnificence." Kayli ran her fingertips down Adam's arm and casually pulled him away from the married woman. It took willpower to keep from digging her nails into his powerful arm. "Keep walking," she whispered.

Away from the crowd, Adam pulled her into an empty room. He found a light and turned it on to reveal a complete theater with rows of seats and a large screen.

"What was that about?" Adam raised his brows.

"Listen." Kayli felt her hands shaking. "What you do with your time is your business, but if you profess to be a Christian, it's best that you not be seen on the arm of a married woman. It's inappropriate, not to mention that your boss, and her husband, certainly wouldn't appreciate it." Kayli crossed her arms to stop the trembling and flopped into an oversized theater chair. She looked around her and sniffed. The room was almost eggplant in color, a deep purple resembling a big, ugly bruise.

Adam pulled her back to her feet. "Are you accusing me of something, Kayli?"

Kayli felt her eyes fill with tears, and she blinked them away. "I'm just saying if you invite a woman to an event, it's appropriate to stay with her. I believe you cowfolks would say, 'Ya got to dance with the girl that brung ya.'"

Adam's smile made Kayli's tears more insistent. He brushed one away from her cheek. "You're absolutely right," he whispered.

"Don't sweet-talk me, Adam. I'm not a fool. If you brought me here as your cover, I will not play that game."

"Kayli, you've got this wrong."

"I won't be played like a pull toy. Whatever disgusting thing you and Andrea have going, keep me out of it. I may not like Mike Williams, but I wouldn't hurt him this way."

He cupped her face with his roughened hands. "Do you really think that's what I'm doing? Kayli, look at me."

Kayli's shakiness became obvious, and she clenched her jaw, which only caused her teeth to clatter. "I don't know what you're doing, Adam. Unlike you I don't have much experience with dating. I guess in my mind I made you out to be something you're not."

He let out a small laugh. "What is it you think I am?"

"I have no idea." Kayli pulled free and turned away from him. "I thought you were a cowboy out of his element in Silicon Valley, longing for a taste of home, but you seem to work this town just fine. Better than I do, that's for sure."

Adam came behind her, resting his hands on her shoulders. "I am a cowboy. Just longing for an apple pie."

"You seem to know your way around this mansion pretty well."

"Kayli, I built it."

"Well, that's no excuse." Kayli lifted her chin.

He whirled her around. "You're jealous." He forced her gaze to his, and she squeezed her eyes shut, rather than face those gorgeous clear eyes. Eyes that appeared so true and sincere.

"I'm not jealous," she railed. "What do I have to be jealous of? And no offense, but if you're the kind who would carry on an inappropriate friendship with a married woman, well, I wouldn't want you anyway."

"But I'm not the type to do that, and you know it."

She gulped. "No." She shook her head. "No, I don't know it. I wish it, but I don't know it at all."

"Let's get out of here. I'll take you anywhere you want to go, but, Kayli, something is here between us. I can't describe it, but I feel it. When you're next to me—don't get me wrong—it isn't lust; it's this unimaginable feeling that I'm destined to know you. I can feel you next to me."

"So you can leave for Montana and let me battle it out with Mr. and Mrs. Williams and their giant conglomerate bakery?"

"You're avoiding the real subject. You live in one of the most expensive areas in America. You can imagine how everyone wants a piece of the pie, as they say."

"Except these people own the whole pie already, and now they want to dip into a little tiramisu, too."

"Competition breeds better product," Adam said confidently.

"Is that how you justify what your building will do to me?"

"I can introduce you to any of these people here tonight, Kayli. You could make enough on the gallery owner's openings alone. You just have to look for other resources."

"What makes you think I want to? I like my business the way it is. I'm not going to change everything into a catering business to assuage your guilt."

"Kayli, stop it." Adam grasped her shoulders. "I didn't ask you out to assuage my guilt, and I'm not going to leave and forget everything I've done to the city of Palo Alto. I'm certainly not going to forget you. Stop avoiding the real issue. What is it between us?"

Kayli felt the undeniable chemistry between them both. An invisible pull that said everything and nothing at all. "You're attractive," she shrugged. "I find you attractive—that's perfectly understandable. You're a fine-looking man." Kayli rambled in her most unaffected voice—when in reality she wanted to explore why she originally thought this man might be her soul mate.

Adam bit his lip, clearly fighting his mirth. "Why were you jealous of Andrea?"

"Because I'm not fond of a man who invites me somewhere and pawns me off on a gallery owner—who is quite handsome, by the way. What if I went off with him and left you alone at this soiree?"

Adam clicked his tongue. "You're absolutely right, and that would prove my country roots. An educated man would never leave the most beautiful woman in the room for an unavailable tyrant of a woman. Just wouldn't happen." Adam shook his head.

Despite herself, Kayli smiled. Squaring her shoulders, she added, "What if I get to know you, like what I see, and you fly back to Montana without looking back?

Love is a decision—haven't you heard that?"

"Then you leave me no choice, Kayli."

Adam approached her, and she felt her heart pound. This kind of attraction wasn't healthy. Maybe she needed to go home and call Robert, retreat to the safety of a friendship and the calm life she knew. She couldn't take this kind of attraction forever; it couldn't be good for her heart. Adam bent as though he might kiss her, and Kayli closed her eyes waiting for his lips to mesh with her own.

"Well, there you are." Andrea's firm voice invaded Kayli's dream, and Adam pulled away.

"You have the most impeccable timing, Andrea."

"Countless remodels are out there waiting to speak to you, Adam."

"Let them wait, Andrea. I'm not taking on any additional jobs, so I appreciate the thought, but—"

"Rachel awaits," Andrea added.

"Among other things."

Kayli felt breathless, torn between her emotions for the man she wanted to trust and driven by fears of who he might actually be.

Chapter 7

The party continued well into the night, but it ceased to be fun at the return of Andrea. To his credit, Adam stole Kayli away immediately, escorting her to his Jeep without an explanation.

"Come to dinner with me tomorrow night." Adam's voice broke the darkness of the car.

"No," Kayli forced herself to say. "I know what I feel, but I also know what I think. I can't throw my brain out the window. That's how women end up married to men who don't keep promises. They believe them when they know they shouldn't. Well, not me. I listen to my instincts."

"Let me tell you about Rachel. I don't want you to question my motives."

Kayli grabbed his hand on the stick shift. "No. Don't tell me a thing. It's better that I just remain ignorant; then I can go on about my life remembering you only as the man who helped Mike Williams seal my fate. This long evening will fade into a distant memory."

She recoiled at the sight of his sad eyes under the map light. "Is that what you want?" His low voice resonated, and she felt the vibrations in her chest.

"Absolutely," Kayli said before truly answering the question in her heart. It wasn't what she wanted at all. But how did she tell this man she barely knew that his absence would hurt her. That his allegiance to Andrea Williams and an unknown woman named Rachel sent an ache through her soul. How sane was that?

"Fine. I don't need a two-by-four through the head. Consider yourself left alone, Garbo. But it's not my choice, Kayli. It will be solely yours." Adam pulled up to the side of the road, and the little cappuccino lights suddenly looked ridiculous to Kayli. She took no pleasure in her quaint decorations. They made her look that much more naive.

She sat frozen, knowing she must move. *Get out of the car,* her brain said, but her heart feared reaching for the door. Walking out of Adam's life forever was a big step, and she wasn't sure she was ready for it. *No, I must stick to my resolve.*

"Is something the matter, Kayli?"

"No," Kayli said too quickly. "I'm leaving." She shivered. "It's a little chilly tonight."

"It's seventy-four degrees."

She shrugged. "Must be the dress."

"It certainly does give one chills." He focused out the window as he said it. His structured profile was outlined, illuminated by the street light. The portrait, so like a great piece of Roman art, sent another flutter through her stomach. He turned to face her, and even in the darkness she could see the intensity of his eyes. Those eyes. "You can run, Kayli, but if you don't see this through, you'll never know."

Oddly she didn't need to ask what he meant. She knew. It was the crazy soul mate thing again. Is this what the Lord had for her? All these wild butterflies in her stomach and searing looks from a handsome stranger? It's what she wanted. She'd always said it. Since she was a little girl, she wanted a man to love her with a fiery intensity. Like Christ loved His Church. The older she became, the more outlandish such a prayer seemed. Yet Adam seemed to be asking her about that very subject. Dare she ignore it when she longed for the answer?

"I'll make you dinner tomorrow night. Complete with an apple pie," she blurted out.

He smiled, letting out a long breath. "Thank you. I'll bring a Bible and lead a devotional after supper. It will keep us out of trouble."

"I would like that. Why don't we see a movie afterward, so we don't get too comfortable?"

"Perfect." Adam brushed the back of his hand along her cheek. "May I kiss you good night, Kayli?"

She nodded. He came closer, and she felt his breath upon her cheek. He brushed his firm lips against hers, and it seemed over before it began. He stepped out of the car and walked her to the doorway.

"Pray about it, Kayli. I don't understand it either."

"I will." She opened the door and closed it quickly behind her. "What am I doing, Lord? He's going to leave for Montana." She dropped her head against the door. "I know I always said I wanted this passionate, immediate kind of romance, but now I'm not so sure, Lord. Now it just feels dangerous."

The phone rang, interrupting her heartfelt prayer. "Hello?"

"Kayli, it's Robert. How was your date?"

"Different. How about yours?"

"Weird. She didn't talk much. I'm not used to being the one who talks."

"That's because you are usually with me, and I have an opinion on everything," Kayli admitted.

"Very true."

"Are you going out with her again?"

"Yes, sometimes things get off to a slow start. I prayed about it, and she has a solid faith, a good family. I think it's worth pursuing."

"Do you think it can start out fast?"

Robert groaned. "What do you mean, Kayli?"

"I mean, what if you were thrown into this short amount of time, and you felt this urgency to get to know someone."

"God doesn't work on a time line. It sounds dangerous."

"It feels dangerous, Robert."

"Then get out."

"It feels dangerous, but it feels right. We're both committed to purity. That's not the issue. My fear is that I'm ready to fly off with a man I hardly know and live amidst the cows. What's wrong with me?"

"Desperation maybe. Your business is in trouble, and it's been a long time since you've seen anyone seriously. Maybe you're not thinking clearly."

"What about arranged marriages? Sometimes brides and grooms never even see each other before the wedding."

"What on earth are you talking about, Kayli? It was just a date. One evening out and a few weeks of your trying to out-bake his mother. I think rambling about marriage is a little frightening. Our pastor says you should know someone at least a year before you contemplate marriage."

"You're right. You're totally right. And besides, no one is asking me to marry him. For all I know, he's got a couple of ex-wives and eight kids. I'm not thinking clearly."

"Right."

"Coffee after church tomorrow?"

"Sure, at our regular place." Robert clicked the phone, and Kayli breathed a sigh of relief at the steadiness of her friend. Of course she was imagining things. It was desperation over her business, nothing more. It had been a long time since she'd had a date. It felt good to be thought of as beautiful. That was it: flattery.

Adam pulled up into his driveway, confused and a bit numb. He felt as though he'd met his wife. He knew it in his heart. Yet how could he explain this fact to a complete stranger? *Hi, God sent me to California to find you. Now please come back to my little cabin in the wilderness and live in a place where they've never even heard of tiramisu.*

He laughed at the thought. He needed to tell Kayli about Rachel. That would seal it. Kayli would run for protection, and he would know how ridiculous these thoughts of marriage were. He wasn't the marrying kind. Hadn't his solitary life taught him that? Andrea said he would never learn to be a partner to anyone. He thought too much of himself. That was probably true, but then again, Andrea wasn't exactly a great judge of character.

His eyes narrowed in disbelief. Andrea stood on his front porch. Her long, violet gown sparkling under the porch light. He sighed and stood tall. This was going to end. "What are you doing here, Andrea?"

"I see you didn't bring your date home. I knew you wouldn't. Still living the monk's life, Adam?"

"What do you want?" He unlocked the front door and walked past her. She followed him in.

"I think you know what I want."

"Is this a joke? You didn't want me when I didn't have the money to pay for your lifestyle."

"Don't be ridiculous. You dropped me, and you know it."

"Lot of good it did me. Look—it's inappropriate for you to be here." Adam remained cool, but his heart pounded. He and Andrea had never had more than a casual friendship with a slight crush. She made it sound like something vulgar and obviously remembered scenes that had never taken place. Living with Mike Williams had changed Andrea, and it wasn't for the best.

"Inappropriate. That's what you said when I tried to talk to you at the party."

"And it was inappropriate then. I fail to see how meeting me alone at my apartment would be any more suitable. You're a married woman, Andrea. Act like it."

"I'm not going to make a bigger fool out of myself, Adam. I came here because I want to know how much it hurt you when I left. I want to hear how you cried when I married Mike. You give me that, and I'll let this go. But if you continue to pretend I was never the one, I won't let it die. I'll let Mike know exactly what we were to each other. What we are to each other."

"What are you talking about?" Now he truly questioned her sanity. Before she seemed bitter and unrepentant toward her husband, but now she seemed incapable of living in reality.

"He's worth more to me divorced than married. That house alone could pay for my lifestyle for an eternity, and I wouldn't have to put up with the slobbering idiot."

"Andrea! Don't say such a vile thought out loud. I haven't been paid for this job yet, and I won't let you imply there's anything between us."

"Why? Because Rachel might find out you were less than a Boy Scout?"

"Because it isn't true. You would let Rachel suffer for your own ego?"

"Tell me how I was the one for you, Adam," she cooed.

He felt his cheek flinch. His mouth would never form such words. But thinking what it might cost Rachel back home in Montana, he swallowed roughly, trying to rid his throat of the terrible lump. "Why would you want me to say that? You belong to another man—that's how God ordained it."

"That's how I ordained it, Adam. I gave up true love for money. You might have thought that was a mistake, but now I can have both. I know you've thought about it. All you have to do is tell me, Adam. Did you think I brought you to California for my health?"

He stared at Andrea with a man's eyes. She was beautiful on the outside, the peak of fitness with elegant, luminous skin, but inside her heart was dead. Frosted over by years of ignoring God's call and neglect by a husband who bought her affections, but now cared little for what she did. Adam tried to keep the contempt from his face and see her as the pathetic figure she was. Cheated on by Mike Williams, who apparently thought she was nothing more than a possession. She was ripe for vengeance. Adam seemed to hold the key to her retaliation.

"I think you brought me to California on a lie. What we had was a long time ago, Andrea. It was special when we were younger, but that was a lifetime ago. You don't really love me. I'm a builder. I will always be a builder. I know you don't respect that."

"But it doesn't matter now, Adam. I have enough money for both of us."

He reached for her hand. "If you think I ever cared about money, you never really knew me."

"I know you need the money now. I know Rachel needs it, and if you want payment from Mike, you'll do what's right."

"No." Adam shook his head. "I would never do what you consider right. I love Kayli."

She cackled. "You can't possibly love Kayli. You've been on what, one date?"

"I don't expect you to understand it. I don't understand it."

She placed a key in his hand. "The guesthouse. Make your choice, Adam. You've got until Tuesday."

Chapter 8

Adam watched Andrea drive away in a black Mercedes. He knelt and prayed vigorously for her. They had been childhood friends, high school crushes, and that's where it should have ended. His ignorance showed in coming to California. He should have known God wouldn't have appreciated the easy route. The fast buck. He would pay for his mistake now. Worse yet, so would Rachel.

Andrea's threat was useless and without merit. Mike Williams was no fool. He would pay up on his contracts or face court. Adam would get his money—eventually. The question was, how long would it take? A scorned husband could make it harder than Adam had time for. He couldn't afford a battle or his boss thinking he'd had anything to do with Andrea's schemes. He prayed over the matter and called Kayli. He wanted to hear her voice. To know all women weren't capable of such lying and wicked games, that a woman out there still enjoyed the simple things in life. One who took joy in decorating the front walk or placed a tiny cow of dough on an apple pie.

The phone rang twice, and Adam breathed a sigh of relief when Kayli's voice sounded alert. "I didn't wake you?" he asked.

He heard the smile in her voice. "No, you didn't wake me. I was reading a novel. How are you doing? You don't sound so good."

"Andrea was here."

"Andrea—was at your house?" Kayli stammered, and Adam felt the heat flare into his face.

He shouldn't have told Kayli. She'd think he had something to do with it, but the alternative was worse.

"She's really a hurting soul." Adam sounded as though he were justifying Andrea's behavior, and he quickly recanted. "I would feel sorry for her if I didn't fear what she might do."

"You should fear what she might do, Adam. Women don't find their way into Mike Williams's heart without a plan. And they don't find their way out without a better one."

Adam scratched his head. "You couldn't have discerned all that from five minutes of meeting the woman."

"Adam, you must be kidding. We women see so much you men don't. First off, women committed to their husbands don't find a way to be alone with another man at a party. Second, a woman of Andrea's means should have nothing to fear in the likes of me. Andrea has a distinct plan, Adam, and you'd be smart to get out of the way if you value your reputation."

His stomach turned. "Are you saying you think it's time for me to leave?"

"No, I don't want you to leave." She let out a breath. "I want you to stay and tell me more of the beautiful rivers running through Montana. I want to hear about the trains to the old mining camps and exploring the ghost towns."

"How much time do you have?" He heard a thump.

"My book just got boring."

They talked of childhoods and dreams and shared hopes until Adam made the mistake of returning to a hard subject.

"Listen, about Andrea."

"I don't care about her, Adam."

"But you need to know. She's up to no good, and I don't want you to believe her." He didn't add that Andrea planned to thwart his payment unless he cooperated. Kayli wouldn't have believed any woman capable of that.

"Adam, one thing I've learned about you in these two weeks. You are not a man who takes the easy route. You have yet to see an apple pie, but you keep showing up, somehow believing one day it's going to be there. "

"It will be. I'm certain of that because I believe in you, Kayli."

"You'd be smarter to believe in God and let Him handle the rest." Her tone had a chill in it, and Adam started.

"What?" Adam looked into the phone, unsure of what Kayli was trying to say.

"You're leaving, Adam. I've got you what, two months, tops? I feel as if for once in my life, I have someone whose opinion I really value. Someone who makes me feel like a princess. Let me live in my little world. Don't remind me you're leaving. Don't remind me a woman named Rachel is waiting back home."

"Rachel is—"

"No," she said, stopping him. "Don't tell me. I told you I want to live in my little world. In two months I'll go back to being Kayli Johnson, struggling pastry chef. Today I want to be Kayli Johnson, princess, or none of this is worth it. I want to be the woman who arrives on the arm of Adam Harper, rugged builder and envy of Mike Williams. A modern-day prom queen."

He felt stunned and tense. What was Kayli telling him? Why did she want him to play this charade? He didn't toy with women's hearts. He was steadfast and true. Yet he looked at the trail of women around him: Rachel, Andrea, and now Kayli. What did it matter if he saw himself as steadfast when others saw him as divided and noncommittal?

"I can't join you for dinner tomorrow night, Kayli." *I'm not worthy.*

He thought he heard a small whimper, but her resonant voice came back to him. "It's just as well." A light click followed.

Kayli arrived at the coffee shop after church. Robert wasn't there yet, so she ordered a nonfat double mocha, anxious to thwart the pounding headache she attributed to caffeine withdrawal and a long night on the telephone.

She wouldn't give Adam Harper the benefit of knowing it was he who caused her pain. Why would she get involved with a man like him anyway? She'd only listened to that chemical fusion between them, their shared hopes for three children and a mom who stayed home. She hadn't given any credence to the facts. She was sure she'd heard God's voice and that He'd been in favor of the courtship; yet she supposed today was proof He wasn't.

"Hey!" Robert waved at her, bringing in another woman. Another era ended. Their Sunday mornings at the coffee shop had been sacred, a time to regroup, and Robert had never allowed someone else to invade their time.

"Hi!" Kayli forced a chipper tone. "Who's this?"

Robert's eyes reprimanded her, forcing her to be polite. "This is Joanie Hanson."

Kayli tried to smile. Joanie was entirely too bouncy for someone who hadn't had coffee yet. "Nice to meet you, Kayli. I understand you and Robert have been friends a long time."

"We have," Kayli said flatly. "But apparently not long enough." She flashed her eyes, and he pulled her by the waist.

"We'll just order coffee, Joanie. Why don't you save our table? Latte?" The redhead nodded. "Great." He drew Kayli into line and stood behind her. "So you want to tell me why you can't be decent to my friend?"

"Robert, this is our time. What's she doing here?"

"I saw her at church after our date last night, and she asked to come along. You can't have your way forever, Kayli. You made your choice about me a long time ago."

"What does that have to do with our friendship?"

"It has everything to do with it. I'm not going to turn down the opportunity for a girlfriend and possibly a spouse in order to be at your beck and call anymore. Your heart was apparently stolen overnight, so you'd best not chastise me."

Shame washed over Kayli like extra foam through a latte. The reason she understood Andrea's actions had nothing to do with being a woman. It was being a woman like her.

"My heart was not stolen." Kayli crossed her arms. "It was temporarily misguided."

"Things are working out with Joanie and me. Why can't you deal with that?" The cut in Robert's words hurt her. Was she so selfish as to deny her best friend a woman of his own? Simply because no man wanted her?

"I suppose I have to." Kayli's coffee came up, and she reached for it. "Tell Joanie I said good-bye. No sense being a third wheel." She turned, making her way through the tables of countless people reading the Sunday paper. She heard Robert call after her, but she ignored him. She offered a phony smile and a wave to the sweet little redhead who'd captured Robert's attention and made her way out the door through the sidewalk tables.

She stopped where she was. That's it! As owner of a local small business, she could get Robert to approve sidewalk tables and café rights before Mike Williams opened his business. The city wouldn't allow two such businesses within a block of one another. Kayli dashed home, determined to beat Mike Williams to the punch and force thoughts away of a dashing builder who made her feel like abandoning thoughts of the future as she knew it: as a successful business owner.

A wife and mother, she sniffed as she walked home balancing her coffee. *I'm not meant for that lifestyle. I'm meant for a higher calling—destined to bring European delicacies to the American masses.* She smiled to herself. That had to be it. That's why the Lord had allowed all of this to happen. Kayli was allowed to feel like putty in Adam Harper's arms so she could know that was a mere whim and wasn't supposed to be her destiny.

She rushed home to make an apple pie. She needed to purge her system of all thoughts and dreams of Adam Harper. Finishing her assignment was a necessary part of flushing him from her mind for good, but not before he knew what he'd be missing.

Chapter 9

Sunday afternoon smelled of cinnamon and warm apples, all the comfort of a familiar quilt. Such a homey scent. Kayli wished it felt that way. The air only reminded her that apple pie was Adam Harper's favorite. He didn't care for her white chocolate truffle or elegant apricot tarts. He enjoyed the simple things in life. Kayli enjoyed the extravagance of life: the different and unique. But would she ever feel the same about excess when Adam enjoyed apple pie in Montana?

Fresh, warm apple pie reminded Kayli of her own mother and their afternoons spent baking. Hot, stinging tears sprang to life. She instantly understood her disdain for apple pie and the reason her bakery had never created one. Some memories were too painful. Her mother had died young and with her, those cozy afternoons. Adam Harper seemed to bring all that emotion bubbling to the surface.

She let the pie cool a bit and placed the disposable pie tin in a custom-made basket. Looking a bit too much like Little Red Riding Hood, Kayli set the pie on her front seat and placed some books around it to prevent its shuffling. Then she squared her shoulders and started her car. She took out Adam's business card and noted the scribbled address on the back. She was on a mission. Adam was about to learn that even the simple things in life could take on an added dimension with Kayli at the helm.

Kayli studied the address on the card then the boxy units in front of her. Adam lived in an old yet desirable part of town. His apartment was on the first floor of a tired-looking building with perfectly manicured lawns. Enough upkeep and neighborhood to keep his rent high, she supposed.

She knocked on the door, not expecting him to be home on such a bright and sunny afternoon, but he answered swiftly. "Kayli." She couldn't tell if he was happy to see her or not, but it didn't matter. This was the end.

"I brought you your pie." She pulled out the tin with a towel. "It's still warm so be careful. You can keep the towel." Turning to leave, she felt him grasp her forearm with his free hand.

"I don't want the towel."

She faced him. "Fine. I'll take it." She reached for the towel, but he wouldn't relinquish it from his grip.

"I have to go back to Montana." His voice held no inflection. "It's Rachel."

The game stopped. "You're leaving? You said two months."

"What does it matter? I take it this is my good-bye gift regardless of what state I'll be in." He raked his hand through his hair, his glass-green eyes fighting back emotion. It broke her heart to watch this steely man lose his normally unnerved stature. His tie from church draped near the phone carelessly, his face blanched. Kayli now understood the freshness of his pain.

"Adam, what's happened?"

"My mother took a turn for the worse."

"Your mother?"

"Rachel. She's the woman who married my father when my mother walked out on us. Technically she's my stepmother, but in my heart she's the only mother I ever had."

"Rachel's your mother?" Kayli's relief could not have gone unnoticed. She nearly cried from the joy that permeated her heart. Perhaps she wasn't there to say good-bye after all.

Adam continued, "She would never take the name of Mother from me. She hoped my mom would return to me someday. She kept that hope alive in me, though I know now she's my mother. She's in a rest home in Montana." He dropped his head. "I knew I should have taken care of her. I should never have left, but I couldn't make any money to care for us, Kayli. I had to work. The rest home costs are tremendous."

Kayli searched for words. He'd done so much. Didn't he understand that? She didn't have to know the details to know he'd done everything he could. She reached for him and pulled him into an embrace. "It will be okay," she heard herself say. "Mike Williams won't withhold payment when he knows the circumstances." But even Kayli didn't believe that.

Adam shook his head. "I didn't listen to my conscience once. I won't ignore it now." He stood tall, gazing at her with a look that said more than words ever could. He squinted, the worn lines from his constant smile reminding her of his capacity for joy. How did she know what this man meant with only his eyes?

"Yes, you need to go." What was she saying? She didn't want him to go. Her business, her condominium, her bills, her future—suddenly none of it seemed important. None of those things made her feel the way Adam did.

He shrugged. "Tom can take over for me until I get back. I have to pray for the best." He stooped and kissed her cheek, then found her lips and pressed his firmly to hers. Nothing prepared her for what coursed through her body. This was it. She'd never hesitated before when she knew what she wanted. No man would ever make her feel this way. Of that she was certain. Her soul mate did indeed exist, and she felt numb thinking he might walk out of her life forever. She couldn't let that happen.

"Are you coming back?" She clutched his forearm, as if to force him to stay.

A black luxury car rolled into the apartment drive, and Kayli separated from Adam immediately. Andrea Williams got out of the vehicle, dripping with platinum baubles and wearing an orange silk pantsuit. Kayli swallowed hard, stepping in front of Adam protectively. This might be her last moments with Adam, the only opportunity she would have to tell him to return to her, and Andrea was stealing what belonged to her. This precious time.

"What do you want?" Kayli asked rudely.

Andrea lifted an eyebrow. "Since I'm not at your house, suffice it to say, I don't want anything from you. It's my employee I wish to speak with."

"Andrea, go home," Adam said.

Shock registered on Andrea's face. "Adam, we have business to discuss, and it won't wait until Tuesday."

"We have nothing to discuss. I work for your husband. If he has something to say, tell him to call me in Montana."

"Montana? You can't leave for Montana! You have a restaurant to finish."

"I have other, more pressing responsibilities."

"Adam," she said in a low, threatening tone, "you don't want to do this to me."

Kayli lost the momentum to breathe. "What do you mean, Andrea? What do you think is between the two of you?" An uneasy swirl started in Kayli's stomach and moved to her throat, stifling any further words.

"I'm the one who got away—isn't that right, Andrea?" He sniffed. "The one who didn't wither under her seductive glance. She doesn't want me. She only wants to feed her ego, to know I'm still hovering about, wishing I could have her." Adam tossed his head.

Andrea's eyes widened, as if she didn't know what Adam might be talking about. "That's not it, and you know it."

"Well, Andrea, I don't wish it. As a matter of fact, I count my blessings every day that the Lord saved me from you. I'm a man who knows what he wants, and I knew a long time ago that I didn't want you." Adam flinched, as though such ugly words pained him, but he obviously felt the cost necessary.

Kayli swallowed hard, wishing there was something she could say, support she could offer.

Andrea looked to Adam venomously. "You needn't bother coming back to California, Adam. If you leave for Montana, Mike will never take you back. It's obvious he can't trust you."

Adam crossed his arms in front of him. "With all you've seen Rachel go through, you would let her be thrown out into the street to satisfy your own vengeance? I can't believe it, even of you, Andrea."

"Rachel told me I'd never amount to anything, and I find it interesting that I should be ultimately responsible for her fate." A low cackle escaped, but it didn't sound as though Andrea took any pleasure in it. A short sob could be heard soon after, and Andrea's cold expression mingled with pain.

"Don't do this, Andrea. It's been over for a long time, and you know that. I love Kayli, and whether you admit it or not, you love Mike."

The fire returned. "You can't possibly love her. You don't know a thing about her."

"I know I've been given a message about her, that she loves the Lord and is committed to the sanctity of marriage."

"Five years of my life I devoted to you, waiting for you to ask me to be your wife."

Adam visibly swallowed. "That was wrong. I was wrong. I knew when we wrote to each other in college. A man knows, and I was too weak to say good-bye. I hope someday you'll forgive me, that you and Mike will work things out." He grabbed her hand, and Kayli wished she could crawl under a nearby rock rather than witness Andrea's soul-piercing cry. Adam's words threw Kayli's heart into turmoil as well. Yes, she loved him, too, as ridiculous as it sounded. But would he play her for years on end as he'd done with Andrea? She shivered.

"You would commit to this woman after knowing her two weeks?"

Kayli's heart pounded waiting for his answer. Was he committing?

"It's not knowing her for two weeks; it's what I know about her." Adam rested his gaze on Kayli. "She loves the Lord, she's committed to Him, and everything she does rises out of that. I know. I have a leading, and I know." They shared a look, and Kayli knew she would never forget that intensity. Whatever happened in her lifetime, another man would never look on her with such overwhelming devotion.

Andrea laughed derisively. "Do you expect her to live in the sticks with you, Adam? She lives in one of the most cosmopolitan areas in the world. Does she love you enough to live in a log cabin near Glacier? Where the clothes come only in flannel?" Another evil laugh followed. "You're dumber than I thought."

Kayli thought about all the luxuries of life: her little convertible, her carefully decorated condominium, her taste for espresso met on every street corner. How would she survive in some little backwoods town with a man she barely knew? She needed to pray, to get away from this and the emotion. Her entire future hung in the balance.

"I need to go home." Kayli gathered her basket and darted for the car. She didn't look back, fearing where it might lead. If she looked into those green eyes again, she would throw out reason, casting away her doubts. Doubts were important; they protected a person. Look at Andrea. She hadn't listened to her doubts, and now she was desperately pursuing another man after her marriage. That was exactly the kind of crazy thing a heavenly man like Adam caused one to do.

"This is all too complicated. I'm a pastry chef, nothing more. Why did I think that some handsome prince was going to sweep me off my feet? I have more smarts than that." The car wanted to steer itself back to Adam's, but she forced the wheel to her condo. This was a time for prayer. Deep and strenuous prayer.

The next day, work pacified Kayli, tearing her mind from the reality that Adam might be gone for good and why she should care. He was a stranger. Nothing more.

Mrs. Heiden remained quiet in her comments. So quiet it unnerved Kayli.

"You might as well say what you're thinking, Mrs. Heiden. He's gone now. Your opinions were apparently right."

"He'll be back."

"What do you mean?" Kayli stopped brushing her pastry and focused on the older woman.

"A man doesn't look at a woman as Adam looked at you and forget it. He knows."

"He knows what?"

The elder woman busied her hands with a wet rag. "My husband used to say that a man knows when he meets his wife. All the rest is merely formality."

"Mrs. Heiden, I can't believe you would believe in such a romantic notion. It's preposterous."

"Maybe, but I can only go on what my husband said, and I think Adam is the same kind of take-charge man. He saw what he wanted. I'm certain of that."

"So if that's true, where is he?"

"Preparing for marriage."

Kayli laughed out loud. "You're right. I suppose he's ordering his tux as we speak."

"That's not what I mean. I mean he's taking care of business, so he can focus on caring for a wife. Open your eyes, Kayli."

"His married ex-girlfriend is still after him, pursuing him with a vengeance. You don't see a problem there?" Kayli asked.

"Only for her."

"I can't believe you're saying all this, Mrs. Heiden. You're usually so practical. Where did that common sense of yours go? And I thought you said he was too good-looking for his own good."

Mrs. Heiden sat down at a small table near the front of the store and stared out the window. "I had forty-three years with my husband, Kayli. It wasn't long enough. I don't want to see you waste your time. If you seek the Lord in this, you'll know you knew from the first day that this is who you wanted."

"Wanting something doesn't make it the right thing." Kayli was arguing for argument's sake.

"True enough, but ask your heart, Kayli."

The shrill tone of the phone reached her, tearing such thoughts from her mind. Adam's warm, familiar voice met hers.

"I miss you," he growled.

"When are you coming back?" Kayli asked unwillingly, afraid of the answer.

"Rachel went home to the Lord, Kayli." Her heart clenched at the sorrow she heard in his voice.

"Oh, Adam, I'm so sorry!" Kayli wished she could embrace him and soothe his pain away, but his distance felt like a world between them.

"God was gracious. I got to see her, to tell her what she meant to me, how much I loved her. She would have loved you, Kayli." He sighed and lowered his voice. "I told her all about you, and she smiled through the whole description, nodding her head."

"It's a compliment that you think she'd like me." Her comment sounded so vacant. She longed to let him know she'd been praying, that she cared, but she came off as austere and disconnected. "What's next for you?"

"I'm coming back to California. We'll decide then."

"Decide?" Kayli choked, her heart throbbing at the possibilities.

"On marriage. I've wasted enough time in my life. You're welcome to say no or wait or whatever you feel, but I'm certain of this, Kayli. I'm coming home to marry you if you'll have me. Rachel told me to act if I was sure. I'm sure."

"Home is where?"

"California. There's nothing to keep me here now. Only bitter memories and a real mother who never loved me. Maybe someday I'll have the strength to tackle that problem, but not yet."

"I'll be waiting," Kayli whispered through stiff lips, afraid to hope he meant what he said.

"I know you're thinking this isn't the best time, and I've been through a trauma, but I know, Kayli. I'll be there in a week, and we'll make plans. I'll call you tonight."

"Adam?"

"Yeah?"

"Are you sure?"

"I've never been more certain about anything. I love you, Kayli Johnson. Become Mrs. Harper and make me the happiest man alive."

Her eyes filled with tears. "You'll have to ask me in person if you're serious."

"Until tonight." He clicked the phone, and Kayli sobbed from pure emotion, leaning her face against the door post and mourning a woman she never met. A woman who shared her love of Adam. Mrs. Heiden surrounded her with a comforting arm.

"I remember it well, Kayli." Mrs. Heiden's own eyes filled with tears. "There is no rational explanation for such a bond."

The two women laughed together. Kayli wondered at what her future would hold but no longer feared it.

Chapter 10

Adam took a deep breath. Flying over the golden hills of California, along the deep blue ocean, brought a renewed peace to him. No, the landscape wasn't nearly as dramatic as his beloved Glacier, but the Golden State was now his home. He'd tossed phone cards out like they were scrap metal from a wrecking yard, but in return he'd learned Kayli was a mystery he would continue to discover in their life together. His first inclination was correct: Kayli's dreams and aspirations matched his own. Whatever path they took, they'd take it together.

Landing smoothly at San Jose International Airport, Adam stepped onto the tarmac, breathing in the cool Bay Area air. Then he saw her. Kayli's deep brown hair flowed in the afternoon breeze, her soft highlights echoing the sun's rays. She waved, her smile growing larger, and his stomach lurched.

He breathed in deeply, but he halted at the sight of Andrea standing beside Kayli. Andrea crossed her arms, anticipating his arrival with seemingly precise motives. Free of carry-on luggage, Adam quickened his pace, meeting Kayli's rustic brown eyes with joy. Momentarily the world around them disappeared, and he pulled her into his arms. The scent of her hair, a mixture of coconut and suntan oil, forced a grin. He was home.

"I missed you," he whispered the words into her hair, lacing his fingers through the soft mesh of tendrils. "But I'm free, Kayli. I wish Rachel was here to meet you, but I know she's smiling on us. She had a solid faith and taught me to love God in the darkest of circumstances." He looked at his feet for a moment. "If I didn't know better, I'd say she released herself so I could go on with my life. She was that type of woman."

"She must have been if she raised you."

"How's business?" Adam asked avoiding Andrea's gaze and crossed arms.

"It's okay. I have more business now that I'm putting the tables out, but I fear Mike Williams's Sunday hours are going to hurt me. I won't do that, though it costs me big financially." She waved a hand in the air. "It's not important. God will provide. If Rachel believed that, I have to as well."

To her credit, Andrea let them have their moment together before she approached. "Quite a cozy greeting. It makes me all tingly inside." Andrea let her eyes roll back in her head to show her sarcasm.

"I heard the restaurant is coming along nicely. Mike sounded pleased when I talked to him on the phone." Adam smiled.

"I'll leave you alone, Adam, but I need one last favor."

His grin died. What would Andrea say in front of Kayli? He uttered a silent prayer, hoping for the best. "I'm fresh out of favors, Andrea."

"Please. I thought about what you said. I do love Mike, as much as it pains me to say so. I want to be his wife. But I want him to want me as well. I thought maybe if I had another man's attention, I'd get his."

Adam placed his arm around Kayli's waist, pulling her closer. "I want the same thing for you, Andrea, but you're going about it wrong."

"I've made a fool of myself, and we're going to counseling. I came to meet you to ask you not to tell him about the pass I made at you. We have enough to work on for the time being."

Adam looked down at Kayli, grateful they shared a faith in God and a higher calling than simply a secular marriage certificate. "As long as you keep working, my tongue will remain stilled."

"Thank you." She nodded at the two of them. "Sorry to interrupt your time, Kayli. You two are a striking couple." A tear escaped Andrea's eyes, but she turned away quickly.

Adam searched Kayli's expression, and they seemed to share a desire to let the conversation drop.

"So what have I missed?" Adam asked.

"Well, Robert is still dating that woman, and she actually went to the *Star Trek* convention with him! He thinks I'm crazy for falling for you over the phone, but I know better."

"He's not familiar with my irresistible voice apparently."

"Apparently."

They walked arm in arm into the airport, retrieved Adam's small suitcase, and stepped into her waiting car in the nearby lot. "May I drive?"

"Certainly," Kayli answered.

Adam drove through all the high tech buildings and passed the concert amphitheater, before arriving at the golf course on the San Francisco Bay shoreline. Pulling into a parking spot, they parked before the small lake with several brightly colored sailboards gliding in the wind. He watched Kayli smile and went around the car to help her out. The soothing sound of pure silence permeated the afternoon breeze. The caw of a seagull broke the stillness every few minutes, but otherwise they were completely alone.

He sat Kayli on a bench and knelt before her. "This is crazy. I'm sure you think I'm crazy, but I love you, Kayli Johnson, and, come what may, I'm committed to you. Employed, unemployed, California, or Montana, one thing will remain constant, and that's my love for you."

Kayli smiled, nibbling on her lip nervously. He touched her cheek and pulled out the red-velvet box. It opened with a squeak, and he watched Kayli's expression light up. "This was Rachel's. She wanted you to have it, and I want you to have it."

"I can't take it, Adam. It's for your wife."

"Kayli," he said, laughing. "I'm asking you to be my wife. I want us to be married."

Choking sobs emanated from his future bride. She covered her face, to hide the emotion, but Adam pulled her hands away. "Is that a yes?"

She nodded. Again and again. "It's a yes!" She grabbed his face and covered him with kisses. "Mike Williams can have whatever he wants, as long as I get you."

His throat grew tight, but he wanted to shout with joy. To sing, to dance. Something to show his emotion. So he broke into song to the Lord while Kayli giggled.

"You'll always have my heart, Kayli. Once I tasted that apple pie, I knew life didn't get any better than this."

Kayli smiled, almost an evil grin. "You ate it before you left?"

"The whole thing."

"Well, you little sneak."

"And it was better than my mother's. Rachel laughed contentedly when I told her that."

"You told her?"

"She would have read it in my face if I hadn't. Although she said my taste buds might have been colored by my feelings."

"I certainly hope so."

"Who would have thought I'd have to come to a European bakery in California for American apple pie?"

"America is a lot of things, Adam, but it's certainly like you, sweet as apple pie."

ELLEN'S INFAMOUS APPLE PIE

This recipe is the best apple pie I've ever tasted, and it is a must for my husband at Thanksgiving and Christmas. My husband's mother, Ellen Billerbeck, perfected this recipe, and it is incredible! Many thanks to her for sharing this recipe and raising such a wonderful son to enjoy it with.

INGREDIENTS:
- 1½ cups sugar (use a tad more if apples are really sour)
- Dash of salt
- ½ cup flour
- Dash of nutmeg
- 2 heaping teaspoons cinnamon
- 6 pippin apples (look for brown crown for the best sugared apples)
- 2 ready-made piecrusts
- 1 lemon
- ¼ stick butter, sliced

DIRECTIONS:
Preheat oven to 350 degrees. Combine sugar, salt, flour, nutmeg, and cinnamon in a bowl. Peel and cut apples in small wedges. Roll out one ready-made piecrust , or your own, and place in a 9-inch pie pan. Layer sugar mix, apples, lemon, and butter. Keep layering until all ingredients are used. Then place second piecrust on top, cutting a hole in the top to allow the mixture to vent. Place a cookie sheet under the pie pan to avoid boil-overs and messy ovens. Bake for 1 hour; then lower temperature to 300 degrees and bake for 30 more minutes.

CUPCAKES FOR TWO
by Birdie L. Etchison

Dedication

To my mother, Naomi Leighton, one of the best cooks ever!

Chapter 1

Cynthia Lyons grabbed her luggage and wheeled it toward the street where a taxi waited. She slung her carry-on bag over her shoulder, pushed a lock of blond hair out of her eyes, and ran to the curb.

"I need to get downtown in thirty minutes. Here's the address." She thrust a small piece of wadded up paper in front of the driver's nose. "Is that possible?"

"Get in, lady. We'll try, but no guarantees."

He started to get out to help with the luggage, but she waved him away. "I'm used to taking care of things myself. Thanks anyway."

Seconds later, the taxi pulled away from the cars parked three deep and was soon in the throng of Portland, Oregon, commuters.

"You aren't from here, are you?"

"No. Is it that noticeable?" Cynthia took a deep breath, willing herself to relax. A job interview shouldn't ruffle her. She had lots to offer a bed-and-breakfast operation.

He looked at her in the rearview mirror. "If you were, you wouldn't have asked if I could make it. It's a straight shot once I get on I-84 heading west."

"That's great. I have an appointment," she said, "and one can't be late for a job interview."

"No problem. We'll make it with time to spare. Traffic is light."

"Thanks" was all Cynthia could manage as a sudden feeling of regret—or was it alarm?—went through her. It was ludicrous leaving Martinez, California, as she had. Stealing away, practically in the middle of the night, leaving her business to Jan, her friend and associate. If only Max had just left her alone. She thought that chapter of her life was over, but he'd returned, acting as if things would pick up as before—and wouldn't take no for an answer. Her thoughts turned to that day when they'd argued.

"Max, we have nothing in common. I need to find someone who believes as I do."

"Are you back to that church thing?" He'd laughed as he said it, showing how unimportant her belief was to him. He was ruggedly handsome and, at six feet three inches, towered over her, almost taking her breath away. "Why does that have to get in the way? It sure doesn't need to."

"I'm not going through it again, Max. Please don't come around anymore."

"And I'm not giving up, not by a long shot." He stood in the doorway, his eyes narrowing. "I'll be back." He left, banging the door hard.

"But you're over him," Jan argued. "You said so yourself just last week."

"I am, and yet I'm not." She'd paused over the box she was packing.

"It's dumb and crazy! Taking off when you have this fantastic business going."

"Which you'll keep going just fine." Cynthia had glanced up, pressing a kink out of the lower part of her back. "Where's your confidence, girl?"

Jan taped the top of the box closed. "I just want you around, that's all."

"I'll probably be back. Give me a year to do *something* else, *somewhere* else, and you'll find me here on your doorstep."

Jan impulsively hugged her. "Oh, I hope so."

Cynthia had stored her bed and other items she wanted to keep, packing her clothes and her favorite recipe collection. If the job didn't pan out for the bed-and-breakfast in Astoria, she would just find something else. She'd circled an ad about a full-time position in a cooking school in Portland, and there'd even been one for an online cooking instructor. Not that she'd *ever* consider doing anything online. Did people get paid for online classes? She knew she could work anywhere. It was just that the job in Astoria sounded so great.

Cynthia recalled the ad: "Victorian House. View of Columbia River. Elegant. Full house expected through fall."

It was August now, and she was prepared to be busy for four months, maybe longer, as some might want to get away for the holiday season. She loved decorating for Christmas.

Cynthia stared at her finger where a beautiful two-carat solitaire had been. Her heart should be healing, still. . . . One didn't get over a relationship overnight. If she knew all that, why did it continue to hurt? Cynthia thought of a quote she'd read in the newspaper. A person wrote to an advice columnist, asking: "Why does love hurt so bad when it's gone?"

"It doesn't," was the answer. "It only hurts when it's still there." Cynthia guessed it was still there.

The taxi wove in and out of traffic. Cynthia's thoughts came back to the present. She glanced at her watch. She had twenty minutes, but the way the driver was going, they'd be there in time, though perhaps not in one piece.

"We'll soon cross the Broadway Bridge. Be there in five minutes, miss."

Cynthia stared at the skyscrapers looming ahead on the horizon. Portland's skyline was impressive, definitely larger than Martinez, the small, east-bay town where she had lived most of her life. On her own since her mother died six years ago, she still missed Mom more than she'd ever thought possible. Memories of Mom's gentleness, her guidance, and the fact that she was home with her Lord were the only things bringing peace to Cynthia now.

She glanced out over a river as the steel grating on the bridge jiggled the taxi and tickled the soles of her feet. The driver turned and stopped at a traffic light at the end of the bridge.

"That's the Willamette River. You pronounce it Wa-lamm-et, not Will-a-met."

"Oh, I know that," Cynthia said with a chuckle. "I'm from California, after all."

He looked at the slip of paper and double-parked in front of an immense building with interesting cornices and huge pillars.

THE GARFIELD, a sign said. OFFICE SPACE, STUDIO APARTMENTS, and LOFTS FOR LEASE.

"This is it?"

He nodded. "That's the address you gave me."

This time Cynthia let him assist her with the large suitcase, then wondered what to do with a suitcase and the carry-on when she went in for the interview. She should have thought of that before now.

Cynthia gave the driver a good tip and headed up the steps, pulling her bags behind her. Surely there'd be a place to leave her things. A corner of the waiting room, perhaps.

She dug in her purse for the name and phone number. *Gabe Taylor*. Cynthia hoped there would be a register inside. She pushed the door open and struggled with her luggage. A man hurried past, then returned to hold the door open.

"Coming to stay, I see," he said with a jovial look.

"Actually, I'm looking for Gabe Taylor's office. Would you happen to know where it is?"

"Sure. It's the third floor up, office to the left; far end."

Cynthia got into the elevator after a woman came out, wondering if the tall beauty might have applied for the position as manager of the bed-and-breakfast.

The woman smiled, one of those half smiles people do when they catch you looking at them, then hurried by.

Cynthia found the name she was looking for etched in silver on the door and turned the knob.

She had hoped the receptionist would show her a place to stash her luggage, but there was no waiting room. As the door came open, she almost fell into the room as the suitcase slipped from her grip. A young man at a desk with his feet propped on top nearly fell over backward in his surprise.

"Hey! Don't you knock before entering a room?"

Her face felt hot. "I. . .that is, I assumed there was a waiting room and a. . ." She blushed even more. "I'm so sorry."

"You're here about the position?"

"If you mean the manager of the bed-and-breakfast, yes."

"Have a seat."

His eyes were a deep brown, and she felt herself becoming lost in his steady gaze.

Glancing at her luggage, a slight smile turned up at the corners of his mouth. "Planning on staying awhile I see. You must be Cynthia Lyons."

She held out her hand. "And you're Gabe Taylor."

He nodded. "I'll just take your résumé and get back to you tomorrow."

"I can wait," Cynthia said. She wanted to add that she had nowhere to go, but thought better of it.

He sat, looked at the folder, then back at her, then at her résumé again, as if he didn't know what to do.

"I need to know today, if possible. It will determine whether I rent a car and start out, or stay in Portland to begin looking elsewhere."

"I see." He leaned back and seemed to study her more closely. "Do you usually call the shots when you go on an interview?"

Cynthia felt the color rise in her cheeks again. "No. This is an exception, as I think I'm perfect for the job and can't wait to get started. I'm sure there's lots to do."

Gabe couldn't believe he was even considering hiring this woman. She had a lot of nerve, coming in here and exerting her way like that. She stood no bigger than a minute and, diminutive as she was, he sensed she was strong and determined—good qualities when running a business. And he needed someone like that, especially since he planned on leaving for New York soon—permanently.

He started reading again, fingering his chin as he read. "You had your own catering business?"

"Yes. Cynthia's Catering has been quite successful. My specialty is a variety of desserts. I make the most fancy cupcakes you ever saw—decorating the tops with special designs, all edible, of course. A friend is running the business in my absence. I also have letters from satisfied customers, should you care to see them."

He waved his hand. "No, that won't be necessary. What concerns me, however, is that you're not looking for a long-term job." He looked up, meeting her gaze again.

"Oh, no," Cynthia said. "I want it to be permanent. I just meant my business is in good hands."

"You had orders from some big names in the Bay Area?"

"Yes. Like I said, there are letters—"

"No, I don't want to see any letters." Gabe looked at her thoughtfully. "What I need to know is what you might have on the menu for a typical Sunday brunch."

Cynthia leaned back. "Probably my Egg Blossoms with Hollandaise, or French

Toast Soufflé. Either one gets rave reviews and is absolutely delicious."

Gabe arched an eyebrow. "And is this going to cost me an arm and a leg?"

Cynthia straightened her shoulders. "Surely you want something to bring people back! I assure you I use only the best ingredients. Butter, cream, the finest of sugar—"

"I'm sure you're right—I mean about bringing them back. And word of mouth works wonders in this business."

He tapped the form with a pencil, then finally pushed his chair back. "Okay. You're hired. Strictly on a trial basis, you understand."

"Of course."

"And I expect a full report each and every Monday morning."

She raised her chin, almost in defiance. "No problem there. I keep close and accurate records."

"So, if you're ready, and I assume you are, we'll take off and head to Astoria."

"We?"

"As a financial advisor, I'm my own boss, and I made no appointments until later this afternoon."

"I see."

Cynthia couldn't help wondering if he had other job applicants to interview, but decided not to ask.

"I suppose you're wondering about other interviewees?"

She glanced away. "The thought did cross my mind."

"The ad you saw was the second one I ran. On a whim I put it in the *San Francisco Chronicle*. Seems nobody wants to take on a B and B this time of year. It's the end of the season. The rainy season is ahead. Now come spring, customers will be banging the door down."

"I like the rain," Cynthia said. "It's soothing."

"Then you should love Astoria." He paused at the door. "Why would you leave California this time of year, anyway?"

The knot grew in Cynthia's throat. It was her business, and she didn't think she needed to explain anything to him. He needed someone to operate his B and B, and that was all that mattered.

She looked up. "It's a personal matter, but it won't interfere with my work. Not in the least."

"Very well, then. I ask for two-weeks' notice. I have someone who ran the B and B for the past few weekends, but she does it only as a favor."

A favor? Cynthia wondered about that. She guessed there was more to this than he was willing to discuss. Not that she cared. She wasn't here to fill anyone's shoes. It was simply a job.

"Let me get my coat, and we'll be off."

Cynthia closed her eyes for a brief moment, thanking God for getting her here safely, for helping her land the job, and also for this man who was getting to her more than she wanted him to. There was something about his face, the thick thatch of hair that appealed to her, but she didn't like the thoughts going through her head. She was definitely not ready for romance.

Chapter 2

The parking lot was two blocks from Gabe's office, and as Cynthia struggled to keep up, Gabe forged ahead, pulling her larger suitcase behind him.

"You'll like the bed-and-breakfast," Gabe said, once they were inside his Mercury and heading west.

"How long have you owned the B and B?"

He grinned. "Forever. I grew up in it."

"Oh." She glanced at his profile and suddenly saw not a bigwig financial advisor, but a man who still had the small town in him though he tried to appear otherwise.

"I was raised in a little town, too," Cynthia said.

He gave her a quick glance, his eyebrow raised. "I didn't think there was such a thing in California."

"Very funny. Actually, Martinez is a wonderful place, and I wouldn't trade the memories of Mom and me walking to the park on Saturdays, listening to concerts every summer, and visiting the farmers' market Thursday afternoons."

"And your mother? Where is she now?"

Cynthia felt her insides tighten. Would she ever get over the loss of her mother? "Mom died the year I started my catering business. I wish she knew how successful I am at a job I love."

"And just maybe she does." He smiled again and she felt a jolt. Gabe must be a Christian, or he wouldn't have made that comment.

Cynthia smiled. "I like to think so. What about your parents?"

"Both gone. I don't remember my father at all. He died when I was five, then Mom a few years ago, and just last year Grams died. She was a strong, determined person, as you might have guessed."

"Yes. And so it was handed down to you."

"Yeah, that's my life story in a nutshell."

They drove silently while a gospel CD played from the car stereo. Her life had changed so much. After losing her mother, she'd dropped out of college and started cooking for one of the restaurants in her neighborhood. She'd met Max, who pushed her into the catering business. "Anyone who cooks with flair, as you do, should cook for a living." Max found her clients, all businesspeople, but Cynthia preferred cooking what she liked, not what they ordered. Still Max prodded her.

Then she found herself pulling away, wanting a different lifestyle than he did. *It all seems so long ago now.*

Gabe hummed one of the tunes while Cynthia watched the countryside fly past. Gabe looked in her direction a few times, and she felt good as she hummed along.

"I see you like the CD."

"I enjoy music. Always have."

Gabe put on the blinker and pulled up in front of a small restaurant nestled in a wooded setting. "This is my favorite eating place, speaking of small towns. It's by far one of the best between Portland and Astoria."

The café was located beside a small stream. The sound of the brook soothed Cynthia, and she felt the tension leave her body. There was something so relaxing about the water.

The waitress came, and they ordered coffee and large bowls of clam chowder.

The coffee was hot, the chowder seasoned and full of clams. Cynthia decided it was similar to her recipe. She'd have to commend the chef.

As if reading her thoughts, Gabe asked, "How does this match up to what you make?"

"Excellent," Cynthia said, setting down her soup spoon. "I'm glad we stopped."

Gabe leaned forward. "You have an interesting manner," he said, catching Cynthia off guard with his sudden statement.

"Oh, and why is that?"

"You seem to be easily pleased."

"And most of your friends aren't?" she had to ask. Was he alluding to previous girlfriends? Cynthia wanted to know, though it was none of her business. She found herself more than casually interested in this person sitting next to her. He was nothing like Max. His earlier haughty, all-business mood had given way to a captivating manner, and she discovered she wanted to know him better. That would be impossible since he lived in Portland. Their business transactions would probably be via the phone or computer.

"I'll pay for my meal," Cynthia offered, but Gabe waved her off.

"This was my idea, and I'll handle it, including the tip."

Nearly an hour later, they pulled into Astoria, and Cynthia gasped when she saw the immense Columbia River. Earlier she'd caught glimpses of it as they drove along the highway, but now the river beckoned with its vast miles and miles of blueness. Hills resembling green velvet on the Washington side of the river appeared to touch the sky overhead. Cynthia took a deep breath. "It's beautiful."

Gabe grinned. "If you like this, wait until you see the view from Taylor's Bed and Breakfast."

Gabe turned and drove straight up a hill. Astoria reminded her of San Francisco.

Contrary to popular belief, people living in the Bay Area did not go into San Francisco often unless they worked there. With her business, she'd hired a driver part-time to deliver her meals.

"So, what do you think? I know our hills don't compare to San Francisco's, but we like them."

"Oh, I love the hills. It's a gorgeous spot, and I can see it's the perfect vacation place for travelers."

"Except when there is snow or ice. That holds us captive, but it happens rarely, so don't worry about it."

Gabe hopped out and took a deep breath. "I tend to forget how clean the air is here. I love this town."

Then why did you leave? Cynthia wanted to ask.

Cynthia stared at the huge house that seemed to tower over her. The dead-end street turned into a hill of green brush. The B and B, a turn-of-the-century Victorian, was painted a deep scarlet. The bay windows were outlined in navy blue, while a sky blue shade accented the gingerbread. A turret on the north side added to the charm. A small yard drew shade from a huge maple that dominated an overgrown flower garden. Already Cynthia's mind whirled with ideas for improving the yard.

"What do you think?" Gabe was at her side, his gaze meeting hers, waiting for an answer.

"It's perfect!"

"Wait until you see the inside."

Steps led up to the wraparound porch, and Gabe produced a set of keys; then they were inside.

Cynthia loved older homes. She marveled at the winding stairway, the highly polished wood, a carved banister, and the rose wallpaper leading up to the next floor. The foyer was perfect with a window bench and a rack for wraps and umbrellas. The area rug was starting to fray, but that was a minor problem.

"Do you want the grand tour now or to just discover it on your own?"

"Now, please."

They climbed the stairs to the second floor, which had four bedrooms. Two were spacious with their own private baths, while the other two rooms shared a bath. Old-fashioned light fixtures gave the appearance of gaslights from long ago.

"It's charming," Cynthia said, clasping her hands.

"The four-poster beds have been in the family for three generations. Just before she died, Grams ordered these matching feather comforters, ruffles, and shams."

"I want to stay in each room a night," Cynthia said. "They're so spacious, and the view—people will love that!"

"I didn't tell you an important part," Gabe said, interrupting Cynthia's reverie.

She turned from the window. "And what is that?"

"You're going to need help. I usually hire high school girls, but Rainey found them unreliable. Sometimes they show up for work, sometimes not."

"Rainey?"

"The person I mentioned who helped me out."

He appeared uncomfortable, and she wondered if Rainey could be an old girlfriend.

"Perhaps the wages weren't high enough, so there was no incentive to do a good job," Cynthia said.

Gabe frowned. "If I pay more than the minimum, I won't make a dime."

Cynthia looked out the window at the river. "I wouldn't worry about it. Things will work out."

"So, do you still want the job?"

"I do, Mr. Taylor. I really do."

They finished the tour, and Gabe showed Cynthia where the fuse box, furnace, and water valve were located. "Everything's been updated, but you just never know." He opened a long cupboard in the kitchen. "Here are candles in case the electricity goes off, and hurricane lamps are on the table in the parlor."

"Does the electricity go off often?"

Gabe nodded. "We have some great storms here, so be prepared." He handed Cynthia his business card. "Contact me if anything goes wrong. And there's always e-mail."

Gabe brought in Cynthia's suitcase, toting it to the small room off the kitchen. He paused in the doorway, as if he needed to add something. His expression said he wanted to stay, and she found herself not wanting him to leave. He had an almost lost look as he ran his hand through his thick hair.

"I'll be in touch. Almost forgot. The computer's in the alcove off your bedroom."

Cynthia walked over, offering her hand. "Thanks for the job. I'll take good care of things here."

He left suddenly, and then came back in. "About a car. The Chevy is over at Rainey's. I'll stop by to ask her to drop it off here. I'd just go get it, but," he said, pausing to look at his watch, "I have a four o'clock appointment."

Cynthia walked out on the porch and said good-bye. A light mist was falling, and it looked like fog rolling in across the river. It made her suddenly feel bereft.

She leaned against the door and closed her eyes. A lot had happened since she'd caught the flight from Oakland. She had much to be thankful for. She lifted her face. "Thank You, Lord, for bringing me this job in such a lovely spot. I ask for Your guidance, and may I do a good job for Mr. Taylor—Gabe. Amen."

Cynthia opened her eyes. "Oh, and Lord, please take away this feeling that is surfacing. Gabe cannot possibly have any interest in me. Let me just do the job and not think about him. Thank You. Again, amen."

After unpacking and slipping into her favorite navy blue sweater, Cynthia explored the food cupboard. Supplies were low, and already she had a list going in her mind. *Guest book needed. Flowers for the foyer, new rugs, new drapes for the living room, and the floors need work.* Was Gabe going to agree to her suggestions? At the thought of his lopsided grin, she felt a sudden surge of energy. Tomorrow she'd go to town to explore.

⚜

Gabe drove the four blocks over to Rainey's and asked her to drop off the car.

Rainey pushed her hair behind her ear. "Don't you want to come in for a spot of tea?"

Gabe shook his head. "Thanks, but no. Need to get back for an appointment."

Rainey looked away, and Gabe felt the old familiar thread of guilt. He'd hurt her, he realized, but he did not love her and knew that wouldn't change. What they once had was the remnants of a first love. After high school graduation, Gabe left Astoria. He had big plans. Rainey went to the local college, got her teaching degree, and was content to stay here. They'd grown in different directions. There was nothing wrong with that. They'd talked about it and agreed to stay friends. So why did he feel guilty when she looked at him?

She gave him an impulsive hug, promising to drop the car off the next day. "And, Gabe, take care of yourself."

"You, too." He looked back briefly and waved.

Gabe drove down the hill toward Highway 30. As Cynthia Lyons' face came to mind, he felt good, almost lighthearted. She was a gem—something told him so—and he knew the B and B was in good hands. She'd been so enthusiastic—like a child on Christmas morning. He could move to New York now and fulfill his dream to make it in the big city.

As he drove over the miles, he kept thinking about Cynthia. There was something that drew him to her, and he wasn't sure what it was. How different she was from Natalie Wiegant. Elegant, efficient Natalie. They'd been dating two years now, and the relationship seemed to be going nowhere. He thought of her in her expensive designer suit, high heels. . . and those beautiful violet eyes. She could have been a model but had chosen finance for a career. Natalie attracted attention wherever she went, and it had been fun attending a host of parties and being part of the in scene.

They'd had a disagreement last week, and her words still stung.

"You're just a mama's boy, Gabe. You need to start moving."

"Moving?"

"Yes. Remember your New York dream?"

"Of course."

Natalie had sauntered across the room—she never just walked—and pointed. "I think you can take the boy out of the small town, but you can never take the small town out of the boy."

Gabe tried to shake the words as he drove on, his thoughts scattered. He had to prove Natalie wrong. And now that the B and B was taken care of, he could and *would* move on.

Gabe hadn't prayed much lately—he wasn't sure why. Busyness. Worry. Trying to get everything together for the New York move. As he approached the industrial area of Portland, he prayed aloud: "Lord, is this new path the right one? How am I to know? Does anyone ever know?"

Cynthia Lyons came to mind again. She intrigued him, but her boldness bothered him. Yet it was that boldness that made her perfect for the job. If she liked the B and B, and every indication pointed to that, she might be there for years. He could live his dream, keep in touch, and come home for a few weeks each summer.

His apartment seemed emptier than usual, and Gabe thought about being back in Astoria, watching while a certain person walked through the house, exclaiming over every feature. He'd felt joy being around her, and for the first time in a long while, he realized how much his life had lacked the very essence of joy. Was Cynthia Lyons bringing joy into his world again?

His head was saying, "New York, New York," but his heart was saying, "Cynthia, Cynthia." It was not a good sign.

Chapter 3

The next morning Cynthia called her friend Jan, back in Martinez, to tell her the news. "I got hired, Jan. I'm now the manager of the most wonderful B and B ever, with a magnificent view. You've got to come see it."

"Hey, good for you!"

"You busy?"

There was an audible sigh.

"Is something wrong?" Cynthia asked.

Her good friend chuckled. "No, it's just that I have lots of orders for this coming weekend. Oh, and I got a call from an online cooking school. They are looking for an instructor to handle a column on sweet treats. Just once a week. You post recipes and go in a chat room to answer questions."

"Sweet treats?"

"You know, desserts."

"Why not just call them desserts?"

"Guess they wanted something different. How do I know? You can call or not; it's up to you."

"Are you feeling overwhelmed? Do you want me to move back?"

"Before you even start your new job? Don't be silly. The little gal you hired will work out just fine. Oh, and Max called, demanding to know where you were. I said I hadn't heard from you—which was true. Finally got rid of him."

A funny ache went over Cynthia. Max had been a part of her life for so long. She found herself thinking of only the good times, not the difficult ones, and wondered if that was what other women did, following a breakup.

"How's he doing?"

"I didn't ask. Look, call me tomorrow," Jan said. "I have to go shopping."

"Yeah, me, too," Cynthia said. "I'm looking forward to it. You wouldn't believe this quaint town. I hope I can find Portobellos."

"Think you'll stay for a while?"

Cynthia felt a sudden lurch. "You know, I think I might."

"And everything's okay?"

"Yeah, except—"

"*Except?*"

"Mr. Taylor is brusque, but cute."

"Whoa, girl. You know you can't go from the frying pan to the fire."

"Don't worry. The feeling isn't mutual."

"So, you going to follow up on the cooking class?"

"Yeah. Sounds interesting. Guess I should at least check it out."

Cynthia jotted down the website and e-mail address. "Thanks, Jan. I'll let you know what happens."

A short time later, Cynthia sat at the computer and keyed in the website.

Online instructor needed. We need someone who makes scrumptious desserts. There is a cry from several would-be bakers wanting to learn how to make fantastic Sweet Treats. E-mail for more information.

The instructions were clear:

We want simple, easy-to-do recipes.
Post a cooking lesson once a week.
Offer at least three recipes. Nothing exotic, but down-to-earth home cooking.
Give specific instructions.
Measurements must be exact.
Close with a request for questions.
Go online once a day; say every evening at six. If there are questions from online cooking students, answer the questions.

The idea intrigued her. There was not the slightest doubt in her mind that she could do it. It wouldn't interfere with her work here at the B and B. Her evenings would be free; she would post her recipes, field questions, and still have energy to handle guests and bake her specialty cupcakes and bread. Yes, God certainly knew how to answer prayer—by giving her not one, but two jobs.

There was more. The sponsor wanted six sample recipes, plus a few tips. Cynthia pored over her recipe books that evening and finally selected six:

Apple Crisp—because it's far easier than trying to make piecrust.

Bread Pudding—an old standard, uses something everybody has on hand.

Chocolate Chunk Cookies—an old standard, but better than the traditional ones.

Berry Cobbler—to make when berries are in season, but can also be made with berries found in the frozen section of any supermarket.

Pudding Cake—an elegant dessert for company in a variety of flavors.

Pound Cake—something Grams made.

They wanted simple. Cynthia knew simple. She had learned simple at her grandmother's knee. Grams loved to cook, and Cynthia had watched, standing on tiptoes, as Grams showed her how to make piecrust, cookie crust, crisps, buckles, and flans. She'd made an apple crisp when she was six. That would be her first recipe to put online. She began jotting down a few hints.

Buy Granny Smith apples for cooking, as they are tart and crisp. They make for great desserts. The biggest job for this recipe is peeling the apples, quartering to get the core out, and the slicing. Try to make uniform slices. And for those who are going to ask—no, you cannot, you MUST NOT use canned apples.

Cynthia jotted the recipe from memory:

Slice up 6 apples into a baking dish. I prefer a round glass bowl, but anything works. Apples brown quickly, so you might want to make the topping before peeling apples.

Topping: Use 1½ sticks butter that has softened. This means taking it out of refrigerator two hours before. And it must be butter. Real butter. No margarine and no whipped butter. 1½ cups white sugar, 1 tsp. cinnamon, and ½ tsp. nutmeg. Mix these together until crumbly. Pat that over the top of the apples. Bake at 375 degrees for approximately an hour. It depends. If you like your apples not to be cooked up, take crisp out after 45 minutes.

Serve with whipped cream or ice cream. Best served while warm. So, plan on taking crisp out of oven an hour before you serve dinner.

Cynthia posted a few cooking tips and a hint of what would come the following week.

By the time she had finished, it was almost noon. She was behind on the schedule she'd set up the night before. Schedules were a must if she were to accomplish several tasks.

The next thing was the grocery list. She'd buy two pounds of Granny Smith apples to test her recipe, and while in the apple section, she'd select five or six Braeburns for the table. She'd found the perfect cut glass fruit bowl in the pantry. Cynthia always had a bowl of fruit on the counter of her kitchen. It cheered her. Thinking of how juicy the apples tasted brought a smile to her face.

But now she jotted things down on a task list. Fresh flowers were another must. She needed a bouquet for the foyer as guests arrived, for the middle of the large table, and one for each bedroom—carnations, preferably, as she could easily find them in colors to match the décor of the rooms.

Cynthia wanted to replace the drapes but knew there might be resistance there. Gabe would not see the need. Still, she put it on her list. She'd cover one thing at a time.

Cynthia went to the office. Crammed behind the kitchen, the office had undoubtedly been a storage room in the earlier days. She'd like to return it to a storage room and put the office in the alcove off her bedroom. The computer was already there, and there was room. It was the perfect place, besides being airy and sunny. She needed sun. According to the weather forecaster, there'd be showers today, and this was *August.* Rain in August! Unheard of in California. She supposed she'd get used to it. But why would people want to vacation if the weather was lousy? Yet there were two bookings for this weekend; one Friday night, the other on Saturday. Both would stay two nights.

Dressing in corduroy pants with a red sweatshirt, Cynthia was finally ready for shopping. The phone rang, just as she grabbed her backpack.

"Cynthia? Gabe here. How's it going?"

Cynthia took a deep breath. "Yes, everything is fine, but it's raining. The sun comes out, and then it disappears."

He laughed. "Tell me something I don't know."

"Does it always rain here in the summer?"

"Without fail."

"Nobody will come."

"They will. Did you notice the games in the closet? And the assortment of videos?"

"Yes, but—"

"They're for people to play when they can't go outside. There's also a new movie house with six theaters downtown. It's just like Portland."

"I haven't been out to explore yet, but intend to go now."

"Any questions?"

Cynthia cleared her throat. "I'd like some new everyday china, as what you have is a hodgepodge of things."

"Didn't seem to bother Rainey."

I'm not Rainey, she wanted to say, but held her tongue.

"The drapes also need replacing. I think they've been there for a long time—"

"That's what gives the house its charm," Gabe interrupted.

"I don't mean to buy something modern, but replace these with new ones. We can use the same fabric and color. I'm sure we could find a seamstress who'd take on the job."

"Try vacuuming them. I'm sure there's lots more wear in them."

"Okay, I'll try it." She wanted to mention flowers and the guest book, and possibly a new throw rug, but thought she'd better wait. They'd definitely lock horns.

The items Gabe addressed were unimportant. He suggested she keep a running itinerary of her days; e-mail him any charges she made; and to call immediately if there were problems.

Problems? What sort of problems was he referring to? She supposed she would find out soon enough.

Cynthia felt as if she was putting brakes on her feet as she started down the hill. She glanced at the clouds scudding across the sky, which had been blue moments earlier but now looked dark and threatening. She hoped Rainey would bring the car over soon. She guessed if it rained too hard, she'd just call a taxi, if they had one in such a small town.

Her list was in her backpack, and she thrust her hands into her pockets and hurried on. The air was brisk, but definitely not cold. At home she'd be in shorts and a tank top by now. One thing was certain: she'd have to buy some jeans and sweaters as she hadn't brought but two warm outfits with her.

The first stop was the florist. Large bunches of roses in every color imaginable filled huge baskets on the sidewalk leading into the store. Inside was a flurry of action with one young girl talking to a customer while an older lady brought out a bouquet of salmon gladioli. Her dark hair was pulled back into a ponytail and tied with a red scarf.

The woman stopped and smiled. "Good morning, can I help you?"

Cynthia nodded. She could stay in this place forever. It was almost as good as her kitchen when it smelled of baking bread and cakes.

"How early must I order flowers?"

"If you put in an order today, I can have them tomorrow. All our shipments come from Portland, just two hours away."

"Yes, two hours away. I came from there yesterday."

"Oh!" Her cheeks flushed as a smile crossed her round face. "You're new to Astoria. Welcome!" She held out a hand. "I'm Mary, and this is my flower shop. Just opened up last March."

"It's wonderful."

Cynthia explained she was the new manager of Taylor's Bed and Breakfast, pointing up the hill.

"Yes," Mary said. "I've lived here all my life and know the Taylor family well. I just went into this business as it's been a longtime dream of mine."

Cynthia smiled. "I think fulfilling dreams is important in life. I wish you every success."

"How is Rainey doing, anyway?"

Cynthia tried not to look surprised. Was something wrong with Rainey? And who was this woman who had helped Gabe out?

"I don't know," she mumbled. "We haven't met yet." *Is there something I should know?*

"She's been ill, I understand. She'll come around when she's on her feet again."

"I hope so. She's bringing me a car, Mr. Taylor said."

"Gabe," Mary said. "We all go on first-name basis around here. And Gabe is one of us, whether he likes to think so or not."

Cynthia wondered about the remark as she moved on into the store, admiring the various displays of fresh flowers and a few plants. She wanted to buy everything she saw.

"I'd like to order fresh flowers to be delivered on Friday." Cynthia hesitated and looked at Mary's face.

"I'll go with the lilies in that pink tone. They're so fragrant."

"That they are."

"Okay, and yes, we deliver, but I'm wondering, is this order for the B and B?"

"Yes. Is that a problem?"

"Gabe's never ordered flowers before."

"It's a must. He'll agree."

"Okay. I'll write it up."

Since Cynthia was walking, she bought only a few things on her grocery list. She'd come again tomorrow. And maybe she'd bring some of her bread or a plate of cupcakes for Mary. She'd make the ones with flowers on top.

Just as Cynthia started to climb the hill toward the B and B, the sky opened and rain soaked her before she got there. Thankfully she'd had her items in a plastic bag and not a paper one. This wasn't the usual "mist." It *was* going to take some getting used to.

Chapter 4

Rainey dropped the car off the following day. If she rang the bell, Cynthia had not heard it. She was busy responding to the online instant message from the cooking guru.

"We're going to call your class The Lion Cooks. A little play on words. What do you think?"

"Sounds fine to me," Cynthia answered. "I'm looking forward to it."

"We'll start on Tuesday. Is tomorrow too soon?"

"I look forward to it!"

Cynthia shut the computer down and went outside to look at the side yard again. She needed to prepare the ground for the bedding plants she wanted. A little color would help immensely. A dusty blue Chevy sat in the driveway, and then she noticed the envelope under the doormat. The keys. But why hadn't Rainey come in? She looked up the street in the hopes of seeing someone walking, but there was no one. For once the sky was a cloudless blue, and the air felt warm. She went back inside to check on the bread rising in the pans. Soon the kitchen would be filled with the fragrance of rosemary and dill. She'd just turned the oven on when the phone rang.

"Did you get my e-mail?"

"Well, and good morning to you, too."

"Good morning."

"I did."

"And?"

"I'll mail the amount by the end of the day. Oh, and Rainey dropped off the car."

"Good. Did she come in?"

"No, which I thought strange."

"You'll meet her one of these days. She's kind of a loner."

"I gathered that."

"I'm coming down this weekend," he said then.

"You are?"

"Thought you might need someone there."

"I know I can handle it." Her pulse raced, though she told it not to.

"I'm sure you can, too."

That night Cynthia went to the message board, looking for responses from online students. She found several. She didn't realize how little some of the readers knew.

"Does it matter what kind of apples I use?" was the first question. "I have these red ones; I don't know what they are."

"I have a can of applesauce, can I use that?" was another.

And yet another: "Do I need to peel the apples?"

Then: "My husband prefers peaches. Can I make a crisp with peaches?"

Cynthia replied:

You can use any apples; it's just that Granny Smiths are the best for cooking. Applesauce is not going to work. You need fresh apples. And, yes, please peel them.

You can make peach crisp. Ripe peaches would be the best, but canned can also be used. Use half the sugar, though.

Quick breads are next. I hope you have loaf pans. If not, buy one or two now. Buy the regular size, not the small ones.

Bon appétit!

Cynthia Lyons

On Wednesday Gabe phoned again. "What is this huge floral expense?"

Cynthia braced herself. "A bed-and-breakfast should have fresh flowers to greet the guests, and a bouquet in their room. It sets forth the right ambience."

"And I say the view is what brings them there—and will bring them back."

"I know. That, too."

"Maybe you'd better run things by me before you buy."

"Okay. Sure."

Rainey came over the next day. She knocked first and then opened the door. "Hello, anyone here?"

Cynthia dried her hands—she'd been peeling veggies to add to a stew that she'd be eating the rest of the week. "Yes, I'm here. In the kitchen." She held out her hand to a young woman who was tall and had broad shoulders but looked about the same age as Cynthia. She knew immediately who it was.

"Hi, I'm Rainey."

"You should have just come in—you must know this place better than I do! I'm Cynthia and so glad to meet you."

"Mary said you were hoping I'd stop by. Been sick, but feeling better now." Her eyes swept over the room, and Cynthia knew Rainey was noticing she'd moved some things around.

"It's different," Cynthia said. "I hope you like it."

"Yes, it's just that Gabe doesn't like change. Has he seen it yet?"

"No, but I guess he will on Friday. He said he's coming down." Cynthia gestured toward the kitchen. "Come on in, and I'll put the kettle on for tea, or whatever you'd like. There's cola in the refrigerator."

"You are a dynamo," Rainey said, "and I'll have tea."

Cynthia pulled out a kitchen chair and put the heat on under the kettle, "I like to keep busy, that's true.

"Gabe was lucky to find you."

"I am lucky the B and B needed a manager, and I couldn't have found a more beautiful spot."

"Astoria is wonderful. We who live here tend to take it for granted."

"Can't get used to the rain, though. I mean it's summer! Look at the clouds—and they just hang over, making it cool and damp."

"It's always been that way. You just get used to it."

"Maybe you do, but I must admit I miss the sunshine in California."

"And the busy freeways, the fires, and floods?"

"You're right. Tell me, did I hear that you and Gabe went to school together?"

Rainey's long, slender fingers wrapped around her cup of tea. She lifted it to take a drink then lowered it onto the saucer. "I have known Gabe since kindergarten. Our mothers were best of friends."

Cynthia wanted to ask if they had been boyfriend and girlfriend, but didn't.

"Yes, I loved him. Might as well tell you now, as you'll hear it through the grapevine. I know he loved me once, but his dream was to move on to Portland and begin his business there. Astoria is too small."

"Maybe he will change his mind." Cynthia squeezed a spot of lemon into her tea.

"No, there's Natalie now. She has him wrapped around her finger, as the saying goes. She's not right for him, but he can't see it. She smells of success, and that's what he's looking for now."

"And what do you do?"

"Teach. At the grade school. Music and art."

"That certainly sounds successful to me."

"Small time, though. Small school. No challenge. But I like it here. Don't imagine I'll ever move. At least I don't have the inclination now."

Later, over a bowl of beef stew, Cynthia thought of the wistful look on Rainey's face. She loved Gabe. When she spoke of him, her eyes lit up, but she'd accepted the fact that what they once had was a thing of the past. Just as Cynthia realized her first boyfriend had left her behind. First love was intense and could be so crushing.

Cynthia went over her notes for the second online class. Quick breads. She had posted a request for favorite comfort foods. She knew she'd get things like mashed potatoes and macaroni and cheese, but when she asked specifically for desserts, chocolate in any shape or form topped the list, but pudding was second. And there were so many kinds of puddings.

Puddings. They were a favorite with the pioneers. Simple; not too many ingredients, usually something they had in the pantry. If you have four ingredients, you can make several puddings.

The phone rang. A reservation for a month away. After marking the calendar, Cynthia mixed up batter for cupcakes. She'd purchased a large mixer with a stand the second day after taking the job. She couldn't live without a mixer that whipped up things in one minute instead of taking ten. She didn't put that on the charge; she'd take it with her wherever she went. The way things were going, Gabe might look for someone who didn't care what the B and B looked like and had no designs to improve it.

Cynthia wasn't into clothes and jewelry, but she insisted on having comfortable, beautiful surroundings—like the bedroom she was supposed to sleep in. It had drab beige walls, white curtains, and a white bedspread with a pink fringe. She hated the whole room. She ordered a new throw rug for beside the bed; a colorful patchwork quilt, pillows with shams, and a dust ruffle; curtains in a cozy, warm lilac; and found a picture for the wall over the bed. It was a small child on his knees beside his bed, reciting: "Now I lay me down to sleep. . ." A Monet print with irises was on the opposite wall. Now she could sleep here. She put down her expenses, not charging for the two paintings.

Gabe called the next morning. "What's this quilt, ruffled sham, and curtains expense? I thought all the rooms were fine the way they were."

"That's for my room."

"*Your* room! Who is going to see your room?"

"I am," Cynthia said, trying to keep her cool.

"Surely your walk-through with guests does not include your room," he said, as if not hearing her.

"Of course my room is off limits, but I cannot sleep in an all white room! Makes me think of a hospital."

"Seemed to be okay for Rainey—"

"Perhaps you should hire her back."

"She can't work now. She's a teacher."

"Well, I'm sorry, but I had to make a few changes, and I thought you'd understand."

"Within reason, yes."

"Tell me what amount that might be."

There was a long silence, and she could hear him leaning forward in his chair and then the sound of shuffling papers. "I have no set amount, Miss Lyons, but just within reason."

"So the Persian rug I ordered for the front hallway is not within reason?"

"Persian rug? In the hallway? Isn't that where the forest green rug is now?"

"Yes, but it's stained and half of the fringe is missing."

"Miss Lyons, I think I better go over the place with you so I can see for myself how many changes you want to make." He cleared his throat. "And it just might be possible that I can get a better deal on prices. Did that thought ever occur to you?"

"Oh, I'm a bargain hunter, Mr. Taylor. A dear lady in Mary's church made the quilt. We bartered."

"Bartered?"

"Yes, I'm baking bread for her son's restaurant. You know that cute, cozy one down on Marine Drive?"

There was another long silence. "How about the curtains?"

"Made by another friend. I had to supply the material, so that's the expense you see."

Cynthia heard Gabe's chair scrape again, a deep sigh, and then a voice that sounded clipped. "I *will* be down this Friday."

"I can handle it. Really I can. Don't you trust me?"

Another pause. "It isn't that. I just need to know what else you want done. It needs my approval. It *is* my house, after all."

"Will you be here in time for dinner?"

"Dinner?"

"Yes. I can cook for two as easily as one."

"Well, I hadn't thought about it. What time would dinner be?"

"After the hors d'oeuvres."

"Okay. Sounds good. What will you cook?"

"I don't know yet. Is there anything you *cannot* eat?"

"Just liver."

"It won't be that as I don't care for liver, either."

Cynthia pored over her recipes that night and decided on the salmon chowder. She'd also make her parsley breadsticks and apple crisp for dessert. It'd make a well-rounded meal.

Should she invite Rainey? That would be a pleasant surprise for Gabe, and it might be nice to have an ally—that is, if Rainey agreed with Cynthia's plans.

Two more guests registered for Saturday, Sunday, and Monday nights. This would make Gabe happy. He might forgive her the expense of the Persian rug. She found it at a secondhand store but hadn't told him that. He'd find out soon enough. Anything was an improvement over the green thing that had been there forever. Of course it matched the heavy green velvet drapes at the bay windows. No amount of cleaning, shaking, or pounding had helped. They had to be replaced.

Cynthia hummed as she made a list of ingredients she needed. The salmon chowder had been a favorite when she'd catered. Not that it was the main dish, but many people preferred a chowder or soup instead of salad. It worked especially well when she offered a tray of cut-up veggies and some nice dip or spread. She decided to include hummus, as well.

Rainey declined the invitation when Cynthia called.

"I have a faculty meeting—yeah, I know. Weird time to have it on Friday evening, but nobody on this board is normal."

"If you can get away, come for the snacks and dessert."

Gabe had told her from the first that there'd be no wine served. "I prefer nonalcoholic drinks," he'd said. "If guests have to have that glass of wine, they can go elsewhere to have it." Cynthia agreed with this reasoning.

At three, Cynthia was ready for her guests. The guest book lay open and waiting for people to sign. She'd found a wonderful fancy pen with a long feather. The rooms were clean; the house smelled of fresh bread. Soon it might smell like salmon, but that was okay. There was no better smell than that of onions cooking with a wonderful fish or beef.

Cynthia sat on the front porch in the chair looking out over the view. A barge went down the river, and she wondered what it would be like to have the job of navigating a barge up and down the waterway. She thought it would be boring but supposed the people who ran it loved the river and could not imagine working on land.

Gabe arrived before the guests from Missouri. She waved and then stopped. Someone was in the car with him. Had he mentioned he was bringing anyone? No, she was sure not. It was probably the girlfriend Rainey mentioned. That was fine. Cynthia would see what her ideas were on what was needed in the house. She might want Gabe to spend even more money.

They got out of the car, and Cynthia went down the steps to greet them.

Chapter 5

Cynthia watched while Gabe went around and opened the car door. A long-legged woman emerged and stood with her long, golden hair gleaming in the sun.

"This is Natalie," Gabe said. "Natalie, this is Cynthia Lyons, the new manager of the B and B."

Cynthia offered a hand to the graceful woman who towered over her. Natalie wore a stylish suit with a diamond pin in the lapel.

"I've heard a lot about you, and you've been here less than a week?"

"Yes, that's right." Cynthia looked back at Gabe, who appeared suddenly uncomfortable.

"Cynthia is a caterer, also," Gabe offered.

"Yes, darling," Natalie trilled, "you told me that on the way here." She turned and looked at the old Victorian house. "So this is the place I've heard so much about." She smiled dryly again. "Gabe's been raving about the B and B for so long. I finally had to see the new diva who is changing everything and giving him a headache."

Cynthia felt her composure slip. *Does this woman have a knack at making one feel bad, or what?*

"Yes, well, I've done what I can." Cynthia walked around to the side of the house. "I put in a new flower garden—petunias, pansies. . . What do you think?"

"I prefer roses," Natalie said, "not that I've ever planted any. I'm far too busy with my consulting firm." She studied one long fingernail. "I hear roses are a lot of work."

Gabe looked at the riot of color and nodded. "Petunias are what Grams always planted. How did you know?"

Cynthia smiled, glad that Gabe had taken time to look at the bright spot. "I didn't, but I was told by the local nursery person that petunias thrive here."

"When do we see the house?" Natalie asked, walking up, linking her arm with Gabe's. She gazed at him with a look Cynthia couldn't quite decipher. It definitely was not adoration.

"Yes, let's go inside," Cynthia said, leading the way as if it were her own house. "I'll put on the kettle for tea or make coffee. We can have a snack now or wait for the guests."

"I say let's have a tour first and then decide," Gabe said.

"You know, darling, I really don't want to stick around to wait for guests. After the tour, I'd like to go to that place on the waterfront. It's highly recommended in the cooking magazine I subscribe to."

"Yes, well—"

"I have salmon chowder for dinner," Cynthia said. "It's a new recipe, and it's just out of this world for taste—"

"My dear, I think you've played the Suzie Homemaker role nicely, but don't overdo it—at least not on my account. I can't even boil water and don't need someone to make me remember how awful I am at cooking."

Cynthia felt as if she'd been slapped. She wasn't trying to impress the woman at all. It hadn't been her intention. She liked to cook, and better yet, liked to share the food she prepared.

"Whatever you have planned is fine," Cynthia said. "Perhaps the guests coming in today will want a bowl of chowder."

"Perhaps they will."

Gabe had not said a word, but Cynthia heard his sharp intake of breath. He might have spoken, but Natalie was far too busy chatting.

Gabe said he thought the floors were wonderful, but she need not have gone to that much trouble. He also liked the way she'd changed the living room around. That surprised her, as he was the sort "who didn't like changes."

"I've seen it," Natalie said, "so that should keep you happy." She glanced at Cynthia. "You're doing a good job, I see, which is good as Gabe won't be around to come checking on you every week, or twice a week—whatever it's been. He's going to New York to live come November."

"You are?" Cynthia blurted out, then realized it was none of her business what Gabe did with his life. He was her boss; she had a job, and that's all that mattered. Why did she care what he did? A small lump formed in the bottom of her stomach when she realized that he was going away and probably looking forward to it. Yet she thought she could detect a "small boy" part about him that maybe he didn't know was even there.

"Natalie, I don't think you need to go around telling my plans—"

"I didn't know you were going to New York," Cynthia said. "Not that you shouldn't, but isn't it tough getting a job there?"

"I have connections," Natalie said, purring like a kitten, taking his arm again in that possessive way she had. "Gabe will do well. He has a friend who will show him the ropes, and he'll be on Wall Street in no time."

Gabe's face went blank, and Cynthia wondered what he was thinking about. She didn't know him well enough to interpret all of his expressions, but she'd guess that he might not be completely sold on the idea.

"I know," Gabe said then. "Since Natalie wants to try out this restaurant with its four stars, we'll do that, and then come back to meet the guests."

"Oh, darling," Natalie interrupted, "I do get bored so quickly in small towns. You know that."

Cynthia looked away. How could the woman be bored in a spot this beautiful? Had she even noticed the view? The beautiful home she was in? She hadn't mentioned the touches Cynthia had worked so hard on—the napkin rings on the already set table, the bloom of flowers in the hall, the gorgeous Persian rug in the foyer. She had not noticed a thing, not even the cooling apple crisp on the counter.

But Gabe had noticed the crisp and insisted on having "just a tiny taste."

One taste led to another until Cynthia had dished up at least a third of the apple dessert.

"This is just like my Norwegian grandmother used to make," Gabe said, polishing off the last spoonful.

"And I just so happened to get that from Nonie, who was my Norwegian grandmother," Cynthia said. "I'm glad you like it."

"No, dear," Natalie said when Cynthia again offered her just a small portion. "It's my figure, you know. I don't eat sweets these days."

"I'm sorry to hear that," Cynthia said. "I find eating one of my true pleasures of life."

Gabe grinned, and Cynthia smiled back. She knew he liked eating, but she also surmised he wouldn't say so, not wanting to invoke another barbed comment.

"I'll be here waiting for the Hendersons," Cynthia said, walking the two to the door. "They are from Missouri and wanted to see what it was like in our wonderful Pacific Northwest, or at least that is what they said online."

"Well, you take care of your guests," Natalie said, patting Cynthia's hand as if she were a small child. Cynthia moved back, saying nothing.

Glad they were gone, she put Gabe's bowl and spoon in the dishwasher. She would invite the guests to share the chowder with her. Why not? If they wanted to go out, that was fine, too, but she had an idea that they might just want to relax tonight and enjoy the conversation. She had put together a scrapbook showing sights to see in Astoria. They could look around on Saturday since they were staying two nights before heading down the coast toward Lincoln City and another B and B called Ocean Lake.

Cynthia let her thoughts return to Gabe and Natalie. Natalie was the right person for some man, but was Gabe the one? She couldn't quite put her finger on how she felt about it, but she didn't think Gabe and Natalie were a good match. Not that it was any of her business.

"Mind your own business, Cynthy," her mama used to say. "It doesn't matter what the neighbors are doing or how they talk to one another. It's their life, not yours."

"I'm just curious," was Cynthia's pat answer. It was true. She loved people and wanted to know what made them tick.

She thought back to the time she'd taken a dish of freshly baked brownies to a new neighbor. The door slammed in her face, the voice behind it telling her to just leave, not to bother them again. Crushed, she'd hurried home and bawled her eyes out.

Her mother had comforted her, explaining that not all people were friendly, no matter how hard one tried to be a good neighbor. Cynthia kept to herself for a few months, but soon she was noticing people and things and was "meddling," as her mother often called it.

Was she meddling now? Why should she care what Gabe did? If he wanted to marry this beautiful, outspoken woman, what was it to her? It was absolutely none of her concern. She had a job, and she would do the job the best she knew how. If it didn't work out, she'd return to San Francisco, and perhaps Max would have a new love interest by then. She would make it, no matter what happened. She was a winner. She knew it, and she was going to keep telling herself that very thing. How could she be anything else with God on her side?

Gabe was never quite sure when it first hit him that Natalie bugged him. Was it her bossiness? She liked to think she had all the answers and her way was the best. When she'd first mentioned moving to New York and finding a job on Wall Street, he realized it had been a dream in the back of his mind. He'd often thought he'd like to live in New York, the financial capital of the world. Somewhere along the way, he had started changing. It didn't seem as important to him. Then Natalie came along and started the fire going again. "Of course you can be a success there," she had said. "I'll be going soon, and I want you to come with me."

He had fallen for the woman completely. So different from Rainey—his old sweetheart from school days—they had broken off their relationship long before he moved to Portland. She had stepped in, helping him out until he found someone to take over the B and B permanently. Rainey was wonderful, and he would always love her like a sister, but he knew they could never be husband and wife.

Could he be a husband to Natalie? He wasn't even sure Natalie wanted that. She seemed content to see him twice a week, to have someone accompany her out for an evening on the town, whether it was a dinner in a fancy, upscale restaurant, or one of the Broadway shows or concerts. She had never mentioned marriage, nor had he. And now that he thought about it, as he sat across from her at the Pelican, he knew he would not be with her forever.

She complained often, like now.

"How this place got four stars is beyond me," Natalie said while they drank coffee. "I have certainly had better coffee in a two-star corner café in downtown Portland."

"Shh," Gabe said, leaning forward. He tried to take her hand, but she pulled away.

"And why shouldn't they know?"

"Let's just enjoy the evening," Gabe said.

It went from bad to worse. Natalie insisted the salad dressing was "store-bought."

"I've never had such tasteless blue cheese," she whined. "Why, there aren't even any chunks of cheese!"

"We can always go back to have salmon chowder," Gabe suggested.

"Oh, you'd like that, wouldn't you!"

Gabe soon gave up. There was no appeasing her. He would stop trying. He had learned when to talk and when to keep silent. Was that the kind of relationship he wanted? Somehow he didn't think it would be that way with Cynthia. And then he smiled to himself. But Natalie caught it.

"What's funny? You're smiling."

"Oh, am I?"

"Thinking about that country bumpkin back there," she said, pushing her salad aside. "I think she's just right for that job, but don't get any ideas, Mr. Taylor. She sure can't help your career as I can."

"I wasn't thinking about my career."

"Perhaps you should." Natalie leaned forward.

But Gabe didn't want to think about it. For some reason he longed to go back to the B and B and wanted to meet the Hendersons, picturing them as a down-to-earth couple from the heartland. Perhaps they even had a farm. They would love Cynthia—especially her cooking.

The sautéed prawns came before Natalie could say anything.

"This is all we get?" she asked the waiter.

"It says six to eight on the menu, I believe, ma'am."

Natalie took a bite and shoved her plate aside. "This has certainly not been a pleasant experience," she snapped. "I think whoever wrote that article in my cooking magazine must be the owner. I'd like a chance to write a piece—"

"Natalie, please," Gabe was saying. This was still his hometown, though he hadn't lived here for the past seven years. He still knew most of the people, and if he remembered correctly, the waiter was someone he had known in high school.

"Gabe, if you won't say something, then I must."

Gabe pulled out some money, put it on the table, and told the astounded waiter—George, or whatever his name was—to keep the change.

"You can go on complaining, but you're going to be alone." He turned away. "I'll be in the car waiting."

Natalie followed, brushing past the waiter on her way out the door.

"You humiliated me," she screamed once they were on the sidewalk. "You should have backed me up!"

"What was there to back up? I thought everything was fine."

"Maybe you won't make it in New York then."

"And maybe I won't!"

He held the door open and almost slammed it before she got her high-heeled foot completely in. He so wished he'd never talked her into coming. He'd been trying for months to get her to come to Astoria, but she was always too busy or wanted to try yet another new restaurant in Portland. Well, this was a first and a last. He sure wouldn't make this mistake again.

"I suppose you're going to pout all the way back to Portland," Natalie snapped, staring straight ahead.

"No, I'm not. We're stopping back at the B and B, and I'm having a bowl of salmon chowder."

"Oh no you're not!" Natalie's eyes blazed.

"I'm driving and I say I am."

"I couldn't possibly stand to be in the same room with Miss Perfect anymore."

"Okay. Sit in the car then. I'll try to be quick."

That is what she did as he went inside. A navy blue car with Missouri plates was in one of the parking spots, and he heard Cynthia's voice carrying from one of the upper bedrooms. His heart did a funny lurch as she came down the stairs, asking the guests to wait until she returned. He figured she probably thought it was another guest.

"Gabe!" Her eyes widened as their gazes met. "But, I thought—"

"I know. Natalie didn't like the food, and I'm back here, wanting to meet the guests and hoping there's enough chowder for me."

"Of course. Come on up while I finish their tour. They can select their favorite room, and then I'll put the chowder on. Surely Natalie will come in?"

"No, I don't think so."

The next hour was pleasant, and the chowder was better than Gabe could have imagined. He had a winner in Cynthia Lyons. He had thought so before, but after tonight, he knew so. You didn't have to hit him over the head to make a point.

Cynthia knew the couple would take the Garden Room. As they brought in their suitcases and hauled them up the narrow staircase, she went down to put the chowder on. They had agreed they would like to have a bowl of salmon chowder and then join Cynthia and the owner. She'd hastily explained that he was in town briefly and would like to try her new recipe.

"I've only had salmon once," Mr. Henderson said. "Wasn't too happy with it. Guess I'm a beef and potatoes type guy. Most of us farmers are, you know."

"But we would love to try it again, now wouldn't we, Chester?" Mrs. Henderson said.

The four sat around the smaller of the two tables and had thick wedges of Cynthia's bread with bowls of steamy salmon chowder.

"So what do you think?" Cynthia asked after everyone had had at least two spoonfuls.

"This is wonderful," Mrs. Henderson said.

"I agree. It's sure got a good flavor."

"I've never tasted anything like it," Gabe said.

"And?" Cynthia asked. "That's good or not?"

Gabe grinned. "Good, of course."

They were just polishing off the chowder when a horn honked. Gabe's eyebrows lifted. "Oh, I think that's my friend in the car."

"Well, why didn't she come in?" Mr. Henderson asked. "Does she have the plague or something?"

"No. We just had a spat, and she insisted on staying in the car."

Gabe felt for his keys just as they heard a car start, and when he looked up, he realized he'd left them in the ignition.

"She didn't drive off and leave you, did she?" Mrs. Henderson asked.

Gabe shrugged. "Nah. She'll be back. She's gone down to the corner store, probably."

But Natalie did not return, and after they had the cheese and fruit platter Cynthia had prepared, Gabe said he'd have to rent a car.

"If we were going that way, we could take you," Mr. Henderson offered.

"I could take you, I suppose," Cynthia offered and then remembered she had two more guests coming in.

"No, the rental car will work fine."

Long after the Hendersons had settled down for the night—at nine they said it seemed like eleven because of the time change—Cynthia went online to see if there was anyone in the chat room or if there were any questions.

"Dear Lion, I made the apple crisp tonight, and my husband ate half of it! I want some more apple recipes. Thank you, Laurie."

Cynthia quickly replied, then shut off the computer. This was going to be fun. And she loved the people who were staying the weekend. But what she couldn't get out of her mind was Natalie and the way she had behaved. And even more, she thought about Gabe, wondering if he was truly happy with the situation. Somehow she felt he belonged here in Astoria, where his heart seemed to be.

Gabe had two hours to think as he drove east toward Portland. Going through the familiar towns gave him small comfort. He had felt embarrassed tonight with Natalie making a spectacle over the dinner. Why was she so negative about things? He thought again of Grams and the lessons he'd learned at her knee. Her voice seemed to come to him now in the darkness and stillness of the car as he sped over the miles to his Portland apartment.

"Don't ever hurt anyone intentionally," Grams had said. "And if someone hurts you, give them the benefit of the doubt. But if they are taking advantage of you, stand up for your rights. God will give you the strength to do that, if you but ask."

Is this what Natalie is doing to me now? Am I letting her do it because I need her help with my goals to become a top financier?

A full moon shone overhead, and Gabe remembered his childhood, walking along the riverbank, looking at the stars overhead, wondering if he would be someone someday.

"But you are someone," Grams said. "God doesn't make junk. Just be true to your inner self. Be the best you can be."

Gabe breathed a prayer, the first he'd said in a long while.

Lord, I need Your guidance. I need insight. Is Natalie the right person for me? If so, why does Cynthia's face keep popping into my mind? Could I be blinded by the need to succeed instead of leaning on You?

It was late when Gabe arrived at his apartment. He saw the Mercury parked on the street, and Natalie stood on the sidewalk, her arms crossed.

"Give me the keys," he said.

"I suppose you're angry."

He didn't look at her. "Not angry, but my eyes were opened tonight."

"Meaning?"

"Meaning that you and I don't have a real relationship. Meaning that I won't be seeing you again."

"And all because of one incident where I lost my temper?"

Gabe sighed. "No, Nat, it's more, much more than that. I don't have enough time to explain it, not that you'd listen if I did—"

"So, that's it? You're breaking things off with me just like that?"

Gabe didn't have to look to know that her eyes were blazing.

"You'll feel differently tomorrow."

"I wouldn't count on it." He moved toward the porch.

"Well, if that's how you feel—" She removed the ruby ring he had given her on her birthday and flung it at him. "I hope you have a wonderful life with Miss Goody Baker!"

Gabe said nothing but strolled up the steps and put the key in the lock, sudden relief filling his being.

Chapter 6

August turned into September and then October. Cynthia kept busy with the online cooking classes and the B and B, which was full during the week, not just on weekends. She had hired a young woman whose husband was out of work to help clean and make up the beds after the guests left. Cynthia had not taken an order for cupcakes in over a month, but she still delivered her special bread once a week to the restaurant in town. Mary delivered fresh flowers twice a week, including small bouquets for each bedroom.

Cynthia was happy with the way things were going, but there was an unexpected ache that went through her. It had to do with Gabe. Soon he'd be gone to New York, and the thought unnerved her, though she wasn't sure why.

New drapes hung at the bay windows, though they were pulled back and held with a matching bow. Gabe had agreed to replace two more rugs and let her take out the wall-to-wall carpeting in the bedrooms. She hated the carpeting. It didn't add to the feel of the Victorian home. But the biggest and most wonderful surprise was when Gabe brought the small fountain to put in the parlor. It added charm, and its trickling sound mesmerized everyone. She remembered the afternoon with fondness.

"This is to appease you as I said no to the outdoor fountain."

"Oh, it's wonderful! I can't wait to set it up."

"Has the raccoon been back?"

That was the reason he'd said no to a fishpond or a waterfall. Both attracted wild animals, and there were certainly some in the hills behind the Victorian.

"I saw footprints yesterday."

Cynthia had mixed feelings about chasing the animal away. The first time she'd caught a glimpse, the raccoon limped off. Later she saw where his right foot was mangled. "Probably from a trap," Gabe said.

The guests had left by noon, and no one was expected that evening. One free night. Cynthia felt heady.

"When do you go back?" she asked. She liked the way his shoulders hunched over the fountain project, the sunshine from a nearby window gleaming on his hair. She had the sudden urge to touch him but stepped back.

He stood, rubbing his back. "I can't lean over for long. It's an old football injury."

"I can do this," Cynthia said.

"I know." Gabe's face suddenly looked flat. "I don't think there's anything you *cannot* do."

"I didn't mean it to sound that way."

"I know," he repeated.

He took her arm suddenly. "Let's go outside; soak up some sun."

Cynthia followed him out the door and down the steps. A riot of color from the impatiens and petunias nearly took her breath away. "I love this spot."

"I know. It's beautiful now, and I appreciate how you've brought it to life. Come sit for a minute."

Cynthia had talked him into the concrete deacon's bench. It was ideal for inclement weather and the dampness Astoria experienced year-round.

She put pads on the bench each day, bringing them in at night or at the first sight of rain. Funny how the small misty showers bothered her no longer. She found she liked how the rain made everything greener and cleared the air.

"I suppose you'll be moving on one of these days," Gabe said.

Cynthia met his steady gaze and looked away again. "I don't know why you think that."

"Someone with your obvious flair for decorating needs to find a better-paying job."

"I'm happy with what you pay me. After all, I don't have rent to pay, and the food is covered. I think it's a good deal."

"How's the online cooking class going?"

"Great." Cynthia thought of her latest posting. Peach Treats. "I keep getting new students. The latest is a guy who wants to impress his girlfriend."

"A guy, huh?"

"Men do like to cook, you know. Why do you suppose all the classy restaurants have male chefs? When they cook, they do it with flourish. They're never afraid to try new things."

"You try new things."

"Yes, I do."

"What treat do you have today?"

Cynthia laughed. "Oh, so is that a hint?"

Gabe stood. "I really need to get back to Portland," he said abruptly.

"Without a slice of peach pie?"

"Peach pie?"

"Made first thing this morning. I had to try this new piecrust."

Gabe stayed another hour, having two pieces and taking a slice with him when he left. Cynthia cleaned off the table. Something was bothering Gabe; it was so evident. She'd tried to get him to talk, but he wouldn't. He'd broken things off with

Natalie; that had happened right after that visit when she'd driven off in the car. No, it was something else. Had he met another woman?

With the rest of the afternoon free, Cynthia checked the phone, making sure it would pick up messages, and headed out, her sweater over her shoulders. She took the last piece of peach pie to Mary. Mary always appreciated her cooking, about as much as Gabe. She'd found a true friend in Mary.

As Cynthia got to the bottom of the hill and onto Main Street, a familiar car went by. Gabe. And beside him sat Rainey. *Rainey?* Was he seeing her again? Friends, he'd said more than once, but was it really only that? Rainey was laughing, and it looked as if they were driving back to Portland together.

"Hey, haven't seen you in a few," Mary said. "How did you like the last flowers I sent? I thought the dahlias were especially colorful."

"Gorgeous. I've never seen such a variety of colors and blooms." Cynthia set the sack on the counter. "Peach pie. Tell me if you like the crust. It has just a smidgen of cornmeal."

"Cornmeal?"

"Yeah. Saw the recipe in *Sunset* magazine."

"Can't wait to try it, but I'll wait until I get home and put my feet up and have a cup of java with it."

Cynthia turned to leave.

"Hey, what's up? Don't you feel like talking, or are guests coming in this afternoon?"

"No, I have a few hours. I just wanted to walk down by the river."

"Is something wrong?"

Cynthia opened her mouth to speak but closed it again. How could she tell Mary what was in her heart—how she had fallen in love with her boss, a man who clearly got agitated with her for things, and who thought of her only as the woman who ran his bed-and-breakfast with precision and dignity?

"You don't have to tell me if you don't want. That's okay. I think I know anyway."

Cynthia spun around. "You *know?* But you couldn't know."

"Could so."

Cynthia looked at her friend, the only real friend she had here. "I will muddle through it, as I do all my problems."

"It may not be as bad as you think."

"Meaning?"

"It concerns Gabe. And I think he's equally smitten but won't admit it. Not yet, anyway."

"He's going with Rainey again."

"They're friends."

"Yeah, you said that before."

"It's true."

"Well. . ." Cynthia paused in the open doorway. "I just don't think you know what I'm thinking about."

"It's a business deal," Mary said then.

"A business deal?"

"Yes. And that's all I'm going to say about It."

A business deal? What would that be about? Did it have something to do with Gabe's going to New York?

The walk along the river was tranquil. A large ship was anchored, and a barge moved slowly toward Portland. One day she wanted to go on the excursion boat that traveled back and forth from Portland, across the Columbia River, to the Washington side, where hills all green and woodsy seemed to meet the sky. Cynthia had driven over once just to see the hills up close. It was beautiful. But what wasn't beautiful in the Northwest?

Cynthia strolled past the old railroad depot. It sat empty and neglected, as if waiting for someone to come along and refurbish it. She could see a restaurant going in. Many cities across the United States had turned their old train stations into works of art. She'd seen one in Bennington, Vermont, when traveling there with her mother just a year before she died. Her one dream was to travel back to the place of her birth, and so they had. Dreams should be fulfilled, if possible.

Cynthia touched the red brick. It would be standing long after she was gone. The old building had possibilities. She had ideas, but nothing with which to do anything.

Cynthia knew she was a dreamer. She'd always been a dreamer. Her mother told her she was like her father. She wished she'd known him better. She wished they could have shared their dreams. Did he see old, dilapidated buildings and imagine them as magnificent structures again? Did he drive through a town and imagine what it would be like to live there? Did he enjoy the sunrises and sunsets as much as she did?

Max had laughed at her dreams. He never understood. He wanted to please her, but in the end he had stopped trying. The fact that he denied there was a God was something Cynthia couldn't tolerate. Why, God was everywhere she looked. He guided and directed her. How could anyone deny His existence?

A breeze blew in from the west. The Pacific Ocean was not far away; its tides ruled the mouth of the Columbia. The waves picked up as she turned and headed back up the hill.

The phone was ringing when Cynthia returned to the B and B.

"Hello, Taylor's Bed-and-Breakfast. May I help you?"

"Cynthia?"

Her heart lurched. "Gabe? I thought you were on the road."

"I am."

"And?"

"I felt I left with things unsaid."

"I saw you go by with Rainey. She's going to Portland with you?"

"No, I dropped her off at the edge of town at a friend's."

"Oh." Now Cynthia felt dumb.

"What's playing in the background?"

"Willie Nelson," Cynthia said.

"Willie Nelson? You like his music?"

"It's a tape Mom gave me one Christmas. There are a few songs that make me think and put things into the right perspective."

"I see. Cynthia, I—"

"Yes? What?"

"Oh, never mind. I wanted to run something by you, but I think it can wait. Take care."

The phone went dead before she could say good-bye.

"We never learn until it's too late," Willie sang, his words filling the now vacant sitting room. Why did that song haunt her so?

Two reservations came in, and soon Cynthia was busy in the kitchen. She wanted to try something new with cupcakes. She'd have cupcakes in the next online class. There was so much one could do with cake.

The doorbell rang. Cynthia dried her hands and hurried to answer. Mary's husband stood there, a smile on his face. "I know this isn't the regular delivery day, but these are special."

"Special?"

"The order just came in on the phone."

"Well, aren't you the speedy one to deliver so fast?"

"Wait until you see the card."

"The card can't be as special as these peonies. They are beautiful!"

Cynthia recognized Mary's spidery handwriting on the small enclosure. It was addressed to her, not the B and B.

I don't think you realize how much your help means to me. Have a wonderful week. Gabe Taylor.

Cynthia smiled. Only Gabe would add his last name as if Cynthia didn't know who he was. She found the lovely milk glass vase in the pantry and filled it with water, adding a teaspoon of sugar. Peonies didn't have a long life, but she wanted these to last as long as possible.

⚜

Gabe called Mary's Bouquets after leaving Astoria. He should have stopped at the store, but the idea hadn't occurred to him until he dropped Rainey off.

"You're in love, Gabe," Rainey had said, looking up at him with a sudden smile.

"Don't be ridiculous," he snapped.

"Yeah, I'm right."

The Mercury stopped, and she opened the door. "You don't want to admit it, but your fast reaction in denying it is all the more reason I believe it."

"Rainey, I'm just getting over Natalie—you know that."

"So?"

"I can't possibly consider even looking at another woman, let alone have a relationship."

"What? You didn't have a relationship with Natalie. She talked and you jumped. Is that what you call a relationship?"

"I thought it was at the time."

"Still going to New York?"

"Of course. Bought the airline ticket last week."

Rainey smiled again. "Anything can happen, Gabe. *Anything.* Trust me on this."

Gabe drove off in a huff. He hated it when she insisted she could read his mind. She was almost as bad as Natalie.

Cynthia. Was it true? He found himself thinking of her endlessly. When he tried to push the thought aside, her smiling face came back to haunt him. How could he be so foolish to fall for someone now? Someone like her?

Someone like her? The thought suddenly hit him. What did he mean by that? Any man could consider himself lucky to have a woman like Cynthia. She was smart, an innovative cook, fixed things, had a good mind... She wasn't a beauty, but she had a good, homespun quality about her, someone his grandmother would have loved on the spot. And Grams was picky about whom she liked and didn't.

He picked up his cell phone and dialed Mary at the florist shop.

After passing through the small town of Clatskanie, Gabe considered all the reasons why this was not the time to fall in love. It had not been long enough since his relationship with Natalie. Was he over her? And Cynthia had been with a man in California—Max, he thought she'd called him. It could be that she was still in love with him. Besides, he remembered reading that one should wait four years before another relationship. *Lord, is that true? Do I want to get involved with this woman?*

"*And why not?*" a voice seemed to say.

Yes, why not?

Gabe didn't take rejection well. For that reason, he had to take things slow. Then

101

he thought about New York. He had always dreamed of living there, of getting a slice of the fast lane. How could he not go now? His friend Jeff expected him. Natalie had closed the door on any help, but he wondered if she could have helped him much anyway. No, he must go. It was a done deal.

❖

The traffic was worse than usual as Gabe drove through the streets of downtown Portland. He loved the town, but the traffic was one huge headache. He longed for Astoria and its quiet nature—the lack of cars, trucks, and noise. Noise always had bothered him. He missed the bellow of a ship's horn, the *clackety-clack* of a train on the tracks. These sounds put him to sleep at night, made him long to travel, to leave the town of his childhood, and go to the city.

Here he was about to leave and go to one of the largest cities in the world. How would he fare? Would he like it as much as he once thought he would? He guessed he would never know until he tried it.

❖

Cynthia's latest cooking class had been a success.

"Noodle pudding? I would never have thought of noodles as being dessert. Thanks for the interesting and delicious recipe."

Cynthia smiled, remembering a visit to a neighbor when she was five. Gloria lived alone and had a wooden leg. The wooden leg intrigued Cynthia. It was the only reason she went with her mother. She hoped to see what a wooden leg looked like. She recalled going into a house that was dark and musty smelling. They entered the kitchen, where the woman sat. "She never gets up to answer the door," her mother explained beforehand. "It takes too long to walk with crutches, you know."

"But if she has a wooden leg, can't she walk on it?"

"Yes, of course, but it's much easier not to."

When they entered the cluttered kitchen, the smell of vanilla emanated from the oven.

"You're just in time to take my noodle pudding out of the oven," Gloria said. "And then you can share it with me."

"I brought cookies," Cynthia's mother said, holding up a small white bag. "They came from the bakery over on Tenth."

"Oh, how delightful. Please set them up on that counter." Gloria pointed.

Cynthia watched while her mother opened the oven door, pot holder in hand.

She wondered what a noodle pudding could be. It didn't sound like anything she'd like.

"We'd be delighted to have a small dish with you," her mother said.

"No," Cynthia started to say, but her mother elbowed her, and Cynthia changed her no to a "yes, thank you."

"Noodle pudding comes from my grandmother, who loved cooking."

Cynthia kept trying to see the wooden leg, but both legs were covered with denim. Cynthia brought two bowls to the table while her mother brought the third bowl and cream she'd found in the refrigerator.

"This is just wonderful that you want to share with us."

Cynthia nodded. "Yes, thank you very much."

Cynthia knew she'd have to hold her nose to get the pudding down. But on the third bite, when she breathed suddenly, a sweet taste filled her mouth, and she ate the rest with gusto.

"I do need this recipe," Cynthia's mother said, and Cynthia nodded in agreement.

Gabe's face came to mind again, but she pushed it aside. He had sent her flowers. Why, she didn't know, but it wouldn't be for the right reason, not the reason she hoped for. She'd enjoy them, anyway.

Cynthia decided to make another noodle pudding and take some to Mary and her family. She was just removing it from the oven when the doorbell rang. No guests were coming, and Mary was still at work.

Rainey stood with jacket in hand. "It does make one sweat coming up that hill," she puffed.

"Come on in. I heard you went to visit a friend."

"Oh, so Gabe called you."

"He did."

"And sent you flowers?"

"Yes, but how did you know?"

Rainey slipped out of her loafers and placed the jacket in a small heap on top of her shoes. "Gabe said I should stop to see the new changes. He seems quite happy about everything."

"Not that he wanted to spend any money—"

Rainey laughed. "That's Gabe all right. He's tight, but that's good in a way. Means he has a good business head on him. He should do fine in New York."

New York. How Cynthia wished she had never heard about it. It made an empty hollow feeling inside her, one that wouldn't go away.

"After a tour, you can have some noodle pudding with me."

"Noodle pudding!" Rainey exclaimed. "Is that a dessert?"

"Yes. I believe it's Armenian. A woman in my old neighborhood used to bake it a lot."

"I'll try anything once," Rainey said, following Cynthia up the stairs.

"It *is* beautiful," Rainey said. "Gabe said you had the magic touch, and I can see he is right."

"I'm glad you think so."

After standing and enjoying the view from the north bedroom window, the two went back downstairs to the kitchen. Rainey accepted the bowl and claimed it was delicious. "So this goes on your website?"

"Oh, not mine," Cynthia said, removing the bowls. "I just send in my column once a week, and then each night I see if anyone has posted a question or comment. Sometimes they send recipes for me to try."

"And you're not too busy with the work here?"

"Usually not."

Rainey left, and Cynthia's thoughts included Gabe again. She hoped Gabe had arrived home all right. She wished Portland wasn't a two-hour drive away. Yet the distance hadn't stopped him before. But New York, that was another matter. It was time to shift gears and go online to see if there were more messages. She turned on the computer and relaxed when she heard its steady hum.

Chapter 7

In the past few months, Cynthia had covered quick breads, puddings, cookies, crisps, flans, and cakes. Her next lesson was to hone in on decorative cupcakes. She had never made any for Gabe, and she now regretted it. Gabe had left for New York two weeks before, and she had not heard a word. Funny how quickly she'd become used to hearing from him, having him drop in, feeding him some of her cooking, and sending him home with a goodie to enjoy the next day. He always called, thanking her. If only they didn't spar so much. Cynthia was a strong person; she'd always known that. She liked having control. A lot of changes had been made to the B and B since she came. The latest was the remodel of one bedroom, which was now pet-friendly.

At first Gabe said no to every suggestion. And so she'd worked and finished one thing at a time. When he saw it, he liked it. He just didn't like it when the bills came in.

"I'm not made of money, you know."

Cynthia laughed. "No, but think of all the money you saved on labor."

Every Friday morning she mowed the lawn and edged it. Some places would expect to pay a gardener, and she'd tactfully pointed out that fact.

The ongoing bill was for the flowers that Cynthia insisted on ordering. The house must look inviting. Word of mouth brought others to the B and B.

Cynthia looked out at the view of the river she'd grown to love. She couldn't think of living anywhere else. It was serene except when the winds came and blew up a storm. When the water was choppy and frothy, she imagined what it must be like to be out in a boat then.

Cynthia dropped Gabe a snail mail note at the end of his first week in New York.

Just wanted to tell you that we had a full house last weekend. More people coming for midweek. Then it should start slowing down, though I don't know why. The weather is glorious. But I really am writing to see how you're doing. Do you love New York? I've always wanted to go, but maybe it's one of those dreams I'll never fulfill.

She wanted to say she missed hearing from him, missed seeing his face, but the words stayed inside her, along with the hollow emptiness.

Why didn't he write? Even if it were just a sentence or two, she'd at least know he was doing okay.

Cynthia made a potpie and invited Rainey over.

"I just wanted to visit. . .see if you had heard from Gabe," she said before Rainey slipped out of her sweater.

"I have not. And I assume you haven't, either."

"Did he always want to go to New York?"

Rainey nodded, taking a piece of the Mexican fudge Cynthia offered her. "Yes, he did. Talked about it as far back as I can remember."

"Then it's good he's doing it. I think life is too short not to do what you've always wanted to do."

"And you?" Rainey asked. "What's your heart's desire?"

Cynthia poured tea and motioned for Rainey to sit at the small table in one corner of the kitchen.

"I think I'm pretty much doing it. I've always liked to cook. I started the catering business, as you've undoubtedly heard about, and now I'm managing one of the loveliest B and Bs in the Northwest. I bake what I want when I want, and I am now teaching others a love of cooking—or hope that I am."

Cynthia grabbed a plate off the sideboard and showed Rainey her latest creations. "These are cupcakes I've made for a party."

Rainey's eyes widened. "I like the butterfly design on this one. They're all too beautiful to eat."

"No, they're to be eaten."

"How did you learn this?"

"By trial and error."

The two women talked, and Cynthia found out a lot about Gabe that she had only guessed at before.

"His grandmother doted on him; he could do no wrong."

"I surmised that."

"His father died when he was too young to remember, but my father remembered him as being loud and lusty."

"Gabe certainly isn't loud," Cynthia interjected.

"I know. He never has been." Rainey sighed audibly. "I have loved him for so many years, first as a boyfriend, and now as a brother. He'd do anything for me."

Cynthia wondered if it was really a brother/sister relationship. Some of the best relationships were ones where the two were good, solid friends. You then built more on that foundation. She hoped someday she'd find someone like that. She knew it would never be Gabe. They disagreed on a lot of things, and though she found him attractive and felt she was falling in love with him at one point, she realized they couldn't make a go of it.

Long after Rainey left, Cynthia thought about her life and what she would now do differently. And she couldn't think of a thing except having a male companion. She missed that very much. There was a show in Astoria she longed to see, but it was no fun going alone. She went out to eat once in a while, but not often, as it was usually a disappointment. She supposed she was like a writer who no longer read a book for enjoyment, but edited every line. Still, a night out could be fun, and someone to help carry the groceries in could be nice. Someday she might realize that dream. There was always hope.

Cynthia cleaned the few dishes up, checked the computer for e-mail—just in case Gabe had written—then started her next column. She liked to keep ahead two weeks in the event she got too busy to do one sometime.

Cynthia turned the last light out and went to her small bedroom at the rear of the house. Sometimes she wanted to be on the tip-top floor as the view was magnificent. But, the innkeeper always had the smallest bedroom.

A sky full of stars was just outside her window, and she marveled in this most wonderful creation. She never tired of looking at the sky and the stars. The moon was but a sliver, making her think of a piece of pie.

Cynthia couldn't sleep, not even after reading a couple chapters in Hebrews. Usually she felt comforted from the faith verse, but not tonight. Her mind kept going back to Gabe and how she felt when he was around. The times they didn't get along were when they argued over the telephone. When he was here, she could ply him with one of her entrees or a fancy dessert, and he was happy. Sometimes they walked down the street to stroll along the river. There they talked about a lot of things, but never business. They left the B and B behind. She liked thinking about those times, knowing they wouldn't happen again. Gabe had carved out his niche; he would stay in New York and forget his simple life in Astoria, and Cynthia had to accept that fact and get on with her life.

Chapter 8

Cynthia had boxes of cake mix lined up in a row: chocolate and vanilla, two favorite flavors. She also had butter, powdered sugar, food coloring, vanilla extract, and lemon. There were also cupcake papers, which she usually didn't use, but she knew they would be easier for the girls to handle while icing and decorating their cupcakes.

"How do I get myself into these things?" she said to Jan, who had called wanting to know how things were going.

"Because you're a glutton for punishment," Jan retorted. "At least that's what my mom used to say."

"It seemed like a good idea at the time."

Cynthia had met the local Junior Girl Scout leader at the florist shop.

"We're having a celebration coming up in honor of Juliette Lowe, our founder. We have a skit, a program showing what we do, but we need to make some money. I keep trying to come up with an idea. Do you have any?"

"No, afraid not," Mary said, as she wrapped a silver ribbon around a bouquet of scarlet mums.

Cynthia walked on into the shop and, as always, had to put her two cents' worth in. "I think it would be fun to have a cupcake raffle. It's not as expensive, the girls could make fancy cupcakes, and people would bid on them."

The leader's face lit up, and she said it was a good idea, but who would help the girls?

"I could. Since cupcakes are my specialty, I have lots of photos and ideas."

"Trust me," Mary said with a nod. "Cynthia Lyons is a wonder when it comes to food. I say go for it!"

Here they were now, ten girls with frosting on the counter, floor, on everyone's apron, and even on a few noses. But the cupcakes were coming along nicely. Each brought a cake mix, to go along with what Cynthia already had, and a box of powdered sugar. Cynthia provided the flavorings and decorations. She had a plate of cupcakes for an example, and the girls each chose which one they liked best. The ladybug always won, hands down.

They baked the cupcakes—each girl would do a dozen, and Cynthia would finish up with the rest and donate those to the raffle. The girls would have one hundred and twenty, and Cynthia would add another hundred or so. That should help toward the expenses of summer camp.

Cupcakes adorned the counters, the top of the stove (now cooled off), and trays on the dining room table. Cynthia had bought pink boxes from the bakery, so the girls could take their cupcakes to the sale in a nice box. She hoped people paid more than they were worth.

Cynthia finished frosting the first dozen—it didn't take her long. The girls crowded around, marveling at how fast she worked.

"I've frosted cupcakes for years; I better be fast."

The door opened and she turned, startled. Nobody ever just came in, not even Mary or Rainey.

It was Gabe. Her heart flip-flopped as she wiped her hands on her apron, now smudged with greens, yellows, and reds.

"Why, Mr. Taylor, what a surprise!" She wondered if her face was red as a flush heated it. "I thought you were in New York."

He came into the room and as their eyes met, there was a sudden longing in his gaze—if she was reading it right. Of course she could be wrong. She had been wrong many times in the past where men were concerned.

"This is Troop 44, and I'll let each girl introduce herself, and, girls, Mr. Taylor owns this house. We have him to thank for letting us use the kitchen."

Gabe smiled and nodded as each girl said her name.

"Are there any samples?" he asked, a grin spreading across his face.

Cynthia looked at her masterpieces. "Actually, these cupcakes were made for a raffle tomorrow night. The proceeds go into the girls' camp fund. Now if you'd like to buy one, you can do that."

"Just give him one," Martha said. "He looks extra hungry."

Cynthia nodded. "I suppose I could do that. Let him pick out his favorite?"

"No, I'll buy since it's for a good cause."

Cynthia had not finished all of her cupcakes yet. The frosting was hardening, but that was no problem. She'd just add a teaspoon of hot water and finish the job.

Gabe bought six cupcakes and set a ten-dollar bill on the table. "I hope this is enough."

"That's more than adequate," Cynthia said. "I'll have coffee ready in a jiff, that is if you want to eat one now."

"Does a bear live in the woods?" He grinned.

One of the Scouts wrinkled her nose. "What does that mean?"

"Of course a bear lives in the woods," another girl answered, "so of course he wants a cupcake. That's what he means."

Gabe pulled out a chair. "You never cease to amaze me," he said to Cynthia.

"What's it going to be next? You'll invite all the politicians over for dinner?"

"Ha-ha!"

The girls put their cupcakes in their boxes, and soon parents came and picked them up. Gabe had started on his third cupcake. "These are not only works of art; they're tasty, too."

Cynthia wondered why Gabe was here. One didn't usually fly to New York, work a few weeks, and fly home. Had something come up that was too important not to attend to over the phone? Was he selling the B and B because he wanted to buy a place in New York? Wouldn't Rainey have mentioned it when she saw her yesterday?

"You're wondering what brought me back."

"As a matter of fact, yes."

"So am I."

Cynthia raised an eyebrow. "Is this supposed to be Twenty Questions?"

Gabe got up then, wiping the frosting off his chin, and it hit her again how much he was like a little boy. She wanted to run her hand through his hair, wanted him to lift her face to his, but she must stifle the feelings. He'd found someone in New York and had come home to pack up the rest of his things in Portland and would probably sell the B and B by the end of the season, which was soon. She felt a lump come to her throat.

"So, are you going to say why you're here, even if I think I know why?"

"Oh, you think you know, do you?"

"Gabe, just come out with it. You're buying a place in New York and selling the B and B. Never mind the fact that it's been in your family for three generations. Never mind the fact that you have an efficient manager who would give her eyeteeth to live here forever. . . ." She stopped in midsentence, realizing what she'd said.

He stood staring at her, as she tried to recover as quickly as possible. "I shouldn't have said that last part. I'm sorry—"

"Sorry?" Suddenly he was there, taking both her hands, removing her frosting-encrusted apron, and pulling her to him. "You'd like to live here the rest of your life? Is this true?"

"Well, I. . ." She looked up into his dark eyes and forgot everything that was on her mind. Only the things in her heart mattered now.

"You are wanting me to kiss you."

Before she could respond, his mouth covered hers, and she felt herself lean into him as if she belonged there, as if she had always belonged there.

"So, that's settled."

"What's settled?" Cynthia stepped back, her hands gripping the sides of her skirt. Usually she wore jeans, but this morning, feeling she wanted to look like an old-fashioned girl, she had donned a skirt with a white ruffled blouse. The apron also had ruffles. It lay discarded on the back of a chair where Gabe had tossed it.

"I have something to show you."

"In Portland? I can't leave. Guests are coming today."

"Not in Portland. It's five blocks away, close enough to walk."

Cynthia wondered what Gabe was talking about. She looked at the frosting dried and congealed in the bowl now. She had to finish the cupcakes first. Would he understand? "Give me fifteen minutes, okay? So I can finish? You can put those that are done in one of the pink boxes—"

"Are you always going to be this bossy?"

Always? Did he say always? Always conjured up good thoughts in her mind. Happy thoughts. Forever belonged to always. She glanced back at him and found herself in his arms again, being kissed not just once, but twice. Finally he released her.

"I missed you so much when I was in New York."

"I missed you, too. Your calls complaining about the latest expense, you suddenly turning up without calling first. . ."

"You do like being bossy, making the decisions, having your own way."

"Now, just a minute. Everything I did for this B and B made it better, and you know it."

"I like it when you get angry. Do you know your mouth gets all small, and your eyes actually flash? I noticed it the first time we met in my office. I said to myself that day, 'Here is trouble.'"

"You did not."

"Did so."

"You never acted like that. I thought you couldn't stand me."

"I was fighting the feeling. You were getting in the way of my dream, my passion to go to New York and become somebody."

"You already are somebody."

"I know. I discovered that while I was gone. It doesn't matter where you are; you're still the same person. And I also knew that God brought you into my life for a reason, and if I didn't get back here, someone else might come along and snatch you up."

Cynthia's head whirled with the suddenness of it. It was happening too fast.

She looked at the frosting and back at Gabe. "This can wait. I've had interruptions before."

"This interruption will be worth it."

"I'm sure it will."

She changed from flats to tennis shoes and grabbed a sweater from the foyer coat rack.

"Where are we really going?"

"To see a house."

"To see a house," Cynthia repeated. She had trouble keeping up with his long stride, until he realized and slowed down. "Here, let me take your hand. That will keep me in pace with you."

Soon they stood in front of an old Victorian, and Cynthia gasped. It looked to be the same vintage as Taylor's B and B. But the paint crumbled, shutters were hanging askew, and the roof was in dire need of repair.

"Whose house is this?"

"Mine."

"Yours? But you never told me you had another house."

"I know, because it wasn't mine. I bought it yesterday; I put down the money after taking out a second mortgage on the bed-and-breakfast, which qualified for a nice loan, thanks to you."

"You really own this house?" Cynthia's mind was reeling.

"Yes. I've loved this house all my life; it's the twin to the bed-and-breakfast. The owners wouldn't sell, though I asked every year. And then Rainey saw that the son who inherited it died of sudden cancer, and she checked around and discovered that his heirs wanted to sell, the sooner the better."

Cynthia looked at the old Victorian, then back at him. "And you're opening another bed-and-breakfast?"

"Yes. That's my plan. But it will take major work, and I need someone who is good with interior design, but I guess she's too busy cooking with everyone in Astoria."

"Gabe! It was a one-time thing. The Girl Scouts, you know?"

"I know. And it's what I've come to admire about you in these past four months. You are so giving and generous and loving to everyone."

His eyes told Cynthia he was once again teasing her, and she playfully pushed him.

"I like all those traits, even the bossiness, as a bossy person gets things done. But the most important one is the loving, and anyone who would help the Girl Scouts make money for their camp is all heart."

A car pulled up and Rainey got out. "I thought you'd be here when nobody answered the door at the B and B. Hello, Cynthia."

"You knew about this?"

Rainey smiled. "Friends know everything, don't they?"

But you still love him, Cynthia wanted to say. Sometimes you can't have what you want most, but life goes on, and soon another window opens; she hoped that was true for Rainey. Rainey was a good, thoughtful person. She needed to find someone, too.

"I'll hear if the deal went through tomorrow," Gabe said then. "And I'm setting up an office right here in Astoria, believe it or not. Didn't think they'd ever need a financial advisor, but the time is right; our town is growing, and I think I'll do just fine here."

He turned toward Cynthia and took her hand again. "Rainey, you know my heart. I fought my feelings toward this woman, but you said to just let it go and see what happened. Go to New York. Pursue your dream. Well, the dream changed. And here I am."

Cynthia looked back at the house. Already she had an idea about the color for the outside paint. Light pink, scarlet, and aqua. She'd seen the colors in a magazine once, and they would make this house stand out like the beauty she once was. There would be lots of scraping and peeling, and it would take time, but the end result would be worth it. The flower garden would be in the front of this house, not on the side. There was more room between the house and sidewalk for a huge plot of flowers and a picket fence.

"I think we should go inside," Cynthia said then. "You lead the way, Gabe. I'll take notes about colors and wallpaper and flooring."

Gabe shrugged. "See what I mean about being bossy, Rainey? She gets to call all the shots, and somehow I think I'm going to like that part." He grinned as he paused on the first step. "Maybe I should carry you over the threshold now, but it wouldn't be appropriate since you don't have a ring yet."

Cynthia shook her head. "This is going too fast. I still can't believe any of it. Maybe I better pinch myself."

"You do that," Gabe said, leaning over and kissing the end of her nose. "Hey, tastes like frosting."

They laughed and then went inside the house. Cynthia thought of the frosting and cupcakes she'd just left. Already she knew what she'd do. She'd cut off the side of two cupcakes, frost them together, and put two hearts on top. Her and Gabe's hearts.

Cynthia liked the comfort of his hand holding hers and glanced up and smiled again. It was time for the dream to begin. God had such perfect timing, as always.

NOODLE PUDDING
(sometimes called Kugel Pudding)

8 ounces wide egg noodles
1 cup crushed pineapple, drained
2 tablespoons sugar
1 cup cottage cheese, small curd
¼ cup butter, melted
½ cup brown sugar
3 eggs, beaten
1 teaspoon vanilla
⅓ cup raisins

TOPPING:
1 tablespoon butter
¼ cup graham cracker crumbs
1 tablespoon sugar

Cook noodles (slightly overcook them). Combine remaining ingredients, except topping, with cooked noodles in a large bowl. Place mixture in a buttered 9x13-inch baking dish. Combine topping ingredients and add to top of noodle mixture. Bake at 350 degrees for 1 hour. A dollop of whipped cream is optional.

BLUEBERRY SURPRISE
by Wanda E. Brunstetter

Dedication

To my friend Jan Otte,
whose sweet treats have brought joy to so many people.
And to my daughter, Lorine Van Corbach,
a talented musician, who has fulfilled
her heart's desire of teaching music.

Chapter 1

Rain splattered against the windshield in drops the size of quarters. The darkening sky seemed to swallow Lorna Patterson's compact car as it headed west on the freeway toward the heart of Seattle, Washington.

"I'm sick of this soggy weather," Lorna muttered, gripping the steering wheel with determination and squinting her eyes to see out the filmy windshield. "I'm drained from working two jobs, and I am not happy with my life."

The burden of weariness crept through Lorna's body, like a poisonous snake about to overtake an unsuspecting victim. Each day as she pulled herself from bed at five in the morning, willing her tired body to move on its own, Lorna asked herself how much longer she could keep going the way she was.

She felt moisture on her cheeks and sniffed deeply. "Will I ever be happy again, Lord? It's been over a year since Ron's death. My heart aches to find joy and meaning in life."

Lorna flicked the blinker switch and turned onto the exit ramp. Soon she was pulling into the parking lot of Farmen's Restaurant, already full of cars.

The place buzzed with activity when she entered through the back door, used only by the restaurant employees and for deliveries. Lorna hung her umbrella and jacket on a wall peg in the coatroom. "I hope I'm not too late," she whispered to her friend and coworker, Chris Williams.

Chris glanced at the clock on the opposite wall. "Your shift was supposed to start half an hour ago, but I've been covering for you."

"Thanks. I appreciate that."

"Is everything all right? You didn't have car troubles, I hope."

Lorna shook her head. "Traffic on the freeway was awful, and the rain didn't make things any easier."

Chris offered Lorna a wide grin, revealing two crescent-shaped dimples set in the middle of her pudgy cheeks. Her light brown hair was pulled up in a ponytail, which made her look less like a woman of thirty-three and more like a teenager. Lorna was glad her own hair was short and naturally curly. She didn't have to do much, other than keep her blond locks clean, trimmed, and combed.

"You know Seattle," Chris said with a snicker. "Weather-wise, it wasn't much of a summer, was it? And now fall is just around the corner."

It wasn't much of a year, either, Lorna thought ruefully. She drew in a deep breath and released it with a moan. "I am so tired—of everything."

"I'm not surprised." Chris shook her finger. "Work, work, work. That's all you ever do. Clerking at Moore's Mini-mart during the day and working as a waitress here at night. There's no reason for you to be holding down two jobs now that. . ." She broke off her sentence. "Sorry. It's none of my business how you spend your time. I hate to see you looking so sad and tired, that's all."

Lorna forced a smile. "I know you care, Chris, and I appreciate your concern. You probably don't understand this, but I need to keep busy. It's the only way I can cope with my loss. If I stay active, I don't have time to think or even feel."

"There are other ways to keep busy, you know," Chris reminded her.

"I hope you're not suggesting I start dating again. You know I'm not ready for that." Lorna pursed her lips as she slowly shook her head. "I'm not sure I'll ever be ready to date, much less commit to another man."

"I'm not talking about dating. There are other things in life besides love and romance. Just ask me—the Old Maid of the West." Chris blinked her eyelids dramatically and wrinkled her nose.

Lorna chuckled, in spite of her dour mood, and donned her red and blue monogrammed Farmen's apron. "What would you suggest I do with my time?"

"How about what you've always wanted to do?"

"And that would be?"

"Follow your heart. Go back to school and get your degree."

Lorna frowned. "Oh, that. I've put my own life on hold so long, I'm not sure I even want college anymore."

"Oh, please!" Chris groaned. "How many times have I heard you complain about having to give up your dream of teaching music to elementary school kids?"

Lorna shrugged. "I don't know. Dozens, maybe."

Chris patted her on the back. "Now's your chance for some real adventure."

Lorna swallowed hard. She knew her friend was probably right, but she also knew going back to school would be expensive, not to mention the fact that she was much older now and would probably feel self-conscious among those college kids. It would be an adventure all right. Most likely a frightening one.

"Think about it," Chris whispered as she headed for the dining room.

"I'll give it some thought," Lorna said to her friend's retreating form.

Evan Bailey leaned forward in his chair and studied the recipe that had recently been posted online. "Peanut butter and chocolate chip cookies. Sounds good to me." Cynthia Lyons, his online cooking instructor, liked desserts. Yesterday she'd listed a recipe for peach cobbler, the day before that it was cherries jubilee, and today's sweet treat was his all-time favorite cookie.

Evan was glad he'd stumbled onto the Web site, especially since learning to cook might fit into his plans for the future.

He hit the PRINT button and smiled. For the past few years he'd been spinning his wheels, not sure whether to make a career of the air force or get out at the end of his tour and go back to college. He was entitled to some money under the GI bill, so he had finally decided to take advantage of it. Military life had its benefits, but now that Evan was no longer enlisted, he looked forward to becoming a school guidance counselor, or maybe a child psychologist. In a few weeks he would enroll at Bay View Christian College and be on his way to meeting the first of his two goals.

Evan's other goal involved a woman. He had recently celebrated his twenty-eighth birthday and felt ready to settle down. He thought Bay View would not only offer him a good education, but hopefully a sweet, Christian wife, as well. He closed his eyes, and visions of a pretty soul mate and a couple of cute kids danced through his head.

Caught up in his musings, Evan hadn't noticed that the paper had jammed in his printer until he opened his eyes again. He reached for the document and gritted his teeth when he saw the blinking light, then snapped open the lid. "I think I might need a new one of these to go along with that wife I'm looking for." He pulled the paper free and chuckled. "Of course, she'd better not be full of wrinkles, like this pitiful piece of paper."

Drawing his gaze back to the computer, Evan noticed on the website that not only was Cynthia Lyons listing one recipe per day, but beginning tomorrow, she would be opening her chat room to anyone interested in discussing the dos and don'ts of making sweet treats. Her note mentioned that the participants would be meeting once a week, at six o'clock, Pacific standard time.

"Good. It's the same time zone as Seattle. Wonder where she lives?" Evan positioned his cursor over the sign-up list and hit ENTER. Between the recipes Cynthia posted regularly and the online chat, he was sure he'd be cooking up a storm in no time at all.

When Lorna arrived home from work a few minutes before midnight, she found her mother-in-law in the living room, reading a book.

"You're up awfully late," Lorna remarked, taking a seat on the couch beside Ann.

"I was waiting for you," the older woman answered with a smile. "I wanted to talk to you about something."

"Is anything wrong?"

"Everything here is fine. It's you I'm worried about," Ann said, squinting her pale green eyes.

"What do you mean?"

"My son has been dead for over a year, and you're still grieving." A look of concern clouded Ann's face. "You're working two jobs, but there's no reason for it anymore. You have a home here for as long as you like, and Ed and I ask nothing in return." She reached over and gave Lorna's hand a gentle squeeze. "You shouldn't be wearing yourself out for nothing. If you keep going this way, you'll get sick."

Lorna sank her top teeth into her bottom lip so hard she tasted blood. This was the second lecture she'd had in one evening, and she wasn't in the mood to hear it. She loved Ron's parents as if they were her own. She'd chosen to live in their home after his death because she thought it would bring comfort to all three of them. Lorna didn't want hard feelings to come between them, and she certainly didn't want to say or do anything that might offend this lovely, gracious woman.

"Ann, I appreciate your concern," Lorna began, searching for words she hoped wouldn't sound harsh. "I am dealing with Ron's death the best way I can, but I'm not like you. I can't be content to stay home and knit sweaters or crochet lacy tablecloths. I have to keep busy outside the house. It keeps me from getting bored or dwelling on what can't be changed."

"Busy is fine, but you've become a workaholic, and it's not healthy—mentally or physically." Ann adjusted her metal-framed reading glasses so they were sitting correctly on the bridge of her nose. "Ed and I love you, Lorna. We think of you as the daughter we never had. We only want what's best for you." Her short, coffee-colored hair was peppered with gray, and she pushed a stray curl behind her ear.

"I love you both, and I know you have my welfare in mind, but I'm a big girl now, so you needn't worry." Lorna knew her own parents would probably be just as concerned for her well-being if she were living with them. She was almost thankful Mom and Dad lived in Minnesota, because she didn't need two sets of doting parents right now.

"Ed and I don't expect you to give up your whole life for us," Ann continued, as though Lorna hadn't spoken on her own behalf. "You moved from your home state to attend college here, then shortly after you and Ron married, you dropped out of school so you could work and pay his way. Then you kept on working after he entered med school, in order to help pay all the bills for his schooling."

Lorna didn't need to be reminded of the sacrifices she'd made. She was well aware of what she'd given up for the man she loved. "I'm not giving up my life for anyone now," she said as she sighed deeply and pushed against the sofa cushion. Ann didn't understand the way she felt. No one did.

"Have you considered what you might like to do with the rest of your life?" her mother-in-law persisted. "Surely you don't want to spend it working two jobs and holding your middle-aged in-laws' hands."

Lorna blinked back sudden tears that threatened to spill over. She used to think she and Ron would grow old together and have a happy marriage like his parents and hers did. She'd imagined their having children and turning into a real family after he became a physician, but that would never happen now. Lorna had spent the last year worried about helping Ron's parents deal with their loss, and she'd continued to put her own life on hold.

She swallowed against the lump in her throat. It didn't matter. Her hopes and dreams died the day Ron's body was lowered into that cold, dark grave.

She wrapped her arms around her middle and squeezed her eyes shut. Was it time to stop grieving and follow her heart? Could she do it? Did she even want to anymore?

"I've been thinking," Ann said, breaking into Lorna's troubling thoughts.

"What?"

"When you quit school to help pay our son's way, you were cheated out of the education you deserved. I think you should go back to college and get that music degree you were working toward."

Lorna stirred uneasily. First Chris, and now Ann? What was going on? Was she the victim of some kind of conspiracy? She extended her legs and stretched like a cat. "I'm tired. I think I'll go up to bed."

Before she stood up, Lorna touched her mother-in-law's hand. "I appreciate your suggestion, and I promise to sleep on the idea."

" 'Delight yourself in the Lord and he will give you the desires of your heart,' " Ann quoted from the book of Psalms. "God is always full of surprises."

Lorna nodded and headed for the stairs. A short time later, she entered her room and flopped onto the canopy bed with a sigh. She lay there a moment, then turned her head to the right so she could study the picture sitting on the dresser across the room. It was taken on her wedding day, and she and Ron were smiling and looking at each other as though they had their whole lives ahead of them. How happy they'd been back then—full of hope and dreams for their future.

A familiar pang of regret clutched Lorna's heart as she thought about the plans she'd made for her own life. She'd given up her heart's desire in order to help Ron's vision come true. Now they were both gone—Ron, as well as Lorna's plans and dreams.

With the back of her hand, she swiped at an errant tear running down her cheek. *Help me know what to do, Lord. Could You possibly want me to go back to school? Can I really have the desires of my heart? Do You have any pleasant surprises ahead for me?*

Chapter 2

What did the ground say to the rain?" Lorna asked an elderly man as she waited on his table. He glanced out the window at the pouring rain and shrugged. "You got me."

"If you keep this up, my name will be mud!" Lorna's laugh sounded forced, but it was the best she could do, considering how hard she'd had to work at telling the dumb joke.

"That was really lame," Chris moaned as she passed by her table and jabbed Lorna in the ribs.

The customer, however, laughed at Lorna's corny quip. She smiled. *Could mean another nice tip*.

She moved to the next table, preparing to take an order from a young couple.

"I'll have one of the greasiest burgers you've got, with a side order of artery-clogging french fries." The man looked up at Lorna and winked.

Offering him what she hoped was a pleasant smile, Lorna wrote down his order. Then she turned to the woman and asked, "What would you like?"

"I'm trying to watch my weight," the slender young female said. "What have you got that tastes good and isn't full of fat or too many calories?"

"You don't look like you need to worry about your weight at all." Lorna grinned. "Why, did you know that diets are for people who are thick and tired of it all?"

The woman giggled. "I think I'll settle for a dinner salad and a glass of unsweetened iced tea."

When Lorna turned in her order, she bumped into Chris, who was doing the same.

"What's with you tonight?" her friend asked.

"What do you mean?"

"I've never seen you so friendly to the customers before. And those jokes, Lorna. Where did you dig them up?"

Lorna shrugged. "You're not the only one who can make people laugh, you know. I'll bet my tips will be better than ever tonight."

"Tips? Is that what you're trying to do—get more tips?"

"Not necessarily more. Just bigger ones." As she spoke the words, Lorna felt a pang of guilt. She knew it wasn't right to try to wangle better tips. The motto at Farmen's was to be friendly and courteous to all customers. Besides, it was the

Christian way, and Lorna knew better than to do anything other than that. She'd gotten carried away with the need to make more money in less time. *Forgive me, Father,* she prayed.

Chris moved closer to Lorna. "Let me see if I understand this right. You're single, living rent free with your in-laws, working two jobs, and you need more money? What gives?"

"I've given my notice at the Mini-mart," Lorna answered. "Next Friday will be my last day."

Chris's mouth dropped open, and she sucked in her breath. "You're kidding!"

"I'm totally serious. I'll only be working at this job from now on."

"You don't even like waiting tables," Chris reminded. "Why would you give up your day job to come here every evening and put up with a cranky boss and complaining customers? If you want to quit a job, why not this one?"

"I decided to take your advice," Lorna replied.

"My advice? Now that's a first. What, might I ask, are you taking my advice on?"

"One week from Monday I'll be registering for the fall semester at Bay View Christian College."

Chris's eyes grew large, and Lorna gave her friend's red and blue apron a little tug. "Please don't stand there gaping at me—say something."

Chris blinked as though she were coming out of a trance. "I'm in shock. I can't believe you're actually going back to college, much less doing it at my suggestion."

Lorna wrinkled her nose. "It wasn't solely because of your prompting."

"Oh?"

"Ann suggested it the other night, too, and I've been praying about it ever since. I feel it's something I should do."

Chris grabbed Lorna in a bear hug. "I'm so happy for you."

"Thanks." Lorna nodded toward their boss, Gary Farmen, who had just walked by. "Guess we should get back to work."

"Right." Chris giggled. "We wouldn't want to be accused of having any fun on the job, now would we?"

Lorna started toward the dining room.

"One more thing," Chris called after her.

"What's that?" Lorna asked over her shoulder.

"I'd find some better jokes if I were you."

The distinctive, crisp scent of autumn was in the air. Lorna inhaled deeply as she shuffled through a pile of freshly fallen leaves scattered around the campus of Bay View Christian College.

Today she would register for the fall semester, bringing her one step closer to realizing her dream of teaching music. The decision to return to school had been a difficult one. Certainly she was mature enough to handle the pressures that would come with being a full-time student, but she worried about being too mature to study with a bunch of kids who probably didn't have a clue what life was all about.

By the time Lorna reached the front door of the admissions office, her heart was pounding so hard she was sure everyone within earshot could hear it. Her knees felt weak and shaky, and she wondered if she would be able to hold up long enough to get through this process.

She'd already filled out the necessary paperwork for pre-admission and had even met with her advisor the previous week. Today was just a formality. Still, the long line forming behind the desk where she was to pick up her course package made her feel ill at ease.

Lorna fidgeted with the strap of her purse and felt relief wash over her when it was finally her turn.

"Name?" asked the dark-haired, middle-aged woman who was handing out the packets.

"Lorna Patterson. My major is music education."

The woman thumbed through the alphabetized bundles. A few seconds later, she handed one to Lorna. "This is yours."

"Thanks," Lorna mumbled. She turned and began looking through the packet, relieved when she saw that the contents confirmed her schedule for this semester.

Intent on reading the program for her anatomy class, Lorna wasn't watching where she was going. With a sudden jolt, she bumped into someone's arm, and the entire bundle flew out of her hands. Feeling a rush of heat creep up the back of her neck, Lorna dropped to her knees to retrieve the scattered papers.

"Sorry. Guess my big bony elbow must have gotten in your way. Here, let me help you with those."

Lorna looked up. A pair of clear blue eyes seemed to be smiling at her. The man those mesmerizing eyes belonged to must be the owner of the deep voice offering help. She fumbled with the uncooperative papers, willing her fingers to stop shaking. *What is wrong with me? I'm acting like a clumsy fool this morning.* "Thanks, but I can manage," she squeaked.

The young man nodded as he got to his feet, and her cheeks burned hot under his scrutiny.

Lorna quickly gathered up the remaining papers and stood. *He probably thinks I'm a real klutz. So much for starting out the day on the right foot.*

The man opened his mouth as if to say something, but Lorna hurried away. She still had to go to the business office and take care of some financial matters. Then she needed to find the bookstore and locate whatever she'd be needing, and finally the student identification desk to get her ID card. There would probably be long lines everywhere.

Lorna made her way down the crowded hall, wondering how many more stupid blunders she might make before the day was over. She'd been away from college so long; it was obvious she no longer knew how to function. Especially in the presence of a good-looking man.

Evan hung his bicycle on the rack outside his lake-view apartment building and bounded up the steps, feeling rather pleased with himself. He'd enrolled at Bay View Christian College today, taken a leisurely bike ride around Woodland Park, and now he was anxious to get home and grab a bite to eat. After supper he'd be going online to check out Cynthia Lyons' cooking class again. Maybe he'd have better luck with today's recipe than he had last week. Evan's peanut butter chocolate chip cookies turned out hard as rocks, and he still hadn't figured out what he'd done wrong. He thought he'd followed Cynthia's directions to the letter, but apparently he'd left out some important ingredient. He probably should try making them again.

As soon as Evan entered his apartment, he went straight to the kitchen and pulled a dinner from the freezer, then popped it into the oven.

"If I learn how to cook halfway decent, it might help find me a wife," he murmured. "Not only that, but it would mean I'd be eating better meals while I wait for that special someone."

While the frozen dinner heated, Evan went to the living room where his computer sat on a desk in the corner. He booted it up, then went back to the kitchen to fix a salad. At least that was something he could do fairly well.

"I should have insisted Mom teach me how to cook," he muttered.

As Evan prepared the green salad, his thoughts turned toward home. He'd grown up in Moscow, Idaho, and that's where his parents and two older sisters still lived with their families. Since Evan was the youngest child and the only boy in the family, he'd never really needed to cook. His sisters, Margaret and Ellen, had always helped Mom in the kitchen, and they used to say Evan was just in the way if he tried to help out. So when Evan went off to college, he lived on fast foods and meals that were served in the school's cafeteria. When he dropped out of college to join the air force, all of his meals were provided, so again he had no reason to cook.

Now Evan was living in Seattle, attending the Christian college a friend had recommended. He probably could have lived on campus and eaten whatever was available, but he'd chosen to live alone and learn to cook. He'd also decided it was time to settle down and look for a Christian woman.

Evan sliced a tomato and dropped the pieces into the salad bowl. "First order of business—learn to cook. Second order—find a wife!"

Over the last few days, Lorna's tips from the restaurant had increased, and she figured it might have something to do with the fact that she'd given up telling jokes and was just being pleasant and friendly, without any ulterior motives.

"I see it's raining again," Chris said, as she stepped up beside Lorna.

Lorna grabbed her work apron and shrugged. "What else is new? We're living in Washington—the Evergreen State, remember?"

Chris lifted her elbow, let it bounce a few times, then connected it gently to Lorna's rib cage. "You're not planning to tell that silly joke about the ground talking to the rain again, I hope."

Lorna shook her head. "I've decided to stick to business and leave the humorous stuff to real people like you."

Chris raised her dark eyebrows, giving Lorna a quizzical look. *"Real* people? What's that supposed to mean?"

"It means you're fun-loving and genuinely witty." Lorna frowned. "You don't have to tell stale jokes in order to make people smile. Everyone seems drawn to your pleasant personality."

"Thanks for the compliment," Chris said with a nod. "I think you sell yourself short. You're talented, have gorgeous, curly blond hair, and you're blessed with a genuine, sweet spirit." She leaned closer and whispered, "Trouble is, you keep it hidden, like a dark secret you don't want anyone to discover."

Lorna moved away, hoping to avoid any more of her friend's psychoanalyzing, but Chris stepped in front of her, planting both hands on her wide hips. "I'm not done yet."

Lorna squinted her eyes. "It's obvious that you're not going to let me go to work until I hear you out."

Chris's smile was a victorious one. "If you would learn to relax and quit taking life so seriously, people would be drawn to you."

Lorna groaned. "I want to, Chris, but since Ron's death, life has so little meaning for me."

"You're still young and have lots to offer the world. Don't let your heart stay locked up in a self-made prison."

"Maybe going back to school will help. Being around kids who are brimming over with enthusiasm and still believe life holds nothing but joy might rub off on me."

"I think most college kids are smart enough to know life isn't always fun and games," Chris said in a serious tone. "I do believe you're right about one thing, though."

"What's that?"

"Going back to school will be good for you."

Chapter 3

Lorna settled herself into one of the hard-backed auditorium seats and pulled a notebook and pen from her backpack. Anatomy was her first class of the day. She wanted to be ready for action, since this course had been suggested by one of the advisors. It would help her gain a better understanding of proper breathing and the body positions involved in singing.

She glanced around, noticing about fifty other students in the room. Most of them were also preparing to take notes.

A tall, middle-aged man, who introduced himself as Professor Talcot, announced the topic of the day—"Age-related Changes."

Lorna was about to place her backpack on the empty seat next to her when someone sat down. She glanced over and was greeted with a friendly smile.

Oh, no! It's that guy I bumped into the other day during registration.

She forced a return smile, then quickly averted her attention back to the professor.

"I'm late. Did I miss much?" the man whispered as he leaned toward Lorna.

"He just started." She kept her gaze straight ahead.

"Okay, thanks."

Lorna was grateful he didn't say anything more. She was here to learn, not to be distracted by some big kid who should have been on time for his first class of the day.

"Everyone, take a good look at the seat you're in," Professor Talcot stated. "That's where you will sit for the remainder of the semester. My assistant will be around shortly to get your names and fill out the seating chart."

Lorna groaned inwardly. If she'd known she would have to stay in this particular seat all semester, she might have been a bit more selective. Of course, she had no way of knowing an attractive guy with gorgeous blue eyes and a winning smile was going to flop into the seat beside her.

I can handle this. After all, it's only one hour a day. I don't even have to talk to him if I don't want to.

"Name, please?"

Lorna was jolted from her thoughts when a studious-looking man wearing metal-framed glasses tapped her on the shoulder.

She turned her head and realized he was standing in the row behind, leaning slightly over the back of her seat, holding a clipboard in one hand.

"Lorna Patterson," she whispered.

"What was that? I couldn't hear you."

The man sitting next to Lorna turned around. "She said her name is Lorna Patterson. Mine's Evan Bailey."

"Gotcha!" the aide replied.

Lorna felt the heat of embarrassment rush to her cheeks. *Great! He not only saw how clumsy I was the other day; now he thinks I can't even speak for myself. I must appear to be pretty stupid.*

As she turned her attention back to the class, Lorna caught the tail end of something the professor had said. Something about a group of five. *That's what I get for thinking when I should be listening. Maybe I wasn't ready to come back to college after all.* She turned to Evan and reluctantly asked, "What did the professor say?"

"He said he's about to give us our first assignment, and we're supposed to form into groups of five." A smile tugged at the corners of his mouth. "Would you like to be in my group?"

Lorna shrugged. She didn't know anyone else in the class. Not that she knew Evan. She'd only met him once, and that wasn't under the best of circumstances.

Evan Bailey was obviously more outgoing than she, for he was already rounding up three other people to join their group—two young men and one woman, all sitting in the row ahead of them.

"The first part of this assignment will be to get to know each other," Professor Talcot told the class. "Tell everyone in your group your name, age, and major."

Lorna felt a sense of dread roll over her, like turbulent breakers lapping against the shore.

It's bad enough that I'm older than most of these college kids. Is it really necessary for me to reveal my age?

Introductions were quickly made, and Lorna soon learned the others in the group were Jared, Tim, and Vanessa. All but Evan and Lorna had given some information about themselves.

"You want to go first?" Evan asked, looking at Lorna.

"I—uh—am in my junior year, and I'm majoring in music ed. I hope to become an elementary school music teacher when I graduate."

"Sounds good. How about you, Evan?" Tim, the studious-looking one, asked.

Evan wiggled his eyebrows and gave Lorna a silly grin. "I'm lookin' for a mother for my children."

"You have kids?" The question came from Vanessa, who had long red hair and dark brown eyes, which she'd kept focused on Evan ever since they'd formed their group.

He shook his head. "Nope, not yet. I'm still searching for the right woman to be my wife. I need someone who loves the Lord as much as I do." Evan's eyebrows drew together. "Oh, yeah—it might be good if she knows how to cook. I'm in the process of learning, but so far all my recipes have flopped."

Vanessa leaned forward and studied Evan more intently. "Are you majoring in home economics?"

Evan chuckled. "Not even close. My major is psychology, but I've recently signed up for an online cooking class." He smiled and nodded at Lorna instead of Vanessa. "You married?"

Lorna shook her head. "I'm not married now." She hesitated then looked away. "My husband died."

"Sorry to hear that," Evan said in a sincere tone.

"Yeah, it's a shame about your husband and all," Jared agreed.

There were a few moments of uncomfortable silence, then Evan said, "I thought I might bring some sweet treats to class one of these days and share them with anyone willing to be my guinea pig."

Vanessa smacked her lips and touched the edge of Evan's shirtsleeve. "I'll be looking forward to that."

"It's time to tell our ages. I'm twenty-one," Tim said.

Vanessa smiled and said she was also twenty-one.

Jared informed the group that he was twenty-four.

"Guess that makes me the old man of our little assemblage. I'm heading downhill at the ripe old age of twenty-eight," Evan said with a wink in Lorna's direction.

With the exception of Evan, they're all just kids, she thought ruefully. *And even he's four years younger than me.*

Vanessa nudged Lorna's arm with the eraser end of her pencil. "Now it's your turn."

Lorna stared at the floor and mumbled, "I'm thirty-two."

Jared let out a low whistle. "Wow, you're a lot older than the rest of us."

Lorna slid a little lower in her chair. *As if I needed to be reminded.*

Evan held up the paper he was holding. It had been handed out by the professor's assistant only moments ago. "It says here that one of the most significant age-related signs is increased hair growth in the nose." He leaned over, until his face was a few inches from Lorna's. As he studied her, she felt like a bug under a microscope. "Yep," he announced. "I can see it's happening to you already!"

Jared, Tim, and Vanessa howled, and Lorna covered her face with her hands. If the aisle hadn't been blocked, she might have dashed for the door. Instead, she drew in a deep breath, lifted her head, and looked Evan in the eye. "You're right about my nose hair. In fact, I'm so old I get winded just playing a game of checkers."

She couldn't believe she'd said that. Maybe those stupid jokes she had used on her customers at the restaurant were still lodged in her brain.

Everyone in the group laughed this time, including Lorna, who was finally beginning to relax. "The other day, I sank my teeth into a big, juicy steak, and you know what?" she quipped.

Evan leaned a bit closer. "What?"

"They just stayed there!"

Vanessa giggled and poked Evan on the arm. "She really got you good on that one."

Evan grimaced. "Guess I deserved it. Sorry about the nose hair crack."

He looked genuinely sorry, making Lorna feel foolish for trying to set him up with her lame joke. She was about to offer an apology of her own when he added, "It's nice to know I'm not the oldest one in class."

✂

Lorna didn't know how she had survived the morning. By the time she entered her last class of the day, she wondered all the more if she was going to make it as a college student. *This is no time to wimp out,* she chided herself as she took a seat in the front row. *Choir is my favorite subject.*

The woman who stood in front of the class introduced herself as Professor Lynne Burrows.

She's young, Lorna noted. *Probably not much past thirty. I would be a music teacher by now if I'd finished my studies ten years ago.*

"Do we have any pianists in this class?" Professor Burrows asked.

Lorna glanced around the room. When she saw no hands raised, she lifted hers. "Have you ever accompanied a choir?"

She nodded. "I play for my church choir, and I also accompanied college choir during my freshman and sophomore years." She chose not to mention the fact that it had been several years ago.

The professor smiled. "Would you mind playing for us today? If it works out well, perhaps you'd consider doing it for all the numbers that require piano accompaniment."

"I'd like that." Lorna headed straight for the piano, a place where she knew she'd be the most comfortable.

"If you need someone to turn the pages, I'd be happy to oblige."

Lorna glanced to her right. Evan Bailey was leaning on the lid of the piano, grinning at her like a monkey who'd been handed a tasty banana. She couldn't believe he was in her music class, too.

"Thanks anyway, but I think I can manage," Lorna murmured.

Evan dropped to the bench beside her. "I've done this before, and I'm actually pretty good at it." He reached across Lorna and thumbed a few pages of the music.

She eyed him suspiciously. "You don't know when to quit, do you?"

He laughed and wagged a finger in front of her nose. "Just call me Pushy Bailey."

"Let's see what Professor Burrows has to say when she realizes you're sitting on the piano bench instead of standing on the risers with the rest of the choir. You *are* enrolled in this class, I presume?"

Evan smiled at her. "I am, and I signed up for it just so I could perfect my talent of page turning."

Lorna moaned softly. "You're impossible."

Evan dragged his fingers along the piano keys. "How about you and me going out for a burger after class? Then I can tell you about the rest of my faults."

"Sorry, but I don't date."

He snapped the key of middle C up and down a few times. "Who said anything about a date? I'm hungry for a burger and thought maybe you'd like to join me. It would be a good chance for us to get better acquainted."

Lorna sucked in her breath. "Why would we need to get better acquainted?"

He gave her a wide smile. "I'm in choir—you're in choir. You're the pianist—I'm the page turner. I'm in anatomy—you're in anatomy. I'm in your group—you're in my—"

She held up one hand. "Okay, Mr. Bailey. I get the point."

"Call me Evan. Mr. Bailey makes me sound like an old man."

"Evan, then."

"So will you have a burger with me?"

Lorna opened her mouth, but Professor Burrows leaned on the top of the piano and spoke first. "I see you've already found a page turner."

Lorna shook her head. "Not really. I've always been able to turn my own pages, and I'm sure you need Mr. Bailey's voice in the tenor section far more than I need his thumb and index finger at the piano."

Evan grinned up at the teacher. "What can I say? The woman likes me."

Lorna's mouth dropped open. Didn't the guy ever quit?

"You're pretty self-confident, aren't you?" The professor pointed at Evan, then motioned toward the risers. "Let's see how well you can sing. Third row, second place on the left."

Evan shrugged and gave Lorna a quick wink. "See you later."

"Don't mind him," Professor Burrows whispered to Lorna. "I think he's just testing the waters."

"Mine, or yours?"

"Probably both. I've handled characters like him before, so we won't let it get out of hand." The professor gave Lorna's shoulder a gentle squeeze and moved to the front of the class.

Lorna closed her eyes and drew in a deep breath, lifting a prayer of thanks that the day was almost over. She couldn't believe how stressful it had been. Maybe she should give up her dream of becoming a music teacher while she still had some shred of sanity left.

As Evan stood on the risers with the rest of the class, he couldn't keep focused on Professor Burrows or the song they were supposed to be singing. His gaze kept going back to the cute little blond who sat at the piano.

He knew Lorna was four years older than he, and she'd made it clear that she had no interest in dating. Still, the woman fascinated him, and he was determined they should get better acquainted. The few years' age difference meant nothing as far as he was concerned, but it might matter to Lorna. Maybe that's why she seemed so indifferent.

I'd sure like to get to know her better and find out if we're compatible. Evan smiled to himself. He would figure out a way—maybe bribe her with one of his online sweet treats. Of course, he'd first have to learn how to bake something that didn't flop.

Chapter 4

When Lorna arrived home from school, she found her father-in-law in the front yard, raking a pile of maple leaves into a mountain in the middle of the lawn.

Ed stopped and wiped the perspiration from the top of his bald head with a hanky he had pulled from the pocket of his jeans. "How was your first day?"

Lorna plodded up the steps, dropped her backpack to the porch, and sank wearily into one of the wicker chairs. "Let's put it this way, I'm still alive to tell about it."

Ed leaned the rake against the outside porch railing and took the chair beside her. "That bad, huh?"

She only nodded in reply.

"Is your schedule too heavy this semester?" he asked, obvious concern revealed in his dark eyes.

Lorna forced a smile. "It's nothing to be worried about."

"Anything that concerns you concerns me and Ann. You were married to our son, and that makes us family."

"I know, but I do have to learn how to handle some problems on my own."

"Problems? Did I hear someone say they're having problems?"

Lorna glanced up at Ann, who had stepped onto the porch. "It's nothing. I'm just having a hard time fitting in at school. I am quite a bit older than most of my classmates, you know."

Ann laughed, causing the lines around her eyes to become more pronounced. "Is that all that's troubling you? I'd think being older would have some advantages."

"Such as?"

"For one thing, your maturity should help you grasp things. Your study habits will probably be better than those of most kids fresh out of high school, too. These days, many young people don't have a lot of self-discipline."

"Yeah, no silly schoolgirl crushes or other such distractions," Ed put in with a deep chuckle.

Lorna swallowed hard. There had already been plenty of distractions today, and they'd come in the form of a young man with laughing blue eyes, goofy jokes, and a highly contagious smile.

"My maturity might help me be more studious, but it sure sets me apart from

133

the rest of the college crowd," she said. "Today I felt like a sore thumb sticking out on an otherwise healthy hand."

"You're so pretty, I'm sure no one even guessed you were a few years older." Ann gently touched Lorna's shoulder.

"Thanks for the compliment," Lorna said, making no mention of the fact that she had already revealed her age during the first class of the day. She cringed, thinking about the nose hair incident. "I'd better go inside. I want to read a few verses of scripture, and I have some homework that needs to be done before it's time to head for work."

Lorna stood in front of the customer who sat at a table in her assigned section with a menu in front of his face. "Have you decided yet, sir?" she asked.

"I'll have a cheeseburger with the works."

He dropped the menu to the table, and Lorna's gaze darted to the man's face. "Wh–what are you doing here?" she rasped.

Evan smiled up at her. "I'm ordering a hamburger, and seeing you again makes me remember that you stood me up this afternoon."

"How could I have stood you up when I never agreed to go out with you in the first place?" Lorna's hands began to tremble, and she knew her cheeks must be pink, because she could feel the heat quickly spreading.

Evan's grin widened. "You never really said no."

Lorna clenched her pencil in one hand and the order pad in the other. "Did you follow me here from my home?"

"I don't even know where you live, so how could I have followed you?" Evan studied his menu again. "I think I'll have an order of fries to go with that burger. Care to join me?"

"In case you hadn't noticed, I'm working."

"Hmm. . . Maybe I'll have a chocolate shake, too."

Lorna tapped her foot impatiently. "How did you know I worked here?"

He handed her the menu. "I didn't. I've heard this restaurant serves really great burgers, and I thought I'd give it a try. The fact that you work here is just an added bonus."

"I'll be back when your order is up." Lorna turned on her heels and headed for the kitchen, but she'd only made it halfway when she collided with Chris. Apple pie, vanilla ice cream, and two chocolate-covered donuts went sailing through the air as her friend's tray flew out of her hands.

Lorna gasped. "Oh, Chris, I'm so sorry! I didn't see you coming."

"It was just an accident. It's okay, I know you didn't do it on purpose," Chris said as she dropped to her knees.

Lorna did the same and quickly began to help clean up the mess. "I'll probably be docked half my pay for this little blunder," she grumbled. "I ought to send Evan Bailey a bill."

Chris's eyebrows shot up. "Who's Evan Bailey?"

"Some guy I met at school. I have him in two of my classes. He's here tonight. I just took his order."

Chris gave her a quizzical look. "And?"

"He had me so riled I wasn't paying attention to where I was going." Lorna scooped up the last piece of pie and handed the tray back to Chris. "I really am sorry about this."

Chris laughed. "It's a good thing it went on the floor and not in someone's lap." She got to her feet. "So what's this guy done that has you so upset?"

Lorna picked a hunk of chocolate off her apron and stood, too. "First of all, he kept teasing me in anatomy class this morning. Then he plunked himself down at the piano with me during choir, offering to be my page turner." She paused and drew in a deep breath. "Next, he asked me to go out for a burger after school."

"What'd you say?"

"I didn't answer him." Lorna frowned. "Now he's here, pestering me to eat dinner with him."

Chris moved toward the kitchen, with Lorna following on her heels. "Sounds to me like the guy is interested in you."

Lorna shook her head. "He hardly even knows me. Besides, I'm four years older."

"Who's hung up on age differences nowadays?"

"Okay, it's not the four years between us that really bothers me."

"What then?"

"He acts like a big kid!" Lorna shrugged. "Besides, even if I was planning to date, which I'm not, our personalities don't mesh."

Evan leaned his elbows on the table and studied the checkered place mat in front of him. He had always been the kind of person who knew what he wanted and then went after it. How come his determination wasn't working this time? *Lorna doesn't believe me. She thinks I've been spying on her and came here to harass her. I've got to make her believe my coming to Farmen's was purely coincidental.* He took a sip of water. *Although it could have been an answer to prayer. Somehow I've got to get Lorna to agree to go out with me. How else am I going to know if she's the one?*

A short time later, Lorna returned with Evan's order, and he felt ready to try again. He looked up at her and smiled. "You look cute in that uniform." When she made no comment, he added, "Been working here long?"

"Sometimes it feels like forever," she said with a deep sigh.

"Want to talk about it?"

She shook her head. "Will there be anything else?"

He rapped the edge of the plate with his knife handle. "Actually, there is."

"What can I get for you?"

"How about a few minutes of your time?"

"I'm working."

"When do you get off work? I can stick around for a while."

"Late. I'll be working late tonight."

Evan cringed. He wasn't getting anywhere with this woman and knew he should probably quit while he was ahead. Of course, he wasn't really ahead, so he decided he might as well stick his neck out a little farther. "I'm not trying to come on to you. I just want to get to know you better."

"Why?"

Evan reached for his glass of water and took a sip. How could he explain his attraction to Lorna without scaring her off? "I think we have a lot in common," he said with a nod.

She raised one pale eyebrow. "How did you reach that conclusion?"

"It's simple. I'm in choir—you're in choir. You're the pianist—I'm the page turner."

"I'm not interested in dating you or anyone else."

Evan grabbed his burger off the plate. "Okay, I get the message. I'll try not to bother you again."

She touched his shoulder unexpectedly, sending a shock wave through his arm. "I–I'm sorry if I came across harshly. I just needed you to know where I stand."

He swallowed the bite of burger he'd put in his mouth. "Are you seeing someone else? You mentioned in class that you're a widow, so I kinda figured—"

Lorna shook her head, interrupting his sentence. "I'm a widow who doesn't date."

Evan thought she looked sad, or maybe she was lonely. He grabbed the bottle of ketchup in the center of the table and smiled at her. "Can we at least be friends?"

She nodded and held out her hand. "Friends."

Chapter 5

Lorna awoke with a headache. She had been back in college a week, and things weren't getting any easier. It was hard to attend school all day, work every evening at Farmen's, and find time to get her assignments finished. She was tired and irritable but knew she would have to put on a happy face when she was at work, no matter how aggravating some of the customers could be. One patron in particular was especially unnerving. Evan Bailey had returned to the restaurant two more times. She wasn't sure if he came because he liked the food or if it was merely to get under her skin.

Lorna uttered a quick prayer and forced her unwilling body to get out of bed. She couldn't miss any classes today. There was a test to take in English lit and auditions for lead parts in the choir's first performance.

She entered the bathroom and turned on the faucet at the sink. Splashing a handful of water against her upturned face, she cringed as the icy liquid stung her cheeks. Apparently, Ann was washing clothes this morning, for there was no hot water.

"Ed needs to get that old tank replaced," Lorna grumbled as she reached for a towel. "Maybe I should stay home today after all."

The verse she'd read the night before in Psalm 125 popped into her mind. *"Those who trust in the LORD are like Mount Zion, which cannot be shaken but endures forever."*

"Thanks for that reminder, Lord. I need to trust You to help me through this day."

"I don't see how we're ever gonna get better acquainted if you keep avoiding me."

Lorna sat in her anatomy class, watching a video presentation on the muscular system and trying to ignore Evan, who sat on her left. She kept her eyes focused on the video screen. *Maybe if I pretend I didn't hear him, he'll quit pestering me.*

"Here, I brought you something." He leaned closer and held out two cookies encased in plastic wrap.

She could feel his warm breath on her ear, and she shivered.

"You cold?"

When she made no reply and didn't reach for the cookies, he tapped her lightly on the arm. "I made these last night. Please try one."

Lorna didn't want to appear rude, but she wasn't hungry. "I just ate breakfast not long ago."

"That's okay. You can save them for later."

"All right. Thanks." Lorna took the cookies and placed them inside her backpack.

"I'm going biking on Saturday. Do you ride?" he asked.

"Huh?"

"I'd like you to go out with me this Saturday. We can rent some bikes at the park and pedal our way around the lake."

"I told you. . .I don't date."

"I know, but the other night you said we could be friends, so we won't call this a date. It'll just be two lonely people out having a good time."

Lorna's face heated up. "What makes you think I'm lonely?"

"I see it in your eyes," he whispered. "They're sad and lonely looking." When she made no reply, he added, "Look, if you'd rather not go, then—"

Lorna blew out her breath as she threw caution to the wind. "All right, I'll go, but you're taking an awfully big chance."

"Yeah, I know." He snickered. "A few hours spent in your company, and I might never be the same."

Lorna held back the laughter threatening to bubble over, but she couldn't hide her smile. "I was thinking more along the lines of our fall weather. It can be pretty unpredictable this time of the year."

Evan chuckled. "Yeah, like some blond-haired, blue-eyed woman I'd like to get to know a whole lot better."

Evan studied the computer screen intently. Brownie Delight was the sweet treat Cynthia Lyons had posted on Tuesday, but he hadn't had time to check it out until today. The ingredients were basic—unsweetened chocolate, butter, sour cream, sugar, eggs, flour, baking powder, salt, and chopped nuts. Chocolate chips would be sprinkled on the top, making it doubly delicious. If the brownies turned out halfway decent, he would take some on his date with Lorna. Maybe she'd be impressed with his ability to cook. He hoped so, because so far nothing he'd said or done had seemed to make an impact on her. She hadn't even said whether she'd liked the chocolate peanut butter cookies he'd given her the other day. Lorna was probably too polite to mention that they'd been a bit overdone. This was Evan's second time with these cookies, and he was beginning to wonder if he'd ever get it right.

Evan still hadn't made it to any of the online chats Cynthia Lyons hosted. Now that he was in school all day, his evenings were usually spent doing homework.

Oh well. The chats were probably just a bunch of chitchat about how well the recipes had turned out for others who had made them. He didn't need any further reminders that his hadn't been so successful.

Evan hit the PRINT button to make a copy of the recipe and leaned back in his chair while he waited for the procedure to complete itself.

A vision of Lorna's petite face flashed into his mind. He was attracted to her; there was no question about that. But did they really have anything in common? Was she someone who wanted to serve the Lord with her whole heart, the way Evan did?

The college they attended was a Christian one, but he knew not everyone who went there was a believer in Christ. Some merely signed up at Bay View because of its excellent academic program. Evan hoped Lorna wasn't one of those.

And what about children? Did she like kids as much as he did? Other than becoming an elementary school music teacher, what were her goals and dreams for the future? He needed to know all these things if he planned to pursue a relationship with her.

The printer had stopped, and Evan grabbed hold of the recipe for Brownie Delight. "Tomorrow Lorna and I will get better acquainted as we pedal around the lake and munch on these sweet treats. Tonight I'll pray about it."

The week had seemed to fly by, and when Lorna awoke Saturday morning, she was in a state of panic. She couldn't believe she'd agreed to go biking with Evan today. What had she been thinking? Up until now, she'd kept him at arm's length, but going on what he probably saw as a date could be a huge mistake.

"Then again," she mumbled, "it might be just the thing to prove to Evan how wrong we are for each other."

Lorna crawled out of bed, wondering what she should wear and what to tell her in-laws at breakfast. Not wanting to raise any questions from Ann or Ed, she decided to only tell them that she'd be going out sometime after lunch, but she would make no mention of where. Her plans were to meet Evan at the park near the college, but she didn't want them to know about it. They might think it was a real date and that she was being untrue to their son's memory. She only hoped by the end of the day she wouldn't regret her decision to spend time alone with Evan Bailey.

At two o'clock that afternoon, Lorna drove into the park. The weather was overcast and a bit chilly, but at least it wasn't raining. She found Evan waiting on a wooden bench with two bikes parked nearby.

"Hey! I'm glad you came!"

"I said I would."

"I know, but I was afraid you might back out."

Lorna flopped down beside him, and he grinned at her. "You look great today." She glanced down at her blue jeans and white T-shirt, mostly hidden by a jean jacket, and shrugged. "Nothing fancy, but at least I'm comfortable."

Evan slapped the knees of his faded jeans and tweaked the collar on his black leather jacket. "Yeah, me, too."

A young couple pushing a baby in a stroller walked past, and Lorna stared at them longingly.

"You like kids?"

"What?" She jerked her head.

"I asked if you like kids."

"Sure, they're great."

"When I get married, I'd like to have a whole house full of children," Evan said. "With kids around, it would be a lot harder to grow old and crotchety."

"Like me, you mean?"

Evan reached out to touch her hand. "I didn't mean that at all."

She blinked in rapid succession. "I am a lot older than most of the other students at Bay View."

"You're not much older than me. When I was born, you were only four."

She grunted. "When you were six, I was ten."

"When you were twenty-six, I was twenty-two." Evan nudged her arm with his elbow. "I'm gaining on you, huh?"

Lorna jumped up and grabbed the women's ten-speed by the handlebars. "I thought we came here to ride bikes, not talk about age-related things."

Evan stood, too. "You're right, so you lead, I'll follow."

They rode in pleasant silence, Lorna leading and Evan bringing up the rear. They were nearly halfway around the park when he pedaled alongside her. "You hungry? I brought along a few apples and some brownies I made last night."

She pulled her bicycle to a stop. "That does sound good. I haven't ridden a bike in years, and I'm really out of shape. A little rest and some nourishment might help get me going again."

Evan led them to a picnic table, set his kickstand, and motioned her to take a seat. When they were both seated, he reached into his backpack and withdrew two Red Delicious apples, then handed one to Lorna. "Let's eat these first and save the brownies for dessert."

"Thanks." Lorna bit into hers, and a trickle of sweet, sticky juice dribbled down her chin. "Mmm. . .this does hit the spot." She looked over at him and smiled. "Sorry about being such a grump earlier. Guess I'm a little touchy about my age."

"Apology accepted. Uh. . .would you like to go to dinner when we're done riding?" Evan asked hesitantly.

Warning bells went off in Lorna's head, and she felt her whole body tremble. "I'm not dressed for going out."

"I was thinking about pizza. We don't have to be dressed up for that." Evan bit into his apple and grinned.

That dopey little smile and the gentleness in his eyes made Lorna's heartbeat quicken. She gulped. "I–I—"

"You can think about it while we finish our ride," Evan said, coming to her rescue.

She shrugged her shoulders. "Okay."

"So, tell me about Lorna Patterson."

"What do you want to know?"

"I know you're enrolled in a Christian college. Does that mean you're a believer in Christ?"

She nodded. "I accepted the Lord as my personal Savior when I was ten years old. At that time I thought I knew exactly what He wanted me to do with my life."

"Which was?"

"To teach music. I started playing piano right around the time I became a Christian, and I soon discovered that I loved it."

"You're definitely a gifted pianist," he said with a broad smile. "You do great accompanying our choir, and you have a beautiful singing voice."

"Thanks." She nodded at him. "Is that all you wanted to know about me?"

"Actually, there is something else I've been wondering about."

"What?"

"You mentioned that you're a widow. How did your husband die?"

Lorna stared off into the distance, focusing on a cluster of pigeons eating dry bread crumbs someone had dumped on the grass. She didn't want to talk about Ron, her loss, or how he'd been killed so tragically.

"If you'd rather not discuss it, that's okay." Evan touched her arm gently. "I probably shouldn't have asked, but I want to know you better, so—"

Lorna turned her head so she was looking directly at him. "It's okay. It'll probably do me more good to talk about it than it will to keep it bottled up." She drew in a deep breath and plunged ahead. "Ron was killed in a motorcycle accident a little over a year ago. A semitruck hit him."

"I'm so sorry. It must have been hard for you."

"It was. Still is, in fact."

"Have you been on your own ever since?"

She shook her head. "Not exactly. I've been living with Ron's parents, hoping it would help the three of us deal with our grief."

"And has it?"

"Some."

Compassion showed in Evan's eyes, and he took hold of her hand. It felt warm and comforting, and even though Lorna's head told her to pull away, her heart said something entirely different. So she sat there, staring down at their intertwined fingers and basking in the moment of comfort and pleasure.

"I'm surprised a woman your age, who's blessed with lots of talent and good looks, hasn't found another man by now."

Lorna felt her face flame. She focused on the apple core in her other hand, already turning brown. When she spotted a garbage can a few feet away, Lorna stood up. Before she could take a step, she felt Evan's hand on her arm.

"I'm sorry, Lorna. I can tell I've upset you. Was it my question about your husband's death, or was it the fact that I said I was surprised you hadn't found another man?"

She blinked away unwanted tears. "A little of both I suppose."

She stiffened as Evan's arm went around her shoulders. "Still friends?"

"Sure," she mumbled.

"Does that mean you'll have pizza with me?"

"I thought I had until the bike ride was over to decide."

He twitched his eyebrows. "What can I say? I'm not the patient type."

"No, but you're certainly persistent."

He handed her a napkin and two brownies. "How do you think I've gotten this far in life?"

She sucked in her breath. How far had he gotten? Other than the fact that he was majoring in psychology, wasn't married, and was four years younger than she, Lorna knew practically nothing about Evan Bailey. Maybe she should learn more—in case she needed another friend.

She tossed the apple core into the garbage and bit into one of the brownies. "Where'd you say you got these?"

"Made them myself. I think I already told you that I'm taking an online cooking class. The instructor is teaching us how to make some tasty sweet treats." He winked at her. "I thought it might make me a better catch if I could cook."

Lorna wasn't sure what to say. She didn't want to hurt Evan's feelings by telling him the brownie was too dry. She thought about the cookies he'd given her the other day. She'd tried one at lunch, and they had been equally dry, not to mention a bit overdone. Apparently the man was so new at cooking, he couldn't tell that much himself. She ate the brownie in silence and washed it down with the bottled water Evan had also supplied. When she was done, Lorna climbed onto her bike. "We'd better go. I hear the best pizza in town is at Mama Mia's!"

Chapter 6

Lorna slid into a booth at the pizza parlor, and Evan took the bench across from her. When their waitress came, they ordered a large combination pizza and a pitcher of iced tea.

As soon as the server was gone, Evan leaned forward on his elbows and gave Lorna a crooked smile. "You're beautiful, you know that?"

She gulped. No one but Ron had ever looked at her as if she were the most desirable woman on earth. Lorna leaned back in her seat and slid her tongue across her bottom lip. "Now it's your turn to tell me about Evan Bailey," she said, hoping the change in subject might calm her racing heart and get her thinking straight again.

She watched the flame flicker from the candle in the center of the table and saw its reflection in Evan's blue eyes. "My life is an open book, so what would you like to know?" he asked.

I'd like to know why you're looking at me like that. "You told our group in class that your major is psychology, but you never said what you plan to do with it once you graduate," she said, instead of voicing her thoughts.

The waitress brought two glasses and a pitcher of iced tea to the table. As soon as she left, Evan poured them both a glass. "I'm hoping to land a job as a school guidance counselor, but if that doesn't work out, I might go into private practice as a child psychologist."

Lorna peered at him over the top of her glass. "Let me guess. I'll bet you plan to analyze kids all day, and then come home at night to the little woman who's been busy taking care of your own children. Is that right?"

He chuckled. "Something like that."

"How come you're not married already and starting that family?"

He ran his fingers through his short-cropped, sandy brown hair. "Haven't had time."

"No?"

"I was born and raised in Moscow, Idaho, and I'm the only boy in a family of three kids. I enrolled in Bible college shortly after I graduated high school, but I never finished."

"I take it you're a Christian, too?"

He nodded. "My conversion came when I was a teenager."

"How come you never finished Bible college?" she questioned.

"I decided on a tour of duty with the United States Air Force instead." A muscle jerked in his cheek, and he frowned slightly. "I had a relationship with a woman go sour on me. After praying about it, I figured the best way to get over her was to enlist and get as far away from the state of Idaho as I could."

In the few weeks she'd known Evan, this was the first time Lorna had seen him look so serious, and it took her completely by surprise. She was trying to decide how to comment, when the waitress showed up with their pizza. Lorna was almost relieved at the interruption. At least now she could concentrate on filling her stomach and not her mind.

After a brief prayer, Evan began attacking his pizza with a vengeance. It made Lorna wonder when his last good meal had been. By the time she'd finished two pieces, Evan had polished off four slices and was working on another one. He glanced at Lorna's plate. "Aren't you hungry?"

"The pizza is great. I'm enjoying every bite," she said.

He swiped the napkin across his face and stared at Lorna. It made her squirm. "Why are you looking at me that way?"

"What way?"

"Like I've got something on my face."

He chuckled. "Your face is spotless. I was thinking how much I enjoy your company and wondering if we might have a future together."

Lorna nearly choked on the piece of pizza she'd just put in her mouth. "Well, I—uh—don't think we're very well suited, and isn't it a little soon to be talking about a future together?"

"I'm not ready to propose marriage, if that's what you're thinking." His eyes narrowed. "And please don't tell me you're hung up about our age difference." Evan looked at Lorna so intently she could feel her toes curl inside her tennis shoes.

"That doesn't bother me so much. We're only talking about four years."

"Right." Evan raised his eyebrows. "You couldn't be afraid of men, or you wouldn't have been married before."

"I am not afraid of men! Why do you do that, anyway?"

"Do what?"

"Try to goad me into an argument."

He chuckled behind another slice of pizza. "Is that what you think I'm doing?"

"Isn't it?"

He dropped the pizza to his plate, reached across the table, and took hold of her hand.

She shivered involuntarily and averted her gaze to the table. "I wish you wouldn't do that, either."

"Do what? This?" He made little circles on her hand with his index finger.

She felt warmth travel up her neck and spread quickly to her cheeks. "The way you look at me, I almost feel—"

"Like you're a beautiful, desirable woman?" He leaned farther across the table. "You are, you know. And I don't care about you being four years older than me. In fact, I think dating an older woman might have some advantages."

She pulled her hand away. "And what would those be?"

He crossed his arms and leaned back in his seat. "Let's see now. . . You'd be more apt to see things from a mature point of view."

"And?"

"Just a minute. I'm thinking." Evan tapped the edge of his plate with his thumb. "Since you're older, you're most likely wiser."

She clicked her tongue. "Sorry I asked."

"Would you be willing to start dating me?" he asked with a hopeful expression.

She shook her head. "I'm flattered you would ask, but I don't think it's a good idea."

"Why not?"

Something indefinable passed between them, but Lorna pushed it aside. "I have my heart set on finishing college, and nothing is going to stop me this time."

He gave her a quizzical look. "This time?"

Lorna ended up telling him the story of how she'd sacrificed her own career and college degree to put her husband through school. She ended it by saying, "So, you see, for the first time in a long while, I'm finally getting what I want."

"That's it? End of story?"

She nodded. "It will be when I graduate and get a job teaching music in an elementary school."

"Why not teach at a junior or senior high?"

"I like children—especially those young enough to be molded and refined." She wrinkled her nose. "The older a child is, the harder to get through to his creativity."

"Does that mean I won't be able to get through to your creative side?" he asked with a lopsided grin.

"Could be." She folded her napkin into a neat little square and lifted her chin. "I really need to get home. I've got a lot of homework to do, and I've wasted most of the day."

Evan's sudden scowl told her she'd obviously hurt his feelings. "I didn't mean *wasted*. It's just that—"

He held up his hand. "No explanations are necessary." He stood, pulled a few coins from his back pocket, and dropped them on the table. "I hope that's enough for a tip, 'cause it's all the change I have."

She fumbled in her jacket pocket. "Maybe I have some ones I could add."

"Please don't bother. This will be enough, and I sure don't expect you to pay for the tip."

"I don't mind helping out," she insisted.

"Thanks anyway, but I'll take care of it." With that, Evan turned and headed for the cash register.

Lorna stood there with her ears burning and her heart pounding so hard she could hear it echoing in her ears. The day had started off so well. What had gone wrong, and how had it happened?

Evan was already up front paying for the pizza, so Lorna dug into her pocket and pulled out a dollar bill, which she quickly dropped to the table. Maybe she'd made a mistake thinking she and Evan could be friends. He obviously wanted more, but she knew it was impossible. In fact, he was impossible. Impossible and poor.

Evan said good-bye to Lorna outside in the parking lot. He was almost glad they had separate cars and he wouldn't have to drive her home. He didn't understand how a day that had started out fun and carefree could have ended on such a sour note. From all indications, he'd thought Lorna was enjoying their time together, but when she said she'd wasted most of the day, he felt deflated, even though he hadn't admitted it to her. That, plus the fact that she seemed overly concerned about his not having enough tip money, had thrown cold water on their time together.

What had turned things around? Had it been the discussion about their age difference? Children? Or maybe it was the money thing. Lorna might think he'd been too cheap to leave a decent tip. That could be why she'd climbed into her little red car with barely a wave and said nothing about hoping to see him again. Of course, he hadn't made the first move on that account, either.

"I thought she might be the one, Lord," Evan mumbled as he opened the door to his Jeep. Remembering the look on Lorna's face when she'd eaten the treat he'd given her earlier that day, he added, "Maybe I should have followed the recipe closer and added some chocolate chips to the top of those brownies."

Chapter 7

The following Monday morning in anatomy, Evan acted as though nothing were wrong. In fact, he surprised Lorna by presenting her with a wedge of apple pie he said he'd made the night before.

"It's a little mushy, and the crust's kind of tough," he admitted, "but I sampled a slice at breakfast, and it seemed sweet enough, at least."

Lorna smiled politely and took the plastic container with the pie in it. It was nice of Evan to think of her, but if he thought the dessert would give him an edge, he was mistaken. Lorna was fighting her attraction to Evan, and to lead him on would sooner or later cause one or both of them to get hurt.

Probably me, she thought. *I'm usually the one who makes all the sacrifices, then loses in the end.* What good had come out of her putting Ron through college and med school? He'd been killed in a senseless accident, leaving Lorna with a broken heart, a mound of bills, and no career for herself. It was going to be different from now on, though. She finally had her life back on track.

"You look kind of down in the mouth this morning," Evan said, nudging her arm gently with his hand. "Everything okay?"

She shrugged. "I'm just tired. I stayed up late last night trying to get all my homework done."

He pursed his lips. "Guess that's my fault. If you hadn't wasted your Saturday bike riding and having pizza with me, you'd have had lots more time to work on your assignments."

So Evan had been hurt by her comment about wasted time on Saturday. Lorna could see by the look in the man's eyes that his pride was wounded. She felt a sense of guilt sweep over like a cascading waterfall. She hadn't meant to hurt him. As a Christian, Lorna tried not to offend anyone, although she probably had fallen short many times since Ron's death.

"Evan," she began sincerely, "I apologize for my offhanded remark the other day. I had a good time with you, and my day wasn't wasted."

He grinned at her. "Really?"

She nodded.

"Would you be willing to go out with me again—as friends?"

Lorna chewed on her lower lip as she contemplated his offer. "Well, maybe," she finally conceded.

"That's great! How about this Saturday night, if you've got the evening off from working at Farmen's."

"I only work on weeknights," she said.

"Good, then we can go bowling, out to dinner, to the movies. . .or all three."

She chuckled softly. "I think one of those would be sufficient, don't you?"

"Yeah, I suppose so. Which one's your choice?"

"Why don't you surprise me on Saturday night?"

"Okay, I will." Evan snapped his fingers. "Say, I'll need your address so I can pick you up."

Lorna felt as though a glass of cold water had been dashed in her face. There was no way she could allow Evan to come by her in-laws' and pick her up for what she was sure they would assume was a date. She couldn't hurt Ann and Ed that way. It wouldn't be fair to Ron's memory. Maybe she should have told Evan she was busy on Saturday night. Maybe. . .

"You gonna give me your address or not?"

Lorna blinked. "Uh—how about we meet somewhere, like we did last Saturday?"

His forehead wrinkled. "Are you ashamed for your folks to meet me?"

"I live with my in-laws, remember?"

"So?"

"They might not understand about my going out with you," she explained. "They're still not over the loss of their son."

Evan stared at her for several seconds but finally shrugged his shoulders. "Okay. If that's how you want it, we can meet at Ivar's along the waterfront. I've been wanting to try out their famous fish and chips ever since I came to Seattle."

Lorna licked her lips. "That does sound good."

Evan opened his mouth to say something more, but their professor walked into the room. "We'll talk later," he whispered.

She nodded in response.

Lorna entered the choir room a few minutes early, hoping to get her music organized before class began. She noticed Evan standing by the bulletin board across the room. She hated to admit it, but he was fun to be around. Could he be growing on her?

When she took a seat at the piano and peeked over the stack of music, she saw Vanessa Brown step up beside Evan. "Are the names posted for the choir solos yet?" the vivacious redhead asked. "I sure hope I got the female lead." She looked up at Evan and batted her lashes. "Maybe you'll get the male lead, and then we can practice together. Our voices would blend beautifully, don't you think?"

Oh, please, Lorna groaned inwardly. The omelet she'd eaten for breakfast that morning had suddenly turned into a lump in the pit of her stomach. She didn't like the sly little grin Evan was wearing, either. He was up to something, and it probably meant someone was in for a double dose of his teasing.

Evan stepped in front of Vanessa, blocking her view of the board. She let out a grunt and tugged on his shirtsleeve. "I can't see. What's it say?"

Evan held his position, mumbling something Lorna couldn't quite understand.

"Well?" Vanessa shouted. "Are you going to tell me what it says or not?"

He scratched the back of his head. "Hmm. . ."

"What is it? Let me see!"

Evan glanced over at Lorna, but she quickly averted her gaze, pretending to be absorbed in her music.

When she lifted her head, Lorna saw Vanessa slide under Evan's arm, until she was facing the bulletin board. She studied it for several seconds, but then her hands dropped to her hips, and she whirled around. "That just figures!" She marched across the room and stopped in front of the piano, shooting Lorna a look that could have stopped traffic on the busy Seattle freeway. "I hope you're satisfied!"

Lorna was bewildered. "What are you talking about?"

"Professor Burrows chose *you* for the female solo!" Vanessa scowled at Lorna. "Just because you're older than the rest of us and play the piano fairly well shouldn't mean you get special privileges."

Lorna creased her forehead so hard she felt wrinkles form. "Why would you say such a thing?"

"The professor doesn't think you can do any wrong. She's always telling the class how mature you are and how you're the only one who ever follows directions."

Lorna opened her mouth to offer some kind of rebuttal, but before she got a word out, Evan's deep voice cut her off. "Now wait a minute, Vanessa. Lorna got the lead part for only one reason."

Vanessa turned to face Evan, who stood at her side in front of the piano. "And that would be?"

"This talented woman can not only play the piano, but she can sing. Beautifully, I might add." He cast Lorna a sidelong glance, and she felt the heat of a blush warm her cheeks.

Vanessa's dark eyes narrowed. "Are you saying *I* can't sing?"

"I don't think that's what he meant," Lorna interjected.

Vanessa slapped her hand on the piano keys with such force that Lorna worried the Baldwin might never be the same. "Let the man speak for himself!" She whirled around to face Evan. "Or does the cute little blond have you so wrapped around her finger that you can't even think straight? It's obvious you're smitten with her."

Evan opened his mouth as if he was going to say something, but Vanessa cut him off. "Don't try to deny it, Evan Bailey! I've seen the way you and Lorna look at each other." She sniffed deeply. "Is she trying to rob from the cradle, or are you looking for a mother figure?"

Evan's face had turned crimson. "I think this discussion is over," he said firmly.

"That's right, let's drop it," Lorna agreed.

Vanessa glared at Evan. "Be a good boy now, and do what Mama Lorna says."

He drew in a deep breath. "I'm warning you, Vanessa. . ."

"What are you going to do? Tell the teacher on me?" she taunted.

Lorna cleared her throat a couple of times, and both Evan and Vanessa turned to look at her. "We're all adults here, and if getting the lead part means so much to you, I'll speak to the professor about it, Vanessa."

"I'll fight my own battles, thank you very much!" Vanessa squared her shoulders. "Unlike some people in this class, I don't need a mother to fix my boo-boos." She turned on her heels and marched out of the room.

Evan let out a low whistle. "What was that all about?"

Lorna shook her head slowly. "You don't know?"

He shrugged. "Not really. She said she wanted the solo part, you offered to give it to her, and she's still mad. Makes no sense to me." He snickered. "But then I never was much good at understanding women. Even if I did grow up with two sisters."

Lorna pinched the bridge of her nose. How could the man be so blind? "Vanessa is jealous."

"I know. She wants your part," Evan said, dropping to the bench beside Lorna. "She can't stand the fact that someone has a better singing voice than she does."

"I think the real reason Vanessa's jealous is because she thinks you like me, and she's attracted to you."

Evan looked at Lorna as though she'd lost her mind. "I've done nothing to make Vanessa think she and I might—"

"That doesn't matter. You make people laugh, and your manner is often flirtatious."

Evan rubbed his chin and frowned. "What can I say? I'm a friendly guy, but that doesn't mean I'm after every woman I meet."

Lorna reached for a piece of music. "Tell that to Vanessa Brown."

Chapter 8

E van moved away from the piano, wishing there were something he could say or do to make Lorna feel more comfortable about the part she'd gotten. The scene with Vanessa had been unreal, but the fact that Lorna was willing to give up the solo part she'd been offered was one more proof that she lived her Christianity and would make a good wife for some lucky man. It just probably wasn't him.

He took a seat in the chair he'd been assigned and studied Lorna. She was thumbing through a stack of music, her forehead wrinkled and her face looking pinched. Was she still thinking about the encounter with Vanessa, frustrated with Evan, or merely trying to concentrate on getting ready for their first choir number?

Lorna was not only a beautiful, talented musician, but she had a sensitivity that drew Evan to her like a powerful magnet. Anyone willing to give up a favored part and not get riled when Vanessa attacked her with a vengeance made a hit with Evan. Lorna had done the Christian thing, even if Vanessa hadn't. Now if he could only convince her to give their relationship a chance. Maybe their Saturday night date would turn the tide.

Lorna had just slipped on her Farmen's apron when Chris came up behind her. "How was school today?"

"Don't ask."

"That bad, huh?"

"Afraid so."

"You've been back in college for a couple of weeks. I thought you'd be getting used to the routine by now."

Lorna grabbed an order pad from the back of the counter and stuffed it in her apron pocket. "The routine's not the problem."

Chris's forehead wrinkled. "What is, then?"

Lorna rubbed the back of her neck, trying to get the kinks out. "Never mind. It's probably not worth mentioning."

"It doesn't have anything to do with Evan Bailey, does it?"

"No! Yes. Well, partially."

Chris glanced at the clock on the wall above the serving counter. "We've still got a few minutes until our shift starts. Let's go to the ladies' room, and you can tell me about it."

Lorna shook her head. "What's the point? Talking won't change anything."

Chris grabbed her arm and gave it a gentle tug. "Come on, friend. I know you'll feel better once you've opened up and told me what's bothering you."

"Oh, all right," Lorna mumbled. "Let's hurry, though. I don't want to get docked any pay for starting late."

Lorna was glad to discover an empty ladies' room when she and Chris arrived a few moments later. Chris dropped onto the small leather couch and motioned Lorna to do the same. "Okay, spill it!"

Lorna curled up in one corner of the couch and let the whole story out, beginning with her entering the choir room that morning and ending with Vanessa's juvenile tantrum and Evan's response to it all.

Chris folded her hands across her stomach and laughed. It wasn't some weak, polite little giggle, like Lorna offered her customers. It was a genuine, full-blown belly laugh.

Lorna didn't see what was so funny. In fact, retelling the story had only upset her further. "This is no laughing matter, Chris. It's serious business."

Her friend blinked a couple of times, and then burst into another round of laughter.

Lorna started to get up. "Okay, fine! I shouldn't have said anything to you, that's obvious."

Chris reached over and grabbed hold of Lorna's arm. "No, stay, please." She wiped her eyes with the back of her hand. "I hope you know I wasn't laughing at you."

"Who?"

"The whole scenario." Chris clicked her tongue. "I just don't get you, Lorna."

"What do you mean?"

"Evan Bailey is one cute guy, right?"

Lorna nodded and flopped back onto the couch.

"From what you've told me, I'd say the man has high moral standards and is lots of fun to be with."

"Yes."

Chris leaned toward Lorna. "If you don't wake up and hear the music, you might lose the terrific guy to this Vanessa person. If I'd been you today, I don't think I could have been so nice about things." She grimaced. "Offering to give up the part—now that's Christianity in action!"

Lorna crossed her legs and swung her foot back and forth, thinking the whole while how tempted she had been to give that feisty redhead a swift kick this afternoon. She'd said what she felt was right at the time, but it hadn't been easy.

"From all you've told me, I'd say it's pretty obvious the woman has her sights set on Evan Bailey." Chris shook her finger at Lorna. "You need to put this whole age thing out of your mind and give the guy a chance."

Lorna cringed. "That's not really the problem. I think Evan is as poor as a church mouse."

"What gives you that idea?"

Lorna quickly related the story of her and Evan's bicycle ride and how when they'd had pizza, he didn't have enough money to leave a decent tip.

Chris groaned. "Don't you think you're jumping to conclusions? Maybe the guy just didn't have much cash on him that day." She squinted her eyes. "And even if he is dirt poor, does it really matter so much?"

"It does to me. I don't want to get involved with another man who will expect me to give up my career and put him through college."

Evan was excited about his date with Lorna tonight. He'd been looking forward to it all week and had even tried his hand at making another online sweet treat, which he planned to give Lorna after dinner this evening. It was called Lemon Supreme and consisted of cream cheese mixed with lemon juice, sugar, eggs, and vanilla. Graham cracker crumbs were used for the crust, and confectioner's sugar was sprinkled over the top. He hadn't had time to sample it, but Evan was sure Lorna would like it.

At six o'clock sharp, Evan stood in front of Ivar's Restaurant along the Seattle waterfront. He was pleased when he saw Lorna cross the street and head in his direction. He'd been worried she might stand him up.

"Am I late?" she panted. "I had a hard time finding a place to park."

"You're right on time," he assured her. "I got here a few minutes ago and put my name on the waiting list at the restaurant."

"How long did they say we might have to wait for a table?"

"Not more than a half hour or so," he said.

"Guess we could go inside and wait in the lobby."

Evan nodded. "Or we could stay out here awhile and enjoy the night air." He drew in a deep breath. "Ah, sure does smell fresh down by the water, doesn't it?"

She wrinkled her nose. "Guess that all depends on what you call fresh."

"Salty sea air and fish a-frying. . .now that's what I call fresh," he countered with a wide smile.

She poked him playfully on the arm. "You would say something like that."

He chuckled. "Ah, you know me so well."

"No, actually, I don't," she said with a slight frown.

"Then we need to remedy that." Evan gazed deeply into her eyes. "I'd sure like to know you better, 'cause what I've seen so far I really like."

Lorna gulped. Things were moving too fast, and she seemed powerless to stop them. What had happened to her resolve not to get involved with another man, or even to date? She had to put a stop to this before it escalated into more than friendship.

Before she had a chance to open her mouth, Evan took hold of her hand and led her to a bench along the side of the building. It faced the water, where several docks were located. "Let's sit awhile and watch the boats come and go," he suggested.

"What about our dinner reservations?"

"They said they'd call my name over the loudspeaker when our table's ready. Fortunately, there's a speaker outside, too." Evan sat down, and Lorna did the same.

The ferry coming from Bremerton docked, and Lorna watched the people disembark. She hadn't been to Bremerton in a long time. She hardly went anywhere but work, school, church, and shopping once in a while. What had happened to the carefree days of vacations, fun evenings out, and days off? *Guess I gave those things up when I began working so Ron could go to school.* Working two jobs left little time for fun or recreation, and now that Lorna was in school and still employed at one job, things weren't much better. *I do have the weekends free,* her conscience reminded. *Maybe I deserve to have a little fun now and then.*

"You look like you're a hundred miles away," Evan said, breaking into her thoughts.

She turned her head and looked at him. "I was watching the ferry."

He lifted her chin with his hand. "And I've been watching you."

Before Lorna could respond, he tipped his head and brushed a gentle kiss against her lips. As the kiss deepened, she instinctively wrapped her arms around his neck.

"Bailey, party of two. . .your table is ready!"

Lorna jerked away from Evan at the sound of his name being called over the loudspeaker. "We—we'd better get in there," she said breathlessly.

"Right." Evan stood up, pulling Lorna gently to her feet.

She went silently by his side into the restaurant, berating herself for allowing that kiss. *I'll be on my guard the rest of the evening. No more dreamy looks and no more kisses!*

Chapter 9

Farmen's Restaurant was more crowded than usual on Monday night, and Lorna's boss had just informed her that they were shorthanded. With God's help, she would get through her shift, although she was already tired. It had been a busy weekend, and she'd had to cram in time for homework.

Lorna thought about her date with Evan on Saturday, which hadn't ended until eleven o'clock, because they'd taken a ride on one of the sightseeing boats after dinner. She'd thoroughly enjoyed the moonlight cruise around Puget Sound, and when Evan walked Lorna to her car, he'd presented her with another of his desserts. This one was called Lemon Supreme, and she had tried it after she got home that night.

Lorna puckered her lips as she remembered the sour taste caused by either too much lemon juice or not enough sugar. *I doubt Evan will ever be a master baker,* she mused.

She glanced at her reflection in the mirror over the serving counter, checking her uniform and hair one last time, as she contemplated the way Evan had looked at her before they'd said good night. He'd wanted to kiss her again; she could tell by his look of longing. She had prevented it from happening by jumping quickly into her car and shutting the door.

"I only want to be his friend," Lorna muttered under her breath, as she strolled into the dining room.

She got right to work and took the order of an elderly couple. Then she moved across the aisle to where another couple sat with their heads bent over the menus.

The woman was the first to look up, and Lorna's mouth dropped open.

"Fancy meeting you here," Vanessa Brown drawled.

Before Lorna could respond, Vanessa's companion looked up and announced, "Lorna works here."

Lorna's hand began to tremble, and she dropped the order pad. Evan Bailey was looking at her as though nothing was wrong. Maybe his having dinner with Vanessa was a normal occurrence. Maybe this wasn't their first date.

Forcing her thoughts to remain on the business at hand, Lorna bent down to retrieve the pad. When she stood up again, Vanessa was leaning across the table, fussing with Evan's shirt collar.

Lorna cleared her throat, and Vanessa glanced over at her. "What's good to eat in this place?"

"Tonight's special is meat loaf." Lorna kept her focus on the order pad.

"Meat loaf sounds good to me," Evan said.

"You're such a simple, easy-to-please kind of guy," Vanessa fairly purred.

Lorna swallowed back the urge to scream. She probably shouldn't be having these unwarranted feelings of jealousy, for she had no claim on Evan. He'd obviously lied to her the other day, when he denied any interest in Vanessa. A guy didn't take a girl out to dinner if he didn't care something about her. *He took me to dinner on Saturday. Does that mean he cares about both me and Vanessa? Or could Evan Bailey be toying with our emotions?*

Lorna turned to face Vanessa, feeling as though the air between them was charged with electricity. "What would you like to order?"

"I'm careful about what I eat, so I think I'll have a chicken salad with low-cal ranch dressing." Vanessa looked over at her dinner partner and batted her eyelashes. "Men like their women to be fit and trim, right, Evan?"

He shrugged his shoulders. "I can't speak for other men, but to my way of thinking, it's what's in a woman's heart that really matters. Outward appearances can sometimes be deceiving."

He cast Lorna a grin, and she tapped her pencil against the order pad impatiently. "Will there be anything else?"

Evan opened his mouth. "Yes, actually—"

"Why don't you bring us a couple of sugar-free mocha-flavored coffees?" Vanessa interrupted. She gave Evan a syrupy smile. "I hope you like that flavor."

"Well, I—"

"Two mochas, a meat loaf special, and one chicken salad, coming right up!" Lorna turned on her heels and hurried away.

Evan watched Lorna's retreating form. Her shoulders were hunched, and her head was down. Obviously she wasn't at her best. He could tell she'd been trying to be polite when she took their orders, but from her tone of voice and those wrinkles he'd noticed in her forehead, he was certain she was irritated about something.

Probably wondering what I'm doing here with Vanessa. Wish she had stuck around longer so I could have explained. Maybe I should have gone after her.

"Evan, are you listening to me?"

Evan turned his head. "What were you saying, Vanessa?"

"I'm glad I ran into you tonight. I wanted to ask your opinion on something."

"What's that?"

Vanessa leaned her elbows on the table and intertwined her fingers. "All day I've been thinking about that solo part I should have had."

"You're coming to grips with it, I hope."

She frowned. "Actually, I've been wondering whether I should have taken Lorna up on her offer to give the part to me. What do you think, Evan? Should I ask her about it when she returns with our orders?"

Evan grunted. "I can't believe you'd really expect her to give you that solo, Professor Burrows obviously feels Lorna's the best one for the part, or she wouldn't have assigned it to her."

Vanessa wrinkled her nose. "And I can't believe the way you always stick up for that little blond. She's too old and too prim and proper for you, Evan. Why don't you wake up?"

Evan reached for his glass of water and took a big gulp, hoping to regain his composure before he spoke again. When he set the glass down, he leaned forward and looked Vanessa right in the eye. "I'm not hung up on age differences, and as far as Lorna being prim and proper, you don't know what you're talking about."

Vanessa blinked and pulled back like she'd been stung by a bee. "You don't have to be so mean, Evan. I was only trying to make you see how much better—"

She was interrupted when Lorna appeared at the table with their orders. Evan was glad he could concentrate on eating his meat loaf instead of trying to change Vanessa's mind about a woman she barely knew.

As Lorna placed Evan's plate in front of him, she was greeted with another one of his phony smiles. They had to be phony. No man in his right mind would be out with one woman and flirting with another. For that matter, most men didn't bring their date to the workplace of the woman he'd dated only two nights before. *Dated and kissed,* she fumed.

Lorna excused herself to get their beverages, and a short time later she returned with two mugs of mocha-flavored coffee. She looked at Evan sitting across from Vanessa, and an unexpected yearning stirred within her soul. Why couldn't she be the one he was having dinner with tonight? All this time Lorna had been telling herself that she and Evan could only be friends, so it didn't make sense to feel jealousy over seeing him with Vanessa Brown.

Maybe I don't know my own heart. Maybe. . .

"This isn't low-cal dressing. I asked for low-cal, remember?"

Vanessa's sharp words pulled Lorna's disconcerting thoughts aside. "I think it is," she replied. "I turned in an order for low-cal dressing, and I'm sure—"

"I just tasted it. It's not low-cal!"

Lorna drew in a deep breath and offered up a quick prayer for patience. "I'll go check with the cook who filled your order."

She started to turn, but Vanessa shouted, "I want another salad! This one is drenched in fattening ranch dressing, and it's ruined."

Lorna was so aggravated her ears were ringing, yet she knew in order to keep her job at Farmen's she would need to be polite to all costumers—even someone as demanding as Vanessa. "I'll be back with another salad."

As she was turning in the order for the salad, Lorna met up with her friend, Chris.

"You don't look like the picture of happiness tonight," Chris noted. "What's the problem—too many customers?"

Lorna gritted her teeth. "Just two too many."

"What's that supposed to mean?"

Lorna explained about Evan and Vanessa being on a date and how Vanessa was demanding a new salad.

Chris squinted her eyes. "I thought you and Evan went to Ivar's on Saturday?"

"We did."

"Then what's up with him bringing another woman here on a date?"

Lorna leaned against the edge of the serving counter and groaned. "He's two-faced. What can I say?"

"Want me to finish up with that table for you?"

Lorna sighed with relief. "Would you? I don't think I can face Evan and his date again tonight."

Chris patted Lorna's arm. "Sure. What are friends for?"

Lorna peered into the darkening sky, watching out the window as Evan and Vanessa left the restaurant. She thought it was strange when she saw them each get into their own cars, but shrugged it off, remembering that she and Evan had taken separate vehicles on Saturday night. Maybe Evan didn't have time to pick Vanessa up for their date. Maybe she'd been out running errands. It didn't matter. Lorna's shift would be over in a few hours, and then she could go home, indulge in a long, hot bath, and crash on the couch in front of the fireplace. Maybe a cup of hot chocolate and some of Ann's famous oatmeal cookies would help soothe her frazzled nerves. Some pleasant music and a good inspirational novel to read could have her feeling better in no time.

Lorna moved away from the window and sought out her next customer. She had a job to do, and she wouldn't waste another minute thinking about Evan Bailey. If he desired someone as self-serving as Vanessa Brown, he could have her.

Determined to come up with a way to win Lorna's heart, Evan had decided to try another recipe from his online cooking class. This one was called Bodacious Banana Bread, and it looked fairly simple to make. Between the loaf of bread and the explanation he planned to give Lorna tomorrow at school, Evan hoped he could let her know how much he cared.

Whistling to the tune of "Jesus Loves Me," Evan set out the ingredients he needed: butter, honey, eggs, flour, salt, soda, baking powder, and two ripe bananas. In short order he had everything mixed. He poured the batter into a glass baking dish and pulled it off the counter. Suddenly, his hand bumped a bowl of freshly washed blueberries he planned to have with a dish of vanilla ice cream later on. The bowl toppled over, and half the blueberries tumbled into the bread pan, on top of the banana mixture.

"Oh no," Evan moaned. "Now I've done it." He tried to pick the blueberries out, but too many had already sunk to the bottom of the pan.

"Guess I could bake it as is and hope for the best." Evan grabbed a wooden spoon and gave the dough a couple of stirs, to ensure that the berries were evenly distributed. He figured it couldn't turn out any worse than the other desserts he'd foiled since he first began the cooking class. That Lemon Supreme he'd been dumb enough to give Lorna without first tasting had been one of the worst. He'd sampled a piece after their date on Saturday night and realized he'd messed up the recipe somehow, because it wasn't sweet enough.

Two hours later the bread was done and had cooled sufficiently. Evan decided to try a slice, determined not to give any to Lorna if it tasted funny.

To Evan's delight, the bread was wonderful. The blueberries had added a nice texture to the sweet dessert, and it was cooked to perfection. "I think I'll call this my Blueberry Surprise," he said with a chuckle. "Sure hope it impresses Lorna, because I'm not certain I have any words that will."

Chapter 10

Going back to school the following day—knowing she would have to face both Evan and Vanessa—was difficult for Lorna. She didn't know why it should be so hard. Evan had made no commitment to her, nor she to him.

When she arrived at school, Lorna was surprised to see Evan standing in the hall, just outside their anatomy class. He spotted her, waved, and held up a paper sack. "I have something for you, and we need to talk." His voice sounded almost pleading, and that in itself Lorna found unsettling.

"There's nothing to talk about." Lorna started to walk away, hoping to avoid any confrontations and knowing if they did talk, her true feelings might give her away.

Evan reached out and grabbed hold of her arm. When she turned to face him, he lifted his free hand and wrapped a tendril of her hair around his finger. He leaned slightly forward—so close she could feel his breath on her upturned face. If she didn't do something quickly, she was sure she was about to be kissed.

Evan moved his finger from her hair to her face, skimming down her cheek, then along her chin.

Lorna shivered with a mixture of anticipation and dread, knowing she should pull away. Just as Evan's lips sought hers, the floor began to move, and the walls swayed back and forth in a surreal manner. Lorna had heard of bells going off and being so much in love that it hurt, but if this weird sensation had anything to do with the way she felt about Evan, she didn't want any part of loving the man.

Evan grasped Lorna's shoulders as the floor tilted, and she almost lost her balance. Knowing she needed his support in order to stay on her feet, Lorna leaned into him, gripping both of his arms. "What's happening?" she rasped.

"I believe we're in the middle of a bad earthquake." Evan's face seemed etched with concern. It was a stark contrast from his usual smiling expression.

Lorna's eyes widened with dread. She looked down and thought she was going to be sick. The floor was moving rhythmically up and down. It reminded her of a ship caught in a storm, about to be capsized with the crest of each angry wave.

"This is a bad one!" Evan exclaimed. "We need to get under a table or something."

She looked around helplessly; there were no tables in the hall and none in the anatomy class, either. The room only had opera-style seats. "Where?"

Evan pulled her closer. "A doorway! We should stand under a doorway."

The door to their classroom was only a few feet away, but it took great effort for them to maneuver themselves into position. Lorna's heart was thumping so hard she was sure Evan could hear each radical beat. She'd been in a few earthquakes during her lifetime, but none so violent as this one.

A candy machine in the hallway vibrated, pictures on the wall flew in every direction, and a terrible, cracking sound rent the air as the windows rattled and broke. A loud crash, followed by a shrill scream, sent shivers up Lorna's spine. There was no one else in the hallway, which was unusual, considering the fact that classes were scheduled to begin soon. Where was everybody, and when would this nightmare end?

Another ear-piercing sound! Was that a baby's cry? No, it couldn't be. This was Bay View Christian College, not a day care center.

"I think the scream came from over there," Evan said, pointing across the hall. He glanced down at Lorna. "Did that sound like a baby cry to you?"

She nodded and swallowed against the lump lodged in her throat.

"Stay here. I'll be right back." Evan handed Lorna the paper sack he'd been holding.

"No, don't leave me!" She clutched the front of his shirt as panic swept through her in a wave so cold and suffocating, she thought she might faint.

"I think you'll be okay if you wait right here," he assured her. "Pray, Lorna. Pray."

The walls and floor were still moving, though a bit slower now. Lorna watched helplessly as Evan half crawled, half slid on his stomach across the hall. When he disappeared behind the door, she sent up a prayer. "Dear God, please keep him safe."

At that moment, the truth slammed into Lorna with a force stronger than any earthquake. Although she hadn't known Evan very long, she was falling in love with him. In the few short weeks since they'd met, he had brought joy and laughter into her life. He'd made her feel beautiful and special, something she hadn't felt since Ron's untimely death. They had a common bond. Both were Christians, interested in music, and each had a desire to work with children.

Children. The word stuck in Lorna's brain. She had always wanted a child. When she married Ron, Lorna was sure they would start a family as soon as he finished med school. That never happened because her husband had been snatched away as quickly as fog settles over Puget Sound.

She leaned heavily against the door frame and let this new revelation sink in. Was going back to school and getting her degree really Lorna's heart's desire? Or was being married to someone she loved and starting a family what she truly wanted? *It doesn't matter. I can't have a relationship with Evan because he doesn't love me. He's been seeing Vanessa.*

"Lorna! Can you come over here?" Evan's urgent plea broke into her thoughts, and she reeled at the sound of his resonating voice.

The earthquake was over now, but Lorna knew from past experience that a series of smaller tremors would no doubt follow. She made her way carefully across the hall and into the room she'd seen Evan enter only moments ago.

She stopped short inside the door. In the middle of the room lay a young woman. A bookcase had fallen across her legs, pinning her to the floor. Lorna gasped as she realized the woman was holding a crying baby in her arms. The sight brought tears to Lorna's eyes. Covering her mouth to stifle a sob, she raced to Evan's side and dropped down beside him. She noticed beads of perspiration glistening on his upper lip. "Is she hurt badly? What about the baby?" Tears rolled down Lorna's cheeks as she thought about the possibility of a child losing its mother, or the other way around. *Please, God, let them be all right.*

"The woman's legs could be broken, so it wouldn't be good to try to move her. The baby appears to be okay." He pointed to the sobbing infant. "Could you pick her up, then go down the hall and find a phone? We need to call 911 right away."

Lorna nodded numbly. As soon as she lifted the child into her arms, the baby's crying abated. She stood and started for the door. Looking back over her shoulder, she whispered, "I love you, Evan, even if you do care for Vanessa Brown."

The next few hours went by in a blur. A trip to the hospital in Evan's car, following the ambulance that transported the injured woman. . . Talking with the paramedics who'd found some identification on the baby's mother. Calling the woman's husband on the phone. Pacing the floor of the hospital waiting room. Trying to comfort a fussy child. Waiting patiently until the father arrived. Praying until no more words would come. Lorna did all these things with Evan by her side. They said little to each other as they waited to hear of the mother's condition. Words seemed unnecessary as Lorna acknowledged a shared sense of oneness with Evan, found only in a crisis situation.

The woman, who'd been identified as Sherry Holmes, had been at the college that morning, looking for her husband, an English professor. He'd left for work without his briefcase, and she'd come to deliver the papers he needed. Professor Holmes wasn't in his class when she arrived. He'd been to an early morning meeting in another building, as had most of the other teachers. Why there weren't any other students in the hallway, Lorna still did not understand. She thought it must have been divine intervention, since so much structural damage had been done to that particular building. Who knew how many more injuries might have occurred had there been numerous students milling about?

Lorna felt a sense of loss as she handed the baby over to its father a short time later. She was relieved to hear that the child's mother was in stable condition, despite a broken leg and several bad bruises.

"You look done in," Evan said, taking Lorna's hand and leading her to a chair. He pointed to the paper sack lying on the table in the waiting room, where Lorna had placed it when they first arrived. "You never did open your present."

She nodded and offered him a weak smile. "Guess I've been too busy with other things." She pulled it open and peeked inside. A sweet banana aroma overtook her senses, and she sniffed deeply. "I'm guessing it's a loaf of banana bread."

Evan smiled. "It started out to be, but in the end, it turned out to be a kind of blueberry surprise."

She tipped her head and squinted her eyes. "What?"

Evan chuckled. "It's a long story." He motioned to the sack. "Try a hunk. I think you'll be pleasantly surprised."

Lorna opened the bag and withdrew a piece of the bread. She took a tentative bite, remembering the other treats he'd given her that hadn't turned out so well. To her surprise, the blueberry-banana bread was actually good. It was wonderful, in fact. She grinned at him. "This is great. You should patent the recipe."

He smiled and reached for her hand. "I don't know what surprises me the most... the accidental making of a great-tasting bread or your willingness to be here with me now."

"It's been a pretty rough morning, and I'm thankful the baby and her mother are going to be okay," she said, making no reference to her willingness to be with Evan.

"The look of gratitude on Professor Holmes's face will stay with me a long time." Evan gazed deeply into Lorna's eyes. "Nothing is as precious as the life God gives each of us, and I don't want to waste a single moment of the time I have left on this earth." He stroked the side of her face tenderly. "You're the most precious gift He's ever offered me."

Lorna blinked back sudden tears. "Me? But I thought you and Vanessa—"

Evan shook his head and leaned over to kiss her. When he pulled away, he smiled. Not his usual silly grin, but an honest "I love you" kind of smile. "I came to the restaurant last night to talk to you," he said. "I was going to plead my case and beg you to give our relationship a try."

"But Vanessa—"

"She was not my date."

"She wasn't?"

He shook his head.

"You were both at the same table, and I thought—"

"I know what you thought." He wrapped his arms around Lorna and held her tightly. "She came into Farmen's on her own, saw me sitting at that table, and decided to join me. The rest you pretty well know."

She shook her head. "Not really. From the way you two were acting, I thought you were on a date."

Evan grimaced. "Vanessa Brown is a spoiled, self-centered young woman." He touched the tip of Lorna's nose and chuckled. "Besides, she's too young for someone as mature as me."

Lorna laughed and tilted her head so she was looking Evan right in the eye. "In this life we don't always get second chances, but I'm asking for one now, Evan Bailey."

He smiled. "You've got it."

"I think it's time for you to meet my in-laws."

"I'd like that."

"And I don't care how poor you are, either," she added, giving his hand a squeeze.

"What makes you think I'm poor?"

"You mean you're not?"

He shook his head. "Not filthy rich, but sure no pauper." He bent his head down to capture her lips in a kiss that evaporated any lingering doubts.

Lorna thought about the verse of scripture Ann had quoted her awhile back. *"Delight yourself in the Lord and he will give you the desires of your heart."* Her senses reeled with the knowledge that regardless of whether she ever taught music or not, she had truly found her heart's desire in this man with the blueberry surprise.

BLUEBERRY SURPRISE

⅓ cup butter
⅔ cup honey
2 eggs
2 ripe bananas, mashed
1¼ cups flour
2 teaspoons baking powder
½ teaspoon salt
¼ teaspoon baking soda
1 cup blueberries

Cream butter and honey until fluffy. Add eggs, beating well after each. Add bananas and mix well. Combine dry ingredients and add to creamed mixture, mixing thoroughly. Gently fold in blueberries. Pour into a 9x5-inch loaf pan that has been lined with waxed paper. Bake at 350 degrees for 50 to 60 minutes, or until a wooden toothpick comes out clean. Cool, remove from pan, and gently pull away the waxed paper. (Makes 1 loaf.)

Bittersweet Memories and Peppermint Dreams
by Pamela Griffin

Dedication

A special thank you to my crit buds on this project,
and to Lena—who gave me permission to use
the tartar sauce/cake incident, based on the real-life
experience of one of her family members.
As always, this is dedicated to my Lord, Jesus,
who sweetens all the flops in my life,
making masterpieces from the messes.

"Taste and see that the LORD is good."
PSALM 34:8

Chapter 1

W ait! Don't leave without me!"

Frantically waving her arm, Erica Langley darted through the icy drizzle, jumped a puddle, and just made it to the bus as the huge door closed. She pounded on the glass with gloved fingers. The driver opened the door again and raised bushy gray brows as he watched her clomp up the steep metal stairs and produce her ticket.

"Almost missed the bus, lady," he grumbled.

"Sorry." She attempted a smile, one he didn't return.

Clutching her shoulder bag to her hip, Erica caught her breath and eyed the seats on either side of the narrow aisle. The front and middle ones were full. Toward the back she spotted two empty rows, but she didn't think her shaky legs would carry her that far. Six rows down she spotted an empty seat on the left and moved toward it.

"May I?" she asked the elderly woman by the window, wondering why no one had claimed the coveted spot. Places close to the door were usually first to go.

"That seat is taken, but you can sit here, if you'd like." The deep masculine voice came from Erica's right. "The passenger who was sitting beside me just got off."

She turned. Gentle brown eyes—puppy-dog eyes—smiled up at her. The hint of a crease in his right cheek suggested a boyish grin when his smile was full-blown. His auburn hair was cut short but unkempt, as if he'd run his fingers through the damp twirls a few times. Beads of moisture sparkled in the strands as if he, too, had made a recent dash into the cold rain. He moved a couple of magazines and a leather briefcase off the aisle seat next to him.

Erica hesitated, uncertain whether she wanted to be in such close proximity to this attractive stranger. He must be uncomfortable with his long, trim build folded into that confined space. His jeans-clad knees hit the upholstered back of the seat in front of him. And he wasn't slouching.

"I promise, I don't bite." His sober expression didn't match his light words.

Embarrassed to feel all eyes on her—even the driver's, who impatiently looked at her in his long mirror above the wheel—Erica sank into the seat. As the bus rumbled out of the parking lot, she wished she had removed her coat first. To stand up now would be awkward. But judging from the warmth, the heater must be on full blast. Deciding she didn't want to bake, even in such frigid weather, she pulled off her gloves and shrugged her right shoulder out of the coat sleeve. Twisting from side to side, she tried to rid herself of the rest of the red wool garment. A large hand touched her shoulder.

"Allow me." Brown Eyes took her black furry collar and helped her remove her other arm from the sleeve. Then he pulled the coat from under her while she braced her hands on the chair arms and lifted herself a few inches. "Are you sure you want to take this off? You're shaking like a leaf."

Which has nothing to do with the cold. Get a grip, Erica. You're twenty-three, not thirteen. "Thanks, I'm fine." Fully seated again, she reclaimed her coat, laying it over her lap. She leaned forward, lifting her waist-length dark hair away from her back so it wouldn't pull, and brought the thick swathe to rest over one shoulder. With jerky movements she straightened her cable-knit sweater, pulling the hem farther down over her jeans, and settled back for the long ride.

"Nasty weather to be out." *Duh!* She mentally struck her forehead, realizing how stupid that sounded.

"Yeah," he agreed. "But at least we're not getting sleet and snow like they are about fifty miles northeast of here. So what brings you out on a night like this?"

Erica hesitated. How could she answer such a simple getting-to-know-you question when her reasons were anything but basic? Should she relay her desire to find the missing piece of her life's puzzle and explain the driving curiosity that compelled her to brave January's bleak weather for a nine-hour bus trip? Or the curiosity that drove her to find out if too much time and distance would hamper the reunion for which she so desperately yearned? And so anxiously feared.

As Erica studied his face—a strong, dependable face—she realized she could tell him none of these things. How could she speak of her heart's hopes and fears when she herself didn't understand them? He was only a stranger, someone who would pass in the night like the fabled ship. Still, there was something about his easy manner that invited confidence.

"Difficult question?" His words came out amused.

She settled for a standard answer. "I bought my ticket early to get the discount price. Since it's nonrefundable, I didn't want to lose out. You?"

"Going home. I had a business conference, and I'm not crazy about plane travel, especially on a day like today." He held out his hand. "I'm Ryan Meers."

She hesitated, taken aback by his open friendliness, then took the hand and offered a returning smile. "Erica Langley."

He gave her hand a little shake. "Pretty name. Nice to meet you, Erica."

Their conversation was interrupted as the lady who had the opposite aisle seat returned—a young pregnant woman with a tot wrapped in a pink baby sling around her. The child looked as if she couldn't be more than a year old. The woman looked exhausted.

"Here, let me help." Erica reached for the strap of the bulky diaper bag, which was sliding off the woman's arm.

"Gracias." Her lips pulled up in a faint smile at Erica. She wriggled her way into the confined space, one hand over the child lying against her protruding belly, the other clutching the chair back as she dropped to her seat.

"You certainly have your hands full," Erica said sympathetically. "How old is your baby? And when are you due?"

"No hablo ingles." Brow creased, the woman shook her head with an apologetic look.

"Oh." Erica's smile faded. She knew no Spanish.

Ryan leaned across Erica and began speaking in what sounded like fluent Spanish. Indeed, the words poured from his lips as if he'd been born with them. The woman's face brightened, and she nodded with a huge smile, offering a stream of words in reply.

"Baby Elita is ten and a half months old, and Carmen is due in two months, though she hopes little Pablo comes sooner," Ryan explained to Erica.

She cast him an incredulous stare. "With a name like Ryan and the auburn hair to match, you speak Spanish?"

He gave her another one of his lopsided grins. "Actually several languages, though I'm not fluent in all of them. My mother is a French teacher, I took Spanish in high school, and I had a roommate in college whose family transferred here from Germany. I also know some sign language. My aunt signs at her church."

"What? No Gaelic?" Erica felt her own lips turn upward.

He chuckled, a pleasant sound that sent a rumbly sort of tremor straight to the pit of her stomach. "No, no Gaelic." He settled back in his seat. "So tell me, Erica, where are you headed?"

She liked the way he said the syllables of her name. Soft, not harsh as she often heard them. "A small, pin-dot town on the map. From what I understand, if you blink you'll pass it by."

"One of those, huh? I'm from a town like that myself. Population 942. Wait, I take that back. Mindy Jacobs had a baby last week. Make that 943."

Erica laughed. "I've always thought small-town life would be so charming. Close-knit families, friendly neighbors, everyone knowing everyone else."

"And everyone else's business," Ryan filled in wryly. "So what's the name of this pin-dot, small town?"

"Preston Corners."

"You're kidding! That's where I'm headed."

Erica's eyes widened. "Really?" A flicker of something akin to nervous energy lit inside her. "Any chance you know Wes Beardsley?"

"Do I! My nemesis and best buddy all through high school. We played sports together."

"Oh?" Her heartbeat quickened. "What's he like?"

"What's he like?" Ryan repeated the question, as if he didn't understand it. "I don't know. . .he can be a regular card at times. A real ham when it comes to the spotlight. Other times he can be stone-dead serious."

Erica moistened her bottom lip, mentally storing the information. "And what's he look like now? Is he tall? Short? Heavy? Thin? Does he have wavy hair like yours or. . .or is it straight?" She fumbled with the last words when Ryan's brows gathered in a suspicious frown, and she realized how odd her questions must seem.

"His hair's straight. He's shorter than I am. Huskier, too." He fixed her with a sober stare. "He's married, you know. Has a great wife—Stacey—and three kids. He married his high school sweetheart, as a matter of fact. They dote on each other."

"Three kids?" Erica knew about the wife but not the kids. Wes hadn't mentioned them during their phone conversation. A firewood peddler had come knocking on her door, cutting the call short. "What does he do for a living?"

"Why do you want to know so much about him?"

Her gaze fell to her lap. "I haven't seen him in a while. I'm just curious."

"Really. . . Curious?" He crossed his arms and leaned against the bus wall, eyeing her as if she were the typical other woman out to steal his buddy from the family who loved him. "So, what are you to Wes? An old girlfriend he met on summer vacations? A pen pal? A college chum?"

Erica tried to swallow the lump that had risen to her throat. Might as well tell him. Since he lived in Preston Corners, he'd know soon enough anyway.

"I'm his sister."

"His sister?" Ryan's disapproving tone changed to shock then grew wary. "Wes doesn't have a sister. We've been buddies for over fifteen years, so I should know."

Erica released a whisper-soft breath and forced herself to hold his gaze. "I didn't know he had a sister, either. Not until several weeks ago. Actually, he has two of them. Me and. . ." She mentally searched for the name. "Paula. Yes, that's it. Paula Rothner. She's my sister, too."

Ryan only stared. Erica offered a thin smile.

"You're putting me on," he said at last.

"No. It's kind of a long story."

"I'm not going anywhere for the next nine hours. The bus isn't due to pull into Preston Corners until tomorrow morning."

"Okay." She repeatedly smoothed her hand down her leg, as though to remove a stubborn wrinkle in her jeans that wasn't there. Anxiety was written all over her. "I don't remember much about life before first grade," she began slowly, her soft, Texas drawl becoming more pronounced. "Just hazy recollections. But I was never sure if they stemmed from something that actually happened or if they came from a recurring dream I've had for as long as I can remember." She cast a worried glance his way. "Does that sound crazy?"

"No. I've read that a child doesn't reach memory stage until six years of age, though I disagree. I remember my dad tossing me up in the air before I hit kindergarten." He tugged at his ear. "The article went on to say that every part of our existence, from babyhood on, takes deep root in a part of our brain that stores that information. Some people never retrieve the events of their first years. But, depending on the memory, especially if it's a traumatic one, our subconscious mind remembers. And it may revisit us in our dreams."

Erica looked surprised. "You sound well informed on the subject."

"I read that in a psychology magazine. I'm a professional counselor."

"Oh." Her eyes took on a wary respect. "I guess that would explain why you know so much about it."

Erica looked away, and Ryan frowned. Why was it that when people found out what he did for a living, they tensed up? As if afraid he might dive into their personal history, asking them to expose their deepest and darkest secrets.

The swishing of wheels on wet pavement and the tapping of light rain on the window were the only sounds heard in their row. Erica began to twist a strand of long hair around her index finger. As tightly as she wound it, Ryan was surprised her fingertip didn't turn blue.

"If you want to talk about it, I promise I won't make you stretch out and lie down on the empty seats in back."

"What?" Her startled gaze met his.

"Like a psychiatrist's couch. People seem to expect me to suggest such a thing. Though I think that mode of analysis is ancient history for the therapist. I wouldn't know, since I'm only a high school counselor."

"A high school counselor?"

"Yes. We have our own methods. We use candy as a bribe to get the kids to talk." Ryan gave her a teasing grin then dug in his jacket pocket and pulled out a red foil-wrapped candy kiss.

Her eyebrows lifted in amusement as she took it. "Thanks." She opened the foil with a crisp rustle and popped the chocolate drop into her mouth. "Mmm. I love these."

"That one's on the house. But if you want another. . ." He pulled a silver piece of candy from his pocket and held it by its white tag, moving his hand to make it sway like a pendulum in front of her face. "Zin you must tell me your dreeem."

Erica laughed at his mad hypnotist-doctor impersonation. "You know, you're easy to talk to."

"Thanks. That's probably the nicest compliment I've gotten all week." He set the candy kiss in her hand. "And just to put your mind at ease, I was only teasing. I don't force confidences."

"That's okay. Like I said, I feel comfortable talking to you."

"So it's not my profession that makes you nervous?" he asked when she averted her gaze to the seat in front of her and was quiet a little too long.

"Not really. I think your profession is great. Necessary for all the troubled youth our world has today. I've just been a bundle of nerves since I woke up this morning, after having had that dream again last night." She released a tired sigh. "I don't know the particulars—how or why—but I can guess what happened. In my recurring dream or memory or whatever it is, there's a cabin in the woods with a porch along the front. I'm about four years old. Two older children and I are crying and screaming as a woman and a man in uniform pull us down the porch steps. I'm struggling to get away. I keep crying for something, but they won't listen. They put us in their car. I turn to look out the rear window at a young woman standing on the porch, watching as the car drives off. She just stands there and doesn't make any move to stop them from taking us." Erica's eyes closed.

Ryan knew Wes was a foster child. But he'd never supposed him to have blood siblings, since he rarely brought up his past when they were kids and never mentioned having sisters. Two weeks before Christmas, Wes expressed a desire to talk to Ryan, seeming eager about something, but had been interrupted by Peggy and the demand that he pull her loose tooth. After that, the kickoff of the football game took precedence. The subject was never brought up again, since Ryan left a few days later to visit one of his sisters for the holidays.

"Do you think the woman was your mother?" he prodded gently.

"After talking to Wes, I'm sure of it. He called, you know. Said he'd been trying to locate me for years. The couple who adopted me moved around a lot." She frowned. "No one told me about my parents when I was old enough to ask. After I'd been in the state's custody a year, Margaret and Darrin 'came to my rescue,' as they put it—"

"Margaret and Darrin?"

A lonely look filtered over Erica's face, exposing her vulnerability. "My adoptive parents. They didn't want me calling them Mama and Daddy. They said it made them feel old."

Ryan experienced a strong urge to reach out and hold her hand but stopped just short of doing so by lacing his fingers tightly across his stomach. "That must've hurt."

She shrugged as if it weren't all that important, but he could see evidence of the pain in her tense mouth and downcast eyes. "I learned not to let it bother me."

"So Wes told you that you had a brother and sister and that he wanted to meet you?"

She nodded. "I can't begin to describe how I felt. I think he said a retired social services worker helped him uncover my new last name and that he'd found me through the Internet. I don't remember—I was pretty much in a daze after his first few sentences when he introduced himself. But I did feel such a strong relief to know I wasn't alone in the world. Margaret and Darrin were off on another cruise, and I was lonely. Wes invited me to his home for Christmas 'to spend time getting to know one another again,' as he put it, and I felt as if something clicked into place. It felt strange, too, as if I were in a dream and I'd wake up to find the conversation hadn't been real. But I had his voice on my answering machine to prove it!"

Her eyes lit up and she giggled, making Ryan smile.

"I went out that night and bought gifts for him and Stacey. I had no idea what their tastes were. I was just thrilled to discover I had a family. Silly of me, I know." She turned a self-conscious glance toward the back of the seat in front of him.

"No, not silly," Ryan corrected. "Generous and thoughtful, but not silly." This time he followed the impulse to lay his hand over hers and give it an encouraging squeeze. Shock, then pleasure, filled her eyes. Cinnamon-colored eyes that warmed him to his soul. "So why weren't you able to visit Wes at Christmas?"

Her expression clouded, and he wished he could retrieve the question as quickly as he did his hand. "I got laid off a few days later. I was a secretary for a corporation that makes kitchen appliances. They had to cut corners and started with people most recently hired."

"That must have been a blow, especially right before the holidays." Ryan reached for his thermos of coffee.

"It was. I wallowed in self-pity for a while. Then I got a postcard from Margaret, telling me they'd met some friends on the cruise and were extending their vacation. I decided it was time to stop feeling sorry for myself and go and meet my brother." Erica cocked her head as if puzzled. "You know, I've always been a fairly private person. I can't believe I'm sitting here, opening up to you like this."

"It's not so surprising. I'm your one link with Wes right now. You feel closer to him by talking to me. My profession might have something to do with it, too, though sometimes people clam up when they discover I'm a counselor. Others talk to me about their problems and have ever since I was a kid. It influenced my career choice. That and a lot of prayer."

"You're a Christian, too?"

"I wouldn't have made it without God in my life, though I didn't find Him until I was sixteen."

"I probably wouldn't have made it without Him, either." She averted her gaze.

Ryan changed the subject, noting how somber she'd become. "How long are you staying in Preston Corners?"

"Until Wes gets tired of me, I guess."

"I can't see that happening." His soft remark brought color to her cheeks, and he admired her fresh beauty. Thick, sable lashes framed her expressive eyes. Besides the frosty pale lipstick she wore, he could see no evidence of other makeup.

A soft grunt from Carmen's seat brought their attention her way. She was attempting to get out of the chair, baby in tow.

"Is everything okay?" Ryan asked in Spanish.

She shook her head and put a hand to her stomach. "I need to go to the restroom again. Every fifteen minutes or so! This baby kicks a lot—he will be a good fighter. Or maybe a soccer player. But Pablo does no good for his mother's poor bladder. Nor does his sister, Elita."

Ryan chuckled then interpreted for the mystified Erica. "Tell her I'll hold the baby," Erica said, pushing up Ryan's estimation of her by several notches. "It can't be easy for her to juggle the girl and tend to her needs, too."

Ryan related the offer. Carmen turned eyes full of surprise Erica's way, hesitated, then carefully lifted the sling from around her neck and placed Elita in Erica's open arms.

"Oh, isn't she just precious?" Erica cooed as she set the bundle on her lap and looked down at the girl once Carmen waddled off. "She's got eyes like big semisweet chocolate drops, just like her mama. Don't you, sweetheart?" She grabbed one small dusky-colored hand and smiled at the tot, who stared up at her, perfectly content to be in this stranger's care.

Ryan watched as Erica continued to play with and talk nonsense to the child. She would make a good mother someday. He turned his gaze toward the rain-streaked glass and the traffic whizzing by in the next lane. Why that thought popped into his head, when he had little to base it on, Ryan had no idea. But one thing he did know: As tempting as Erica was, as sweet as she seemed, he would keep his vow and not get involved with her. Not with any woman.

Chapter 2

Near midnight, the bus rumbled to a stop by a motel. An all-night café stood nearby. Everyone turned curious eyes toward the driver as he stood and awkwardly faced them. By the expression on his craggy face, Erica sensed the news wasn't good.

"Sorry, folks. The winter storm took an unexpected turn and has hit the next two towns on our route. We might be gettin' some ugly weather here, too. I talked to my supervisor, and he advised me to wait till daylight when the bridges and overpasses are clear of ice. By then the sand trucks will've made their runs over the freeway. You're welcome to sleep on the bus—we got plenty o' blankets and pillows—or if you want a bed, there's a motel over yonder." That said, he quickly reclaimed his seat, as if relieved that his brief ordeal at public speaking was over.

Several passengers grumbled, and some got out their cell phones, but no one complained too loudly. Who could argue with someone who wanted to protect lives?

Erica sighed and settled back in her seat. Texas was like that. Not many knew how to drive in winter weather, so the least amount of snow or sleet shut things down fast. Earlier today, she'd been thankful to learn the bus company hadn't canceled this trip since the storm wasn't forecast for their route. She'd watched the news last night to be sure. But then, Texas weather was so unpredictable.

"Treat you to a midnight snack?" Ryan asked.

Erica smiled, deciding to make the best of things. "Only if we have separate bills."

As they left the bus, she focused on the electric, red vacancy sign broadcasting its message from the motel's office window "over yonder," as their hillbilly driver had put it. She wished she could afford a room, but with the loss of her job, she should watch her money. Her lease would soon be up on her apartment, and she might have to find a cheaper place to live. Regardless, Erica couldn't let Ryan pay for her meal when they were only strangers.

They sat tucked away in a cozy booth of the warm restaurant. Pictures of cartoon armadillos wearing cowboy hats and toting six-shooters in gun belts covered the gray board wall near their window. The table itself bore an old-fashioned newspaper print décor with headlines about bandits, cattle drives, and cowboys mixed in with ads sporting everything from men's hair tonic to ladies' corsets.

They munched on longhorn cattleburgers and tater sticks, and downed a pot of hot, decaffeinated coffee labeled Thick-as-Mud Brew. Afterward, Erica was surprised when Ryan motioned the grandmotherly waitress over to their table a second time and ordered a batch of chocolate-chip pancakes, also asking Erica if she wanted anything more. Grinning, she shook her head, wondering where Ryan stowed all his food. When the waitress brought his order to the table, Erica couldn't hold back a laugh and noticed amusement flicker in the waitress's eyes, too.

A whipped cream smiley face with white bushy eyebrows decorated the top of the chocolate-dotted stack of four pancakes, and a maraschino cherry nose sat in its middle.

Ryan lifted his eyebrows and looked at the waitress.

She grinned. "Normally, I'd just do it up like the picture on the menu, but I couldn't resist. Since you ordered what the little tykes usually do."

Ryan puckered his mouth, as if holding back a laugh at the joke played on him, and the crease mark in his cheek deepened. "Well, you pegged me right, ma'am. I'm a boy at heart, with an insatiable sweet tooth to match. Got any chocolate syrup to go over these?" His golden-brown eyes gleamed as the smile stretched across his face.

"For you, sugar, anything." The waitress moved away, soon returning with the requested item.

"You know," Erica mused, "staring at that work of art makes me wish I'd learned how to cook. I live off microwave dinners, and any time I have a craving for a sweet, there's a bakery down the street from where I live. Still, it must be nice to be able to just whip up something whenever you feel like it."

Ryan doused his pancake stack in a river of semisweet dark syrup and cut off a big bite with his fork. He soaked it in the sweet liquid pool and, wearing a teasing smile, offered it Erica's way. "Want a sample before I demolish this?"

His manner was friendly, as if she were his kid sister, nothing more. Yet to Erica the gesture seemed almost intimate, as if they were boyfriend and girlfriend and not merely strangers sharing a bus seat. Heat warmed her cheeks, and she wished she hadn't spoken.

"No, that's okay."

"You sure? I hate to eat all this in front of you." A chocolate dribble slipped from the pancake and hit the table. Another drip looked well on its way to following it.

Deciding it would be better to just take that one bite than make a bigger mess, or draw any unwanted attention their way, Erica leaned on her elbows toward him and snipped the bite off the fork with her teeth. Despite her caution, she felt the syrup coat the skin outside her mouth. Embarrassed, she hastily licked the chocolate away from the corners, then settled back in her seat and blotted her mouth with a napkin, afterward wiping up the spill on the table. Ryan hadn't moved a muscle, only stared at her. His fork, now empty, was still extended.

"Thanks," she managed. "It's good."

Her words seemed to snap him out of whatever trance held him bound, and he dove into his dessert as though he hadn't just eaten a three-course meal. They made small talk about food, the café, and the area, but Erica sensed a peculiar tension now lingering in the air. Ryan paid to have his thermos refilled with hot coffee for the trip, and then, to Erica's dismay, plucked up both bills from the table before she could reach for her purse.

"Ryan, I said—"

"Please," he interrupted, his gaze gentle. "Let me do this for Wes's little sister. As a welcome to Preston Corners?"

"We're not there yet," she countered dryly. His answering smile disarmed her and made her forget the reason she didn't want him to pay for her meal.

After they both took a quick restroom break, Erica pulled the faux fur collar of her wool coat around her ears. Ryan did the same with his jacket, and they braved the bitter cold wind on their hurried trek back to the bus. The disgruntled driver gave them a nod as they boarded but offered nothing by way of communication.

"I'm beginning to think he's a mountain hermit moonlighting as a bus driver," Erica whispered.

Ryan chuckled but didn't answer.

"So, tell me about yourself," Erica said once they'd settled in their seats. She noticed many chairs throughout the bus were empty, including the row next to theirs, and the rows ahead of them and behind. She and Ryan were sequestered in their own private world, made even more private with the now dim lighting. As though reading her mind, he clicked on the small light overhead.

He turned in his seat until he faced her better. His knees almost brushed hers. Crossing the arm nearest her over his waist, he propped the back of his head against the plastic window shade. "About me, huh? Okay. . . I grew up the only male sibling in a house of five females, all who went through varying degrees of emotional traumas. At different times, of course. Dad was the smart one; he practically lived in his study."

"And I'm sure you were always calm, never once raising your voice or getting emotional?" Erica gave him a mock reproving stare, trying to hold on to the light mood that revisited them. Still, she couldn't help feel envious that he'd had a true home and what she detected as a good relationship with his family, despite his teasing words.

"Nope, never," he said with a straight face. "I was a perfect saint."

"Yeah, right. I'd love to hear your sisters' versions."

"You may just get the chance. Most of them still live in Preston Corners."

His reply made her feel awkward, as though he might think she was asking for an invitation to get to know him better. Flustered, she reached for her handbag, unzipped it, and fumbled inside for what she wanted. She pulled out a brush, her makeup bag, and a crumpled wad of lipstick-stained tissues.

"Looking for something?" Ryan asked, clearly amused.

Her fingertips located a thin box. "Be nice, or I might not share." She opened the cardboard flap and tipped a white square into her palm then handed the box to him. "Want one?"

"I'm not sure." Ryan eyed the offering as if it were poison pellets. "What is it?"

"Cyanide gum," she quipped.

"In that case, I'll take one. I haven't had my quota for the day." He popped a square into his mouth with a grin, and she rolled her eyes.

"Actually, it's a gum you chew in place of brushing your teeth."

"Does it work?"

"I don't know, but it better. I almost missed the bus from standing in line to buy it. 'But for white teeth and fresh breath, I'll do anything.'" She mimicked a commercial she'd heard for the gum and gave him a toothpaste ad smile while fluttering her lashes.

The late hour must be getting to her. Or nervousness. Or insanity. Or all three. Aware she was acting ridiculous, she self-consciously tucked her hair behind one ear.

Ryan's grin faded, and the expression in his eyes softened. "You know what, Erica? I think Wes is going to love you."

⚜

Unable to sleep, Ryan studied Erica's closed eyes. He remembered how they'd widened at his last words, an hour ago, about Wes loving her. As if fearful that he actually might.

Conversation between them grew stilted after that. Erica went in search of a pillow and blanket, claiming she was tired. Once she'd taken her seat, also bringing back with her a pillow and blanket for him, she turned slightly away with a soft "G'night, Ryan."

Had Erica misinterpreted his words and thought he was making a pass? A better question might be why he felt so comfortable with her, as if he'd known her all his life. Was it because she was Wes's kid sister, and he saw some of his buddy in her?

Looking down at her slightly plump form and the dark crescent of lashes resting against her rosy cheek, Ryan rejected that idea. Except for the fact that they had similar eye color and both had straight hair, she looked little like Wes. And her lips were bowed, not thin. Slightly parted as they were now, they looked entirely too kissable. The second time he'd thought about kissing her. The first time was at the café when she'd eaten the pancake bite and he'd experienced a strong urge to kiss the chocolate from her mouth. That had been a mistake. He shouldn't have offered her a sample, though his intention had only been friendly.

He wrenched his gaze from her face and looked over the darkened bus, listening to snores rumbling through the area, the driver's the loudest. Sleet tapped the windows. Ryan shouldn't have drunk so much coffee, either—another item to add to his list of "shouldn't have dones"—or at least a wise choice would have been to have his thermos filled with decaf.

Hearing a soft whimper, he looked at Erica. A vee had formed between her brows, as if a dream troubled her. She whispered something he couldn't understand. He brought his ear closer to her lips, hoping she'd say it again.

"Mama, don't let them take me. . ."

At the faint gasp of words that bubbled out, something powerful clenched his gut. Before he could question his actions, Ryan shifted his pillow and lifted the armrest. He wrapped a protective arm around Erica's shoulders, gently moving her so that her pillow rested against his side. Then, reaching above, he turned out the light.

Daylight streamed through the window, beckoning Erica awake. She rested against something solid and warm. Opening her eyes, she saw that her pillow was a blue patterned sweater. A blue patterned sweater that moved up and down with each breath of its owner, and something equally solid and warm looped around her upper back.

Gasping, she straightened and looked into Ryan's amused eyes.

"Good morning," he said. "We should be nearing Preston Corners soon."

Her face going hot, Erica pulled away, and he moved his arm from around her. Slowly he pumped it up and down, as if lifting a ten-pound weight, and massaged his elbow, obviously trying to remove the stiffness. To cover her embarrassment, Erica plucked her pillow from the floor and smoothed her tangled hair with her fingers. She couldn't believe she'd ended up cuddled against his side. By the sun's position in the sky, she'd slept for a while. She vaguely remembered waking up for a few blurry moments around dawn, when the motel passengers boarded and the bus started back up, but she'd drifted off to sleep again. Had she lain against Ryan the entire night?

Carmen gave her a knowing smile, flustering Erica all the more. Ryan's words hit her then.

"Did you say we're nearing Preston Corners?"

"In less than an hour, I expect, though we're traveling slower than normal because of the weather. We passed Little Rock not long ago." He smiled. "Welcome to Arkansas."

She swallowed, her gaze going to the window and the hilly terrain with its masses of snow-flocked pine and hardwood trees flying past. Much different than the flatlands of central Texas. Like a whole new world. Had it been a mistake to follow her heart on a whim? Had she acted rashly once again—something Margaret often accused her of doing?

"Anything wrong?" Ryan asked.

She shook her head no, then nodded yes. "What if he doesn't like me?" she murmured. "What if I'm nothing like he remembers?"

"If my calculations are accurate, you were four and Wes was nine at the time. Besides, what's not to like? I've enjoyed having you as a seatmate, Erica. You're a lot of fun to be with. I've known Wes a long time, and like I told you last night, I'm sure he'll love you."

This time Ryan's encouraging words didn't rattle her. Last night, when he'd said them, she imagined they were coming straight from Ryan's heart and hadn't been about Wes at all. A foolish thought. Why she was drawn to this man on such short acquaintance, she had no idea.

Her gaze went to the winter scenery flashing by the window. Soon a good chunk of her history would be settled forever. Yet now, Erica wasn't sure she was ready to face it.

Chapter 3

At the bus depot, Ryan looked for Wes's blue truck and frowned. "I can't understand why he's not here yet. He would've called the bus company to find out the new arrival time."

Erica's gaze flitted to the pavement, around the nearly empty parking lot, then back to him. She seemed agitated. "I didn't expect him to come. I sort of. . .came without telling him."

"He didn't know you were coming?" Ryan asked, incredulous. "The bus originally wasn't scheduled to arrive until three-thirty this morning. What were you planning to do when you got here?"

"I thought I'd just hang around the depot until a decent time, then look him up in the phone book." She shrugged self-consciously. "Look, I jumped into this without thinking ahead, a foolish habit of mine. If you could just tell me where he lives, I'll phone for a taxi."

Ryan shook his head in amused exasperation. "No taxi. You can ride with me. My car's parked in that lot over there. The transmission was acting up, which was one reason I didn't want to risk driving it all the way to Dallas. But it should make it to Wes's house all right."

Uncertainty crossed her features, and Ryan thought he knew the reason. To go with him would pair them alone together for the first time. She only had his word that he was Wes's friend.

"Tell you what. I'll give Wes a call, tell him you're here, and he can verify that I'm not the big bad wolf out to accost pretty girls wearing red coats." He grinned at his Red Riding Hood joke.

She rolled her eyes but nodded for him to go ahead.

He pulled out his cell phone and dialed. Wes wasn't home, but Stacey was. After filling her in, Ryan handed the phone to Erica, who took it with a trembling hand.

"Hello? Yes, I'm Erica," she said in a squeaky voice. She listened awhile, glanced at Ryan, and nodded. "I met him on the bus." A flicker of a smile played with her lips, and she looked away. "No, but he did tell me that he wasn't a wolf. . . . Really. . ." She drawled, then giggled and shot another look Ryan's way.

Just what was Stacey telling her?

"Thanks. I will. I'm looking forward to meeting you, too. You and Wes both.

Bye." She handed the cell phone back to him. "She seems nice."

"Yeah, she's great. What'd she say about me?"

She appeared amused. "Just that I'm safe in taking you up on your offer for a ride."

"Is that all she said?"

"All you need to know." Grinning like a kid with a juicy secret, Erica grabbed her suitcase and overnight bag and moved toward his car.

With a wry smile, Ryan turned off his phone, shut it, and picked up his own suitcase. He was glad she'd relaxed but wished it hadn't been at his expense. Knowing Stacey as he did, he had a feeling a lot more was said about him.

An hour later, Erica willed herself not to start pacing again. Stacey was a regular fireball—and as sweet as they came. After Erica's arrival, she gave Erica a warm hug, then hurried back to the kitchen to finish preparing Wes's lunch. He'd be home from his job at his construction firm any minute. The older kids were at school, so Erica hadn't had a chance to meet them yet, and baby Lance was taking his nap. Ryan thumbed through some books in a walnut built-in bookcase, having stated that he wanted to see Wes's face when his buddy caught sight of Erica. She didn't mind. She preferred having Ryan there. His presence calmed her, at the same time stimulating her in a way she didn't understand. For the past eight years she'd dated on and off but had never found Mr. Right. Had she met him on a bus?

The sound of wheels crunching up the rocky drive alerted her. Erica clutched the armrests in a death grip, her gaze fastened to the front door. She didn't breathe as boots clomped up the porch and the door swung open, revealing a husky, dark-haired man with a beard.

"Ryan!" he greeted. "I didn't know you were back in town. How was the convention?"

"As conventions go, all right, I suppose. I got back today. And I brought someone with me." Ryan looked at Erica where she sat in a far corner of the room. The newcomer followed suit.

"Hello," he said, his expression curious as he rubbed his whiskered jaw. "So, you're a friend of Ryan's?"

Erica only sat and stared, as if she'd been cast in cement. Yet inside, her emotions exploded like sticks of dynamite.

Ryan put his hand to the newcomer's shoulder. "Wes, surely you recognize your baby sister?" he said quietly.

For a moment Wes only stood there. Then his eyes widened, and he dropped the rolled-up newspaper he held. It fell to the glossy hardwood floor. "Erica?" His voice deepened to a low rumble.

Unable to stand, she managed the briefest of nods. He took a few uncertain steps her way, sudden moisture glistening in his eyes, the same cinnamon color as hers with the same flecks of dark red. "I'm your brother," he said, kneeling on one leg before her. "I'm Wes."

The earnestness on his rugged face, the longing for acceptance answered Erica's own deep need. "I know," she whispered, tears filling her eyes.

They reached for each other at the same time. Softly crying and laughing, brother and sister held to one another tightly, and the wound that came about when they were torn apart as children began slowly to mend.

After dinner, the family and Ryan sat in the living area around a blazing fire. The tenseness of the unknown had eased, and Erica now felt relaxed.

"If she's Daddy's sister," round-eyed Peggy asked, "what does that make her to me?"

"Our aunt, stupid," Peggy's nine-year-old brother replied. "Same as Aunt Paula."

"I'm not stupid! Just because you're a year older doesn't mean you know everything, Billy Beardsley!" She stuck out her tongue at him.

"Kids," Stacey warned, "if you two don't stop this bickering, you're going to bed. And there's no name-calling in this house, either." Her green gaze pierced her son, who was a miniature of her in looks and coloring, whereas Peggy favored her father and had the same cinnamon-colored eyes. Eight-month-old Lance looked up from a nearby playpen, his hair surprisingly blond and his eyes light brown.

Stacey's gaze sailed to the clock above the mantel, and her brows rose. "Oops, my mistake. It's already past bedtime."

"Aw, Mom," Billy complained, "can't we stay home from school tomorrow, since Aunt Erica came to visit?"

"You'll have plenty of chances to spend time with her. Now, tell everyone good night, and then it's off to bed with both of you."

Two sets of grumbles met her demand, but one stern look from Stacey silenced them. After depositing hugs and kisses to both men, Peggy whispered something in her father's ear. His eyes glistened and he nodded.

Shyly, the girl approached Erica. "Can I hug you good night, too—I mean since you're my new aunt and all?"

Pain shot through the bridge of Erica's nose at the sudden onslaught of tears. "Of course you can."

Peggy tentatively slipped her arms around Erica but moved away before Erica could reciprocate, as if a sudden case of bashfulness had hit. Billy held out his hand. "I'm too old for all that mushy stuff. Night."

Holding back a laugh, Erica managed as serious a face as Billy's and shook his hand. "Night."

"Hope you have lots of peppermint dreams," Peggy added with a smile.

"Peppermint dreams?" Erica asked.

"That's what I call sweet dreams from God," Peggy explained. "Dreams Jesus gives to make us happy."

After the kids scrambled giggling from the room, Stacey spoke. "Back to Christmas; I'm so sorry you weren't able to contact us." Her gaze flew to Wes, who lay stretched out in an easy chair, his stocking feet propped on the matching ottoman. "But trust my husband to omit necessary information, like our phone number."

He shrugged. "Hey, I was nervous, too. Give a guy a break." He winked conspiratorially at Erica, and she felt a pleasant tingle at the bond they now shared. "I guess I should've called back when we didn't hear from you, but I got to thinking maybe you didn't want to have anything to do with us after all, and I didn't want to push. Just so you know it, Paula's planning to visit again sometime before spring. She's a Realtor in Florida and is married to a pilot. They have six kids, so she won't be able to get away anytime soon. I hope you can stay with us awhile."

"I don't know. My lease *is* almost up on my apartment. I guess I could call Margaret and ask if she would send someone to collect my things. But are you sure I won't get in the way?"

"Never," Wes assured. "We've got a lot of lost years to make up for."

"And we have a nice guest room with its own bath," Stacey inserted. "Consider it yours."

"Thank you." Erica smiled, touched by their kindness. She was glad to be connected to such a family. "Can I ask you a question, Wes?"

"Sure, honey. Ask away."

The endearment warmed Erica. "I've had a disturbing dream since as early on as I can remember. I was wondering if you could enlighten me about any of it." She told them her dream, noticing how sober Wes grew.

"Red Baby," he said gruffly.

"What?" The words sounded familiar, though Erica didn't know why.

"The name of your Raggedy Ann doll. You took it everywhere. Wouldn't part with it. I don't know why they wouldn't let you take it with you that day, unless they couldn't find it. That's what you were crying out for. That and Mama."

"Then my dream really did happen?"

He nodded. "Exactly as you told it."

Silence permeated the room. Erica, now somber, stared into the dancing fire. Her gaze wandered to Ryan's sympathetic one and locked.

Stacey cleared her throat and stood. "Well, those dishes won't wash themselves."

"I'll help." Erica started to rise, but Stacey waved her back down. "No, this is your first day here. I had someone else in mind." She looked directly at her husband.

Wes interlaced his fingers and cupped his hands behind his head. "You could ask Mrs. Warner next door. She's got time on her hands now, with her family out of town and all."

Stacey's eyes narrowed. "Mrs. Warner, huh? I don't know, Erica, he looks mighty comfortable, don't you think?" Stacey's lips twisted in a grin as she grabbed a nearby pillow and flung it at her husband's flat stomach. "To work, O mighty king. Before we ate, you offered to help serve your queen in yonder castle kitchen after the festive banquet—remember?"

Wes groaned. "Actually, I'd forgotten."

"Good thing I've got a great memory then," she replied sweetly. Stacey shot a look between Ryan and Erica, then back to her husband, her eyes widening in emphasis. She couldn't have been more obvious if she'd pulled Erica out of her chair and shoved her down on Ryan's lap.

"Oh, all right," Wes grumbled with a soft wink at Erica as he followed his wife to the kitchen. "A monarch's work is never done."

An uneasy silence filled the room, broken only by baby Lance's gurgling conversation with a stuffed giraffe in his playpen.

"Mommy!" A call came from the hall. "Are you coming to tuck us in?"

"In a minute, sweetie," Stacey's voice sailed from the kitchen, and she giggled. "Wes, stop that!"

Ryan abruptly stood. "Well, it's back to the old grindstone for me tomorrow. Tell Wes and Stacey I had to leave, would you? I'll let myself out."

"Sure. Good night." Erica wondered if she should walk him to the door anyway. Would he try to kiss her if she did? Somehow, she doubted it. Except for yesterday when he'd taken her hand for a few, brief seconds—and later, when she'd fallen asleep all over him—Ryan had kept his distance and hadn't touched her. Maybe Erica was reading more into the situation than was there.

The thought discouraged her. Was she falling for him?

Chapter 4

Erica cut another heart from the red foil to glue on the poster that would hang in the children's hospital playroom. She'd been at Preston Corners almost four weeks now, each day bringing her closer to her new family. The one bee in her honey had to do with Ryan.

Though he'd come over on Monday nights to watch football with Wes and on Sundays to eat dinner with the family, he'd never once asked her out. Erica knew she hadn't imagined the interested look in his eyes when she'd caught him watching her—many times. Nor his embarrassed flush and uneasy grin before he turned away.

"Stacey, what's wrong with me?" Erica tossed the scissors aside.

Stacey quit sprinkling silver tinsel bits on the glue covering some pink construction paper. "Wrong with you? There's nothing wrong with you. You're a born artist, and these decorations are sure to make every child at the hospital smile. I like the goofy faces you drew on the heart people."

"I'm not talking about this." Erica waved a hand over the kitchen table covered with craft supplies. "I'm talking about Ryan."

"Ahh," Stacey said and nodded sagely. "Let me guess. He hasn't made a move yet?"

Erica fidgeted. "That sounds as if I *expect* him to think of me as more than a friend." She frowned. "But what else am I to assume? He comes over all the time, and we talk. A lot. He acts interested in me, and I've caught him watching me a number of times."

"Want big brother Wes to ask his intentions?" Stacey lifted her brows in a teasing way.

Erica blew out a frustrated breath. "Thanks a lot, Stacey." She didn't need banter right now. She needed advice.

Stacey dusted off her hands, producing a shower of shiny silver particles that floated to the table. "Okay, all kidding aside. Remember what I told you on the phone the day Ryan brought you here? That he could in no way be classified as a ravenous wolf, and a more apt description would be a meek lamb?"

"Yes, but I thought you were joking."

"Well, to a certain degree I was. But it's a known fact that Ryan's never made the first move when it comes to women, though it wasn't always like that. In the conversational department, he's in his element. When it comes to anything else, he backs off. Fast. After his junior year in high school he quit dating, though I'm not sure why. Believe me, Erica, you're not the first woman I've heard complaints from."

"He's had a lot of admirers, huh?"

"Scads. With a face and body like that, and the fact that he's a lovable ex-jock with a sympathetic heart and a penchant for listening to problems—for listening at all, for that matter—is it any wonder?"

"I suppose not." Erica concentrated on cutting another heart from shiny paper, determined not to let Stacey's revelation upset her. "So he's Mr. Perfect. Like in that old Milton Bradley Mystery Date Game where you open the door, hoping to get the smiling guy in the tux?"

Stacey laughed. "Hardly! I've known Ryan as long as I've known Wes. He's a dear, but his place is a wreck. Takeout containers all over the room, discarded clothes slung over chairs. He makes an effort to do a quick cleanup when company calls, but it's obvious he doesn't live that way. He needs a woman to pick up after him. His sisters cleaned up his messes while he was growing up. Didn't do him any good, if you ask me."

"I've heard bachelors can be messy," Erica defended him.

"Maybe, but there's more. Sometimes his discussions on psychology can be about as effective as going under anesthesia. Really mind-numbing."

Erica didn't think they were all that bad, and she'd heard a number of them.

"Basically all I'm saying, Erica, is if a woman weighs the good with the bad and finds she's willing to put up with all of it, then she's also going to have to be willing to make the first move."

"The first move?" Erica had no experience in that area. Her dates had been simple, usually ending with a kiss at her front door. But she'd never initiated any of them.

"Yep," Stacey said with a decisive nod. "The first move."

Troubled, Erica lowered her gaze to the table. She noticed a piece of paper lying atop a stack of magazines. A website was scrawled underneath the caption "The Lion Cooks."

"What's this?" she asked.

"Hmm?" Stacey looked up from spreading more glue on construction paper. "Oh, an online cooking course I thought about taking. It offers dessert-making classes. I can't now, of course. Not since they called me back to work at the hospital because Janine is going on maternity leave. The drive there is one hour both ways. I won't have any extra time for cooking classes. But I'm glad the adoption finally went through for Janine. She's waited a long time for that baby."

Erica hoped the unknown Janine treated her child with more love and kindness than Erica had received from her adoptive parents. She fingered the paper, and her mind returned to the Ryan situation. How hard could it be to learn to bake and whip up a few scrumptious desserts with which to tempt him? Margaret had never allowed Erica in the kitchen during her childhood, claiming she didn't want her to make any messes. Yet at the memory of how enthusiastically Ryan devoured the chocolate-chip pancakes at the restaurant, Erica was ready to give baking a try. Maybe this could be considered a "first move."

"Mind if I sign up for the course?"

"Be my guest." Stacey smiled. "My great-granny always said, 'A way to a man's heart is down his gullet and through his belly.' And Ryan has a big sweet tooth."

Erica smiled at how well Stacey read her true intentions.

"Auntie Erica? Are you sure you're s'posed to put that in there?" Peggy's voice was doubtful. "That's not what Mommy uses when she makes cookies."

Drawing her brows together, Erica studied the empty can in her hand, then gave the child a confident smile. "My online cooking instructor said it's okay to substitute ingredients we don't have. So I don't see why not."

Erica felt more at ease with her new family every day, but not enough so that she was going to ask them to buy the required ingredients for her homework recipes. With no car at her disposal, a solo trip to the supermarket was out of the question, as well. Anything she needed and didn't have she would locate an adequate substitute for, since Stacey had given her free rein in the kitchen. Erica's high school teachers once labeled her "creative." Now was the time to put some of that creativity to use.

She hesitated, feeling as if she'd forgotten something. Had she put in salt? Oh well. A little more wouldn't hurt, even if she had. Ryan liked things salty, too— like chocolate-covered pretzels. But where was the teaspoon she'd used?

She looked all over the counter. No measuring spoon. Nor did it show up in the silverware drawer. Which must mean that she hadn't used the salt yet. Cupping her palm, she studied its middle. That seemed about right for a teaspoon-sized amount. She poured the white grains into her hand and tossed them onto the dough in the bowl.

Noting Peggy's uncertain expression, Erica smiled. "It'll be fine. Wanna stir?"

Eagerly Peggy nodded and reached for the wooden spoon. After a number of rotations with the utensil, she relinquished the blue ceramic bowl to Erica, who scraped the lumpy batter into miniature mounds on a greased cookie sheet and slid it onto the top rack of a preheated oven. Erica couldn't help noticing that Peggy didn't ask to lick the spoon or the bowl. Wasn't that the first thing kids usually wanted to do?

A few minutes later, Billy sauntered into the room, a St. Louis Cardinals baseball cap on his head. "Yuck! What's that smell?"

Erica frowned. Obviously the kid didn't like oatmeal. "I'm baking cookies. Don't worry, you don't have to eat any."

"Good!" The boy grabbed a baseball mitt from the counter and a ball, tossing it in the air as he headed out the back door.

Peggy tugged on Erica's sleeve. "Billy's just mad 'cause he got in trouble today at school and has detention tomorrow."

Erica smiled. "I'm not upset. Not everyone likes the same things. And that'll leave more cookies for us to enjoy."

Peggy wrinkled her brow, as though she wasn't so sure, then walked over to pick up her doll that was sitting in the chair "watching" them. "Will you play house with me?" she asked.

"Later, okay? I don't want to risk the chance of me not hearing the timer and having these burn." Erica looked at the rag doll. "You know. . .I used to have a doll something like that when I was a little girl."

"What happened to her?"

Erica stared at the painted cloth face a moment, feeling uneasy, as if an old unwanted memory was trying hard to resurface. Hurriedly she looked away and stared through the oven window at the baking lumps of dough. "I don't know." Her voice came out hoarse.

Peggy was quiet for so long that Erica looked over her shoulder. The child had left the kitchen, leaving Erica to her thoughts. She wasn't ready to face the details of her past, whatever they might reveal, and forced herself to think of something more pleasant—like the pleased, adoring look that was sure to be on Ryan's face when he tasted the cookies she'd spent an hour making for him.

The doorbell rang, and she smiled.

Chapter 5

Ryan—what's wrong?" Erica leaned across the table. "Are you okay?"
He had the most peculiar look on his face, as if he'd been frozen in time.
His eyes had widened, and he slowly chewed the large bite of cookie in his
mouth as if it were concrete and not crumbs.

"Nothing," he mumbled between slow chews, barely moving his lips as he spoke.
"Can I, uh, have some water?"

"Sure."

Erica retrieved a small tumbler, filled it, and handed it to him. He slugged it
down like a man who'd just spent a week traveling through the desert and had come
to his first oasis.

"Is anything wrong?" she asked when he lowered the cup.

"No, everything's fine." His voice still came out raspy. He set the rest of his
cookie on a napkin, walked over to the sink, refilled the glass, drank it down, and
refilled it again. "Uh, Erica, what kind of nuts did you use?"

"The recipe called for walnuts, but we didn't have any. I read it was okay to
substitute pecans, but we didn't have any of those, either. So I, um, used peanuts."

"Ahh. Salted ones?"

She nodded. "I figured with oatmeal it would work, and you do like salty foods,
right?"

He gave her a strange look. "Sometimes." He drank down the rest of the water.

Erica studied her hands clasped on the table. Maybe she *had* put in too much salt.
The teaspoon she'd used had been found on the floor earlier, hidden by the throw rug
partially covering it. And the peanuts probably made the cookies even worse.

"Feel like going to the Dairy Drizzle?" Ryan set the empty cup on the counter.
"We could drive down for a couple of large chocolate shakes. My treat."

"In the wintertime?"

He grinned. "That's the best time of year for ice cream desserts."

The man had just downed three glasses of water and was still thirsty for a shake?
Those cookies must have really been bad!

Erica gave him the best good sportsmanlike smile she could muster. "Make mine
a hot chocolate, and I'm with you a hundred percent."

Once outside, Erica took a deep breath of the bracing air. It sparked a feeling of playfulness in her. "Let's walk. It's only two blocks."

Ryan agreed. They moved along the wet sidewalk, which had been brushed free of the powdery snow that dusted the ground. The setting sun was magenta-pink, glowing like a tropical disk that just touched the uppermost tips of the greenish-black pines. Layers of rose-tinged, ivory clouds moved in long, gentle waves around and below the neon sun. To Erica, it looked as if a foretaste of summer filled the sky, while the earth stubbornly retained winter. Just ahead, the forested Ozarks produced a picturesque backdrop, and a church steeple could clearly be seen nestled midway up the snowy hill.

"I love this place," she enthused, her breath misting in the cool air. "It's so small-town Americana, like a Norman Rockwell painting. It's as if time passed by this small corner of the world and left it ageless."

Ryan looked up at the wooded mountains. "We've gone so far as to put a computer in the library, but in many respects, Preston Corners hasn't changed all that much in fifty years. You should have been here for the tree-lighting ceremony at Christmas. It's a big event the whole town turns out for, and the mayor awards the honors of pulling the switch to the most outstanding citizen of the year. This past December, the privilege was given to sixteen-year-old Twila Miller, for saving a child she was babysitting from his burning home."

"Have you ever been given the honors?"

"Once." He seemed embarrassed to say it.

Smiling wide, Erica tugged at her furry coat collar, bringing the edges together. She closed her eyes, absorbing the scent and feel of her surroundings. "I wish I could've seen it. In fact, I wish I could stay in Preston Corners forever."

"You like it that much?"

"Oh, yes! I've lived in many states, but here. . .well, I feel like I've come home."

"Maybe you should stay then."

Ryan's quiet words startled her, and she spun to face him. The snow muffled sound, making it easy to hear a voice, even one spoken in low tones. But she'd heard his words clearly enough, whether he'd meant them to be heard or not.

"Do you want me to stay, Ryan?"

He shoved his hands into his jacket pockets. "Sure, if that's what you want."

They were alone on the sidewalk, no neighbors in sight. Feeling suddenly daring but a little anxious, too, Erica closed the distance between them until she was within touching distance. "But what do you want?" she insisted softly.

"Whatever you want." He looked beyond her, avoiding her eyes.

Clamping a tight lid over her fear of being rejected, Erica spoke. "Well then, if you really mean that, what I want is for you to stop treating me like I'm nothing more than Wes's kid sister—when I think what you really want is to kiss me as much as I want you to."

Sudden flames burned within his eyes, rivaling the heat she felt in her face at blurting the bold words. Yet after weeks of his coming around to see her, and not always Wes, what was Erica to think? Especially considering the longing in his eyes when she'd caught him looking at her, time and again.

"So now you're playing counselor?" His voice sounded as if he needed to clear it.

She'd already stepped over the line of embarrassment. Might as well rush all the way in and hope she wasn't acting too much the fool. "I'm just telling you how I feel, Ryan. I think you like me as much as I like you. But for some reason you don't want to admit it."

He inhaled a swift breath, and she wondered if she'd made a mistake. What if she'd misread his actions?

An eternal moment stretched between them. Just when Erica was ready to escape back to the house, he gently brushed his gloved fingertips across her jaw, pushing back a thin strand of long hair that had connected with the corner of her mouth.

"I do like you, Erica. But let's take this slow and easy. Please?"

How slow was slow? And easy? Patience was never an easy virtue for Erica, but she nodded, trying to understand his point of view. Okay, maybe she *was* trying to push things between them too fast. She'd never had any real and lasting relationships with either her adoptive parents or her few former boyfriends. Maybe her desire to experience the joy of a truly loving relationship spurred her into jumping in the middle of love's shining sea, when she should just carefully wade out through its shallow waters. The waters beyond could be tumultuous if one wasn't prepared—hadn't her school chums told her that? She didn't want an icy and unexpected wave to overtake her before she could get a grip on her life or her feelings. She wanted the waters to ease around her, warm and inviting, like being immersed in the hot springs up to her neck.

Wes and Stacy had taken her for a daylong trip to the hot springs weeks ago, and Erica loved them. That's what she wanted her experience with Ryan to be like—a love that was warm, tender, and soothing, like the springs. But one that was bubbling up, effervescent, and alive, too! Until then, she would just have to be patient. Too bad they didn't offer a course on patience online, like they did cooking classes.

"How about we get that hot chocolate?" Ryan asked, breaking Erica from her thoughts. He held out his hand for her to take.

Confused, Erica studied him, caught his faint smile, then returned it and clasped his gloved hand. "You're on."

The lighthearted mood back, they strolled down the sidewalk. Feeling silly, Erica swung their clenched hands between them in exaggerated arcs as if they were two young kids, until she had him laughing and they were both bantering again.

Later that night, once Ryan left, Erica jotted an e-mail to Cynthia, her online cooking instructor.

> *I blew it, Teacher—I really blew it. I don't think I'm cut out to be another Sara Lee or Betty Crocker. Just call me Butterfingers—or better yet—The Cookie Cremator. This "substitute queen" really blew it.*

She went on to type out all that happened then sent the post. She was surprised when the computer bell dinged not five minutes later, telling her she had mail. It was from Cynthia.

> *Erica,*
>   *First rule of baking, and one that will save you a great deal of embarrassment in the future: always sample your creations before serving them to guests.*

Erica felt the blush heat her face. She should have known better. Ryan had walked into the kitchen at the same time the cookies came out of the oven, and Erica was so excited about her treat for him, she'd offered them without taste-testing first. She read the remainder of the post.

> *Don't feel bad. Every cook—especially one so new to baking as yourself—has her moments. I could tell you of a few embarrassing mistakes that I made when I first started, like the time I lifted the beaters while the mixer was still going. But I better not say more, lest you lose respect for your teacher. And I do understand your reasons for needing to substitute, but try not to do too much of that if you possibly can. If you're unsure about the suitability of your substitute, please contact me. I would be more than happy to help or offer any suggestions I can.*
>   *Happy cooking! (And it will get better. I promise.)*
>   *Cynthia Lyons*

Erica smiled. The woman was such an encourager. Maybe Erica would make it through this course, if not with flying colors, then with crawling ones. She groaned at her lame joke and punched out a reply to Cynthia.

Chapter 6

Hearing a knock at the door, Ryan pushed the mute button on the TV remote and went to answer. "Wes," he said with some surprise when he saw his visitor, whom he'd seen only that morning. "Everything okay?"

Wes walked into Ryan's apartment, hands in his jacket pockets, and eyed the place as if he'd never seen it before. Ryan moved to pick up his jacket that he'd tossed over the chair and shoved his shoes under the coffee table with his socked foot. Empty, food-speckled cardboard containers from Ming-Lee's Chinese Restaurant were strewn over the coffee table from dinner, and he swiped them together, walking with his armload to the kitchen trash.

"What's up?" he asked once he returned. Wes still hadn't taken the seat Ryan cleared for him. Ryan looked at the brown vinyl cushion to make sure nothing else was there. He was no housekeeper, as all his friends knew, and generally picked up around the apartment once a week since he was rarely home. His sisters jokingly called him a hopeless slob, but he didn't think he was as bad as all that.

"I need to talk with you about Erica." Wes remained standing a few feet inside the door. He seemed uncomfortable, and Ryan thought he understood. Wes must need counseling. Maybe things between him and his newfound sister weren't as smooth sailing as Ryan had assumed from seeing them together these past weeks.

Ryan adopted his understanding, counselor expression. "Come on in the rest of the way and sit down." He reclaimed his sunken spot on the vinyl couch.

Wes finally moved and took a seat on the matching chair. He leaned forward, elbows on his knees. "You've been over to see Erica a lot lately."

"Yeah?" Taken aback, Ryan copied Wes's sitting position, waiting to see where this conversation was going.

Wes compressed his mouth. "I'm just wondering where all this is leading and what you've got in mind."

In disbelief, Ryan stared at his old friend some seconds before he answered. "Let me get this straight. You're asking me what my intentions are toward your sister?"

"That about sums it up."

"Wes, this is me you're talking to. Your best buddy from high school." Ryan tried to remain calm, though he felt justifiably upset. "We've known each other since we were in Little League together. We go to the same church, and for the past five years,

I've come to your house every Sunday to eat dinner with your family. And now you're telling me that you don't *trust* me?"

"It's not that I don't trust you." Wes began to bounce one leg in his nervousness. "It's just that I care about Erica. Stacey said she's uncertain about everything right now and is trying so hard to fit in with our family. I feel sorry for the poor kid. I know she's scared to face the past. Whenever I bring it up, she cuts me off and changes the subject." A trace of a smile lifted his thin lips. "She's trying hard to please you, too, what with those awful desserts she makes. No one wants to hurt her feelings and tell her she's no cook. So we force the food down anyway. But she does it all—the cookies, the pastries, the pies—for you. Stacey told me that's the only reason Erica enrolled in the cooking class. To please you."

Ryan squirmed. He hadn't known that. He remembered the tart, stringy rhubarb concoction that followed last Sunday's meal and his polite comment that he was too full, after taking the first awful bite that made his lips pucker. In the future, he resolved to be a more gracious guest. Even if he had to get his stomach pumped afterward, he didn't want to hurt Erica's feelings.

"Normally I wouldn't have told you and risk embarrassing Erica should she find out. But I don't want her hurt, Ryan. You haven't exactly dated anyone since high school, so your sudden interest in Erica is puzzling, to say the least. You were a regular Fonz in our sophomore and junior year, dating a different girl every weekend. The sudden switcheroo from wildly popular with the chicks to sworn off them for good confused me."

Ryan's face heated. He didn't like to be reminded of his past. "So what you're saying, basically, is that for you to see me with Erica sets off all sorts of mental alarms because you think I may have resorted to my old ways? The big bad wolf's waiting for his chance to gobble up your little sister?" Ryan was unable to keep the bitter sarcasm from his voice. Again, he forced himself to maintain self-control. After all, Wes didn't know the entire story. Ryan never told him.

"Wes, I'm a practicing Christian now. I wasn't then. I'm also a high school counselor and need to keep my reputation squeaky clean. If I didn't abide by what I tell those kids, then I wouldn't be much of an example, would I?"

Wes placed his palms on his knees and stood, evidently tense. "I know all that, but you're confusing Erica. Stacey's had a number of talks with her, and Erica doesn't know how you feel about her or even where the relationship is going, if there is one. Her words, not mine."

"So what do you want me to do about it?"

"Tell her."

The answer was so obvious Ryan should have figured it out himself. Yet to tell Erica would mean to break a confidence, to share a secret. And the only way he would do that was to seek permission first, obtained through a long-distance phone call. The thought made him suddenly tired.

"You're right. I should've said something long ago."

Wes chuckled, and Ryan looked up from staring at the faded ring on the coffee table. "What's so funny?" Humor escaped him at the moment.

"I do believe this is the first time I've ever counseled you, old buddy."

Ryan grinned. "Even counselors need advice sometimes."

"No hard feelings?"

"None taken."

"Good." Wes moved to the door and put his hand on the knob. He looked over his shoulder. "See you at dinner Sunday?"

"Not this time around. I need to take care of some things."

"I understand."

Once Wes left, Ryan sank back into the cushions and stared at the ceiling. It would be better for Erica if he made himself absent for a while. He enjoyed her company, but after learning what he had, he didn't feel right about continuing his visits. She wanted them to be more than friends, and Ryan just couldn't allow that to happen.

❧

Erica moved through the small crowd flocking the bake sale tables of the church cafeteria and spotted Stacey. "Have you seen Ryan?"

"No." Stacey's gaze fell to the plate of brownies in Erica's hand. "Just find any old spot to put those down."

"Oh, these aren't for the sale. The ones I made for the fund-raiser are over there already. I put these aside for Ryan."

Stacey's brow wrinkled. "Erica, Wes and I think there's something you should know. . . ."

Erica looked past her, catching sight of a tall auburn-haired man in a beige polo shirt near the glass doors. "There he is. Sorry, Stacey, but I need to catch him before he leaves." She weaved through the hungry buyers and hurried out the door, catching up to Ryan on the sidewalk.

"Oh—hey, Erica."

Wasn't he glad to see her? He seemed tense. "Are you coming over for dinner?" she asked. "I haven't seen you in weeks."

"I suppose I could. I do need to talk to you about something. Or we could talk now."

"Now's not a good time." If they talked now, he wouldn't come for dinner, Erica somehow knew. "I should go collect the kids from children's church. Stacey has her hands full with the bake sale. So, I'll see you later." She gave him a bright smile and hurried away, then realized she still held his plate of brownies. She would just give them to him after dinner.

The next few hours plodded by for Erica, but Ryan did come to dinner. He was quieter than usual, though he laughed at Billy's corny jokes and gave the proper amount of interested admiration to the new dress on the doll Peggy shoved toward his face. After the dishes were cleared away, the family scattered, leaving Erica and Ryan alone. Sure their absence was intentional, Erica suddenly felt nervous. Quickly, she retrieved the plate of brownies from the counter and set it in front of him.

"I made these for you," she explained.

He looked at the dark squares beneath the pink cellophane for so long Erica wondered if he'd heard her. Finally, he lifted a corner of the plastic wrap and picked up the smallest brownie. Substitutions had been necessary again, but this time Erica was pleased with the results.

Ryan took a nibble and chewed. Surprise lifted his eyebrows, and he took a much bigger bite. "These are all right." He sounded as if he didn't quite believe it.

"Oh, I'm so glad you think so!" Erica smiled in relief. "I had to substitute again. We didn't have vegetable oil, so one of the girls in my online cooking class told me that applesauce works just as well."

Ryan took another bite and stared at the brownie as if puzzled. He sniffled softly, as though his nose was starting to run. "It doesn't have any apple taste to it. But it does have a flavor that's unique."

"That's probably the carrots."

"Carrots?" Slowly, Ryan lowered the brownie. He sniffled again, harder this time.

"Stacey didn't have applesauce, either—the baby ate it all. And since this recipe was for an assignment, I had to bake it this week. So, because Lance's baby food is like the consistency of applesauce, I figured a jar of carrots would work just as good. Carrot cake is delicious, so I thought it would work okay. . . ." Her words trailed off, uncertain.

The strangest expression came over his face. "It did work, except for one thing. I'm allergic to carrots."

"Allergic?" Years ago, a former classmate of Erica's had been rushed to the emergency room because of a severe reaction to shellfish. Erica knew food allergies were nothing to tamper with. "Oh, Ryan, I'm so sorry! Do you need me to take you to the hospital?"

"No, I'm okay." He pushed the plate of brownies far from him, as if even being near the dark squares could make it worse. "The reactions I've had have never been severe. Just annoying."

His voice sounded funny, as if his nasal passages or throat were getting clogged. Were his eyes watering?

"Maybe if you drank some water it would help? And if you went outside, maybe the fresh air would help clear your sinuses?"

"Maybe." Ryan rose from the table to fill a glass with water. He drank it down and refilled it two more times.

Spring warmed the days, though it was still cool enough for a sweater. Erica excused herself to grab one, then joined Ryan in the spacious backyard. An abundance of green-leafed oaks, maples, and gum trees filled the surrounding area. Instead of a fence, a high row of bushes acted as a boundary line all around. Ryan stuck his hands in his pockets and moved across the grass. Erica walked beside him.

"Have you decided what you're going to do yet?" Ryan asked. "About living here?"

At least he sounded a little better. "I thought, for now, I might apply at Jewel's Mini-mart. They're looking for a cashier."

"Then you've decided to move to Preston Corners?"

"Yes. Wes and Stacey want me to, and I do, too. When I'm ready to dig deeper into the past, if I'm ever ready, I want them nearby. It'll only take a week or so to make arrangements to move my things here. When I can afford it, I saw the most darling apartment complex near Wes's." She looked at him and gasped. "Oh, no!"

"What's wrong?"

"Your face!" She stood within a foot of where he was standing and reached out to touch his jaw. "You've got a patch of little pink bumps on your cheek."

"A rash," he said weakly and lifted his fingers to scratch it. "Sometimes it happens when I accidentally ingest carrots or any member of the parsley family. Avocados, too."

"You don't know how sorry I am about all this." Before she could think twice, Erica moved to place a sympathetic kiss on the unaffected area at the corner of his mouth near the growing rash. She felt him startle, but otherwise he didn't move. She pulled back to look at him. "Forgive me for poisoning you?"

"Erica, that's a little harsh. Besides, there's nothing to forgive. You didn't know."

They were standing so close she had to tip her head back to see his face. She lifted her hand to his opposite cheek. "At least this side's okay," she whispered.

"That's good." His reply came low. They stared at each other a long moment before his head began to lower. At the brush of his lips across hers, her heart jumped. As he allowed them to linger, an electric-like warmth tingled through her. Suddenly he jerked back, as if the physical contact now alarmed him.

"Ryan?" She felt confused. "What's wrong?"

"Nothing's wrong." His voice sounded angry as he moved a short distance away.

Feeling duly rebuffed, she snapped, "So it's me you don't like? I'm sorry. I guess I had it all wrong."

"I do like you, Erica—too much. That's the problem. And please stop saying you're sorry." He briskly rubbed his pink cheek with his fingertips.

"Maybe you should go put something on that," Erica suggested, pity taking the sharp edge off her anger. She felt bad for her outburst. Anyone suffering as he was wouldn't have kissing on his mind.

"It can wait. There's something I need to say." He stood, uneasy, as if trying to figure out how to begin. "My sister got pregnant when she was a senior in high school. It was a secret closely guarded by our family, even in this small town. Wes didn't even know about it."

Erica drew her brows together. So why was he telling her?

"She moved to the city to stay with friends of my mom's until the baby came. Then she gave her away in an open adoption. Once Susan returned home, her boyfriend—a guy I'd idolized—didn't want anything to do with her, so she tried to commit suicide. My parents put her in a mental hospital a hundred miles away and told everyone she was off visiting relatives. My sister screwed up her life in more ways than one, though I could never call Taylor a mess. She's in high school missions now. Her adoptive family sends Susan pictures each birthday and keeps her informed, which is how I know all that."

Erica frowned during Ryan's awkward spiel. So Ryan's sister had given away her daughter, too, though the circumstances were much different than Erica's. Still, Erica didn't understand what this had to do with the present. "Why are you telling me this, Ryan?"

He shoved his hands in his pockets and studied the bushes nearby. "When Susan snapped and I saw the bandages on her wrists, I swore I'd never end up in a situation like hers. I'm ashamed to admit it, but I treated the girls I dated in high school just as badly as Susan's boyfriend treated her. Using them to get what I wanted and not giving any thought to what could happen next. When I thought my sister was going to die, and I saw how badly her heart was broken over the jerk, I wondered how many girls I might have hurt, too. I became a Christian during that time, and I vowed to myself and to God that I'd never date again. That I would wait until He shows me who to marry, if I'm to marry." He looked at her again. "I was wrong to have kissed you, Erica. I don't want to complicate things between us."

"There's no need to make a federal case of it, Ryan. It was just a simple kiss."

His eyes were sober. "Was it?"

So he had felt the connection, too. Yet she was determined not to let him see how he'd hurt her. "Why didn't you tell me this before today?"

"I had to call Susan and get permission to tell her story. She's happily married now and living in Tennessee, but she's not at home much and is hard to get ahold of."

"But—when you told me that you wanted to take it slow and easy. . ."

"You're right. I shouldn't have put it like that." He sneezed.

She looked at his jaw and frowned. "The rash is spreading. You really should go take care of it."

"I need to get home anyway. I'll put something on it then and take some antihistamines, too. But before I go, please tell me things are still okay between us. I never meant to hurt you, and I certainly never meant to lead you on."

"I know. The fault's as much mine as it is yours. I shouldn't have jumped to conclusions."

Erica smiled through her disappointment. Yet she couldn't help be envious of the unknown woman Ryan would one day marry.

Chapter 7

Ryan pulled his car into Wes's drive, noticing Erica peek out the window then quickly draw back. He couldn't blame her for not wanting to see him. Not after last week.

When he was a teenager, it had been difficult to keep his self-made vow to God. As the years progressed and any temptation arose, he learned to take it to the Lord in prayer and forget about it. Until this past January, when he'd met Erica on the bus, he'd been successful. Now Erica taunted his thoughts daily. Nor had he been able to get their sweet kiss erased from his memory bank.

Ryan left the car and knocked on the front door. "Hey," he said, when she opened it a short time later.

"Hey back." Her words sounded uncertain. Obviously she wondered what he was doing there.

"Ready to go?"

Surprise touched her eyes. "You're coming with us?"

"Actually, I'm taking you. Wes couldn't get off work, so I offered."

"Oh." She hesitated before sending a wisp of a smile his way. "Then I guess I'm ready."

Ryan wished there were something he could say or do to smooth things between them, but it was probably best to say nothing. Hopefully, any tension would ease up soon.

The forty-five-minute drive passed with little said. Using Wes's directions, Ryan found the place and pulled into a clearing in the woods. An abandoned cabin stood there. Erica clutched the door handle, though she made no attempt to get out.

"It's just like I remember in my dream," she said, her voice faint. "When Wes told me our old cabin wasn't far, I knew I had to come. To see for myself. I thought I was ready for this. . .now I'm not so sure."

"You going to be okay?" Ryan asked, noticing how she had paled.

She gave a faint nod. "I had the ministry team pray with me Sunday. For courage to face whatever I might find and for God to help me put any missing pieces together."

"Then He will."

She sucked in her lower lip, her doubtful gaze still on the ramshackle building.

He reached over to squeeze her hand. "Sometimes we have to confront our pasts to be able to go on in the present and live fulfilling lives. But remember, Erica, it's only the past. It can't hurt you. Not unless you let it."

"I know." She took a deep breath and held it. "I never told anyone this, but I had a friend in fourth grade. Before we moved, I used to pretend her parents were mine. . . that when her mother baked cookies, it was for me—her little girl. And when her father played softball with us, that he was my daddy, too. I even called them by those names, though I sensed it made them uncomfortable."

Raw pain filled every nuance of her expression. "Margaret and Darrin never loved me. They adopted me to do a good deed and be elevated in their social circle of the community. Oh, they saw to every material need I had. I went to elite private schools and had the best education money could buy. The nicest clothes, a roomful of expensive toys—everything a child could possibly want. At least that's what I was told often enough." Her words were mocking, bitter.

Before Ryan could respond, Erica wrenched open the door and got out. He followed suit, coming around to her side of the car. She turned tormented eyes his way.

"Why'd she do it, Ryan? Why'd she sign away her own children?"

"I thought Wes told you—"

Erica gave an impatient wave of her hand. "Oh, yeah, sure. He told me that when he found her years ago, she told him she did drugs. I know all that. But it doesn't excuse the fact that my mama gave us away to strangers! Like unwanted secondhand shoes!"

Erica rushed toward the porch. Before reaching it, she picked up a good-sized rock and hurled it at the cabin. Thankfully, her aim wasn't the greatest. It just missed the window. Ryan hurried to stop her before she could try again.

"Erica, listen! You have every right to be angry—I understand. Believe me, I do. But this isn't the way to deal with your anger."

"Take your hand off my arm, Ryan," she seethed between her teeth. "I want to break every window in that horrible place, then watch it burn to the ground!"

She struggled to get away. He wasn't getting through to her, so he did the only thing he knew to do, the only thing he wanted. He drew her close and held her tightly. At first she fought—hard. Finally, when she saw she wasn't getting anywhere, she wilted against him. Her agonized sobs pierced the air, making painful stabs at his heart.

"Shh, it's okay," he murmured, planting a few kisses atop her head until she stilled. He pulled back, wishing he had a handkerchief. With his thumbs he wiped away her tears. "Feel any better?"

She shrugged.

"Let's sit down." Once they settled on the top porch step, he looked at her. "I know that right now all you feel is the pain. But, Erica, deep down I think your mama loved you."

"Yeah, right." She grew rigid, but he put up a hand to stop the rest of her terse words.

"Let me finish. She told Wes that on one occasion—when she woke from her drug stupor and realized two days had passed—that during that time anything could've happened to you and the others without her knowledge. She realized then that she wasn't fit to raise you. She thought she could get over her drug habit the first time someone called social services. But after two years and countless failures, she gave up and signed the papers."

Erica's hands on her lap tightened into fists. He didn't know if it would do much good to continue, or even what he could say to get through her self-made blockade. But he tried again. "I think she must have felt what Moses' mother felt when she put him in that reed basket and sent him down the Nile for his own good. Like Moses' mother, your mother knew that life with her was dangerous to her children. She made the ultimate sacrifice, Erica. For you."

"Sure she did." Erica compressed her lips and blinked, as if trying to keep more tears at bay. "I wish I could believe that. I really, really do. But I can't." She shot to her feet and wandered down the porch steps to the periphery of tall pines circling the mountain cabin.

Ryan longed to know what was on her mind. *Please, God,* he sent up a silent prayer. *Show her what it is that she so desperately wants to know, and reassure her as only You know how.*

After a time of walking near the fringe of trees, Erica retraced her steps to the house. Before turning at the south corner, she looked at Ryan, as if about to say something, then stopped. Her brows came together, and she lowered her gaze to the bottom of the porch. All of a sudden, she fell to her knees on the grass and dropped down on all fours.

"Erica?" Puzzled, Ryan moved her way. When he reached her, she had wriggled halfway under the crawl space of the porch, only her jean-clad legs showing.

"Oh! It's here. Oh, Ryan. . ."

She backed out, holding a misshapen grayish clump of material with a scrap of faded red around its middle. One black button eye remained, the painted smile from the circular doll face barely discernible. Only a few pinkish-white pieces of yarn were still attached to the cloth head.

"Red Baby." She said the name as if it were a coveted treasure she held and not a mildewed scrap of rags. Sitting back on her legs, she brought it to her chest and stared at the trees, her eyes going distant. The gentle breeze played with her long hair, lifting the top strands as if in a caress. Suddenly she turned wide eyes his way. Ryan knew he'd never forget the expression on her face as long as he lived.

"I remember," she said in awe. "Mama told us that some nice people were coming to take us to better homes. I cried and told her I didn't want to go. She held me on her lap and cried with me, then pushed me away and ordered me not to cry, that she was only doing it for my own good. I ran out of the house, angry, and hid under the porch with my doll. I was determined no one would find me. But I got hungry and sneaked into the kitchen for an apple. That's when they came."

Tears trickled from her lashes. "Oh, Ryan, you must be right. Mama cried with me and held me. She didn't want me to go, either. So she must've loved me some. . ."

Emotion clutched Ryan's throat. He crouched beside her and laid a gentle hand on her shoulder. "I'm sure she did, Erica. After all, how could she keep from it?"

At his quiet words, shock filled her eyes. He stood to his feet, wishing he could retrieve the hasty comment. He knew he loved her. But it didn't matter what he wanted. He'd made a vow.

"Are you ready to go?" he asked gruffly. "We have a long drive ahead."

She nodded. "I think I'm finally laying my ghosts to rest." A soft smile lit her face. "I'm going to make it, Ryan. I'm truly going to make it."

"Of course you are." He helped her up and squeezed her hand, allowing the contact to last no more than a second. Then he turned and walked to the car.

After a silent and uncomfortable drive, they finally approached Wes's house. Erica noticed a shiny red car in the driveway. She watched the front door to the house fly open, and a chic woman with short, frosted blond hair came hurrying down the steps. Erica had no more than opened her car door and stepped out when the woman—shorter than her by almost a foot—gave her a breathless smile.

"Erica?" she asked. "But of course, you're Erica! You and Wes have the same eyes."

Before Erica could reply, she found herself engulfed in a heartfelt hug, surprisingly strong coming from such a petite woman. Stunned, Erica shot a look at Ryan, but he only shrugged.

"I'm Paula Rothner," the woman laughingly explained as she pulled back. "Your long-lost sister."

Tears pricked Erica's eyes. "Paula?"

The woman nodded, clasping Erica's upper arms. "I was ten last time I saw you. Oh, but you still have the same sweet face!"

"Paula. . ." This time Erica returned the tight hug. Any lingering gray clouds that had revisited her at the return of Ryan's emotional distance blew away from her heart. "We weren't expecting you until day after tomorrow, but I'm so glad you came early."

Paula's shining eyes surveyed Erica from head to foot, then darted to the faded clump of material she held. Her brows drew together in puzzlement. "What is that?"

Erica looked at the dilapidated doll. "I found it under the porch of our old cabin. It's my old doll."

"Red Baby? To think it was there all that time. . ." Paula's expression sobered. "Stacey told me you went to the cabin."

"I had to see it."

"I understand. Let's talk over coffee. Stacey and Wes went for some takeout fried chicken." Paula looked at Ryan for the first time. "You must be Wes's friend—Ryan, isn't it? I've heard a lot about you."

"All good I hope."

"Let's just say that I never knew someone as 'meek as a lamb' could look so strong."

Ryan groaned. "Maybe I don't want to know the rest. Stacey's always loved to tease me, ever since high school. I never knew if it was because she was an only child or if it's because she's two years older than me."

Paula's eyes twinkled. "She ordered me to tell you to stay for dinner."

He hesitated as though he might accept, then shook his head. "I can't. Saturdays are laundry days, and I have plenty. I'm sure you have a lot of catching up to do, without me around."

Erica felt a stab of disappointment and managed what she hoped was a dazzling farewell smile, as if she didn't care whether he stayed or not. "Okay, then. Thanks for the ride, Ryan. See you around." She turned her back on him and walked toward the house, ignoring Paula's curious upraised brow.

"Yeah, see you. . ." Erica couldn't help but hear the confusion in his voice. Knowing she'd behaved immaturely, and remembering how sweet he'd been at the cabin when she was falling apart, she looked his way. He hadn't moved from his spot.

"Thanks, Ryan." She gave him a genuine smile this time. "For being the best friend a girl ever had."

He stared at her a few seconds before replying. "Any time, Erica." His smile was faint as he turned to go.

She had tried to make amends for her bad behavior. Why did he still seem upset?

Once inside, Erica put water on the stove to heat. Paula spotted a pan on the counter, and with a spoon she reached for a messy dessert square. One small chunk had already been taken out.

"Don't eat those!" Erica blurted, startling Paula into snatching back her hand. "I forgot to throw them away," she meekly added.

"Throw them away?" Paula eyed the yellow, white-powdered topping in confusion.

"I'm taking an online cooking class," Erica explained, feeling the blush rise to her face. "And I didn't have a lemon, so I substituted lemon juice. Only I didn't know that when it's concentrated you're only supposed to use a little. Three tablespoons are equal to one lemon, I found out. Only I didn't know that at the time, because Peggy had torn off the label, and all I had to look at was a green bottle."

Paula raised her brows at Erica's haphazard explanation. "So how much did you put in?"

"Um. . .one cup for each lemon." The words were reluctant. "And the recipe called for two lemons, so the bars are really tart, not to mention runny."

Paula tried to suppress a smile, but it ended in a laugh. She put her arm around Erica's shoulders. "Don't feel bad. I'm no cook, either."

"Really?"

"Yeah. It must be an inherited trait or something."

Both women giggled, and Erica set about making some raspberry herb tea. "Do you use sweetener?"

"Just a teaspoon of honey. Not the jar." Paula winked to take the sting off her joke.

Erica rolled her eyes and grinned. She prepared both cups, taking them to the table. "Now that we're finally together, I have no idea where to start."

"Tell me about what happened today," Paula suggested. "And how you found Red Baby."

Erica sobered. "Okay. Maybe you can help fill in the blanks."

For the next several minutes, Paula listened, her eyes sympathetic. "How hard it must have been for you, not knowing! I was older so I remember more than either you or Wes do." Paula looked down at her tea and stirred it. "Mama not only had a drug problem, she drank. Sometimes she was so wasted, she couldn't do the simplest things. I took care of you and Wes when Mama would pass out." Her lips lifted in a slight smile, and she stretched her hand across the table to cover Erica's. "You were my live baby doll; I loved you so much."

Erica returned the smile.

After a moment, Paula withdrew her hand. "Twice, someone called social services, and they came. I was so glad to get out of there and live a normal life with normal people, even if it was only a foster family. But they were nice."

Erica's mouth dropped open. "You were glad Mama gave us away?"

"No, sweetie, maybe glad is the wrong word. Relieved might fit better, though I missed you and Wes a whole lot. It would've been perfect if we could've stayed together. Just the three of us. I guess I loved Mama, too, but even at ten, I knew something was wrong with her and with the way we lived."

Paula released a soft breath. "Mama got married young, she told me once. When

Daddy ran out on her, it's like she completely folded. She never finished high school and couldn't get better work than to sack groceries. With her drug habit, the money went fast, and we never had enough food on the table. Then there were those weird, perverted boyfriends of hers that always came around." Paula shuddered. "Let's just say, sometimes it's better not remembering."

Erica stared at her flowered mug. "But she did love us?"

"I don't know. I guess. She never physically abused us, though she slapped my face on a few occasions when I sassed her. She just never was able to take care of herself, much less three kids." Paula shook her head, as if to dispel her thoughts. "I learned long ago not to think about those days. Even the Bible mentions something about not looking behind and only looking forward."

"If I'd done that, I wouldn't be here," Erica argued.

"Maybe. But I believe God had a hand in all of us finding one another again. We're all Christians—thankfully all raised by Christian families—and God is our Father and leads us. He's the One who brought you home, Erica. All I'm saying is that I don't think we should look too closely at what happened before. Let's just live in the present and forget the rest."

Erica thought about Paula's words. Margaret and Darrin could hardly be called Christians. Erica had accepted the Lord through their maid's counsel. Yet her sister was right. Now that the past had been dug up and laid bare, it was time to lay it to rest.

"Paula, have you talked to Mama since Wes found her?"

Her sister fidgeted with the handle of her mug, looking at it as she ran one coral fingernail up and down the curve. "No. Why?"

"Wes has her number in New Mexico, and I'd like to call her. Do you want to get on the extension?"

Paula's expression was one of surprise.

"I think you're right, and we do need to let go of what happened," Erica admitted softly. "But I want to talk to Mama again. I never had much of a home life, so this is important to me."

"But why involve Mama? We have each other now."

"Wes's pastor said that a big part of forgetting is forgiving. He's right. How can I carry a grudge about the past and forget it at the same time? There's no way. Wes has already forgiven Mama. Let's you and I do the same."

Paula's brow creased. "I hadn't realized I still had any bad feelings toward her until today. But I'm not sure I'm ready to talk to her yet, either."

"Will you at least try? Or, if you can't, will you just listen to what she has to say?"

"You realize that could be painful?"

"Yes. But how will we know if we don't try? I'd like for us to call her together.

That way we'll be here to support one another if it doesn't turn out well."

Paula was quiet a moment. "I guess you're right. It's time."

Erica hurriedly located the number written in the address book by the wall phone and made the long distance call. Now that she'd reached this decision, she didn't want to delay. Cowardice might set in if she did. Paula might change her mind. Erica could almost hear the rapid beats of her heart as she waited. One ring. . .two. . . then three. . .

Disappointed, she was about to hang up on the fifth ring when a woman's husky voice answered. "Hello?"

Erica froze, her mind reeling. She sank to a nearby chair.

"Hello?" The woman seemed perturbed now. "Is anyone there?"

"Mama?" Erica croaked.

A pause. "Who is this?" The woman sounded almost angry.

Oh, dear God. . .did I made a mistake and dial a wrong number?

Resisting the impulse to slam the receiver back on its hook, she clutched the phone more tightly. "It's, um, it's Erica. And—and Paula's here, too. We're at Wes's house."

She impatiently nodded toward Paula, who'd moved to the family room, staring at the cordless as if it were a live snake ready to strike. Finally, she picked up the receiver. "Hello, Mama." Her voice came out in a flat monotone.

"Paula?" the woman said in a raspy breath. "And Erica?"

Erica nodded then realized what she was doing. "Yes."

"My Paula and Erica?" The woman was clearly crying.

"Yes, Mama. It's me." This from Paula, who sounded subdued.

"Oh, my babies. I'm so sorry. You'll never know just how sorry. . ."

Erica smiled through her tears. She knew.

Chapter 8

Three weeks later Erica watched as Wes pulled up to the bus station. "You're sure about this?" he asked with a frown. "You're welcome to stay."

She forced a smile. "It's time I went home. I can't impose on you and Stacey forever."

"But I don't understand why you changed your mind about living here. The job at the mini-mart probably wasn't the greatest anyway—I'm sorry that they'd already found someone. But, like I said, they're looking for a secretary at the church. That's right up your alley." He cast a studied glance around the parking lot.

"I know, but after talking with Mama, I realize I need to have a heart-to-heart with Margaret and Darrin, too. Maybe their reasons were wrong for adopting me, but they did take care of me all those years. I need to at least thank them for that. I never did." There was another reason for her sudden getaway, one Erica didn't want to voice. Her heart was tied to Ryan's, and living in Preston Corners had become too difficult. She admired Ryan's decision to wait for the wife that God handpicked for him, and she loved him too much to try to change his mind. Every time he came to Wes's house—twice a week for the baseball game and Sunday dinner—was bittersweet torture for Erica. What was worse was when he stayed away, as he'd done this past week. Maybe, in time, she would consider living in Preston Corners. But not yet.

Wes helped her with her luggage, making sure the bus employee stowed it properly. He asked her if she had her ticket for the fourth time and generally treated her like the big brother he was. And she loved every bit of it.

"You're coming back for Thanksgiving and Christmas?" Wes asked. "It's the earliest Mama can get here with her husband. He sounds like a nice guy. He's the one who helped her get into the drug rehabilitation program, you know. Now they both head a drug support/help group in their community. You really have to come back, Erica. Christmas in Preston Corners isn't something to miss. Peggy and Billy can take you sledding on the hill behind our house, if we have snow. And Stacey makes one mean turkey with all the trimmings. You can even make a dessert to go with it, if you really want to."

He seemed edgy, talking more than usual and about things she already knew. She studied him curiously. "Wes, you're acting weird. Is everything okay?"

"Sure. Except that my little sister is leaving us."

Erica accepted his tight bear hug. "I'll be back," she said into his shoulder. "Now that you've found me, you'll have a hard time getting rid of me."

"As if I'd want to try." His smile was wide in his beard. "You know, Erica, Ryan wasn't too happy when I told him you were leaving. I thought there might be something between you two. . ."

"No. Please, tell him good-bye for me." So Ryan wasn't too happy? Still, that hadn't stopped him from keeping his distance.

"You have my number?" Wes asked as they walked to the bus door. He shot another look around the parking lot.

"I think Stacey wrote it on every available piece of paper she could find and stuck them all in my luggage. I'm surprised she didn't embroider it on the throw pillow you guys gave me for a birthday present."

He grinned and scratched his beard at her exaggerated teasing. "If you'd have put the idea in her head, she probably would have."

"I never knew my birthday was in June until Paula told me. Margaret always gave me a party in August, the month they adopted me."

"Erica, did they abuse you?" Wes's voice grew gruff. "You never said much about your life with them."

She let out a long sigh. "No, not physically, anyway. More like emotional neglect. It's in the past, and I'd rather not talk about it. I've forgiven them, too."

Admiration shone in his eyes. "Ryan was right. It's awful you had to grow up living with those people, but it's helped to shape you into a woman of character. I'm proud to call you my sister."

Wes's words floated through Erica's head minutes later as she sat on the half-empty bus, waiting for it to depart. She put her carryall on the seat beside her, not wanting company. For Wes she had been brave, but now, with no one around to see, she slipped into the doldrums.

Oh, how she would miss Ryan! He, on the other hand, was probably breathing a huge sigh of relief that he wouldn't have to sample any more of her cooking disasters. Her last flop two weeks ago had been her worst. No wonder he hadn't come around last Sunday.

The chocolate cake layers had turned out flat—like pancakes—and she'd used two containers of fudge icing to try to give them a lift. Erica had laid her fork down after the first strange-tasting bite. Surprisingly, Ryan continued to eat the cake, though with a martyred expression on his face. Halfway through, when he asked what she'd substituted this time, she told him she'd had all the ingredients for once, then named each one. His face seemed to turn a little green on the last item she mentioned, and Stacey laughed outright. Erica felt the blush rise to her cheeks again.

How was she supposed to know that cream of tartar wasn't the same thing as tartar sauce? To make matters worse, she'd confused the recipe amount with the ingredient above it and had put in a half cup instead of a teaspoon.

Sighing, she propped her elbow on the armrest and laid her cheek in one hand, turning her head to stare out the window for a last glimpse of Preston Corners. From her place in the sixth row, she heard the pressurized sound of the door shut, then several seconds later, open again. Footsteps clomped up the metal stairs. Obviously the latecomer had almost missed the bus, as she had that long-ago day in January. Had it really been five whole months since she'd sat beside Ryan on a seat much like this one and admired his gentle brown eyes?

"Excuse me. Is this seat taken?"

Erica's heart skipped a beat. With disbelief, she turned to face the tardy passenger.

"No?" Ryan smiled, took her carryall off the aisle seat, and sank into it, setting down the sack he carried. "At least we have better traveling weather today. Sunny. Warm. Though it's a bit humid, isn't it? Probably because of all that rain we got last night."

"What are you doing here?" Erica managed.

He pulled a wrapped box from his sack. "I missed your birthday and wanted to get this to you. Happy birthday."

Tears clouded her eyes. She blinked them away as he laid the box on her lap. When she didn't move, he pulled the yellow ribbon holding the flower-sprigged wrapping paper together.

"You really shouldn't have, Ryan."

"Hush and open your present."

With trembling fingers, she undid the flaps at both ends and slid a shirt box from the confines. She offered him a puzzled look, but he only nodded. "Go on."

Erica lifted the box top, pulled back the tissue, and stared. A tear escaped and fell to the pinafore covering the green calico dress of the Raggedy Ann doll in her lap.

"Interesting thing about those dolls," Ryan said close to her ear. "They come with a message printed on their chests."

Erica didn't remember that. "They do?"

"Go ahead and take a peek. I don't think your new Red Baby would mind."

Feeling incredibly foolish as well as strangely anticipatory, Erica lifted the dress over the doll's white bloomers. Emotion catching her throat, she cupped a hand over her mouth at the embroidered message that met her eyes: A red heart held the words "I love you."

Suddenly she heard the sound of tires crunching over gravel. Her gaze jerked to his expectant one. "Ryan! The bus is moving. You need to tell the driver to let you off."

He blew out a short breath and shook his head with a wry grin. "Not quite the response I was hoping for. Maybe this will prod you into saying the right thing." He lifted the doll—to reveal a black velvet box nestled in the tissue.

Erica's eyes widened as she looked from the box to Ryan then back again. She swallowed. Did this mean what she thought it did?

His fingers went to her chin, gently forcing her gaze to meet his serious one. "Erica, I was a fool. All along the Lord was showing me His will regarding you, but I'd been so accustomed to running away I couldn't see it. Not until our kiss. That really started me seeking Him. Then when you called me your best friend that day we went to the cabin, well, I knew I wanted much more than to just be friends with you. Still, God had to show me the truth."

Erica felt dazed. "The truth?"

"That you're the one He handpicked for me. Maybe your personal quest brought you to Preston Corners, but God had a hand in it all along. For my benefit, as well as yours." He clasped her hands, his expression tender. "I love you, Erica Langley."

"Really?"

Ryan nodded. *"Je T'aime. . ."* He brought her hand to his mouth and kissed the back of her fingers. *"Te amo. . ."* He kissed her other hand. *"Ich liebe dich. . .*and if you want me to say it in sign language, I'll tell you I love you that way, too. Just please tell me I'm not too late, and you'll be my wife."

Erica never knew joy could produce itself in so many tears.

"Erica?" he prompted, as if concerned.

"Before I give you my answer, I think I do want you to say it in sign language," she said staunchly, though she felt deliriously giddy. "I'm not convinced yet."

With a wide grin, Ryan took her in his arms and kissed her breathless.

Loud clapping and wolf whistles filled the bus, breaking them apart. They cast self-conscious glances at the smiling people in the seats around them. Then they looked at each other. Erica stared up into Ryan's shining eyes, knowing she could gladly look into them a lifetime. "Okay, Ryan, you've convinced me," she whispered. "I'll marry you."

Ryan gave her another kiss, this one brief but tender. Erica giggled, swiping one hand over her tear-wet cheek. "When you make up your mind about something, you don't collect dust, do you?" she asked.

"I've waited a lifetime for you, Erica. How could I wait another moment?"

The words warmed her soul, but reality beckoned. "Shouldn't you get off the bus before it leaves the city limits? I'll come back to Preston Corners soon." Nothing could keep her away now.

"I made arrangements to take some time away, though I'll bet Wes thought I'd never get here. He flagged the driver to wait when he saw my car careen around the corner."

"Wes?" she said incredulously, then remembered his extreme interest in the parking lot while they were saying good-bye. "So, he knew all along you'd show!" She grinned. "The weasel. Playing it up and making me think we wouldn't see each other again for a very long time."

"He probably was beginning to wonder when I was so late. I had to go through the third degree when I told him of my feelings for you several days ago. But we now have his blessing." Ryan smiled. "I'm going back with you to help you pack and get your affairs settled. I have a friend in the area I'll stay with. Then I'm personally escorting you back to Preston Corners, where you belong."

Erica didn't argue. She'd felt this place was home almost since the moment she saw it.

"Don't you want to see your ring?" Ryan asked.

"Oh—of course I do!"

Ryan popped open the jeweler's box. He pulled out the diamond solitaire and slid it onto her extended finger. Awed, Erica looked at the beautiful token of his love, then tightly interlaced her fingers with his—though what she really wanted was to throw her arms around him and kiss him again. Yet they'd given the other passengers enough of a show for one day. She lifted his strong hand clasped with hers and contented herself with kissing one of his knuckles.

"Ryan Meers, I love you," she whispered, certain no one could be as happy as she.

Epilogue

With winter's breeze chilling her face, Erica stood beside Ryan at the front door and watched their guests leave. Paula herded her troop into a mini-van, then slid inside next to her husky husband. Their mother hesitated beside a silver Buick's car door, which her tall, dignified-looking husband held open for her, and looked over her shoulder once more to wave. Erica smiled and waved back at the beautiful brunette, whom she'd been surprised to see she so strongly favored at their first face-to-face meeting—the day before Erica's wedding.

This past year, after three weeklong visits and countless phone calls between them, Erica and her mother had grown close. Erica was happy to see that even Paula was loosening up around their mother, though she still seemed sullen at times. But for the most part, they were all friends.

"You'll see them tomorrow," Ryan teased, tightening his arm around her waist. "They'll be here another week."

"I know," Erica sighed happily. "It's just that every moment is so precious. Sometimes you don't know how blessed you are until it's all taken from you. But thankfully, what got ripped away from me was restored." She looked up at him, her gaze adoring. "And you've been such a rock of support through it all. I've loved every moment of our married life together, Ryan."

He grinned and brushed his lips against hers. "Care to go for a few more rounds, Mrs. Meers?"

"I'm game if you are. At least sixty more years or so. This has been a wonderful first anniversary."

The baby started crying, and both Ryan and Erica turned to look. Margaret, with her perfectly coiffed hair and expensive clothes, appeared totally out of her element with little Charla.

"I don't think she likes me." Margaret awkwardly held the bald-headed baby up in the air a foot away from her.

"Sure she does," Erica said. "Just jiggle her against your shoulder. She loves that."

Margaret did so. The baby stopped crying and nestled her head against Margaret's neck. Erica smiled at the look of surprised contentment that crossed Margaret's face. During their heart-to-heart talk over a year ago, Erica learned some things about her adoptive mother. Margaret had been abused as a child and struggled with low self-esteem all her life; she didn't know how to show love to others. In an uncharacteristic emotional moment, Margaret assured Erica that, despite Margaret's inability to show it, Erica had been loved and wanted.

The baby fell asleep, and Darrin moved toward Margaret. "Put her in the bassinet. It's time to leave these kids alone."

Ryan lifted his eyebrows in Groucho Marx style at Erica, and she giggled.

At the door, she turned to Margaret. "I'm so glad you could come. Of course, you must also come to Christmas dinner at Wes's tomorrow. We're eating at one o'clock and then later we're all going to the tree-lighting ceremony together. Wes has been elected to light the tree this year for all the volunteer work his construction firm has done for the community."

Margaret seemed uncertain. "Are you sure we won't be imposing?"

"Oh, no! Stacey asked me to remind you. After all, you're family, too."

Ryan agreed as he picked up his plate from a nearby table, where a tabletop fiber-optic Christmas tree rotated in its stand. He took a bite of the last piece of anniversary cake.

Tears glistened in Margaret's eyes. "Thank you for inviting us. Your entire family is wonderful. It's amazing to see how much good has come about in all of your lives, despite everything that's happened. In fact. . ." She looked at her husband, and he gave a nod. "Would you mind very much if Darrin and I went to church with you tomorrow? I'd like to learn more about this God of yours that you said made it all possible."

Erica's heart felt near bursting with joy. "Oh, I'd love for you to come!" She stepped forward to hug the astonished Margaret, who still wasn't accustomed to physical displays. Margaret gave an uncertain smile then walked away with Darrin, who also got a quick hug first.

"I think she's coming around," Ryan said as he moved beside Erica and observed them drive away in their Lincoln Towncar. "I think they both are."

"Oh, I hope so." Erica closed the door against the cold and watched Ryan fork another bite of dessert into his mouth. "I'm glad you like the cake. I just wish it wouldn't have fallen. It was supposed to look like a pinwheel. Not a broken wheel. I guess a cake decorating class will be the next course I take. I wonder if Cynthia's offering one."

"Well, no matter how it looks, it tastes great! You've improved a lot over the year, hon. But it sure is different. It looks like a child's cake with all that carnival-like festivity on top—but Christmassy, too."

"Didn't I once hear you say something about being a kid at heart?" Erica teased and looked at the slice on his plate. "The semisweet chocolate pieces remind me of the bittersweet memories I had of my childhood. And the crushed peppermint glaze on top?" She snapped a good-sized bit off the red-and-white speckled dark chocolate triangle perched atop the fudge icing.

"Hey!" Ryan laughed in mock protest.

Smiling, she continued her explanation, holding up the chocolate piece. "It reminds me of something Peggy once said about God giving us peppermint dreams—what I think of as a bright future. This cake is symbolic of His sweetening my life and bringing good out of the bad. And giving me His best when I met you." She gave him a peck on the lips then popped the huge chunk of melting chocolate into her mouth, hitting the outside of her lips and making a mess of herself, giggling.

"All right, you!" Ryan set his plate down and grabbed her hands before she could wipe away the streaks. He bent toward her, trying to dart light licks to her cheeks to get the chocolate off her face—while she shook her head from side to side to evade his silly efforts, laughing like a child being tickled. A few hit their mark—when suddenly, his mouth targeted hers, and he gave her a long, delicious kiss that made Erica forget all about childish games.

"The baby's asleep," he murmured.

"Mmm," she agreed with a smile, her arms still looped around his neck.

Ryan kissed the sensitive spot near her ear. "One last thing, before I forget all about that cake, Mrs. Meers. What were those nuts you used? They had a strange flavor I've never tasted before."

Erica let out a nervous, uncertain giggle, and Ryan straightened to look at her. She lifted her brows sheepishly. "Um. . .nuts?"

He released a heartfelt groan. "Never mind. I don't want to know."

She let out another giggle, and bending down, Ryan captured it with a kiss.

Dark Chocolate 'n' Peppermint Dream Cake

A fun "cake makeover" to add zip to any plain cake, Erica and Ryan's anniversary cake is good for all occasions. A chocolate-lovers' dream, it's been a favorite in our family for years.

1 box cake mix (chocolate or white)
1 can chocolate fudge frosting
1 (8 ounce) bag semisweet baking chocolate chips
Several pieces hard peppermint candy, crushed
½ cup slivered or sliced almonds (optional)

Bake cake according to directions on box. Cool and frost. Sprinkle with nuts if desired. Melt semisweet chocolate using low heat. Spread evenly over cookie sheet covered with waxed paper and freeze. After 5 minutes check chocolate. It should be firm enough to score, but not totally solid. Using a round inverted cake pan as a guide, cut a circle in the chocolate toward end of cookie sheet, then score the circle as if cutting a pie, making 8 triangular "pieces."

Score remaining chocolate by making 2 parallel lines approximately 5 inches apart (or height of cake). Within those lines, make cuts 2–3 inches apart, so that you end up with a row of rectangles. Repeat above steps for next row. When all chocolate is scored, refreeze.

Once chocolate is solid, carefully break along scored lines. Spread triangles on top of cake at slight angle, to resemble a pinwheel, with only one long edge digging into frosting.

Use rectangles to "fan" around side of cake, anchoring edges into frosting. You should end up with a 3-D effect. If chocolate begins to melt, freeze until solid, then resume decorating. Sprinkle crushed peppermint over top and sides of cake.

Cover cake and store in refrigerator. (The peppermint will slightly melt to give a glazed effect.)

*Warning: This cake mysteriously disappears overnight when chocolate-lovers are in the house.

CREAM OF THE CROP
by Tamela Hancock Murray

Dedication

To Daddy
A sweet man who loves sweet treats

Chapter 1

Gwendolyn Warner opened the heavy door to the office marked EXECUTIVE SUITE. She was greeted by a large desk situated toward the back of a plush room. Each wall was decorated with framed ads for DairyBaked Delights' products. On either side of the desk and behind it were doors labeled with the names of the president, CEO, and vice president. The chief executive officer's door remained ajar.

She looked at the business card in her hand. *Rhoda Emerson, Chief Executive Officer, DairyBaked Delights*. The person she was supposed to see. She looked at the sign once more and confirmed she was in the right place. Good. At least she wouldn't be late for her interview. This job was too important. She couldn't blow her chances by being late. She had to appear smart, creative, self-assured, and capable.

No one was sitting behind the desk, so Gwendolyn decided to settle in one of the two red upholstered chairs with a magazine and wait to be called. She had arrived fifteen minutes early, as was her usual method.

In her best effort to look nonchalant, she retrieved a woman's magazine from her black leather tote. The cover promised articles revealing how to drop ten pounds in two weeks and how to create fabulous desserts, along with photos of the latest celebrity hairstyles. None of these items interested her. Gwendolyn wanted to study the photographs inside. Besides, she had to do something except sit on the edge of the seat, legs crossed at the ankles, hands holding on to her knees for dear life. No, she couldn't afford to look too anxious.

Absorbed in her magazine, Gwendolyn startled when a male voice boomed from behind the president's door.

"I never authorized hiring a new photographer for our ad campaign! We could save money by using old file photos."

Save money? She clenched her teeth. Uh-oh. Maybe she wouldn't get this job after all.

A calm, steady reply came from a female voice. "But this photographer comes to us with fine references, education, and credentials. And since she's just started her own studio, her fees should be very reasonable."

"Using old file photos would be even more reasonable," the man snapped.

Shaking her head, Gwendolyn decided she would vote this man least likely to suffer a stomach ulcer from suppressing his emotions.

"I'd like to know who decided to override my authority in this matter. I thought I was supposed to oversee all ad campaigns," he bellowed.

Gwendolyn's chest tightened. *What is this? With my background, I thought that I'd be a shoo-in to photograph the new DairyBaked Delights ad campaign.* Anxiety clenched its ugly grip around her midsection.

"Sebastian, I suppose I did. But I wanted a new photographer, and so I made the decision," the female voice answered, still maintaining calm.

Sebastian. Where have I seen that name?

She looked around the room and read the name on the door in the back of the room. Sebastian Emerson, Vice President.

A small gasp escaped her lips. So the VP didn't want anything to do with her? How could she conquer such a formidable adversary? Her interview prospects for this job seemed to be waning quickly.

Heavenly Father, I pray it's Your will for me to get this job. If it is, let this Sebastian man see that he needs to support me in my work. In the precious name of Your Son, amen.

She knew her prayer was selfish, but she felt that such a desperate petition was needed. If she didn't get this high-paying assignment, Gwendolyn would have to admit to her brother that she couldn't make a living on her own as a photographer.

Through years of hard work and sacrifice, Bruce, who was fifteen years her senior, had established a successful photography studio. Gwendolyn had been his assistant since high school. At first, Bruce was proud that his kid sister was part of his business. Gwendolyn was a miracle baby, born in her mother's forty-fifth year. By that time, Bruce was a teenager and had become accustomed to his status as an only child. With so many years between them, Bruce had always been protective of her, but he never related to her as an equal.

Still, she had imagined he would be proud when, after discovering a love for photography in his studio, she announced that she wanted to follow in his professional footsteps. But when she left Northern Virginia to earn her degree in photography at a small college in the southwestern part of the state, Virginia Intermont College, his lack of enthusiasm was palatable. He preferred not to talk about her studies, except to remind her how many years he had worked to establish himself in a brutally competitive field. He was worried about how she would pay back the college loans. A reasonable worry, to be sure, since her field was so uncertain. But he had succeeded without a university degree. She had hoped that, in time, he would come to consider her an asset, someone who could partner with him in his work. Instead he regarded her as a rival, sending her on the least desirable assignments and booking her portrait sessions on the times he knew she had a Bible study or a church choir rehearsal scheduled. After three years of trying to prove herself, she knew she had no choice but to strike out on her own. Her decision magnified Bruce's feelings that she was nothing more than a competitor to be squelched. If Gwendolyn failed and had to beg him to take her back, he would be sure to make her life even more miserable.

Failing was not an option she wanted to contemplate. She had to succeed.

A female voice brought her back into the present. "I'm the one who authorized the new hire."

Gwendolyn glanced again at the sign on the door and confirmed that the office belonged to the CEO, Rhoda Emerson, the woman she was scheduled to see.

"And your father agrees with me," Mrs. Emerson said.

Your father? So Sebastian is Mrs. Emerson's son. Maybe I can win this one after all. She felt a smile of triumph form on her lips.

She could sense from his persistence that Sebastian wasn't going down without a fight. "I thought we would just use the outtakes from our last photo shoot. The ones that Ebba took."

"No. I let you have your way last time, but not now. Even the best of Ebba's remaining pictures aren't what she would want to appear in any DairyBaked Delights ad. I won't hear of it."

"Ebba was the only one who could handle Pansy," Sebastian pointed out.

Pansy. That must be the name of the cow.

"I'm sure this photographer will do just fine with Pansy," Mrs. Emerson argued. "I've been assured there will be no problem."

Gwendolyn swallowed. Her experience with animals was limited to the pets little children would bring in to Bruce's portrait studio to be photographed. Their owners usually took care of them.

Lord, please help me!

"He'd better be good with animals. Pansy has been our symbol since the company started." Even though she'd never met him, Gwendolyn could almost see Sebastian folding his arms across his chest. "I'm not giving Pansy up for anybody."

"No one is asking you to. And you may as well know now, the photographer is not a he. It's a she. Gwendolyn something or another," Mrs. Emerson answered.

Gwendolyn wrinkled her nose. Some ally, if she couldn't remember her last name.

"And I'm sure she'll know what it takes to reach the next generation," her ally continued. "When I was young, there weren't so many choices. Now everyone has so many options in every area of life. That includes what type of commercial baked goods to buy. Not only do we have to compete with traditional bakeries, but many grocery stores have their own top-notch bakeries as well. Not to mention the big mail order bakeries. And all of them use every possible medium to remind consumers how many choices they have."

"You forgot to mention the biggest new kid on the block—the Internet," he reminded her. "Why do you think I recommended that you ask for Internet rights to the photos?"

"Oh, the Internet. Yet another thing I have to worry about." Gwendolyn heard Mrs. Emerson sigh. "How will I ever reach kids today?"

"You can start by not referring to young adults as kids." Sebastian retorted. "I know this is a new generation. But must we be like everybody else and use blatant sex appeal to sell our product? The people who buy our products respect us for not pandering to the lowest common denominator. We don't want to lose our base of established customers!"

Blatant sex appeal? No one had told Gwendolyn that the shoot would have anything to do with sex appeal. All she knew was that the ads would involve a cow and some baked goods. Even though creativity was her business, Gwendolyn had a hard time picturing an ad with a cow and a cake as being sexy.

A feeling of grudging admiration for Sebastian welled up inside her. At least he tried to hold on to some standards.

At that moment, a chubby matron who Gwendolyn surmised was the executive secretary entered from the hallway. Spotting Gwendolyn, she hurried to close Mrs. Emerson's door before setting a stack of paperwork on her desk. "May I help you?"

She stood. "I'm Gwendolyn Warner. I have an appointment with Rhoda Emerson."

"Oh. So you're the photographer. Sorry to keep you waiting. I had to step out of the office." The matron looked more embarrassed than the situation warranted. Perhaps she knew Gwendolyn had overheard an argument. "Uh, I'll let her know you're here."

"Thanks." Still wanting to appear calm, Gwendolyn returned to her seat.

The secretary quickly entered the CEO's office and then emerged a few moments later. She gave Gwendolyn a brief nod. Gwendolyn's heart began to hammer. *What will I do if they decide not to hire me? Oh, I can't think of that now.*

Fixing her face into a pleasant mask, Gwendolyn set her shoulders straight, smiled politely, and swept into the CEO's office with the confidence that had served her well during many interviews and difficult photo shoots.

Gwendolyn had taken care to appear in dressy pants, flat shoes, and a crisp white cotton shirt that bespoke a healthy pride in appearance yet told onlookers that her clothes wouldn't encumber her work.

Gwendolyn knew she had made the right decision to wear her favorite gray wool trousers when she saw Mrs. Emerson attired in a soft but businesslike suit the color of charcoal. Short but loose bleached-blond curls and soft makeup gave her a youthful appearance but did not quite camouflage the fact that she qualified for senior citizens' discounts. Though Gwendolyn had heard Mrs. Emerson could be tough, she sensed the older woman possessed a gentle side behind her businesslike veneer.

Gwendolyn scanned the office, in search of her antagonist. He was nowhere in sight. An interior door offered a clue as to how he had made his escape.

Coward!

Mrs. Emerson broke into her thoughts. "Thank you for meeting with us today," she said, extending her hand.

"Us?"

"Yes. My son, Sebastian, will be in momentarily," Mrs. Emerson assured. "In the meantime, I've already looked over your sample photos. I must say, they are quite impressive."

"Thank you, Mrs. Emerson. I do my best to create memorable photographs." She handed the older woman a formal portfolio of her best photos. "I also have examples of my most recent work here, if you care to see them."

"Certainly." Mrs. Emerson took the portfolio. "Please, call me Rhoda." She sat down in the executive chair behind a large desk, but not before motioning for Gwendolyn to take her seat in a nearby leather chair. Gwendolyn watched as Rhoda flipped through the book. "Hmm," she said.

"You have a question?"

"I notice that your professional portfolio includes weddings and portraits, but no commercial ads."

Gwendolyn swallowed. She knew when she agreed to the interview that Rhoda might mention her lack of commercial experience, but this woman cut right to the chase! "I was an assistant at Bruce Studios for five years," she answered.

At that moment, the young photographer was glad to see that Rhoda apparently didn't make the connection that Gwendolyn and Bruce shared the same last name. "You might know us. I mean, them." Calling the people at Bruce's studio "them" instead of "we" seemed strange. "They" were her work family. And her friends. She cleared her throat.

"Yes, I am familiar with them. Your association was one of the main reasons why I was willing to give you a chance."

Oh, great. I'll never get out from under his shadow.

Rhoda flipped through to the last picture. "And, I do like the artistic shots you included."

Rhoda's compliment gave Gwendolyn courage. Maybe she did have a grain of talent, after all. "Thank you, ma'am."

"Oh, don't 'ma'am' me." She waved at Gwendolyn as if the gesture would cause the offending reference to disappear. She shoved a box in her direction. Gwendolyn's inspection revealed that it contained individually wrapped brownies.

"All right, Rhoda." Gwendolyn selected a tempting piece of cake loaded with frosting and chocolate chips. "Thank you." She nodded toward her portfolio as Rhoda continued to flip through the pages. "My education is mentioned on my résumé. College gave me an opportunity to take artistic photos, as well. The type of creative photography that makes a print ad successful."

"I see." She set the portfolio on her desk. "All of that is very commendable, but I want you to know here and now that I have my limits. I want to reach the next generation, but not at the expense of our current customers. I look at the magazine ads. This artsy stuff can be a bit much sometimes. I will not accept any campaign that doesn't mention our product. And I don't want to see black and white photos of anemic-looking couples crawling all over each other. I've heard the old adage that sex sells, and perhaps it does. But I won't resort to that tactic to convince customers to buy our products."

Obviously, despite Rhoda's willingness to argue with Sebastian, her son's opinion held powerful sway. She resolved to remember that. "I hadn't planned on that type of ad for you," Gwendolyn assured Rhoda. "I'm afraid some other manufacturers have cornered the market on those. I understood I would be working with a cow and a cake."

"Oh, and don't forget Bernie. The Saint Bernard."

"A–a Saint Bernard?"

"Of course. We always use Bernie in our winter campaigns—unless you have a better idea."

"No, no," Gwendolyn hastened to assure her. Racking her brain, she remembered seeing a Saint Bernard in past ads for DairyBaked Delights. Their popular slogan, "DairyBaked Delights to the rescue!" flashed though her memory.

"We're quite attached to Bernie," Rhoda said. "My father was fond of his Saint Bernard, so he liked to use him in the ads way back when. I've kept up the tradition as a nod to the past."

"I like that."

Rhoda sent her a pleased smile. "If you're as good as I think you are, I'll be giving you more latitude later. That's why I want you to know the rules right off the top. Love of our product is more important than art, I believe."

Gwendolyn's first love was art, but she couldn't express disagreement with her prospective client. She searched for a common denominator. "I think it does help to be familiar with a product you're selling."

"Then I trust this is not the first time you've tried one of our products."

She chuckled. "No. I'm afraid I succumb too often to your baked goods. And I do thank you for making sugarless CreamDreams. They've gotten me through many a chocolate craving."

"Have they now?" Rhoda grimaced. "I'll tell you a secret, but you didn't hear this from me. I don't like the sugarless stuff. But our customers sure seem to."

"I enjoy all your products. That is why I jumped at the chance to photograph an ad for DairyBaked Delights," Gwendolyn said.

"Really?" Rhoda's expression displayed her approval.

"Really." Gwendolyn nodded. "Even though I want this assignment, I wouldn't lie to get it."

Job 32:21–22 popped into her mind. *"I will show no partiality, nor will I flatter anyone; for if I were skilled in flattery, my Maker would soon take me away."*

For the briefest of moments, she considered sharing the verse with Mrs. Emerson. Just as quickly, the thought vacated her head. No need to appear any more self-righteous than she already had.

"Good." Rhoda's expression softened from that of a tough businesswoman to a mother hen's. "I didn't think you looked like someone who would resort to deceit."

"Never." Seeing Rhoda's friendly expression, she decided to take a chance. "I'm a Christian."

Rhoda's face lit up. "Even better." She leaned forward and lowered her voice. "We're not supposed to ask, you know." She leaned even closer and lowered her voice another notch. "I do believe you are the perfect photographer to take us into our next phase of development. Don't tell anyone, but we're planning to—"

An interior door to their left creaked open. Startled by the unexpected intrusion, Rhoda and Gwendolyn both nearly jumped out of their chairs as they looked in the direction of the sound.

Rhoda leaned back, swiveled her chair, and smiled too broadly. "There you are, Sebastian." Her voice was louder than necessary.

Gwendolyn shot her gaze to the door through which Sebastian entered the office. She stood in anticipation of a handshake and mustered a smile for her opponent.

Chapter 2

Gwendolyn had to compose herself from taking in a noticeable breath of surprise and pleasure upon spying her adversary. Sebastian Emerson appeared nothing like the bellowing troll she had heard protesting her existence. Despite his reminiscence of Grandpa and his old-fashioned attitude of thrift, Gwendolyn could see by his youthful appearance that Sebastian had not yet celebrated his thirtieth birthday. Sebastian was one of the rare men who was several inches taller than Gwendolyn. A dark suit nipped at the waist accentuated his broad chest and shoulders, suggesting hours spent lifting weights. Deep brown hair was cropped to perfection. She couldn't resist staring up into Sebastian's gray-blue eyes.

A spark of interest ignited as he returned her look, only to fade as he apparently remembered he was supposed to be against her. "So you are the photographer." His voice was curt.

So much for a friendly greeting.

His mother gave Sebastian a warning look before turning to Gwendolyn. "This is my son, Sebastian Emerson."

"How do you do, Mr. Emerson." Remembering that most men don't offer their hands in greeting to a woman unless she makes the gesture first, Gwendolyn extended her hand. Sebastian might have been a rival, but she wouldn't stoop to abandoning her manners.

He took her hand. His grip proved to be firm and businesslike, though more warm and pleasant than she expected. "You may call me Sebastian. Mr. Emerson is my father." The smile Sebastian gave her in return was warm enough to make Gwendolyn wonder if Rhoda's son could somehow be molded into a real human. He even went so far as to motion Gwendolyn to one of the seats situated in front of his mother's desk, then sat beside her.

"Gwendolyn," said Mrs. Emerson, who had seated herself in the spacious executive chair behind her desk, "Sebastian is our VP."

"Supposedly," Sebastian muttered.

Gwendolyn knew her expression betrayed her surprise at his comment. She tried to contort it back to normal.

"Unlike yourself, the VP didn't find out about the new ad campaign until this morning," Sebastian said in an aside to Gwendolyn.

"Sebastian doesn't like surprises," Rhoda explained. "But never mind that. The important thing is the photo shoot. Gwendolyn, as we discussed earlier, you'll be working with Pansy during the first shoot. You are familiar with Pansy, I'm sure."

"I assume she's the dairy cow who's been your symbol for a while."

"Exactly. You and Pansy will be selling these." Rhoda handed Gwendolyn two stuffed toys that had been sitting on her desk. One was a white-and-brown cow, and the other was a Saint Bernard with a small plastic barrel that mimicked wood around his neck.

"How cute!"

"We think so." Rhoda smiled. "This little toy is free with three proofs of purchase and $1.99 postage and handling. Not a bad deal, don't you agree?"

"Not a bad deal at all."

"I was told you're good with animals," Rhoda said.

She hesitated. "I haven't had the opportunity to work with a cow," she had to admit, "but I look forward to meeting Pansy."

Gwendolyn cut her glance to Sebastian long enough to ascertain his response to her answer. Instead of the disapproval she dreaded, she caught him in a tender look, studying her as though he were eager to memorize her features. His unspoken message sent embers that made her skin tingle hot before he focused his attention back to the business at hand.

"As I'm sure you know," Rhoda droned, "we're hoping the new campaign will increase our fall sales well into winter."

Gwendolyn nodded. "People love to have lots of baked goods to serve when they entertain."

"Especially over the hectic Thanksgiving and Christmas holidays," Rhoda agreed. "And we do have a superb line of kosher products for Hanukkah as well. I'm sure you realize that many of today's women don't have time to do their own baking."

"And that's where DairyBaked Delights comes to the rescue," Gwendolyn pointed out.

Rhoda chuckled. "I'm glad to see you've just about memorized our ad copy."

"I make it my business to know as much as I can about my clients."

"You're a young woman after my own heart. It sounds as though we're off to a great beginning. And if the first shoot increases our sales," Rhoda added, "we'll be calling upon you for a second shooting. Then you'll be well on your way to a long-term position as our photographer for DairyBaked Delights."

"That would be wonderful." Gwendolyn cut her gaze to Sebastian long enough to see if he would object. Thankfully, he said nothing. She breathed an inward sigh of relief that she hoped didn't show on her face.

Rhoda stood. Sebastian and Gwendolyn followed suit.

Rhoda eyed her from head to toe. "You certainly are statuesque, more like a model than a photographer. It's a wonder you stay behind the camera. You're as pretty as many of the girls in the glamour magazines."

"That hardly matters, Mother," Sebastian reminded her.

"Don't pay any attention to my son," Rhoda told Gwendolyn. "He seems to have some difficulties dealing with humans."

"Don't we all, at one time or another?" Glancing at Sebastian's physique, its fine tone evident even under his suit, Gwendolyn had a sudden thought. "Sebastian, have you ever considered modeling?"

"You have the job, Miss Warner. There's no need to resort to flattery." Though she knew Sebastian wanted her to think he had been insulted by her remark, Gwendolyn noticed his face held a shadow of pleasure.

"I'm sorry."

"Sebastian," Rhoda chastised, "you are the one who ought to apologize for being so ungracious. I taught you better than that."

"I know." He set his handsome face in Gwendolyn's direction. "Sorry. Thanks for the compliment."

"Maybe my compliment was my way of saying that I just want you to be comfortable with the way your company is presented to the public." She hoped her explanation, despite its incoherent logic, absolved her from her unintentional expression of interest in her new boss. "Your mother has already told me that she doesn't want anything too artsy or with blatant sex appeal."

"Right." He nodded.

"I think what you have in mind is just the approach for your product. However," she continued, "you've seen the trend of company leaders going directly to the public." *And none of them are nearly as attractive as you are.*

Her idea took her by surprise. Gwendolyn lost her train of thought. "And I—I—"

"You what?" he asked. "You're suggesting that I should appear in our ads?"

"That's not such a bad idea, Sebastian," Rhoda intervened. "Why don't you consider it?"

"No thanks. Vanity is not one of my weak points." Sebastian surveyed Gwendolyn, his eyes glimmering. "Judging by how you're thin as a reed, you must not ever indulge in baked goods."

"Then you don't know me very well." She placed her hand on her hip. "I have a huge sweet tooth."

"You wouldn't know it to look at you."

She decided not to acknowledge his backhanded compliment. "I can prove it. When we shoot the ad next week, I'll bring the best dessert you ever put in your mouth!"

Sebastian's eyebrows arched. "Really?"

"Yes. And if you don't like it, you can fire me." She extended her freshly manicured hand for a shake to seal the deal. When he grasped her fingers, the touch of his warm flesh sent renewed sparks through to her heart. She hoped the gentle squeeze he gave her hand wasn't a figment of her imagination.

Clutching her portfolio, Gwendolyn headed to the car. In case they were watching, Gwendolyn kept her step light until she slid behind the driver's seat, well out of the range of prying eyes. After placing her portfolio in the passenger seat, she crossed her arms over the unfeeling steering wheel and laid her forehead upon them.

"Now what will I do?" Gwendolyn wailed to the horn. "I have no idea how to cook!"

Chapter 3

Standing in front of her bathroom mirror on the Saturday night before Monday morning's photo shoot, Gwendolyn looked at her face one last time as she prepared to wash most of its color down the drain. Light foundation, golden brown eye shadow, brown mascara, coral lipstick, and peach-colored blush accentuated her features. After she removed such enhancements, she noticed that she looked younger than her twenty-five years. Did she look like a professional photographer—one who owned her studio—not just a wannabe spending too much of her savings to finance a dream that might prove to be nothing more than pie in the sky?

She sighed. Putting the shoot together—a vision based on her own idea—had proven expensive and time consuming. Thankfully, her assistant, Fernando, was still in college and eager to work cheaply in exchange for experience and a good reference. Fernando had spent the entire week setting up the scene in the small warehouse space she had rented so Pansy wouldn't ruin her studio in the city. Not to mention she couldn't imagine a cow roaming the streets of the nation's capital.

Besides hard work, Fernando offered her some amusement. Taking advantage of his dark wavy hair and olive complexion, he had changed his name to Fernando from what he considered a less than glamorous moniker, Chip. In keeping with the change, he often tried to act as though he had just gotten off the boat—or, rather, the jet—from Milan.

To her relief, the warehouse was already prepared for Pansy's arrival in two days. She pictured the scene. A backdrop depicting snow was in place. Artificial snow was ready to be fanned over the scene to create the effect of a winter storm. The look was so realistic that a pleasant shiver traveled up her spine as she remembered happy times playing in snow. She had envisioned just how she would situate the cow and the model she had hired. She felt nervous about Sebastian's mandate regarding sex appeal. With his concerns in mind, Gwendolyn had spent hours poring over photos of available models. She selected a beauty of understated elegance—a brunette with the right kind of wholesomeness. Surely Sebastian would be pleased.

Not too pleased, I hope.

Her cheeks flushed hot. *I'm not jealous. No way. Now where did that thought come from?*

Determined not to dwell on her traitorous heart, she concentrated on how she would impose an image of the product itself onto the scene after the photos were shot.

She sent up a prayer to cover the photo shoot, added her thanks for Fernando, and reminded herself that she'd be giving him a nice Christmas bonus should the DairyBaked Delights account prove profitable.

Freshened in body and spirit, Gwendolyn decided to indulge in a cup of herbal tea before going to bed. Waiting for the water to heat, she sat at the table in the portion of the kitchen that doubled as a dining area in her small apartment. A batch of the latest fashion and beauty magazines heaped on the counter was too tempting to ignore. These popular publications were those in which she dreamed her photos would appear. Instead, she was fighting for a chance to photograph ads for a tiny bakery situated beyond the growing suburbs of the nation's capital city, in the middle of what was still Virginia farmland.

Certainly, the advertising campaign had enough money behind it to offer her a break. Even the first photo shoot guaranteed she would appear often over the next few weeks in the *Washington Post*, the *Richmond Times–Dispatch*, plus smaller local newspapers. Rhoda had even said the ad would be run in color in at least two Sunday editions of both of the larger papers. DairyBaked Delights planned to place a full-page glossy in several regional magazines. Such exposure should have excited Gwendolyn, yet it wasn't enough. She knew her brother wouldn't be impressed unless she surpassed his success by making the big time. That meant going to New York, Paris, and Milan to shoot photos for famous fashion designers and internationally known products.

"Although," she muttered, "Rhoda did mention something about the next stage of development. I wonder. . ."

She shook the thought out of her head. No need to think up grandiose schemes.

Turning her attention back to the magazine, she studied the avant-garde look so many of the two-page glossy ads touted. *I can take photographs that are every bit as eye-catching and creative as these. As a matter of fact, I'm even better than most of these photographers.* She lifted her chin in defiance, though the eyes in the photographs only offered vacant stares in return.

"Charm is deceptive, and beauty is fleeting; but a woman who fears the Lord is to be praised." The words of Proverbs 31:30 mocked her.

"Lord, why must You chastise me? You know I love You. Don't I have a right to my own dreams? Is it really wrong to want a little success in this world?"

But what is success?

The question disturbed her. What is success, really? Unwilling to search her soul for the answer, Gwendolyn pushed the question out of her mind.

She turned over a page and saw an ad for whipped topping. A luscious-looking slice of pie stared at her from the page.

She gasped. "Oh no! I forgot all about the dessert I promised Sebastian!"

Panic gripped her. Where would she find a recipe? She had no cookbooks and no experience. "Where's Mom when I need her?"

She picked up the phone and called her sister's house, where Mom and Dad were visiting.

"But of course I don't have my cookbooks here with me," Mom answered after Gwendolyn told her about the dilemma.

"Mom! I thought surely you'd be making dinners for them. You always tell Sarah how much you want her to learn to cook like you do."

"I know, but it seems ever since they visited New Orleans last summer, Josh has taken a liking to Cajun food. That's just not my thing. Although. . ." Her voice suddenly became too cheerful. "I do enjoy eating it while I'm here. Sarah has mastered seafood gumbo, and it's quite spicy."

Gwendolyn knew her mother's code word—spicy—meant that she'd be hitting the antacid later. "Hmm. Sarah just walked into the room, huh?"

"Yes indeed!" Mom sang.

"Well, you're doing the right thing to be a good mother-in-law to Josh. I'm sure he appreciates it."

"I know he does. And I really do love Sarah." Even though Sarah was in the room, Gwendolyn knew her mother meant the compliment.

Gwendolyn talked to her sister, her brother-in-law, their two kids, and Dad. Making dessert was getting quite expensive. Finally Mom got back on the phone with a new suggestion. "Why don't you call your friends, honey? I'm sure someone must have a good recipe."

Gwendolyn laughed. "My friends? You mean the ones who eat fast food every night? They think cooking means you zap leftovers in the microwave. I don't think so."

"You have a point," Mom conceded. "I have another idea. You're always talking about how great the Internet is. Why don't you try there?"

Gwendolyn snapped her fingers. "The Internet. Hmm. I suppose I could do a search and come up with something."

"I'm sure you could."

As Gwendolyn contemplated the possibilities, the notion that she might find something worthwhile grew. "Great idea, Mom! You're the best. Call me when you get home, okay?"

Moments later, a search yielded results. "Cynthia Lyons' Online Cooking School. Hmm."

She studied the teaser for the school. Pictures of dishes Cynthia taught her students looked good enough to serve at the best gourmet restaurants. "I can't believe this class is free." Gwendolyn looked at a picture of a cookbook. "Maybe I'll buy a copy of her book. In the meantime, I'll see what help I can get by e-mail."

Dear Cynthia,

Hi! I'm a new student who just enrolled in your school tonight. They said I could e-mail you so here I am!

I'm in a pickle. Cute food-related joke, isn't it? I'm in a desperate pinch. Sort of like needing a pinch of salt. Hey, I'm on a roll! (Maybe a cinnamon roll? Ha-ha.) Anyway, I need a recipe quick!! I promised my new boss I'd make him a super dessert. Problem is, I don't have a good recipe! I need to have the dessert by Monday morning. So really, I need to make it Sunday night at the latest. Not much time!

Can you give me any suggestions? It needs to be something easy. Cooking is not my forte. I guess if it was, I wouldn't need your school!

Thanks for your help.

Gotta dash—like a dash of pepper! Ha-ha!

Yours,

Gwendolyn Warner

Now, if only Cynthia Lyons, whoever she was, would come through!

The next day after church, Gwendolyn eagerly checked her e-mail. A message from Cynthia awaited!

Dear Gwendolyn,

Welcome to the class! I trust you will enjoy learning new ways to cook. I do happen to have a recipe I'll be happy to share with you. It's for key lime pie. Not too exotic, but different enough that your new boss should be favorably impressed. You can use graham cracker crust, but if you really want to wow him, you might try a traditional piecrust. Nothing beats a flaky, homemade piecrust, especially if your boss's mother or grandmother made her own pies.

"She sure did—and does!" Gwendolyn assured the absent Cynthia. "At least, that's what I'm willing to bet since he's the son of a bakery owner."

She kept reading.

The recipe I've included is foolproof. I've used it many times myself, and my students have all been pleased with it.

Happy cooking!

Cynthia

Gwendolyn printed out the recipes and examined them both. Neither looked too difficult. "Excellent!" She lifted her fist in the air with triumph.

She cleared a section of the kitchen counter and got out her ingredients for the piecrust. How hard could making a piecrust be? She had watched Mom make piecrusts for years. All she did was throw together a little flour, water, and a few other ingredients, chill the dough awhile, and roll it out. Voilà! A beautiful crust. She could certainly do the same. Mom would be so proud!

She noticed that Cynthia's recipe called for vinegar. "Vinegar, huh? Hmm," she wondered. "Does a 't' mean a teaspoon or a tablespoon?" She measured out a teaspoon. "That hardly seems like anything. I'd better try a tablespoon. And I think I'll add a little more for good measure."

The dough rolled up into a nice ball, just as the recipe promised. Gwendolyn placed the bowl in the refrigerator to chill for two hours. She'd take a break and make the pie filling, then roll it out and be all set.

Not until later when she was preparing to complete her cooking task did Gwendolyn realize that she should have made sure she had plenty of eggs on hand. The recipe called for four eggs, but she only had three left.

"That shouldn't matter," she reasoned. "Eggs are so tiny. I'll just use what I have." She looked at the clean counter. "But first, to roll out the pie dough."

She set the oven temperature to 400 degrees to cook the crust. After dividing the dough in half, she attempted to roll it out. Why wouldn't the roller run smoothly over the dough? Why was it sticking to the roller, and to the counter? What a mess! Then she remembered she was supposed to flour the rolling pin and the counter.

Gwendolyn rolled and rolled, but her crust didn't look anything like her mother's. The dough was the ugliest she had ever seen. And the thickness varied from place to place. The buzzer let her know the oven had reached the preset temperature.

"Well. It'll just have to cook until it's right." She placed her ugly piecrust in the oven and hoped for the best. "Besides, no one will care once the filling's in."

Even though she used only three eggs, the pie filling didn't seem any worse for the lack of one little egg.

"This sure is soupy," she noticed after adding the juice. "Oh! It says a half cup, not a cup." She shrugged. "Oh, well. It should congeal just fine anyway. But I wonder why it isn't green like a lime. I've never seen such an anemic color. It looks more like a watered-down lemon than anything else. This won't do at all."

Gwendolyn thought about what to do. "I know." She snapped her fingers and searched her cabinet. "There it is. Green food coloring." She was glad she had helped her niece color Easter eggs the previous year. "I'll use some of that."

She added one drop to the pie mix and stirred, but it didn't turn the nice shade of green she expected. She added another, and another, and several more, stirring after each round. Instead of a beautiful shade of emerald green, the mixture turned a strange shade of aqua. "This is bound to look better once it's done cooking." Cheerfully she placed the pie into the center of the oven and waited.

Lord, I know this is trivial, but please let this pie turn out okay.

When the pie came out at the appointed time, Gwendolyn nearly shrieked. The color hadn't improved at all. If anything, cooking brought out the blue even more. Even worse, the crust was black around the edges. Gwendolyn tried to flake off as much of the burnt portion as she could with a butter knife, resulting in minimal, if any, improvement.

She groaned. "What am I going to do?"

Her kitchen clock told her the hour was almost midnight. She had no choice. Her new boss would feast on this very pie the next day.

The next morning, Sebastian stood beside his kitchen sink and drank a tall glass of orange juice blended with a raw egg. "Wonder if Gwendolyn drinks juice for breakfast?" he muttered.

At that moment, he realized he had been thinking of the photographer with chocolate-colored hair and matching eyes ever since he'd met her. "Gwendolyn. Gwendolyn Warner. Why does she haunt me? Why do I wonder about everything about her—even what she eats for breakfast?"

The only answer was Sebastian's basset hound whimpering for his own breakfast.

"Aren't you glad you don't have to worry about such nonsense, Cookie? All you have to think about is sleeping and getting fed every day." Sebastian poured his pet a healthy portion of premium dog food and set the hound's monogrammed bowl on the floor. "Here you go, boy," he said, giving Cookie a quick rub behind the ears.

As the dog chomped his food, Sebastian journeyed into the largest of three bedrooms in the house he occupied. The four-year-old house had been custom-built on a parcel of land that had been part of Grandpa's farm before he started the bakery business. Though modest, when Sebastian approved the plans, he knew the house would be too large for a bachelor. He had not built the home for himself, but for the wife and family he hoped to have one day. Still, Sebastian was in no hurry for One Day to arrive. Though women pursued him, even calling to arrange dates, Sebastian had not found any of them alluring enough to cause him to break his quiet stride of life.

Opening the door to his walk-in closet, Sebastian pondered several suits, shirts, dress pants, and jeans. On the days he had sales calls to make, the decision to dress in a suit was automatic. Sebastian mused that perhaps a suit was no longer required in a world of casual Fridays, but he clung to tradition out of pride, stubbornness, and, though he was loath to admit it, a desire to be different.

Yet today was not a usual business day for the VP. Today he was scheduled to visit a photo shoot, just to be sure it was going according to plan and, as Mother liked to say, "To remind them that DairyBaked Delights is paying the bill."

Sebastian had been present during other shoots, but those had only involved Reginald and Bernie. The animals wouldn't have cared if Sebastian appeared in a bath towel. But an elaborate set, with a professional model—well, that was something altogether different.

Having finished his breakfast, Cookie joined his master in the bedroom. The dog nuzzled against Sebastian's bare leg.

"You're no help at all." Nevertheless, Sebastian chuckled and gave his buddy a playful pat on the head.

Cookie waddled to his customary position on the oval beige rug beside Sebastian's bed, closing his eyes for an early morning snooze.

"Decisions, decisions." Sebastian pulled a dressy blue shirt off a cedar hanger. Standing in his shirttails, he debated whether to wear a pair of dark blue chinos that had been faithful friends since the day they were purchased. "No one else will be wearing a suit," he told Cookie. "I'll fit right in."

The dog opened one eye. Looking at his master, he wagged his tail in approval.

Sebastian twisted his mouth. "On second thought, I am the one paying the bill." The idea prompted him to don a dark blue suit and matching tie. "There. That's better."

As he perfected a Windsor knot, Sebastian had a horrifying thought. "Cookie, do you realize this is the first time I've ever put on more than one change of clothes for work?"

"Ummm hmmm," Cookie seemed to say.

"What do you think has happened to me, boy?"

He whimpered.

"Yeah, maybe you're right. Although I never thought I'd go for such a tall, thin woman. She looks like a model." He pursed his lips. "The kind of model my sister always admired." Bittersweet images of his older sister came to mind. "Do you think I'm making a big mistake, boy?"

This time, not even Cookie gave him an answer. Sebastian was on his own.

Meanwhile, Gwendolyn waited anxiously for Pansy to arrive. Just that morning, someone named Hal, who said he boarded Pansy and Bernie, called to ask for directions from his farm in Haymarket. So someone else would be bringing DairyBaked Delights' mascots. Had Sebastian forgotten all about the dessert? Strange, she felt sorry that she might not be seeing him after all. If he didn't show, at least after the shoot she could console herself with a big slice of pie. Somehow, the thought didn't comfort her as much as she thought it might.

Two hours later, Sebastian arrived at the warehouse. He was glad he didn't have to venture all the way into Washington. Though the city offered excitement, he had no desire to enter the frenzy full-time. Trips to the Corcoran Gallery of Art and plays at the Kennedy Center gave Sebastian the cultural infusions he needed without the everyday hassle of urban living.

Gold hands on the black face of his watch confirmed that Gwendolyn must already be an hour into the photo shoot. Rushing, lest he miss the entire session, Sebastian pulled into the first generous parking space he saw and made his way into the dumpy building. He didn't have to note the room number. A catchy tune would have led Sebastian in the direction of Gwendolyn's studio even if he had not visited in the past. He knocked on the door loudly enough to be heard over the music. As he waited for a response, he noticed that the song, a tune he didn't recognize, mentioned Jesus. And not as a swear word. The singer was praising His name!

The volume was turned down so he could no longer hear the words, just a faint tune. He heard footsteps as someone approached the door, and then Gwendolyn answered.

"Mr. Emerson! I was wondering when you would show up."

He looked around, pretending to search for his father. "Dad? Are you here?"

"Sorry." Her face blushed a pretty shade of peach. "Sebastian."

"I would have been here sooner if not for the traffic. I-66 was terrible," he responded, referring to the highway used by commuters heading into Washington from the western suburbs.

"No matter. We haven't started yet. You arrived at just the right moment," she smiled and gushed, leading him into the room where the photo session was to occur.

He looked at his watch. "You haven't started yet?"

"The model is still in hair and makeup."

"Still?" Sebastian glanced once again at his watch.

The melody of her laugh echoed in the studio. "You're spoiled since Pansy doesn't need much preparation to look cute. But hair and makeup for real models takes forever!"

"I see," Sebastian muttered, even though he didn't. As he followed Gwendolyn to the set, he noted her slim figure and gorgeous mane of hair. "I'll bet if you were the model, you wouldn't take more than five minutes," he blurted.

She turned her head just enough so he could see her eyes and answered. "Are you kidding? I'd take all day!"

"I find that hard to believe." Sebastian found himself enjoying the light banter. Already, Gwendolyn had made him feel relaxed, as though he, not she, should have been feeling nervous. She seemed just as at ease as she had the first day they met in his mom's office. Nothing he said or did ever seemed to intimidate her. He found her self-confidence both impressive and charming.

Glancing about the room, he noticed Pansy contentedly chewing her cud. A handsome young man was stroking the side of her neck. A vague feeling of jealousy ripped through Sebastian, taking him by surprise. "Who is that?"

"Oh, I'm sorry," Gwendolyn apologized. "That's Fernando, my assistant."

Fernando sent him a cocky grin and waved.

"I'd be lost without Fernando," Gwendolyn said.

"I'm sure." Sebastian had taken an instant dislike to Fernando. No man had any business being that handsome. He couldn't help wondering if Gwendolyn shared his opinion.

"Do not listen to my beautiful boss lady, Mr. Emerson," Fernando protested in a strange accent that seemed to mock a character in a mafia movie. "She flatters me."

Unwilling to think about Fernando any longer, Sebastian looked for Bernie. As soon as their eyes met, the dog let out several loud barks and rumbled until the cage shook.

"Settle down, boy!" Gwendolyn coaxed.

"Where's Hal?" Sebastian wondered.

"He went out for a latte. He'll be back before we get started."

"He'd better be. Hal's the only one who can keep Pansy under control."

Gwendolyn picked up a petit four and began applying petroleum jelly to the outside with a miniature paintbrush.

"Now what?"

"You've never seen your other photographers at work, have you?" Her voice held an edge that revealed her suspicion.

What could he say? He had always trusted Ebba. "The last photographer we had was in place before I was even born."

"Oh. She just retired, huh?"

"After a long career, yes. And I never once heard her say the first thing about petroleum jelly."

"I'm sure she used it. She just didn't tell you, that's all. It's nothing sinister. Petroleum jelly will make the chocolate coating on your petit fours look even more scrumptious, especially under the right lighting. You'll see."

Sebastian pointed to an oversized fan. "What is that for?"

"For the shots of falling snow, of course." Gwendolyn nodded toward a set depicting a ski slope. "When the time is right, we'll turn the fan on low and use artificial flakes to create a gentle snowfall."

Sebastian pictured the campaign Gwendolyn had explained to his mom. Mom had okayed the idea and then passed on the info to Sebastian without getting his approval first. So what else was new?

Still, he had to admit, he liked the idea. The model would be positioned, half sitting and half lying, as if she had just fallen in the snow. Pansy would be in the background, taking in the whole situation with her big brown cow eyes. Wearing a barrel around his neck replicating the ones on the stuffed dogs, Bernie would look at the model as if he were her best friend. A few petroleum jelly-painted petit fours would be placed in the snow, as if they had fallen from Bernie's barrel. Gwendolyn had suggested this as a way to show the consumer the product itself.

He pictured the caption, in red script:

Want to win her over?
Let DairyBaked Delights come to the rescue.
P.S. Bring the dog.

"I'm sure I'll be pleased," Sebastian said with a nod.

"Good. I think this ad will get everyone's attention and convince people to buy your goods for holiday entertaining."

Just then, the model appeared. She was wearing ski garb the color of raspberry jelly. Her face was made up in a flamboyant style. Her lips were the color of raspberries, and her dark hair was streaked with the same color. She did remind him of a bonbon.

"Here she is," Gwendolyn said. "What do you think?"

Fernando didn't hold back his opinion. "She is beautiful, is she not?" He brought his fingertips to his thumb, then touched them to his lips. Making a kissing noise, he drew his hand back toward the model in an exaggerated gesture. *"Bella!"*

Sebastian felt his breakfast threaten to make an encore appearance. Fernando's character seemed to be a guise, not the true persona of a full-blooded Italian male.

Sebastian looked at the model but visualized Gwendolyn instead. *"Bella,"* he whispered.

"Is anything wrong?" Gwendolyn asked.

"No. Nothing." Actually, everything. Sebastian realized he had been staring not at the model or anything else in the room he was supposed to be observing. Ever since he stepped into the room, he could only concentrate on Gwendolyn. He had to leave. He had to, before he made a complete and utter fool of himself.

"Everything looks as though it's going smoothly," he managed. "I see no need to stay and watch the entire shoot. But I shall expect exceptional results." With a curt nod, Sebastian set out to make his exit. In his haste, his knee tripped the latch to Bernie's cage. Enthralled by unexpected freedom, the dog bounded for the set.

"Stop, Bernie!" shouted Gwendolyn. "You'll ruin everything!"

Chapter 4

The dog wasn't listening. Jumping on the fan's pedestal, he pressed the switch with his massive right paw. A second thump with his left paw sent the fan's blades from a gentle spin to full speed. Mighty gusts of wind filled the room. Picking up white plastic bits from an open container in its path, the wind swirled them into a frenzy until the inside of the studio resembled a blinding blizzard.

Before the unexpected burst of wind, Fernando had set a few petit fours in the artificial snow that had been placed on the make-believe ski slope. But the platter of petit fours that Fernando held proved to be the dog's goal. Bernie bounded for the treats. His slobbering mouth made contact with the edge of the thick china, knocking it to the floor. Unprepared, Fernando lost his balance and landed on the floor, jelly-covered candies cascading all over his indigo shirt and black pants.

The petit fours that flew from the platter onto the model landed on her hair. Gravity taking them downward, they left trails of jelly clinging to her smooth locks. Flying artificial snow adhered to the gunk. The final effect gave the impression her hair had been visited by snails that left behind slimy, snowflake-filled trails. Gooey treats spiraled downward and landed on her outfit, leaving greasy brown blotches wherever they hit before making their final free fall to the floor.

Having vanquished his enemies, Bernie bounded for the petit fours and engulfed a mouthful of treats. The pause in the dog's leaping seemed to bring Fernando to his senses, propelling him to shut off the fan. The blizzard ceased.

"You brute!" Fernando screamed as he got up and assessed the spots of jelly and chocolate on his clothing. "Now my beautiful silk shirt and best pants are a disaster!" His dark eyes narrowed as he looked in Gwendolyn's direction. "Someone will have to pay me every last cent it costs to replace this!"

By this time, Gwendolyn had helped the model recover and was ready to put a consoling hand on the assistant's shoulder. "It's all right, Fernando. It's only a shirt."

"Only a shirt! But it is my favorite shirt!"

Sebastian interrupted with a more immediate concern. "Don't let Bernie eat the treats. He could die!"

"He could?" Gwendolyn asked.

"Yes. My dog, Cookie, got into an open box of truffles last Christmas and became violently ill," Sebastian said as he attempted to corner Bernie. "His vet said dogs don't have the enzyme needed to digest chocolate."

"Not to mention, no creature should be eating petroleum jelly," Gwendolyn added, trying to grab Bernie's collar. "Those are props, Bernie."

"Now, now, Bernie. You don't want to eat that." Sebastian's coaxing failed to convince the animal. The dog's response was to lunge onto Sebastian, the surprise impact knocking him to the floor. Bernie's front paws held him down by his shoulders and his back paws rested on Sebastian's legs.

"Get off my knees! That hurts!"

Wagging his tail, Bernie complied, but not before drooling chocolate, raspberry jelly, bits of chocolate cake and vanilla cake, mauled cherries, coconut, caramel, and petroleum jelly all over Sebastian's suit and hair. Only a quick turn of his head saved Sebastian's face.

"What's going on here?" Hal interrupted.

"Get your dog!" Fernando commanded.

Hal set his latte in an empty corner on the floor and rushed to calm the excited animal before confining him to his cage. Hal's cooing words to assuage the animal seemed to have a soothing effect on the humans as well.

Looking about the trashed studio, Gwendolyn seemed to be making mental calculations as to the amount of damage caused.

"How did he get out of his cage? I had it locked," Hal said as Bernie entered his portable kennel.

"My knee hit the latch," Sebastian admitted. "I'm just glad you got here when you did, Hal."

"So am I," Gwendolyn agreed. "But Hal's arrival was too little, too late, I'm afraid. This place is such a mess, I don't think we'll be able to shoot today."

Her edict resulted in a collective groan.

"When will we be able to reschedule?" Sebastian wanted to know.

"I'm afraid I won't be able to reschedule a shoot now until next week. First, the studio must be cleaned. Then I'm booked with other jobs from tomorrow until next Tuesday."

"I'm sorry," Sebastian said. "Please reschedule whenever you can."

"I'm sorry, too. I know I promised your mom—"

"Never mind. It was mostly my fault. I'll explain everything to her." He looked at the disaster that the studio had become. "Hire a cleaning crew. DairyBaked Delights will cover the expense."

"That is very generous of you, Mr. Emerson," Fernando said.

"Yes, thank you. That will save Fernando and me a lot of valuable time, and allow us to reschedule your shoot sooner," Gwendolyn added.

Fernando cleared his throat. "About my shirt. . ."

Though he felt no special generosity toward the young man, Sebastian knew he had to make amends. He took out his wallet, withdrew five twenty-dollar bills, and handed it to Fernando. "Will that buy you another silk shirt?"

He nodded several times in rapid succession. "Yes! Thank you!"

"Good. I'm glad to have at least one person happy today. I'll see the rest of you later." Humiliated by his error and disgusted by the mess the dog had slobbered on him, Sebastian rushed out the door, determined nothing would stop him this time.

He hadn't even gotten to the elevator when he heard Gwendolyn calling him. "Sebastian! Wait!"

He pretended not to hear. *Not even Gwendolyn can console me now.*

"Sebastian!"

He was cornered. "What is it?"

Her eyes bespoke her sympathy. "Look, I'm really sorry about today."

"Sorry? Why are you sorry?" he snapped. "You and your staff will be paid for today even though you didn't snap the first picture, and you'll collect your fee for your work next week."

Her mouth opened as if she were about to deliver a rebuttal, but she didn't speak. The hurt look on her face, still smeared endearingly with chocolate, was too much for him to resist.

"Now I'm the one who's sorry. I didn't mean that."

"I know. At least, I think I know." From Sebastian's perspective, her smile lit up the entire building.

"I'm just kicking myself for being such a klutz that I've thrown off the whole day." Sebastian looked at his ruined suit and let out an audible sigh. "I just want to go home and forget this morning ever happened."

Gwendolyn cocked her head toward the model, who had begun wiping off her face. "You could be her." She lifted a strand of her own dark hair, which had become saturated during the effort to calm Bernie. "Or me. Want to help me clean this out of my hair?" To his surprise, rather than being angered as Fernando had been, Gwendolyn giggled like a young girl flush with the excitement of her first slumber party.

"You think this is funny?" he asked.

She stopped laughing long enough to ask, "Don't you?"

Gwendolyn's resilient spirit was difficult to resist. "I suppose we do look pretty amusing. And we probably smell even worse. At least I'm sure I do. Clothes can be replaced, and we humans are washable, aren't we?"

"As far as I know." He grinned in spite of himself.

"Fernando is a player, and he wants to be ready for his next impromptu date," Gwendolyn told him. "He always carries more than one change of clothes. Maybe he has a pair of pants and a shirt you can borrow."

He looked down at his long legs. "I don't know. He's a lot shorter than I am."

"Who cares what the clothes look like? As soon as you get home, you can change and enjoy your day off."

"Enjoy my day off?" he scoffed. "Not when I've got to face Mother and tell her I've run up a huge bill with no pictures to show for it."

"That's all right. You don't have to pay me."

"No, I insist." Sebastian tipped his head to one side and shrugged. "You shouldn't have to pay for a lost day and a cleaning bill when the accident wasn't your fault."

"Maybe you'll feel better after eating my dessert," she suggested.

"Dessert?"

"Don't you remember? I promised to make you dessert."

"Oh, that." Embarrassment covered him as he remembered how rudely he had challenged her. "You didn't really have to do that."

"Didn't I?"

"All right, I suppose I did seem pretty serious about the whole thing last week. If there's enough dessert, maybe we can share it with Fernando and Hal later. A good dessert should put us all in a better mood."

After cleaning the goo from her face and hair and sponging off her soft white sweater and black pants as best as she could, Gwendolyn was ready to serve her dessert. She retrieved the pie and a container of whipped cream from the compact refrigerator and headed toward the table where everyone sat, awaiting a treat.

When she noticed Sebastian, she nearly dropped the pie. Following her suggestion, he had borrowed a shirt and a pair of pants from Fernando. Since the wild floral-patterned shirt was three sizes too small, Sebastian was forced to keep the buttons on the front and cuffs undone. Gwendolyn had to admit her new boss possessed a chest her male friends in the modeling business would envy. She summoned her willpower to keep from staring.

Fernando's blue jeans constricted Sebastian's taut abdomen and full thighs so that he shifted in his seat every few minutes. Their ill fit wouldn't have been noticeable to the casual observer, except that the jeans were hemmed well above his ankles. If Gwendolyn had seen Sebastian without knowing why he was wearing such a getup, she would have guessed he had been stranded alone on a desert island since he was twelve years old and had been wearing the same outfit since his ship wrecked.

Trying to maintain her composure, Gwendolyn placed the dessert on a table where it wouldn't be visible to the rest of the group. Only the model had excused herself. Gwendolyn wasn't surprised that she passed on dessert.

The burned piecrust hadn't improved in appearance overnight. The color looked bluer than ever. She tried to cover her mistake with whipped topping, but some of the color was still visible from the gaps in the top. Giving up, she brought the dessert to the table.

Sebastian was the first to speak. "Uh, what kind of pie is that?"

"Key lime, of course!" Gwendolyn smiled so broadly she could almost feel the corners of her lips touch the sides of her ears. She looked around the table and noticed that everyone's expressions looked as though they were watching a circus performer rather than anticipating a piece of delicious pie. "Why? Is something the matter?"

Fernando answered. "It is a most. . .interesting. . .shade of. . .teal."

Gwendolyn examined the pie. "Teal?"

Sebastian nodded. "I'd have to say he's right. Sort of a teal green."

"Oh. It must be the food coloring. Yes, I was hoping for a more true green, but it turned out a bit odd. But it will still taste wonderful, I'm sure." She knew she sounded like a television commercial.

"You added food coloring?" Fernando asked.

"Yes. I didn't like the way it looked after I made it. I thought it looked anemic. More like a really, really pale lemon than a nice fresh lime. I was hoping to make it the color of the limes you see in the stores. You know, a nice, pretty shade of green." She shrugged. "Oh, well."

"Oh, well?" Hal grunted. "Sorry, but I think I'll pass. Say, Sebastian, got any more of those petit fours left?"

"I used them all," Gwendolyn snapped.

"Oh." Disappointment colored Hal's tone. "I saw some pumpkin cake in the coffee shop. I think I'll grab me a piece of that before I head on out to the farm."

Fernando's eyes darted from side to side, and he squirmed in his seat.

"You don't have to eat it, Fernando," Gwendolyn said, swallowing to overcome her hurt feelings.

"Are you sure you don't mind? Uh, lime never was my favorite flavor, anyway. I never even liked those lime lollipops they give away at the bank." He grinned. "I always asked for grape. Still do, as a matter of fact."

"Care to go next door with me?" Hal offered.

Fernando gave Gwendolyn a pleading look before he answered. "If it's all right with everyone. . ."

"Cowards!" Sebastian teased.

Funny. That's what I used to think about you. To her surprise, Sebastian seemed almost likable.

"But we will be cowards eating pumpkin cake!" Fernando countered as he and Hal headed out the door.

After their exit, Sebastian turned to Gwendolyn, a smile lighting his handsome features. "Looks like we've been deserted, pun intended."

"Cute." Gwendolyn screwed her mouth into a wry grin.

"I thought so."

She looked at the door. "Go ahead." She tried not to choke on her words. "I suppose you want to go with them."

"Not at all."

"Really?"

"Really." The light in his gray-blue eyes showed her that he meant it. "I want to try your pie. After all, you promised to make the dessert, the least I can do is eat it." He winked. "Who knows? Maybe you've invented a new product for DairyBaked Delights!"

Relieved that the troll had permanently retreated to his lair beneath the bridge, Gwendolyn placed her hands on her hips. "You don't mean that."

"Perhaps not about the new product. But I do want to try the dessert."

"Well, I don't want to try it," Gwendolyn admitted.

"Why not?" Sebastian challenged. "What happened to your spirit of adventure?"

"It doesn't extend to food gone wrong."

"Aw, come on. I can look at this pie and tell you put a lot of work into it. We've got to try it."

"Well, okay." She cut into the pie. The knife slid through the filling without a problem, but the crust was another matter. In her attempts to cut through it, she ended up stabbing it in frustration.

"Whoa!" Sebastian said. "You don't have to kill the pie, do you?"

"No." She stopped stabbing. "But apparently I need to kill the crust."

He chuckled. "Let me help you with that." When he drew closer to her, she caught the aroma of his clean skin. A pleasant woodsy scent of a brand of cologne she couldn't identify emanated from his neck. She wished he could linger, just so she could breathe in his warmth and closeness longer.

"She's putting up quite a fight," he observed.

"Who?" Gwendolyn blurted.

He gave her a strange look. "The piecrust, of course. She's a tough one. Why, who did you think I was talking about?"

"No one," she spouted. "Nothing. I don't know. I'm just not used to anyone calling a piecrust 'she.'"

He chuckled. "I guess not." He placed a slice of pie on her plate. "Well, you gave it the old college try, but I am the conqueror!" He lifted his hands in the air in mock victory.

She laughed in spite of herself and watched him struggle to cut a second piece.

Moments later, he scooped up a dollop of filling. "Ah, there's nothing like toothpaste pie." He placed a spoonful in his mouth. "Mmm, good!"

"Toothpaste pie?"

"Sure is."

She studied it. "You know, come to think of it, the color is a little like the spearmint flavor I use. Well, it won't taste like spearmint. That I can guarantee."

He nodded. "Actually, it tastes great."

As the flavor of lime burst into her mouth, she had to nod in agreement. "You're right. It does taste good. But it looks so awful, and the crust is so tough; I have to say, I failed. I could just die." She looked into Sebastian's steely blue eyes. "And I know what this means. Both my dessert and my photo session flopped. You win," she conceded. "I'm fired."

Chapter 5

Seeing the photographer's distress, Sebastian realized that in spite of how badly the shoot had gone, and regardless of the fact that the dessert had been a flop, he didn't want to fire her. Feeling ashamed, he recalled how boorish he had been to Gwendolyn when they first met. Although the company was well in the black financially, Sebastian remembered when they weren't, and he still hated to waste money. Mother didn't always exercise the same caution. Sebastian had taken out his anger with his mother on the young woman when she was doing nothing more than appearing for a job interview. She hadn't deserved the treatment he'd given her, and he knew it.

Still, pride made him resist. "Do you think you deserve to be fired?"

Gwendolyn gulped. "Not really." She bowed her head, causing her long lashes to form lush crescents on her pale cheeks. "But I was foolish enough to make a promise I knew I couldn't keep. Now I have to accept the consequences."

He nodded once. How could he fire someone who possessed such humility?

Her coral lips curved into a frown. "Besides, it's not like you'd be losing any good pictures if you let me go now."

Sebastian saw her shoulders sag in defeat. She busied herself by piling the dessert plates she had brought into a neat stack, her chocolate-colored eyes avoiding his.

She was beautiful. That couldn't be denied. But for Sebastian, her appearance had become secondary to the fiber of character she displayed.

"I won't let you go." As soon as the words escaped his lips, Sebastian realized that he sounded more like a suitor than a boss. For once, he hoped they weren't of like minds. Otherwise, she might see he had just admitted he wished he could captivate her forever.

Matthew 12:34 came to mind: *"For the mouth speaks what the heart is full of."* Thinking of this eternal truth, he was all too aware an expression of chagrin passed over his features.

Her gaze met his, her delicate features marked with questions.

Sebastian changed his expression to one that would brook no nonsense. He tried to give his voice an edge of authority. "What I mean to say is, Mother will be upset enough by today's fiasco as it is. How could I tell her I fired her handpicked photographer on top of everything else?"

Gwendolyn let out a little "oh" that indicated his answer was a disappointment. Sebastian couldn't deny a triumphant feeling that she might return his interest.

Gwendolyn was quick with a comeback. "I'd like to be a fly on the wall when you tell her!"

Her remark stung as surely as if she had slapped him across the cheek, but he couldn't let her know. "So you'd like to see me squirm?" He arched his eyebrow to indicate he was an accomplice to her joke.

"Not really," she admitted. "Although you've certainly seen me embarrassed enough."

"Perhaps." He stirred the dessert with his spoon. "I must confess, this is the best toothpaste pie I've ever eaten."

"My guess is that it's the only toothpaste pie you've ever eaten."

He decided that no reply was necessary. In the company of Gwendolyn Warner, the prospect of toothpaste pie seemed pleasing indeed.

❦

The phone was ringing as Gwendolyn slipped the key into the scratched brass doorknob of her apartment door.

"Coming!" she called to the telephone as though it would respond with more than an urgent summons. After shutting the door and setting down the leftover dessert, she ran the few steps necessary to reach the other side of the living room and picked up the receiver before the answering machine responded.

"You sound winded!" Her mother's familiar voice succeeded in conveying both chastisement and concern.

"Hi, Mom. I just got in from the photo shoot."

"So how did it go?"

Gwendolyn set her keys on the arm of the thirty-year-old couch, a gift from her parents' attic. She plopped on top of a giant sunflower set against a worn background of avocado green. "You don't want to know."

"Oh, don't I?"

"What you really want to know is how the dessert went over."

"You know me so well." Mom chuckled. "Of course I don't even have to ask about the photo shoot. I know it went swimmingly. They always do."

Gwendolyn bit her lower lip and shot a wordless prayer heavenward asking forgiveness for her lie of omission. If she revealed too many disasters, her mother might decide to arrive in Washington the next day and straighten things out in her capable way. "About the dessert. . ."

"What about it?"

"Well, let's just say your title of Best Cook Ever is still safe. Very safe."

Mom's throaty laugh filled the phone line. "Oh, I wouldn't be so sure. With a little practice, you'll soon surpass me."

"Oh, I already have. In the category of toothpaste pie."

"Toothpaste pie? Whatever do you mean?"

Gwendolyn grimaced as she remembered the teal green filling and tough crust. "That's how the pie could best be described."

"But toothpaste?"

"I added food coloring, and. . .let's just say it didn't turn out the nice shade of green I expected."

"And you got this recipe from a woman who runs a bed-and-breakfast? Remind me not to eat there!"

"No, Mom. The recipe was good. Cynthia Lyons' website recipe didn't tell me to add food coloring. I did that on my own. And, thinking back, I might have made a mistake or two on the piecrust ingredients. And besides, Cynthia recommended that I use a graham cracker crust. Foolish pride made me try something I didn't know how to make. So I can't lay any of the blame at Cynthia's feet—or on her keyboard." She chuckled at her own humor.

Mom laughed the same way she always did whenever she read the comics in the Sunday paper. Their shared amusement cheered Gwendolyn.

"So are you still going to stay with the class?"

"Sure. I have a lot to learn. Obviously."

When she hung up minutes later, Gwendolyn's initial excitement about the job returned. She thought about the next photo shoot. Her stomach danced the twist. The emotion took her aback. She told herself her reaction was only delight about keeping her job. Other possibilities were too unsettling to contemplate.

❧

The following night, Gwendolyn logged on to the cooking course. Apparently feeling more ambitious than usual, Cynthia had challenged everyone to submit a favorite cake recipe. She offered to hold an online chat for anyone interested in talking about recipes. Gwendolyn sent her grandmother's recipe for sour cream cake, then got the go-ahead from Cynthia to try it.

"Yay!" Gwendolyn typed on the screen. "I hope I can do Nanny proud."

"I'm sure you will," Cynthia answered.

"I don't always succeed in my attempts," Gwendolyn typed.

Someone named Subqueen chimed in. "Well, I can't talk. You should have seen the lemon bars I made the day I met my sister for the first time! Lemon soup bars are what they should've been called—and talk about tart!"

Gwendolyn grinned. Apparently Subqueen was just as bad a cook as she was! Suddenly she didn't feel so alone anymore.

Someone else typed, "I'll bet your lemon bars were better than what I recently ate. I called it 'toothpaste pie.'"

Toothpaste pie! Her heart felt as though it had fallen to her feet. She looked at the classmate's screen name: CreamyDream.

It has to be Sebastian. She felt tears threaten. *After he tried to make me feel better today, here he is, making fun of my pie, where he thinks I won't see.* She swallowed and stuck her lip out with the false pride of someone who was hurting. *So what? Who cares what he thinks?*

She grabbed a tissue and kept reading.

"In spite of the color, the wonderful woman who made the pie had a great sense of humor," CreamyDream wrote. "It truly was one of the best desserts I ever tasted."

"Because of the woman who made it, huh, CreamyDream?" LzzyGurl typed.

CreamyDream replied with an emoticon smiley face.

Gwendolyn couldn't believe her eyes. "Because of the wonderful woman who made it?" Sebastian was talking about her? Her tears disappeared just as quickly as they came.

Obviously Sebastian hadn't recognized her screen name. She thanked Cynthia and logged off, whistling a happy little tune.

As soon as he saw IPhotoU log off, a sick realization hit Sebastian in the stomach.

IPhotoU?

Could that be Gwendolyn's screen name? No. No. He hoped not. But somehow, in his heart, he knew IPhotoU was Gwendolyn.

He groaned. How could he have made fun of her pie—however good-naturedly? He must have come across as a crank and, as a result, left hurt feelings in his wake. Sebastian felt devastated. Gwendolyn was the only woman to crack his tough exterior in years. He had been focused on the family business for the past five years. His personal life had been on hold. Finally, a Christian woman he thought he might grow to love—and he had ruined everything.

Over the next couple of days, Gwendolyn found her thoughts returning again and again to her new job. Yet as soon as she thought about how she could make the next photo shoot a success, images of Sebastian popped into her head. They persisted no matter how she pushed them aside.

In the evening, she tried to concentrate on devotions, focusing on Romans 8:28: "And we know that in all things God works for the good of those who love him, who have been called according to his purpose."

As she contemplated the passage, the words *love* and *purpose* leapt out at her. She set her Bible, still open to the passage, on her lap.

Lord, why do I feel You are trying to show me something in granting me this job? Are You finally telling me to pursue modeling full-time, or do You have something else in mind? Why is it when I think of this job, my mind dwells on Sebastian? You know nothing like this has ever happened to me before. I need Your help, Lord, to sort out my feelings and to see how they fit into Your plan for my life.

Though the Lord didn't respond with a definitive answer, Gwendolyn noticed her spirit being strengthened. The feeling was like water being added to a half-empty cup. The pouring came from the Lord. The filling increased her confidence that the Lord would soon reveal His will.

Chapter 6

I can't believe Aunt Jeanette didn't realize I'd have to drive forever to get here," Gwendolyn grumbled as she finally pulled her compact car into the parking lot, miles from her apartment. But she couldn't waste such a marvelous Christmas gift—a year's membership to a new gym facility with aerobics classes, racquetball and tennis courts, two hot tubs, an Olympic-sized pool, and huge rooms filled with state-of-the-art exercise machines.

She was in a better mood once she'd dumped her coat and gym bag in a locker and headed for the treadmills. She had just entered instructions for a thirty-minute run at five miles per hour, hoping to work her way up to six within a few weeks. Soon she felt the presence of a fellow runner jump on the machine next to hers. Cutting her glance to the right, she nearly tripped when she recognized Sebastian Emerson.

He returned her stare. "Gwendolyn?"

"In the flesh," she puffed, regaining her stride.

"What are you doing here?" Sebastian managed to press buttons as he spoke.

"I could ask you the same thing. I've been a member for over two months, and I've never seen you here before."

"But we didn't know each other before." His machine increased its speed to 6.3 miles per hour. "I hardly recognized you. Uh, you don't mind if I run beside you, do you?"

"Why would I? You're a member here, too."

They ran alongside each other without speaking until Sebastian finally ventured her name again. "Gwendolyn?"

She snapped her head in his direction. "Yes?"

By this time, he was becoming a bit winded, although not enough to alarm her. "Uh, I have a question. Do you take online cooking classes?"

She nodded.

His lips twisted into a frown. "Cynthia's?"

"Yes."

He groaned. "You were on the chat the other night, weren't you?"

She nodded. "I was surprised to see you on the list. I would have pegged you as someone who knows how to cook all sorts of sweets."

"No. I work in the front office, not in the bakery itself. My grandfather was trained in Germany. He was a baker's apprentice before he came to America as a young man in 1948. I can hardly boil an egg, myself. So I thought I'd learn." He wiped his face off with a small white towel.

Feeling left behind, she set her treadmill a couple of notches higher. "Cynthia's place is a good start. I've learned a lot already."

"So have I. But now I wish I hadn't taken it."

"Why?"

"Because of what I said the other night. Look, if you hate me, I understand. I'm sorry," he said in between huffs of breath. "Especially about what I said about your pie."

She felt her heart soften. How could she not forgive Sebastian, when he was willing to come to her and confess his mistake? She decided to focus on the positive comment he had made about her. "And the wonderful woman who made it?"

His face became redder. Gwendolyn had a feeling the flush wasn't the result of increased exertion. "I'm sorry."

"So you didn't mean what you said?"

"About the pie?"

She heard herself breathing harder. Her throat became sore as air flowed over it through her open mouth. "No. About the wonderful woman."

"Of course I meant it."

So he meant it! "Why are you taking classes?" she asked, her huffing matching his.

"No special reason. I live alone, and I get tired of eating out of the microwave, I guess."

She laughed. "Me, too. In that case, why don't we try out some of the recipes together?"

His eyes brightened. "Really? You'd like that?"

"Yes."

"How about Thursday?"

"Sure. You can meet me at my apartment. I'll e-mail CreamyDream my address." She sent him a sly grin.

"Why don't we go out to dinner first, and then come back and try out our desserts?" he proposed.

"That means I have to get dressed up?"

"Not at all." Sebastian gave her a quick glance. "You're even more beautiful without makeup."

Unwilling to let him see that she was flattered by his remark, Gwendolyn focused on three big screen televisions just in front of them. Each was tuned to a network station. Closed captioning provided dialogue, since the sound was turned off in deference to the rock music blaring from the gym's radio.

"If only that were true," she denied.

He shook his head in rebuttal but changed the subject. "I thought you lived nearer to D.C."

Gwendolyn brightened. "I do. This membership was a Christmas gift from an aunt who has no concept of metro traffic. But it's worth the drive. Lucky you if you live nearby."

"I could almost walk it."

"Then you could probably run it." Gwendolyn was still huffing, but Sebastian was now gliding as though he were on a Sunday promenade.

"So could you. Although you don't need to work yourself to death exercising."

Remembering his earlier remarks about her slight figure, Gwendolyn bristled. "I like to keep in shape, that's all."

"Then you must be in shape enough to join me in a game of tennis."

Wary of another challenge after the pie fiasco, Gwendolyn searched for an excuse. "Isn't it a bit cold?"

"Not on the indoor courts."

"I didn't bring my racquet."

"They have loaners at the front desk." A triumphant grin indicated he enjoyed his checkmate. "And don't tell me you have to get home. It's still early."

Sebastian had anticipated her trump card and played it before she could. "All right. You win."

"Not yet. But I will."

"So you're not afraid you might lose the match to a girl?"

"Should I be?"

"Maybe. Although I might let you win. Wouldn't want to do permanent damage to your male ego." Grabbing the white hand towel she had thrown over the treadmill's display, Gwendolyn patted the sweat from her face as the treadmill slowed for a one-minute cooldown. "I'll get a racquet and meet you on the court."

"Ad one!" Sebastian called before he delivered a robust serve. He had won five games to her four. The game in progress had ended up in a deuce, so they were playing for two advantage points to determine the winner. If he earned the last point, Sebastian would win the set.

Gwendolyn had positioned herself well, just in front of the baseline in the backcourt. Despite her teasing, she discovered early in the set that she needed to fight for every point. Sebastian had proven his talent for placing the ball where Gwendolyn would have to expend the most effort to return it. This time was no exception; the ball barely cleared the net, well into the service area.

She dashed for it. Her forehand stroke sent the ball higher than her intent. Taking advantage of her mistake, Sebastian charged the net and leapt high in the air, returning the ball with a forceful overhand smash, a power stroke too difficult to return.

"Good game." She extended a congratulatory hand.

Sebastian grinned. "Thanks for letting me win." His hand made contact with hers, causing that spark again.

With regret, she broke the grasp. "You're welcome. Although I could have played a better game with my own racquet," she protested teasingly.

"Excuses, excuses." He shook his head in mock sympathy. "You'll have to bring your racquet next time."

Next time. Why did that sound so good?

A few moments later, she and Sebastian approached the desk so she could exchange the borrowed racquet for her membership card. Gwendolyn was taken aback by a query from the woman at the desk. "You're Gwendolyn Warner? The model?"

She nodded.

"I saw your ads for Lustre Lipstick." She studied Gwendolyn but protested as she returned her card. "You don't look like Gwendolyn Warner."

"No one does." Turning on her heel, Gwendolyn exited, an obviously amused Sebastian following beside her.

"Good retort. I think she was stunned."

"I stole that line from Cary Grant." She stopped in front of her car.

Sebastian's eyebrows shot up. "But I don't get it. I thought you were a photographer."

"I am. But I did some modeling awhile back." She kept her voice curt to discourage inquiry. Her modeling days were over. She hurried over to her car.

"This is your car?" His voice betrayed his surprise.

Gwendolyn opened the door of the ancient Ford Aspire. "I *aspire* to something better, but this is all I can *afford,*" she quipped.

A chuckle was her reward. "Don't tell me you plan to give Cary Grant credit for that line as well."

"No. I made it up all by myself. Although I won't promise someone else hasn't thought of it, too."

"You mean, such brilliance might be duplicated?" As she laughed, he changed the subject. "So when will you be back?"

"Tomorrow or the next day."

"That soon?" He appraised her figure in a way that reminded her of a personal trainer. "You really don't need all this exercise."

"I want to stay healthy."

"Yes, but I don't think you will add a day to your life. The Lord is in control."

"I agree."

His mouth dropped open in apparent shock. "You do?"

"Yes." She placed her hands on her hips. "Just because I used to be a model doesn't mean I don't read the Bible."

"Then I owe you an apology. I jumped to the wrong conclusion." He thought for a moment. "So tell me, how can a Christian woman pursue a career devoted to vanity?"

His unforeseen question left her with no quick response. Instead, she felt an unwelcome surge of anger. "It was nice playing tennis with you, Sebastian. See you another time." Without looking back, she jumped behind the wheel of the car. Ignoring his protests and apologies, she sped out of the lot.

Sebastian's question about reconciling her Christianity with her profession was provocative. Too provocative.

She wasn't sure she wanted the answer.

Chapter 7

The next Thursday, Sebastian knocked on Gwendolyn's apartment door. Even though she had left the gym in a huff, she hadn't called to cancel their plans to have dinner together.

"Coming!"

Good. So she hasn't conveniently forgotten. His heart thumped at the melodious sound of her voice, muffled though it was through the door. An instant later, Gwendolyn appeared before him. Her hair was styled in loose curls that framed her creamy complexion and dark eyes. She had chosen a soft coral sweater and black dress pants with low heels. As always, she looked beautiful.

"Come on in." She stepped to the side and eyed the dessert. "Can I take that?"

"Sure." He hesitated. "About the other night—"

"I'm sorry," they said in unison. At the realization, they chuckled.

"Look," Gwendolyn said, "I shouldn't have peeled out of the parking lot like that. I was being childish. You posed a perfectly reasonable question, one that I don't have an answer for. I was too embarrassed to face the facts, so I ran away. Can you forgive me?"

"I'm here, aren't I?" he responded only half-jokingly. "No one has all the answers. Least of all me. If I came across as challenging you, I'm sorry. As Mother told you, I have trouble relating to humans sometimes."

The cordial look on her face was his reward.

Gwendolyn lifted the transparent green plastic container to eye level and examined the contents. "What is this?"

"Noodle pudding."

"Oh, yes. I remember that recipe. I didn't have the nerve to try it."

"I tasted it," he admitted, following her into the small kitchen just off the side of the common area. "I think it's pretty good."

Gwendolyn set his container on the kitchen counter, then pointed to a closed cake container. "I made Nanny's sour cream cake."

"Mmm. Now that sounds good. I don't remember her posting that, though."

"She didn't. It's from my own grandmother. I've called her Nanny ever since I was two years old."

"Oh, a family heirloom."

"The recipe is, anyway. I'm not so sure I'd want to eat a family heirloom," she joked. "I think it turned out okay. It looks good, anyway." Gwendolyn lifted the cover to reveal a perfectly formed Bundt cake.

"Looks good. No frosting, huh?"

"Doesn't need any. Besides, that's what makes it so portable. Not a lot of sticky icing to contend with."

"True." He rubbed his chin. "Looks like something DairyBaked Delights could package."

Gwendolyn let out a musical laugh. "I could just see Nanny now, if she thought her cake might go national—"

"Maybe even international."

Only an instant flew by before she gasped. "So that's what your mom was about to tell me? You plan to go international?"

"That's a long way off. We've just come out of a corporate reorganization and are just recovering from that. Plus, we haven't even broken into the Midwest market in the U.S. yet. So don't say anything."

"Your secret is safe with me." Gwendolyn cut off a slice of cake and placed it on a blue and white dish. "Here," she said, handing him the dessert. "Life is short. Eat dessert first."

"But won't we spoil dinner?" Despite his protest, he took the dessert and sat down at the small kitchen table.

"Maybe. But I can't wait to try the noodle pudding."

"And we can have more dessert after we get back from dinner, huh?" he ventured.

"Of course!" She took the seat beside his.

He grinned. Gwendolyn's love for life was making her more and more attractive to him. He took a bite of cake. "Say, this is good!"

"Thanks. And so is your noodle pudding. So, have I made up for the toothpaste pie?"

"And then some! Oh, I almost forgot," Sebastian said. "Bernie got into an altercation with one of Hal's cats and got a scratch on his face. The vet said he'll need at least a week, maybe a little longer, to heal well enough to appear in a photo."

"Another week? But—"

"I know. We'll miss Thanksgiving."

"I don't suppose we could shoot it without him."

"Not a chance."

"So what will we do?"

He shrugged. "We'll just catch the latest trend. We'll run an old Thanksgiving ad and call it a classic."

"I'm sure people will enjoy that." Gwendolyn seemed to be trying to hide her disappointment.

"But I don't like that idea as well as running something fresh." Sebastian let out a resigned sigh. "Maybe everything's turned out for the best. Since the new photos will be geared to spring, we won't have to worry about plastic snow."

"After what happened last time, I'm not sure I ever want to work with plastic snow again, anyway."

"Maybe the beach."

"Whatever you say. You're the boss."

Sebastian cringed at the designation. Could it be possible that she couldn't see his real feelings for her?

Gwendolyn expected him to escort her to his car but, instead, he offered his arm so they could walk to the restaurant. She remembered the only steak restaurant within walking distance. "You must be taking me to the John Paul Jones."

He nodded. "Ever tried it?"

"Are you kidding?"

"Why would I be kidding?"

She avoided his gaze. "The truth is, I can't afford it."

"Perhaps DairyBaked Delights will change that."

Gwendolyn smiled to herself. *At least he's finally decided he likes me—as a photographer, anyway.*

They chatted as they waited for dinner to be served. Gwendolyn was pleased to discover it was easy to talk to Sebastian. Even more importantly, they agreed on the things that mattered in life.

She felt her heart softening toward him, glad he was proving to be somewhat human after all. Quite a far cry from the first day they met, when Gwendolyn was certain she could never like such a stuffed shirt.

The steak placed before Gwendolyn was so large, a portion of the fatted tip hung over the edge of the plate. Thankful for the concept of doggie bags, Gwendolyn was just about to reach for the steak sauce when Sebastian's hand touched hers.

"Care to say a blessing?"

"A blessing?" Gwendolyn was accustomed to muttering a few words of thanks for meals consumed in private, but never in public. She perused the room and noticed every table was full.

"We don't have to, if you're embarrassed."

A sense of shame engulfed her. "I guess I shouldn't be."

Sebastian flashed her a smile and took her hands in his. Their comforting warmth left her feeling secure. The prayer he spoke was barely above a whisper. "Our Father, we thank You for Your bountiful provision and the time we have this night to share in it. In Christ's name we pray, amen."

He gave her hands a squeeze before releasing them. Feeling self-conscious all the same, Gwendolyn darted her glance over the room. None of the other patrons had noticed their gesture. To her surprise, her relief was mingled with disappointment. Perhaps their willingness to pray before a meal could have inspired others. Biting into the savory meat, she resolved not to be shy about saying blessings in public in the future.

"Enjoying your steak?" Sebastian seemed pleased.

"Mmm!" was all Gwendolyn could muster with her mouth full. Nodding, she dug into the baked potato slathered in butter and sour cream.

"I must confess, I'm surprised to see you eating so well." He took a sip of coffee.

She swallowed, an unpleasant thought occurring to her. "Please don't tell me this is a test."

"Of course not. What would make you think that?"

"You know perfectly well." Putting down her fork, Gwendolyn realized the voice that exited her lips was more snippy than she had intended, yet she couldn't stop herself from continuing. "Sebastian, you have no idea what my life has really been like. You seem to think I'm too thin."

"Says who?"

"You did. The day I first met you in your mom's office, and you asked me if I ever touched a piece of chocolate."

"Oh." He stared at his empty plate.

"You just don't understand."

Mimicking her, he put down his own fork and leaned forward. "Then why don't you make me understand?" His voice held no dare.

"I'll try." She sighed. "All through school, I was teased and taunted for being a bean pole. Until ninth grade, I was taller than anybody else in class, including the boys. After they started catching up to me in height, I hoped and prayed the teasing would stop. But it didn't, because then they decided I was too skinny." Remembering those lonely times, she clutched her stomach. "I would go home every night and drink milk shakes until I was about sick, hoping to gain weight. But no amount of high-fat foods, or anything else, helped. I was known as 'the bean pole' until graduation day."

"Your classmates don't get extra credit for originality."

"They didn't have to. I got the point."

"I'm sure you did." Sebastian's mouth softened, and he shook his head slightly in a gesture of sympathy. "You're right. I had no idea. That must have been terrible for you."

"It was." She sighed.

"But you judge others. You just had to hire a model yourself."

"True. But I always try to judge favorably. And when I look for friendship, I don't go by looks."

"Maybe God was trying to teach you something through your high school experiences," he pointed out.

She nodded. "I learned a lot."

"Good. So you're not still doing crazy things like drinking yourself silly with milk shakes, are you?"

Gwendolyn shook her head. "No." She smiled in spite of herself and swept both arms over her body. "Can't you tell?"

"No. You're perfect. Perfect just the way you are."

"I wouldn't have known it. . ." The faraway look on Sebastian's face caused Gwendolyn to lay down her imaginary sword. "What's the matter, Sebastian? What are you thinking about?"

He shook his head as if returning from Oz. "Nothing."

"I know that's not so. I told you about my miserable school experience. The least you can do is tell me about yours."

"I wasn't the one who was miserable."

"Then you were the bully." Having seen the competitive and disagreeable side of Sebastian, this wasn't a stretch for Gwendolyn to imagine.

"Actually, I wasn't." He half-smiled. "I was thinking about Candy."

"Candy? Oh, you mean your petit fours."

"No. My sister, Candy."

"Sister?" Gwendolyn didn't bother to conceal her surprise. "I had no idea you had a sister."

Sebastian extracted a photo from his wallet. Faded with time, it was the portrait of a sprightly blond teenager. Gwendolyn speculated that Rhoda must have looked much like Candy when she was that age.

"So beautiful," Gwendolyn said with unabashed admiration.

"And so thin. At least in this picture." He studied it. "Too thin. And do you want to know why?" His eyes narrowed as his voice took on a hard edge. The misty eyes were gone. "Because of people like you. Skinny people. People who never knew what it was like to be fat."

"But, Sebastia—"

"Can you imagine what it must be like for a girl to be overweight, especially when her parents own a bakery?"

Gwendolyn stiffened as she thought back to her own experiences. "Yes, I can."

"I doubt it. Because even though people teased you, at least you're built like a model. Just think about what it's like for a plump girl to see people like you everywhere she turns. Women she's supposed to emulate, to admire, to adore. And she can't be like them. Because she isn't made that way."

"Look, I never said everyone should be like me."

"You don't have to. Just your photographs are enough." He let out a sigh. "I'm not saying you're to blame. You're in an industry that demands thinness."

Reaching for his hand, she managed to touch it before he pulled it away, clasping both hands around his cup of coffee.

She retreated and stirred her own coffee. "Obviously you're upset. And understandably so." Gwendolyn caught his gaze. "Tell me about her."

"Candy was one of those girls who was chubby as a child and even more plump as a young teenager. People would say, 'You have such a pretty face.'"

"How thoughtless."

He nodded. "Maybe they wouldn't have been so insensitive had they known how much worse their taunts made her feel." Sebastian folded his arms across his chest. "Anyway, she wanted to be popular, and finally, with Mom's help, she dieted until she was almost as thin as you. Unfortunately, it worked. She became popular."

"Why is that so unfortunate?"

"Because if her weight loss hadn't changed things, maybe she wouldn't have been so determined to keep the weight off. At first, the popularity and praise seemed great. She seemed more secure than ever. But eventually she became addicted to the praise and began to agonize over every fluctuation in weight. She worked harder than ever to stay reed thin. She kept on losing more and more weight. Before our eyes, she went from looking healthy to a waif. It was awful."

"It must have been," Gwendolyn agreed. "But it seems her weight loss was motivated by kids at school, not the media."

"Think again. I noticed Candy's open admiration for models in magazines and thin actresses in movies and on television."

Gwendolyn held her breath, bracing herself for whatever news he had to share.

"Over a period of two years, Candy finally lost so much weight that she had to be hospitalized. Thankfully, she recovered."

"I'm so glad to hear that."

He nodded. "She's fine now, but she doesn't want to have anything to do with the bakery."

He leaned closer. "I convinced Mom and Dad not to use human models in DairyBaked Delights' ads for many years. I don't want my family to do anything to contribute to any other young girl's loss of self-esteem—or health."

Gwendolyn felt her own eyes mist. "So that's why you were so opposed to me using a model."

"Yes. And now that I think about it, I'm still opposed to it." Without warning, Sebastian threw down his napkin. "Gwendolyn, this evening's over. I'm taking you home."

Chapter 8

Over the next few days, as much as she wanted to talk to Sebastian, Gwendolyn sensed that he needed to work out his issues for himself. She made no contact with him but concentrated on her work. Photographing reed-thin models, she couldn't help wondering if Sebastian was right about unrealistic media images.

The knowledge that Sebastian was angry with her was even worse. Almost a week had passed with no contact from him. His silence made her wonder if she was supposed to show up for the scheduled photo shoot for DairyBaked Delights. But each day that she didn't hear otherwise was another day she could hope the assignment was still hers.

Even if Sebastian never could be.

During evening devotions, she sought answers through prayer. She hoped the Lord would grant her peace or lead her to the right verse of scripture. But she found none. Perhaps her mind, or heart, was not yet open to His leading.

The day before the second photo shoot for DairyBaked Delights, Gwendolyn was thumbing through the day's mail when she spotted an envelope bearing the return address of Kline and Birmingham Studios, Inc., in New York City.

Hands trembling, Gwendolyn opened the envelope.

Dear Miss Warner:

After reviewing your portfolio, we believe your photographs and previous work experience show you have the potential to become a name in the photography profession.

I would like to meet with you at your earliest convenience so that we may discuss how your association with our studio may be of mutual benefit. Please contact me at your earliest convenience to schedule an interview.

Sincerely,
Irma Horton
Kline and Birmingham Fashion Photographers

Surprised, Gwendolyn slowly sat on the couch. She read and reread the letter, unable—or perhaps simply unwilling—to believe it. After Gwendolyn had memorized every word, she was still not ready to let go of the letter. She began to stare at the paper, a quality rag bond in a gentle yellow, its red letterhead suggesting youthful vigor and energy, much as she pictured a big, vibrant New York studio.

This was the letter she'd been wanting for years.

But instead of elation, Gwendolyn felt unable to move. Weeks ago, she would have taken the news as a sure sign that God was answering her prayers and telling her He wanted her to be a commercial photographer. Now, she wasn't so certain.

She remembered a verse she once memorized for Sunday school, Deuteronomy 13:4: *"It is the Lord your God you must follow, and him you must revere. Keep his commands and obey him; serve him and hold fast to him."*

She knew what she had to do. And tomorrow she would set her plan in motion.

Gwendolyn donned a pair of black wool trousers, an emerald green angora sweater, and a strand of pearls with matching earrings and bracelet. As she touched lipstick in Coolly Coral to her lower lip, the doorbell rang. "Coming!" She glanced one last time in her dresser mirror. Satisfied with her reflection, she darted to the door to discover her visitor was Sebastian.

"Why do you look so surprised? You did look through the peephole this time, didn't you?"

She gritted her teeth in embarrassment. "I guess not."

"You really must change your habits." His voice was teasing but soon became serious. "And I should change mine. I want to apologize to you for my behavior the other night. My sister's reaction to media images happened years ago. I shouldn't hold you personally responsible for something you had nothing to do with."

"No, I understand. What your family went through was traumatic, and I am part of a profession that perpetuates those images. I'm so sorry your sister was hurt. But I'm glad you told me about her. From now on, I'm going to be very careful about what assignments I accept, and what creative direction I take with those I do accept."

"I can't ask for any more than that." He smiled. "I come bearing gifts."

"I wondered why you were hiding your hands behind your back."

"I have a surprise." He presented Gwendolyn with a narrow white box about three feet in length. Gwendolyn guessed the box concealed a bouquet of flowers. "So, am I invited in?"

Playing along, she put the box up to her ear. "Well, since I don't hear a ticking sound. . ." Flashing him a smile, Gwendolyn stepped aside for him to enter.

"You thought I was still angry."

"Not only angry, but determined to fire me," she observed as she shut the door.

His lips pursed. "I'm sorry about that. Because I definitely want you to stay on as my company's photographer—if you'll still have us."

"Yes!"

"In that case, these are yours." He handed her the box.

"You mean, you were going to take this back if I said no?"

He grinned. "Well, Mom likes gifts, too."

"Oh, you!" she teased.

Opening the box, Gwendolyn inhaled with delight when she discovered a dozen long-stemmed red roses. "These are beautiful!" Selecting one that was on the verge of blooming, Gwendolyn stroked a silken petal with her fingertip.

With her unspoken permission, he followed her into the kitchen so she could put the flowers in a vase. "I admit, after our conversation the other night I was ready to see Mom and demand we buy out your contract. But thankfully, I decided to wait until I cooled off. Then after a lot of soul-searching, I came to my senses. And I'm thankful you were gracious enough to accept my apology." She felt his gaze upon her as he watched her arrange the flowers. "You're dressed mighty well for so early in the morning. I hope this doesn't mean you have a shoot scheduled with Sara Lee."

"Hardly," she answered. "As a matter of fact, I was on my way to see your mother."

His eyebrows furrowed. "You were?"

She nodded. "I was going to tell her that I didn't want to use a human model in the ads if you were opposed to one."

"Really? You were really going to tell her that?" His mouth dropped open as though he didn't believe it were possible. "What I think matters to you that much?"

"It always has." Gwendolyn tried not to cringe when she recalled Sebastian's opposition to her the first day they met. She leaned against the counter and folded her arms. "But more important to me is what the Lord thinks. And I have to tell you, I've been struggling with this career."

"Really? But you seem so committed."

"I am. At least, I thought I was." *Until I met you.*

"If it's such a struggle," he asked, "then why do you pursue it?"

"I sort of fell into it, and at the time it seemed as though it was the right thing to do. You see, my brother is a professional photographer."

"He is?"

"I was his assistant before I broke out on my own. I didn't make a big deal about being related to him for obvious reasons."

"So creative talent runs in your family."

"I like to think so." She nodded. "But your comments about models hit home with me in more ways than one. Remember, I used to be a model myself. Nothing big, mind you."

He looked her over from head to toe, but his admiring glance made her feel loved. "So I haven't seen you in any of the big magazines? I'm sure if I had, I'd remember."

She chuckled. "Thanks, but I think it was God's plan for me not to be a huge success. While he was learning his craft, my brother used me as his subject many times. Of course, he wanted exposure for his pictures, so my photos eventually wound up with local people who thought I'd make a good model. Some of them had the power to follow through on their instincts. I've done lots of runway shows for retailers around here."

"I can't imagine you looking snooty and prancing around."

"Oh, yeah?" Lifting her nose and straightening her lips, Gwendolyn narrowed her eyes just so. She could see from the expression on Sebastian's face that she had succeeded. Slouching ever so slightly as she inserted a hand in each front trouser pocket, Gwendolyn strode around the small living room.

"Bravo!" Sebastian clapped. "But didn't you list a lot of bridal shows? I think I'd be put off if I were your groom." His mouth twisted into a wry grin.

Gwendolyn affected a fake Eastern European accent. "What do you mean by that? Do you not consider it an honor for me to step on you with my spike heel?" Though her shoes boasted modest stacked heels, Gwendolyn twisted a heel into the carpet.

Sebastian crossed his arms over his face in mock surrender. "Scary!"

Giggling, Gwendolyn placed her hands on her hips. "I'll show you something a lot less scary. Here's my 'happy bride' look." She affected a pleasant expression that fell just short of giddy. Pretending to wear a full-length skirt, she cavorted around the room, her manner and style giving her the effect of one floating upon a cloud.

"I have to give you credit. Modeling seems to require a degree of acting. I can't believe you never made the big time."

She paused, thinking back on her career. "I could have made a decent living. I think that's one reason why my brother, Bruce, was so mad at me for abandoning modeling for photography. I went from being his asset to becoming a rival. He thought I was wasting money on getting a photography degree when I could have dropped out of high school to be a model."

"He didn't really advocate that, did he?"

"No," she admitted. "College was another matter. Tuition, you know."

"I know. But schooling is never a waste, at least in my book." He chuckled at his pun.

"Cute," she said with a grin.

"So you want to be a famous fashion photographer?"

"I once thought I did. I even thought that since I hadn't made any real effort to be a model at first, perhaps that was God's plan for my life. But now I'm not so sure."

"I remember when the dessert flopped. You didn't try to worm your way out of our agreement. You were ready to accept the consequences." He looked into her eyes. "Maybe you were having doubts?"

She shook her head. "Not then. I wanted that job desperately. Quitting was the last thing I wanted to do. But if you had held me to our agreement, I would have left that day. Keeping my word is more important to me than any job."

" 'Charm is deceptive, and beauty is fleeting; but a woman who fears the Lord is to be praised,'" he said.

"Oh, the Proverbs 31 woman." Gwendolyn waved her hand dismissively. "If you expect me to live up to her, I'm afraid you're in for a rude awakening." She chuckled. "Although I'm glad to see you're reading your Bible."

"Yes, more so than usual," he admitted.

"Me, too." Her voice took on a faraway quality. "Searching for answers."

"Did you find yours?"

"I think so."

"Good. I think I found mine, too." Stepping toward her, he took her hands in his. "Gwendolyn, I've come to realize that just because Candy couldn't face her problems in a healthy way doesn't mean everyone else is like her."

"I know. But I've been contemplating what you said, and I feel the same way you do. I wouldn't want what I do for a living to contribute to anyone else's problems."

"That's just it. I see now that people make decisions about their lives every day. Maybe seeing someone thin will inspire them. Or make them depressed." When he let out a sigh, she knew he was thinking about his sister.

"What you told me about your sister made me think a lot. As I told you before, I really don't want to be responsible for something like that."

"I know you don't." Sebastian paused as though he were contemplating what to say next. He looked her in the eyes. "You live a healthy lifestyle, right?"

"I try."

"You don't crash diet or go on binges or do other unhealthy things to stay thin, do you? Or drink milk shakes just to put on a pound or two?"

She shook her head.

He chuckled. "As long as you're being responsible about the way you eat and exercise, you can't be expected to shoulder the blame for people's reactions to your image, whether you're in front of or behind the camera. Just as I have no control over whether someone has an allergic reaction to chocolate." He gave her hands a light squeeze. "Honor God by doing your best and then leave the outcome in His hands."

"What about using beauty to sell products? That seemed to be a concern of yours."

"Who was I kidding? People want to see beautiful models." Sebastian caught her gaze and held it. "And if the truth be known, I want to see a beautiful model—and photographer—every day. Her name is Gwendolyn Warner."

Gwendolyn became conscious of her heartbeat. She didn't want to spoil the moment, but she had to allay her fears. "Sebastian, I have to know. Do you really want to see Gwendolyn the famous photographer, or Gwendolyn the local portrait photographer?"

He didn't hesitate to answer. "I've spent a lot of time thinking about that very question since I last saw you. Do you want the truth?"

Feeling scared, she whispered, "Yes."

"I'd like to see Gwendolyn as a happy and fulfilled woman, regardless of the career she chooses."

She breathed a sigh. Sebastian's words had set her free. Free to be the woman she wanted to be.

"Sebastian, there's something I have to tell you." Stepping back, she let go of his hands.

"Oh?"

"I've been asked to interview with a studio in New York City. I think the meeting is just a formality. I expect them to offer me a contract."

He hesitated for only a split second. "Then go. Make your dreams come true."

"Do you really mean that?"

"Yes, I do." He clasped her hands once more. "But will you come back to me?"

"That's just it, Sebastian. I no longer want to go. I don't want to leave."

"Really?" His gaze grew soft. "Because of me?"

Did she dare admit the truth? She looked into his eyes and decided that she could take the risk. "Yes. Because of you."

"In that case, will you be more than my photographer? More than my friend?"

"Yes! If that's what you want."

"That's what I wanted from the moment I saw you." Wrapping his arms around her waist and shoulders, Sebastian pulled her closer to him.

Feeling the warmth of his lips as they drew closer, Gwendolyn lost herself in his kisses—the first of many to come.

Sour Cream Pound Cake

1 cup butter
½ cup lard or vegetable oil
3 cups sugar
1 cup sour cream
6 eggs
3 cups flour
½ teaspoon salt
½ teaspoon baking powder
3 teaspoons vanilla extract
2 teaspoons lemon juice

Cream butter and oil. Add sugar and sour cream to mixture and beat until well mixed. Add eggs one at a time, beating well after each egg. Sift flour, salt, and baking powder in large bowl and add to mixture. Add vanilla and lemon juice, mixing well. Pour into greased, floured Bundt pan. Be sure to use a traditional Bundt pan, because the recipe doesn't work as well with tube or loaf pans. Put in cold oven, baking at 300 degrees for 1 hour and 30 minutes.

APPLE ANNIE

by Joyce Livingston

Dedication

Several years ago as a surprise for Mother's Day, my youngest son, Luke, took his wife Tammie and me (his three children and his father, too) to Apple Valley Farm in Northeast Kansas, where we all enjoyed a marvelous dinner in the Apple Valley Farm Restaurant and a melodrama in the Apple Valley Farm Barn. This yearly trip to Apple Valley Farm has become a Mother's Day tradition, one Tammie and I look forward to every year, and Luke never disappoints us.

Although Apple Annie's story is set in Idaho, many of the things about the restaurant and the barn have been inspired by Kansas's own Apple Valley Farm. With thankfulness and a mother's love, I dedicate this story to Luke.

I'd also like to thank Millie Miller of Edmund, Oklahoma, for giving me the recipe for the Sinfully Decadent Awesome Caramel Apple Pie, the specialty of Apple Annie's Restaurant.

Chapter 1

A nnie, Brad's here." The waitress hurried to the window and pulled back the red-and-white-checkered curtain. Her eyes sparkled as the red minivan pulled across the parking lot and came to a stop.

Annie lifted a handful of menus from the big iron kettle and shuffled them in her hands. "That man! I don't know why he refuses to park in one of the handicapped stalls."

"Because it's for handicapped people! I doubt Brad ever thinks of himself as handicapped, or even physically challenged. Isn't that what they call it these days?" the waitress asked. The two women observed the electric lift lowering on the clean van. "I've never seen a man with two legs any happier than Brad. He makes everyone around him feel good. Wish I had his attitude. I'm sure my customers would appreciate it!"

The phone rang, and she scurried to answer it, but Annie lingered at the window. Brad Reed had shown up at Apple Valley Farm the first night of their new season. Several nights a week since then he had returned and always asked for the same table—the table for two, crowded into the far back corner next to the old woodstove. And he always topped off his meal with a wedge of what he called "sinfully decadent" Awesome Caramel Apple Pie. Even the waitresses had taken to calling the famous pie "sinfully decadent" when they described it to their customers.

Annie smiled. Sinfully decadent. No doubt the apple pie was the only sinfully decadent thing going on in Brad's life. Not with the way he was always talking about God. She enjoyed visiting with the man, but she had to admit he made her feel a pang of guilt sometimes at her own lackadaisical attitude toward God. The guy was too good to be true. Surely something dark and dank lay beneath that winning smile. One would think, from his constant pleasant demeanor, that he hadn't a care in the world.

From the window she watched him struggle to move from the seat into the electric wheelchair, roll onto the steel platform, and lower himself to the ground. Then he pushed the button to return the lift to its place before sliding the door closed. It was amazing how much effort it required for him to get out of his vehicle. With all the trouble it took, it seemed as if he would forget it and stay at home, parked in front of the TV with the remote in his hand. Feeling like a voyeur, she let

277

the curtain drop, lest he see her. The last thing she'd want to do was embarrass him.

As he maneuvered the chair up the ramp, she pushed open the door with her famous Apple Annie smile, the one her customers had come to expect. "You made it. I was afraid with the forecast of heavy rain, you might decide to stay home tonight."

A broad smile lit up the man's face. "A little rain stop Brad Reed? Never. I thought you knew me better than that. Besides, I'd never make it through the weekend without—"

She lifted her hand and stopped him. "I know. Our sinfully decadent Awesome Caramel Apple Pie. You're incorrigible!" She stepped back out of the way while three waitresses left their stations to crowd around their favorite customer, oohing and ahhing over him as if he were a celebrity. *That man is a magnet.* She watched them fuss over him, taking turns arguing about who would serve him.

"As much as I love all this attention, I think you girls better get back to work. You know what a slave driver Apple Annie is." His tone was teasing, and even his eyes seemed to be laughing. "But you're great for my ego. Let's do it again sometime—when Apple Annie isn't watching!" The girls giggled and returned to their stations, glancing over their shoulders and smiling at him.

He shrugged his broad shoulders and lifted his brow at Annie. "Sorry. Some women just can't leave a handsome, eloquent, attractive man like me alone."

The girls tittered and giggled to one another from their places, filling glasses, taking orders, and conversing with the customers already seated at their tables.

"Good thing you told my crew to get back to work. I was about to fire the whole bunch of them." Annie smiled and handed him a leather-covered menu. "You're a terrible distraction, you know." She gathered her long calico skirt about her and led him toward his usual table.

"Can I help it? It's sheer animal magnetism. If God created me irresistible, who am I to fight it?" He followed close behind her, the wheelchair's motor making a gentle hum.

"Yeah? You're blaming God? I'd say some men are conceited on their own. And whoever told you that you were handsome and irresistible?" She didn't turn to look at him, but she knew he was smiling.

"Only every waitress who works for you!" His hearty laugh was infectious.

She glanced over her shoulder at him. "You men are all alike!" The man was a charmer, she had to admit. No wonder he had all the Apple Valley women clamoring after him.

"If I'm such a distraction, maybe you'd better sit down and have dinner with me and keep me out of trouble." She pulled away a chair, and he rolled past her into the space. "They have great food here."

She gave him a nudge then bent and rested her hand on his shoulder. "You should know. I think at one time or another this summer you've tried everything on the menu."

He gave her a sad puppy-dog look that made her laugh. "On the menu maybe, but not your magnificent buffet. I hate to admit it, but in this rolling chariot of mine I have trouble manipulating the food onto the plates and the plates onto the tray and the tray onto my lap and the—"

She tossed her head and held up both her hands. "I get the message! Loud and clear! You need a little help, and you think I'm the one for the job. Right?"

"Exactly. Will you have dinner with me, Apple Annie?" Brad winked then reached out and took hold of her hands. He stroked them gently with his thumbs as he gazed up at her.

She noticed that his eyes were the same color as the thick chocolate fudge sauce they served on the dessert bar. She could never resist that sauce, even though she knew she'd suffer the consequences later for indulging, and her bathroom scales would be only too willing to remind her.

He had never touched her before, other than an occasional handshake, and for some reason it unnerved her. She wanted to back away; yet she enjoyed the strong, masculine feel of his fingers closing over hers.

"Dinner? Here? Now?" she asked. She felt awkward.

Her first impulse was to say no. Most days she didn't take time to eat until after the dinner crowd had gone. But it was still early, and most of them hadn't even arrived yet. With only a piece of dried toast and a hurried glass of iced tea for lunch, she had to admit she was a bit hungry.

"Please?"

"Only if you'll let me help you with the buffet. We're trying out a new potato dish tonight, and I'd like your opinion." She pulled her hands from his grasp and adjusted the red satin bow that held her dark, thick ponytail. Why did she say yes? Normally she shied away from eating with patrons, afraid of showing partiality.

"Deal." He stuck out a hand. "Let's shake on it before you change your mind."

She put her hand timidly in his and once again felt the strong, warm touch of his fingers as they squeezed her hand. Then he pulled the lever under his right hand, and the chair backed slowly away from the table. "Lead the way. I'm famished."

Annie crossed the restaurant to the buffet line and lifted a green tray from the tall stack. "What kind of salad would you like?"

Brad rubbed his chin and surveyed the enticing array of salads. "I've never tried the red cabbage. Is it good?"

She laughed and spooned a small bowl full and placed it on his tray. "You tell me, after you've tasted it."

"Look—I've got an idea," he said, his gaze never leaving her delicate face. "Why don't you choose the rest of the meal for me? I'm not a picky eater—but I'm sure you know that, as many times as you've seen me making a pig of myself in your restaurant. I'll take potluck—whatever you choose, except for those." He leaned forward and pointed toward a fancy white dish containing bright green Brussels sprouts. "If former President George Bush can refuse to eat those awful things, so can I!"

She rolled her eyes. "And you said you weren't picky."

"I'm actually more picky about my women than I am my food," he said with a lifted brow and a sideways grin.

"Hmph. What women? I've never seen you with a woman."

He turned up his mouth, his brown eyes riveted on hers. "Umm. You're right. At this time of year most of the good-looking women who chase me are at the beach concentrating on their suntans. And I have an awful time maneuvering this chair of mine in the sand."

A giggle slipped out before she could stop it. "Good excuse."

"Maybe I'd better find me a woman who doesn't want to fry herself and get skin cancer. Want to volunteer?"

She raised her brows and looked at him. "Yes, but only for tonight." Then she laughed, something she seldom did now with the demands of running a restaurant, the Big Barn Melodrama Theater, and the orchards. With all these responsibilities, her life had become much too serious and busy.

"Only for tonight?" He inched the chair forward a bit. "I hate one-night stands."

"I thought you said women found you irresistible!"

He threw up his hands. "Maybe I stretched the figures a bit!"

"Well, you've just met a one-nighter." She selected a colorful bowl of fruit salad and placed it on his tray. "Tomorrow you'll have to find a replacement. I don't have time to play the dating game with you."

"Then, sweet lady," he said with exaggerated emotion as his fingertips touched her arm, "we have but one glorious night together. Let us make the most of it."

She gave his hand a swift rap and an accusing grin. "Unquote! Our melodrama actors use that line every night in our theater. You're plagiarizing!"

"Can't blame a guy for trying!" He shrugged then watched her select a thick, juicy slice of roast beef, adding a large helping of mashed potatoes and brown gravy and a beautifully browned cloverleaf roll.

When she was finished filling his tray, she followed him to the table. Once his chair was in place, he took the tray from her and removed each item. He kept his gaze on her as she walked back to the buffet line, filled her own tray, and returned.

She set their trays on a nearby table. "I'll get the coffeepot."

Brad laid his hand on her wrist. "No, let me get it. You work too hard. You deserve to be waited on once in awhile."

She wanted to refuse his offer, but she feared she might offend him if she reminded him how much easier it would be for her to do it. So she sat down, leaned back in her chair, and spread her napkin across her lap. "I take decaf."

"You got it!"

Annie watched Brad weave his chair in and out among the tables until he reached the drink station. How would he ever carry that pot back to the table? She jumped to her feet and rushed toward him, not wanting him to be embarrassed by an impending catastrophe. But before Annie could get to him he reached up and pulled a towel from a shelf, wrapped it around the hot stainless steel pot, and locked the coffeepot securely between his thighs.

He gave her a sheepish grin, turned the chair around, and rolled toward her. She stood there gaping. "You didn't think I could do it?"

"I—wasn't sure." Now she was the one who was embarrassed, and she didn't like the feeling.

He lifted an arm, pushed up the sleeve of his polo shirt, and flexed his biceps. Using that exaggerated deep voice again, he said, "Woman. Me, Tarzan. You, Jane. And don't you forget it!"

Annie relaxed and enjoyed the evening more than she had in a long time. Brad had become like a dear old friend. She had missed male companionship. She hadn't had much of it with boyfriends, but before his illness she'd had her dad, the only real hero in her life.

"Mind if I pray and thank God for our food?" Brad broke in as she reached for her fork.

His question surprised her. Not that she'd been on that many dinner dates, if that's what her college dates to pizza hangouts could be called; but none of her escorts had ever asked to pray before the meal. She glanced around to see if others were watching and, finding them occupied with their own conversations, lowered her fork. "Sure—if you want to."

He reached across the table and took her hands. To her astonishment, instead of bowing his head, he lifted his eyes heavenward. "Good evening, God. It's me, Brad, and Annie is here with me. We're sharing a great meal. We've come into Your presence to thank You—for this food and the hands that prepared it, for the air we breathe, and the life and health we enjoy every day. We may not know how or why things happen the way they do sometimes, but one thing we know. You are in control. Bless this food now and forgive us for neglecting to praise and thank You for all You do for us."

He paused. "Do you mind if I pray for your dad? I've heard he's having quite a struggle with Alzheimer's."

She met his gaze, and the warmth and concern she saw there made her heart tighten with pent-up emotion. She could only nod. His hands tightened around hers, and for a moment she thought she was going to cry. This man was genuinely concerned about her dad.

"And, God, we bring Annie's father to You, asking that somehow You will touch him and heal his mind. And be with Annie and her family as they often find themselves locked out of his memory, and give them comfort as they recall better times. Amen."

She bit her lips and pressed her eyelids shut against the tears that threatened to erupt.

Apparently Brad noticed. "Want to hear the story about the chicken who got hit by a car as he crossed the road?" He unfolded his napkin and grinned.

She wrinkled her nose. Their conversation had shifted abruptly from one of sadness to the ridiculous. "Sounds kind of gruesome."

"Not the way I tell it." He spread the napkin across his lap and smoothed it out with his hands.

She dabbed at her mouth with her own napkin then returned it to her lap, her eyelids still pressing back unshed tears. She was eager to listen to whatever foolish tale he would tell to take her mind off her father's illness. "Okay, I'm game. Tell me about the chicken who got hit crossing the road."

"Well, a man was driving down the road. But before he could stop his car, a chicken ran out in front of him, and he hit it." He wadded up his napkin and let it drop onto the table. "The guy rushed out of his car, scooped up the chicken, and took it to a nearby veterinarian. The doc took one look at the poor chicken and confessed, 'I'm not sure I can do anything for him, but I'll try.'"

Brad folded the napkin in half then rolled the two opposite sides toward the center and held it up for her to see.

" 'This look like the chicken you hit?' The man shook his head. 'I'm afraid not.'"

He folded the napkin in half again, bringing the four rolled ends up together in his hands. He stuck an index finger into the end of each roll and pulled out the loose end, creating four spiraled-out segments.

"The veterinarian held the chicken up and again asked the man, 'Does this look like the chicken before you ran over it?' Again the man shook his head."

With a vigorous laugh Brad held onto the ends of two of the spiraled rolls and let the other two ends drop free. 'Doc!' the man cried out. 'That's the chicken! You fixed him as good as new!'"

Annie's mouth dropped open, and she clapped her hands. "That looks exactly like a chicken, but without the head! How did you do that?"

"My own personal magic!" Brad grinned with satisfaction as she laughed at his ridiculous joke. "I'm full of chicken jokes. Want to hear another one?"

"I'm tempted." She giggled and pointed to their full plates. "But I think we'd better eat first, before everything gets cold. Try those potatoes and let me know what you think."

He scooped up a big helping of the cheesy potatoes and savored them slowly, then waved his fork at her approvingly. "Mmm, excellent. With only one leg I'm certainly no Galloping Gourmet, but I say they definitely should stay on your menu."

She nodded. She was glad he liked them, but his comment about his leg took her aback for a moment. "Then they'll stay."

Annie enjoyed every minute of the meal and the light, easy conversation. Most nights she ate alone, after everyone else had finished for the day. Before she knew it she'd cleaned her plate, leaving only an olive and a small piece of bread. It had been months since she'd eaten such a hearty meal. She finished the last of her coffee, folded her napkin, and placed it on the table.

Brad frowned. "You don't have to go yet, do you?"

She pushed back her chair and stood to her feet. "Yes, but maybe we—"

"Maybe we could have our sinfully decadent Awesome Caramel Apple Pie, and then you could go?" He gave her a hopeful look and a wistful smile.

"Sorry, but I have to go now." She hated to leave the man and his wonderful sense of humor. "I was going to say maybe another time, but right now I've got to seat the dinner crowd. I'm afraid you'll have to eat your pie alone."

For only a moment his face lost its resident smile. "I hate eating alone. That's why I come here as often as I do. I may sit at a table for one, but this place is always filled with happy people. It rubs off on me, and I hardly notice only one person is sitting at my table—me."

She detected a certain sadness in his eyes, one she'd never noticed before. "Well, if you're not in a hurry to get home and you don't mind eating late"—she saw his face brighten—"I guess I could have that pie with you after the evening performance in our theater. But it'll be after ten o'clock," she cautioned, glancing at her watch.

He swung his arm across his chest with a flourish and bowed as low as one could from a wheelchair. "Ma'am, I'd be proud and honored to join you in a humble piece of pie—" He stopped and scratched his head. "Or was that a piece of humble pie? Hmm, I never can remember."

She gave him a playful swat as a large group of patrons entered, their eyes scanning the restaurant for its well-known hostess. "Brad, I have to go. I guess since you're going to have pie with me later you'll be staying for the melodrama in the barn. I'll see you there."

"Sure, I'll be there. Wouldn't miss it. And, by the way, my mother raised me to be a gentleman, and gentlemen always rise when a lady leaves the table," he told her with a warm smile. "I want you to know I may be sitting on the outside, but I'm standing on the inside."

She smiled, too. "You never have to worry about standing up for me. I've always known you were a gentleman. And you're wonderful company. No wonder all those women chase after you. See you later." And she hurried off to greet her customers.

Brad watched as she gathered her skirts about her and made her way through the crowded restaurant. He wondered how beautiful, vibrant Annie Johnson had managed to stay single. At least, she wasn't wearing a wedding ring, and she'd never mentioned a husband during their dinner conversation. Or even a boyfriend. Though he'd known her only a few months, by his standards she was pure gold. If he ever found a woman like Annie, he'd— His glance fell to his empty trouser leg. What woman would want a one-legged, handicapped man?

Chapter 2

"Hey, Lady, want a ride?"

Startled, Annie spun around. Most of her dinner patrons had headed for the barn to attend the evening's performance of the latest melodrama. She hadn't expected anyone to be waiting when she opened the door.

"I didn't mean to frighten you," Brad explained as he rolled toward her. "I'm sure you've been on your feet all day, and I thought I'd give you a lift up to the barn."

She stared at the man. "Lift? How? There's only a path."

He shot back a smile as he patted his lap, his eyes twinkling. "Right here."

"There? You're kidding, aren't you?" One corner of her mouth turned upward in a slight smile. Thinking back, she couldn't remember ever sitting on a man's lap, other than her father's or her uncle's.

He held out a hand. "No, I'm not kidding. Climb on. I'm a safe driver. I promise not to exceed the speed limit."

Annie watched as he skillfully maneuvered the chair, coming to a stop beside her, facing the barn. Surely he wasn't serious.

"You're afraid I'll drop you or we'll run into a tree, aren't you? Don't worry—I've been driving this little jewel for years." He patted his lap again. "Come on. I'll bet none of your other boyfriends offered you a ride in a wheelchair. This could be the experience of a lifetime. You wouldn't want to miss it, would you? This baby will do every bit of three miles per hour."

She shifted her purse from one hand to the other. He was right. She was afraid. The path to the barn was up a gentle hill most of the way. What if—

"Annie, you'll be safe." His tone was reassuring. "I promise. It'll be fun."

She accepted his hand but kept her feet on the ground. "Have you ever—"

"Carried someone like this? On my lap?"

She nodded.

"Sure I have. My nephews. My nieces." He tugged on her hand, but she stood fast.

She tilted her head and raised a brow. "How old were they?"

"Well, the oldest niece was seven, but the oldest nephew was—" He paused.

"Brad! How old was your nephew? And be honest," she cautioned. "I want the truth."

"Ah—nine?"

She withdrew her hand and slapped at his arm playfully. "Nine? You've only carried a nine-year-old child on that chair, and you expect to carry me? Forget it."

Brad reached for her hand again and squeezed it tenderly. "Did I mention he was a very big nine year old?"

"You're incorrigible!"

"But lovable, right?" His brown eyes gleamed.

She ignored his question. But, yes, no doubt about it, he was lovable, in a big brotherly sort of way. "You promise you won't drop me?"

"Try me."

She slipped carefully onto his lap, his one arm circling her tiny waist as he pulled her to him. He smelled nice, like shampoo and after-shave, and she found herself melting against him as her arms wound around his thick neck. To her surprise she felt safe.

"Put your feet on the empty footrest," he told her.

"Are you sure it won't crowd you?"

He snickered. "Annie, I need only one footrest—remember?"

She blushed.

"Ready?" His face was so close to hers that their cheeks nearly touched.

She closed her eyes and leaned into him. "Ready, I think. Just be careful, okay?"

Brad adjusted his grip about Annie's waist as his right hand moved to press the lever. The chair moved forward slowly. Annie, the woman he'd fallen helplessly in love with the first night he'd visited Apple Valley Farm, was in his lap, her arms hugging his neck. How many times had he dreamed of being this close to her? Of holding her? Kissing her? The tendrils of her lovely dark hair touched his cheek. If only she were his. If only—

"Brad? Did you hear me?"

"Ah—sure, Annie. I'd never let anything happen to you. I promise."

He maneuvered the chair up the packed dirt trail to the Big Barn Theater, part of the Apple Valley complex. The complex included not only the restaurant and the theater but also a large orchard and the family home as well.

"Annie," he asked, feeling the awkwardness of their silence as they rolled along, "how long has your family owned Apple Valley Farm?"

"Forever. My great-great-great-grandfather homesteaded this ground and started the orchards, but it was my grandfather who started the restaurant and my father who converted the big barn into a theater. Why do you ask?"

He slowed and pushed the lever slightly to the right to miss a rock in the trail before answering. "Just curious. Now you're the sixth generation, and the mantle is being passed on to you? Now that your father is sick?"

She loosened her hold about his neck. He hoped it was because she was feeling more secure and not because she wanted to move away from him. "Yes, he signed the property over to my older sister, Valerie, and me when he was diagnosed with Alzheimer's. He didn't want any problems after he—"

She paused. He know it was difficult for her to think of her father in those terms, and he almost wished he hadn't asked.

"Sister? I didn't know you had a sister. I've never seen her around the restaurant, have I?"

She shook her head. "She's actually my half-sister, by my dad's first wife. We've never been close. I rarely see her."

Brad stopped at the bottom of the ramp near the theater to let Annie off his lap. Just then the lead actor in the melodrama, the villain, came running toward her.

"What's wrong?" Annie asked.

Between breaths the man told her the pianist had phoned, his car had broken down, and he couldn't make the evening performance. "We have a packed house. Shall I tell our customers we'll give them a rain check? I don't know what else to do."

Annie stared at the man. "I–I guess we'll have to. We have no one else to take his place."

"Is the music score on the piano?" Brad asked.

"Yeah, I saw it there a few minutes ago when I went to check on him, before his call came in." The man was wringing his hands. "Why?"

Brad rolled up next to Annie and tugged on her hand. "I'll play if you want me to. I've seen the play at least ten times. I think I can follow it, if you don't mind a few mistakes and you let the audience know I'm only filling in."

Her eyes widened. "Really, Brad? You'd do this? I didn't even know you played."

"I play mostly by ear, but I can read music, too. I'm better at playing country gospel than anything, but I'm sure I can handle the melodrama music."

Annie turned to the man. "Make sure the chair is pulled away from the piano. Brad's going to be our guest pianist tonight."

When it was time for the preshow, Brad skipped the songs the regular pianist played and performed a couple of his favorite ragtime tunes, much to the delight of the audience. Annie took center stage, welcomed each person who had come, and introduced Brad.

He nodded, turned back to the piano with a reassuring grin toward Annie and played the introduction to the first act. The footlights dimmed, and the play began. In the semidarkness, out of the corner of his eye, he saw Annie slip past him and drop into a chair only a few feet away. He grinned to himself. *I'd do anything for Annie, even if it means embarrassing myself in front of a crowd.*

Annie watched Brad's fingers move over the keys. He was handling the music score as capably as the regular pianist. How kind it was of him to volunteer. She and the cast were grateful, as was the audience of young and old alike. She laughed as they hissed and booed the villain and cheered the hero and heroine. Brad's fingers never missed a beat, and by the look on his face, she was sure he was enjoying himself.

At the conclusion of the performance, each actor and actress received well-deserved accolades, but Brad alone got a standing ovation. Annie watched with pride as members of the audience crowded around him to express their appreciation. Without him they would have had no evening performance at Apple Valley Farm.

He waited by the ticket counter until Annie was ready to go back down the path to the restaurant. He beamed as she climbed onto his lap without an invitation.

"Oh, Brad, you were wonderful." She wrapped her arms about his neck and held on tight. "How can I ever thank you?"

A coy smile tilted the corners of his mouth. "Give me time. I'll find a way."

She chattered on, scarcely hearing his answer. He had turned a possible catastrophe and box office loss into a huge success, and she was grateful. Caught up in describing his performance at the piano, she didn't notice the way Brad hung on her every word and drew her closer about the waist.

"You know," she said with a confident smile, "I could get used to this—riding with you. It's kind of fun, and it sure beats walking." Immediately she wished she could withdraw her words. She was sure that staying in the wheelchair, with no other option, was anything but fun for Brad. "I'm so sorry," she said sincerely. "I only meant—"

He pulled back on the lever, and the chair came to a sudden halt, forcing Annie to hold tightly to Brad. "Annie, believe me—you have nothing to be sorry about. I'm sure you think your words upset me. They didn't. I know your heart's right."

"I have a habit of speaking before I think," she mumbled.

Brad smiled and lifted his hand. "Forget it, Annie. I already have." With a little pressure on the lever, the chair moved forward again. "I tried crutches a couple of times, but after a few falls I decided I felt more secure in this wheelchair. Besides, with my hands full, I had no way to carry my briefcase, and a good lawyer can't go anywhere without his briefcase. He needs it to make him look official, even if it's empty!"

She grinned at him, thinking again of the evening's performance. "You're something else, Brad." Then she asked quietly, "Did you ever consider a prosthesis?"

The smile never left his face. "An artificial leg? Never! A buddy I knew in high school had one of those weird things. He never did get used to it. I figured, why bother?

I hear those things aren't too comfortable, and I'm a sissy when it comes to pain."

They reached the door to the restaurant. "Hey, I worked up an appetite playing that piano. I'm ready for pie. How about you?"

"You bet. I'm famished too."

The restaurant was empty except for two young women scrubbing the floor. Annie scooted off Brad's lap and waved her hand. "Pick out a table, and I'll get our pie."

Brad selected a table near the front, unrolled his napkin, and waited.

A few minutes later Annie walked to the table carrying two large pieces of pie. "Can you live without coffee? They've already washed all the pots and put them away."

He chuckled and pushed back her chair with his foot. "I'll struggle through, but I could use a big glass of water."

"Done." Annie took two glasses from a shelf, filled them with ice and water, then returned to the table. "I don't need this pie, you know. If I eat with you very often, I'd have to waddle instead of walk."

"Fat chance," he countered, laughing at his own unintended pun. "That body of yours could use a little fattening up. And I like that comment about eating with me."

She gave him a playful frown. "Thanks for that left-handed compliment."

"Whoops. And you think you have a habit of speaking before thinking? Guess it's my turn to ask for forgiveness. I know it didn't come off like it, but I meant that as a compliment. You have a great shape—" He slapped his jaw. "I'm digging myself in deeper, aren't I?"

Annie picked up his fork and handed it to him with a giggle. "Shut up and eat."

They laughed and talked their way through their pie, Brad being his usual comedic self and Annie his appreciative audience.

"I can't eat another bite," Brad said, rubbing his stomach.

She looked at his plate then at him. "It's a good thing. Your plate is empty."

He gasped. "So it is!" His eyes twinkled.

Annie dropped her fork and stared at her own plate. "I can't believe it. I've eaten all of mine, too. I never eat an entire piece of pie. Especially this one—it's so rich." She pointed her finger at him. "And it's all your fault, you and that witty tongue of yours. You kept me laughing so hard I didn't realize how much I was eating." She pinched at her waist. "Yuk! I can feel those pounds creeping on already."

She picked up their dishes and carried them into the kitchen as Brad made his way toward the door.

The two girls had finished cleaning up and left, so Annie turned out the lights and flipped on the burglar alarm. Then she followed Brad out, locking the door behind them.

She extended her hand. "Good night, Brad. And thanks for a wonderful evening.

I've loved every minute of it."

Instead of shaking her hand, he took it and pulled her to him. "Me too. But as I told you, I'm a gentleman, and I won't let you walk to your car alone. Hop on."

She gave him a shy smile, slipped an arm about his shoulder, and slid easily onto his lap. "I thought you'd never ask."

They rode silently to her car with Annie's head resting on Brad's shoulder. He waited while she located her keys and opened her door.

She turned to him and smiled again. "I've enjoyed your company. I hope we can do it again sometime."

Brad grabbed her hand and brought it to his lips. "How about tomorrow night?"

She pulled her hand away and placed it on her hip. "Come on, Brad. Be honest. Is it me or my apple pie you like?"

"Well"—he paused and rubbed his chin—"that's a hard question. But if I had to make a choice I'd pick—"

Annie clamped her hand over his mouth. "Don't say it. I have a feeling your answer is going to be my apple pie."

Brad cupped his hand over hers and gently pulled her fingers away, kissing the palm of her hand. "Annie, as much as I love your Awesome Caramel Apple Pie, it takes a distant second to you." His laugh echoed across the empty parking lot. "But I have to admit—you're both appealing."

Her laughter joined his. "Is that appealing with an a? Or a peeling with two e's?"

"Both. Good night, Annie. Lock your doors and be careful driving."

She slid under the steering wheel and put the key in the ignition. A quick turn and the engine started. "Then I'll see you tomorrow night?"

Grinning, he backed his chair away from her car. "Count on it."

Brad watched the car move out of the parking lot and onto the street before twisting the lever on his chair to the right and heading toward his van. "Well, old buddy," he said aloud as he lowered the ramp and rolled up onto it, "you've done it. Opened your heart to a woman, something you vowed you'd never do." *You know she's only toying with you,* an inner voice told him. *A beautiful, vivacious woman like Annie Johnson doesn't want a broken, incomplete man. A woman like that can have any man she wants, and that man isn't you. You can't even stand up and take her in your arms or walk by her side. You're a fool, Brad Reed—a stupid, gullible fool. And if you don't back away from this woman now, before you fall any further in love, you'll get hurt. And hurt bad.*

Chapter 3

Annie glanced at her watch. Seven-thirty and no Brad. Hadn't he told her he'd see her at the restaurant the next evening? Was he sick? Did he have an accident? She pulled back the checkered curtain and scanned the crowded parking lot for the fifth time.

"Where's Brad?" One of the waitresses stepped behind the register to ring up a ticket. "Several of our customers have asked about him. They thought it was neat the way he played the piano last night. I hear he was pretty good."

Annie glanced out the window again. "He was good. And he said he'd be here tonight."

The waitress walked up beside her and peered out. "Do you suppose something is wrong? He's here every Thursday night—without fail!"

"I don't know," Annie answered, recalling how much fun she'd had riding on Brad's chair. "Maybe he made other plans."

"Maybe he found a girlfriend," another waitress added cheerfully as she joined the two at the window. "He's a great-looking guy, and he's also one of the nicest men I've ever met. A girl would be lucky to snag a man like Brad."

"He's handicapped though," the first waitress reminded them. "Not every woman could handle that. I'm not sure I could."

Annie listened and for the first time considered what it would be like to date a handicapped man. While she enjoyed riding on Brad's chair, what would it be like to have a boyfriend who was stuck in a wheelchair? To be unable to stand on tiptoes to kiss him or beside him with his arm about her waist. She shook the thoughts from her head. Why should she concern herself about such things? Brad was only a friend, nothing more. Perhaps he'd found a girlfriend. Well, more power to him. A good man like Brad deserved to be happy. She hoped he wouldn't fall for some woman who would toy with his emotions and leave him heartbroken.

It was nearly a week before Brad appeared again at Apple Valley Farm. And although his greeting to Apple Annie was cordial, the old spark she'd seen in him was gone. He sat at his regular table, focused his attention on his dinner, consumed his pie, and left, barely saying good-bye.

Annie watched with heightened interest as he maneuvered his chair across the lot. What had happened? He'd been warm and friendly; now he barely acknowledged her presence. Even the waitresses had noticed. Brad wasn't himself, and everyone was concerned. Had she offended him in some way?

She turned away once the van was out of sight, determined to ask him the next time he came in. If there was a next time.

Brad watched Apple Valley Farm disappear in his rearview mirror. He had promised himself he would stay away, but he'd felt compelled to see Annie one more time, and she was every bit as beautiful as he'd remembered. Much too beautiful to be interested in him. *Oh, God!* He laid his hand on the stub of his missing leg. *Why did You ever let me meet Annie Johnson?*

Annie sat by the bed holding tightly to her father's hand. The nurse was taking his temperature. Today was one of his better days. He had recognized her and called her by name when she walked in carrying a bouquet of daisies. She didn't mind his calling her by her mother's name, but it broke her heart to see him confused and disoriented.

"You're nearly normal, Mr. Johnson. That's good!" the nurse told him with a pleasant smile. She was staring at the tiny numbers on the thermometer. "The sun is shining, and your lovely daughter is here. This must be your day."

The man smiled back and squeezed Annie's hand. "This is my Annie," he told the nurse proudly, remembering her name again.

"You're mighty lucky to have a daughter who cares about you, Mr. Johnson." The woman moved to the window and with one pull raised the miniblinds to the top. Warm sunshine filled the room. "She your only daughter?"

The frail man nodded.

Annie frowned and put a hand on his shoulder. "No, Dad, I'm not your only daughter. Remember? Valerie is your daughter, too."

"Valerie?" he repeated. He gazed blankly at the flowers she'd placed in a vase on his bedside table.

"I didn't know you had another daughter, Mr. Johnson." The nurse smoothed his covers then patted his weathered hand. "Is she as pretty as this one?"

Mr. Johnson's gaze never left the daisies.

"My sister, actually my half-sister, doesn't live here. She lives in New Orleans, so Dad doesn't see much of her," Annie explained.

The nurse filled Mr. Johnson's water glass then gave him his medication. "He'll probably doze off. That pill usually makes him sleepy, but the doctor gave orders for us to give it to him at this time each day."

"I understand, and besides I need to get back to work. I'll stay until he falls asleep."

The nurse stepped over to the door. "You two have a nice visit. I'll be back later to check on him."

Annie thanked her then turned her attention to her father. He seemed to be failing more each day. Only three months ago they'd carried on lively discussions about Apple Valley Farm, politics, the stock market, and a myriad of other things her father was interested in. Now the conversation was one-sided. She talked. He smiled. She wondered how much of what she was telling him was getting through. If only Valerie would contact him—before it was too late for him to recognize her. How many times had she called in the past six months to ask about him? Twice? Three times?

She took a comb from the drawer and stroked it through his thinning gray hair. "Oh, Dad, I need you," she whispered softly. "Running Apple Valley Farm is almost too much for me. Come back to me, please."

For a second she thought she saw a light flicker in his eyes at the mention of his beloved Apple Valley Farm. He was the fifth generation to run the farm, and now she was the sixth.

Not by choice, but by obligation.

I'm going to phone Valerie this afternoon, she promised herself. *Maybe she'll come for a visit.*

It was nearly three o'clock before Annie was able to get away from her duties long enough to make the call. Valerie answered on the fourth ring.

"Val, it's me. Annie. How are you?"

"What's wrong? Is Dad okay?" the woman asked quickly without greeting her sister.

Annie twisted the phone cord around her finger. She and her older sister had never been close. Annie's father and Valerie's mother had divorced when Valerie was only four. The two girls hadn't even met until Annie was ten, and they rarely saw one another after that. But they had corresponded occasionally through the years, through birthday and Christmas cards mostly. Her father had never talked much about his first marriage, and now it was almost too late to ask him about it. But Valerie was his daughter, and she deserved to know how he was, even if she didn't feel the need to pick up the phone and call.

"He's—fine. At least as fine as a seventy-three-year-old man with Alzheimer's can be. He's failing rapidly, Val. Most days he doesn't even recognize me and calls me by Mom's name. If you want to see him—"

Valerie interrupted. "Funny you should call. I've made plans to come, Annie. I'll be there tomorrow. I already have plane tickets. I need to talk to you about something."

"Oh? What?" *What could she want to talk to me about?* Annie brightened. *Perhaps she wants to help out with his care.*

"I'll tell you when I see you. Can you pick me up in Boise at two? If not, I can rent a car. I think I can find the place okay."

Annie frowned. "Sure. I'll be there."

"Fine. See you then."

The dial tone sounded. Annie stared into the phone. Valerie had hung up.

"What's up with you, Son?"

Brad grinned at the diminutive woman. She was sipping tea from a delicate rose-trimmed teacup. "What makes you think there's anything up with me?"

"A mother can tell those things. There's something going on in your life. Is it a"—she paused and eyed him suspiciously—"woman?"

He felt a flush rise to his face. "Is it that obvious?"

Mabel Reed's eyes sparkled as she reached out her hand and cupped her son's chin. "It is when you've had so few women in your life. Who is she? And when can I meet her?"

His expression sobered. "She's not in my life, Mom. I'm merely her friend. Nothing more on her part. There's no way she'd be attracted to me. Not with—"

Her finger pressed his lips to silence. "Don't say that, Brad. Many handicapped men have full and satisfying married lives. Some women out there are—"

"I don't want any of those women, Mom. I want Annie. But an active, vibrant woman like her could never love me. She needs a whole man." He sighed and leaned back in his chair. "One who can walk by her side, not roll along in a wheelchair."

Mrs. Reed pulled her chair closer to her son. "You've got to get over this, Brad. You're a handsome, brilliant man with a lot to offer. The woman who gets you is going to get a real prize."

"Booby prize, maybe."

"Tell me about her. Is she pretty?" his mother prodded, ignoring his remark. "Does she love the Lord?"

"She's beautiful, Mom. And smart. And witty."

"And what about her relationship with God?"

He glanced down at the table. "I think she's put God in the closet. Her life seems to be too busy for Him right now, what with her responsibilities and all. You've probably heard of her business," he added proudly.

"Oh? What business is that?"

"Apple Valley Farm."

His mother arched her brows. "That wonderful restaurant where they serve some type of caramel apple pie? I've never been there, but several of my friends have, and they rave about it. This girlfriend of yours works there?"

Brad smiled at the mention of Annie's famous pie. "Not only does she work there, but she also owns it. And, as much as I'd like to claim Annie, she is not my girlfriend."

"Have you ever asked this Annie out?"

"No, but we had dinner together at her restaurant. I'm just one of her many admiring customers." Brad leaned over to pick up the teapot and filled both their cups with steaming hot water. "You should see Annie, Mom. Everyone calls her Apple Annie, and she greets each of her customers at the door wearing some sort of fancy long dress with apples all over it and a long white apron. And she has apple things all over the restaurant. Apple tablecloths, apple salt-and-pepper shakers, apple pictures, apple figurines. Even her napkins have apples on them. It's a great place. I'll take you there sometime."

She touched his face affectionately. "Oh, Brad, this is really serious, isn't it? I've never seen you like this. You're really in love with this Annie, aren't you?"

Brad rubbed his forehead. "Yes, Mom. I'm hopelessly in love and can't do a thing about it."

She rose to her feet, bent over her son and wrapped her arms about his shoulders, then kissed his cheek. "You can't not do anything about it, Bradley. You have to tell her how you feel."

He blinked hard then looked into her eyes. "And take a chance on losing our friendship? No, things would never be the same between us if I did that. I'll have to be content with things the way they are."

His mother sank back into her chair and sipped at her tea. "Brad, I can only guess at what life is like for you. To be confined to a wheelchair with no hope of ever getting out of it, and I'm sorry. So sorry. Why did you take a job in the orchard that summer, instead of working at the grocery store? Why did that loader malfunction at that particular time? And why did my son happen to be standing behind it when it did?" She pulled a handkerchief from the cuff of her sleeve and dabbed at her eyes. "You were so young. Only fifteen, with a promising life ahead of you. Why would God let such a thing happen?"

Brad stared at the floor. How many times he'd asked himself those same questions. *Why? Why? Why?*

"But, despite the pain and suffering and the trials you've gone through, you have such a great attitude. And you've grown up to be a responsible man with a successful business and a promising future. And, best of all, you haven't turned your back on God."

"God has been good to me, Mom. If it weren't for Him and the comfort He's brought me when I've been at my lowest, I don't think I could have made it. That, and the support I received from you and Dad."

Mrs. Reed set her cup on the table, a warm smile on her face. "You deserve the love of a good woman. Don't let this chance at love get away from you, Dear. Ask Annie out on a date. Give her a chance." She gave his arm a little nudge. "You and I both know you won't be content simply being her friend. You're already in too deep for that. If you love her as I think you do, go to her. Court her. Let her know how you feel."

Brad evaluated her words. Everything she was saying was true. Although he'd never experienced the love between a man and a woman before, he was sure his part of the equation was true love. But dare he let Annie know of his feelings for her?

Maybe.

But not yet.

It was nearly five-thirty before Brad got home from his office. By six o'clock he'd showered, shaved, and, with great effort, changed into tan trousers and a pale blue polo shirt. He sat debating about whether he should eat his dinner at the nearby steak house or go to Apple Valley Farm as his heart told him to. He had gone there so often lately that he wondered if he might be wearing out his welcome. Maybe he'd skip a night and go to Apple Valley next week. But, he reasoned, if he did settle for steak instead of going, he'd be missing a chance to be around Annie.

His mind was still not made up when his phone rang.

"Is this Bradley Reed?" he heard a woman ask between sobs. "I'm afraid I have bad news."

Chapter 4

No Brad again tonight?" one of the waitresses asked Annie as she stood in the doorway greeting her customers. "It's past the time he usually comes."

"I haven't seen him," Annie called back over her shoulder as she led a party of six to their table. Where was Brad? Had she offended him in some way? It wasn't like him to stay away like this. Maybe he'd found a restaurant he liked better.

"Hey, is that one-legged man going to play the piano for tonight's melodrama?" one of her regular customers asked when she walked past his table. "That guy sure knows how to play the piano. We really enjoyed him."

Annie shook her head, irritated that he would use those terms to describe Brad. "I'm afraid not. That was a one-time thing. He was kind enough to fill in for our regular pianist. But I'll tell him what you said the next time I see him." *If I see him a next time,* she reminded herself. *Where is Brad?*

Brad propelled his chair from the van and wheeled into his mother's apartment. "Where is she?" he called to the next-door neighbor who was waiting for him at the door.

The woman pointed her trembling hand toward the narrow hall. "In her room. She wouldn't let me call an ambulance. She wanted you."

Brad rolled quickly past her down the hall and into his mother's bedroom. She was sitting on the edge of the bed cradling her arm close to her body, crying.

"I did something so stupid," she said.

He hurried to her side. "What happened? Are you all right?"

"It—it was the electric teakettle," she told him between sobs. "I—forgot to unplug it before I took it—to the table, and when the cord tightened—it pulled out of my hand and threw boiling water onto my arm."

Brad could see the horror written on her face, and he knew she had to be in excruciating pain. He took hold of her hand and carefully pulled it toward him, revealing a scarlet red burn that was already forming watery blisters. "Oh, Mom. You should've let your neighbor call 911. We need to get you to a doctor."

Three hours later, Brad was sitting by his mother's hospital bed watching the even rise and fall of her chest as she lay blanketed in white, her bandaged arm on a pillow at her side. The burn was every bit as bad as he'd suspected. The doctor had even indicated some skin grafting might be necessary in the future. But at least she was alive. He shuddered to think what might have happened if the scalding water had splashed onto her face or into her eyes or—it was too frightening to think about.

He stayed with her until he was sure she was asleep. The doctor had said he wanted to keep her in the hospital for several days because of her age, in case of complications with her burns. She was given something to relieve her pain and help her sleep. He had wanted to stay with her, but they'd advised him to leave, saying she would probably sleep through the night.

He checked his watch as he rolled through the hospital's double doors, suddenly realizing he hadn't eaten supper. As he turned into a fast-food drive-through, his mother's words came back to him—the words she'd spoken that very day: *"Don't let this chance at love get away from you, dear. Ask Annie out on a date. Give her a chance. You and I both know you won't be content simply being her friend. You're already in too deep for that. If you love her as I think you do, go to her. Court her. Let her know how you feel."*

⚜

Valerie's plane arrived at two o'clock the next afternoon, and Annie was there to meet her as promised. After casual greetings and obligatory hugs, they picked up her luggage, climbed into Annie's van, and headed for Apple Valley Farm.

"I'm glad you've come. But don't be upset if he doesn't recognize you," Annie warned as they drove along. "Some days he remembers; some days he doesn't." She pulled past a slow moving truck then fell back in line with the other traffic.

"Do you think he'll ever—?" Valerie stopped and fiddled with the clasp on her purse, as if to avoid looking at Annie.

"Get well?"

"Yes."

"No. I wish I could say there was hope for him. But, according to his doctor, he'll get progressively worse and eventually—" She gulped hard, unable to put his foreordained destiny in words.

"That's what my doctor said, too, when I described Dad's condition to him."

"It's so sad." Annie's voice broke with emotion. Only recently had she started to accept what the doctor had confirmed about her father's condition. "There's no hope."

Valerie stared out the window solemnly. "It's a good thing he was smart enough to sign the property over to the two of us before he got like this."

Annie smiled. She remembered the day her father had called her into his office and shown her the papers he'd had the attorney draw up, turning over everything to his two daughters. "That's our dad."

"It was all legal, wasn't it? Without any loopholes I don't know about?"

Annie glanced at her sister then back to the road. "Legal? Of course. What do you mean by loopholes? I don't understand."

"I mean, he didn't put any stipulations on it that I'm not aware of, did he?"

"Stipulations?" Annie repeated, wondering what her sister could be implying. "I guess I don't understand your question."

Valerie tilted her head. "I mean, is there any reason why we couldn't sell the farm?"

Annie stepped on the brake. The vehicle slowed and came to a sudden stop on the shoulder of the road. "Sell Apple Valley Farm?" she asked incredulously as she spun around toward the woman. "What kind of question is that?"

"I hadn't intended to bring it up before we got to the house, but I need the money, Annie. And it seems to me we have only two choices. Sell the farm, restaurant, and theater and split the proceeds, or—" The two sisters locked their gazes and their wills.

"Or?" Annie asked, her face burning. The very idea that Apple Valley Farm would leave the Johnson family infuriated her.

"Or we can have it appraised, and you can buy out my half and keep Apple Valley Farm for yourself."

Annie couldn't believe what she was hearing. Sell Apple Valley Farm? "But—" she stammered, "it's our heritage. We're the sixth generation to run the farm. Our grandfathers—"

Valerie held up her hand between them. "Your heritage, maybe. Not mine. I've barely seen my father since he and my mother divorced. That place means absolutely nothing to me, except for the money it represents."

Annie wanted to slap her. How dare she talk like that? Their father had put his life's blood into Apple Valley Farm. She could understand Valerie's not wanting to pull up her stakes in New Orleans to move to Idaho, but sell the farm? Never! "I can't believe what I'm hearing. If Dad ever heard you talk this way he'd—"

"He'd what?"

Her haughty tone made Annie's stomach turn.

"It's too late for him to do much about anything. He's already turned everything over to the two of us. You can't take something like that back. We're the legal owners now. It's out of his hands. No court in the land would give it back to him."

Annie's hand flew out seemingly of its own accord and hit Valerie's cheek with a loud smack, reeling her back against the seat. She regretted it the minute she'd done it, but it was too late. She had slapped her half-sister.

The two sat staring at one another—Annie grasping for words, her sister holding a hand to her reddening cheek.

"What was that for?" Valerie finally muttered, her face filled with anger.

"How dare you talk like that about our father? He took care of your mother and you all those years. I know. I saw the canceled checks when I took over the book work for him. He paid dearly for that divorce. And from what I've heard, none of it was his fault. Your mother cheated on him." Her accusation was sharp, and like the slap she regretted her words the minute she'd voiced them. Her father had told her those things in confidence.

"My mother cheated on him? That's not the way I heard it!"

Annie drew in a deep breath. She had to control her feelings. Railing at her sister was getting neither of them anywhere. None of what they were discussing could be proven either way. "Let's not discuss this, Valerie. Neither of us was there. And it all happened years ago."

Valerie stared straight ahead, rubbed at her cheek, and remained silent.

Annie fumbled for words. If they were to resolve any of this, the two of them had to get along. "I'm—I'm sorry for slapping you. But you have to realize you're speaking of the loving, caring man who raised me. The man I respect more than any other man I know. I have to defend him, even from you, his other daughter."

"I'm sorry. I was only telling the truth."

"The truth as you know it," Annie added. "Now could we drop this discussion? Please? We need to hurry to get to the care home and see Dad before I have to head back to the restaurant."

"Okay, but I want my share of the money, Annie. And I want it as soon as possible. Let's go see Dad, and we can discuss this later. But, believe me, I'm serious about this. I want out of Apple Valley Farm."

Annie had to clasp both hands together to keep from slapping Valerie again. She bit her lip until she nearly drew blood to avoid saying the things she had on her mind. No way would she let Apple Valley Farm leave the family. But how would she ever keep it? She was barely breaking even as it was. A few dollars one way or the other would put her either in the red or in the black.

Unfortunately, in the early stages of his illness, before they knew he had Alzheimer's disease, her father had let the farm lapse into disrepair. Then, to cover his losses when the stock market dropped, he took out several big loans, which now needed to be repaid. But, by the time Annie discovered the poor financial condition, the harm was done, and she had no other choice but to try to set things right and repay the loans. If her father had been in his right mind, he would never have let things get out of hand like that. There was absolutely no reserve to buy out her sister's portion.

"As you said, we'll discuss this later." She pulled the car back onto the road, and they continued in silence toward the care home and their father.

Their visit was pleasant enough. Their father was slightly more alert after his afternoon nap, and once he even called Valerie by her name. But in his next sentence he called her by Annie's mother's name, which didn't set too well with his elder daughter.

No mention was made of selling Apple Valley Farm, for which Annie was grateful. Not that her father would have understood anyway.

She drove Valerie to the farmhouse, with her assurance that her sister would walk to the restaurant for dinner later, then hurried to greet her customers as Apple Annie. Only tonight, Apple Annie found it difficult to smile. The mere thought of losing Apple Valley Farm set her nerves on edge.

It was nearly eight before Valerie showed up at the restaurant. Annie selected a small table in the far corner of the restaurant, the same table for two where she and Brad had eaten dinner, where they could talk without being interrupted.

"You've done wonders with this place," Valerie conceded as she ate her dinner salad. "Where in the world did you find so many apple things? Everywhere you look are apple pictures, apple figurines, apple this, and apple that. I'm amazed. And your customers seem to love it. And that garb of yours!" She pointed toward Annie's costume and laughed in a way that Annie sensed was slightly mocking. "That's priceless!"

"It's all part of my long-range marketing plan, Valerie. I went to college for four years to learn marketing. I figured I'd put that education to good use," Annie explained. She was proud of what she had done to build up the restaurant's clientele. But Valerie made it sound like a big joke.

Valerie stabbed a cherry tomato on her fork and waved it around. "Well, it's lucky for me—apparently your cute little idea seems to have increased the restaurant's business. That'll mean more money for both of us when we sell it."

Annie grasped the edge of the table with her hands to keep them from flying to her sister's neck and choking her. "We are not selling Apple Valley Farm," she said through clenched teeth. "Positively not!"

"Oh? You have the money to buy out my half?" Valerie raised her brow.

Annie glanced around her, but those nearby were enjoying their dinner and paying little attention to anything else. "Look, Valerie. I am not going to lose Apple Valley Farm. It is staying in the Johnson family. Period!"

Valerie dropped her fork onto her plate, grabbed Annie's wrist, and leaned so close their foreheads nearly touched. She spoke in a hushed but angry voice. "I want my money, and I want it now. I don't care if you have Apple Valley Farm or Joe Blow has it. It means nothing to me. If you want to keep it, fine. But you'll have to come up with my half. I've already spoken to an attorney—one right here in Apple Valley—and he assures me if you cannot buy me out, this place will have to be put on the market. The rest is up to you."

Annie wiped her mouth with her napkin, stood up, and placed her napkin on the table. She appeared calm on the outside, but inside she was seething. Countless words crossed her mind, but she knew she wouldn't change anything by saying them.

Valerie watched her guardedly, as if she expected a thunderous outburst. But when her sister remained silent, she added, "My attorney wants to meet with you at ten tomorrow morning—at the restaurant. Then I'm flying home."

Annie took a deep breath and let it out slowly. Valerie hadn't come to see their father. She had come only to lay claim to her half of the farm. She was thankful her father would never know that. "I'll be there," she said dryly as she turned and walked away, leaving her sister at the table.

It was nearly eleven before Annie returned to the farmhouse. She was glad the door to the room she had given Valerie was closed. She'd had enough confrontations with her already. Carrying on a congenial conversation was impossible now. The battle lines had been drawn. Only the weapons had to be chosen.

She set her alarm for six and was out of the house before the door to Valerie's room opened, although she was sure she could hear her moving around inside.

At least she could have managed to see our father again before she left, she told herself angrily. She climbed into her van and headed for the care home. *But it seems all she's interested in is his money.*

"Well, you're up early," one of her father's caretakers said as Annie passed her in the hallway. "Your father had a good night, and I'm sure he'll be glad to see you."

Annie nodded and hurried into his room, where her father greeted her with a big smile. He was sitting on the edge of his bed drinking a glass of juice.

"Hi, Daddy," she said cheerfully, hoping she wouldn't have to explain why Valerie wasn't with her. "I love you." She kissed his forehead then hugged him.

"I love you," he returned, taking her by surprise.

"I came to see you yesterday. Do you remember?"

He nodded, but his face held a vacant smile.

"The nurse said you had a good night."

Again he nodded.

Oh, Daddy, I need you, she said in her aching heart. *I don't know what to do, and there's no one to talk to about this.*

"Is she here?" he asked, his expression still wearing its pasted smile.

Annie's heart sank. He remembered Valerie's visit. "No, sorry."

"When did your mother leave?" he asked as he took another sip of the juice.

"Mother? Leave?" It suddenly hit her. He wasn't talking about Valerie after all. He was thinking about his wife. "She—she's been gone a long time, Daddy. Don't you remember? We buried Mama in the Apple Valley cemetery several years ago."

He placed his glass on the tray, raised his legs onto the bed, and leaned back into the pillows. "I'm going to see her, you know. She's waiting for me. She's with God."

Annie blinked then shut her eyes. "I know, Daddy. I know."

She pulled her chair up close and stroked his fragile hands until he drifted off. "I miss you, Daddy," she told him in a whisper. "I promise you I won't let Apple Valley Farm get away from us."

Brad was awake and up long before his alarm sounded. All he could think about was his mother. He entered her room at Apple Valley Memorial Hospital before seven and sat watching her sleep, wishing somehow he could bear her pain for her. When she began to stir, he pulled the white blanket up about her shoulders as best he could then put a kiss on the tip of his finger and transferred it to her cheek. She looked so small, so helpless, lying in that sterile bed surrounded by a dozen bouquets sent by her friends and neighbors. He had been extremely concerned about her, but the doctor had assured him she was doing well but should remain in the hospital for a few more days.

He moved her glass of water where she could reach it more easily, then turned and rolled toward the door. It was time to get to his office.

"Brad?"

He spun around to find his mother's eyes open. "Yes, Mom?"

A faint smile played at her lips. "Are you going to see that young woman of yours tonight?"

"I thought you were asleep." He rolled up beside her bed. "I've put your glass where you can reach it. Is there anything else you need before I leave?"

"You're not answering my question."

Brad thought it over before responding. "Yes, I am. I'm going to her restaurant for dinner."

"Court her, Son. Like your father did me. No woman can resist a loving, caring man like you. Don't let your handicap keep you from her. Even if she says no and turns you away, at least you tried. Nothing ventured—"

"Nothing gained. I know. Dad used to tell me that all the time. It's the reason I finished my college education. He drilled it into me."

"Go to her," she said softly, her words drifting off. Her eyelids closed, and she fell back into a deep sleep.

Brad smiled at his mother. In many ways Annie was like her. Beautiful. Tenacious. Ambitious. Gentle. Caring. He could go on and on about the attributes of the two women he loved. He closed the door behind him and headed for his office.

He had been at his desk for only a few minutes when his cell phone rang.

"Brad Reed."

"Oh, Brad, I'm so glad I reached you. This is Annie. I got your number from one of the waitresses. I need you. Can you come to Apple Valley right now?"

Chapter 5

B rad smiled into the phone. Annie Johnson was the last person he'd expected to be on the other end of the line. "Now? You want me to come now?"

"I'm in trouble, Brad. I didn't know who to turn to, with Dad so ill. I've been so busy running things here since I've come back home that I've hardly taken time to make friends with anyone."

"Sure, I'll come—if you need me." He glanced at the stack of unopened mail on his desk and the pile of call slips left over from the day before when he'd stayed with his mother at the hospital. "Give me thirty minutes."

"Oh, Brad. I can't thank you enough. Please hurry."

Brad placed the phone in the receiver then called his secretary. "An emergency has come up. Call and reschedule my appointments." He shoved a few file folders into his desk drawer, put his cell phone in his pocket, and rolled toward the double doors leading to the elevator. "If you hear anything from the hospital or my mother's doctor, call me on my cell phone."

His secretary hurried to keep up with him. "But where are you—"

The elevator doors opened, and Brad rolled inside, calling back before they closed, "I'll check with you later. Please take care of things for me, okay?"

It seemed to take him forever to reach Apple Valley Farm. The traffic was unusually heavy for a weekday morning. Finally, he drove into the parking lot and pulled up near the front door. Annie ran out to meet him. She was wearing a light pink pantsuit, instead of her Apple Annie costume. To Brad, she was the most beautiful woman he'd ever seen.

"I'm so glad you're here." Her face was pale, and her breath came in short gasps. "I knew I could count on you."

"It isn't your father, is it?" Brad asked, his own mother's accident fresh on his mind.

Annie stood beside the door of the van as the ramp lowered his wheelchair onto the pavement. Her eyes were puffy and red from crying, and he wanted nothing more than to take her in his arms and comfort her.

"Let's go inside where we can talk." She grasped one of the chair's handles and walked along beside him. "We don't have much time."

Talk about what? And why don't we have much time? he wondered.

They reached Annie's office then, where they wouldn't be disturbed by the employees who were getting ready for the lunch crowd.

He took her hands in his. "Okay," he said gently. "I'm here. Tell me what's upset you so much."

She glanced nervously at her watch. "My sister and her attorney will be here at ten. That's less than an hour away."

He frowned. "Your sister? Her attorney? Why are they coming here?"

Annie pulled her hands from his and started pacing the room. "I probably should have a lawyer representing me, but I don't know any lawyers in Apple Valley. That's why I called you. I thought perhaps you could help me find a good one—someone who wouldn't bleed me to death."

He leaned toward her and took her hands in his again. "Annie, settle down," he said calmly. "Breathe. It can't be that bad. Tell me what's going on."

Annie drew in a fresh breath of air and swallowed. "She's demanding her half of everything on Apple Valley Farm. The restaurant, theater, orchards, the house—all of it," she blurted out. She let go of his hands and sat down in the chair beside her desk.

"How can she do that? Your father is still alive. Doesn't he own everything?"

Annie shook her head. "No. When the doctor diagnosed Alzheimer's, Dad had papers drawn up giving everything to my stepsister and me. Equally. He knew he would reach the point where he would be unable to make a decision and wanted everything to be clean for us girls."

Brad rubbed his hand across his forehead. "I didn't even know you had a sister."

"Half-sister," she said. "By my father's first wife."

"And she's decided she wants her half now?"

She nodded again. "She gave me two choices. Sell everything or buy out her half." She lifted her tear-filled gaze to his. "I can't raise that kind of money, Brad. I'm barely scraping by as it is."

"She sounds pretty selfish."

Annie bit her lip. "She is. And she barely said hello to Dad when we visited him yesterday." She glanced at her watch again. "Oh, Brad, I'm sure I'm going to need an attorney to represent me. I wish I'd known which one to call. That's why I phoned you. I need someone here with me who's on my side."

Brad rolled his chair up next to hers and slid his arm about her shoulders. "You have an attorney, Annie. One who'll fight for you like a mad dog."

She turned and looked at him. "Who?"

"Me."

Annie stared at Brad. "You? I don't understand."

He smiled at her. "Do you realize you've never asked me what I do for a living? And then the night I told you I don't think you heard me. I'm an attorney. I have my own law firm." He gave her a jaunty salute. "Brad Reed, attorney-at-law. At your service, ma'am."

Her eyes widened with surprise. "You're an attorney?"

"You bet," he said, pulling a business card from his inside pocket. "And a mighty good one, if I do say so myself."

Her expression sobered. "I don't have much money to pay you."

He took her hand, lifted it to his mouth, and kissed it. "I'll take it out in Caramel Apple Pie."

Annie let out a sigh of relief. "You're incorrigible."

"I think you've told me that before." Brad kissed her hand again then became serious. "We have work to do. Tell me everything you know about this so we'll be prepared when they arrive."

For the next twenty minutes they discussed her sister's demands and Annie's options.

"I have one final question for you, Annie." Brad placed his pen on the legal pad where he'd been taking notes. "I want you to think it over carefully and make sure your answer reflects how you feel."

Her eyes widened.

"You've been to college to prepare for a career, and from what you've told me you'd never intended to come back here to live. Then your father got sick, and you were forced to come back."

"I wasn't exactly forced." She twisted her ring on her finger. "I mean, Dad needed me. That was reason enough."

"But once your father—" He hesitated. "I hate to say it, but we have to face reality. Once your father is gone, or he's lost his mental faculties, your obligation will be fulfilled. Isn't that right?"

She nodded. "I guess so."

"Then this is my question, and I want you to think about it long and hard before you answer. Are you sure you want to stay on Apple Valley Farm for the rest of your life?"

Annie's mouth dropped open, but no words came out.

"One more thing, Annie." He cupped her chin in his hand and looked into her eyes. "God has a plan for your life. He allows us to make our own decisions—He's given us a free will—but His way is always the best." He slipped an arm around her shoulders and gave her a firm hug. "I'd like to pray with you about this. Okay?"

She nodded then bowed her head.

"Lord, it's me again. Annie has a real problem and needs Your guidance in this matter. You know the details, and You know what's best for her. Help her make the right decision."

He drew her close to him, and for the first time in a long while, she felt secure. She was no longer alone. Brad was there.

"And, God," he continued, "most of all, draw Annie close to You. Reveal Yourself to her and help her want to draw near to You. I praise Your name. Amen."

Annie rested her head on Brad's shoulder. He asked so little of her yet was willing to give so much. Who was this man who had come so suddenly into her life? And why was he willing to drop everything and run to her aid when she called him? She knew she should pull away. Their prayer was over, but something about his nearness comforted her. She didn't want the moment to end.

It was Brad who moved away. "I'm going to get us some coffee while you consider my question. Take your time. Your answer is very important." He rolled to the drink station and filled two cups, placed them on a tray on his lap, and rolled back. Then he pulled his chair up beside her.

Annie added cream to her coffee and stared into the swirling mix. She had never thought about it that way. She realized that any decision she made now would influence the rest of her life. Was keeping Apple Valley Farm in the Johnson family that important? Important enough to dedicate her life to it? To give up the career for which she'd spent four hard years preparing?

She watched Brad out of the corner of her eye. Strong, handsome, confident Brad. Life had dealt him a terrible blow; yet he'd succeeded in spite of it. Would she be strong enough to stand by the decision she must make with such grace and style as he had?

He remained silent, occasionally jotting a few notes on his legal pad, other times looking away as if in deep thought.

Annie placed her elbows on the table and cradled her chin in her hands, her eyes closed. Was it pure stubbornness that made her want to hold onto the farm? Was it her hard feelings toward her stepsister, who hadn't raised one finger to help her since their father had become ill? What were her motives?

She turned toward him, her eyes misty with confusion. "What would you do, Brad? If you were me?"

He took her hand. "I'm not you, Annie. This has to be your decision. You're the one who will have to live with it."

"But committing to something for the rest of my life at my age? I've barely begun to live. There's so much out there I haven't experienced."

He pushed a lock of hair from her forehead and smiled into her eyes. "Many people make a lifetime commitment when they're much younger than you. Marriage is a lifetime commitment, too."

Marriage? Annie pondered his words. What an unusual parallel. He was right, though. But how many of those marriages ended up in divorce? Over fifty percent? And couldn't she sell the farm later?

"Annie, I'm not saying your commitment has to be forever. Of course, you could decide to sell the farm later on. What I'm saying is, no lender will even talk to you about financing unless you are committed to a long-range plan. Your age will go against you. You've run the farm in the absence of your father, but other than the few months you've been on your own, you don't have a track record with the business."

She drew back at his words, tears clinging to her dark lashes. "Are you saying I don't have a chance to keep this place?"

"No, Annie, I'm not saying that at all. But you have to be prepared for the battle ahead of you. Not only the one with your sister, but the one you'll have finding someone to finance your sister's half. If you intend to keep this place, you must be committed."

Why does life have to be so complicated? she wondered.

"Think what you could do with the money your half of the sale would bring. You could write your own ticket. Establish your own marketing firm. Wherever you choose. Be your own boss."

She looked at him. "Now are you saying we should sell this place?"

"No, not at all. I want you to consider all the ramifications before you make a decision."

An awkward silence filled the room. The only sound she heard was an occasional bang or thud coming from the kitchen.

"I want to keep Apple Valley Farm," she said finally. "It's my heritage. I've already used my marketing skills here, and they're paying off." She leaned back in the chair and smiled at Brad. "I'm sure of it. I could never let this farm out of the family without at least making a stab at keeping it for my children. If I'm ever lucky enough to have children."

"Oh, I'm sure you'll have children one day," he assured her.

Annie smiled. "I'll have to find a man who'll have me first."

"You'll find him all right. In fact, he may be closer than you think."

She scarcely heard Brad's words as she started to think of ideas for building up Apple Valley Farm's business.

"I'll be there for you, Annie—if you want me to represent you as your attorney. You know that, don't you?"

She suddenly realized how difficult it must have been for him to get away from his office on such short notice. "Can you? I mean, don't you have other clients you should be taking care of? I don't want to cause—"

"You let me worry about that, okay? Right now you have my full, undivided attention."

A faint smile crossed her lips. "Thanks for praying with me. It helped."

"My pleasure. But, Annie, you need to be on praying ground with God to expect answers to your prayers. Are you?"

His question stopped her. "When you put it that way, I'm—not sure," she answered hesitantly. She felt uncomfortable with the direction their conversation was taking. "Do we need to discuss religion now? When we should be concentrating on—"

"Annie, dear Annie. Nothing is more important than having a right relationship with God. I brought this up now because you are probably facing one of the most difficult battles you'll ever encounter in your life."

He put the cap back on his pen, slipped it into his shirt pocket and smiled. "Keeping Apple Valley Farm is going to take a miracle from God."

"There you are!"

The two at the little table turned quickly at the sound of Valerie's voice.

Chapter 6

Annie feigned a smile and hurried to greet them, but her heart wasn't in it. Her sister's threatening words kept ringing in her ears: "*I want my money, and I want it now. I don't care if you have Apple Valley Farm or Joe Blow has it. It means nothing to me.*"

"I hope you've decided to sell, Annie," Valerie said curtly as she gestured toward the short man behind her carrying a large briefcase. "It would simplify matters."

Annie ignored her remark and gestured toward Brad who had rolled his chair up beside her. "Valerie, this is my friend Brad, and he—"

"You're going to need more than a friend, Annie," Valerie said sharply. She looked at the handsome man then the chair. "You're going to need a good lawyer."

"Looks to me like she's already got one. The best one in the state, I'd say." The man behind her crossed the room to Brad and extended his hand. "Nice to see you again, Brad."

"Yes, as I was about to say when you interrupted me, Valerie—Brad is not only my friend but my attorney. He'll be representing me in this matter."

Valerie cleared her throat nervously then nodded toward the man. "I see. Well, Ben Calhoun will be representing me."

Annie motioned to one of the servers to bring a coffeepot while they sat down around one of the restaurant's larger tables. Once everyone's cup had been filled, Brad began.

"As I understand it," he said, enunciating each word as he looked directly into Valerie's eyes, "you've given my client two alternatives. Sell the entire estate known as Apple Valley Farm and the two of you divide the proceeds evenly. Or you expect Annie to buy out your half. Is that correct?"

Valerie nodded.

Annie smiled to herself. Her sister seemed intimidated by Brad's authoritative manner. And to think two hours ago she didn't even have an attorney.

Brad placed the yellow pad on the table and studied it for a few moments. "I also understand you have done nothing toward the maintenance or operation of Apple Valley Farm. Is that correct?"

"Doing those things was impossible for her. I want to remind you she was living out of state," Ben Calhoun interjected.

"How about the care of your father, Ms.—"

Annie felt a flush rise to her cheeks. She hadn't told Brad her sister's last name. "Malone," she whispered, leaning toward him.

Brad smiled at Annie, and she felt her heart grow warm. Then he nodded toward Valerie. "Ms. Malone."

Valerie bristled. "No. As Ben said, I live out of state. Taking care of him was impossible."

Brad narrowed his eyes and leaned forward in his chair. "Was my client also living out of state when her father became ill?"

Valerie hesitated, glancing about the room. "I guess. She was attending college. But—"

Her words dwindled off while the three of them waited for her answer. "I was–ah– busy. I couldn't be here," she mumbled.

"Oh? Your employer wouldn't give you time off?" Brad prodded, his eyes never leaving her face. "You were holding an important position of some kind?"

Valerie fidgeted with a button on her blouse. "No. I mean—I don't work—outside the home, that is."

"May I ask what kept you so busy that you couldn't come when your father needed you?"

"I—ah—" She looked helplessly at her attorney, but Ben Calhoun sat listening, apparently as interested in the answers to Brad's questions as he was.

Brad pressed on. "You were saying?"

"I have—social obligations," she blurted out, avoiding his penetrating gaze. "And I have headaches."

Brad leaned back in his chair and locked his hands behind his head. His smile seemed almost, but not quite, threatening. "Then, of course, you'll want to make sure my client is reimbursed for taking the full responsibility of the maintenance and operation of Apple Valley Farm, as well as the constant care and responsibility of taking care of her ill and aging father."

Valerie grasped her attorney's arm. "Do I have to do that? Can they make me?"

But before he could answer, Brad spoke. "We can't make you do anything, Ms. Malone. But I assure you, if this is taken to court, which my client is prepared to do, any judge will look favorably on the person who has abandoned her own life to take care of her father and do whatever was necessary to keep his business in operation. Especially a business that has been in the family for six generations."

Valerie shoved herself back against the chair and crossed her arms. "It isn't fair."

"That's what I thought when you came waltzing in here yesterday demanding your half of Apple Valley Farm," Annie blurted out while trying to keep her tears from surfacing.

Brad lifted his hands. "Look—I don't think anyone here wants to take this thing to court. Between the four of us, we should be able to find an equitable solution."

He turned to Valerie. "I'll do some figuring and come up with what I feel is a reasonable amount for the services Annie has provided. Of course, that'll come off the top of whatever is determined to be a reasonable fair market value of the estate. And it will include the wages Annie could have earned at some New York marketing firm with the degree she received in college."

Valerie hit the table with her fist. "But that could be thousands of dollars!"

"Yes, I'm sure it will be, Ms. Malone. Must I remind you she's done it all without your lifting one finger to help? I'm sure the nursing home has kept a record of all your father's visitors over the past year. How many times has your name appeared on that list?"

Annie wanted to stand up and cheer. Brad was saying all the right things. Things she'd wanted to say but hadn't had the courage. But she was sure the nursing home guest register was something he'd made up to frighten Valerie. She had never seen such a list.

"Aren't you going to say anything?" Valerie yelled at her lawyer.

Ben Calhoun shrugged his shoulders. "Brad is only saying what any judge would say. I thought you wanted an equitable settlement. That's what he's talking about. What more do you want?"

"I want what's rightfully mine!" she shouted, her face red with anger. "Half! And I want it now!"

"I'm sorry, Ms. Malone," Brad told her in an even voice. "The wheels of justice don't roll that fast. I can assure you that coming to an agreement with my client will facilitate matters much more quickly than any court hearing." He capped his pen and put it in his pocket. "Your attorney can expect to hear from me in a few days."

The two men shook hands; then Brad extended his hand toward Valerie. "You'll have to excuse me, Ms. Malone. If it were possible, I'd rise to shake your hand, but unfortunately I'm not able."

Valerie backed away, refusing his hand and not saying a word.

Annie moved quickly to her sister's side. "Please, Valerie. I have no idea how I can raise that kind of money, and I can't fathom the idea of selling Dad's beloved Apple Valley Farm. Won't you reconsider? I could send you a check every month. Everything above the actual cost of running the place. Wouldn't that help?"

Valerie put her hands on her hips and glared at her sister. "Like I told you, Annie—I want what's mine, and I want it now! Put up or shut up!" With that, she turned around and headed for the door, knocking over two chairs on her way.

Ben Calhoun said a hasty good-bye, grabbed his briefcase, and followed her out the door.

Annie leaped onto Brad's lap and threw her arms about his neck. "You were wonderful! I couldn't have asked for a better lawyer."

"Don't get too excited, Annie. It isn't over yet," he reminded her, making no attempt to pull away from her grasp.

Annie suddenly realized how foolish she must look, plunking herself onto his lap like that, but she couldn't help herself. Only a few hours earlier she had been terrified, with no one to turn to for help. Then Brad had come to her rescue. Warm, comfortable Brad. He always seemed to appear in her life at the right time. She leaned away from him, looked into his eyes, and found she didn't want to turn away. Something about Brad was so—manly. Yes, that was the word. And he always smelled nice. As if he'd come fresh from a shower. His gaze held her captive.

Brad pulled her to him and cradled her head on his shoulder. "I'd do anything for you, Annie. Absolutely anything," he murmured as his lips sought hers.

"Sorry—I forgot my hat."

Annie pushed away from Brad to find Ben Calhoun hovering over them.

"I—didn't mean to interrupt," he stammered awkwardly. He grabbed his hat from the table and hurried back toward the restaurant door.

Brad burst out laughing, and Annie blushed as she pushed herself off his lap and stood, smoothing the wrinkles from her shirt.

Then she turned and smiled at him. "Will you be my guest for dinner tonight? I feel like celebrating."

"You bet I will!"

⁂

Brad spent the afternoon in his office. He worked on the proposal he would present to Ben Calhoun, setting aside the papers of his more important clients for later. Right now, Annie was his prime concern.

By four o'clock he was sitting beside his mother, holding her hand, and reading to her from the Bible. Afterward he told her about his morning with Annie.

"I'm anxious to meet this woman," she told him as he prepared to leave. "Any woman who can put that kind of smile on my son's face has to be some kind of woman. I've never seen you so happy, and it's about time."

"I'm in love, Mom," he confessed as he filled her water glass. "Hopelessly in love." He paused then leaned forward and lifted his empty trouser leg. "But Annie could never love me. She has one invalid to care for already. Why would she want two?"

His mother frowned and patted his hand. "Don't use that word, Son. You're not an invalid. You've always taken care of yourself. And since your father died, you've taken care of me. I'm sure your Annie doesn't think of you as an invalid. Don't let that stand in your way. Let her know how you feel. At least you'll find out for sure where you stand with her."

Brad grinned at his mother. "Where I stand? Was that an intended pun, Mom?"

She swatted at him with her uninjured hand. "You! That's another wonderful thing about you, Brad Reed—your delightful sense of humor. I can't even remember a time, since right after your accident, that I've heard you complain. About anything! You can't say that about most men. Any woman should be proud to be your wife."

"You are my mom. You are supposed to say nice things about me."

"Brad, be serious. You love this woman, and I can't imagine her not loving you. Don't let her get away."

"What I'd like to do is ask her to marry me," he said shyly, avoiding his mother's eyes. "Foolish, huh? Guess I'm a dreamer where Annie is concerned."

"Then ask her. Before some other man does. If she's as good a catch as you say she is—well, don't wait too long."

"I wish I had the courage."

Mrs. Reed pointed toward the door. "Be gone with you. Go to that young lady of yours and show her how much you care." She smiled. "And I'll be praying God will give you courage."

He kissed her hand and called back over his shoulder as he rolled toward the door. "You and God? With a team like that, how can I miss?"

Annie spent more time than usual fixing her hair and applying makeup. She hadn't been able to get Brad off her mind all day—the professional way he'd handled Valerie and her attorney, and the ridiculous way she'd thrown herself into his lap. She smiled as she flipped through the menus, making sure each one had the nightly special attached to it.

"You're mighty happy tonight," one of the waitresses told her. "Is that a new pair of earrings?"

Annie reached up and touched her ears. "No, not new. I only wear them on special occasions."

A second waitress joined them. "Special occasions? Is this your birthday?" She gave Annie's arm a playful pinch. "Maybe you have a date!"

Before Annie could respond, the door opened, and Brad rolled in, a bouquet of red roses in his lap.

Both waitresses glanced from the flowers to Brad to Annie then disappeared, whispering and giggling as they went.

"Hi." Brad grinned and handed the bouquet to her. "These are for you."

Annie buried her face in the lush, red-velvet blooms and breathed in their fragrance. No one had given her flowers since her college days. "I love them. Thank you, Brad. You are so thoughtful. I'll put them in—"

Suddenly they heard a loud rumbling noise from the parking lot.

Annie hurried to the window, pulled back the curtain, and peered out. "It's that motorcycle gang again!" she groaned. The waitresses and some of the customers dashed to the window, too.

"What motorcycle gang?" Brad asked as he rolled up beside her and stretched forward to see.

"They were here earlier this summer and caused a lot of trouble. I think they'd been drinking. They knocked over chairs, threw food at each other, and used words I'd never heard before. Most of my customers feared for their safety and left. I had to call the sheriff to get them out, but they nearly wrecked the place before he arrived."

Brad's eyes widened. "He arrested them, didn't he?"

She shook her head and shouted over the noise. "No, he told them if they left, he would let them go. And he did!"

The room became quiet as the rumble of motors ceased. Annie watched the gang members stalk across the parking lot to the door of the restaurant.

"I'm not going to serve you again," she said to the rough-looking man who was apparently their leader. She stood in the doorway, her arms folded across her chest. "You and your friends are not welcome here."

He stuck his thumbs in his belt loops, jutted out his jaw, and stared at her. "You sure that's a good idea? Me and my men are hungry. Our money's as good as theirs." He gestured toward the customers who sat in their chairs like statues.

She lifted her chin. "As I said, you are not welcome here. Now go."

Staff and customers alike watched the scene before them, but no one moved to help Annie.

"What if we don't want to? What're you gonna do about it? Hit me with a wet noodle?" He threw his head back and let out a boisterous laugh. "Or maybe call my old pal, the sheriff?"

Brad rolled toward the man. "Look, Frank. Why don't you and your men find another place to have your supper? Miss Johnson has already told you you're not welcome here."

The gang leader ran his hand over his face. "Hey, Brad, old boy. How you doin'? Ain't seen you since—"

"Since my client sued you for damages, right?"

The man rolled his eyes. "You got lucky. The judge was on the take."

Brad tightened his jaw. "Frank, turn around and get out of here, okay? No one wants you here. Crawl on your cycle and take it on down the road."

The man he called Frank leaned into Brad's face, nose to nose. "And who's gonna make me? You? I can take half a man like you with both arms tied behind my back."

Annie caught her breath. "Brad! Don't antagonize him. I couldn't stand it if anything happened to you because of me."

Without turning to look at her, still nose-to-nose with the burly man, Brad told her calmly, "Don't worry. Frank and I understand each other. Don't we, Frank?"

The man backed away. "That mean you're gonna tell your little woman to let us stay?"

"Nope, I'm telling you to get out of here. Now."

Frank narrowed his eyes beneath his shaggy brows, his rowdy laugh echoing through the room. "Guess that means you're gonna make me, right?"

"You wouldn't fight a one-legged man, would you?" one of the male customers called out. "That would be mighty cowardly."

"If I fight you and win, will you and your men leave?" Brad asked Frank, ignoring the other man's remark.

"How could I fight you? You can't even stand up!" he said, scowling.

"Brad, don't!" Annie rushed to his side.

He turned to her and smiled briefly. "Clear off that table behind you, Annie," Brad instructed. "Take everything off, even the tablecloth."

Frank frowned at him.

"How about arm wrestling, Frank? That sound fair to you?"

The man rolled up his sleeve and flexed his huge biceps. "Sure you want to tangle with this?" he asked with a smirk.

"I win—you leave," Brad said.

Frank laughed bitterly. "But what do I get when I win?"

"I'll buy your supper," Brad said as he rolled up to the table Annie had cleared. "Steak, lobster, whatever you want. I'll even throw in a piece of Annie's Awesome Caramel Apple Pie."

Annie could hear her heart pounding in her ears. How could he joke at a time like this?

Brad motioned to the chair opposite him. "Come on, Frank." And with a wink toward Annie he added, "Put up or shut up!"

Frank stepped over to the chair.

Chapter 7

Annie tried to swallow around the lump in her throat. What was Brad thinking? She guessed Frank weighed at least thirty pounds more than Brad, and he was probably taller, too. And it was obvious by the size of the man's muscles that he worked out regularly and was in great shape. He could take Brad in—she refused to think about it.

She stared at Brad. He was sitting at the table looking calm and cool, waiting. He was fit, too. But how could he ever expect to hold his own against that man? She glanced at the phone. Should she call the sheriff before things got out of hand? He didn't do anything the other time—why should this be any different? Why waste her energy?

Frank pulled out the chair, threw his long leg over its back and sat down, his huge hands gripping the table's edge. "Hey, man. Last chance to back away. Sure you want to do this? I'd hate to see a grown man cry," he taunted. "Especially in front of your little girlfriend."

Brad leaned back and locked his hands together over his chest, keeping his eyes on the man. "I'm sure someone will give me a tissue if I break out in tears. Don't worry yourself about it." He leaned forward again, nearly touching Frank's nose with his, and narrowed his eyes. "I think the question is—are you sure you want to do this? I'm the challenger—remember?"

Frank shot a look at his comrades who stood watching in silence. "One of you guys keep your cell phone handy. Old Brad here is gonna be needin' an ambulance. I owe him big-time. Twice!" he added, holding up two fingers.

"Aren't you ready yet?" Brad asked impatiently. "Let's get this show on the road."

Frank appeared to be not only up for the challenge but eager for it. He cracked his knuckles then placed his right elbow on the table, holding his muscular, tattooed arm in an upright position. "You wanna do two falls out of three? Or go for broke with one?"

Brad's gaze never left Frank's. "I issued the challenge. You decide."

Annie couldn't remain silent any longer and rushed to Brad's side. "No, don't! Please. Stop this right now. I don't want—"

"It's okay, Annie," Brad reassured her. Still looking at Frank he reached out and touched Annie's hand. "Frank and the boys have promised to leave when this is over.

Everything's going to be fine. Trust me."

Frank laughed coarsely again. "Sure about that, Brad, old boy? I think the best advice you could give your little girlfriend would be to start getting a table ready. I'm gonna have me a nice big steak after I beat the—" He stopped and grinned at Annie. "Excuse me, ma'am. I nearly forgot I was in the presence of a lady."

"Let's get on with it," Brad told him. "One? Or three?"

Frank sized up his opponent before answering. "I'm not sure that arm of yours would hold up for more than one round." He nodded his head and scowled, then stationed his elbow on the table. "Let's make it one."

Brad smiled, and Annie wondered if this was his strange way of psyching out the competition. It certainly wasn't a smiling matter to her. Frank could break Brad's arm. Then where would he be?

One of the waitresses stepped up to her. "Don't let him do it. He'll get hurt, and losing could devastate him. Think how embarrassed he'll be with everyone watching. You've got to stop this."

Annie's shoulders drooped. She couldn't bear the thought of what might happen to him if he lost. "I've tried. Brad won't give up, and I'm sure Frank won't either."

Frank motioned to Annie. "We need a starter. You're it."

She gasped and stared at the man. "No, I couldn't!"

"Do it, Annie," Brad told her, his gaze still locked on Frank. "All you need to do is count to three and say go!"

"But, Brad—"

"Do it, Annie. Now." His tone was firm.

Annie moved to the side of the table, her heart pounding furiously, as the two men adjusted the position of their elbows on the table and locked hands. "Oh, Brad, be careful. I couldn't stand it if he hurt you. You're too important to me."

Brad stared into Frank's dark gaze. He had faced him once before as an opponent—in a courtroom. The man had been charged with beating up an innocent bystander and stealing his car. He had won the case, and Frank had ended up in jail. He knew Frank carried a grudge against him and was out to get him, and he knew the man was strong. Men in prison spent much of their time working out. But he was strong, too. And he had to protect Annie. He might not be able to stand toe to toe with Frank, but at least he had a chance of defeating him hand to hand.

God, he breathed out to his Father in prayer, *if I ever needed Your help, it's now. I can't let Annie down. Give me the strength to defeat this vile man. He can't win. Please, God. I know I can't have Annie, but I have to do this for her. I love her.* He tightened his jaw, lifted his chin, and nodded for her to start the count.

Annie's eyes widened with fright, as did most of the onlookers'. She reached over and squeezed Brad's shoulder then started counting.

"One."

Brad swallowed.

"Two."

He sucked in a deep breath and held it.

"Three."

His fingers tightened around Frank's.

It seemed as if she would never say it.

"Go!"

Brad felt Frank's paralyzing grip on his hand, and the two men began their struggle for victory over the other.

The restaurant was silent.

It seemed as if the clock on the wall had stopped ticking.

Men stared.

Women hid their eyes.

Annie cried.

One second it seemed as if their locked hands were going Frank's way. The next second, Brad's. Back and forth they went. On and on, each hoping to outdo the other.

Annie caught her breath then wrung her hands as the minutes ticked by.

Brad watched Frank's eyes for any sign of weakness, but all he saw was dogged determination. He suddenly became aware of all Frank had to lose. He was the head of the gang. For him to be defeated would be a disgrace. Especially by a man in a wheelchair. *God, give me strength. With Your help I know I can do this!*

With one powerful grunt that seemed to come from the deepest part of his being, Frank gave a hard lunge of his wrist, and their hands moved toward his side of the table.

Then Brad saw what he had been looking for, a flash of satisfaction on Frank's face. A quick window of weakness. With all his might and one final gasp of fresh air to fill his lungs, he pushed Frank's hand across the imaginary line, and it was over. Frank's arm hit the table. Hard.

Brad had won!

Annie rushed to Brad's side, jumped onto his lap, and threw her arms about him. "Oh, Brad, you did it! You did it! And you're all right. I was so afraid—"

"I did it for you, Annie." He took a deep breath and looked into her eyes, his face covered with perspiration. "I told you I'd do anything for you. Doesn't this prove it?"

She kissed his cheek, and Brad breathed a prayer of thanks to God. For he knew without God's help he could never have defeated Frank.

Brad looked across the table into the man's face. Frank hadn't moved. He was still sitting there, staring at him, dazed.

"I'm sorry you went down like that in front of your friends," Brad told him so softly that only the three of them could hear. "I hope now you'll keep your end of the bargain and leave without any trouble."

Frank stuck out his hand. "I may be a troublemaker, but my word is good. You beat me fair and square." He gave him a slight grin. "Both times."

"I had the advantage, you know."

The man frowned. "Advantage? What advantage?"

Brad gave his hand a hearty shake. "I asked God for help."

Frank looked at him. "That so? Me and the man upstairs aren't exactly on speaking terms. Guess he liked you better."

Brad smiled. "Mind if I send you a Bible? I have your address, unless you've moved since your trial."

Frank stood up and shrugged his broad shoulders. "Sure. Send it to me. I can always use a little kindling for my fireplace." He turned and headed for the door alone. His gang was already in the parking lot starting their motorcycles and heading out.

"I guess this cost him his place as a leader. I doubt his men will have much respect for him after this."

Annie leaned her head on his shoulder and patted his cheek. "Oh, Brad, you were wonderful. My brave Brad. My hero!"

Brad beamed. He'd never been called a hero. If it would impress Annie, he'd fight Goliath, even without the help of a bag of stones. "God helped me," he said. He enjoyed the attention she was lavishing upon him.

"But Frank was so strong. I never thought you'd stand a chance of winning!"

He pulled a handkerchief out of his pocket and wiped the perspiration from his face. "I neglected to give Frank one small bit of information he might have found useful."

She leaned back with a puzzled look. "Information? What?"

He grinned. "I've been the YMCA's undefeated arm-wrestling champion for five years in a row. And I've taken first in the state competition the past three years. I've whipped several men bigger and stronger than Frank."

She cupped his chin in her hand and looked into his eyes. "Even if you'd lost, you'd still be the winner to me. No one has ever stood up for me the way you did. I lo—" She stopped herself, a shy smile on her face.

Just then a dozen or more of the restaurant's male patrons gathered around Brad to congratulate him. As much as he enjoyed their praises, he felt sadness when Annie slid off his lap and stood.

After the men had returned to their tables, Brad rolled into the restroom and washed his face and combed his hair. He smiled at his reflection in the mirror. He had won!

※

Annie was waiting for him at their little table, her heart filled with admiration. His damp hair lay in ringlets over his forehead, and his face was flushed from all the effort he'd put into defeating Frank. He was the handsomest man she'd ever seen. Why hadn't she noticed it before? Her heart did a somersault as he rolled up beside her. What a strange feeling she had in the pit of her stomach at the mere sight of him.

What was happening? Yesterday he was her friend. Today he was— She smiled warmly as their elbows touched. What was Brad to her? Her attorney, of course. Now her defender. But he was more than that. Much more. Brad was—Brad! The most wonderful, caring, unselfish man she'd ever met, and she found herself wanting to spend every minute with him.

They enjoyed a relaxed dinner together. For once Annie let her staff do the work while she lingered beside Brad. Since it had been such a hard day, she decided to go home and let those helping at the theater close for the night.

"Hop on—I'll give you a ride," Brad said at the door.

She climbed onto his lap immediately and put her arms about his neck. When they reached her car, she kept her head on his shoulder. She felt as if she wanted to stay there forever. It was a beautiful moonlit night—a perfect night for lovers. She smiled inwardly. *Lovers? The two of us?*

"I guess you're tired," Brad said finally, breaking the spell. "I'm going to meet with Ben Calhoun in the morning. I'll call you after we've talked."

Annie kissed him lightly on the cheek and stood up. "Thanks, Brad—for everything."

"You're welcome." He waited until she started her car then rode the lift up into his van and waved good-bye.

※

He watched the taillights of her car disappear in the distance and then turned the key in the ignition. He had nearly blurted out how much he loved her but was glad he hadn't. Sure, Annie was grateful for what he'd done to Frank, but admiration and gratitude were a far cry from love. Why would she want him when she could have her pick of men? Whole men. Not a half man like him—as Frank had called him.

No, he had to prepare himself. As soon as Annie and her sister's estate was settled she would have no more use for him. He'd better start distancing himself from her now. He wasn't sure he could handle her rejection. Yes, it was time for him to get out of Annie Johnson's life.

It was nearly ten o'clock when Brad entered the Apple Valley Farm restaurant two days later. Annie was finishing her bank deposit and hurried to meet him. "Oh, Brad, I've barely slept the last two nights. All I could think about was you and the way you stood up to Frank. I was so proud of you."

He pointed to his half-empty pant leg. "Stood up? That's a stretch of the imagination, isn't it?"

Her hand covered his, but he pulled away. "Why do you always put yourself down? You're a wonderful man. You needn't apologize for anything. Look what you've done with your life. Look what you've accomplished despite—" She stopped.

He rolled up to a table and motioned for her to sit beside him. "I've brought bad news. I presented the figures to both your sister and Ben Calhoun. And while she didn't dispute them, she made it very clear she wanted the farm sold and her half of what was left after all your expenses were taken out. She was adamant about it. I don't think she'll back down."

Annie stared at the table, unable to speak.

"And I've checked with several of the banks where I regularly do business. None of them is willing to lend you the money to pay her off, considering your outstanding loans. I tried—I honestly tried. It looks as if you have no choice but to sell."

He felt like a villain as he watched the look of horror spread over Annie's face. "The worst part is that your sister already has a buyer. Someone has placed a firm bid on Apple Valley Farm. And it's a good one. I think she had that in her pocket before she came here."

Annie leaned against the table and held on to it for support. Her stomach churned. "A buyer? So soon?"

"Yes, and you have only three days to accept, or their offer will be withdrawn."

Annie rubbed at her temples. "Is–is it really that good an offer?"

"I'd say it's an exceptionally good offer, considering the last appraisal your father had on the place," he conceded. "Even taking the portion out for your expenses, you'll both come out extremely well, but you'll lose the farm."

She lifted a misty gaze to his. "And you think we should sell at that price?"

He stroked his chin. "I'd say it's probably as good as you'll get, considering the economy and the reluctance of the lenders to finance you. It's your decision." He reached into his pocket and pulled out an official-looking document. "I've brought the signed contract. All you have to do is read it and sign it. I've read every word. It's a legitimate offer. But the final decision is yours."

Annie reached for it with trembling hands. "There's no other choice, is there?"

Brad lowered his head and answered softly, "No, I'm afraid not."

Annie dropped into a chair and through bleary eyes scanned the words. With Brad's assurance that he had read the document, she took the pen he offered and signed her name.

"I'll take this to Ben this afternoon. As you no doubt read, I insisted on the closing to be three months from now. That should give you plenty of time to wrap things up here and remove your personal items. Your sister has agreed to those terms." He took her hand in his and slowly rubbed his thumb over it. "I'm sorry, Annie. I had hoped we'd be able to dissuade Valerie."

She turned her head away and blinked several times. "You did all you could. I know that. And I can never thank you enough."

Brad stared at her for a moment then withdrew his hand, backed away, and moved toward the door. "I guess that does it for us. It's been a pleasure knowing you, Annie. You take care now." And he rolled out of the door.

Annie stood frozen to the floor. Whatever was he talking about? "It's been a pleasure knowing you"? What did that mean? His words sounded so—final! As if it were over between them. She pulled herself back to reality. As if what were over? Nothing was going on between them, was it?

She hurried to the window. The platform on Brad's van was lifting him inside. She had to catch him!

"Brad! Brad!" She rushed outside and across the parking lot, her apron strings waving behind her. "Wait! I love you!"

Brad rolled down the window and leaned out, a questioning look on his face. "Annie? What did you say? I couldn't hear you."

She rushed to the window, cradled his cheeks in her hands, and kissed him on the mouth. "I said I love you, you silly goof. I'm losing Apple Valley Farm, but I can't lose you, too! Did you think I'd be stupid enough to let the only man I've ever loved get away from me that easily?"

Brad stared at her. "You? Love me? Really? Are you sure?"

She let go of him, rushed around the van, opened the passenger door, and then clambered onto his lap. "Quit talking and kiss me." She slipped her arms around his neck.

Brad sighed and laughed at the same time. Then, reaching alongside his seat, he released the lever and pushed the seat back as far as it would go. "Whew, it was pretty close quarters there for a moment. I don't think the engineer built these seats for two!"

She grinned and kissed him again.

Then he sobered. "Don't toy with my emotions, Annie. Please."

She leaned back against the steering wheel and stared into his eyes, wondering if she'd misread his attentions. "You–you mean you don't have feelings for me? I was so sure—"

He tightened his lips and swallowed. "Oh, I have feelings all right—I've tried to hide them. I think what you're feeling now is gratitude because I've helped you through some rough spots. What I want and need is—your love. Real love." He paused and turned his head away. "A love to last a lifetime. Not your pity."

"Pity? Why would I pity you? You're the most together person I know." She touched his chin, forcing him to turn back to her. "I want that same kind of lifetime love. And I want it from you."

His hand went to the stub of his leg that had been left behind after his accident. "I'm not the man for you. Not with this."

Annie's fingers ran down his arm to his hand, to the stub veiled by his trousers. "This is one of the reasons I love you. I think what you've gone through with the loss of your leg has made you more of a man than the most whole man I know. But—" She frowned.

"But what?"

"But I wonder if I'm enough woman for you. Maybe you don't love me as I've hoped you do. I mean, you're so close to God, and I feel"—she swallowed— "separated from Him. I'm not sure He'd accept me, the way I've turned away from Him all these years."

Brad pulled her close. "He's only a prayer away. All you have to do is ask for His forgiveness. It's that simple."

"I will, and I'm ready. I've seen Him working in your life, and I want that same closeness you have with Him. I know He loves me, but—I need to know how you feel about me. Do you think you could ever love me, Brad?"

He nestled his face in her hair then let his lips trail across her cheek and finally rest on her lips. "Love you, Annie? I'm so crazy in love with you that it hurts. I've loved you since that first night I came to your restaurant and—"

"And tasted my sinfully decadent Awesome Caramel Apple Pie?"

Brad pulled away long enough to murmur with a mischievous smile, "Exactly."

That evening a smiling young woman, dressed in her freshly starched Apple Annie costume, pushed open the door for her favorite dinner customer, Brad Reed. Only this time, instead of handing him a menu, she sat on his lap and kissed him—to the applause of the staff and other patrons.

Brad considered the setting and decided this was the perfect time to propose. He pulled a small, black-velvet box from his jacket pocket, opened it, and held out a beautiful diamond solitaire ring. "Apple Annie," he said, speaking slowly to make sure she understood every word, "will you marry me?"

"Yes!" she exclaimed and held out the ring finger of her left hand. "I thought you'd never ask!"

Everyone in the restaurant clapped again.

Brad grinned. "Now can I have that piece of pie?"

The next week was filled with mixed emotions for Annie: deep sadness when she told her employees of the sale of Apple Valley Farm and great joy as she planned for her wedding to Brad.

Brad. Dear, sweet, lovable Brad. How could she have ever hoped to face her future without him? Her only regret was that her father wouldn't be alert enough to get to know the wonderful man she would be marrying. They'd decided to put their wedding on hold until after the closing of the farm, wanting nothing to cloud their special day.

Annie heard Brad's van pull into the parking lot. She glanced at the apple-shaped clock on the wall then watched him make his way to the restaurant's door. Why was he here at ten in the morning? He'd told her he had an early appointment at his office. She filled two cups of coffee and walked over to a table, motioning him to join her. Something was wrong. She could see it on his face.

"The deal on the farm fell through," he blurted out as he reached for her hand and pulled her onto his lap. "I'm sorry, Annie. Ben assured me the man's credit was impeccable. He couldn't raise the money."

She leaned against him and sighed. "What does that mean? Where do we go from here?" The words were scarcely out when she heard loud thuds coming from outside the restaurant.

Brad slipped his arms about her and held her close. "A man is putting up a for-sale sign. Your sister insisted on it."

Annie's hand went to her chest. "Is that—necessary?"

"She seems to think so, and legally we can't stop her."

Annie looked at the sparkling diamond on her finger. "This will delay our wedding, won't it?"

Brad nodded.

"It isn't that I wanted to leave Apple Valley Farm," she said with a sigh. "I just wanted the whole sordid mess to be over. Will this never end?"

The next week several prospective buyers paraded through the restaurant. None of them fit the description of the kind of person Annie would want to take over her beloved farm. Each day her sadness about leaving the place seemed to offset the joy of her engagement to Brad. Her life was a roller coaster of highs and lows. The brightest spot in her day came when her wonderful Brad entered the restaurant for his supper. His mere presence caused her gloom to disappear, if only for a few hours each night.

"Annie!" He rolled through the door toward her, waving a piece of paper in his hand. "Look! A new offer!"

She hurried to him, took the paper, and began to read. But what she read didn't make sense. Her name, Anastasia Johnson, was listed on the buyer's line.

She looked up at him. "I don't get it. What does this mean?"

Brad patted his lap, and she climbed onto it. "You're buying Valerie's half of Apple Valley Farm! It's all yours—lock, stock, and apple!"

She scanned the paper again. "But I've been turned down by all the banks. How could this be?" His laugh soothed her heart. How could she be sad when she was engaged to a man like Brad?

"Hey, Sweetie, you're marrying a lawyer. Haven't you heard all those lawyer jokes? We're a bunch of smart cookies."

She jabbed her elbow into his ribs. "Cut the funny stuff, Reed. Explain in plain English, not lawyer terms."

"I had misgivings about that first offer when it came in. I did a little checking on my own, and from what I found out I was reasonably sure the deal would go sour. So I called a few of my close friends who owed me favors and had a little money lying around, and I offered them a good use for it. With what I had and what we collected, we've made up an association of investors. We even have a name for ourselves—AARP."

She raised her brow. "AARP? Now that's original. Seems I've heard of another organization with those initials."

Brad grinned. "Apple Annie's Rescue Partners. Catchy, isn't it?"

She sobered. "You're serious, aren't you? You've done this!"

"As I told you in the beginning, dear Annie, I'd do anything for you. I love you with all my heart."

"No joke?"

"No joke. This is the real thing."

Chapter 8

I t was a beautiful fall day. The sky was blue, and the birds were singing in the trees. Annie Johnson-soon-to-be-Reed was very happy. She stood in the window of her upstairs bedroom and gazed out at the rows and rows of lush green apple trees in their orchard. The trees stood like soldiers. Their branches, now relieved of the weight of the fall crop, were lifted heavenward toward their Creator.

Annie felt a peace with God she hadn't dreamed possible. She was grateful to Brad for his patience in explaining the scriptures to her and leading her to his Lord. She was grateful to him also because now, with God's help, she possessed two very important things in her life: the wonderful man she was about to marry and her beloved Apple Valley Farm. Only one other thing would complete her happiness.

Babies!

The young couple had been so busy taking care of the farm and the restaurant, visiting with their parents, and planning their wedding that they'd scarcely had time to sit down together and enjoy one another's company. They had discussed financial and personal affairs, but the subject of children had never come up.

Annie thought she knew why. She suspected Brad didn't want children because he feared he might not be the father he'd like to be, confined to his chair, unable to run with them or play sports with them. Perhaps she had avoided the subject because she didn't want to face the answer. If that's the way it had to be, fine. She would learn to live with it. Brad would be enough for her. But she had to know now—before they exchanged their vows. She hurried to her bedside table and dialed Brad's number. He answered on the first ring.

"Are we going to have babies?" she blurted out, barely giving him time to say hello.

"Babies?"

"Yes. Are we?"

"Don't you think we should get married first? I'm kind of old-fashioned, you know."

She could almost see him smiling over the phone. "Brad, be serious. Do you want babies?"

"Do you?"

"Of course, I do. I want your babies. Oodles of them!"

"Umm, oodles? I'll have to think about that one. By the way, how many would oodles be?" She could hear the laughter in his voice. "How about only a dozen?"

She smiled into the phone as she twisted the cord about her finger. "Then I take it you do want children?"

"If you promise they'll all look like you."

"I'd rather they look like you."

"Well," he said, his tone more serious, "I can promise you they won't be born with only one leg. It's not hereditary, you know—not in the genes!"

"I love you, Brad Reed, you crazy nut!"

"That's why you called me? To ask if I wanted children?"

"Isn't that enough?"

"Don't you know it's bad luck to speak to the groom on the phone on his wedding day?" he asked. She could hear muffled laughter in the background.

"That isn't what they say, and you know it!"

"Lady, anything you say or do is good luck to me. The kind of luck God brings, not the world."

"I know. I love you. See you at the church in a few hours."

"Church? Is today our wedding day? I was going fishing."

"You're—"

"I know. Incorrigible." He paused. "Annie? This is going to be our wedding night. Our first night together. Some things may seem a little—uh—strange. Are you sure you're up to it?"

Her grip tightened on the phone. He would never admit it, but she knew he was concerned that she might find the stub of his leg repulsive. "Sure, I'm looking forward to it. You needn't worry. Everything will be fine, the best night of our lives."

She heard a chuckle on the other end.

"Whew, I'm sure glad to hear that. I guess it's okay then if I bring my teddy bear and wear my funky nightshirt. The one with Big Bird on the front."

She laughed into the phone. Life with Brad would not only be wonderful; it would be funny. And their children would have a loving father.

The little country church was filled to overflowing. Even Annie's father was there, seated by Brad's mother, who had offered to keep an eye on him. Huge clay pots of blooming lavender chrysanthemums with big white satin bows decked the front of the sanctuary. White and lavender satin bows graced each end of the old oak pews, where the couple's friends and family sat waiting for the wedding to begin. On either side of the lectern, tall brass candelabra stood, each holding twelve tall lavender candles, their wicks glowing, filling the church with a warm amber glow. Everything in the room spoke of peace and serenity.

Everything but one.

The groom.

He watched the closed door to the foyer, anxiously waiting for his bride to appear, sure she would change her mind at the last minute.

The music began, and the audience stood as Annie stepped into the open doorway. At that moment Brad knew if he'd had two good legs he could not have contained himself. He would have rushed down the aisle and pulled her into his arms. She was so beautiful. He couldn't believe she was going to be his—for as long as they both should live. Squinting against the tears he felt rising to the surface, he lifted his face and thanked God for the wife to whom he was about to pledge his life. He was sure no man had ever been happier than he was at that moment.

Annie, in her mother's wedding gown of antique white satin, checked off for the hundredth time the items a bride should have at her wedding: a blue garter, a handkerchief borrowed from Brad's mother tucked into the tip of her sleeve, the old comb her grandmother had worn in her hair, and a brand new pair of white satin slippers. She was ready.

She stepped into the doorway of the chapel, tears of happiness welling up in her eyes. She gazed with love at the man seated at the other end of the long white runner on the floor. The runner seemed to draw a path right to him as he sat there smiling at her. She wanted to lift her skirts and dash to him, slip into his lap, and hold him close to her. But she knew such unorthodox behavior would throw their wedding into pandemonium. Instead she fought the impulse and fell into the expected one-slow-step-at-a-time bridal march.

Since neither Brad nor Annie had young relatives, they had no flower girl or ring bearer and chose rather to meet one another at the altar. Annie had wanted her father to give her away, but because of his illness, she felt it best for him to sit in a pew and watch. Her maid of honor was her old college roommate, and Brad's best man was an attorney friend.

As they repeated their vows to one another, Annie thanked God for bringing Brad into her life at the right time, a gift above all others.

Finally, after the soloists had sung and the couple had exchanged vows, Pastor Moore challenged Annie and Brad to live their lives for each other, putting God first in all things. Then he pronounced them husband and wife.

Annie gave her bouquet to her bridesmaid then slipped onto Brad's lap for the traditional bridal kiss. Brad lifted the shimmering veil that covered Annie's face, pushed back a lock of hair, and kissed her. Lightly, at first, but then the kiss deepened—as if neither one remembered the audience looking on, witnessing their happiness. Annie and Brad would remember that kiss for the rest of their lives.

Pastor Moore turned to the friends, family, staff, and business acquaintances who filled the church and with a broad smile said, "It is my pleasure to introduce to you, Mr. and Mrs. Bradley Reed."

The groom drew his wife close and pushed the lever forward, and Brad and Annie Reed rolled up the aisle in his wheelchair, love for each other shining on their faces.

"Are you ready to go home, Sweetheart—to Apple Valley Farm?" Brad asked tenderly when they had reached the privacy of the church's foyer.

"Oh, yes, dearest love, my precious husband." She longed to be alone with him as his wife.

The wheelchair came to a sudden stop, and Brad snapped his fingers. "Oh no!"

Annie stiffened. What could have happened to cause him such anxiety?

"I have to go back to my apartment!" he exclaimed. "Now!"

"Whatever for?"

He grinned. "I forgot my teddy bear and my Big Bird nightshirt!"

SINFULLY DECADENT
AWESOME CARAMEL APPLE PIE

This terrific recipe was given to me
by Millie Miller of Oklahoma City.

1 high-quality, ready-made, deep-dish apple pie
    with lots of apple filling
1 small jar caramel ice cream topping
1 cup chopped pecans

Bake pie for 20 minutes according to package directions. Remove from oven and make deep holes in the top, filling each hole with a spoonful of caramel topping. If you have any topping left, spread it over the top. Sprinkle chopped pecans on topping. Return pie to oven for approximately another 20 minutes and bake until the topping bubbles and apples are tender.

Note: Be sure to put a large piece of foil or a cookie sheet under the pie when baking since it may boil over.

ANGEL FOOD
by Kristy Dykes

Dedication

To my hero-husband, Milton,
who is my collaborator in the deepest sense of the word—
he's believed in me, supported me, and cheered me on
in my calling to inspirational writing.

If I speak in the tongues of men and of angels, but have not love,
I am only a resounding gong or a clanging cymbal. . . .
If I give all I possess to the poor. . .but have not love,
I gain nothing.
1 CORINTHIANS 13:1, 3

Chapter 1

A ngel Morgan still couldn't believe her good fortune. She put the paint roller in the tray and looked around—dreamily—at the building that was now hers, compliments of her late great-aunt Myrtle Jean. It would soon be an elegant, upscale restaurant called Rue de France.

"No fair." Angel's mother, crouched above the baseboard and, smiling, kept up with her steady strokes. "No slacking on the job."

"I, Myrtle Jean Morgan, being of sound mind"—Angel made her voice crack like an old lady's as she held an imaginary will in her hands—"do bequeath to my great-niece Angel Morgan my building in Nine Cloud, Florida, to do with as she sees fit. I also bequeath a sum of money to be used wisely. . . ."

"You could've been an actress." Her mother shook her head, her eyes twinkling.

"I wonder if I'll ever get used to being the owner of my very own restaurant." Angel felt a sense of wonder and awe. She stared out the tall Palladian-style windows she'd worked so hard on yesterday, removing years of grime and neglect. Now they sparkled in the summer sunshine. She would get to the glass door this afternoon, if time allowed. "Pinch me so I'll know this is real, Mom."

Her mother, agile even at sixty-seven, plunked down her paintbrush, dashed over, and playfully pinched Angel on the upper arm.

"Ouch, I was just kidding." Angel laughed as she rubbed the spot, then grabbed her mother in a bear hug. "Oh, Mom, I'm so happy."

"And I'm happy for you." Her mother's voice choked up with emotion. "If anybody deserves this, it's you, hon. It's a blessing from the Lord. You know that, don't you?"

Angel nodded and slowly released her, then walked back to her paint roller. If her restaurant was going to open on time, she'd better keep painting.

Her mother resumed her painting as well. "Of course, you're one of the hardest working people I've ever seen—"

"I'm a chip off the old block."

Her mother waved her hand in the air, as if she was shy of compliments. "How do you say *excellent work* in French?"

"*Travail excellent.*"

Her mother swept her hand around the large, high-ceilinged room. "That's what you've done here."

"Thanks, Mom. I couldn't have done it without your help."

"But the Lord's help, most of all. He's gifted you with determination. . .and fortitude. . .and creativity—"

"Now you're embarrassing *me*."

Admiration shone in her mother's eyes. "You are *so* creative, hon. What a nifty idea, to give the downtown business owners a free lunch right before your opening day. . ."

"In only two weeks, I'll get to meet the important people of Nine Cloud."

"Your father used to call people like that The Brass. He said they dressed to beat the band."

Angel laughed. "Well, I'm going to be dressed to beat the band that day." She glanced down at the paint globs on her clothes.

"Knowing you, you will be."

"That reminds me. I need to design an invitation for the free lunch and get it in tomorrow's mail. I'm lucky I learned desktop publishing in a PR class—"

"You're blessed, you mean. Luck doesn't come into play for a Christian."

"I *am* blessed, Mom. I've got the greatest mom in the world. You've been my cheerleader since I was a kid."

"A champion's worth cheering for."

Angel's eyes misted over. As the white walls turned goldenrod, she thought about her childhood that had been dear and sweet and pleasant—but only because her mother had worked like a Trojan to make it that way. Other women might've given up, but not her mother. Angel's father had died when she was eight, and her mother had found a job as a school-cafeteria cook to support them.

God's the reason we're making it, her mother often said. *He's the most important thing in life.*

Angel sighed contentedly, thinking about her twenty-four years. She'd determined early on to make something of herself, to go somewhere beyond the crackerbox house she'd grown up in on the wrong side of the tracks, and she'd worked hard to see that happen. In high school, she hit the books while her friends enjoyed football games and parties. She did the same in college to maintain a four-year scholarship. For the past two years, she'd worked—slaved actually—in an upscale restaurant to learn about the business firsthand.

The only thing she hadn't attained from the grit and gruel and grind of hard work was her great-aunt's bequest. It had caught her by surprise. Now her dream was about to come true. She was a restaurant owner, and the money would flow in, and she would buy a beautiful home for her and her mother, and nice cars, too. And her mother would never have to work again.

She pushed the paint roller up and down the eleven-foot high walls. Paint one section. Move paint tray with foot. Paint the next section, move paint tray, *ad infinitum* it seemed. But that was okay. Every paint stroke brought her nearer to her goal, and that made her happy.

She paused for a moment and worked her shoulders in circular motions. The only thing that could make life any better for her right now was for Mr. Right to come on the scene. She'd been looking for him for years.

The friends she'd grown up with were all married and either had babies or were pregnant. One had met her husband in church when they were both a mere sixteen. The others met their guys in their early twenties. Not so for Angel. She'd had lots of dates and one relationship that looked like it might lead to marriage. But *her* man—Mr. Right—had never materialized for her.

She scanned the room, pleased with her work. All of the walls were rolled. She put down her roller, poured paint into a small plastic pail, grabbed a paintbrush, and climbed a ladder. As she painted the edges of the wall up near the crown molding, she was careful with her strokes so she wouldn't get golden yellow paint on the wood.

She glanced down from her perch on the ladder, saw her mother, and thought about the love between her parents, something her mother had endearingly talked about Angel's entire life.

Angel wanted that kind of love—if and when it came to her. She breathed in deeply. *I long for the day when True Love knocks at my door.*

"Angel? I called you two times."

"Hmm?" Angel stopped painting and turned, balancing carefully on the tall ladder. "Sorry. I was—"

"Daydreaming." Her mother chuckled, her midsection—the only rounded part on her lean body—jiggling.

"You know me."

Her mother gave a knowing nod. "You're a pie-in-the-sky, Pollyanna girl. But that's okay. I always said you could have as many daydreams as you want, as long as you turn them into reality someday. And that someday has arrived. I'm proud of you, hon. Now, somebody's knocking at the door. Weren't you expecting some equipment to be delivered? Do you want me to answer it? Or do you want to?"

Cyril Jackson III knocked on the door of old Miss Morgan's building. He had about twenty minutes before an appointment and wanted to welcome the new business owner to Nine Cloud.

A few minutes passed, and he knocked again. He knew people were working inside. He could see them—or at least vague forms—through the dirty glass of the door. One was high up on a ladder. The other was in the far corner, crouched near the floor.

So why wouldn't they answer the door? Or at least call out to let him know they were coming? Surely they'd heard him knock. He wished they'd let him in. This June sun was as hot as an August one, and he swiped his forehead, then knocked again.

As he waited, he glanced down the street and saw the three downtown buildings he and his father, Cyril Jackson II, owned in the long row of buildings lining Main Street.

He felt a sense of place and peace in the quaint, small-town atmosphere of his hometown in central Florida, things big-moneyed developers were seeking to create all over the state. Master-planned communities, they called them.

Just last week, he and his father had ridden over to see a city built out of nothingness near Disney World. It had two-story houses surrounded by white picket fences, a main street with awnings over the sidewalks, and neighborhood schools. These were things Nine Cloud had had all along.

He and his father laughed when Cyril read aloud the snazzy brochures—written by advertisers to lure people to move to the friendly, relationship-laden Southern town—exactly what Nine Cloud was and always had been. Of course Nine Cloud didn't have a hotel like this new town, or street singers at Christmastime, or fancy restaurants and shops, or famous authors visiting the bookstore, or art festivals.

But Nine Cloud had history. . .

. . .and heritage. . .

. . .and pride.

He had to be honest with himself, though, as he glanced at the peeling paint on some of the buildings. Nine Cloud *did* need some refurbishing. But more than a physical transformation, Nine Cloud needed a spiritual transformation. He was praying for several situations. He was interceding for Ted White, owner of White's Hardware, to accept the Lord. And Joe Freeman, the funeral director, needed to get back in church. He dropped out last year when his son died. And some of the teenagers in Nine Cloud were getting into trouble—drinking and things. They desperately needed God.

Lord, he silently prayed, *give the folks of Nine Cloud a new glimpse of You.*

He saw one of the vague forms coming toward the door. "Finally. Somebody's going to answer."

The door opened two inches at most. "Yes?" A young woman stood in the narrow opening, paint streaks in her blond hair, on her T-shirt, her cut-offs, and her ratty tennis shoes. She brushed her fingers through her hair as if to freshen it up, and more paint joined the paint that was already there.

Good thing your paint's the same color as your hair, ma'am.

"Would you. . .um. . .like to come in?" The young woman opened the door only an inch more.

Haven't you ever heard of Southern hospitality, lady? You're supposed to throw open the door in welcome.

"If you come in, you'll have to be careful where you step. Paint's everywhere."

"I see that." He stepped inside, enjoying the air-conditioning immediately, and closed the door behind him. This was probably Miss Morgan's great-niece. He'd heard via the town grapevine that Miss Morgan had willed her building to her. Yes, it was the great-niece. He remembered seeing the striking blond at the funeral.

She held out her hand, then looked down at it and withdrew it. "I'd shake your hand, but. . .um—"

"Paint."

"Yes. Paint."

"Cyril Jackson, here." He dipped his chin in politeness. "I own Main Street Café, right down the street."

She looked sheepish, didn't speak.

"And you're the owner of the new restaurant, Rue de France, right?" he asked.

"You know the name of my restaurant?"

He tipped his head sideways. "You've got a flyer out front. In the window."

"Y–yes. . .of course."

"A French restaurant in Nine Cloud. . ." He stopped himself. He wouldn't be rude enough to voice his thoughts. But he couldn't help thinking them. Hadn't she done any demographics? Marketing studies? Why would she start a French restaurant in Nine Cloud? It sounded like a flop to him.

An older woman with a friendly face walked up and shook his hand. "I heard you two talking. I'm her mother. Nancy Morgan's my name. It's nice to meet you, Mr. Jackson."

He exchanged greetings with her.

"I'm going to go hunt some sweet iced tea, hon," the mother said. "I've worked up a thirst. Would you like some?"

"Sounds good, Mom."

"Try Main Street Café." Cyril pointed to his left. "On down the street. We always have sweet iced tea on hand. And try our fudge-covered brownies. Mama Edwards makes them every morning."

"I will," she called as she bustled out the door. "Thanks for the suggestion."

Cyril looked around. The two women were doing a nice job on the place. The ceiling had been redone. And the brick wall had some type of fancy paint treatment on it that showed traces of its original finish. And the yellow color on the rest of the walls blended nicely with the oak floors, or what he could see of them under the drop cloths.

The young woman stood there, not saying a word.

"Well. . ." He cleared his throat. Was she never going to introduce herself? "I know your mother's name. And I know your restaurant's name. But I don't know *your* name."

Her face reddened. "I'm. . .Angel Morgan." She stuck out her hand, then nervouslike, as if remembering the paint, quickly withdrew it.

"Angel." He rocked on his heels. Appropriate name. Blond hair. Blue eyes. Wonder if she had wings and a halo? "Angel, welcome to Nine Cloud."

Angel berated herself as soon as Mr. Jackson walked out the door. She'd acted like a moron instead of the smooth businesswoman she was. She hadn't even displayed proper etiquette.

"I don't know why the cat got my tongue. But I just couldn't think, let alone talk." He seemed so. . .austere. And unfriendly?

She'd wanted to make a good impression on the business owners of Nine Cloud. That was the first step to success. She'd intended to meet them at the free lunch she was going to host, when she'd be dressed in nice clothes.

"And here I am, covered in paint." With a glance at her paint-stained cut-offs and remembering her lack of manners, she knew she'd shot that chance with *this* businessman. And *that* made her frustrated with herself.

She knew who *he* was as soon as he'd said his name. When she'd talked with the attorney who executed Aunt Myrtle Jean's will, he mentioned several business owners, including the one on Main Street who would be her chief competition!

"Mr. Cyril Jackson." She let out a smirk. "The Third." A name for him came to mind. "Mr. Brass," she accused. Then another named surfaced, one she hadn't heard since elementary school days. She couldn't resist saying it now. "Mr. Hooty-Toot."

Chapter 2

Cyril sat down in his usual spot in the white-steepled church in the center of town. He'd just finished teaching his middle-school boys' Sunday school class, and he welcomed the quiet time during the organist's prelude.

A couple of the boys had been unusually rowdy this morning, horsing around and making their usual obnoxious remarks. Jason Baxter had tried Cyril's patience in the worst way. But Cyril didn't let him know he'd irked him. Instead, he quietly breathed a word of prayer and asked for wisdom, then continued with the lesson.

When Jason first started attending the class, someone told Cyril his mom had a drug problem, and his heart had gone out to him. He had donated money through the church to be used to purchase groceries and necessities for Jason and his mother. Every Sunday, he brought doughnuts and juice to his class, and he gave the boys freebies—prize items boys of his age enjoyed.

Cyril occasionally took them on outings, showing them a good time while trying to live out the Gospel before them, hoping they would make a decision for Christ. A couple of them had done this, but Jason had never responded.

Cyril had done a lot to help Jason, to no avail it seemed. He'd tried to find out what made him tick, tried to get him to open up, but the boy was like a stone wall.

Lord, he silently prayed, *be real to these boys. Give them the strength and will to live for You. Help them put You first in their lives. And, Lord, help Jason realize his need of a Savior. Let him know You're real and You're there for him. Somehow, speak to his heart. Lord, use someone to get through to him.*

Later, as Pastor Kyle preached, Cyril deemed his sermon a masterpiece. Pastor Kyle and his wife were in their late twenties, unlike the church's former pastor who had been much older. Even though he was young, Pastor Kyle was a gifted speaker.

Lord, let someone respond to Your Word today.

At the close of the service, Pastor Kyle gave a salvation appeal.

A woman walked down the aisle, a stranger. She knelt at the altar, and an altar worker came and knelt beside her.

Jason came barreling down the aisle, tears streaming down his face. He knelt beside the woman.

Cyril's heart lurched when he saw Jason. *This must be his mother.* He remembered his prayer. He'd asked God to use someone to get through to Jason. And God had used his mother! *Thank You, Lord.*

Cyril quickly made his way to the altar and knelt beside Jason. A little while later, he knew the angels in heaven were happy. The Bible said they rejoiced when a sinner found the Lord.

And Cyril was rejoicing, too.

After the service, Angel spotted Mr. Hooty-Toot coming down the church aisle. She waved and smiled like a kid opening Christmas presents, and he waved back. She would dazzle him this time—for her restaurant's sake. No cat-getting-your-tongue stuff today.

"Why, hello, Mr. Jackson," she said, as he approached, her voice dripping with friendliness. *Hello to the owner of Main Street Café, domain of down-home cooking.* She'd already heard some locals say his restaurant served soul food, what with its home-style fare and its superb black cook, Mama Edwards. "It's good to see you."

"Call me Cyril." He held out his hand.

She shook it heartily. "Only if you'll call me Angel."

"Sure thing. I almost invited you to church the other day when I stopped by your restaurant and almost asked if you were saved—"

"Of course I'm a Christian, Mr. Hoo—" She caught herself. "Mr. Jackson."

"It's Cyril—"

"I received a pin every year for perfect Sunday school attendance when I was growing up, over in Orlando." She didn't tell him her mother had agreed to be her chef at Rue de France *if* Angel started going to church again.

"Perfect attendance in Sunday school? Learning Bible stories? Memorizing scriptures?"

She nodded. " 'I can do all things through Christ who strengthens me,' " she quoted.

"Now that's what I call *real* soul food."

Angel smiled to be polite. But she didn't want to talk about the Lord right now. She wanted to talk about Rue de France—at every opportunity that came her way. The Lord had His place, of course, but for right now, at this pivotal time in her life, when she'd put all of Aunt Myrtle Jean's money on the line, she needed to push her restaurant.

"You look like you zoned out. . . . I asked if you're ready for your opening day?"

"Opening day?" Angel felt all aglow. "As ready as ready can be. The curtains are hung, the furniture's in place, the menus are beautiful, and the table service is Paris perfect at Rue de France."

"Why'd you decide on a *French* restaurant?" He rocked on his heels, his expression unreadable. But his disdain came through loud and clear.

"I spent a week in April at a Paris cooking school. It was the grand prize for a contest I entered, and I fell in love with France while I was over there. When I decided to open a restaurant, it seemed the way to go. *Vive le difference, monsieur!*"

"Bone jeer, mad a moe sale." He dipped forward in a mock bow.

She didn't think his exaggerated redneck drawl was funny. But she would continue being nice. She couldn't afford to do otherwise. "I'm offering a free lunch to downtown business owners the day before my official opening day. I put the invitations in the mail yesterday. It's on a Monday, two weeks from tomorrow. I hope you'll come by."

His eyebrows went up, then down. "I'll put it on my calendar."

For several moments, she churned out information like she was a publicist, using words and phrases like *upscale* and *elegant* and *patterning after the Paris restaurant where I'd studied*. She didn't care about her shameless self-promotion. Everyone in Nine Cloud would soon see that Rue de France was worth bragging about.

"I plan to serve mostly fine French cuisine," she said, "though I'll have some sandwiches, too. My signature dessert will be *Charlotte au chocolat.*"

"Sounds divine. *Angel's* food is di–vine." He dragged out the last word.

She gripped her purse, viselike. Was he making fun of her restaurant? He'd already made fun of her French. Did he think his restaurant was superior? Probably so. "I hope you'll soon say my food *tastes* divine."

"Sure thing." His affirming words didn't match his tone.

Irritation bubbled inside her like fudge in a pot. Talk about a condescending attitude. Forget he was a mover and a shaker in this town. The word *influencer* lit up like neon lights in her brain, but she turned them off with an imaginary flick of the wrist. Forget he was single—the attorney had told her that tidbit of info about Mr. Cyril Jackson III. Forget he was a Christian—he'd just told her he was. Forget her quest for Mr. Right.

In her mind, he was Mr. Hooty-Toot.

Cyril felt a little guilty as he watched Angel shaking hands with Pastor Kyle in the church foyer. He'd maintained a stiff reserve with her and kidded her condescendingly. But her pushy ways brought it out of him. Whatever happened to genteel Southern charm in women? Where were the angelic ways he'd anticipated when he'd met her and learned her name?

Thinking quickly, he determined to make up for his behavior by asking her to lunch. He would display some Nine Cloud friendliness. He could do that much. It was professional courtesy to extend oneself to a fellow business owner. And besides, she was one good-looking woman.

He made his way down the church steps and into the parking lot. He saw her getting in her car and caught up to her just as she shut the door. "Angel?"

She looked up at him as she put on her seat belt. "Yes?"

"Care to get some lunch with me?"

Her brows drew together contemplatively.

"We could talk about Nine Cloud. . .and your plans for Rue de France."

She brightened. "That sounds great."

"What's your choice? B&B Cafeteria? Or Jim's Steak House? Those are the only two restaurants open on Sundays in Nine Cloud."

"Either one's fine with me. Why don't I follow you?"

"You're on."

Five minutes later, Cyril pulled into the parking lot of Jim's Steak House, knowing Angel was following. He searched for a parking place amidst a sea of trucks and a few cars. With their gargantuan tires, some of the trucks were nearly as tall as hundred-gallon drums.

Half of Nine Cloud must be inside. For some reason, every pothole he hit—he counted seven in all—seemed to jar him like they were jarring his car. Probably because Angel was hitting them, too, he decided. She'd gone to considerable trouble to fix up her aunt's old building, and she was probably thinking Jim of Jim's Steak House needed to repave his parking lot.

He walked up to the restaurant with Angel at his side. He grabbed the handle of the glass door, but it was so heavy he couldn't get it open. Obviously, the swing mechanism was in disrepair. He gave it a hefty pull and finally opened it. She walked inside, and he followed her, the door bumping him on the backside.

She slid in on one side of a booth, and he slid in on the other. "Thanks for suggesting this." She opened the dog-eared menu. "I appreciate your friendliness. I'd be eating alone today if you hadn't asked. I don't know too many people yet."

"I'm sure that'll change—"

"Oh, yes."

"You said you're from Orlando?"

"Yes. When I decided to open a restaurant in Nine Cloud, I decided to live here, too. I fixed up the apartment on the second floor of Aunt Myrtle Jean's building. I'm liking it, though downtown is dead in the evenings. But since I'm on the premises twenty-four-seven, it'll be a big help in running Rue de France."

"The restaurant business can be all-consuming, so be careful."

She shrugged. "I'm game. I'll do anything it takes to see it succeed. I've dreamed of owning a restaurant for a long time. I'm ready to work my heart out, as my mother puts it."

Cyril felt something gooey on his fingers, saw the shininess of pancake syrup on the menu—and now on his hand. He pulled his napkin out from under the fork and wiped the goo from his fingers. *She has vim, vigor, and vitality*—an old saying of his grandfather's—and he admired her already. "You said your mother's going to be your cook?"

"My chef. She'll be driving over to Nine Cloud every day. But it only takes about thirty-five minutes. I tried to get her to move in with me, but so far, I haven't been able to convince her. She says her little bungalow in Orlando is just fine for her. Someday, though, after the business takes off, I'm going to buy a nice home in Nine Cloud and get her to live with me. I want to take care of her in her later years, like she took care of me when I was growing up."

He noted the wistful look about her, enjoyed the soft side he was seeing.

They placed their orders and didn't say much for a few minutes, just listened to the songs on the jukebox.

"She thinks my tractor's sexy," crooned the country singer. "She likes my farmer's tan."

When they made eye contact, they got tickled. He laughed, and she giggled, and her eyes twinkled, and his shoulders shook in mirth.

"What a song," he said, shaking his head.

"I never listen to country music. But it's a hoot."

The waitress brought their drinks and salads.

"Thanks," they said in unison, still laughing.

Cyril asked the blessing over the food.

Angel took a sip of her sweet iced tea, then picked at her salad and finally took a bite.

He was enjoying looking at Angel across the table. Living in a small town, going to a small church. . .well. . .pretty women—especially those with drive and ambition—didn't come along too often. She'd practically dropped down from. . .heaven? *Her name is Angel,* he thought with a smile. He'd been praying for a good mate. He'd asked the Lord for the last two of his twenty-five years—soon after he and Sheree broke up—to send him the right mate. He'd dated several women during that time, though none seriously. *Angel is. . .fine.*

He tried to distract his thoughts and concentrated on his salad. What wasn't brown was wilted. Two miniscule pieces of tomato were the only other ingredients. He pushed the bowl aside and took a long swallow of his sweet iced tea. At least the tea was good.

Angel pulled a napkin from the stainless steel dispenser and took a swipe at something on the table, then wadded it up and put it aside.

Cyril wondered what she was doing. Then he spotted a dead fly—belly up—on his side of the table, between the ketchup bottle and the filthy window. She must've found a fly, too. He went through the same procedure, the napkin swiping and wadding.

They got tickled again.

"Sorry about that," he finally said, still laughing.

"It's not your fault." She fished in her purse and pulled out a bottle of hand sanitizer. "This isn't your restaurant."

"No, but I know who owns it." He drummed his fingers on the table. " 'Course, Jim pays a manager to see that things like this don't happen. But even managers have to be managed."

She didn't say anything, just poured some sanitizer in her palm.

He held out his hand, and she poured some in his. He admired her for not chiming in with criticism of Jim's restaurant, though it would've been well deserved. He believed in sticking up for fellow business owners. Apparently she had this philosophy, too, and he admired her all the more.

The waitress brought their entrees and left like she was going to a fire.

Cyril needed butter for his roll. He looked across the restaurant but couldn't see their waitress. Another waitress approached. "Ma'am. . ."

The waitress whizzed by without stopping.

He looked left and right, searching for their waitress, for any waitress. He saw their waitress approaching. "Ma'am. . ."

She whizzed by.

He broke his roll in half and took a bite. Forget the butter. "You said your mother's a cook—"

"The best."

He smiled. "What line of work is your father in?"

"He passed away—"

"I'm sorry."

"I was only eight years old when it happened. . . ."

"That must've been hard."

She nodded. Like she was lost in time, she held a forkful of rice and gravy in midair. "I still remember the day he died." She put down the fork and blinked hard, as if trying to ward off tears. "I was born when they were in their forties—"

"So that means your mother's in her. . .what? Early sixties?"

"She's sixty-seven."

"No way. She can't be."

Angel smiled. "I guess hard work—and raising a child in your forties and fifties—keeps you looking young."

"I'll say. How old was she when you were born?" He laughed. "I guess I'm asking how old you are."

"I don't mind telling you. I'm twenty-four. Mom was forty-three when I was born. And Dad was forty-five. That doesn't sound out of the norm today—"

"Lots of people have children later in life."

"Right. But when I was born, it was fairly unusual. Mom and Dad got married when they were eighteen. They'd been together a long time when I came along. Mom always said they weren't just husband and wife, they were best friends, too." She smiled. "You know what Southerners say. They were so close, they were like white on rice."

He laughed at the familiar cliché.

Her eyes seemed to glow. "They called me their miracle baby." She had a distant, far-off look. "They were the most wonderful parents. . .loving and caring. . .and fun, too. Every afternoon when Dad got home from work, he'd sit with me on the porch swing. And Mom would be in the kitchen, cooking up a storm. And when she'd call us in for supper"—she breathed in deeply—"why, I can still smell the aromas. Chicken frying in the skillet. Biscuits baking in the oven. . ."

He sat quietly, envisioning the homey scene she was painting with verbal brush strokes. And he could feel the sense of nostalgia she was creating, and it was a good feeling.

She blinked hard again. "Dad was a car mechanic. We made it even though things were tight. But after he died, Mom needed to find a job so we could survive, she said. She was elated when she got the job at my elementary-school cafeteria. She said she would be able to be near me all day long. She retired two years ago." She paused.

"But here I've been babbling like a parrot," she continued, "and I haven't even let you say a word. Sorry."

"No need to apologize. I was enjoying it." He really was. He saw why she was so. . . pushy, he'd called it earlier. No, she was driven, he decided. By necessity.

"It's your turn to talk. Tell me some things about you."

He drained his tea glass then looked around for their waitress. Where was the woman? He spotted her near the cash register, jabbering on her cell phone. He stood up, loped across the aisle to an iced-tea station, whisked up a pitcher, and then loped back to the table. In short order, he refilled both his and Angel's glasses. He sat down and set the pitcher on the table to keep it handy.

"Did you grow up in Nine Cloud?" she asked.

He nodded. "I'm a native. Born and raised here."

"When I tell people I'm a native of Orlando, they always say, 'I bet you've seen a lot of changes.'" She smiled. "You can't say that about Nine Cloud, can you?"

"No. Nine Cloud's been the same since I was a kid. No malls. No huge housing developments. And no superstores." He chuckled.

Angel studied the tabletop, ran her finger over a chipped-out place in the laminate.

"Let me guess what item you'd like to add to my list about Nine Cloud."

She looked up, questions in her sky blue eyes.

"No progress."

"I didn't say that."

"You were thinking it."

"How could you know that?"

"I just do." He wiped his lips with a napkin—a fresh one pulled from the container—then pushed his plate back. He'd finished eating and wanted to get to know her better. "And you know what? You're half right."

"I am?"

"I've been here all my life, and I'll admit, Nine Cloud needs some spiffing up here and there. In fact, it needs more than that. It needs refurbishing. Especially our downtown. I'm not blind. But renovation costs are sky high. And most business owners are barely making ends meet now. They don't have the money to kick in the tens of thousands it would take."

"But if we all got out and used our elbow grease—"

"That won't cut it—"

"It would help...and if we'd put on things like...like craft festivals to draw people... and if we'd erect historical markers and then promote them so people would come see the landmarks and shop at our businesses—"

"But Nine Cloud doesn't want to draw hordes of people—"

She rolled her eyes. "People equal money."

"I know that. I'm a businessman. But you need to attend a town-council meeting sometime. Nine Cloud doesn't want to attract people. They think developers would start building scores of new neighborhoods and shopping centers, and we'd lose our small-town atmosphere if that happened—"

"That's not necessarily so." She went on and on with other ideas, not missing a beat. "And if everybody would bring their businesses up-to-date. . ." She looked around the restaurant.

Cyril's eyes followed hers. With a sweeping glance, he noticed things he'd never focused on before—dilapidated furnishings, peeling wallcoverings, brown water-stained ceiling tiles.

". . .and up to par."

He squelched the *bah, humbug* rolling up his throat but couldn't prevent the low *tsk-tsk* escaping his lips. Who did she think she was, to move to Nine Cloud and two weeks later tell folks their town was archaic? And *then*, to top it all off, to tell them they needed to change it? Oh, yes. She was Miss Pushy.

And I'm drawn to her like a magnet to metal!

As Angel drove home, she couldn't keep from thinking about Cyril. Correction. His Lordship. She'd looked up the meaning of his name last night. *Lord.* That's what it meant.

At lunch today, when she'd mentioned her innovative ideas for improvement and growth for Nine Cloud, His Lordship resisted every one. And like a cloud blotting out sunshine, a coolness had settled over them.

"You're behind the times, Mr. Cyril Jackson III—just like your town. And just like your old-fashioned name."

Chapter 3

"My, we served a lot of people today." Angel ate the last bite of her signature side salad—apples, celery, pineapple, and pecans served on Romaine with a tangy dressing drizzled over it. She leaned back in the Bentwood chair, enjoying the delectable flavors. "We must've had forty in here."

"The day will come when we'll have forty paying customers." Across the table, her mother stood up and gathered her dishes. "And more."

"And I don't think that day is too far off." An eternal optimist, Angel knew Rue de France was about to explode with success.

"Me neither."

Work awaited, and Angel raked scraps of food from her dinner plate onto her salad plate.

"With the way you've decorated this place, and the good food you're serving, and the excellent service you give to customers, well, you're going to have a thriving business." Her mother added Angel's dishes to her own stack, then made her way toward the kitchen.

"I can't wait to see that happen." Angel looked around at the French-style décor she'd created. Yellow walls. Blue and white striped tablecloths made from fabric bought at the *Marche St. Piere* in Paris. White lace curtains at the tall Palladian windows. Blue and white plates on wall shelves here and there. A blue and yellow tapestry rug in front of the door.

She sighed. The place had a soul, or *âme*, as the French called it. It was the most important thing to get right in any venture, French people were noted for saying. And she believed she'd gotten it right. Rue de France seemed to reach out and hug a person.

Her thoughts shifted to a year or two down the road, and the home she would buy, and the new car she would give her mother, and the other amenities in life that success would bring—all because of Rue de France. Life was grand. And would get grander.

She stared out the windows that fronted Main Street, watched people ambling by, saw the tattered awning over White's Hardware Store, noted the peeling paint on the bookstore. If only Nine Cloud would do some downtown renovation, like what a lot of other small towns were doing. Forget reconfigured streets for more convenient parking and lush landscaping for beauty, and park benches for ambience—things that needed doing and would certainly bring in more customers. Just do some cleaning, painting, and fixing.

She picked up her stemmed water goblet, made her way to the kitchen, and opened the broom closet to get an apron. Way in the back, behind several, was the apron she'd purchased in Dallas at the National Restaurateurs' Convention, the one with the cute words on it.

Kiss the Cook.

She recalled HAM—her three new friends, Haley, Allison, and Monica—a thought as pleasant as a bite of *Charlotte au chocolat*. They were a barrel of laughs. When Haley found out the gift shop didn't have anymore Kiss the Cook aprons, she begged Angel to pass the apron around until they all got a turn to wear it. HAM was in agreement. They said they were all needing help finding romance.

She pulled out the apron and ran her fingers over the words on the front.

I sure haven't been kissed in a long time.

For some reason, Cyril Jackson appeared in her mind's eye. Because he'd been here for lunch today? But it was more than that, she had to admit, despite her earlier feelings about him. *He is handsome, and he is a Christian,* she thought with a little thrill as she envisioned his dark hair and eyes and his tall, regal bearing and his upstanding reputation. Everybody liked him and looked up to him.

Her mother was wiping the stainless-steel island with a wet cloth. "Cyril Jackson went out of his way to talk with me today. Several times, I might add."

"He did?" Angel's heart fluttered. *He talked to me several times, too.*

Her mother nodded. "He's a nice young man."

Angel smiled as she leaned against the doorway and looked into the dining room, her gaze wandering to the front of the restaurant. A warmth seeped into her soul, and she knew it wasn't from the sunshine streaming through the sparkling windows.

What if Cyril turns out to be Mr. Right?

She certainly hoped to get to know him better. And see where things would lead. A childhood song fluttered through her memory.

" '*Qué será, será*, whatever will be, will be,' " she sang. " 'The future's not ours to see. *Qué será, será.*' "

Her mother gave her a knowing look. "Whatever will be, will be?" Her eyes gave off their familiar twinkle. " 'The future's not ours to see,' " she sang softly. " '*Qué será, será.*' " She paused and looked toward the ceiling. "Lord, please bring about Your will for Angel in the romance department, whatever it is."

Angel sighed as she put the Kiss the Cook apron over her head and tied the strings at the small of her waist. In her heart a hope grew, as surely as the magenta-colored phlox were growing in their window boxes outside.

Late that afternoon, Cyril sat in his office that was housed in the building beside Main Street Café, working on his books. To offset an expected downfall in business at his café due to Angel's free lunch today, he'd come up with a good plan. Early that morning he'd faxed outlying businesses and offices and offered free delivery for lunch.

His manager had just informed him that his idea was a smashing success. Though they'd had few customers in the café during the noon hour, his profits were excellent. In fact, the profits were better than they'd been for a single day in a long time.

Figuratively, Cyril gave himself a pat on the back. "Maybe I'll do that every day." But delivery help was hard to find in the middle of the day. All the teenagers were in school. On second thought, maybe he'd do it once a week, maybe twice.

He smiled. "I need to go thank you in person, Angel Morgan, for the extra money in my cashbox."

Ten minutes later, he walked down the sidewalk to Rue de France. He couldn't wait to see the sunshiny woman in her sunshiny restaurant—even though he'd eaten lunch there less than three hours ago.

And he stepped up his pace.

Angel looked at her watch as she dried her hands on the colorful kitchen towel. Three thirty. Her mother was probably getting into Orlando now. Good. Mom would be home before the bad traffic started.

She hung the towel on a rod, then made her way into the dining room and straightened the chairs from the lunch crowd.

A knock sounded at the door.

Who could that be? Hadn't she displayed the CLOSED sign? A glance that way showed her it was in the window. A peek at the front door showed Cyril Jackson standing there, smiling at her.

"Cyril. . .I'm coming." She dashed across the dining room, zigzagging around tables, her heart as light as a cheese soufflé. She swung the door open wide. "What brings you here for the second time today? Come on in."

He stepped inside and closed the door behind him. "I could easily say your food drew me back." He touched his midsection. "That was some kind of eating at lunchtime. What'd you call that dessert you served us?"

"Charlotte au chocolat."

"It was delicious." He looked at her apron and smiled.

She glanced down and realized she still had on her KISS THE COOK apron. Her face grew warm, and her heart turned a flip-flop. Did he think she was on a hunt for a man? Hadn't Haley said people would think that?

"Interesting apron." He chuckled.

She whisked it off and slung it over her arm. "Would you. . .um. . .like a piece of pie? I. . .um. . .just pulled three out of the oven. For tomorrow's lunch crowd."

"I'll have to run some extra laps tonight if I do." He touched his midsection again. "That Charlotte stuff at lunch, and now pie?"

"It'll be worth it. It's my mother's recipe. It's not fancy but it's good. It's called chocolate chip pie."

"You talked me into it."

"Come on back." She waved for him to follow her as she turned and headed for the kitchen. They made small talk as she scurried around. She brewed a fresh pot of coffee, placed two wedges of pie on the Eiffel Tower dessert plates she'd purchased at the Paris Chinatown, and garnished them with dollops of whipped cream and fresh mint leaves.

Cyril helped her carry mugs and silverware to the dining room, and they set the table together.

Shortly, they were seated at a table that overlooked a lace-covered window, Angel's heart singing.

Cyril put two tiny sugar cubes in his coffee. "Does each piece equal one teaspoon of sugar, or what? We don't use these things at Main Street Café." He grinned.

"Umm. . .it's supposed to, but you might need to add an extra cube. I don't think they're quite a teaspoonful."

He added another cube, then heavy cream from the dainty-footed pitcher. He stirred until his coffee reached a light golden color. "You know the proverbial saying. . ." She giggled and nodded as she shook out her cloth napkin. "I've heard it a million times in the restaurant business—"

"Me, too."

"You like your coffee like you like your women—"

"—blond and sweet." He finished the saying for her, his eyes roaming her long hair.

She could feel her face heating up, like it did when he'd caught her wearing her Kiss the Cook apron.

"I came by to say thank you, Angel."

"Thank me? For what?"

He told her about his business plan at lunchtime and how successful it was.

"That's a great idea," she exclaimed, when he finished telling her the details. "I'm always on the lookout for new things to try. The PR classes I took in college help me think along those lines. You know. Promo for the business and all."

"I think it goes way beyond classes. I think it's inborn in you."

She shrugged. "I admit I'm full of ideas. My mother calls them daydreams."

"You want me to pray?" He looked down at his pie. "I don't think I can resist any longer."

She smiled. "Sure." She bowed her head as he led in a blessing for the food.

He put his napkin in his lap, took a bite of pie, and swallowed it slowly, like he was savoring it. Then he became animated. "Angel!" His eyes widened. "*This*"—he tapped the plate with his fork—"should be your signature dessert!"

"It's good, isn't it?" She ate a bite and took a sip of her coffee.

"It's fabulous."

"But I wanted something French sounding."

He ate another bite, then another. "This pie'll make you want to slap your grandmaw." He chuckled.

She laughed at the Southern euphemism. "My father used to say that all the time. Except when my mother fixed chocolate chip pie. Then he'd say, 'This is lip-smacking good.'"

"I'll agree with that. And it makes you want to. . .kiss the cook." He was looking right at her, all traces of amusement gone from his eyes.

She averted her gaze, stared down at the table, noticed his plate was empty. "You want more?" She made a movement to stand, but her legs were Jell-O.

He gestured for her to stay seated. "Much as I'd like to, I'd better not."

She sat back down.

"But I'll sign up for another piece *real soon*, okay?"

Real soon held promise. She nodded and took another bite, fancifully envisioning the *real soon* appointment with Cyril. A picnic by a pond? A private, candlelit dinner for the two of them in Rue de France? Nothing could please her more. Perhaps the *real soon* appointment would grow into *frequent* appointments. *Dates* was the better word.

There I go again. Daydreaming.

As Cyril made his way down the sidewalk after leaving Rue de France, there was a spring in his step. A thought hit him, an old saying he'd heard his grandfather say many times. *In the spring, a young man's thoughts turn to fancy.*

No. That wasn't it. *In the spring, a young man's fancy turns his thoughts to love.*

That wasn't quite it either, but it was close. And so were his sentiments. He smiled.

And it's not even spring.

Chapter 4

Angel picked up her cell phone on the first ring and smiled. It was Cyril. "Hi."

"Hi, Angel."

For several minutes, they talked—about everything and about nothing. If she were a cat, she would be purring. He asked how her day had gone. She asked the same.

"Are you free on Saturday afternoon?" he asked. "Would you like to get a bite to eat with me?"

She was so excited, she could've reached through the phone and hugged him. *He's asking me for a date. And a date leads to dates. And dates lead to a relationship.* There she went again, daydreaming. But that was the only way to succeed in life, in her opinion. Daydreaming led to goals. And goals led to plans. "A man with a plan" went the business adage for success. Only she was a woman with a plan, both for her business and for finding Mr. Right.

"I thought about driving over to the beach and eating some seafood. Jack's Crab Shack isn't fancy, but it has some gooooood"—he drew it out Andy Griffith-style—"food."

"I'd love to go."

"Great."

"What time? And is it casual or dress?" *Slow down, Angel.* She laughed. "I guess *shack* tells it all."

"Oh, it's informal all right, but it's as good as all get out."

"I love seafood."

"We might walk on the beach after dinner. Is that okay with you?"

She took a deep breath to steady her heart. "I'll look forward to it, Cyril." *Will I ever!*

❧

Angel checked her appearance in the full-length mirror one last time. Twisting this way and that, she knew her attire was perfect for their date at the beach. Red cowl-necked shirt. Red and black print cropped pants. Black open-toed heels that could easily be removed when she and Cyril walked in the sand.

She pulled out her lightweight black sweater and put it by her purse so she wouldn't forget it. She might need it. Even though it was July, brisk breezes could stir up quickly on any given evening on the beach and particularly tonight. It had been rainy the last two days, bringing the soaring temperatures down.

Twenty minutes later, she was sitting beside Cyril in his car as he drove toward the coast. In the backseat was a basket holding wedges of chocolate chip pie in plastic containers. She'd brought along his *real soon* request.

"What's in the basket?" he'd asked when he picked her up.

"A *pique-nique a la Provencale,*" she'd said with a French accent.

Now she glanced over at him as they drove along, the soft FM music filling the car. She liked his hearty laughter. And his winsome ways. And. . .and. . .him. Period.

Cyril, are you Mr. Right? She hoped so. It had nothing to do with a quick decision. Though she'd known him only a little over a month, she'd waited her entire adult life for the right man to come along, someone whose goals and morals matched hers. She felt good about Cyril—despite their awkward beginning. In fact, she felt more than good. She felt. . .wonderful.

After Angel and Cyril finished eating at Jack's Crab Shack—both of them ordering fried shrimp and finding out it was their favorite seafood—they did just as he'd said. They walked on the beach, the waves lapping gently at their bare feet, creating a pleasant sound.

As she expected, the weather turned a little cool. She untied her sweater from around her neck and pulled it on to ward off the chill. But her heart was as warm as brownies pulled from the oven.

"Cold?" He rested his hand lightly on her shoulder.

She thought her heart would jump out of her chest. "No, not now." Not after his warm touch. For long minutes, neither said a word. She was glad. She was reveling in what was transpiring between them—a pleasantness, and maybe something more.

"Thanks for dinner," she finally said.

"Glad you could come. I'm enjoying the evening with you."

"Same here." She paused. "I've told you a lot about me, but you hardly told me anything about yourself."

He shrugged. "Not a whole lot to tell."

"Try me."

"I grew up in Nine Cloud. I went to elementary school, middle school, and high school here."

"Did you play any sports?"

"Basketball."

"And after you graduated, you. . . ?"

"I went to University of Florida. I wanted to go to our denominational college, but UF was my father's alma mater, so I went there to please him. When I finished school, I came home to help run our family business—"

"Which is. . .besides Main Street Café?"

"We've run the café into the third generation now. But we dabble in other things. . . we have some land. . .and some citrus groves. . .things like that."

She'd heard they owned a large chunk of land that bordered Nine Cloud to the east and west. People in town called it the Jackson land.

"Dad's had me involved in several of our businesses since I was a kid." He smiled. "I've picked my share of oranges and grapefruits, believe me."

"Someday, when I own a home in Nine Cloud, I want an orange tree in my yard. And a tangerine tree, too."

"I have a trio of citrus trees in my yard—orange, tangerine, and grapefruit. And my grapefruit are pink grapefruit. The best and sweetest."

"The best?" She scrunched up her nose, thinking of the sour fruit that didn't appeal to her, cook though she was. "I guess pink grapefruit is the way to go, if you've got to eat grapefruit."

"You don't like it?"

"Well, let's just say it's not my favorite citrus fruit. It's so sour, and you feel like you're wrestling with an alligator to get the meat out of the membranes."

"If I ever fixed one for you, you'd like it. It's all in the cutting and serving of it."

"Okay. You're on."

"All right. As soon as my grapefruit's ripe, I'll fix one for you."

"Deal."

He stopped on the beach and she stopped, too. "We've walked a long way."

She glanced behind them, saw the lights of restaurants and hotels far down the beach. Above them, a full moon shone down. Her heart skipped a beat.

"We need to head back," he said.

"Okay."

They turned and started up the beach. Angel was chilly, but she'd be willing to stay out here for hours to be with him. Thankfully, he'd already led them out of the water, and they were now walking on dry, powdery sand.

"I told you about my school life," he said. "But I didn't tell you about my church life."

"I'd like to hear it."

"My mother accepted Christ when I was a kid. I'll never forget that time. It was like somebody gave her a gold mine. She was that excited. I guess she needed some joy." He shook his head. "My father was an alcoholic."

"Oh my."

"He wasn't a down-and-outer, though. Our family's enjoyed financial success for generations back. But he was a social alcoholic. And that's as bad as the other kind because he always had a drink in his hand. Or at least it seemed that way. Ever seen those old comedy videos of Dean Martin clowning around with Frank Sinatra?"

"I'm not sure. . ."

"You know who Dean Martin is, don't you?"

"Yes."

"I've seen them all my life. My father loved Frank and Dean. Anyway, on these videos, Frank's always cutting Dean down about his drinking, and Dean's always cutting Frank down about his carousing with women." He drew a deep breath and slowly released it. "You could safely say Dad was a combination of the two of them."

Angel didn't know what to say. Her father had treated her mother like a queen. They'd enjoyed the love of a lifetime, a unique and sacrificial love. A *faithful* love. She'd been raised in a safe, secure, and loving environment. "I'm. . .I'm so sorry."

He reached for her hand as if he needed the touch of a human being. He grasped it firmly in his. "It wasn't a good life for Mom. Of course I didn't know about these things when I was growing up. She kept them from me. But I knew things weren't good at our house. A kid's no dummy. He can sense things. There were arguments, though Dad was the main one doing the arguing. And when he wasn't arguing, he was away. And there was the weekend drunkenness, and my mother not being able to count on my father for anything, it seemed. And then. . .and then she left him—"

"They divorced?"

"She should've divorced him, I guess. But when I was ten, she told him she was leaving for a while to think things through. She took me with her, and we went to the coast. She and Dad had a condo on the beach, and that's where we stayed. It was during the summer, so she didn't have to worry about school."

He let go of her hand as they walked. "A neighbor in the next condo struck up a friendship with Mom. Mom and the woman—Kendra—started having coffee together a few mornings a week, and Kendra started talking to Mom about spiritual things—"

"Did your family go to church before that?"

He shook his head. "Mom had a vague knowledge about God, but she'd never experienced a relationship with Him. One day Kendra told her you could *know* you would go to heaven when you died, that you didn't have to just *hope* you did. And then she explained salvation. Mom later told me no one had ever done that for her. It was like a lightbulb went on in her head. All of a sudden, she had an overwhelming desire to know God—"

"Sounds similar to my mother's experience."

"Kendra asked Mom if she'd like to invite Christ into her heart, and she said yes. Mom came over to the sofa where I was sitting and grabbed my hand. Tears were pouring down her face. We knelt down in front of it, and Kendra led us both in prayer, and we asked the Lord to be our Savior. It was like a sunburst of joy hit Mom's soul, and I could tell from that moment she was a different person. And I was, too. I remember the feeling distinctly, even though I was only ten at the time. It was like a ton fell off my shoulders. The weight of sin."

"Wow."

"We moved home the next day, and Mom told Dad what happened. At first, things didn't change—for him, I mean. He still drank, though he didn't leave for trips as often. And he still had a quarrelsome nature. But Mom had this newfound joy—and hope—and so our house was different. Anointed, I'd call it. Mom started going to church and got involved, and I did, too. We attended Sunday school, and I joined the boys' program on Wednesdays."

"What about your dad? Did he mind?"

"No. He said he didn't care. He said since her religion made her so happy, he was all for it. And what I'm about to tell you next may sound dramatic. Or it may *not* sound dramatic. I've heard all kinds of conversion stories. I've heard of people seeing visions of Jesus. . .and I've heard of people visiting revivals and being changed by the power of Christ. . . ."

Angel nodded. She'd heard—and seen—stories like those, too.

"And then there are stories like Mom's—of someone sharing the truth in love. But Dad. . .well, one day Mom and I got in the car to go to church, and she was backing out of the driveway. . .and Dad comes running out of the garage and jumps in the passenger seat. She told him we were going to church, and he said, 'I know.' She didn't say anything, and I didn't either. He went to church with us—to Sunday school, too—get that. And at the close of the pastor's message, Dad walked to the altar and told the pastor he wanted what my mother and I had. Dad prayed for Christ to come into his heart. From that day to this, he's never drunk a drop of liquor. And he's lived a life for the Lord ever since."

"That *is* dramatic."

"It's a miracle."

"For sure." Angel marveled at the story. It was amazing.

"There's no telling what would've happened to our family if Kendra hadn't told Mom about Jesus. I don't know where I'd be right now. I might be just like Dad was." He paused, as if deep in thought. "That's why I tell everyone I meet about the love of God. That's why I'm sold out to Him—hook, line, and sinker."

They reached the place where they started walking on the beach earlier, near Jack's Crab Shack. Looking over a sand dune and toward the parking lot that was lighted by streetlights, Cyril could see his car in the nearly deserted lot. It was late.

He opened the car door for Angel. "Have a seat, and stick out your feet."

She laughed. "You're a poet and don't know it." She proceeded to do as he said.

He chuckled. "I'll be right back." He walked to the trunk, then came back to her door. He poured water from a jug over her feet, handed her a towel, and waited while she dried them.

"Thanks." She handed him the towel. "That felt good."

"What? Walking on the beach with me? Or rinsing your feet?"

She laughed. "There you go again with your poetry."

He chuckled as he made his way to his car door, gently shaking the towel in the breeze, got in, rinsed and dried his feet, then cranked up the car.

"I *did* enjoy walking on the beach with you." Her voice was soft as she reached down and slipped on her shoes. "It was. . . wonderful."

"And so is this. . ." He reached for the basket in the backseat, then put it between them. "Let's eat your pie now, okay?"

"Sure."

"But let's get some coffee to go with it. That all right with you?"

"What goes better than pie and coffee?"

You and me. He wheeled into a small restaurant, dashed inside, and in a jiffy was pulling out of the parking lot and onto the highway, two cups of coffee sitting in the built-in cup holders near the dashboard. "You don't mind if we go to one other place before we head back, do you?"

"No. Not at all."

"The condo I was telling you about earlier? Where Mom and I found the Lord? We walked past it tonight. We still own it."

"Your old stomping grounds."

"Yes. I guess that's why I love the beach so much. It holds happy memories. I'm going to show you another place we own."

"Another condo?"

"No. A house." He sipped his coffee as he drove for a good ten minutes. He turned onto a narrow, private road. At the end of the road, he pulled up to a house that fronted the ocean, the headlights allowing them to see in the darkness. The house was weathered and beaten looking, and the yard was full of sandspurs. "Dad bought it the first of the year—for the land really. It's a little run-down—"

"It looks like a wonderful place to retreat to. Sort of like a hideaway."

"We're not sure what we're going to do with it." He cut off the engine, rolled down the electric windows, and turned the radio to a soft level. "We'll either remodel it or demolish it and build something in its place."

"A little TLC, and it'd be beautiful."

He laughed. "There you go again. You and your bright ideas." He looked at her, then slowly reached up and caressed her cheek with the back of his hand, first the right side, then the left. He couldn't resist. Then his hands were on the bottom of the steering wheel again, but he kept looking at her intently. "I'm getting to where I like your ideas, Angel. . ." *And you.*

She looked down at the basket in her lap and traced the print of the napkin.

"I apologize for my forwardness," he said. "I shouldn't have done that—"

"Yes, you should have."

He was surprised at *her* forwardness. But he liked it. He reached over, cupped her chin in his hand, and gently turned her face toward him, forcing her to look at him. Even in the moonlight, her eyes were as blue as the ocean and just as mesmerizing.

"I guess I should apologize," she said.

"For what?"

"For this—" She reached over and gave him a warm hug, snuggled to him for long moments, then settled back in her seat. "I—I guess it's the. . .the beach in front of us. . . and the waves lapping gently. . .and. . .and the moon shining down. . . ."

"Whatever made you do it, I'm glad."

⚘

Late that night, Angel pulled the sash of her terrycloth robe tightly about her waist, then brushed her hair that was damp from the shower spray.

She'd taken a hot shower, but it hadn't been to warm up, as she'd thought about earlier when they were walking on the beach. His nearness in the car had done the job.

And it not only warmed my heart, it ignited it.

She remembered the tender moment when she'd hugged him. Then she'd withdrawn from him. He seemed old-fashioned in many ways, and she didn't want to appear forward—which she wasn't.

Hadn't she hugged him for the reasons she'd told him? Hadn't the romantic setting pulled it out of her? Yes, but it was more. It wasn't entirely the romantic setting. It was. . .him.

Chapter 5

"I just don't understand small-town mentality," Angel complained to her mother as they cooked. "Why these people don't flock to a French restaurant is beyond me. Don't they realize the uniqueness? Why, how many small towns do you know of that have French restaurants?"

"Maybe it's too much of an oddity to them, hon." Her mother stood at the stove, stirring a honey-colored sauce. "Maybe you need to adjust the menu."

"I've already stopped serving *rouget*—"

Her mother smiled. "Nine Cloud people couldn't seem to adapt to whole red mullet staring up at them from their plates—"

"Wonder why?" Angel laughed. "You'd think rednecks would like red fish."

"Rednecks?"

Angel sighed. "I was joking. Nine Cloud has lots of sharp people. Only *some* of them are hicks." She was thinking of some of the church members. But they were sweet hicks, she had to admit. "And forget the *gigot d'agneau* with *herbes de Provence*. That went off the menu after the first month."

"Lamb *is* a little wild tasting, if I do say so myself."

Angel giggled. "I've got a secret."

"You don't like it either?" Her mother's eyes danced in merriment.

Angel shook her head no. "But I wanted it on the menu because it sounded sophisticated."

Her mother laughed heartily. "Well, at least the sandwiches sell well."

"Those sandwiches are the only thing keeping this ship afloat. But I don't know for how long."

Angel's eyes misted over, but she willed herself not to let the tears fall. She'd been open since June—for two months. If business didn't pick up soon, she might have to close Rue de France. And she couldn't bear the thought.

⁂

Late that afternoon, Angel sat at a table in the dining room, doing office work. She glanced out the window and noted the awning over White's Hardware Store. It had another tear in it, compliments of last night's rainstorm and high winds. Maybe now, Mr. White would see the need to replace it.

"Why can't you people see the need for progress?" she said through gritted teeth.

She spotted the peeling paint above the awning. "Decrepit. Antiquated." She couldn't think of any more adjectives. *In desperate need of repair.*

"Repair?" Into her mind flashed a picture of the pastor at church. Last Sunday, Pastor Kyle had announced he wanted the congregation to take on a different kind of project. He wanted their church to rebuild a destitute family's house. And he was proposing to do it in a short amount of time with the help of lots of workers. He had put out a heart-stirring plea for volunteers to sign up.

She would like to help. But there were only so many hours in the day. Rue de France consumed all her time except for the hours she managed to squeeze out to be with Cyril. She smiled at *that* thought.

"The church rebuilding project? My plate's too full for that."

Chapter 6

Standing between the two back pews, Angel gathered her purse and Bible. She was in her usual hurry to get to Orlando and spend the afternoon with her mother. She spotted Cyril rising from his pew near the front. He'd asked her several times to sit with him. They'd spent a good bit of time together lately, and he said he wanted to be with her in church, as well. But she told him if she sat in back, she could dash out and get on over to Orlando to be with her mother. He understood, he said.

She felt a tap on her shoulder.

"Isn't your name Angel Morgan?"

She turned around and saw a petite, seventyish lady in the aisle.

The elderly lady's clothing cried passé, but her manner made up for it with the sparkle on her countenance. "Sweet thang—that's what I call my grand young'uns, so I hope you don't mind me callin' you that. Anyway, we're as tickled as can be that you're attending our church."

"Thank you. I enjoy the services."

She gave Angel an air kiss on the cheek, then a boisterous hug. "The Apostle Paul says to greet the brethren with a holy kiss, but I'm sure he meant the sistern, too." She let out a jolly laugh.

Angel smiled as she breathed in deeply. The elderly lady's hug smelled like the lavender in the French countryside she'd come to love during her time in France.

The lady stepped into the pew in front of Angel, plopped down, and turned to face her. "Like I said, we're mighty glad to have you in church with us. I seen you every Sunday, but this is the first chance I had to say hello. I never can get back here in time."

Angel told her about spending Sunday afternoons with her mother.

"I know. Somebody told me that. That's right commendable. Well, I won't beat around the bush. I come back here on a mission."

"A mission?"

"Yessiree Bob. Pastor Kyle asked me to start a new Sunday school class, and I'm wondering if you'd be a member?"

Angel made a mental note. Put a bouquet of fresh lavender—or some sort of purple flowers at least—in the center of each table in Rue de France.

"I knew your great-aunt. I visited her regularly after she became a shut-in. I was saddened to hear of her passing."

"Thank you, Mrs. . . ?"

"Sister Wilkins."

"Pleased to meet you, Sister Wilkins." Angel smiled at her.

"Same here, sweet thang. In this new Sunday school class I'm starting, we'll be studying a book called *The Dedicated Life for Christ*. The course'll run for three months. Unless we get to enjoying our self so much that we keep going. You know how Sunday school is. Everybody wants to share. I'm sure a-hoping you'll become a member of my class."

"I. . .I'm not. . .sure. . ."

"Oh, there's Cyril." Sister Wilkins clasped hold of Cyril's hand as he walked by.

He stopped in the aisle.

Sister Wilkins pawed over his hand as she looked up at him, her eyes as twinkly as stars. "How's our resident bachelor today?" She winked at Angel. "Do you know this young lady?"

He smiled at Angel. "I certainly do."

Angel looked away, thinking of the romantic times they'd had recently. Her breathing was so short, she was afraid it was jiggling her cotton top.

"Cyril, I was just telling her"—Sister Wilkins gestured at Angel—"about my new Sunday school class. I was asking her if she'd join it." She turned to Angel. "I checked, and you aren't enrolled in any of our Sunday school classes, so I thought you'd be a prime prospect. Cyril here"—she thrust her hand toward him—"is joining. Pastor Kyle's doing a rotation thingy in Sunday school and asked Cyril to take a break from the middle-school boys and help me get this new class a-going. Will you commit to us?"

Angel hated being put on the spot like this. *If I join this class, the next thing you know, they'll be asking me to do other things. . .*

"I know you'll find it interesting. And we need to become more dedicated to Christ. All of us. Studying how to do it will help. . . ." Sister Wilkins's voice trailed off, question marks forming in her faded blue eyes.

Angel fiddled with the zipper on her purse. Sister Wilkins was speaking the truth. Angel couldn't deny it. And her mother would readily agree.

"Won't you please come?"

Angel's cell phone rang, and she was glad for the interruption. She whipped it out of a side compartment of her purse and noted it was her mother. She turned to Sister Wilkins. "If you'll excuse me, I'll only be a moment."

"Go right ahead, sweet thang."

Angel took the call and told her mother that yes, she would pick up some butter and that she would be on her way in a few minutes. Then she closed her phone.

Sister Wilkins shifted in the pew, the scent of lavender wafting through the air again. "We all need to make time for the work of the Lord."

Angel squeezed the tiny phone in her hand. The work of the Lord? All she knew right now was the work of Rue de France. Well, the *lack* thereof. With hardly any customers, she was consumed with worry, not work.

" 'Only one life, 'twill soon be past, only what's done for Christ will last.' That's an old poem—"

"I know. My mother quotes it all the time."

Sister Wilkins rose to her feet, wincing in pain. "I got a hitch in my get along." She laughed as she touched the small of her back. "Just don't get old, folks. Just don't get old."

Cyril made eye contact with Angel, and they both laughed with Sister Wilkins, enjoying her antics.

"Well, I know you got to go. I heard you a-telling your mother you were on your way. So I won't keep you." Sister Wilkins smiled. "But I hope you'll join my class."

Cyril nodded. "I second that."

"I. . .well, I'll have to see."

"Food for thought, right, Angel?" Cyril's penetrating gaze seemed to pierce the sinews of her soul.

Angel slowly nodded. My, he looked serious. What was he thinking?

"Well, what do you think, Cyril?"

Cyril looked down at Sister Wilkins but didn't say anything. He was too busy ponderating, as his grandfather liked to say.

"I thought she was a perfect prospect for my class. I thought she'd commit. I really did. . . ."

He couldn't concentrate on what Sister Wilkins was saying as she jabbered on. All he could think of was Angel. She was pretty. Check. And she was single. Check. And she had get-up-and-go. Check. And they'd had such good times together lately. Check.

But she's not interested in Kingdom doings.

Uncheck.

Cyril clearly saw that now. Every time they'd been together in the last few weeks and the subject of God or the church had come up, Angel hadn't had much to say.

Disappointment that was sharper than a hunger pang hit him in the gut. No, the heart.

Chapter 7

Angel sat in her living room, surfing restaurant sites on her laptop on yet another dateless Saturday night, trying to glean ideas.

The proverbial saying, "Absence makes the heart grow fonder," was certainly applicable here. She couldn't keep her thoughts off of Cyril. Apparently, that wasn't the case with him. What was going on? They'd had many Saturday night dates in a row. Now she only saw him in church or downtown when their paths happened to cross.

"Well, I guess that leaves me some free time to devote to the church rebuilding project."

She picked up Pastor Kyle's letter she'd received in today's mail and reread it. He was pleading for volunteers. When she saw the part about the four children in the family and no father, tears came to her eyes. That meant a single mother working her heart out to make a living and raise the children. That sounded familiar. She knew what it was to be in need. And she knew what she had to do.

She put the letter down, picked up her cell phone, and called the pastor. She told him she wanted to sign up for the project and mentioned her areas of expertise. When she found out only nine other people had volunteered, she was flabbergasted. But she didn't say anything.

Their conversation came to a close, and she clicked off her cell phone with more force than necessary. "Ten volunteers for a project this massive? That figures." She was feeling sarcastic tonight—not her usual *modus operandi*. But it couldn't be helped. She'd moved to Nine Cloud with high hopes, only to have them dashed.

The townspeople resisted progress. . . .

Her restaurant wasn't doing well. . . .

And her budding romance had turned out to be no romance at all. She didn't know what had happened with Cyril and her. Whatever had been afloat had sunk like a capsized ship.

On second thought, maybe she *did* know what happened. He was *always* talking about God and church, and it irked her sometimes. Maybe he sensed that about her, and maybe that irked *him*. After all, he was Mr. Evangelist.

Now, when she saw him, she felt awkward and uncomfortable. Before, she'd been so happy every time she was with him. She thought it was the start of a meaningful relationship.

"Relationship? Ha." She closed her laptop, made her way to her desk, and sat down. "Cyril Jackson III, you're too heavenly minded to be any earthly good." *At least any good to me.*

She grabbed a pencil from the penholder and drew a house on the back of Pastor Kyle's letter. She put a front door on it, windows on either side, and flowers out front, all stick drawing, kindergarten-style.

"I don't know what the future holds for me concerning Mr. Right." She couldn't keep the acrimony out of her voice.

"But one thing I *do* know. I'll work my heart out for this poverty-stricken family." She had a strong back and a good eye for righting things. She could hammer nails and paint walls and gather debris. And anything else they requested of her.

Meantime, she would work her heart out for Rue de France, too. She *would* see success, come what may. It was the driving force in her life.

"Hi, Cyril. This is Pastor Kyle."

"Well, hello, Pastor Kyle." Cyril pointed the remote and hit the Mute button. *Wonder why the pastor is calling?* He would see him in the morning at church. "What can I do for you?"

"I noticed you were the first one to sign up for the church rebuilding project. I wanted to express my thanks."

"I'm looking forward to it. This family. . .what's their name?"

"The Hendersons."

"The Hendersons are going to be mightily blessed. But the ones who work on it will get the biggest blessing. I'm convinced of that."

"You're right, Cyril. It's more blessed to give than receive, the Good Book says."

"Amen. Who's going to head up the project?"

"That's why I'm calling. Will you. . .be the team captain?"

"I. . .uh. . ."

"You have business savvy. . .and Roy Johnson signed up to be a volunteer. . .and he can give you good advice. He's got his contractor's license now. . .and he's—"

"Why don't you make him team captain? He's much more knowledgeable about building than I am."

"I feel like the Lord wants you to do it."

"You do?"

"I do."

"Well, I can't argue with the Lord, can I?" Cyril chuckled.

"No."

"All right. I'll do my best."

"I knew you would."

"Well, I guess I'll see you in church in the morning, Pastor—"

"One other thing, Cyril."

"What's that?"

"Will you give one of the volunteers a call?"

"I'll call all of them, once I figure out a game plan."

"I mean tonight."

"Tonight?"

"Yes."

A pause. A glance at the TV screen. "Sure, Pastor. Who is it?"

"Angel Morgan."

Angel volunteered for the rebuilding project? Well, shut my mouth, as Sister Wilkins would say. Cyril had tried to get Angel to sign up for the project, just as he'd tried to get her to join Sister Wilkins's Sunday school class, to no avail. He said it would please the Lord. No takers. He said it would be rewarding. No takers. He said it would be fun. No takers. He finally got the message. Angel just didn't have her priorities right. That was when he decided to cool things for a while.

"Angel wants to help," Pastor Kyle went on. "She said she can paint walls and trim. And she can drive a pretty good nail. And she said if it's needed, she'd like to help pick out paint colors and things like that. I'd like you to call her tonight, and let her know we appreciate her volunteering."

Cyril quickly summed up the situation. Pastor Kyle must be trying to get him and Angel together. Cyril had had a friend-to-friend conversation with him recently. He'd told the pastor he and Angel had gone on a few dates. He also mentioned he was disappointed in her and hadn't taken her out in several weeks. "*The Lord wants you to pray for her,*" Pastor Kyle had told him

"Cyril? Did I lose you?"

"No, Pastor."

"I feel—"

"—the Lord wants me to call her?" Cyril interrupted good-naturedly.

Pastor Kyle laughed. "No. This time, I'm the one who feels that way."

Cyril joined in his laughter, for some reason feeling good about the future of his and Angel's relationship. "Okay. I'll do it."

"Keep me posted."

"Oh, I will, Pastor."

Angel heard her cell phone ring. She pushed aside her stick drawing of the house

and picked up her phone. She was surprised to see Cyril's number. "Hi, Cyril."

"Hi, Angel. How are you?"

"Fine." *Not really.*

"Pastor Kyle said you signed up for the church rebuilding project."

Angel did a double take. Why'd the pastor call Cyril and tell him she'd volunteered?

"I'm going to be heading up the project. I'm calling it Project Hope."

"My, Pastor Kyle works fast. I just called to tell him I wanted to sign up."

"I'm glad, Angel."

She remembered when he'd tried to get her to volunteer. But that wasn't her reason for doing it. "When I got his letter, I knew I had to help."

"The church appreciates your help. And I know it'll mean a lot to the Henderson family. I've decided to have a planning meeting next Saturday night. Can you make it?"

What used to be our date nights. "What time?"

"I'm firming up plans now. I'm thinking about luring volunteers by providing a meal at my café. If I decide to go that route, I'll probably start it at five thirty."

"That's a great idea. As they say, the way to a man's heart is through his stomach."

A pause ensued.

"Cyril? Are you there?"

"Yes."

"I thought we got cut off." *What was going on?*

"I'm here." Another pause. "Angel, if I decide to have the eating meeting, would you be willing to make some of your chocolate chip pies for dessert?"

She was caught off guard. Of course she didn't mind bringing dessert. She loved to cook. But his request seemed a little odd to her—

"That's okay. You don't have to. I'll get Mama Edwards to make us something, some kind of cake maybe—"

"I'll be glad to bring the pies. How many are you expecting?"

He let out a smirk-laugh. "We have ten on the volunteer list right now, but we need twenty or twenty-five at least, to pull this off. Pastor Kyle wants the house completed in ten days' time, if possible."

"I'm a positive thinker. I'll bring six pies. Each pie serves eight, so that'll be enough for thirty people and *lots* of seconds for the big eaters."

"Angel. . .you rock, as the middle schoolers say."

The cat had her tongue for a moment. Her heart fluttered. *You rock, Cyril.* "Glad I can help."

❧

"Man, who made this pie?"

"This stuff is pure heaven."

"Oh, that my wife could cook like this. . ."

"Can I have another slice?"

"Whadayacallit?"

"Musty."

"*Musty?*"

"I *must* have some more." Hand waving in the air. "Seconds, please."

"Is there a name for it?"

"Whoever made it oughta call it Heavenly Pie."

"Oh man, that's hitting the nail on the head."

"Yep. Heavenly Pie."

"What a divine thought." A geehawing chuckle. A stab in the ribs. "Get it?"

"I sure do." A last bite. A swig of coffee. "And I'm gonna get me some more."

"Ladies and gentlemen." Cyril tapped a fork on his glass, making a *ping* sound. "If you're finished with your dessert, please find a seat on the other side of the café. The busboy will clean our tables while we have our meeting. But before you get to moving about, I'd like to introduce you to Angel Morgan. She's the lady behind the Heavenly Pie."

The crowd applauded.

"Angel, would you stand up?"

Angel stood and smiled.

"She owns Rue de France, the French restaurant down the street."

They applauded again.

"I hope you'll try her fare. Everything I've eaten at her restaurant is top-notch. She serves entrées. . .and sandwiches. . .and desserts. . .and Heavenly Pie, of course."

"There was a motive to your madness." Angel smiled at Cyril as she gathered her empty pie pans while he turned off the lights.

He shrugged then grinned. "Wouldn't you say it was a good one?"

She nodded. "Maybe after tonight, I'll have a few more customers."

"I hope so. They sure loved your Heavenly Pie."

"Heavenly Pie, is it?"

"Somebody came up with that tonight—"

"I know. I heard them."

"I already told you, you should make it your signature pie for Rue de France."

"I really like that name. Heavenly Pie." She'd give his suggestion some consideration. "I think your idea is brilliant, Cyril."

Chapter 8

Angel drove toward the Hendersons' house where she'd been working for a week. Every spare minute away from Rue de France, she spent at Project Hope. She had spread wallboard mud on the new walls, then taped and sanded them—with instructions from one of the volunteers, of course. She carried debris—strips of carpet, pieces of mildewed walls, sections of old cabinets, even a commode—to the trash receptacle outside.

She gave decorating guidance to Ms. Henderson as she made selections of paint colors, cabinets, countertops, and new furniture.

Angel had done everything they'd asked her to do, had been glad to do it. She couldn't wait to hang the curtains and help decide the furniture placement in the rooms. That would be the crowning touch. The icing on the cake.

This evening, she would be painting, so she wore her paint clothes—the same ones she'd worn when she painted Rue de France—a T-shirt, faded cut-off jeans, and old tennis shoes. She might as well be comfortable.

She pulled into the small grassless front yard. Laying new sod would be the last thing they'd do. She envisioned the heavy snow she saw on last night's news in some other part of the country. Here in Central Florida, it was mild year round, and even though it was October, the sod would be rich and full and green from the day they laid it. She pictured the young Henderson children playing in this filthy dirt pit and then later, their joy at playing on the soft green grass.

To her right and left, she saw rows of houses like the one they were rebuilding, with hardly any space between them. She heard people talking loudly on porches up and down the street. A horn blared in the distance.

Somebody was singing at the top of their lungs, and babies wailed.

Next door, a woman screamed, as if in agony. "You cain't leave me. I cain't stand it if you leave me."

Deeply touched, Angel shook her head. But at least the church was rebuilding one house. She recalled Pastor Kyle's sermon illustration on one of the Sundays he put out a plea for volunteers. It was about a young boy standing on a seashore, throwing back stranded sea creatures that lined the shore by the thousands. A man asked him why bother, and the boy said, "I'm saving this one and this one and this one."

Tears stung her eyes as she got out of her car, her mind on the family they were helping.

"Hiya." A young girl, maybe twelve or thirteen, jumped down from the front porch and made her way to Angel's car. "Like my new do?" She made a primping gesture.

Angel recognized the girl as a member of the Henderson family. She'd seen her a couple of times during the project. "Looks just like Oprah's hairstyle, Shanika. Or at least the way she was wearing it on her last magazine cover. I think she has a new— what'd you call it?"

"Do—"

"—a new do every day or two."

Shanika nodded. "She has her own private hairdresser."

"That style looks nice on you. And aren't you wearing some makeup?"

Shanika dropped her gaze, shylike. "Yes, ma'am. Part of this program was makeovers for Mama and me. They did me today. Mama gets done Saturday. We got some new clothes, too." She touched the lapel of her crisp white shirt, ran her hand down her stylish new jeans.

"I see that."

"I'm supposed to help you paint tonight. You need a hand with your stuff?"

"Sure." Angel gestured at paint trays and rollers in her backseat and picked up as many as she could hold.

Shanika gathered the rest of the items, and they walked toward the house, picking their way around the huge trash receptacle and various building supplies.

"We sure are glad y'all put a new swing on our porch," Shanika said as they walked up the front steps. "Our old one had some cracked boards down the middle. Kinda caught you in a ticklish spot, if you know what I mean." Shanika's dark brown eyes sparkled. "Thank You, Lawd, for a new swing."

That cracked Angel up—Shanika's cute mannerisms. It took her awhile to quit laughing. "I love a porch swing."

"We do, too. Mama says she doesn't really need to watch soap operas. She can sit right here on the porch and see them day and night."

Angel laughed again. This girl was delightful. She would like to take an interest in Shanika's future, give her guidance and advice, that sort of thing. She'd like to see her make something of her life.

When they got inside the house, Angel could see they were among the first to get there. A quick glance out the kitchen window told her Cyril's car wasn't there yet. Perhaps he'd stopped to pick up something. She was looking forward to seeing him.

While Shanika changed her clothes in the bathroom, Angel made her way into a bedroom and put down her paint supplies. Working on Project Hope had given her a great sense of fulfillment. And it gave her opportunities to be in close proximity to Cyril.

Now *that* was icing on the cake!

Angel glanced at her watch and noticed a smudge of paint on it. She wiped it off. Good thing it was her old one.

Nine o'clock already. The evening had gone by quickly. She and Shanika were finishing up the third bedroom. Shanika was at her side, rolling paint on the wall in fast, even strokes. Though the girl was young, Angel could see she was industrious. She'd go somewhere in life, this girl.

Shanika leaned her paint roller on the side of the tray, opened a can of paint with the special instrument, and then poured more paint into the tray. She closed the can, whisked her roller through the paint, and started painting again.

"Shanika?"

"Yes, ma'am?"

"You're a hard worker."

" 'We'll work till Jesus comes, we'll work,'" Shanika belted out in song. " 'Till Jesus comes, we'll work, till Jesus comes, and we'll be gathered home.'" She giggled. "That's an old hymn Mama likes to sing, especially when she's trying to get us to help her clean house on Saturday mornings."

Angel smiled at her. "You have a dramatic flair, too. That's a winning combination. Hard work and personality." Shanika reminded her of Oprah, with her honey-colored skin and beautiful hair and expressive eyes. "What do you intend to do with your life?"

"Oh, I don't know. . ."

"What're your interests?"

"I love to read."

"That's good. My mother always said reading expands your world. Do you want to go to college?"

Shanika stopped painting. Her eyes lit up. "Someday I'd like to be a teacher. And maybe a principal." She shrugged her shoulders. "I hope I can go to college."

"You hope? Of course you can. If a person puts her mind to it, she can do anything she wants to."

Shanika resumed her painting.

"I guess you know about Oprah's rise to fame?"

"Yes, ma'am. She started out with slim pickings, but now she's got plenty of money. And houses and cars. And TV shows. And she makes movies. And she owns a magazine. And—"

"—and she's smart and. . .generous. . .and gifted. . .it seems like she has the power to do just about anything. I guess you could say she's got it all."

Shanika didn't respond.

"Who knows? Maybe you'll be the next Oprah, Shanika. Now that's what I call success."

"No, ma'am."

Angel was surprised. "What?"

"Oh, I'm not saying Oprah isn't successful. Everybody knows better than that. She's on the"—she paused like she was thinking—"pinnacle—that's one of my spelling words this week. She's on the pinnacle of success. She's riding the high wave. She's not only rich and smart and generous and gifted, it seems like she's got something about her I can't explain. . ."

"I'd say it's an ethereal quality. Whatever it is, it draws people to her."

Shanika nodded vigorously. "But none of that's *real* success, in my book."

"What is *real* success, in your book?"

Shanika held her paint roller in midair. She took on a theatrical stance, putting a hand over her heart and clamping her eyes shut. " 'If I speak in the tongues of men and of angels, but have not love, I am only a resounding gong or a clanging cymbal. If I have the gift of prophecy and can fathom all mysteries and all knowledge, and if I have a faith that can move mountains, but have not love, I am nothing. If I give all I possess to the poor and surrender my body to the flames, but have not love, I gain nothing.' "

Angel was momentarily stunned. "You're. . .quoting. . .1 Corinthians 13?"

Shanika opened her eyes. "It's called the Love Chapter."

"I know. Where'd you learn it?"

"At my church. I help teach a children's Sunday school class. I help them memorize scriptures."

"That's amazing."

"No, ma'am." Shanika dipped her paint in the tray and put it to the wall, then kept up with her steady strokes. "It just takes practice." She smiled. "Practice to learn it, and then practice to live it."

Angel swallowed hard. "Shanika. . .you're something. . .you know that?"

Shanika shrugged.

"You didn't answer my question, though."

Shanika gave Angel a sideways glance.

"What is *real* success, in your book?"

"What I just quoted. The love the apostle was talking about is the love for the Lord. Jesus said I am the way, the truth, and the life. Nobody comes to the Father except by me. Putting Jesus, His work, and His Word above all else—*that's* what *real* success is, in my book."

Angel took a deep breath and slowly released it. Rue de France was the center of her world—not Jesus Christ. And before Rue de France, other things had crowded out the Lord. She'd pushed Him aside in her feverish quest for success.

But you did it for a good reason, came a dark voice. *You wanted to take care of your mother.*

And that's right and good and worthy, Angel responded in her heart.

But what about 1 Corinthians 13? The Love Chapter? An enlightening voice.

Love? I've got plenty of love.

Not the right kind.

A warring seemed to be going on in Angel's soul as thoughts ricocheted through it. *Sure you have love. Look. You're involved in this project.*

What's your motive? I'm not only interested in what you do, but why you do it.

But I empathized for the family. A truthful answer. *I identified with them. I gave of myself in this project.*

"If I give all I possess. . .but have not love, I gain nothing."

Angel winced. What had Shanika said about the love 1 Corinthians talked about? That it was referring to the Lord and putting Him first? *That's real love,* Shanika had said.

The nugget of wisdom hit its mark, piercing Angel's heart. *Lord,* she prayed in anguish of spirit. *What should I do?*

Put Me, My work, and My Word first in your life.

I will, Lord, I promise I will.

She was so happy, she hugged Shanika in a sisterly hug. "Thank you, Shanika."

Shanika looked puzzled.

"For bringing me manna from heaven." The manna was light and sweet and good, and Angel envisioned big fluffy dumplings raining down from the sky. The thought made her smile with a newfound joy.

Shanika quietly went back to her painting, as if she possessed the wisdom of the ages.

Angel thought about the irony of the situation. She wanted to give guidance and advice to Shanika, and Shanika ended up giving them to her.

She saw her vision again. Manna. A fitting vision for a cook. *Lord, thank You for speaking to me through this young girl. Forgive me for not putting You at the top of the list in my life. Help me to do better.*

"Please help me achieve *real* success," she said aloud.

"What'd you say?" Shanika stopped painting and looked at her.

"I was. . .well, I was praying."

"That's something I do all the time. Morning, noon, and night. It's what my mother taught me to do."

"Mine, too. And from here on out, I'm going to do more of it."

Chapter 9

Cyril came out on the front porch and restacked building supplies in preparation for tomorrow's work. He saw Angel in the yard cleaning some paintbrushes and rollers under a faucet by the light of the spotlight someone had hung on the eaves. She'd worked hard on this project, and he admired her. He wished—

"Cyril? I need to talk with you." Angel turned off the faucet.

"What's up?" He figured she needed to know something about tomorrow's assignment.

"Can we talk when everyone's gone? I need to tell you something important. I'll meet you here, on the front porch, if that's okay with you?"

"Sure." *This must be serious, by the tone of her voice.* He recalled passing by the room where she and Shanika were painting, and he overheard Shanika quoting a Bible verse. *Hmm...*

Fifteen minutes later, when the last person left, Cyril went through the house locking the windows. He stretched his tired muscles as he turned off the lights. He was used to exercise but not this kind of labor. But every ache was worth it. To him, this was a part of working for the Lord. He recalled a scripture where Jesus taught that if we offered a cup of cold water in His name, we were doing it as unto Him.

I've done this project for You, Lord.

He made his way through the front door and locked it behind him, then glanced around and saw Angel sitting on the porch swing.

"Have a seat." She patted the space to her right.

He sat down beside her and pushed hard with his foot, and the swing went back and forth. He laughed. "Reflex, I guess. You sit on a porch swing, and you want to get it going."

She nodded. "You should've heard Shanika tonight. She was telling me her mother would rather sit on the porch than watch TV." She started laughing.

He looked over at her. What did she mean? And why was she laughing?

She stopped laughing and proceeded to explain what Shanika had said about TV and soap operas and porches. "I'm bungling this." She tried again. "I can't seem to capture the essence of what she said." She smiled. "Oh, forget it."

"You wearing on my nerves, girl," hollered someone from next door. "If you don't change them clothes, I'm gonna beat your buns."

"There!" Angel's face was animated. "That's what Shanika was talking about."

He laughed, and she joined in.

"Shanika was so cute, the way she said it."

He sat there, enjoying the moment and enjoying being with her.

"Cyril, I wanted to tell you, I learned something new tonight."

"I did, too. Roy showed me how to lay ceramic tile." From his sideways glance in the dim light cast by a street light, he could see she was itching to talk. But he figured he'd have a little fun with her. "First, you trowel the adhesive on the floor. It's real thick, like peanut butter, and then you lay the tile on top of that, and you put little spacers between them. And then you let it dry for a good twenty-four hours. And then, when it's dry, you go back and put in the grout—"

"I don't mean to interrupt you but—"

"You can't wait to tell me about your conversation with Shanika, right? Other than the one about the porch. . .and soap operas?"

They both laughed.

"Did you hear us talking?"

"I heard her quote from 1 Corinthians 13. That's all. I was on my way outside to get more tile from Roy's truck."

Angel told him how she and Shanika had been teamed together, how impressed she'd been by her, how she wanted to give the young girl guidance and advice. But the tables turned, and Shanika gave Angel the best guidance of all.

"The best guidance?"

"I've got my priorities right, Cyril." Angel looked over at him, her eyes brighter than the stars that filled the night sky. "Shanika helped me see what's important in life." She continued talking, giving him the details.

"That's wonderful." He'd been praying for Angel ever since Pastor Kyle recommended it, and this was news that thrilled him. Now, maybe they could—

"I've been ministered to tonight, Cyril. By a young girl." She told him about the manna from heaven she'd pictured at Shanika's wise words. "I learned so much from her."

"Sometimes in our Christian walk, we struggle with things, and—"

"*You* have struggles?"

"Of course I do. We all do. We're human. The important thing is to let the Lord speak to us *in* our struggles."

"He sure spoke to me. Out of the mouth of babes. . ."

"When the Lord speaks to us, whether it's through a person, or through His

Word, or in prayer, or however He chooses to do it, well, it's like you described. It's like—"

"—manna to our souls." She laughed. "I guess you could say I got some soul food tonight. Food from heaven. And food from Shanika."

"Food for Angel." He took her hand, drew it to his lips, and kissed her fingers. "How about"—his voice grew husky—"angel food?"

Chapter 10

Angel's heart beat a little trill when Cyril tapped on the kitchen doorway of Rue de France at the stroke of noon. Her heart did that every time she saw him. She wanted to be with him every minute, and she was sure he felt the same way, though neither had said the magic words—*I love you*—yet.

"Come on in," she said.

"I figured you were back here." He made his way toward her.

"Shouldn't you be eating at Main Street Cafe?" He had his own restaurant. And this was lunchtime. And business was business. And he'd eaten lunch here for four days in a row.

He drew her to him and put his cheek to hers. "There's a motive to my madness," he said into her hair.

She returned his embrace warmly, longingly. She remembered when Cyril had said that phrase after her pie was such a hit at the Project Hope planning meeting. After that, her business had picked up. Though people weren't lining the sidewalk to get into Rue de France, she was having a better flow of customers.

"A person can eat ham and butter beans just so much." He winked at her.

She smiled, knowing Main Street Café had lots of menu choices, all of them delicious. She led him into the dining room and gestured at a table.

"Okay. I admit it." He pulled out the chair and sat down. "I thought maybe if I eat here a lot, it'll influence more townspeople to try Rue de France."

She handed him a menu, then leaned down and straightened the sweetener packets on his table. "Thanks, Cyril."

"But the real reason I came back today. . .is because I can't stay away from you." He trailed his finger up the back of her hand.

Oh, Cyril. . .I'm sure you're Mr. Right. She almost shouted out *Thank You, Lawd*, Shanika-style but managed to restrain herself.

"What's good today?" He looked down at the menu.

You. She recommended some choices, stumbling over her words, her heart still hammering.

He placed his order.

She headed for the kitchen. *I think True Love just knocked at my door.*

The days progressed into weeks, and the weeks into months.

Happy days...

Happy weeks...

Happy months.

Cyril procured a grant for downtown refurbishment and got the townspeople on board, and Nine Cloud got spiffed up. Paint. New awnings. Flowering shrubs in planters. Benches. Even new streetlights.

"Charming," people were saying.

"Good for business," Cyril always commented. "And no new housing areas yet," he added with a laugh.

Cyril saw the Lord perform spiritual transformations. Ted White from White's Hardware recognized his need of a Savior. Joe Freeman from the funeral home experienced a heart healing and came back to church. Some teenagers found Jesus and gave up their drinking.

Cyril was thrilled for Angel when Rue de France took off. She gave the Lord the credit.

"The Lord blessed me because I put Him first and everything else second," she liked to say.

Besides her hordes of lunchtime customers, she came up with the brilliant idea of teaching French-cooking lessons on Monday and Tuesday nights. She advertised in area newspapers and now had a long waiting list. She'd told him it was fast becoming the mainstay of her business.

"Ideas are spinning in my head like tops on their axes," she frequently said with a smile. "Ideas that are working." She was putting on afternoon dessert hours on Thursdays and Fridays that were a hit with the ladies, where she served a variety of dainty desserts, including tiny wedges of Heavenly Pie. And she catered ladies' events like bridal and baby showers and birthday parties, both at the Rue de France and in private homes.

But the best thing that happened in Nine Cloud was Cyril got to see Angel every day. He went somewhere with her every Saturday—to the shore, the park, the river, a play, a concert. It didn't matter where they went or what they did. They were together. A couple.

He proclaimed his love for her first. He did it the night of their first kiss...which happened to be...Valentine's Day.

She would never forget the night as long as she lived. . . .

They sat under a full moon on a bench facing the ocean, where people passed by on the boardwalk behind them.

"May I kiss the cook?" he asked.

She felt like laughing at his reference to her apron but nodded instead—vigorously, her heart pounding like the ocean waves.

He kissed her gently at first, and then their lips stayed together for a span of time, both of them seeming to revel in the moment that would stay in their memories forever.

He pulled back and looked deeply into her eyes. "One more question."

"Yes?"

"May I tell the cook I love her?"

"Oh, yes."

"I love you, Angel."

"I love you, too, Cyril." She adored his old-fashioned ways, how he'd waited months to kiss her and tell her he loved her. Thrill shivers coursed through her. And during those months, she'd come to realize she was old-fashioned in some ways. But not quite as much as he was. She reached up, drew his face toward her, and kissed him hungrily, like she didn't ever want to let him go. "I love you, I love you, I love you."

"Now that's the *crème de la crème*," he said, when he came up for air. "Did I say that right?"

Her answer was another kiss.

❦

The next morning, Cyril called Pastor Kyle. "I want you to be the first to know."

"Know what?" Pastor Kyle had a smile in his voice.

"I told her I loved her."

"Then I'm guessing you'll be needing a preacher?"

"I'm thinking June, if she'll agree."

Chapter 11

The March evening couldn't have been any more perfect. Or romantic. Angel took a bite of lobster, then glanced at Cyril. From their table by the window at the superb beachside restaurant, they had a perfect view of the ocean. And the food was nearly indescribable. That was saying a lot from someone who'd studied cooking in France.

Cyril had presented her with a bracelet corsage when he'd picked her up. It was made of lavender and could've come straight from Paris, it was so French looking.

On the drive to the beach, they had enjoyed a pleasant camaraderie. But something scintillating yet sweet had swathed around them like gossamer.

Now, sitting in the restaurant, she felt a draft of cool air from the air-conditioning vent and pulled her black net shawl around her shoulders. In her movement, their knees touched under the table, and thoughts of love filled her heart.

"A penny for your thoughts?" Cyril squeezed a wedge of lime into his ice water, then placed his hand over hers on the table.

"I. . .um. . ."

"You? Angel Morgan at a loss for words? That kicks in a memory for me. The cat got your tongue the first time we met."

She nodded. "I wanted to meet business owners dressed like a businesswoman. Instead—"

"You were covered in paint—"

"I felt so stupid, I forgot my manners—"

"And I was pretty smug-acting, wasn't I?"

"You could say that. In fact, that night I secretly started calling you Mr. Hooty-Toot."

"You didn't?" He looked playfully thunderstruck.

She nodded, exaggeratedly so. "After I looked up the meaning of your name, I decided Mr. Hooty-Toot was apropos."

"Why? What's it mean?"

"Lord. You were acting so. . .lordly."

He chuckled. "What does *your* name mean? I'm sure it means angelic being. But anything else?"

"Messenger."

He swung his head from side to side, like he was deep in thought. "Couldn't be more appropriate. Angel, you're my messenger of love."

Angel wondered where Cyril was going as he passed the turn to the highway that led back to Nine Cloud. Then she knew. He was taking her to the beach house where they ate her pie on their first date.

He turned onto a narrow private road, then pulled into the driveway. His headlights showed a refurbished house, the dull weathered boards now painted a crisp sandy beige, the professional landscaping beachy and inviting.

"What happened here?" She was delighted with the changes. When she'd first seen the house, she thought it would make a perfect beach hideaway if only someone would give it some TLC.

"We decided to remodel it when we were making the changes to Nine Cloud."

"It's beautiful, Cyril."

"We knocked down some walls and added a big room on the back. The ocean view is fantastic."

"Can I see the inside?"

"Sure. Come on." In a flash, he was at her door, opening it. "But it's not furnished. Or decorated. That comes next."

At the front door of the house, he stepped inside, found the lights, and flicked them on. "Come on in." He held the door open for her.

She walked into a large room that was big enough for several conversation areas. "This is going to be beautiful when it's all done."

He pointed to a far wall. "That's where the kitchen will be, as soon the cabinetry and countertops are chosen." He pointed to another area. "That'll be the dining room." He walked across the large room and stopped. "This is the addition." He pointed upward, then continued on toward the wall of windows. "Come look out."

She walked over and stood by him in the addition that couldn't be detected as such. It blended in perfectly with the rest of the house. Through the floor-to-ceiling windows, she saw the ocean that looked like black glass in the moonlight. The sight took her breath away.

"We'll probably have several tables and chairs in this area. We'll use it for casual eating and playing table games, things like that."

She looked around the room. In her mind's eye, she could see a limestone or buffed-marble floor. And beach-type furniture—rattan, maybe, or wicker. And paintings that captured the ocean's beauty. And—

"Care to walk on the beach?"

Her heart did one of its familiar trills. "I—I'd love to."

He unlocked the glass door and slid it aside. "After you."

She stepped out onto an expansive patio, and he followed her out. She looked up into the most spectacular sky she'd ever seen.

"You sure aren't saying much tonight." He whispered the words into her hair from where he stood behind her. "Cat got your tongue again?"

Calm down, my heart. "I—I. . ." She started again. "The beauty of this place. . .the ocean. . ."

"I remember the night you said the ocean made you hug me." His voice was husky as he gently turned her to face him. "You said it had something to do with the moon shining down. . ."

She glanced skyward and saw a full moon.

". . .and the way the waves lapped. . . ."

She heard the ocean behind her, a sound that echoed the beating of her heart.

"Come with me." He took her hand and led her across the patio. "Better take off your shoes."

Shivers danced up her spine, and there wasn't even a slight wind. She knew where they were coming from. Cyril and his nearness. She slipped off her shoes, and he did the same.

He led her into the sand, and they walked down the beach, neither of them saying a word, his arm around her, her arm around him.

After a long while, they turned and headed back toward the beach house, both of them talking in soft tones—words of endearment, *amour.*

Aimer eperdument, Angel thought. Love to distraction.

He stopped and kissed her, and she thought her heart would burst from happiness.

He dropped to his knees in the sand.

Her heart was liquid love. "Cyril. . ."

He took her hand in his. "My darling Angel, will you marry me?"

"Yes, yes, yes." She bent down and kissed him.

"To have and to hold?" he quipped.

"From this day forward."

"Forever and ever?" He stood up and took her in his arms.

"Thank You, Lawd!"

Chapter 12

Their June wedding couldn't have been any more perfect.

They had the rehearsal dinner at Main Street Café.

They got married in the white-steepled church in the center of town.

They repeated their vows in front of Pastor Kyle.

They held the reception at Angel Food—formerly known as Rue de France—with the guests spilling out onto the grassy town square.

The wedding cake was a Parisian version, with fondant icing and edible lavender flowers cascading over it.

The groom's cake wasn't a cake at all. It was Heavenly Pie—lots of them—Angel Food's new signature dessert. It was rich like their love but laden with chocolate.

And Nine Cloud was on cloud nine!

And their honeymoon? They spent it at the beach house Angel had just decorated. She named it *Le demeure d'amour*. The abode of love.

Heavenly Pie

1 (9-inch) prepared piecrust
1 cup chocolate chips
½ cup butter or margarine, melted
2 eggs
1 cup sugar
¼ cup flour
1 teaspoon vanilla
1 cup pecans, chopped
Whipped topping

Line bottom of piecrust with chocolate chips. (Don't be tempted to use more.) In a separate bowl, mix remaining ingredients with a fork, then pour over chocolate chips. Put foil strips around edges of pie. Bake at 350 degrees for 45 minutes or longer, until brown on top. Inside should be soft but not runny. Serve warm (by oven or microwave) with a dollop of whipped topping. Refrigerate. Stays good several days. (But you probably won't find this out because it'll get eaten before then.)

JUST DESSERTS
by Aisha Ford

Dedication

To my family...
I love you more than words will ever be able to express.

Chapter 1

Monica Ryan paced her office at her restaurant, The Pie Rack, waiting for Adella to click back over from call waiting. Despite having been on the phone for the past half hour, Monica estimated she and Adella had only clocked about ten minutes of actual talking time.

Thanks to the fantastic technology of Adella's cell phone service, Monica didn't have to wait in silence. Instead, she got to listen to a nice variety of swoony love songs. Not that she had anything against swoony love songs, but after twenty minutes, Monica was certain the music would start to wear on anybody's nerves!

Impatient, Monica sighed and sat in the rolling chair at her desk. Adella Parker was an old acquaintance from high school, and there was heavy emphasis on the word *acquaintance.*

In the ten years since they'd graduated, Monica had seen Adella around town a few times and generally heard about her appearances at high society parties and benefits.

The closest encounter Monica ever really had with Adella was running against her for senior-class president. She'd beaten Adella by a huge margin, but Adella hadn't really seemed to care.

Supposedly, her father, the CEO of a multibillion-dollar company, had thought it good leadership practice for Adella to try running for office. However, Adella's ideal job description was more along the lines of carefree heiress than serious politician.

Fast-forward ten years later, and Adella still played the role of a carefree heiress, but now she had a new title to add to the list: bride-to-be.

"Hello. Hello?" Adella unexpectedly shouted into the receiver.

"Yes, yes, I'm here."

"Monica?"

"Adella?" Monica cleared her throat and spoke louder. "I'm here—it's me, Monica."

"Oh, good. I thought I'd lost you for a minute. Like I was telling you before, we love everything you sell at the bakery, and we'd want to have you do a dessert buffet at the engagement party—with lots of those sweet potato pies, but we're trying to keep costs down."

"I'm sure we could work out some type of. . .something," Monica said, vaguely wondering if Adella even knew what *keeping the costs down* actually meant.

Nothing in the society news columns of late indicated that Adella's family fortunes were dwindling.

But nonetheless, the job would be great exposure for The Pie Rack, and short of Adella being a bridezilla a million times over, Monica knew there was no good reason she would turn down the job.

"Fantastic," Adella said.

"Well, thanks so much for calling," Monica said, hoping to wrap up the call. Business was business, and there was no way she wanted to get sucked into talking about the "good old days" of high school.

Her old yearbooks and scrapbooks, safely hidden in the attic, were full of the pictorial evidence that the good old days were not that good at all—at least not her senior year.

"Just one more thing," Adella said, interrupting Monica's thoughts. "I was reading one of my bridal magazines the other day, and it says that if possible, I should try to find a caterer who can do both the meal and the dessert. Is there any way you could pull that off?"

Monica sighed as quietly as possible, hoping to reign in the urge to cut a potentially difficult client loose before the situation got too complicated. "Honestly, Adella, we really do only specialize in desserts—"

"But didn't your family own a restaurant when we were in high school?"

"Yes, we did, but due to. . .circumstances, we're only in the dessert business now."

This time it was Adella's turn to sigh. "To tell you the truth, that's not exactly the type of catering setup I was hoping for. Just to make things easier on myself, I'd like all of the food to come from the same vendor."

"You're planning this party yourself?" Monica blurted out before she could stop herself.

"I am." Adella giggled, then grew serious. "I know everybody thinks I'm a clueless society girl, but the minute Byron proposed, I just knew that I wanted to be in charge of every tiny detail of this entire experience. You get married only once, so I'd like it to be perfect, you know?"

"Wow. I don't think I would have so much fun planning every detail of my own wedding, but I admire your determination."

"Oooh!" Adella squealed. "Are you getting married, too? How come you didn't tell me sooner?"

Why did Adella have such an uncanny ability to turn the conversation to uncomfortable topics? "No, no, I'm not engaged. You sound like one of my relatives now," Monica said, trying to keep the mood light. "I was just saying that if, I mean, *when* I get engaged, I doubt I would enjoy being the sole planner for the event."

"Oh, I understand how you feel," said Adella. "It seemed like it took forever for Byron to propose to me, too. How long have you been waiting for that special someone to pop the question?"

There was no special someone, and there really never had been, unless you counted Gil. "And that won't ever count, at least not now," Monica murmured.

"What was that?" Adella asked.

"Oh, I'm sorry, I guess I was thinking out loud."

"Don't worry about that, I know you're probably having a busy day—oops! Call waiting—it's Byron, let me put you on hold for one tiny little second."

Before Monica could protest, Adella placed her on hold again—with more swoony love songs!

"That's fantastic, honey. It might be just what The Pie Rack needs to get us back on the map."

This was all the encouragement Monica needed to hear. Spending the better part of an hour listening to Adella ramble on and on had been worth it just for this.

"Thanks, Dad. The only catch is, her parents want to keep the costs down so they can splurge on the wedding."

"No problem there; we can give them a good deal. The exposure alone will be worth it."

Monica shifted her cell phone to the other ear and pondered how to tell her dad the second part of the agreement. A gust of wind blew so hard that her car veered slightly into the next lane. Monica tightened her grip on the wheel and wondered how she would break the rest of the news to her dad.

"Did you sign papers yet?"

"Not exactly. We talked over the phone, but the contract will be contingent on us providing the entire menu for the party."

"What do you mean?"

"It means, we get top billing, but we have to provide all of the food for the party."

"And how are we supposed to do that, since we only serve desserts?"

Monica could hear the frustration building in her father's voice and instantly regretted telling him the news over the phone. She should have told her mom first, and then they could have broken the news together.

"Well, I'll be. . .that Amos Butler got the best of me again, didn't he?"

"Bob. . .calm down," Monica heard her mother saying in the background. Usually, when her father got started about Amos Butler, his former business partner, there was no stopping him.

"Dad, it's not a lost cause. It'll be okay. She's given me three days to find a caterer who will provide the entrees, and we can still do the dessert, and everything will be fine."

"And how are you supposed to do that?"

"I'm totally capable of finding someone. Remember the National Restaurateurs' Convention I went to last summer? I made some good contacts there and got to know some local restaurateurs better. I'm sure I can find someone local who'll be willing to agree to this deal."

"I don't like the sound of it, but I trust you. Do what you can do. If not, we'll do fine without the job."

"Thanks for understanding, Dad. Any other time I might have turned the offer down flat, but for some reason I couldn't say no."

"Humph. Three days is a ridiculous deadline, so you'd better get on the phone and start calling folks now."

"I will do my best just as soon as I get home from the gym."

"The gym? You're not even at work?"

"Actually, I'm on my way to the gym now, but I'll call you later with an update about how the search is going."

"Monica, I know you're in charge of the company, but maybe this is something you should have discussed with me first. After all, if it doesn't work out, then you're putting the company name on the line."

Monica could see his point, but part of being in charge was making mistakes, wasn't it? And what about taking risks? Didn't all the entrepreneurs who prospered take big risks at one time or another? She could tell this conversation was not going to end well or soon, if her dad had his way. The best course of action for now would be to get off the phone.

"Okay, Dad, I promise we can talk about this later. But right now isn't the best time. It's really windy outside, and I'm having a hard time steering the car, so I probably shouldn't be talking on the phone."

Bob grunted in reply, but Monica knew he wouldn't protest further. One of his pet peeves was driving near people who seemed to be distracted because they were talking on the phone. Both of her parents constantly lectured her about her habit of driving and chatting. Their remedy for the situation had been to buy her an earpiece for the phone, but Monica usually forgot to put it in the car.

"All right. Get off the phone and call me later. Even though I wonder if going to the gym when you've got so much to do is a good use of your time."

"Love you, Dad." Monica hung up quickly, before her dad could give her a speech on the virtue of diligence at work.

How could a man who never took a day off from work in over forty years possibly understand her need to blow off steam by doing something other than standing over a stove, concocting new recipes?

Just over a year ago, when her mother had finally convinced him to retire, Monica and her mom were both at their wits' end, because her father found a way to come into the office nearly every day.

Over the past few months, she'd managed to convince him that the place was in good hands, but the last thing she needed was for this deal with Adella to fail. If that happened, she might as well move right out of her office, because her dad would be back at work quicker than Adella could click over to the other line.

Pulling into an empty parking space, Monica decided now was a good time for a quick prayer.

"Lord, looking back, it feels like maybe I did the wrong thing to say yes to the deal with Adella. If it was a mistake, please show me a graceful way to bow out before I get in over my head. But if this is something that will be good for business, then I'm asking You to help me with all of the details—and please keep my dad calm in the process."

A loud, forceful bang on the passenger-side door of the car interrupted her thoughts. Monica quickly glanced over to see what was going on.

The man parked next to her had opened his door and rammed his door into hers. With an apologetic look on his face, he mouthed, "Sorry," and bent down to examine the damage.

"Great, just what I need. Instead of getting my cardio in, I get to sit here and haggle with this guy over insurance information."

She yanked her gym bag out of the backseat and steeled herself to get down to business. Tall and handsome, with an air of confidence, he looked like the type of guy who would try to convince her that any damage wasn't his fault, and then brag to his friends about how he'd put one over on some naive woman at the gym. He almost reminded her of Gil, but underneath that borderline arrogant exterior, Gil was truly a nice guy. At least, he had *seemed* nice—he and his backstabbing family.

"Well, no one's going to walk all over me today," Monica muttered, stepping out of the car and hefting the bag over her shoulder. "I already messed up with Adella, but this pushover is reformed as of right now."

Feeling mildly disgusted that she had thought about Gil twice today, when she'd gone years without even saying his name, Monica had a feeling her dad was right. She should have stayed at work and skipped the workout today, but since she found herself in this situation, she was determined to get a satisfactory resolution, no matter what antics this guy tried to pull.

As Monica walked to the other side of the car, the man stood up and grinned. "Amazingly, it looks fine to me."

"Are you kidding? It sounded like you hit the door with a sledgehammer." *Don't back down,* she told herself.

He shook his head and motioned to the door. "Nope, not even a scratch. And, for the record, I didn't hit it on *purpose*. It's this January weather," he said, gesturing midair. "Right when I got out of the car, the wind picked up and took the door with it."

As Monica reached the door, he stepped back so she could examine it for herself. Bending over, she saw no sign of scratches or dents.

Embarrassed for being so nitpicky, she stood up, feeling a sheepish grin spread over her face. "I guess you're right. So no harm done."

"Right. . .right," he said, speaking slowly and staring at her so intently that she grew uncomfortable under his scrutiny.

Her first impulse was to jump in the car and drive away, but she recognized something distantly familiar about this stranger.

Forgetting her manners, Monica stared back, straining to get a better look at him, despite the dim light outside.

"Monica?" he said.

Was it really? No way.

"Monica!" he said again, this time, more assured.

"Gil?" Monica wondered if the long day at work had stressed her to the point where she was merely imagining him. What if other people in the parking lot were watching her converse with nothing but air. Or maybe she had simply fallen asleep at her desk.

Before she could ponder more possibilities, the man presumed to be Gil took a step forward and enveloped her in a hug.

It was Gil. This was not a dream.

Chapter 2

I t really has been a long time, hasn't it?"

Monica nodded, sipping her banana-berry yogurt smoothie. "Part of me can't even believe we're sitting here together." She quickly considered how that might have sounded and tried to think of a way to clarify her thoughts. "Not. . . together, together. Just, together. . .here. . .you and me, you know?"

The corner of Gil's mouth twitched, but if he found her statement uncomfortable, he hid it well.

"I know. I mean, it almost feels like I'm meeting you for the first time."

Except for the hug. Nobody would hug a stranger like that. Monica pushed the memory of his cologne aside and tried to concentrate on her smoothie instead.

"So tell me everything that's been going on with you," he said.

Monica chuckled. "How much time do you have? Because recapping ten years is going to take more than a few minutes.

"I've got time," he said, a glint of laughter in his eyes.

"No, you don't," she protested. "Besides, that would leave no time for you to talk. What have you been up to?"

He shrugged. "This, that, and everything. I went away to college while I was getting my business management degree, and I came back and worked at the restaurant during the summer. By way of an interesting turn of events, I discovered I was just as good at managing talent as I was at managing in the food business, so I moved away for good, became a talent manager for gospel musicians, and then came back a year ago to pick up where I left off. It seems that my dad heard your dad was retiring and decided to play copycat."

The mention of their fathers gave Monica pause. Suddenly, her smoothie wasn't as appetizing. What would her dad say if he knew she was sitting in the café at the gym, sipping a banana-berry smoothie across from the son of the man who had almost ruined all that he had worked to build?

As she glanced around to see if she saw any familiar faces, Monica felt like a criminal.

She pushed her smoothie aside and stood up. "Well, it was nice seeing you again."

Gil stood, too. "Wait, that's not fair. You didn't tell me what you've been up to."

Monica lifted her gym bag and took a step away from the table.

"Hey, I know what happened with our parents wasn't. . . ideal. But I think we can at least make the decision to be friends with each other, can't we?"

Monica took a step back toward the table but kept her keys in her hand, ready to escape at a moment's notice. Yes, she wanted to befriend Gil again, but she didn't want to disappoint her family. There was a fine line here; she didn't want to cross it. Especially not now. The last thing she needed on her already-full plate was an old family feud.

"You know what? I think my dad was wrong." Gil stood and took a step closer. "And honestly, ever since then, business hasn't been the same."

"And you connect that to what happened between our dads?"

Gil shrugged. "I can't say for sure, but I know things have been tough. Right now I don't know how much longer we. . . My dad begged me to come back and see if there's a way to keep from shutting the place down."

"Oh, Gil, I'm sorry." Ashamed at her own selfish thoughts, Monica sat back down. "I. . .I didn't know. Really, I didn't. My dad doesn't even like to talk about your family."

Gil sat down across from her. "I really didn't want this conversation to be the Butler-family sob story. That's why I asked what was going on with you."

Monica hesitated, wanting to be honest but not seem as if she were bragging.

"It was tough in the beginning, right after our parents split the company. But my dad was determined to make a dessert café succeed. It's been hard work, but we're finally getting to a place where things are starting to look up. We're actually shooting a commercial in a few weeks, and we have a spot scheduled on a local TV show soon."

"That's great. You guys deserve it."

"We've worked hard for it."

A long silence passed between them, and finally Monica broke it.

"So what are your plans for your dad's business?"

Gil shook his head. "My honest opinion is that we should close it before we lose too much more, but he's got it in his head that we can hold on until we can get some kind of breakthrough. I don't have the heart to tell him it's not that probable. The big chains are just chipping away at our profits, day by day." He looked down at the table and was quiet.

Monica put her hand over his. "I'm so sorry. I know what it feels like to keep advertising and hoping word of mouth will spread and seeing nothing happen."

"Brainstorming for hours on end, looking for the one elusive idea that might change the course of things—and not finding it and feeling helpless," Gil spoke up, finishing her thoughts.

All at once, she remembered her situation with Adella and realized that she could solve her problem and extend an olive branch to Gil and his family in their time of need.

Quickly, she explained the terms of the deal and asked if he might be interested in partnering together to fulfill the terms of the contract.

"I still can't believe you're even asking me, I mean, after everything."

"Maybe this opportunity will give our families the boost in business we need and provide us all with the chance to heal," she answered.

"Are you sure? Really? Catering Adella Parker's engagement party with you?"

"Do you think you can do it?"

"At this point, I'm willing to try anything to make my dad happy," said Gil.

"Then that's it. We'll work at it together and hopefully. . ." Monica paused, not knowing exactly how to finish her thoughts.

"Hopefully," Gil said, breaking the silence, "our families will be friends again."

Chapter 3

Gil went straight to his family's restaurant, Amos's Smokehouse, as soon as he left the gym and spent the next several hours in the office poring over his parents' old recipes, hoping to find some dishes that would work for Adella's party.

He couldn't wait to tell his family about this exciting venture, but he dreaded the look on his father's face when he found out that partnering with Bob Ryan's company was part of the deal.

Gil slumped over the desk, resting his hands in his forehead. Maybe this wasn't such a good idea after all.

Should I call Monica and tell her this isn't the good fit I thought it would be?

Gil picked up his phone but couldn't bring himself to dial her number. If he had to cancel the deal, he should at least do it in person, right?

And then what would she think of him? After he'd failed her in their relationship so long ago, how could he go back on his word now?

There was also the undeniable fact that she was still just as beautiful as she had ever been, if not more. Following through on this deal would also give him the chance to reconnect with her and maybe rekindle the romance that had just budded when the spilt happened.

Most people who had known the Butler and Ryan families for many years always speculated that one day he and Monica would get married and expand the family business.

He and Monica had grown up as best friends by circumstance, spending most of their free time at the restaurant, simply because their parents were there. As they grew older and entered the phase where they began noticing the opposite sex, they both dated other people but remained close friends.

Then, the summer before the last year of high school, after their parents decided to open a second location, things changed. It was as if all of a sudden, a curtain was lifted, and they saw each other in a different light.

Their families were elated that the two of them were finally dating, and deep down inside, Gil felt he had found the woman he wanted to spend the rest of his life with. He never told Monica how serious he felt, partially because it would have been awkward at their young ages, and partially because just after Christmas, their parents had the big disagreement.

At first, he and Monica had continued to date, because their fathers often disagreed on how to run the business. Despite their many arguments, Amos and Bob always came to some kind of compromise. But this time had been different.

First, the problems increased when Gil's father issued the ultimatum—either sell the struggling second location or part ways. Monica's father had refused, because he felt that they hadn't given the second restaurant a chance to build a clientele.

Gil's father saw dwindling dollar signs and worried that the place was losing too much too fast, and wanted out immediately.

Suddenly, they no longer ate family dinners together, their fathers stopped speaking to each other at work unless it was absolutely necessary, and then Monica's father did the unthinkable—he quit.

Gil didn't blame Monica's dad for his gumption. While he loved his own father, Amos Butler had a tendency to run his household and his business like a bully—his way or no way. Most of the time it worked, but it seemed that now his heavy-handed tactics had backfired.

After Amos realized Bob was serious, he decided to make sure Bob knew he was making a big mistake by legally and permanently severing ties with him.

Lawyers were called in to organize the deal, and it was agreed that the Butlers would keep the original restaurant location, the original recipes, and the well-recognized name, while Bob Ryan decided he would assume ownership of the not-so-successful location, taking only the sweet potato pie recipe.

Amos had openly mocked Bob for not putting up more of a fight and demanding more. Bob refused to argue any longer and moved across town to be closer to his business.

Gil and Monica continued to date, but the situation grew increasingly awkward as Gil's father looked for a way to wield more control over Bob Ryan.

Out of sheer frustration that he had been unable to get Bob to change his mind, Amos Butler forbade his family to have contact with any of the Ryans—and for Gil, that meant no more dating Monica.

He remembered the day he had gone over to her house to explain the situation. He promised her it was temporary, and soon enough, things would be back to normal.

But soon enough never came. They saw each other at school and different social events but didn't really talk. After a couple of months with no change in the atmosphere, Gil had an argument with his father and decided he didn't care about the rule any longer. In a huff, he drove to Monica's house, only to have her father answer the door and inform him that now Monica was forbidden to talk to him.

By that time, graduation was coming up and when Gil heard Monica was going to the prom with one of their mutual friends, he gave up on the relationship.

Instead, he spent his last few months of high school with an eye to the future, hoping to move as far away from St. Louis as possible.

But now that he had the authority to make decisions like this for the company, along with the chance to see where this relationship might go, there was no way he was going to let his dad talk him out if it.

Monica paced the floor of her living room late that night, wondering how in the world she would explain this new turn of events to her parents.

At least half a dozen times since her chance encounter with Gil, she had picked up her phone to call them but always lost her nerve before she could fully dial the number.

"Lord, did I mess this up even worse?"

She turned on the TV to try to mask the growing rumble of doubts running through her mind, but that did little to help.

Despite the impulse to back out of the agreement with Gil, she couldn't help but wonder how things might have been between them had their fathers not had that argument ten years ago.

Would they have remained high school sweethearts and gotten married after college and stayed on to manage the restaurant together? Would they have had children by now?

"Stop it," Monica said, turning off the TV. "You just ran into the man; stop imagining what could have been and focus on what is."

She picked up her phone again, this time, wondering if she should just call Gil and cancel the whole deal.

No. She wouldn't do it. She couldn't, not after the way she had run into him under such unusual circumstances. Maybe it was more than coincidence they had met today. Wasn't partnering with Gil the best idea after she had prayed and asked for a solution to catering Adella's party?

Yes, if nothing else, God had provided an answer to her prayers. As for their families reconciling, Monica didn't have the same high hopes Gil had expressed, so there was no use in letting her mind wander to the what-ifs of what might have been.

Yes, he was still just as good-looking, but that had nothing to do with their deal. From the way he talked, he had been able to put the family business aside long enough to establish a life away from work, something Monica had never really been able to do.

While his family had the benefit of working with an established restaurant, Monica's family had been working overtime for the last ten years to play catch up. Though he had been cordial and very friendly today, he had given no indication that he was interested in more than a work relationship. And why should he? Monica couldn't imagine why he wouldn't have a girlfriend or even be nearly married right now.

Monica turned on her laptop and started typing out preliminary notes for the party menu. She and Gil had agreed to meet again tomorrow afternoon to compile their ideas and finalize the menu before she met with Adella again.

While she typed, Monica thought about how her father would take the news. There was really no way to ease into such a potentially inflammatory announcement.

Thinking back to the days after the split, Monica remembered her father spending hours working overtime and even taking a second job just to keep The Pie Rack afloat, just to prove to himself that Amos Butler was wrong.

Would the news be a bit more bearable if he knew how desperately Gil's family needed this job, or would he remember how alone they felt after Amos had laughed and told him that a dessert café was a ridiculous idea?

And worse yet, would her father be angry with her for even speaking to Gil? Not long after Gil's dad had stopped him from seeing Monica, Gil had come over to visit, but Monica's dad had refused to let her see him, and told her she wasn't allowed to speak to Gil any longer.

That decree had been uncomfortable back when she was seventeen, but out of respect to her parents, she'd obeyed and considered her romance with Gil to be over.

Now that she was almost twenty-eight, she doubted the rule still held, but if her dad remembered, explaining her way out of it would be uncomfortable to say the least.

"I'll tell them first thing in the morning," Monica decided, turning off her computer.

It was no use trying to work right now. Too much had happened today, and she couldn't see a real rhyme or reason to any of it.

Her new plan for the evening didn't get much attention. Monica decided she would go to bed early, get a full eight hours of sleep, and deal with all of the pesky little details in the morning.

Chapter 4

Monica's dad slapped the arm of his easy chair for emphasis. "There is no way The Pie Rack will do business with Amos Butler."

Monica slumped on the sofa in her parents' living room. So far, not so good. "Dad, please, just give it a chance. Remember, yesterday you told me to do whatever I needed to do to make this catering job a reality. Maybe this is a good thing."

"I don't even want to discuss this further," Bob said, crossing his arms over his chest. "Get on the phone right now and call that boy and tell him I said no."

"I can't do that, Dad. They need this job just as badly as we do, if not more."

"No. No, and what are you even doing talking to him? Didn't I tell you not to associate with them any more?"

Monica chuckled nervously, hoping she could make her dad calm down. "That was ten years ago, Dad. I think I might be able to make a few decisions on my own."

"No good can come of this."

"If we don't take this deal with the Butler's, we can kiss the engagement party good-bye. Where else am I going to find someone to partner with before tomorrow?"

"That's what I told you yesterday. Three days is a ridiculous deadline." He shrugged then continued. "Just call Adella and tell her we can only do dessert. If she says no, then we can't do it."

"Dad, it's been ten years since we've spoken to this family, and I just ran into Gil out of nowhere yesterday. Do you think this is God's way of telling us it's time to bury the hatchet?"

"Or maybe this is God's way of telling us we're not supposed to be catering this party." He held up his hands in protest. "Don't bring God into this. I've forgiven the Butlers, and I'm not holding any grudges. But that doesn't mean I'm going to sit back and let his son break my daughter's heart again. Who knows what they're up to this time?"

"Dad, I'll be fine. This isn't about me and Gil."

"I know that's right, because I won't let it be about that. How do you think I felt when my best friend stooped low enough to tell his son he couldn't see my daughter any more. You cried for two weeks straight."

"I was seventeen. Everything was a big deal then."

"No. That's the end of it. I'm the boss, and I say no. This won't work. We can't trust those people."

"Bob," her mom said, speaking for the first time since Monica had explained the situation. "Since you're officially retired, Monica is technically the boss, and I think you should let her make the final decision."

Both Monica and her dad turned to stare at her mom.

Monica was surprised because her mother generally deferred to her father's final decision in all things business related.

"Phyllis, please let me handle this," Bob said. "I know what I'm doing."

"I'm not saying you can't handle it, but think about how you've taught Monica to run the company. You've always said you wanted her to be prepared to do this on her own, and now when she has the chance to prove herself, you swoop in and take over again."

"I'm not taking over, I'm providing business advice."

"You gave her an ultimatum, not advice. It was an order. Don't you remember last week when Reverend Molson preached about casting your cares on the Lord?"

"Yes, but that has nothing to do with this situation."

"In a way it does. If you cast your cares on God to fix a situation, then you trust Him to do it. You give it to Him, and you don't keep taking it back just so you can make sure He's doing things right."

"Monica is not God, Phyllis."

"I didn't say she is. My point is that if you trust her to run The Pie Rack all by herself one of these days, you should trust her to make decisions you don't necessarily agree with without jumping in to stop her."

"Monica, I understand what your mother's saying, and I do trust you, but I can't allow this to happen while I sit here twiddling my thumbs. It's too risky."

Monica felt a surge of courage and spoke up again. "Dad, isn't that what Amos Butler told you about the second restaurant? And didn't he say the same thing when you took the pie recipe and decided to open a dessert café?"

"That was different."

"Was it really?" Monica asked.

"How so?" asked her mom.

Bob shook his head. "No, Phyllis. I just don't trust them. They have to be up to something else."

"I honestly don't feel like that, Bob," said her mother. "If nothing else, I think we should go ahead and do this. If it doesn't work, then we cut our losses, but I don't want us to teach Monica that she should never take chances. Most things worth anything involve taking a chance."

"Like what?"

Phyllis grinned. "Like you asking me out back in college when you thought I would turn you down."

Bob nodded in agreement. "Now you're right about that. It took me two months to work up the nerve."

"Like I didn't notice that you followed me around all the time and just happened to turn up at every event I went to."

Bob laughed. "So I wasn't exactly as subtle as I thought."

He grew quiet, and Monica didn't interrupt his thoughts, even though she felt like she could come up with a hundred reasons why she should be allowed to make the final decision.

"All right, Monica," he said finally. "You decide. Like your mother said, we do trust you, and even though we might not agree with every decision you make, you will eventually be the sole owner of The Pie Rack, and I know you'll do a good job. If you think this is a good risk to take, we stand behind you."

"Oh, thanks, you guys!" Monica exclaimed, and hugged both of her parents. "I promise this will be the best risk I ever take."

"You think so, honey?" her mom asked, smiling. "You know marriage is a big risk, too. So is starting a family."

Bob frowned. "Who said anything about marriage?" He cleared his throat. "Monica, honey, you can make all the business decisions you want, but just don't get any ideas about marrying that boy. I can barely stomach the idea of doing business with a Butler, but I draw the line at being related to them."

Phyllis grabbed his arm, pulled him up out of his chair, and led him toward the kitchen. "Bob, you're cranky because you haven't eaten. Let me fix you some breakfast."

"You're trying to change the subject, but I'm too hungry to argue," he said.

"Guys, I wish I could stay and eat with you, but I've got to get to work. I've got a lot to do today," Monica said.

"Just remember," her dad said, "this is strictly business. Don't come in here announcing you're engaged to Gil Butler."

Phyllis laughed. "Monica, have a good day at work, honey." To her husband she said, "And, Bob, stop being ridiculous. Who said anything about marriage?"

Bob rolled his eyes. "You did, and don't think I forgot."

Phyllis winked at Monica. "Don't pay any attention to him, honey. Go to work and do a good job."

"Out of the question. Absolutely not. How can you think of joining forces with the enemy?" Amos Butler jumped out of his seat and paced the floor of Gil's office.

Gil laughed out loud. When he needed to, his dad could certainly turn on the dramatics. Sometimes he wondered if his father hadn't gone into the wrong profession. Amos Butler, Oscar-winning performer, sometimes seemed far more accurate than Amos Butler, restaurateur.

"Dad, calm down. This is current day St. Louis, not some old western film. The Ryans are not the enemy. If anything, they could say the same thing about us."

"They're not the enemy to you? So how do you see it?"

"What they are right now is a welcome breath of fresh air for our struggling restaurant. We need them more than they need us for this deal. If we say no, Monica will find another company to fill the void."

"I'm not that desperate."

Gil pushed away from the desk and stood up. "Okay, fine. You may not be that desperate, but I am. You dragged me back here to run this place, but you won't let me fully utilize the managing skills I learned in school. Every time I have an idea, you shoot it down. Too frivolous, too risky, too bold, not bold enough."

"I'm the one who built this business."

"Yeah, you built it with the help of your best friend, who you ditched in order to save a few dollars. And where did it get us?"

Amos said nothing but stared out the window, his jawline twitching.

"I'll tell you where it got us." Gil pulled up the monthly balance sheet on his computer and swiveled the screen so his father could see it. "In the red." Gil instantly regretted doing so, because he had managed to sidestep the question of how much money they *hadn't* made for the past couple of months.

The corner of Amos's mouth twitched, but no emotion filtered through his stoic gaze. He shook his head. "It's a mistake. Stop doing the bookkeeping on the computer and go back to paper."

"No. It's not a mistake."

"You got that. . .Internet on this computer?" Amos asked, tapping the screen with his finger.

"Well, yeah, but. . ."

"That's the problem," his dad interrupted. "You probably got some kind of virus. That's what's messing up the numbers."

"No, Dad, there's no virus on this computer. The antivirus program works just fine. And I've double- and triple-checked the numbers. There's no way around it. We can't blame the computer."

Amos folded his arms over his chest. "Go back to paper. Pencil, paper, and calculator are all you need. I did it that way, and it worked just fine before you insisted on having computers. I put you through college doing the bookkeeping on paper."

Gil sat down in the chair across from his dad. "Dad, I'm sorry to break the news like that. I was angry and trying to prove my point. But I have double- and triple-checked those numbers, on the computer and on paper. We've been in the red for a little over a month, and I don't see a way out. If anything, this job will give us what we need to get back on stable footing again."

"It'll put us in the black again?"

Gil nodded slowly. "If we're very careful with our spending, yes. In the meantime, we need to start exploring more options to either make more or spend less."

"I won't sacrifice quality!" Amos barked.

"That's not what I'm asking you to do."

His dad sighed loudly and leaned back in his chair. "Then what *are* you asking?"

"Just for your permission to work on this project with Monica. It doesn't mean you're bound by contract to do anything else with the Ryans, but it could mean the difference between us having what we need to stay open long enough to turn things around."

Amos stood up and looked at the ground.

Gil's heart ached for his dad. Over thirty years of running his own business and the man had very little to show for it.

When Gil had been away, he could push this reality aside, but now that he lived here, he, too, felt the burden of wondering how to turn things around.

He wished desperately he had the perfect formula to bring in more customers and revenue, and with every passing day, he felt less and less confident in his own abilities to get the job done.

The bright moment in all his time here recently had been running into Monica. Yesterday, after they parted, he'd been full of optimism and hope about where their relationship might go, but this morning he'd awakened to more realistic thoughts. Now, just thinking about her brought on such a flood of emotion that he found himself pushing the thoughts aside rather than processing them, simply because the memories filled him with such regret.

Where would they be now had their parents not parted ways? Would they be married, maybe even have kids?

But the more pressing question was, why would Monica want anything beyond a business relationship with him? His father had almost ruined her family financially. Now the shoe was on the other foot.

Why would she want to date a man who had nothing to offer but a failing business? True, his music-management projects had been successful, but she didn't know that.

All she saw when she looked at him was a business failure. He had seen it in her eyes when he'd tried to explain why he had come back to St. Louis. She'd probably only offered the job because she felt sorry for them.

And yet, as desperately as he wanted to reject the work if her offer was out of pity, there was no way he could turn her down. Plain and simple, his family needed the money. If only his father could agree and give his blessing.

As if overhearing his thoughts, Amos spoke up. "Monica, huh?"

"Excuse me?"

"Is this more about getting your old girlfriend back or saving the restaurant?"

Gil shrugged. "I don't know. Both, I guess, but if I had to make an educated guess, I'd say that after everything that happened, there's no way she'd even think about dating me again."

"You're probably right about that," his father agreed. "But if you promise to put as much energy into fixing the business as you will into winning this girl back, then I won't stand in your way."

"You're sure about that? You're not going to change your mind and make me look like I was trying to sabotage them? I know how hard it is for you to stay away from work, even though you're supposed to be retired. Do I have your guarantee that you will not ruin this for me?"

Amos shrugged. "A few months ago, I might've, but now that I got a look at those spreadsheets, it doesn't look like I have much of a choice, do I?"

"Not necessarily, Dad. I want more than anything to try this, but I will let you make the decision."

Amos moved to the door. "I gotta get over to the YMCA and meet your mother for this spinning class, and if I'm late, I won't hear the end of it for days. As far as the deal with the Ryans, you make the choice. I trust you."

"Thanks, Dad. I promise that I will give this my all."

"I know you will. But leave some energy for pursuing that girl, too." He laughed softly. "Because if she *is* interested in you, it's not going to be for money."

Chapter 5

S o we're done?" Gil wanted to know.

Monica glanced around the restaurant where they had met for a late lunch. The dinner crowd was starting to trickle in, and their waitress would probably love for her and Gil to leave so she could seat someone else at their table.

"I believe we are. And, hey, look at it this way, this was probably the longest lunch meeting on record. We started at two, and it's almost five o'clock," Monica answered.

Gil stretched his arms over his head and yawned. "It has been a long meeting, but the time seemed to fly by. Now what's the next step?"

"Tomorrow evening, I'll run this by Adella, and if she likes it, we're all set."

"And. . .you'll keep me updated?"

Before Monica could answer, her cell phone rang. Checking the caller ID, she saw it was Penny Phelps, the host of a local TV show that was widely watched. In two weeks, they would come by to profile The Pie Rack for the "Hidden Treasures" segment they showed each day.

"I need to take this," she told Gil. "Do you mind?"

"Not at all." He pushed the papers they'd been working on aside and took a bite of his salad.

"Thanks," Monica said, flipping the phone open. "Hello?" She angled slightly away from Gil so as not to be rude.

"Monica? Penny Phelps here, calling about your appearance on *St. Louis Morning*."

"Yes, yes, I got a confirmation from the camera-crew assistant a few days ago, and we're all set for the Thursday after next."

"Yes, I know," Penny said. "But I have another opportunity for you, if you'd be interested."

"Really? I guess I'm definitely interested," Monica said. "What does it involve?"

"Funny you should ask," Penny said. "We just learned our guest for tomorrow's taping of the 'Daily Recipe' segment has a nasty flu and won't be able to make it. Apparently, baked potato soup is not something she can even *think* about without tossing her. . .well, you get the picture."

"So. . .you want me to make the soup for her?" Monica asked, puzzled.

"Not exactly. I was looking through the upcoming features segments and saw

410

that you guys are famous for your signature sweet potato pie. I'm wondering if you'd be willing to come on and demonstrate it for the viewers. If anything, it'll drive more customers to your place in advance of your 'Hidden Treasures' segment."

"I'd love to. Just name the time and place."

"And you don't mind giving up your recipe?" Penny probed.

"Honestly, I can't give them the *exact* recipe we use, but we do have a good recipe we give to our patrons all the time. I could definitely use that one."

"Perfect," said Penny. "Now, you should be at the studio at 7:00 a.m. tomorrow, and bring all the ingredients for your recipe, as well as a couple of already prepared pies—one to display and one for us to taste after we finish the demo. Anything else you need to know?"

Monica racked her brain to search for additional questions but couldn't think of any. "Nothing off the top of my head, but if I think of something, is it okay to call you at this number?"

"Sure, it's my cell, so I always have it on me. I believe we're set. Thanks for the favor, and I'll see you in the morning."

"Great. See you then." Monica hung up the phone and turned to face Gil, who was looking at her expectantly.

"You sound like some kind of big shot," he teased. "What's going on?"

"Oh, wow, this is the most exciting thing!"

"Really? Was it Adella calling to say she wants us to cater the wedding, too?"

"No," Monica answered, shaking her head. She instantly remembered that Gil's business wasn't doing so well, so she reigned in her exuberance in order to not seem like she was rubbing her company's success in his face.

"Penny Phelps just asked me to demonstrate a pie recipe on her show tomorrow."

Gil grinned widely. "That's fantastic. When will it be on?"

"I'm pretty sure it's live. Oh, wow. I'm going to be on live TV. I wonder if I need to come with hair and makeup done or will they do it for me?" Monica sighed in frustration. "Of course I would come up with questions like this after she hangs up."

"If it's live, I guess I'll be getting up early to watch you. It's not every day you see a good friend on TV."

Good friend. His words jarred her a bit, but she determined not to show it. What right did she have to be disappointed? Their short-lived romance had been finished for a decade. At least he still wanted to be friends. That said a lot, considering how he could actually be content to never talk to her again.

Besides, her parents were counting on her to not let her judgment be clouded by emotions while she and Gil worked on this project. So he was making it very clear he was just her friend.

Fine, I can deal with that, she decided. *But why does he have to be so blunt about it?*

At least have a little compassion for a girl's feelings, huh?

"Earth to Monica," Gil said, laughing. "Is it just me, or have you gone into full-speed brain fog since Penny called?"

"Sorry about that. I guess I'm trying to mentally pull together everything I need to get done for tomorrow."

"Let me help you," Gil said, opening to a blank page in his notebook. "Here's your 'to-do' list. Just say whatever you need to get done, and I'll write it down. That way, you won't lose track of any thoughts while you're trying to get your list together."

"You're volunteering to be my scribe?" she teased. "I have to warn you, I can be a little long-winded sometimes."

"Oh really?" he asked, arching his eyebrows. "That's funny. Must be my luck because my favorite girlfriend was also very talkative."

Monica was taken aback. Was this his way of telling her he was in a relationship?

Gil must have sensed her confusion, because he hurriedly continued speaking. "Yeah, actually you remind me of her a lot. I dated her my senior year of high school and we haven't really talked since then. Well, actually, I ran into her yesterday, but didn't get to ask her anything important, like whether or not she was dating anyone. . . or if she would let me take her out to dinner tonight?"

"Dinner?" Monica echoed, feeling pleased that he actually seemed to be showing some interest in her. He was certainly taking an indirect route to asking her out, but she couldn't help but find it kind of cute.

"Yeah. Apparently, she got some really exciting news about her job today, and wanted to take her out to celebrate." Gil leaned a little closer to her. "Give me some advice. Should I ask or do you think she would laugh in my face?" In a stage whisper, he added, "We didn't break up in a very ideal way."

"Since when have you ever seen an ideal break up?" Monica countered.

"So I should go for it? Do you think she would say yes?"

Monica tilted her head to the side and pretended to be thinking. "I think she would definitely say yes, except she might not have time—at least not tonight."

Gil frowned in an exaggerated fashion. "So that's a no?"

"I wish I could, but I have so much to do. I have to be at the studio at 7:00 a.m. But I've got stuff to finish at the office this afternoon, and I've got to bake a couple of pies and then get ingredients together for the demo, find something to wear, and make sure I have everything together for the meeting with Adella tomorrow night."

"I can think of one item you can strike from the list," Gil said triumphantly.

"Really? Which one?"

"Baking pies. The last I heard, the bakers at The Pie Rack make several dozen pies every day. Just pick up a couple from the restaurant."

Monica shook her head. "I can't. I know I'm probably being too hands-on, but

I feel like if I'm going to demonstrate it, I need to bring pies I actually did myself."

"Then let me bring takeout over, and I can eat it while I watch you cook."

"Gil, are you inviting yourself over to my house?" she asked, pleased that he wanted to spend more time with her.

"Guilty as charged."

"I heard that girl you wanted to take to dinner really, really likes sesame chicken."

"Then I will be at her house at seven on the dot with sesame chicken."

Monica quickly jotted down the directions to her condo then gathered up her notes and headed back to work. If her dad had been less than thrilled about this morning's announcement, the call she was about to make would more than make up for the shock of having to work with the Butlers for the engagement party.

Chapter 6

"Wow, do you have like an army of kids in the neighborhood, or is cooking for hundreds of people just a hobby of yours?" Gil asked, taking in the sight of Monica's kitchen.

"Excuse me?"

Gil pointed to the kitchen table and countertops, which held industrial-sized packages of baking ingredients. "Do you bake cookies for your neighbors in your spare time? I can't think of any other reason why a single woman would need this much flour."

Monica laughed and walked to her refrigerator. Swinging the door open to reveal a nearly empty interior, she said, "Ha, ha, my comedian. No, I don't have all this stuff just sitting around every day. I brought these ingredients home from the bakery so I could work on the pies tonight."

"Well, that makes much more sense," he said.

"I can't believe you thought I have all that stuff just sitting around. You should see my cabinets—they're even more empty than my fridge."

"What do you eat? Air?"

Monica put a finger to chin and feigned deep thought. "Let's see. . .my weekday dinner preparation usually consists of stopping at the grocery store on my way home from work to pick up a frozen dinner."

He pointed to a pot resting on the stovetop. "What's cooking now?"

"I just peeled a bunch of potatoes for the pies I have to bake tonight. Hopefully they'll be boiling soon."

"Smells good." Gil held up the bags he'd carried in. "Well, rest assured, this sesame chicken is not from a box in the freezer section. Should I plate it up?"

"No, no, you're the company. Why don't you sit down in the living room, and I'll get dinner on the table."

"Are you sure there isn't anything I can help you do?" he wanted to know. "Can I help you get your ingredients together?"

Monica shook her head. "I was going to do that really quick before dinner. Just make yourself at home, turn on the TV, whatever."

Monica put the takeout into the microwave to heat and began transferring the ingredients into smaller canisters.

"Hey, I have the same laptop!" Gil called from the living room. "Mind if I check my e-mail?"

"Go right ahead. Dinner in about five minutes."

Monica transferred flour into a smaller canister, then pulled dinner out of the microwave and fixed plates for her and Gil.

Walking into the living room to let him know dinner was served, she watched as he clicked on her laptop. To her surprise, she watched in amazement as her bookkeeping program popped up on the screen.

Why in the world was he looking in that program? Wasn't he supposed to be checking his e-mail?

Monica cleared her throat. Gil turned abruptly and closed the cover of the laptop.

"How's the e-mail?" she asked, trying to keep her voice level.

"Well. . .honestly, I didn't quite make it there yet. I. . .I accidentally pulled up some other program."

Monica put the plates down on the dinette table and headed over to where Gil sat with her computer.

"Really? What other program?"

"It looks like your bookkeeping program. I must have accidentally clicked on a different icon, and it just opened." He stood up and walked to the table where their dinner sat. "But don't worry," he added. "I wasn't snooping."

Monica followed him to the table and noticed she'd forgotten silverware. "Let me run back into the kitchen for a minute."

As soon as she entered the kitchen, Monica realized she'd forgotten to finish transferring the salt and sugar to the canisters, so she took Gil the flatware and explained that she would join him in a few minutes.

"I started this job in the kitchen, and I know I won't be able to relax and eat dinner if I leave things undone."

Gil nodded and kept eating as Monica made her escape.

She was vaguely aware of the fact that it was probably rude to make Gil sit and eat by himself, but she needed to do something to keep herself busy and refrain from jumping to conclusions. If she were sitting across from him right now, she would have a hard time reining in her imagination.

While she transferred the ingredients, Monica prayed silently.

Lord, if my dad was right and Gil really is up to something wrong, please show me before something goes wrong for The Pie Rack.

Monica hoped against all hope that he had been telling the truth—that he'd opened the program accidentally and he wasn't snooping.

She pressed the lid back on the sugar jar and took a deep breath before returning to the table.

Gil looked up and smiled. "It was starting to feel a little uncomfortable, sitting here eating by myself. Glad you came back. And I do hope you believed me when I said I wasn't snooping. The last thing I want to do is give you a reason not to trust me."

"Oh, you know me, I have a one-track mind when it comes to my 'to-do' list," Monica said, sidestepping the question.

"Are you baking the pies after we finish?"

"Probably. The longer they sit after you bake them, the better they taste."

"I remember. Our dads took six months to perfect that recipe."

Monica laughed. "I remember that after they finally agreed on the recipe I was so tired of sweet potato pie I could hardly stand to look at one, let alone taste it, for at least a good year."

Gil shook his head. "I never had that problem. And after we stopped selling it, I had to rely on going to friends' houses to taste it."

Monica stopped eating, her fork midair. "You stopped selling the pie?"

"Yeah. After the whole. . .fiasco, my dad got the idea that he didn't want to have anything in common with your dad, so we stopped selling sweet potato pie, and he refused to even have it in the house."

"You're kidding."

"I am not. I remember once, when I was home for Christmas break during my sophomore year of college, I was at my friend Eddie's house. They had a couple of pies from The Pie Rack, and I think I ate an entire pie by myself."

Monica couldn't help but laugh out loud. "Did anyone notice or say anything?"

"I doubt it. A bunch of people were there hanging out, going in and out of the kitchen, and I just knocked that whole pie off, piece by piece."

"That's a great story. How would you feel about taking a pie home with you tonight?"

"I would be eternally grateful."

"Then it's settled." Since they were finished eating, Monica stood and began clearing the table. "If you don't mind hanging around while I make these pies for the show, I'll make one for you, too."

"Absolutely no problem for me. Can I help?"

Monica shook her head. "I work best if nobody is standing over my shoulder when I cook. You can either watch TV or check your e-mail while I get the pie into the oven, and we can talk while it's baking."

"I'll go for the TV, since I already had a difficult time checking e-mail. But hurry up and finish so I don't feel like I'm just sitting around doing nothing while you do all the work."

"I'll try." Monica went to the kitchen, drained the now soft potatoes and began mashing them and adding the other ingredients.

She felt a sense of relief that he had turned down the opportunity to get his hands on her computer again. Surely that meant he really had opened The Pie Rack's financial files by accident.

At any rate, she was also glad that he wanted to stick around and talk to her. Of course, the promise of pie had something to do with that, but wasn't the way to a man's heart supposedly through his stomach?

In record time, Monica mashed, blended, and whipped the ingredients and got the pies ready to bake.

Gil came in the kitchen just as she slid the last pan in the oven.

He walked over to the bowl where she'd mixed everything. "Can I have a taste?"

"No—that's another one of my kitchen rules. No eating anything with raw egg in it."

Gil frowned. "I'm sure I'll be fine. Everything smells good, and it's going to be hard to wait until it's done baking." "You are worse than a little kid," she teased. "Let me see if I can find you something to tide you over until these are done."

Monica checked the drawers in her refrigerator and found she had a couple of single slices of pie she'd brought home from work yesterday.

"Can I interest you in a slice now?" she asked, waving the container under Gil's nose.

"As long as I can warm it up in the microwave, yes."

"It's hot now, but you have to promise me you'll let it sit overnight before you cut it."

"Are you serious?" Gil wanted to know.

"Yes, I'm serious. And if you don't promise me, I will be forced to keep it here tonight, and you can come pick it up tomorrow."

"I don't recall having this rule back when our dads made the pie."

"That's because my dad did a little retweaking of the recipe and the cooking procedure. We discovered that even though it tastes fine right out of the oven, if you let the flavors set up while it cools for several hours, it tastes even better."

"I don't like the idea because I want a piece right now, but I'll do what you said."

"Great."

"So what time can I cut into this masterpiece?"

"Well. . .I'm getting to the studio around seven, and I think we'll be going on the air shortly afterward, so I guess after seven, seven thirty, you can eat it."

"I'll do that. Maybe I'll even get up, cut a piece, and then taste it while you're doing your segment. I'll have to make sure I don't feel superior over the other viewers, since I have a pie that was personally prepared by the beautiful woman showing Penny how to make it."

"You can call me beautiful all you want, but that won't let you cut the pie sooner."

Gil hung his head in mock shame. "I guess you saw right through my attempt to butter you up?"

Laughing, Monica put her hand on his shoulder and steered him toward the door. "Enough about cutting the pie right now. It's not ready yet. Now go home before I change my mind and take it back."

Gil opened the door and paused. "Thanks for the pie and for a great evening. I had fun catching up on old times with you."

"Me, too."

"We should. . .do this again, sometime?"

Monica tilted her head to the side. "Are you trying to get me to bake you more pies?"

"No. I mean, anytime you want to give me a pie, I won't turn it down, but I'm saying I have fun with you. I can't talk to a pie. I miss you a lot more than I realized."

"Same here."

A long silence passed while neither of the two moved.

Was he going to try to kiss her good night? Monica couldn't decide if she should push the door open to signal that the evening was over or lean in to invite a kiss.

Gil moved a step closer and hugged her. It wasn't a terribly romantic embrace, since he was balancing a still-warm pie in one of his gloved hands, but it worked for Monica.

She inhaled the scent of his cologne, mixed with the aroma of pie, and relaxed.

She didn't know how he felt, but she wouldn't mind giving the relationship another chance.

He ended the hug, waved good-bye, and left Monica standing there, watching him get into his car and drive away.

Monica reluctantly closed the door and got ready for bed. She would have liked to call her mom or a friend and analyze her evening with Gil to determine if he had given any indication that he wanted more than friendship right now, but she didn't have time.

If she wanted to do a good job in the morning, she needed lots of rest tonight. The analysis would have to wait.

Chapter 7

Gil got up an hour earlier than usual to get ready for work and watch Monica on *St. Louis Morning*.

Keeping his word, Gil had not touched the pie last night, but his mouth watered as he went to the kitchen to cut a slice.

Gil put the pie on a saucer and turned on the TV just as Penny Phelps introduced Monica.

He watched as Monica went through the motions of mixing the ingredients and Penny chatted and asked questions.

I am so fortunate to know her, and even more fortunate that she wants to be friends again after all that happened, Gil decided.

Remembering back to their hug from the night before, Gil wondered how she would have reacted if he had kissed her. The thought had crossed his mind, and he had almost followed through with action. But at the last moment, Gil had ruled out more than a hug, mostly because it would have been incredibly awkward to attempt a kiss while he held a pie in one hand. But the next time he saw her, there wouldn't be any pie. . . .

When they reached the part of the recipe where Monica produced an already-cooked pie out of the oven twenty seconds after putting in an uncooked one, Gil chuckled. Having grown up around the restaurant business, he had always found the illusion of speedy cooking on TV shows quite funny.

Finally, Monica cut slices of pie for herself and Penny.

"Oh, I can't wait to taste the famous Pie Rack sweet potato pie," Penny gushed. "I've always heard so much about it, but this is my first time to actually have some."

Gil mirrored Penny as she put some on her fork and took a generous bite.

As soon as the dessert hit his taste buds, he realized that the grimace Penny had on her face was involuntary—because he was making the same face.

Spitting the pie onto the plate, Gil tried to figure out what had gone wrong with the recipe.

Penny didn't fare much better. "Water!" she croaked, as Monica looked on with a stricken expression on her face. Utterly confused, Gil watched as Monica finally tasted the pie herself. Unlike him and Penny, Monica did manage to swallow the bite, but it appeared to take a great deal of effort.

Gil took the uneaten pie back to the kitchen and got ready to leave. He didn't know how long Monica would remain at the studio, but wherever she was, he planned to find her and do what he could to help.

Monica rested her head on the steering wheel and cried, not caring if anyone saw her. Penny Phelps had been good-natured about the whole situation, and she assured Monica that the "Hidden Treasures" segment would still air. In fact, the crews were coming in two days to get some footage.

"Mistakes happen," Penny said. "I'm just sorry it was live and I wasn't able to pull it off more convincingly."

As soon as she had tasted the pie, Monica understood exactly what was wrong. Mentally retracing her steps, she realized that in her haste to transfer the ingredients to smaller canisters, she had poured salt into the sugar container.

Any other day, she probably would have caught the mistake before it went too far, but because she was so flustered after catching Gil in her bookkeeping files, she hadn't even noticed.

Gil.

Monica sat up and wiped her eyes, remembering her dad's warning.

"No good can come of this."

He had been right. Now Monica even doubted that Gil was telling the truth last night. Accidentally. "Ha! The big liar," she said bitterly.

Her cell phone rang, and the caller ID read GILBERT.

"Calling to rejoice in my failure?" she said to the phone. "Forget it. Pretending to help me and then trying to sabotage me behind my back does not count for friendship." She turned the ringer to silent mode and ignored the call.

Thoroughly embarrassed, Monica pulled herself together and drove to her parents' house.

Chapter 8

An hour later, having been comforted by her mother and encouraged by her father, who diplomatically refrained from any I-told-you-so statements, Monica headed to The Pie Rack, feeling better emotionally, but mentally more confused than she had ever been when she'd arrived.

Looking in the rearview mirror and noticing that her makeup was a little less than pristine, Monica realized she'd been so flustered after the recipe demonstration that she left her makeup bag at the TV station.

There was no way she felt like showing her face there any time soon, so she decided to make a stop at the pharmacy to replace a few basics.

A woman on a mission, Monica swiftly gathered up mascara, lipstick, powder, neutral eye shadow, and headed to the checkout line.

All of the lanes were crowded, with at least four people waiting. Monica quickly perused the customers' shopping baskets and moved to the line where people were purchasing the fewest items.

While she waited, she thought about the conversation she'd just had with her parents. Strangely, they both found the pie-tasting mishap quite comical, and despite the potential image problem the appearance might cause for The Pie Rack, they both seemed to doubt Gil had deliberately tried to make her ruin the recipe. Though they both seemed concerned that he had accessed The Pie Rack budget spreadsheets, they both agreed to give him the benefit of the doubt that it had truly been an accident.

"But he took a pie home, too," Monica protested. "If he was really my friend, he could have at least tried to warn me before I went on the air."

"I thought you told him to let it sit overnight. Maybe he still has yet to taste it," her mother suggested.

Gil's repeated calls to her cell phone also polished her parents' opinion of his character.

"At least give him a chance to explain himself," her dad advised. "If he's as wonderful as you described him the other day, he just might be feeling pretty terrible right about now."

"I doubt he would keep calling if he'd done something untoward. About now is the time you'd expect someone like that to quietly slink out of sight."

Monica had agreed to give him a chance to explain, but right now she didn't want to think about it. All she wanted right now was to hurry up and get out of the store, so she could reapply her makeup and go to work without looking as bad as she felt.

The woman in front of her in line turned around and said, "I can't believe this is taking so long. What are they doing up there, anyway?"

"Tell me about it," Monica nodded in agreement. "I have to get to work pretty soon."

The woman shook her head and turned back around. With nothing better to do, Monica examined all of the impulse-buy items strategically placed on both sides of where she stood.

The lady in front of her turned around again, as if she wanted to continue the conversation, but Monica pretended to be engrossed in reading the copy on a package of scented hand sanitizer. She wasn't trying to be rude, but neither did she feel much like making small talk.

Although Monica made no move to converse with her, the woman still kept turning around intermittently to glance at her, and she wondered if there was something hanging out of her nose. There was nothing worse than having people stare at you without saying anything.

"Monica, isn't it?" the woman said.

Startled, Monica looked up at her. "I'm sorry?"

"Your name is Monica, isn't it?"

Monica nodded, although she couldn't ever recall having met this woman before in her life.

"I knew I had seen you somewhere before. I'm Leeda Adams."

Monica blinked. The name didn't ring a bell, either.

The woman must have realized that Monica had no recollection of ever meeting her.

"I'm Gil Butler's cousin. We met once when he brought you to a family dinner."

Monica could remember the event itself, but not Leeda in particular. Ten years had passed since then, and Gil had about a million cousins. Well, not really a million, but at least twenty or thirty.

"So how's business for you? Pretty good, I hear, ever since your family ran off with the better location and left Uncle Amos and Aunt Melinda in the lurch."

Monica felt herself growing angrier by the second. First, Gil had indirectly ruined her TV appearance, and now his cousin wanted to accuse her family of initiating the dissolution of the partnership.

Monica didn't have a chance to defend herself because Leeda kept going. "You know, Uncle Amos always said your family would get what you deserved someday, and if it hasn't happened yet, it will sooner or later, because God don't like ugly, that's for sure."

Monica was taken aback by such a harsh statement. Had Gil's family really told people that her family cheated them? The nerve of them! The exact opposite was more honest.

Trying to keep composed, she answered, "I really don't think you should be commenting on matters you don't know anything about."

The line was finally moving now, and thankfully, Leeda's items were already being scanned.

But that didn't stop her from throwing out another nugget of wisdom. "Oh, I know enough, all right, and I know one thing for sure, as long as you let it keep festering, it'll just get worse. What you reap is what you're gonna sow. What you need to do is get together and at least talk it out. And it seems to me a little apologizing might be in order."

Likewise, Monica thought. *Wouldn't it be nice to hear Amos say sorry to Dad for greedily taking the most profit and leaving us to start over financially? Or maybe Gil would like to explain why he was* really *snooping in my files.*

The checker moved swiftly, and within moments, Leeda and her platitudes were gone. And not a moment too soon. Monica didn't know how much longer she could remain civil.

As soon as she finished paying for her purchases, Monica went to her car, reapplied makeup, and thought about her promise to let Gil explain himself.

For the rest of the short drive to The Pie Rack, she fussed under her breath about the nerve of Gil's cousin.

By the time Monica pulled into the parking lot at work, she had calmed down considerably, but there was no way she was calling Gil right now. Leeda had told her that Amos wished The Pie Rack would fail. Was he bitter enough that he'd stoop so low as to send Gil to make it happen?

No, she wasn't going to be calling Gil back anytime soon. The last thing she wanted to do was hear his smug voice right now.

Monica entered the building and graciously accepted the sympathetic glances and pep talks from The Pie Rack employees.

On a normal day, she might stick around out front and chitchat with the waitresses or go back to the kitchen to make small talk with the bakers, but today she did neither. Instead, she went straight to her office.

No sooner than she had gotten situated at her desk, someone knocked on the door.

"Come in!" she called.

The door swung open, and Gil stood in the doorway.

Chapter 9

A long silence passed between them. Monica wondered who had sent him back to her office. As soon as Gil was gone, she intended to find out and have a long talk with that individual about respecting her privacy.

Gil held a vase of roses and he stood still. His usual confidence was gone, as if he could sense that she didn't want him there. "Can I come in?"

Monica wanted nothing more than to tear into him about the accusations his cousin had just made, but just before she opened her mouth, she remembered her parents' advice and pushed aside the impulse to jump to conclusions.

He'd better do some pretty fancy explaining, she told herself.

Gil came in, and Monica fully expected him to take a seat in one of the chairs in front of the desk.

He surprised her completely by putting the vase on her desk, then coming around to her side of the desk and bending down to give her a hug. Although at first she wanted to pull away, Monica didn't. She rested her head on his shoulder and hoped he was being sincere. All of the old feelings she'd experienced after their break up came flooding back, and Monica realized that what she really wanted was to find a way to make sense of this whole mess.

Despite what had transpired ten years ago, and regardless of what his cousin said, the last thing she wanted was to lose him again.

"How are you?" he asked quietly, pulling away from the hug and taking a seat in a chair.

"Completely mortified. It's not every day you make a pie so nasty that Penny Phelps spits it out on live TV."

"I wish I'd tasted the pie last night. At least I could have warned you about it."

Monica could tell he was sincere, and her earlier misgivings melted away. "At least you kept your promise."

"Is there anything I can do to help remedy—" Gil was interrupted by Monica's cell phone ringing.

Monica checked the caller ID and groaned. It was Adella. Her menu presentation was later this afternoon, and Monica didn't know if she had the resolve to handle Adella's personality after all that had already happened. She wondered if Gil might be willing to handle that meeting by himself. All he really had to do was show Adella a list of potential dish choices.

"Hello?"

"Monica, this is Adella." Her tone was clipped and very somber.

Monica wondered if the room was abnormally hot, or if she was just getting nervous. "Hi, Adella. We're still on for the meeting this afternoon? Three o'clock?"

"I don't think so."

"Excuse me?"

"This morning, I was awakened by several phone calls from friends who saw you on *St. Louis Morning* and told me I was making a big mistake to let you cater my engagement party."

"Adella, I can explain that. We had a mix up with some ingredients, and that's why the pie I used this morning didn't taste right. I can assure you that nothing like that will happen for your event."

"Well. . ." Adella hesitated, and Monica glanced at Gil.

He seemed to be getting the gist of the conversation, and he looked worried. Now that he was counting on this job, Monica wanted to do everything she could to make sure it didn't get pulled out from under them.

"You do realize our contract was contingent upon you finding another company to provide the dinner menu, right?"

"Yes, I'm aware of that, and I have found a partner. We've actually written out several sample menus that we were going to show you this afternoon, and I think you'll be more than happy with—"

"Hold on, that's my other line." Adella clicked over and left Monica on hold. But today's music was more along the lines of contemporary jazz rather than the swoony love songs of a few days ago.

Although Adella's frequent switching to another line annoyed her to no end, Monica took the opportunity to quickly explain the seriousness of the situation to Gil.

"I'm sorry I was such a klutz. The last thing I wanted to do was lose this job for us," she told him.

"Don't worry, I doubt she'll actually fire us, because that would mean she'll have to go back to the drawing board."

Monica nodded in agreement. "You're right. But now she'll feel like she can ask for ridiculous concessions, and we'll have to give them to her."

Gil shrugged. "That's the beauty of this business. The customer is always right, so you have to be willing to go the extra mile."

"Your dad always said that," Monica said, remembering.

"Yeah. He still does. I think it's his motto. My mom says she's surprised those weren't my first words."

Adella clicked back over. "Here's the deal. I will be willing to reconsider if you set up a complete menu tasting for me and Byron."

"So you'll come in this afternoon and pick a sample menu, and then we'll set up another date for you to taste everything?" Monica clarified.

"No, the meeting for this afternoon is cancelled. I want you to cook all of your sample menus, and then we'll come in and taste everything and *then* pick the menu we want for the party."

Monica held back a retort. There were easily sixty to seventy dishes on those sample menus. She couldn't ask her staff to work that much overtime, and she doubted Gil wanted to ask the same of his employees.

For once, it was her turn to put Adella on hold. "Could you wait just a moment while I check on something?" she asked.

Adella agreed, and Monica put the phone on mute to discuss the situation with Gil.

"She wants us to cook every item on the sample menus, and then she'll taste everything and decide if she still wants us for the party. Is it still worth it to you?"

"I'm in if you are."

"If you're in, I guess I have to be." Monica picked up her phone again. "Adella, I think we can arrange what you've requested. When would you like to schedule this tasting?"

"How about tomorrow?"

Monica sat up very straight in her chair, indignant that Adella even thought something so complicated could be arranged in a mere day. Trying to remain diplomatic, she spoke quietly. "I'm sorry, but that would be impossible for us. I was thinking more along the lines of a week from now."

"That's too late for me. The party is in three weeks, so if this doesn't work out, I'll have to find another caterer in record time."

Monica hated to agree with Adella, but she made a lot of sense. She would feel the same way if she were in Adella's shoes.

"Okay, I understand. Tomorrow is still impossible for us, but is there another day you would like?"

"Let me check. . ." Monica could hear Adella turning pages, presumably in her appointment book, and she hoped Adella would pick a reasonable time frame.

"Quite honestly, I'm really booked right now. The only other day I have is this Friday."

"We'll take it," Monica said, hoping Gil would be in agreement.

"How does two o'clock sound?" Adella wanted to know.

As if I really have a choice, Monica thought. "Two o'clock is great. We'll see you then."

She hung up the phone and turned to Gil.

"How did it go? Did we save the deal?"

"Maybe. We'll find out on Friday."

"Friday? That's three days away. I thought you were going to insist on more time."

"It was the best I could do. She was this far from canceling the whole thing," said Monica, holding her thumb and forefinger a mere fraction of a millimeter apart.

"Then I guess we'd better get in gear to get all of this stuff ready."

"Yeah." Monica pulled her planner out of her purse and started mentally noting what she would be able to put off in order to make time to get ready for the tasting. She and Gil would have to set up shop at The Pie Rack and work evenings to get the dishes ready.

This time, there would be no room for mishaps. She would taste anything that went to the table before Adella could even lay eyes on it.

Then she realized that two days from now, the crew from the TV station was coming to get footage for the "Hidden Treasures" segment. She'd planned to spend the next two days getting The Pie Rack into tip-top shape. There was no way she could have the kitchen being used as catering central with cameras coming. Everything had to be beautiful and flawless—especially after what had happened this morning. And if she were busy getting The Pie Rack to look immaculate, where would she find time to help Gil?

"Monica? What's wrong?" he asked. "I think you just paled several shades," he said, resting his hand on hers.

"We have a slight emergency on our hands," she told him.

Chapter 10

"Are you sure this is a good idea?" Monica asked. She and Gil were in the kitchen at her condo, warming up finger foods.

"It's not ideal, but we don't really have a choice. And it's about time. This needed to happen eventually."

"Convincing them to help us will be harder than trying to nail Jell-O to a tree."

"In theory, yes. But they are our parents, and they want us to succeed, so they really are our only hope right now. Besides, I know my dad, and ever since he retired, he's been itching to get back into the kitchen."

"My dad, too. But doesn't your dad ever cook at home?"

"My mom lets him in there sometimes, but he prefers the hustle and bustle of a deadline—hungry customers waiting for their food." Gil took the lid off a simmering saucepan full of spinach and artichoke dip.

"Hey, mister, hands off. What did I tell you about messing around with stuff while I'm cooking?" Monica warned, waving a wooden spoon at him.

"I forgot you like to be the queen of the kitchen without anybody 'hovering' over you."

"Exactly. If you want to help, go in the living room and see if anything needs to be picked up."

"That would be fine, except you and I both know the living room is spotless. You're just giving me busy work," he protested.

"Yes, I am. So get out of the kitchen," she said, grinning at him.

A few moments later, Gil returned with a handful of envelopes and a large package. "What should I do with the mail?" he wanted to know.

"Actually, you can give it to me." She'd been so preoccupied over the past few days that she'd let the mail build up and hadn't had a chance to look at it.

Monica took the mail, and gave Gil her spoon in exchange. "Keep an eye on that spinach dip for me? Don't let it stick or burn."

"Oh, so now you let me cook. But only when it's convenient for you."

"Hey, it is *my* kitchen," Monica retorted, taking a seat at the table to look through the mail.

Most of it was the usual, junk mail and bills, but the package caught her eye. It was from Angel Morgan, a friend she'd met at the National Restaurateurs' Convention last summer.

She, Angel, Haley, and Allison had met and bonded when the elevator they were all riding at the convention got stuck.

Monica shook open that package and an envelope fell out, along with an apron.

Angel had purchased the last apron but hinted that she might share it if she found romance.

Monica tore open the envelope and read the letter. It was chatty, highlighting some of the recent happenings in Angel's life.

The last few sentences caught Monica's attention:

Remember the apron I bought? And how you and the girls told me I needed to share it if it brought a man into my life??? Well, God sent a certain gentleman by the name of Cyril Jackson III (and boy is he dreamy!) my way, and we're about as cozy as two peas in a pod. No engagement ring yet, but I have every reason to believe one will be forthcoming!

This cook is getting plenty of kisses nowadays, so I thought I'd send it your way.

Keep in touch, girl, and let me know how the restaurant business is treating you.

Lots of Love,
Angel

Monica held up the apron and laughed at the red lips next to words that proclaimed KISS THE COOK.

It was a little gutsy for Monica's taste—not exactly something she'd normally purchase for herself, but just seeing it brought back the memories of time spent with Angel, Haley, and Allison.

She smiled as she carried the apron into the kitchen with her. She would have to wear it a few times before she sent it on to Allison or Haley.

Gil was still busily stirring away at the spinach dip. He looked up at her and waved her over to where he stood.

"I didn't let it stick," he said, waving the spoon in the air.

Monica looked down at the stovetop and gasped. "Yeah, but you're dripping cream sauce all over my flat-top range. Do you know how hard it is to clean these things?"

She put the apron on the counter and grabbed a sponge, intending to do some damage control.

As she scrubbed away, she sensed Gil standing right next to her. Irritated, she scrubbed even harder. Couldn't he find anything better to do than *watch* her clean?

Sighing loudly, Monica stopped scrubbing and turned to face Gil. "What? Isn't there something else you can do?"

He grinned. "Well. . .if you insist." Before she realized what was happening, he took her in his arms and kissed her.

It was probably the most unromantic time for a kiss, but Monica didn't want it to end. Suddenly, the stress factors of the day—the salty pie, Adella's demands, and the meeting with their families—didn't seem as troubling.

When the kiss ended, Monica and Gil stood silently, not speaking, just looking at each other.

Monica racked her brain to think of something to end the awkward pause and could only come up with, "What was that for?"

Gil shrugged and pointed to the apron. "I was just following the instructions."

At that moment the doorbell rang. Monica hurried to the entryway to find her parents standing on the front porch.

Gil's parents were making their way up the walk, warily eyeing the Ryans.

Monica motioned everyone inside and took their coats. An eerie silence filled the room once again, until Gil's dad spoke over the quiet.

"This better be good."

Gil put his arm around Monica and smiled. "Trust me, Dad, you'll love it."

Chapter 11

Monica stood next to Gil, who was peeking out the hallway window into the dining room. They were at Amos's Smokehouse, watching Adella and Byron sample the food.

He smiled down at her. "How is everything in the kitchen?" he whispered.

"Like a dream. They're in heaven. It almost seems like old times."

"Really? No problems whatsoever?"

"Well, your dad and my dad had a minor 'discussion' about how to season the barbeque sauce—sweet or spicy—but they compromised. How are Adella and Byron liking the spread?"

"They love it, from what I can tell. They're going back for seconds and thirds for some of the dishes."

"Looks like this job is in the bag," she said. "And all because you're such a genius."

"More like our mothers are geniuses," he corrected her.

"How did you figure it out?" she asked again. "The entire time you were talking, I kept praying silently that our dads wouldn't argue. The only thing is, I missed pretty much everything you said. Since then, everything has been such a blur that we haven't even had a quiet moment to talk."

"I know," he said, rubbing her shoulder. "You spent all your time at The Pie Rack and left me here at our restaurant to supervise our parents cooking. I missed you. . . and your kiss-me apron."

"It's not a kiss-me apron. It's a kiss-the-cook apron."

"And you're the cook," he retorted. "So how did the taping for 'Hidden Treasures' go? I got home too late to call you last night."

"Beautifully. The place was spotless, we had a nice crowd of customers, the weather was great, so everything looked sunny and bright on camera, and Penny sat down and ate an entire piece of pie. Before she left, the staff took a picture with her, and they're going to put it up on the wall."

"I'm proud of you," he said. "You didn't let the salty pie keep you down. You got right back up and kept going."

"You're not as proud of me as I am of you," said Monica. "Now finish telling me how you figured out our moms had been communicating all these years." Monica chuckled softly. "I still can't get over the looks on their faces when you said, 'Mom, Mrs. Ryan, is there something you'd like to share about money that only the two of you know about?'"

Gil shrugged. "It wasn't that hard. I was searching desperately for any accounting mistakes in the hope that there might be more money in some other account somewhere. I didn't find another account, but I found several instances of unexplained disappearances of money not long after the split. Then, in this past year, I kept seeing unexplained appearances of money. For a while I got nervous because I thought either my parents were sloppy at balancing the checkbook, or they were cooking the books."

Monica shook her head. "Our dads were stunned, but they couldn't protest so loudly when our moms admitted to sending each other money secretly when things got tough. It was pretty humbling to watch."

"Yeah, all of a sudden, they realized that friendship was about more than who won the argument. The money your mom sent definitely kept us afloat for several months."

"Your mom did the same for us, too. I remember those first few years after the split as being pretty lean, but things could have been a lot worse if she hadn't been helping."

A sudden eruption of laughter sounded from the kitchen.

"Sounds like everything is fine back there," Monica said.

"Yeah, the only thing is, now they're talking about coming out of retirement to work together again."

Monica put a hand to her forehead. "I was just getting used to my little office."

"Actually, they're thinking more along the lines of a catering company. The moms don't want them at a restaurant all hours of the day and night, but all agreed that cooking for different functions now and then might be fun."

Monica shrugged. "As long as they can keep it fun." She peeked out to look at Adella and Bryon again.

"If this goes well, Adella hinted that we might be able to cater her actual wedding. Wouldn't that be fun for our parents?"

"Yeah. I think wedding catering is a good place to start," he agreed. "Maybe one day they can even cater ours."

Monica stepped back and looked at him in amazement. "Gilbert Butler, I know you are not proposing to me right now. For one thing, this is not even a *remotely* romantic setting. We're in the middle of the hallway between the kitchen and the dining room, peeking out of a window."

Gil took a step closer, but Monica kept talking. "Plus, we've only been reacquainted for a few days, we haven't even gone out on an official date, and our parents are just coming off of ten years of not speaking to each other. Not exactly ideal conditions for getting engaged, don't you think?"

"I agree, and that's why I'm not proposing."

Monica suddenly felt embarrassed. Talk about jumping to conclusions. She looked away so he couldn't see her face.

He moved closer and put his arms around her. "I'm not proposing *yet*. But I'm pretty sure I'm falling pretty hard for this girl I broke up with back in high school."

"Really?" Monica said, not caring that she was grinning from ear to ear. "What's she like?"

"She's a little shorter than me, has really pretty, light brown eyes, sometimes she panics when she gets stressed out, and she has this cute little apron that keeps telling me to kiss her."

"A talking apron, hmm?"

"Not really. But, now that you mention it, I think I hear it calling right now."

Gil pulled her closer and kissed her.

When the kiss ended, Monica rested her head on his shoulder. "That's some apron," she said, smiling.

Sweet Potato Pie

1 (9-inch) deep-dish pie shell, frozen
2 ¼ pounds sweet potatoes
Pinch baking soda
4 tablespoons margarine
1 cup sugar
½ tablespoon nutmeg
½ tablespoon cinnamon
¼ cup whole milk
1 egg
½ tablespoon vanilla

Thaw pie shell for 10 minutes; then poke sides and bottom with a fork. Bake at temperature indicated on packaging for 7 minutes or until very lightly browned, then remove from oven. Peel and quarter sweet potatoes. Place in pot and cover with at least two inches of water. Add baking soda to water, and boil potatoes for 25 to 30 minutes or until soft enough to mash. Drain and mash potatoes. While potatoes are still hot, mix in margarine. Add sugar, nutmeg, cinnamon, milk, egg, and vanilla, one at a time, mixing well to fully incorporate after each addition. Pour entire mixture into blender or food processor and blend for 20 to 30 seconds or until mixture has a smooth consistency. Pour filling into pie shell and bake at 400 degrees for 40 minutes or until mixture is well set. Cool for at least one hour before slicing.

APPLE PIE IN YOUR EYE

by Gail Sattler

Chapter 1

Are you sure about this, Lynette?"

Lynette Charleston had never been so sure about anything in her life.

"Yes, Mrs. McGrath. Plenty of other people in the congregation can serve on the gardening committee besides me."

"Then what are you going to do with yourself?"

"Nothing, at least for a while. The church has grown so much in the last few years. Close to six hundred people attend here now. Let's give someone else a chance to participate."

Over the ten years since her father had become pastor of Good Tidings Fellowship, Lynette had been a part of almost everything that needed doing in the church at one time or another. She had served in the nursery, typed the bulletin, played guitar for the worship team, organized events, even cleaned the washrooms. She'd served on the construction committee when they converted some of the storage area into classrooms. She'd actively participated in organizing the social club at Christmas and holiday events. She sang in the choir. She'd occasionally been asked to find and arrange for guest speakers for the ladies' ministries luncheons.

Lynette couldn't remember a time when she hadn't been actively involved in something. Now, at twenty-six years old, she needed to stop being the pastor's daughter and simply become a member of the congregation so she could take some time to focus on her relationship with God.

No more teams, no more council sessions, no more meetings. Especially no more committees.

"I guess I'll see you on Sunday then," the elderly lady said, patting Lynette on the shoulder.

Lynette reached up and patted Mrs. McGrath's hand, as Mrs. McGrath continued to pat her shoulder. "Yes, Mrs. McGrath. I'll see you Sunday."

❧

"Oh no! Look at that! Do you think it's because of the storm last night?"

At Sarah's voice, Rick Meyers glanced at the puddle on the floor of the foyer then looked up. Nothing was dripping now, but the telltale stains on the open beam ceiling told him where the water had come from.

He turned to Josh. "Go get the mop and bucket from the lockup and wipe this

up before everyone starts arriving. Ryan, we've got to see what happened to the roof."
He turned to the group of girls. "Can you young ladies see if there are any more spots
like this and clean them up? Then find buckets or something to catch more drips in
case it starts raining again."

Sarah tugged on his sleeve. "What about our practice for the drama?"

With the dark skies and winds still gusting, Rick knew they should prepare
for more rain that morning. "I've got to check the roof first. Get whoever isn't busy
cleaning up to help set everything up and start without me. I'll be there as soon as I
can."

As he walked with Ryan to dig the ladder out of the storage shed, Rick unclipped
his cell phone from his belt and dialed Pastor Chris's number. Since there was no
answer, he knew the pastor was already on the way. He was amazed he'd arrived
before the pastor on a Sunday morning, especially since he'd picked up some of the
youth group members on the way.

While he climbed the ladder, Rick thought of last night's storm. He had picked
up pieces of soffit and vinyl siding from his backyard this morning. Not all had come
off his own house. Many houses in his neighborhood had suffered damage either
from downed trees or simply from the force of the wind and heavy rain.

Ryan steadied the ladder in the wind while Rick climbed up. Once he reached
the eaves and surveyed the wide expanse, his heart sank. The roof on the old church
building hadn't been in the best condition to start with. In addition to many shingles
being ripped and broken off, some sections of shingles were missing entirely. In more
than one place he could see strips of black tar paper flapping in the wind, exposing
bare wood beneath.

He calculated from his present perspective which one of the gaping spots caused
the puddle in the lobby.

And this was only one side of the roof. He doubted the other side was much
different.

A car entered the parking lot on the other side of the building.

"It's Pastor Chris!" someone called out.

Rick made his way down the ladder and jogged into the building, where he
found Pastor Chris in the lobby staring up at the ceiling while Josh wrung out the
mop into the bucket.

"Quite a storm last night. I was worried about this. Josh says you were on the
roof. How bad is it?"

Rick rammed his hands into his pockets. "Bad."

"Can it be fixed? I got a few drops of rain on the windshield on the way here, so
more rain is coming any minute."

"Yes. The forecast said we'd have more rain this morning, but not as much wind.

As to fixing it, I don't think it's possible. For now we can patch it, and a few spots will have to be tarped, but it will only be temporary. We need a new roof."

"We don't have money in the kitty for this. This is a major expenditure."

"I know we've got a few members who are roofers. Between them and a few volunteers from the congregation I bet we could do the work for nothing."

"Yes, but we need something to work with. Do you have any idea how much the shingles and tar paper to do a roof this size will cost?"

Rick shook his head. "I'm guessing it would be in the thousands for materials alone."

Together they watched the small group of teens scurry to clean up and prepare for the Sunday worship service.

Pastor Chris folded his arms across his chest. "We're going to need a few fund-raisers, not just within our own church. We've got to reach out to involve the whole community for this kind of money."

A few more members of the youth drama club walked in. The main door closed behind them with a bang.

"Hey, Pastor Chris! Rick! Wicked out there. Sorry we're late. We had to pick up some stuff that got blown down before we could leave."

Silence hung in the air until the echo of rain started on the roof above.

Rick and Pastor Chris turned toward each other. "Uh, oh," they mumbled in unison and looked up.

"I hope those girls found a few more buckets," Rick muttered as he pushed the mop bucket to where he thought the water would most likely come down.

Pastor Chris checked his watch. "It's time for me to start preparing for the service. It looks as if I have a few extra things to pray about."

Rick nodded.

As the pastor retired to his office, Rick gathered the drama team to run through their production as best they could before the congregation arrived.

Throughout the service, water dripped into the buckets, distracting and disturbing many of the members. At the close of the service, because of the obvious need, everyone agreed that something had to be done quickly.

Most of the church members stayed behind for an emergency business meeting. A group of volunteers came forward to patch and tarp the roof as soon as the rain stopped and it was safe to do so. The same people also volunteered to follow the guidance of their two professional roofers to save the labor costs when it came time to put the new roof on.

Then came the hard part. Money.

Pastor Chris stood. "I don't suppose I have to say that now we need a fund-raising committee."

Mrs. McGrath raised her hand. "What about the conference? Can't they give us the money?"

The pastor shook his head. "They gave us money less than a year ago to expand the Sunday school classrooms. They have a limit as to how much they can spend on one congregation, and we've already exceeded our allowable expenditures."

Everyone in attendance nodded. Rick remembered what a difference the new classrooms had made. He also remembered how they'd barely raised the money in the first place. The pastor was right; they couldn't ask for more money until they tried to raise it themselves and fell short.

The pastor smiled weakly. "Everyone here knows how committees usually run."

He paused. Many people smiled and nodded, mostly the elders and others who were more involved in activities requiring group organization.

Pastor Chris continued. "The more people on a committee, the longer each decision will take. And as long as it takes to make a decision, it takes even longer to get the project moving. We don't have time to waste now. We need a committee, but we also need to move things along quickly."

Mrs. McGrath raised her wrinkled hand and stood. "Your daughter, Lynette, has the most experience with committees. If anyone can get things moving quickly, Lynette can. And Lynette isn't on any other committees right now."

All heads turned to Lynette.

Rick's heart started pounding.

Lynette.

He couldn't remember a time in his adult life he hadn't loved her. When her father became pastor of Good Tidings, he had been eighteen, and she'd been sixteen. The first day they met, he'd immediately developed a massive crush on her that grew with every passing week. By the time he turned twenty, he was hopelessly and helplessly in love with her and had been ever since.

But Lynette didn't know he existed. At least, she didn't know he existed beyond the realms of the group functions of the church. Many times he'd joined a committee or volunteered for a special event simply because he knew Lynette would be involved. He'd asked her out on a number of occasions, but she had simply replied that she didn't date members of her father's congregation, changed the subject, and gone on to business as usual. Sometimes he'd been part of that business; sometimes he hadn't.

Over the years Rick had tried to forget about Lynette, but he couldn't when he saw her at least once a week. Being one of the few single men in the congregation, many women made it more than obvious that they wanted to get to know him better. But every time he went out on a date, he found himself wondering what it would have been like if he'd been with Lynette. Such thoughts were not fair to the other women who would never be Lynette and could never take her place in his heart.

Therefore, unless a woman could be content simply to share a friendship, he chose not to have an active social life. This also gave him the opportunity to devote all his time and energy to the youth ministry. He would never forget the day he turned his life over to the Lord, because that was literally the day he knew his life had been saved by grace. When he was a child, the constant conflict between his parents had been difficult. When he reached his teen years, the fighting and battles for control of each other and their family had come to the point where he didn't think he could make it through another day. Then a friend had brought him to a youth group meeting. That had become a turning point in his life and made him want to be there for other teens who needed Christ, whatever their reasons.

Through both his leadership and his friendship he'd seen many young people build a firm relationship with Jesus Christ before they were thrown into the adult world. He had been the youth leader for five years, and Rick never wanted to do anything else, unless it was pastoring a church of his own. For that reason he'd been attending Bible college at night, taking courses as he could squeeze in the time between his job and his part in the youth ministry.

In many ways he envied Lynette for having been born into a church family. However, she had chosen to be involved in adult ministry functions rather than with the young people.

One of the senior deacons raised his hand and stood. "I've seen Lynette in action, and she does get results fast."

A round of mumbled yeses echoed from the large group. Almost everyone nodded in agreement.

Pastor Chris smiled at his daughter. "Lynette? Will you head up the roofing fund-raising committee?"

Lynette's eyes widened, and her face paled. "Committee?"

Except for the plop, plop, plop of water dripping into the buckets and the drum of rain on the roof, silence filled the room.

The pastor lowered his voice. "We need you, Lynette."

Eyes still wide, she scanned the entire congregation.

"Come on, Lynette," one of the ladies called. "I'll help you."

"Me, too!" someone else called.

Many people called out with offers to help. However, Rick did note that no one volunteered to actually lead or let Lynette off the hook. He wondered if he'd been the only person in the congregation who'd thought that Lynette seemed tired lately, and less enthusiastic than in the past. A number of times he'd tried to ask her if anything was wrong, but when the conversation became personal, she'd changed the subject.

Pastor Chris raised his hands. "Wait, everyone! I appreciate so many volunteers, but in this case I don't think we should have more than two or three people involved, at least at first, until we get something in place. Maybe before we go any further, we should discuss some ideas as to how to raise this much money and then accept volunteers."

People started calling out their ideas, not waiting for a show of hands.

"Bake sale?"

"Bottle drive?"

"The junior youth could do a car wash?"

"A fund-raising dinner with prizes to draw people?"

"Maybe we could sell hot dogs outside the grocery store one Saturday?"

"What about a craft day for children in the neighborhood? People from all over come to do things with their kids."

Rick frowned. While those were good ideas, none of them could provide the amount of cash needed in a short time—unless the church could combine them.

Rick raised his hand and stood. "I wonder if we could have an event inside the building and extend it into our parking lot, something big that would reach out to the whole community. Then we could do all those things in one day. We could advertise to draw people."

"Yes! The youth group could run the whole thing. A youth fun fair!"

"Uh, I didn't mean—"

Before he could finish his sentence, the group applauded.

"That's great, Rick. Thanks for volunteering with the youth group. And what about you, Lynette? Rather than have a whole committee, how about if you and Rick organize the whole thing? I'm sure it would be much smoother, and faster, with only two people running everything. I know this is rather short notice, but as you can see we're desperate."

All heads once again turned to Lynette, who sat in her chair stiff as a board.

Water continued to drip into the buckets as rain pelted the roof.

"I guess I could. . ."

"Wonderful! Thank you, Lynette and Rick. Do you think you can have a proposal put together for the church board meeting on Wednesday?"

"Wednesday? This Wednesday?"

Rick turned and focused his attention on Lynette. At the same time she turned to him. They stared at each other, not breaking eye contact.

Rick forced himself to breathe. For the first time ever he would be spending time alone with Lynette. Just the two of them and no one else. For years he had prayed for the opportunity to be with her and not be surrounded by a crowd, but he had never in his wildest dreams considered or wanted circumstances like these. This would not be a leisurely chat over a cup of coffee. This project meant hard work, intense brainstorming, and careful planning. As their plans progressed, it would also mean strict supervision of the teens, who would be in their charge.

It was far from the ideal situation, but this gave him the first opportunity in ten years to spend significant time alone with Lynette. Up until now, for all the times he'd tried to talk to her in varying situations, both alone and in a group setting, he'd failed.

If God was leading him toward Lynette, then conversely she should have been as drawn to him as he was to her. He couldn't help but feel she liked him, which was encouraging. But every time he steered the conversation from neutral topics to something more personal, everything changed. She had drawn some kind of unseen line he couldn't cross, because suddenly, instead of drawing closer, she would pull away. For a few weeks he wouldn't see her at all except for church on Sunday, and even then it would be at a distance.

Now, since they were forced to work together, if he handled this correctly he could discover if what had burned in his heart for her all these years was God's will for him—and for her. His questions would finally be answered. But he would also have to accept it if her answers were not the ones he wanted.

Rick swallowed hard. Whatever happened between them now would affect his entire future and the direction of the path for his entire life.

Slowly Lynette nodded at him.

Rick nodded back and turned to the pastor.

"Yes, I think we can have something before the board on Wednesday."

Chapter 2

Lynette hit send to reply to Rick's e-mail confirming their meeting after supper. When the words disappeared from her screen, she rested her elbows on the edge of the desk and buried her face in her hands. She didn't know which was worse, working with another committee or working with Rick.

She didn't think asking God for a little time off was a bad thing. Yet, not only was she expected to work on possibly the most important project of the church's history, she had to do it with Rick.

Over the years she had seen a number of church members succumb to burnout syndrome from pushing themselves too hard for too long. For all Lynette did, so far she hadn't felt overwhelmed. Up until now. She had started to feel herself falling into the pattern. Because of her experience in dealing with people, she thought she could pull herself out of the downward spiral before it was too late. She needed to retreat and spend some time with God, and that meant being away from people for a little while. After some time alone, she could face another committee meeting for the Lord's work and do it with enthusiasm.

The saying that God didn't give people more than they could handle echoed through her mind. For the first time she had to trust that was true, because deep in her heart she didn't know if she could handle so much responsibility one more time. At least not now.

But then, Rick had come up with the community Fun Day concept. Therefore, he had to already have a workable idea in mind or he wouldn't have made the suggestion. As tired as she was, she had to trust Rick to shoulder most of the workload while she did what she did best, which was the behind-the-scenes organization of the project.

Lynette stared at the computer screen so long the screen saver came on.

Rick.

Many of the single ladies in the church had a crush on him, yet to everyone's dismay he remained single. Lynette had always been fond of Rick. He had asked her out a few times, and she was tempted. However, before she agreed to go out on what was obviously meant to be a date, images of what happened to her mother flashed through her mind. In the nick of time her good sense returned, and she turned him down.

Lynette rose from her desk and prepared a simple supper for one. Rick had asked if she wanted to go out to grab a quick bite so they could get down to business, but she wasn't ready for that. She didn't want to be near Rick when she was weak and unsure of herself. Yet now she had been obligated to spend time with him with no one else present.

Allowing herself to give in to what she'd worked so hard to maintain would be a recipe for disaster, both personally and spiritually. She was tired, and it would be easy to let her good judgment wane. Until whatever day they selected for the event, Lynette prayed for God's strength to guide her, because she couldn't do it on her own.

The doorbell rang at the exact second she finished her dinner. She tucked the plate in the dishwasher and ran to the door.

Before opening it, Lynette paused to remind herself not to stray from the topic of church business, regardless of Rick's charm. They were together to raise money for the new roof, and that was all she could ever allow.

When she opened the door, Rick stood smiling in the doorway. "Hi, Lynette. I'm glad you could find the time to do this tonight. You looked so tired yesterday that I was almost surprised you agreed to it."

Lynette tried not to be impressed with his sensitivity. "I know, but I always find it so hard to say no when people ask me things. I suppose I have to learn."

He nodded. "It's hard, but I've found it's okay to say no. People do understand."

Lynette wasn't so sure. She had been involved in so many things for so long that people expected these things of her. But Rick wasn't there to discuss people's expectations. He was there to start work on the fund-raiser.

Lynette directed him into the living room. When he sat on one end of the couch, she sat at the other end.

"So, Rick, what do you have in mind? Have you selected a day? How many of the youth will be involved?"

"Uh—so far I have no idea what we're going to do, I don't know what day is best, and I haven't talked to the youth group because our meetings are Wednesday and today is only Monday."

"You're kidding."

He grinned. Little crinkles appeared in the corners of his bright green eyes. All of a sudden the supper she thought was so delicious didn't sit too well in the bottom of her stomach.

"Nope. I was just as unprepared for this as you."

Lynette shook her head to bring her concentration back to the problem at hand. "What are we going to do?"

His smile disappeared. "I have a number of ideas. We only have to get a proposal to the church board by Wednesday—not the whole complete plan—but we have to be realistic about this. We can't waste time, because the next time the rains come we'll be in serious trouble. I'll phone the older members of the youth group about whatever we come up with today; then we'll discuss it again. By Wednesday we should have a good idea about what we're capable of producing."

"I think I should warn you that Dad has already found a supplier for the shingles and made a tentative order, pending financing. He's getting a good price through Jeff, who's going to be heading up the actual work."

Rick cringed. "Great—no pressure." He let his sarcasm hang for a few seconds then cleared his throat. "He's right to do it now, but we have to be prepared. I was thinking we should pick the Saturday before Labor Day weekend. That way people will be antsy to go out and do something, but not be out of town or otherwise have made plans."

"That's a good idea. What do you have in mind?"

"I don't know. When I got home after church yesterday, I wrote down what I could remember." He twisted, not rising from the couch, extended one leg, and pulled a crumpled paper out of his jeans pocket. He tugged on the paper to straighten it then began to read. "Bake sale, bottle drive, car wash, kids' crafts."

"I think someone mentioned selling hot dogs."

"Yes, but none of those ideas can raise the kind of money we need. We have to think big. That's why I thought of a community event, but I have no idea how to put such a thing together."

"I guess that's what I'm best at—putting things together. But I usually don't come up with many good ideas by myself."

His grin froze her thinking process. "Don't we make a great team then?"

Lynette jumped to her feet. "Let me get a pen and paper, and I'll start making notes, too."

Once in the kitchen Lynette tried to stop her hands from shaking as she dug through the drawer. She didn't want to be a great team with him, although she had to admit they worked well together. In the past when they'd served on the same committee, she had admired Rick's creativity when they needed to get a job done. He came up with good and unique ideas, most of them workable if she set her mind to organizing the details and mechanics.

Then, when the time came to ask for volunteers, especially with the more difficult tasks, Lynette was more likely to be silent and do whatever was required herself. Rick, on the other hand, was good with people. No matter what task lay ahead, very few people could say no to him. As well, whoever ended up helping did so cheerfully and graciously. His gift for the Blarney made Lynette wonder if he had a little Irish in his background. As much as she didn't want to, she couldn't help but like him.

By the time she made her way back into the living room, she found Rick leaning over her coffee table and scribbling more illegible notes on the small paper.

"I think I've come up with a few more ideas," he said, still writing. "We could make it into a mini-fair. Our parking lot is certainly big enough." He stopped with the pen still touching the paper. "Did you know that the Robindales know someone who has a hobby farm and does a side business of a traveling petting zoo? Since we're a church, I wonder if they'd let us use their portable pen and some animals for free if we let them display their signs in a prominent place on the day of the fair."

For the first time since she heard of the project, a rush of excitement fluttered in her stomach. "I don't know if we could charge money for that, but it certainly would be a drawing feature for the community."

Rick nodded. "We can't have rides or anything, so I'm trying to think of stuff I usually see at the smaller country fairs, like bake sales, displays, and contests with prizes."

The excitement waned. "That would mean we'd have to buy prizes. I don't know if we can afford that kind of expenditure."

Rick shook his head as he wrote something else. "We don't have to. I'll make a few phone calls tomorrow and see if I can get a few donations. I have an uncle who runs a motel in Seattle. I could probably get a grand prize of a weekend for two, along with a couple of passes for the Space Needle. Of course, we'll have to decide what kind of contest is worthy of that kind of prize."

Lynette tapped her index finger to her cheek as she struggled to think. "If we're trying to reach the community, we should emphasize kids' and teen activities."

Rick nodded and stopped writing. "I agree. What do kids like to do?"

Lynette grinned. She'd spent enough time in Sunday school to know the answer to that one. "Young children like to draw, and kids of all ages like to throw things. In fact, I know many adults who like to throw things—they just won't admit it. I'm thinking about a paper-plane-throwing contest, with prizes. What about teens?"

Rick's mouth quirked up at one corner. "Teens like to eat, so my suggestion is some kind of eating contest. The only two things I can think of are hot dogs and pies, but your father is going to be selling hot dogs. We don't want the teens to eat all our profits."

"Then a pie-eating contest is the best choice. One reason I love living in Washington state is because I know so many people with apple trees. Since apples are everywhere this time of year, we could probably get most of the apples for free."

"Sounds good to me," Rick mumbled as he started writing again, which emphasized that Lynette had not written a single thing. She rectified that by picking up her pen and making notes also.

As the evening continued, they discussed everything on Rick's list, which allowed Lynette to make many tentative plans. They also drew a picture of the parking lot and building so they could get a better idea of the space required versus what they had available.

Before she knew it, the clock read 10:30. They still didn't have a concrete plan, but they had come up with a number of good ideas that needed to be discussed with the youth group members before they could present their proposal to the church board.

Lynette followed Rick to the door. "So you know who you have to contact tomorrow?" she asked as she opened the door.

He nodded. "Yes. I'm pretty sure I can get most of the calls made on my lunch break. You're going to call around and scrounge for apples, right? I'll call my uncle about the weekend getaway idea. We should get together again tomorrow. Same time, same place?"

"Yes, I think we should."

Rick smiled. "See you tomorrow, Lynette. Oh, and don't cook tomorrow. I'll bring something. Since I have to work late, I'll be coming straight here."

She almost said no but couldn't justify why not. His coming over with dinner only meant church business, so they could discuss the matter at hand sooner, and nothing more.

All she could do was nod.

"Good. This has been a great evening, Lynette, in more ways than one."

Before she could respond, he turned and left.

Lynette stood in the doorway, watching as he drove away. It had been a great evening. For the first time in a long time she hadn't minded discussing and making plans for a complicated event. In fact she'd actually enjoyed it, which made her wonder if maybe she wasn't as burnt out as she thought.

Chapter 3

Pizza box in hand, Rick knocked on Lynette's door and waited.

When the door opened, Lynette's beautiful smile nearly made him drop their supper. "Hi," he mumbled as he tried to maintain his dignity.

"Hi. How did everything go?"

"As well as could be expected, I suppose. I couldn't get hold of my uncle, and it appears our other plans may have changed a bit. I don't think anything like this ever happens as it was planned the first time around."

Her smile dropped, and Rick immediately felt the loss.

"You should probably come inside before that gets cold." She turned around and walked into the house. He shut the door behind him and followed her into the kitchen.

She spoke over her shoulder as she reached for a couple of plates from one of the cupboards. "If it makes you feel any better, my quest for apples turned out more bountiful than I could ever have planned. What happened to you today?"

Rick set the pizza box on the table and sat down. "Our impromptu youth group meeting was a lesson in organized confusion. We came up with a million ideas, but nothing concrete. Everyone volunteered to do something, but no one knows what. The topper came when Sarah Rondstadt said she knows someone who has one of those dunk tanks, and she's going to ask if we can borrow it. You know what Sarah is like once she sets her heart on something. No one can ever say no to Sarah. That means we have to find someone whom people will pay money to try to dunk and who won't mind being dunked. Do you have any idea how hard that's going to be?"

Lynette grinned. "You told me yesterday you could say no to people."

"This is Sarah we're dealing with. That's different."

She scrunched up one side of her mouth as she opened the pizza box. "A dunk tank isn't necessarily a bad thing. But it does change the spin on the other events we can have around it."

He nodded and folded his hands in his lap. "We got the petting zoo, by the way. The owners told me they require four people to be inside the pen with the animals and children at all times, and the teens are all fighting for who gets first dibs to be with the goats. I also found out how they make money from these things. Since we're a church, we have the animals for free for the day. It's up to us if we want to charge admission, but I had to guarantee those feed bins will be inside the pens. You know, they're kind of like gum-ball machines, but they hold the feed pellets for the animals. Want to imagine how many quarters go into those machines during a day of wall-to-wall children?"

Lynette's cheeks turned pink. "I've been known to put a few quarters in those things, too. But the main thing is the petting zoo will be a draw for the other events where the church will make money."

Rick could well imagine Lynette feeding animals at a children's petting zoo. Her kind and gentle spirit was one of the many reasons he'd fallen in love with her so long ago.

"Ryan suggested the senior teens could do a slave auction, but I turned that down. For our own church members, that's different. But for a community event I'm not going to be sending minors out to the homes of strangers to do work I know nothing about. It doesn't matter how big some of them are; they're still our children."

"Good idea."

"Brad suggested a neighborhood dog show, but we can't have people bringing their dogs if we're having the petting zoo. We can't risk the goats' getting frightened and stampeding or doing whatever goats do when they get scared."

"Oh. I hadn't thought of that. I'd better cross the dog show off my list."

They paused for a word of prayer over their supper then continued to discuss more ideas.

Rick couldn't believe how fast the night progressed, but then he should have expected that every minute he spent with Lynette would pass too quickly.

Before he knew it, he was standing at the door, saying good-bye. "I guess I'll see you at the church tomorrow night. What time? Seven?"

Lynette nodded. "Yes. I'll see you there."

Rick's heart pounded as he stood on the porch. Lynette stood in the doorway, close enough that he could lean over and kiss her, if this had been a date.

Rick blinked and stepped back. This wasn't a date. This was church business, and church business only. While they'd had a pleasant enough evening together, every time he tried to turn the conversation to more personal topics, Lynette had promptly steered the conversation right back to the fund-raiser.

Spending time with her, even in the context of business only, had only intensified what he'd felt all along. Not only did he love her, but more than ever he knew God had put them together.

Now he had to convince Lynette of what God had laid on his heart. Even though she seemed intent on the fund-raiser, he had to move beyond the business at hand and talk about the two of them together—forever, he hoped. Knowing Lynette as he did, Rick also knew he had exactly until the day of the fund-raiser to succeed or fail, because after that she would pull away from him, just as she'd done for years.

Rick cleared his throat. "I guess we'll get together again Thursday night so we can go over what the board says. If they agree with the date we've set, that means we have two and a half weeks to get this whole thing happening."

"That's not a lot of time. Only two days ago it sounded like such a simple thing. It seems to get bigger and bigger as we go on with it."

Rick swallowed and willed his hands to stop shaking. Slowly he reached forward and grasped Lynette's hands, holding them gently within his as he spoke. "I know. There's something else I wanted to talk to you about also."

Within his grasp her hands became rigid. A split second after he spoke, Lynette yanked her hands out of his and backed away. Rick mentally kicked himself for trying to move too fast.

She looked up at him, her eyes big and wide. "Actually, while we're talking about getting together, I think it would be a good idea to meet at the church instead of at my house. That way we'll be right there where it's happening, and we can organize it better. Don't you think so?"

No, he didn't think so, but it didn't appear he had a choice. "I suppose."

She smiled, but her smile never reached her eyes. Once again he kicked himself for trying to move too fast.

"When do you think we should start bringing some of the teens into the planning?" Lynette asked.

If it were up to him, the day before the event. "I don't know. Whenever you think it's best."

She backed up another step, her wide eyes fixed on him like a deer caught in the headlights about to be run over by a truck. "Then let's talk to them right after the church board meeting. I'll see you there. Good night, Rick."

He had barely backed up a step, and the door closed.

Rick wasn't at all sure what had just happened, but he did know one thing. Tonight he would be spending a lot of time deep in prayer.

Rick waited while all the members of the church board read their copies of the proposal. He wondered if Lynette was as nervous as he was, though he didn't know why. Every suggestion they'd made had been outlined into a workable station, and all the stations combined would make a great and varied community fun fair, even without rides.

He'd had no concept of the magnitude of the project before he became involved. The seemingly endless wait for the board's reaction weighed on him like a cloud of pending doom hovering above him, emphasizing that he'd jumped in way over his head.

Mr. and Mrs. McGrath, the head deacons, nodded at each other. Mr. McGrath laid his paper down on the table, clasped his hands to rest them on top of the paper, and turned his face toward Rick and Lynette, who were sitting beside him.

"Can you two pull this off?"

Out of the corner of his eye he saw Lynette flinch.

For the first time he had some doubts. For all their great plans, so far they had no viable donations, no prizes, no booths, and no adult volunteers. All they had for sure was a group of overanxious, inexperienced teenagers, an empty dunk tank, a pen of hungry goats, a few bushels of apples, and a list of great ideas. He supposed that if the whole thing fell through, they could still make some money by charging money for kids to feed the apples to the goats. He also feared that the person who'd end up getting dunked was going to be him.

Rick chose not to follow that defeatist line of thought. He turned to Lynette. "We can do this. Can't we?"

His stomach flipped over when she turned slowly, making direct eye contact with every person in the room except him, stopping at her father.

"Yes, we can do this," she said.

Her father crossed his arms over his chest. "Do you have any idea what it will take to get all this together in two and a half weeks? We'll have to advertise beyond our own small community, to match the scope of the fair. Twenty-five thousand people live in this city, and it takes money to reach them. Like the roof, that kind of money isn't in our budget either. But if you say you can do it, we'll okay the additional expense."

Rick's stomach tightened. Attempting to raise money was one thing, but he hadn't anticipated having to spend money to make money.

"I knew that, Dad."

"Okay then. Everyone, I think we can approve this."

Rick forced himself to smile. Of course Lynette would have already figured all the expenses into the big picture. If Lynette thought they could do it, then they could do it. He hoped and prayed he was up to the task.

Lynette stood. "Oh, there's one more thing, which will probably mean more to the success of this fund-raiser than anything else, including our advertising."

Rick's head spun. He didn't need another complication.

The room fell as silent as it had on Sunday when he was nominated for this project, except this time no drips were banging into the buckets.

Lynette smiled at everyone around the room. "Pray for good weather. We're going to have a fair in the parking lot."

Chapter 4

Lynette slipped her key into the lock and pushed the huge wooden door of the church open. She came by herself to the church often, to be alone with God. Not that she couldn't be alone with God at home, but being in the wide-open sanctuary somehow made the connection more intimate.

In silence she walked through the foyer, pausing to drop her notebook and purse on the table before she entered the sanctuary. Mirroring the shape of the building, the sanctuary consisted of a large rectangular room. As she walked up the center aisle, she ran her hand along the tops of the arms of a few of the pews before she chose a seat in the center.

In turn Lynette took in all the features of this church she loved so much. The old wooden pews showed their age yet were not excessively worn. To the front the simple podium sat before a small raised platform, barely large enough for her father and the worship team of five members. Large narrow windows graced both sides of the long room, letting in the bright sunshine on a summer day or the steady gray of a rainy Pacific Northwest winter.

As she closed her eyes and inhaled deeply, she could still smell the lingering fragrance of the remaining flowers from the Carrions' wedding last weekend.

This building had done its part in the beginning of many happy marriages over the years by providing a place to celebrate a new joining in God's sight. Also before and after every Sunday service the entire building buzzed with happy voices of children playing as their parents visited with their Christian brothers and sisters.

More important than the building were its people. Her father's congregation had grown to such a point where she no longer knew every regular attendee by name. Still, as a body of believers, she loved all the people there with the love Christ had shown her.

Lynette tipped her chin and looked up. The dark wood of the open beam ceiling overhead created an illusion of a greater size to the room, although in practical terms it wasn't the greatest for energy conservation. Often the temperatures were too cool in the winter and too warm in the summer, common for an older building, constructed before people began to think of environmental concerns and the cost of heating. The fact remained that the strength there was the love of the people for each other.

That was why she had to do her best to raise all the money required to fix the roof. These people were depending on her to come through. No one knew her sudden aversion to committees.

In a convoluted sort of way she was glad the committee consisted only of her and Rick. While she had been in group situations with Rick before, she and everyone else knew that performing in the group dynamics of a committee was not where Rick's talents shone. Rick was a leader. Even when she first met him ten years ago, she could see his potential. He had been kind and gentle, but also firm and friendly when it came time to do a job. Years later Rick had matured and met the potential everyone had seen in him in his present ministry as youth leader. Rick loved people, and he loved the Lord. He was everything she could ever want, but she couldn't have him.

Lynette dropped her gaze from the ceiling and stared at the empty podium.

Rick had always held a special place in her heart. For many years she had successfully avoided dealing with how she felt about him, but working so closely with him now made her look at him differently. Over time something had changed so gradually she hadn't noticed, but now she couldn't help but recognize the connection. All they had to do was look at each other, and no words were needed. She knew what he was thinking, and vice versa. As much as she wanted to deny what sparked between them, no matter how hard she tried to fight it, it was there.

Lynette slouched in the pew and buried her face in her hands. "Dear Lord, help me," she said out loud. Her own voice echoed back in the large, empty room.

Before she could collect her thoughts to pray, the thump of the main door closing echoed through the large doorway, along with Rick's voice. "Lynette? Where are you?"

She stood, ran her hands down her sleeves to smooth out a couple of imaginary wrinkles, and left the sanctuary. "I'm here," she called out once she reached the table, where she picked up her notebook. Rick approached and came to a stop in front of her.

Lynette jerked her thumb over her shoulder. "Let's go use Dad's office."

Rick's eyebrows raised. "The office? What for?" He stuck one hand in his pocket and extended the other hand, in which he was holding a clipboard with a crumpled note paper attached to it, toward the couch in the lobby. "Can't we sit here?"

Having to share a couch was exactly the reason she wanted to meet at the church instead of her home. "I think we'll be able to write better in the office. With the desk," she said.

With the desk between us, she didn't say.

He brought the clipboard up and pressed it to his chest. "Is there something wrong? I don't understand."

"Nothing is wrong. I just want to use the office."

His eyebrows scrunched in the middle. "But. . ." He shrugged his shoulders. "Okay. Let's go. We've got a lot of things to discuss. I've got some good news and some bad news."

She almost stumbled then kept walking to the safety of her father's office, where the desk would serve as a safe and effective barrier between them. Only after she sat behind her father's heavy wooden desk and Rick pulled up one of the chairs so he could use a corner for his own writing surface could she dare to ask. "I think I want the bad news first."

"Actually that is just an expression. I don't have good news."

Her heart sank, but she didn't say anything. This project had to be successful. Too many people were depending on them.

"Remember I told you about the dunk tank?"

She nodded. "Yes. If the bad news is that we didn't get use of the dunk tank after all, I don't think that's really such a loss. I can't figure out what we would do with such a thing anyway."

Rick shook his head. "No, we've got it for sure. It's just that Sarah told Trevor about it." Rick laid his pen down and started counting the people off on his fingers as he mentioned them. "And he told his brother who told his friend who told his neighbor who told his uncle who told his sister-in-law who told her boss."

Lynette shook her head as well. "I don't understand why you're telling me this. I don't know any of those people."

"Mary's boss is the mayor."

"So?"

"I don't think you understand the big picture here. At our little church community one-day fair, we're going to be dunking the mayor."

Lynette felt sick, and it wasn't because she was too hungry.

"No. . ." She let her voice trail off. "We can't pull something off on a grand enough scale to include Mayor Klein."

"We're going to have to. He left a message on my voice mail saying he's looking forward to a fun and carefree day as a welcome change to the old grind."

"If the mayor is going to be there, do you think the local newspaper is going to be there, too?"

"Yup. This is good public relations for the mayor, so count on it. But just think, we won't have to spend so much on advertising because his own public relations committee will send out a bulletin to the who's whos and community boards telling them about it. So maybe there is good news in this after all."

Lynette didn't think so. She stood and waved her hands in the air at Rick, coming just short of leaning forward over the expanse of the desktop and wrapping her hands around his neck. "Are you crazy? This means we have exactly fifteen days left to organize and prepare an event that's going to draw the mayor and his entourage and the newspaper!"

"Anyone in the paparazzi will tell you there's no such thing as bad advertising...." His voice trailed off.

All Lynette could do was sink back down in the chair and stare at him across the desk in silence, with her mouth gaping open.

Rick stared back, not saying anything either.

The silence dragged on until Rick sighed, leaned back in the chair, and crossed his arms over his chest. "When did I lose control?"

"As soon as you started taking suggestions from the youth group, I think."

Rick narrowed one eye, pressed his lips together with one side crooked slightly downward and nodded without commenting further.

Lynette also leaned back in the chair and crossed her arms. "I know we've discussed this before, but you said you were able to say no to people."

"I think I might have been wrong."

His deadpan expression was her undoing. Lynette couldn't stop her giggle.

The corners of Rick's mouth twitched, and he started to laugh, too.

The tension broken, Lynette wiped her eyes. "What are we going to do?"

"I think the only thing we can do is go with it and pray for sunshine. Like you said."

Lynette sighed and slid the list and notes in front of her. "Between the mayor and the goats we should attract a lot of people. What else can we do that will make money? Do you think we can have the worship team playing and put an offering box in front of them? Or is that too much?"

Rick tapped his pen to his cheek. "It's obviously a fund-raiser. Whether or not they get any money, it's good exposure to have visitors listen to upbeat Christian music with wholesome and uplifting themes. I'll talk to the team."

"Good idea. If we're going to have lots of people, we're going to need lots of food to sell. Do you know anyone who has one of those popcorn or cotton candy machines?"

"Nope. But I can ask Sarah. For someone who is only seventeen, she seems to know a lot of people who have connections."

Lynette made a tick beside that notation. "I'll have to think of more kids' games. I wonder if we should still have the pie-eating contest?"

Rick leaned forward, and Lynette stopped writing. "I think there's something I forgot to mention."

Lynette buried her face in her hands. "Do I want to know?"

"The mayor asked me to put his name in for the pie-eating contest, which should generate more people entering."

"I wonder how many pies we should make."

"Make as many pies as you have apples. We have to have a pie for anyone who wants to enter, even at the last minute. Besides, we can sell any we have left over."

She made a few more notes, sticking her tongue out of the corner of her mouth as she continued to think. "I'll make a few more phone calls for more apple donations. We should plan out everything we're going to do and assign volunteers today."

At his nod they agreed on all the events and booths. The major draw for young children would be a booth where the children threw their fishing line into a make-believe pond. Two volunteers hidden inside the pond would attach a toy fish and a card with Matthew 4:19 where Jesus called everyone to be "fishers of men."

For the older children they planned a paper airplane contest in which they would give away model airplanes as prizes for the different age categories. Since Rick had finally managed to contact his uncle, they had a prize of a getaway weekend to Seattle, including tickets to the Space Needle. They decided to make that a raffle for which the congregation would sell tickets, as well as having them for sale to the community at the fair.

They also planned games that didn't necessarily award prizes, as well as a bake sale and craft table.

Lynette laid her pen on the desk and ran her fingers through her hair. "This has been great. I think we've made a lot of progress. This weekend we can start constructing the booths and games. At first I had my doubts about this, but I think we can pull this off."

"I told you before that we make a great team. We should get together more often."

Lynette jumped to her feet. "Yes. Well. Oh! I think it's way past our bedtime—we both have to get up for work tomorrow. Let's lock up, and we can be on our way."

"Uh. . ." His voice trailed off.

Lynette didn't wait for Rick to continue. She hustled him out the door and locked up, the whole time yakking and blabbering on and on about anything that entered her head. Anything except getting together with Rick. She didn't want to entertain that thought.

As she slid into her car and closed the door, Rick stood to the side, his arms crossed, watching. His confused expression nearly broke her heart. She knew he liked her. Knowing him as she did and judging from what she'd heard, she sometimes wondered if he fancied himself in love with her.

She knew she wasn't being fair to him. In all the time she tried to discourage him, he never gave up. And now, since they had been seeing each other every day, the situation had become worse instead of better. He left her no alternative but to tell him the reason she couldn't see him outside of church business, no matter how much she liked him.

But not today. Lynette planned to do the cowardly thing and tell him at the end of the fund-raiser when everything was over and she wouldn't have to face him anymore, at least not directly.

Lynette waved in the rearview mirror as she drove off for the safety of her home.

Chapter 5

Rick walked into the church building, stepped around the bucket in the lobby, and headed for the pastor's office, where he knew he would find Lynette.

The woman was going to drive him crazy, if she hadn't driven him there already.

Instead of making it better, the past week had made everything worse. He'd wanted their time spent together to confirm or deny everything he felt for her. He could definitely say he loved her more than ever. He now knew for sure that he wanted to spend the rest of his life with her. He also knew she would be happy being a pastor's wife. The problem was, he didn't think she wanted him to be that pastor.

He couldn't count the times in the past week that he'd tried to talk to her, to slip into the conversation that he loved her and had loved her for a long time. And he'd tried to talk about the future they could have together as pastor and wife.

Every time, as she had countless times over the years, the second he began to address the subjects of love and a future together, she'd changed the subject. Twice she mumbled something he couldn't understand and literally ran away.

Rick had always thought of himself as a good, Christian man, with godly hopes and dreams and a promising future. Obviously Lynette didn't agree.

He stepped into the office to see her comparing figures on a spreadsheet to a calculator tape.

"Hi," she mumbled around the pen in her mouth. "I was adding up how much we have to make. Dad left me all the receipts and estimates. I didn't know we'd have to pay for a disposal bin too. And do you know how expensive it is to advertise?"

Rick pulled a paper out of his back pocket. "Oh. I nearly forgot. Here's the bill for the trophy for the pie-eating contest."

Lynette groaned.

"But I brought a big basket of apples with me."

"Let me guess. From someone Sarah knows."

Rick grinned. "How did you know?"

"Actually, in addition to the four baskets someone brought on Sunday, the Browns dropped off a big bag, too. It appears we have plenty of apples."

"How's the entry list coming?"

Lynette laid the pen down and folded her hands on top of the pile of papers.

"It's a good thing we have all these apples. It looks as if we've got sixty entries, and we want to have some pies to sell after the contest is over."

Rick rubbed his hands together. "Looking good then. Just like you. You're always looking good."

Lynette's cheeks flushed a deep shade of crimson, giving her more appeal than ever. "Stop that. We have work to do. Sit down."

They set to work finalizing the plans for the last booths and events and decided on who would be best suited to do what needed to be done. Before they went home, they divided up the lists so they could each make the appropriate phone calls.

When they were finished, Rick leaned back in the chair and raised his hands, linking his fingers behind his head. "I guess tomorrow we should have the youth group start constructing the props and decorations and things."

"Yes. It'll be a lot of work to build a fake pond, because we'll have to build a frame then somehow cover it. We don't want to run short on time."

Rick studied the calendar on the wall. "Next weekend we'll have to go shopping for all the supplies we need, the table coverings, prizes, groceries, and stuff. Then the weekend after is the big day. We don't have a lot of time, do we?"

"No, we don't. I'd better add the model kits to my list."

Rick sighed. He could see what kind of mood she was in, and today would definitely be strictly business, as would every day this week when they got together with the youth group to begin the building and planning.

But their weekend shopping trip had great possibilities.

"Let's get to it then," he said as he selected a pen out of her father's bin. "We'll have the youth group meet here every night at seven during the week, and I'll pick you up at ten sharp on Saturday morning. The end is near."

For some strange reason he was certain Lynette's face paled.

"Yes," she mumbled and abruptly began making more notes. "The end is near."

Rick was surprised to see Lynette waiting at the curb for him when he arrived at her house for their shopping trip.

"I guess it's silly of me to ask if you've got the list."

She mumbled something under her breath as she fastened her seat belt.

"What's our first stop?"

"First the megastore, then the lumber store; then we have to go to the Chungs' and pick up more apples."

Rick squeezed his eyes shut for a second then shifted into gear. "More apples?" he asked as he pulled into traffic. "You've got to be kidding. How many does that make now?"

Lynette sighed. "I don't have a clue. People have been dropping off bags and boxes of apples at the church all week. I didn't have the heart to tell anyone we had enough."

Rick didn't comment. Right now the apples were the last thing he wanted to think about. Since they would never accomplish all that shopping in two hours, that meant they would be having lunch together. This time he wouldn't be seeing her at her home or at the church. He could take her someplace nice, and most important, they would be on neutral ground.

Finally, they could talk. And it didn't have to be all business.

By the time they finished their first stop it was after one o'clock, and Rick's stomach had begun to make rude noises. Lynette had suggested a fast food restaurant, but he insisted on a little bistro where they could have a more private table in a less hectic atmosphere.

After the waitress seated them and gave them menus, they were finally alone and forced to stay in one place. Lynette had nothing to look at, nothing to fret over, and no place to go.

Or so Rick thought. As soon as he opened his mouth to speak, Lynette picked up the menu, holding it so high he couldn't see her face behind it.

Rick sighed, reached across the table, and pushed it down flat to the table. "Relax, Lynette. Why are you so jumpy? I don't bite. I promise. This is just lunch, nothing more."

"Sorry," she mumbled then tried to pick up the menu again.

Rick kept his hand pressed on it, pinning it to the table. "Why don't you want to look at me? I'd hate myself if I've done something to hurt your feelings and didn't realize it. You must know by now that I like you very much."

Her face paled, and this time it wasn't his imagination. "I know you do. I like you, too."

"Ah. Now we're getting somewhere. I don't see that as a problem, but you've been running away from me as if I've done something wrong. Have I?"

She continued to tug at the menu. Rick grabbed it and pulled it away then rested both menus in his lap.

Her face turned three shades of red. He couldn't help but smile, now that she had no choice but to make eye contact.

Lynette cleared her throat. "I know what you are trying to do."

Rick crossed his arms over his chest, still guarding both menus. "Okay, tell me. What am I trying to do?"

"You're trying to get me to go out with you."

"Is that a bad thing?"

Of all the timing the waitress appeared to take their orders. Rather than admit they'd been playing childish games with the menus, they both ordered a hamburger and fries, even though that was exactly what Rick had been trying to avoid by coming to the bistro.

When the waitress left, Lynette folded her hands on the table and looked him straight in the eye. "Did you see that little dog locked in that car in the parking lot at the megastore? That's so dangerous in this kind of weather. It only takes a short amount of time for an animal to be overcome by the heat in a closed vehicle this time of year. I wish I'd written down the license number so I could report it."

"Yes, but you're trying to change the subject. Why is it a bad thing because I want you to go out with me?"

She turned her head down and stared intently at her hands, which were still folded on the tabletop. "Because I won't go out with anyone from my father's congregation."

Suddenly Rick lost his appetite. If it had been something he'd done or something he could change, he could have dealt with it. It was obvious she didn't expect him to leave the church and his ministry with the youth to go out with her. He had a feeling there was more to it that she wasn't saying. "I don't understand."

She raised her head and made direct eye contact. Rick froze.

"You're taking leadership courses at Bible college. You know what they say about spending too much time with someone of the opposite gender. And I'm the pastor's daughter."

Rick shook his head. "But I'm not counseling you, nor are you counseling me. We don't have that kind of mentoring relationship. So what if you're the pastor's daughter? I just want to go out with you."

"That doesn't matter. You'll notice I've never dated anyone from our own church; it's not only you."

"Why doesn't that make me feel any better?"

"Sorry—it isn't the way I wanted it, but that's the way it is."

Rick leaned forward. He wanted to touch her hands, to hold them while sitting across from her; but she must have guessed what he was thinking, because she stiffened and leaned back in her chair.

"Lots of pastors' daughters date men from their father's congregation. I see it all the time." He lowered his voice. "Sometimes they get married, too."

"That may be true, but sometimes bad things happen. There can be accusations of favoritism and other improprieties."

Rick blew out a quick breath of air. "Improprieties? Oh, come on."

"It's true. Do you know anything of my family's history, before my father came to be pastor at Good Tidings?"

"No, only that you came from another city in another state. Remember—I was only eighteen then. And you were only sixteen. I'll never forget the first time I met you."

Her face flushed for a second, and she shook her head. "The reason we left the other church was because my mother became involved in a big scandal."

Now he really wasn't hungry anymore. "I didn't know that."

"Yes. She'd been doing some bookkeeping for one of the members of the congregation, helping in the interim while his regular bookkeeper was away for some surgery. I'm not sure of the details; it was so long ago. Suddenly rumors started floating around that more was going on than accounting."

He almost hated himself for asking, but he had to. "Were any of the rumors true?"

"No! My mother was devastated by the accusations, but my father stood by her because he knew the truth. But the other man's wife didn't believe him, about why they spent so much time alone together. Most people in the church took sides, and it ended up dividing the church. It was awful."

"Is that why you didn't want me going to your house? You wanted to do everything at the church."

"Yes."

The waitress chose that moment to deliver their lunches. After a short prayer of thanks for their meal, they began to eat, but Rick only ate it because he had to. Everything tasted like cardboard. Judging from the way Lynette toyed with her meal, she felt the same way he did.

"So what happened? Did it get worked out in the end?"

"No. My mother didn't know until it blew up in her face that they were already having marital problems. His wife ended up leaving him, which made the situation even worse. Rather than live in the midst of the speculation and accusations, which only caused more arguing among the church members, my parents decided to leave that particular church. When my father was offered the position at Good Tidings, he jumped at it with no hesitation. You'll also notice that my mother only participates in ladies-only functions or in a large committee."

"But this is different. Neither of us is married." Although he did want both of them to be married—to each other.

Lynette toyed with her fries then laid the fork down and folded her hands on the table. "Is it different? Improprieties still happen between people who aren't married. And people still talk."

"But we're not kids running on overactive hormones. You're twenty-six, and I'm twenty-eight."

"The rumor mill knows no age limit. Not only was my mother an adult, she was married, too. Scandal spreads quickly, and it doesn't have to be based on fact."

"I don't understand how something like that could perpetuate to that degree. I can't help but think that he did something to make it worse. Maybe he had a hidden agenda. What if he was even the one who started the rumor? He could have been using your mother to get his wife to take more notice of him. It wasn't your mother's fault."

"It doesn't matter, Rick. The end result is what counted. The fallout split the church, and my mother was devastated by all that happened. My family ended up having to leave a fellowship they loved, with a lot of hurt feelings. I don't ever want to have to go through that."

His mind raced, but he couldn't think of a thing to say. He wanted to say that their own congregation was above such a thing, but he couldn't. All it took was one person to start a scandal, real or imagined, when someone's feelings were hurt. Rick suspected that the man involved most likely tried to use the situation to his own benefit to salvage or quicken the breakdown of his marriage, but no one would ever know the truth.

He pushed his half-eaten meal to the side. "So where does that leave us?"

"There is no 'us,' Rick. There never has been. But we've always been friends. We can certainly stay friends."

Friends. Rick felt the kiss of death on any relationship he could ever hope to have with Lynette.

"But what about you? Your future?" Rick swallowed hard. The words were almost too hard to say. "If you won't go out with anyone from your own congregation, where are you going to meet people? Do you plan to stay single for your whole entire life?"

"I firmly believe that when the time is right, God will place the right man in my path."

According to Rick, the right man was already in her path. She was looking right at him but couldn't see him.

Lynette pushed her plate to the side. "We should get going. We've got a few more stops to make, and I have plans to go out with some friends for dinner."

Rick didn't ask if she was referring to male or female friends. He didn't want to know if they were from another church.

"Okay," he mumbled as he scooped up the bill, and they headed for the cashier to pay. "Let's get the rest of our shopping over with."

Chapter 6

Rick walked past the church office, waved at Lynette's father, and continued into the kitchen. "I'm here. Are we ready?"

"Yes. I'm so glad you could get the day off too. I can't believe how this project has snowballed. I'll never do this by myself," Lynette said.

Rick glanced toward the back wall. He'd never seen so many apples at one time in his life, not even at the grocery store.

Every day they'd met with the youth group at the church to build and plan the booths and displays. Today was Friday, the day before the fair, and everything was ready. Everything except the pies.

"Yeah. I can see why you took the day off." He glanced again at the wall of apples. "How many pies do you think this is going to make? I hope you know I barely cook, and I've never made a pie in my life."

"That's okay. It's my granny's recipe, and it's the easiest apple pie recipe in the world. Besides, I'm not a good cook either. If I can do it, you can do it."

"How many contest entries did we get? We had seventy a few days ago."

"Ninety-something. But we have to remember there are bound to be some entries from the people who don't come to our church and will come tomorrow. We have to count on that."

Rick rolled up his sleeves. "Tell me what to do."

He watched and listened carefully as Lynette mixed up some vinegar, water, and an egg, combined some flour and stuff with some lard and then dumped the liquid in.

"Watch carefully," she said then reached into the bowl with her hands.

Rick shuddered. "You've got to be kidding. I'm not touching raw eggs."

She grinned, and his stomach did a strange somersault. "Don't be such a wimp."

"Sticks and stones," he grumbled as he drew in a deep breath and slowly stuck his fingers in to start the mixing process.

After considerable poking and prodding, Lynette held up a big ball of pastry dough. "See? When yours looks like this, then you roll it out. Just be careful not to overwork it."

Rick poked the mushy lump in his bowl with one finger. "Overwork it?"

Lynette looked into his bowl. "You mix it until it's like mine; then stop. There, like that. Now it's ready to roll."

He couldn't help but smile as she picked up a rolling pin. "I always thought rolling pins were for chasing errant husbands. Would you like to chase me with that thing someday?"

Her mouth dropped open, and she fumbled with the rolling pin for a few seconds. "Quit it. We have too much to do to be fooling around. This is how it's done."

Rick watched her start from the middle and roll it outward, pressing evenly as she worked. She made him help slice up enough apples to fill the crust, and then they sprinkled flour and sugar and cinnamon on top. To finish it off, he watched as Lynette laid the pastry top on and pressed it down around the edges with a fork.

He grinned. "I can do that."

Without a word, Lynette pointed to a box on the counter, where he found another rolling pin. As he began to roll his lump of dough flat, he snickered to himself. "This is so domestic. Wait until the guys hear about this."

Lynette sighed. "Just keep rolling while you're talking. We're going to keep making pies until we run out of apples. You shouldn't be eating the dough—it isn't good for you when it's raw like that. Don't think I didn't see you eating the apples either."

Rick grinned around the chunk of apple in his mouth then picked up the rolling pin and continued to flatten more pastry dough.

At first he thought rolling out pastry and slicing up the apples was fun, but the more he did, the less interesting it became. Since they could only fit three pies in the oven at one time, it didn't take long for the pies to start lining up on the counter. By the time they filled up one side of the counter with pies, Rick no longer thought making pies was a fun way to spend the day.

By noon his back was feeling the effects of lugging around the heavy bags of flour and leaning over the counter while he worked. Lynette didn't complain, but he thought she was definitely slowing down, too.

He pressed his floury fists into the small of his back. "I think it's time to quit for a while."

"We can't. We've got nearly a hundred done, but we've used only half the apples, and we've baked only eighteen. I don't know what we're going to do. We can't put uncooked pies out for the contest, despite the fact that you seem to prefer them raw."

Rick covered his stomach with one hand. At first he thought he was being funny; but he'd eaten a little too much dough, and now his stomach didn't feel so good. Since it was lunchtime, he hoped some real food would cure what ailed him.

Lynette walked to the fridge. "I didn't want to leave because I knew we'd have pies in the oven, so I made sandwiches for lunch."

"Sounds good to me."

He noticed she had made only two sandwiches. With her father in the same building, in the room next to the kitchen, Rick wondered if she'd left her father out of their lunch plans on purpose.

As they always did, they paused for a prayer of thanks and began to eat.

In an odd sort of way he was having a good day. After Lynette had explained what happened with her family, he could understand why she worked so hard to avoid him, even if he didn't agree. Also, now that he knew, a burden seemed to have lifted, and she acted relaxed with him. In his heart he knew it was because she trusted him not to step beyond the guidelines she'd drawn for their relationship, now that everything was out in the open.

If he had to see a bright side, it would be that she trusted him enough to be honest with him, and she trusted him to respect the lines she had drawn.

He knew he would always want more, but if friendship was all he could have, then Rick intended to be the very best friend he could be. Of course, what he really wanted was the best friendship of all, the special friendship of the bond of a man and wife.

For the balance of the afternoon they continued making more and more pies. He did his best to keep the conversation cheerful, even though both of them were becoming increasingly tired. By the time they were finished, it was suppertime. But more than supper, Rick wanted a nap. He wondered if it was a sign of old age creeping up on him and then shook the thought from his head.

Since they still had pies in the oven, the second the new batch went in, they took off for the drive-thru so they could be back quickly. They talked nonstop the entire drive, neither of them breathing a word about apple pies or anything to do with church business. They simply had fun.

With the arrival of the youth group members, between baking pies, they set everything in order in the lobby, ready to be brought outside first thing Saturday morning.

When all was complete, Rick stood on a chair amidst the mayhem and clutter, stuck two fingers in his mouth and let out a sharp, piercing whistle. The room quieted instantly.

"Attention, everyone! Now for the last job of the day!"

Everyone in the room groaned.

"If anyone here hasn't seen them, Lynette and I made two hundred and seven pies today, and we could bake only fifty-one." He paused while he counted everyone in the room. "There are thirty-two of you here, and I know it's late, but I'm going to give each one of you three pies to take home with a note of how long to cook them. Bring them back, cooked, tomorrow morning at eight o'clock sharp, or earlier if you've been assigned to help with the goats. Class dismissed, and I'll see you all tomorrow."

As everyone left, Lynette counted the remaining pies. "We still have sixty pies to bake. I'm going to be up all night, and I still won't get them all done."

"I'll take half."

She counted on her fingers. "That will still take five hours to bake. The night's too short. We have to sleep."

"Then what about your parents? That's only twenty pies each." Rick paused to calculate three pies per half hour baking time. "No, that's still not good enough. I need a church directory. I'll be right back. You start packing three pies per box. I'm going to be making some deliveries."

Before she could protest that it was too late to be phoning around for favors, Rick took off into her father's office, closed the door, and locked it behind him. In less than twenty minutes he had acquired the help of the eighteen families he needed.

He returned to Lynette in the kitchen. "Let's load up the car. I'm on my way. I'll see you in the morning. And don't forget your three pies."

It took him an hour to deliver all the pies to be baked, which was much better than the original five hours it would have taken if he and Lynette had to bake them all themselves.

As soon as he arrived at home, Rick put his pies in the oven, but they weren't fully cooked by the time he was ready for bed. He waited out the last ten minutes standing near the stove, because he knew if he sat down he would never get up.

He couldn't remember the last time he'd been so tired, but the day's efforts had been worth it in more ways than one. He'd spent the entire day with Lynette, and for the first time in ten years she had made no efforts to get away from him. Not once had she appeared nervous or uncomfortable in his presence. Just as she'd promised, they had spent time together as real friends, sharing and talking about everything with no holds barred. By the end of the day he loved her even more than he did before, if that were possible.

Today a large barrier had crumbled, and with that barrier gone, he knew she loved him as much as he loved her. She just didn't know it yet.

Tomorrow, before the fair was over and life returned to normal, he had to do something about it.

The timer for the oven dinged, and Rick removed the pies from the oven.

Tomorrow would be another day.

Chapter 7

Lynette walked toward the church with all her attention on the clipboard, knowing she had walked this same way so many times that she didn't need to look where she was going. Rick followed directly behind her, carrying the huge box.

"Have you got the trophy?"

"Yup."

"The envelope with the gift certificates?"

"Yup."

"The case of chocolate bars?"

"Yup."

"Fishing rods?"

"Yup."

"Toys?"

"Yup."

"Paper?"

She checked off the colored felt markers without asking. She already knew they were in the Sunday school classroom. Her mom was picking up the hot dog buns and wieners, and her father was picking up the coolers for the drinks.

"Plastic forks?"

"Lynette, I had the same list as yours. I have everything in this box except duct tape. Trust me."

She stopped dead in her tracks. Rick bumped into her from behind, not hard enough to knock her down but hard enough to send the clipboard and pen flying to the ground.

She whirled around. "You forgot duct tape? You have to go back."

"You think I should? I was kidding."

She couldn't hold back her giggle. "So was I. Everything will be fine. Look above. Blue sky."

"How can you tell? It's hardly daylight."

Lynette lost her smile. "Quit being so grumpy. Today is going to be great!"

Rick didn't smile. "I haven't had a decent night's sleep in a week, I was up before the crack of dawn, and I didn't have time to make coffee this morning. Don't give me any of that *great day* stuff."

She tipped her head to one side and patted him gently on one shoulder. "Not a morning person, are we?"

He grumbled something she wasn't sure she wanted to hear. Before she had time to respond, a car turned into the parking lot.

"Sarah and her dad are here. The dunk tank won't be far behind. Hurry. Put the box beside the door and go meet them. The animal pen is due to arrive in half an hour." She checked her watch to be sure. "Where are all the boys? They said they'd be here."

Rick also checked his watch. "They're not due for five minutes. They'll be here in ten."

The four of them carried the boxes and paraphernalia out of the building until the first van full of teenagers arrived. Soon they were followed by a pickup truck loaded with fencing and a few bales of hay.

The youth group members continued to arrive, each bringing the three pies, which Lynette directed to tables set up inside the lobby. The younger boys helped Lynette arrange the tables around the parking lot while the older boys and Rick set up the pen and spread the hay. Those remaining assembled the dunk tank. When everything was together, the boys filled the tank with warm water, and the girls set up the backdrop and erected the fish pond booth, doing their best to make the blue enclosure that would hide the two volunteers inside to resemble a small lake. By eight-thirty the last of the helpers arrived, all the pies were lining the tables in the lobby, and within fifteen minutes all the tables and booths were ready.

"There're the goats!" called out a couple of the girls when the truck and trailer came into view.

Rick checked his watch. "Right on time. This is great."

Lynette wiped her hands on her jeans. "That's what happens when everything is organized efficiently and you have lots of help."

Rick grumbled under his breath again, but this time Lynette didn't have the strength to tease him about his rotten mood. The exhausting pace of the past three weeks had caught up with her; yet she still had many hours of hard work ahead of her. She couldn't afford to slow her pace now. Soon it would be the time they'd advertised they would officially open.

Rick supervised loading the goats into the enclosure, making everything ready. Still, nothing ever went smoothly, despite the most careful preplanning. Even though she felt ready to drop, her insides were still tense, waiting for something to go wrong at the last minute when things seemed perfect.

Once again Lynette tallied up everything around her. The only person missing was the mayor, who would be arriving at eleven, after the fair was in progress.

Rick appeared at her side. Lynette flinched when he picked up one hand and rubbed it between both of his. "Are you okay?" he asked quietly.

She smiled weakly, grateful for his recovery from the morning grumpies, and shrugged her shoulders. "I guess."

He jerked his head toward the building. "Come into the church with me for a minute."

Not letting go of her hand, Rick started walking, giving Lynette no choice but to follow. He stopped when they were inside the door where they could still hear what was going on outside, but no one could see them.

"Turn around," he murmured as he placed his palms on her shoulders then slowly turned her around so her back was to him.

"What are you doing?" she asked, tilting her head to glance over her shoulder at him.

"Shh. You're so tense." At his words, with his palms still on her shoulders, his thumbs pressed into her shoulder blades then began to move in little circles, loosening up the knots in her muscles. With his touch all the tension of the morning and the past few weeks began to drain out of her.

"I don't know if—"

"Shh, I said. Don't talk. Relax." As his thumbs pressed harder, Lynette struggled not to melt. In only two minutes she couldn't have talked if she wanted to.

"We talked a lot about being friends, and as a friend I've been worried about you," he said without easing up on the pressure. "I can't help but wonder why you took on a project like this. Before we got involved in this whole thing, you seemed ready to drop. I even thought you were starting to pull away from the church. The grapevine told me you've dropped out of every committee. I'm glad you're finally learning how to say no to people before you reach your breaking point. It isn't selfish—it's critical to know your limits so you can have an effective ministry. As for this fair, even though it's been hard on both of us, I'm grateful for this time we've been able to spend together. It's meant a lot to me. I hope that when it's over we can stay friends. Or more."

His touch slowed and stopped. Slowly she felt herself being turned around to face him. "More?"

He replaced his hands on her shoulders and raised his thumbs to brush her cheeks. "Special friends, Lynette. I want to be special friends. Forever."

Lynette's heart went into overdrive. For eight years she'd been distancing herself from him, and now she knew he'd loved her all that time. Now that he agreed to be friends she could finally admit to herself that she had loved him for a long time, too, but she'd been too frightened to explore a relationship. After their discussions on what happened with her mother, she had done nothing but think about how she'd let it affect her life and mostly her relationship, or lack thereof, with Rick.

The more she thought about what happened to her mother, the more she suspected Rick was right. The man involved must have perpetuated the rumors for some reason, even if no one would ever know or understand why, or the situation would never have gone so out of control for so long.

Rick had no hidden agenda. For as long as she had known him, he'd been open and honest with her in both thought and deed. Lynette had been the one to put up all the roadblocks. She needed to talk to him about what could lie ahead for them, while she still had the courage to do so.

Lynette raised her hands to touch the sides of his waist. "We don't have a lot of time, so—"

She couldn't finish her sentence. Before she could think, his mouth was on hers. This was not a sweet, gentle kiss. He kissed her as if he meant it, from the bottom of his heart.

So Lynette kissed him back the same way because she meant it from the bottom of her heart, too. She no longer wanted to keep hidden away from him as she'd done for so many years. She had wasted too much time, and she wasn't going to waste any more. She wanted to have that special relationship with him, as he said.

She slipped her hands around his back and held him tighter. His hands slipped to her back, and he pressed her against him. He lifted his mouth away only long enough to whisper her name, tilt his head a little more, and kiss her again.

A sharp whistle cut the air. All talking and banging outside stopped.

Rick and Lynette broke apart and stepped back from each other. As her brain slowly started to clear, Lynette thought she saw Rick shake his head to do the same. Without a word between them, they hurried outside.

Her father stood in the center of everything with his hands raised over his head.

"Attention, everyone! We're ready to start, in plenty of time before the first people get here. While it's still quiet and it's just us, I want to take this time to pray for God's blessing on this day."

Lynette almost smiled to herself at her father's "just us" comment. The "just" consisted of about one hundred and fifty church members.

They all bowed their heads. Lynette struggled to push aside thoughts of what had just happened and concentrate on her father's words as he prayed, which was extremely difficult with Rick at her side.

After a slight pause, her father thanked God for the joined effort of the entire congregation. He then praised the Lord for the blessings of everything from the small donations to the large specialty items that would make the day a special attraction for the community. He prayed for God to be glorified in everything they did and to bless their time with the people of the community. Last of all he prayed for the proceeds to be enough to fix the church roof.

The group called out a boisterous "amen," and everyone proceeded to their stations.

Fortunately for Lynette, one of the teens pulled Rick away toward the goat pen, giving her a chance not to be distracted by his presence. She needed time to think.

Chapter 8

I t's okay." Rick pressed the two pieces of wood together then stood back. "It's still connected, but I think I'll get some twine and reinforce it to be sure. Thanks for bringing this to my attention."

"Glad it's nothing," Andrew said as he ran his fingers over the joint in the portable fence. "I'll go back in with the goats now. I didn't know if they could knock this down."

As soon as Andrew walked away, Rick let himself sag. He couldn't believe what had happened with Lynette. He certainly hadn't planned on kissing her; he'd only wanted to talk about seeing each other after the fund-raiser was over. But when she put her hands on his waist it was too close to a hug, and he lost it.

Then she hadn't pushed him away, nor had she hesitated. She'd kissed him back. Not a light little friendship kiss either. She had kissed him for real. It was there, the connection he'd hoped and prayed for. He'd thought about it and dreamed about it for so long that over the past few days, when she had begun to respond to him, he didn't know if her reaction was real or in his over-optimistic imagination.

But today, ten minutes ago, he certainly hadn't imagined the way she'd kissed him.

He continued to fiddle with the fence, even though it was fine, because he knew he couldn't wipe the sappy grin off his face quite yet. He was a man in love, and she loved him back. He knew it now without a shadow of a doubt.

Today, after everything was over, he could do something about it. Already, fifteen minutes before their advertised opening time, guests started to arrive, which was a good indication for the rest of the day. Soon a steady stream of people flowed in.

By the time the mayor arrived, the place was bustling. Most of the crowd hovered around the dunk tank as Mayor Klein climbed onto the collapsing platform. The newspaper camera caught him giving Pastor Chris a wink and a thumbs-up as he settled into the seat. They also took a picture of Pastor Chris buying the first ticket for a chance to dunk the mayor. The crowd hushed as he aimed the ball for the target, wound up—and missed.

Rick smiled, almost sure the pastor had missed on purpose.

Many people bought a chance to dunk the mayor, who was attracting quite a crowd. A man Rick didn't recognize finally hit the target, and the mayor slipped down into the warm water as the people cheered and applauded. As Mayor Klein came out of the tank, he made a show of pretending the water was cold, toweled off his face, and returned to the seat, which a couple of the church deacons had put back into position.

After a few dunkings, the crowd began to disperse. Pastor Chris remained beside the mayor, encouraging everyone to buy a ball and dunk their fine mayor again. Of course, having a photographer from the local newspaper presenting a potential chance for everyone to be in the paper greatly encouraged people to try their aim.

Since the mayor was in questionably good hands, Rick left on his quest to find Lynette. He made a big circle of all the booths, checking the goat pen, the bake and craft tables. Not finding her there, he moved on to the children's games and contest tables. After he'd checked every booth without success, Rick stood beside the fishing pool and crossed his arms. The only place he hadn't checked was the church building, where all the pies were stored.

"Rick?"

He turned his head without moving. "Yes, Sarah?"

"I have to, uh, go, uh—can you do the fish thing for me?"

Rick nodded. "Sure, Sarah."

As Sarah took off at a run toward the building, Rick walked behind the backdrop, dropped to his hands and knees, and lifted the blanket to crawl into the make-believe lake where he could attach prizes for the children when they threw in their line. A familiar voice came from within.

"Hi, Rick."

He grinned as he crawled inside and let the blanket drop, hiding them from everyone. "Hi, Lynette. I was wondering where you went."

She smiled, and his heart went wild. "I'm down here, a little fish in a big pond. Keep your head up. Those little balls aren't heavy when they hit you in the head, but they can get tangled in your hair. I've recently found that out the hard way."

He ran his fingers through the top of his hair as he parked himself on the padded surface beside her. "I don't think that's possible with me. But I appreciate the warning."

A little ball with a fishing line attached sailed through the air and landed between them.

Lynette giggled. "You can do this one."

Rick quickly clipped on a toy fish with the Bible verse attached and tugged gently on the line.

"Mommy! Mommy! I caught a fish!" a child squealed from the other side of the backdrop.

The line tightened, but Rick didn't let go. He tugged again.

"Mommy! It's a big one!"

Lynette covered her mouth with her hand and giggled again. "I hope the fight is worth it."

Rick released the line, allowing the toy fish to be reeled in.

"I caught one, Mommy! It's so pretty!"

Rick and Lynette smiled at each other.

"I like kids," he said, his voice coming out strangely husky.

She ran her fingers across his chin. "I know."

The tap of footsteps on the cement of the parking lot surrounded them, and voices echoed all around. Yet, behind the backdrop and surrounded by the cloth-covered wire circle, the enclosure felt strangely private.

His throat clogged, but he cleared it. "We have to talk."

"I know."

"About the future."

"I know."

His heart pounded in his chest. It may not have been the ideal place to propose, but if he didn't he thought his heart might burst. "Lynette—"

The blanket lifted, and Sarah crawled in to join them. In the cramped quarters Rick shuffled to the side.

"I'm back. Thanks. Ryan is looking for you. They want to put more warm water in the dunk tank, because Mayor Klein is starting to shiver for real."

Rick gritted his teeth, crawled out from beneath the blanket, and made his way to the dunk tank to do his duty. He hadn't said what he wanted to say to Lynette, but on the bright side at least now he knew where she was.

He made pleasant conversation with the mayor and the pastor while he added more warm water to the tub. As soon as the temperature was pleasantly warm again, Rick made his way to the barbecue, where he found Lynette's mother.

Ever since Lynette had told him what had happened in their other church, he found he respected Mrs. Charleston even more than before. She had handled the situation with class and dignity, and above all she had trusted the Lord with her heart and soul in times of trouble. In retrospect it was only because of the unpleasant incident Lynette had told him about that they'd moved on to Good Tidings, where they were truly happy and the people of Good Tidings were equally happy with them.

Rick reached into his back pocket and pulled out his wallet. "Two hot dogs, please. Loaded with onions."

"Onions? Are you sure? Are these for you and Lynette?"

He nodded.

Lynette's mother shrugged her shoulders and loaded two hot dogs each with huge piles of extra fried onions.

Rick grinned. If they both had onions, they would be safe with each other, but not anyone else.

As he approached the fish pond booth, he watched as Lynette crawled out through the blanket. She stood, glanced over her shoulder, and rubbed her bottom with her hands.

"Hi," he said as he neared her.

Her face flamed, which he thought cute.

"Sitting for so long on the cement like that is hard, even with that padded blanket."

He nodded and handed her one of the hot dogs. "I know. Who's in there now with Sarah? I hope it's not Brad."

"Don't worry—I know better than that. Melissa is with her. I'm not going far so I can see if Brad comes around."

"You're good in church leadership roles, you know."

She took a big bite of the hot dog, closing her eyes to savor the rich onions. "So are you."

"Do you think you could do this kind of thing on a regular basis?"

"Not run community fairs, but, yes, I like being in leadership roles. As long as I remember to take a break every once in awhile. I learned that the hard way, I think."

Rick's heart pounded at the possibilities. He was a volunteer youth leader now, but with a couple of more years of Bible college at night school, he could one day fulfill his dream of pastoring a church of his own.

"I was wondering, one day, do you think—"

"Lynette! I've been looking all over for you!" a voice called out from the masses. Mrs. McGrath pushed her way through the crowd and joined them. "We're almost ready for the pie-eating contest. I noticed that Mayor Klein is signed up, too."

Rick stuffed the rest of his hot dog into his mouth in one bite. "How many entries do we have?" he asked around the food in his mouth.

Mrs. McGrath beamed. "We have over a hundred and fifty."

He nearly choked. Lynette patted him on the back with her free hand.

Mrs. McGrath raised her eyebrows and pressed her wrinkled hands to her cheeks. "Gracious! I just thought of something! Do we have enough pies?"

Lynette nodded and spoke first because Rick still couldn't talk. "Yes. We made somewhere around two hundred pies. But where are all those people going to sit? I planned on bringing out about eight tables and putting them in the middle of the parking lot. We'd better get more out, real fast."

Rick pressed one fist into the center of his chest. "I'll get the boys to start bringing them out, along with more chairs. I'm going to need a calculator to figure out how many tables we'll need to seat that many people."

Lynette turned to him and folded her arms across her chest. "This isn't a difficult question, Rick. One table fits four people on each side and one at each end. That's ten people per table."

He felt his cheeks heating up. "I knew that," he mumbled.

Lynette took one step with Mrs. McGrath and then suddenly stopped and turned back to him. "Do we have enough plastic forks?"

Rick shook his head. "No. Maybe you'd better run off to the store while I get the boys to help me with the tables and chairs."

"But what about Sarah in the fish pond?"

"Don't worry. I'll have Brad with me."

Rick took off in one direction, while Lynette took off in another. While he scrambled to find all the available teen boys from the youth group, he heard the announcement for the last call for the apple-pie-eating contest.

He had finished setting up the last table when Lynette returned with a grocery bag full of plastic forks.

"Are you ready?" she asked.

"Yes. Do you have any idea how much money we've made, just with the pies?"

"Yes." Lynette broke out into a huge smile. "So many people are here. Wouldn't it be wonderful if we made enough money to fix the roof and not have to ask the congregation for any?"

While that would have been wonderful, one thing on his mind would have been more wonderful, if only he could get the chance to talk to her.

"Yes. Now get up to the podium. They're signaling for you."

Chapter 9

Lynette faced the crowd. She estimated that twice as many people surrounded her in the parking lot as on a busy Sunday morning service, which would bring the number to about a thousand people. Her head reeled to think how much their church had been blessed today. And such a gathering usually drew more families to their humble church family.

She cleared her throat and tapped the microphone with her index finger. "Is this thing on?"

Feedback screeched through the speaker system.

Lynette felt her face grow warm. "Oops. Sorry. First of all, I'd like to say thank you to everyone for participating. I think I can say we're all having fun, right?"

A round of applause and cheers was the reply.

She smiled, doing her best to hold back her tears. "Before we get to the crowning event of the day, our apple-pie-eating contest, I'd like to award the prizes for the raffle and the children's contests."

She called out the name of the person who had won the weekend in Seattle and the trip to the Space Needle, but they had apparently already left. Lynette tucked the envelope into her back pocket for safe keeping then gave out the awards to the children. She was pleased to see the prizes equally divided between church members and people from the community.

"Now for the moment we've all been waiting for. Before we start, I'd like to say that for those of you who have entered and don't finish your pie, we have plastic wrap over there." She pointed to four ladies at a faraway table, who waved at the crowd.

"For those of you who didn't enter but still would like a pie, we'll be selling the remaining pies after the contest for ten dollars each. If all the contestants will now proceed to the tables corresponding to your entry number, we'll hand out the pies. Take a seat at one of those tables over there and wait for the signal to begin. The winner will be awarded with this trophy." She held up the huge loving cup for all to see. "Also, since this is a church, the winner will get this lovely leather-bound, gold-embossed, brand-new Bible." She held up the Bible as well.

Considering that the four ladies had to hand out one hundred and sixty-two pies, the process went surprisingly well. Soon everyone who entered was seated and ready for the signal.

Rick appeared at her side. She covered the microphone with her hand. "Rick? What are you doing here? Why didn't you enter the contest?"

He covered his stomach with his hand. "After yesterday I can't even look at an apple pie, never mind eat one. I don't see you in the contest entrants either."

Lynette stiffened. "I have to be the emcee. I can't."

At her reply Rick made a strange snorting sound. She elbowed him in the ribs and uncovered the microphone. "Is everybody ready? Forks down, hands in your laps. The first person to finish, stand and raise both hands in the air, and call out that you're done." She scanned the seventeen tables of entrants, sucked in a deep breath and yelled, "Go!"

Most people in the crowd cheered on someone they knew as men, women, teens, and children alike did their best to gobble down their pies as quickly as they could. Each entrant had been supplied with one glass of water to help wash it down, and one volunteer stood at each table to refill the cups, if necessary.

Lynette could see three men in particular, only one of whom she recognized, down to the last sliced piece of pie.

A forty-fiveish man she didn't know with a bald head and green T-shirt jumped to his feet. "Done!" he yelled at the same time as one of the boys from the youth group started to stand.

"We have a winner!"

The crowd cheered and applauded.

Lynette walked up to him, announced his name to the crowd as best she could, and presented him with the Bible and trophy.

"Thanks," he said as he failed to hold back a small burp.

The crowd around him laughed, and his ears reddened. "I think you might be seeing me and my family here one Sunday soon."

"That is great. It has been wonderful to have you, and congratulations."

With the fair officially over, the crowd dispersed slowly, and volunteers began to pack up their tables. They decided for safety's sake to leave the goats and their pen for when the last volunteers remained so as not to disturb the animals, although Lynette couldn't believe how tame and friendly they were. When the guests had gone and only the church volunteers remained, Rick drained the dunk tank. Lynette and her parents walked around to collect the money that hadn't yet been put away and thank the volunteers for their help and contributions.

As she walked, Lynette's father followed, punching up figures on a calculator.

"Daddy!" Lynette whispered behind him as he added the numbers from the fishing pond into his total. "Why are you doing that now?"

"I couldn't help it," he whispered back. "I can't believe how much money we raised. I think we're going to make everything we need in one day!"

Lynette's breath caught in her throat. "Are you serious?"

He nodded and kept punching in figures.

He followed her to the last table, which was the pie table. One sad, lonely pie remained. "I guess no one wanted to buy the last one," her father mumbled while he waited for her mother to count the money.

He punched in the amount. "I can't believe this. According to my calculations we're only a hundred and fifty dollars short of our total goal. That covers everything, even the cost of the advertising and paying for the gas to get the goats and the pen here."

Lynette's mother sighed and looked at the last pie. "That's too bad. We came so close. If only we could find a way to make a hundred and fifty dollars on this one pie."

Suddenly Brad raised one finger in the air. Lynette hadn't noticed him beside her. But of course since Sarah had been trailing behind her after the fish pond was taken down, she should have known Brad wouldn't be far behind.

"I have an idea that will get you a hundred and fifty for that pie. Maybe more."

Lynette's heart raced. "Really? That would be wonderful! What are you going to do, auction it?" She couldn't see anyone paying a hundred and fifty dollars for a simple apple pie, especially since so many had already been purchased.

"Something close. I'll be right back."

Chapter 10

Rick stacked another piece of the dunk tank into the back of the pickup truck then stopped to wipe the sweat off his brow with the sleeve of his shirt. He gritted his teeth at the action behind him.

Rick turned around to the crowd of teen boys. "Brad, quit talking and get back to work. I'm tired and want to go home, and I'm sure everyone else here does, too."

He saw something being passed to Brad, and Brad took off. He opened his mouth to call after him, but the rest of the boys got back to work, saying nothing about Brad's not helping.

Rick sighed. He was too tired to care. If the boys were okay with Brad's goofing off, then he would deal with him later. Rick wanted only to go home and lie down.

He knew he wouldn't get any sleep. As tired as he was, he would think only of Lynette.

All day long he'd been hoping and praying for a miracle, but with all the distractions and interruptions it didn't happen. He wanted to talk to Lynette while she could remember everything that passed between them when he kissed her. He needed to assure her that whatever passed between them was mutual, and it was real.

He watched while the man who owned the goats herded them into their trailer. Lynette's father handed the man some money to pay for the gas, and the goats were on their way.

Since the goat pen was the last thing left to be cleaned up, a number of the teen girls joined in to help. Some of their parents got involved, and then more people did, too.

It made Rick wonder why they suddenly had too many people volunteering to do the work.

Someone behind him cleared their throat.

Rick froze, with his hands full of hay. He stiffened and turned around.

Lynette stood in front of him with an apple pie in her hands.

"What are you doing here?" he asked.

"This is for you. It's the last pie."

"No, thanks," he mumbled. The last thing he felt like was pie. He'd eaten too many raw apple pieces and far too much raw pastry to be interested in it, no matter how good everyone said the pies were. Besides that, his hands were covered with dirty straw, and he was coated in dust and sweat from head to toe. "You can have it."

As he began to turn around, he couldn't help but notice that everyone seemed to be watching him, as they had slowed down their clean-up efforts.

"Rick?"

He turned back to Lynette. "Yes?"

"All day long I've had something I wanted to say to you, and I never got the chance. I want to say it before I give you the pie."

His heart stopped then started again in double time. Despite the heat and the hard work Rick broke out into a cold sweat.

Lynette's voice dropped to a whisper so low he barely heard what she said. "I love you, Rick."

His stomach flipped over a dozen times. This wasn't the ideal moment for such a discussion, especially in the middle of a crowd and with him covered in hay and who knew what else. But he'd learned the hard way that often the right moments had to be made, rather than waiting for them to happen.

"I love you, too," he ground out. "I've loved you for years."

She cleared her throat again. "Close your eyes."

Rick also cleared his throat, which had gone very dry, and closed his eyes obediently. His voice came out in a hoarse croak. "Lynette, I know this isn't the most romantic setting, but will you marry me?"

He squeezed his eyes tighter and waited. He didn't think it in her character to kiss him in front of a crowd; but then again he wouldn't think she'd ever been proposed to before, so he didn't know what she would do. She had already surprised him by kissing him so profusely in the church, where anyone could have walked in on them.

Instead of a tender kiss to his lips, a slight scratchy substance pressed into his entire face. The scratchy sensation instantly broke up, changing to something slimy pushing against his skin. At the impact he jumped backward. The pressure disappeared. Something clanked to the ground.

Slimy lumps slithered down his face, along with the drier, crusty lumps, which landed with a plop at his feet. Something stuck in his hair and didn't fall down. His eyes remained clamped shut while all the people around him cheered, applauded, whistled, and laughed. Putting two and two together, he remembered Brad walking around to all the church members, teens and adults alike, instead of helping clean up the mess. Now he knew what Brad had been up to. That everyone had teamed up against him to have a pie thrown in his face didn't surprise him. What did surprise him was that Lynette had been the one to do the dirty work.

He pressed the lengths of his fingers to his eyebrows akin to windshield wipers. With a downward motion he swiped down his face to push away what he could of the remnants of the apple pie.

Lynette stood in front of him, her eyes wide and both hands covering her mouth. She was the only one not laughing or smiling.

He cleared his throat again and forced himself to smile, even though he knew it was weak. "I hope that was a yes."

Her eyes widened even more, if it were possible. "Are you mad at me?" she asked through her fingers. "We made it. With that last pie we made all the money to pay for the roof."

Rick smiled and stepped closer to Lynette. He paused to look at his fingers, wiped them off on his jeans as best he could, and reached up to run his fingers through the hair at Lynette's temple.

"Of course I'm not mad, but I must admit I am surprised. I do believe I asked you a question, though, and the question still stands."

Slowly she raised her right hand and touched his cheek. He could feel her fingers trembling, so he reached up and covered her hand with his, pressing her palm to his face, trying his best to ignore the slight slime still coating his skin.

"Yes, that was a yes," she whispered.

Rick thought his heart would burst. He wanted to kiss her well and good, but between the crowd surrounding them and the pie covering his face he couldn't. Instead he leaned forward to brush an appley kiss across her tender lips. Despite the public atmosphere, he didn't move and remained standing toe to toe, gazing into the eyes of the woman he loved.

"That's it!" Pastor Chris called out from somewhere behind him. "Let's all get back to work. We need somewhere to park our cars tomorrow morning."

Around them the sound of movement returned.

Rick couldn't make himself move. One day in the near future he was going to marry the sweetest, most wonderful woman in the world.

A quick smile flittered across her face then dropped. "I guess we should get back to work."

One corner of his mouth quirked up. "I think we've done enough work. Let's take off."

Her eyes widened, and she broke out into a full grin and covered his hands with hers. Her eyes absolutely sparkled. "You're right. We've done most of the work so far, and now it's time for us both to learn to say no once in awhile. Let's let everyone else finish, while we go somewhere and talk. I've wasted too much precious time. I don't want a long engagement—how about you?"

Rick thought he must be dreaming. He would have pinched himself to make sure he was awake, but Lynette was holding his hands steady. Instead he rubbed two fingers together. Since he could still feel some apple-pie slime residue between them, he knew this was really happening. "That sounds like a great idea. I need to clean up first, though. Where would you like to go?"

Lynette gave his hands a gentle squeeze. "Let's go to the coffee shop on the corner. But if they offer me apple pie for dessert, I'm going to say—"

Rick waited for her reply

Lynette grinned. "Yes!"

Lynette's Granny's Apple Pie

Pastry (makes 3 pies)
    5½ cups flour
    2 teaspoons salt
    2 teaspoons baking powder
    1 pound lard
    1 egg
    2 teaspoons vinegar
    Enough cold water to make 1 cup with the egg and vinegar

Mix all dry ingredients with your hands. Cut in lard with a pastry cutter. Make a well and pour in the liquid—mix with your hands—do not overmix. Roll out on a lightly floured surface.

Filling (for each pie)
    4 to 5 apples, peeled and sliced thin
    2 tablespoons flour
    ¾ cup sugar
    Cinnamon to taste (about 1 tablespoon)

Add sliced apples to uncooked pie crust. Combine flour and sugar and sprinkle over top of the apples. Add cinnamon to taste. Top with pastry; press edges with a fork; make slits to vent. Bake for 10 minutes at 400 degrees and continue baking for 25 to 30 minutes, or until golden brown.

About the Authors

Kristin Billerbeck makes her home in the Silicon Valley with her engineering director husband and their four children. In addition to writing, Kristin enjoys painting, reading, and conversing online.

Birdie L. Etchison lives in Washington State and knows much about the Willamette Valley, the setting for the majority of her books. She loves to research the colorful history of the United States and uses her research along with family stories to create wonderful novels.

New York Times bestselling author, Wanda E. Brunstetter has written nearly 70 books, many with Amish characters and settings. Wanda and her husband, Richard, live in Washington State but travel often as she researches her books. When Wanda isn't writing, she enjoys performing with her ventriloquist puppets, gardening, photography, and looking for unusual shells on the beach.

Pamela Griffin lives in Texas with her family. She fully gave her life to Christ in 1988 after a rebellious young adulthood and owes the fact that she's still alive today to an all-loving and forgiving God and to a mother who steadfastly prayed and had faith that God could bring her wayward daughter "home." Pamela's main goal in writing Christian romance is to help and encourage those who do know the Lord and to plant a seed of hope in those who don't.

Tamela Hancock Murray lives in Northern Virginia with her two daughters and her husband of over twenty years. She keeps busy with church and school activities, but in her spare time she's written seven Bible trivia books and twenty Christian romance novels and novellas.

Joyce Livingston has done many things in her life (in addition to being a wife, mother of six, and grandmother to oodles of grandkids). From being a television broadcaster for eighteen years, to lecturing and teaching on quilting and sewing, to writing magazine articles on a variety of subjects. When she isn't off traveling to wonderful and exotic places as a part-time tour escort, her days are spent sitting in front of her computer, creating stories. Joyce became a widow in 2004. In 2008, she married her Sunday school teacher, Pastor Dale Lewis (who had also lost his spouse), and became a pastor's wife, serving daily with him in his ministry. Joyce feels her writing is a ministry and a calling from God, and hopes readers will be touched and uplifted by what she writes.

Kristy Dykes—wife to Rev. Milton Dykes, mother to two beautiful young women, grandmother, and native Floridian—was author of hundreds of articles, a weekly cooking column, short stories, and novels. She was also a public speaker whose favorite topic was on "How to Love Your Husband." Her goal in writing was to "make them laugh, make them cry, and make them wait" (a Charles Dickens's quote). She passed away from this life in 2008.

Aisha Ford is a writer and book enthusiast who lives in the Midwest. She remembers falling in love with a good story as a kid, and reading about interesting characters who had exciting adventures became one of her favorite hobbies. Eventually, reading developed into an interest in writing, and she began creating her own characters and stories. She is grateful, humbled, and excited to have the opportunity to share these characters and their stories with others and deeply appreciates each letter and note and encouraging word she's received from her readers.

Gail Sattler lives in Vancouver, BC, where you don't have to shovel rain, with her husband, three sons, two dogs, and a lizard who is quite cuddly for a reptile. When she's not writing, Gail is making music, playing electric bass for a local jazz band, and acoustic bass for a community orchestra. When she's not writing or making music, Gail likes to sit back with a hot coffee and a good book.

Coming Soon from Barbour Books. . .

8 WEDDINGS *and a* *Miracle*
Romance Collection

Weather the storms of life alongside nine modern couples
who hope to make it to the altar,
though they may need a miracle to intervene.